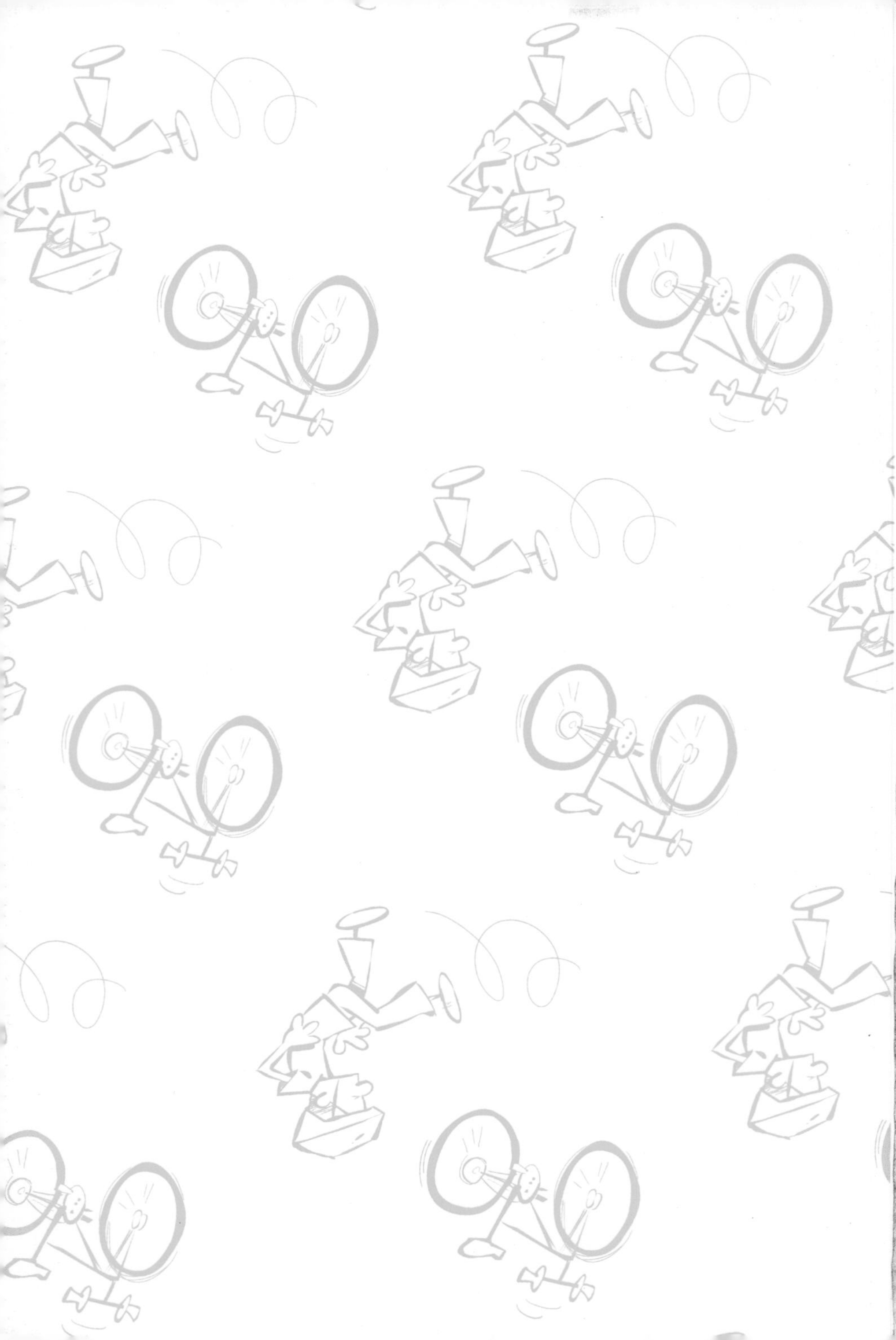

MIDDLE SCHOOL MISADVENTURES

MIDDLE SCHOOL
MISADVENTURES
DANCE DISASTER

JASON PLATT

LITTLE, BROWN AND COMPANY
NEW YORK BOSTON

ABOUT THIS BOOK

The illustrations for this book were done in Corel Painter on the Wacom Cintiq companion and colored in Adobe Photoshop. This book was edited by Rachel Poloski and Esther Cajahuaringa and designed by Megan McLaughlin. The production was supervised by Kimberly Stella, and the production editor was Jake Regier. The text was set in MisterAndMeBook, and the display type is MisterAndMe.

Little, Brown and Company
Hachette Book Group
1290 Avenue of the Americas, New York, NY 10104
Visit us at LBYR.com

First Edition: April 2022

Little, Brown and Company is a division of Hachette Book Group, Inc.
The Little, Brown name and logo are trademarks of Hachette Book Group, Inc.

The publisher is not responsible for websites (or their content) that are not owned by the publisher.

Library of Congress Cataloging-in-Publication Data
Names: Platt, Jason, author, illustrator.
Title: Dance disaster / Jason Platt.
Description: First edition. | New York ; Boston : Little, Brown and Company, 2022. | Series: Middle school misadventures ; 3 | Audience: Ages 8–12. | Summary: "Newell's perfectly comfortable life is turned upside down when Mrs. Hendricks announces the upcoming school dance and he discovers his dad is dating his math teacher." —Provided by publisher.
Identifiers: LCCN 2021011925 | ISBN 9780759556621 (hardcover) | ISBN 9780759556638 (trade paperback) | ISBN 9780759556577 (ebook)
Subjects: LCSH: Graphic novels. | CYAC: Graphic novels. | Dance parties—Fiction. | Dating (Social customs)—Fiction. | Fathers and sons—Fiction. | Friendship—Fiction. | Middle schools—Fiction. | Schools—Fiction.
Classification: LCC PZ7.7.P55 Dan 2022 | DDC 741.5/973—dc23
LC record available at https://lccn.loc.gov/2021011925

ISBNs: 978-0-7595-5662-1 (hardcover), 978-0-7595-5663-8 (pbk.), 978-0-7595-5657-7 (ebook), 978-0-7595-5659-1 (ebook), 978-0-7595-5660-7 (ebook)

Printed in China

1010

Hardcover: 10 9 8 7 6 5 4 3 2 1
Paperback: 10 9 8 7 6 5 4 3 2 1

FOR MY FRIEND JOI

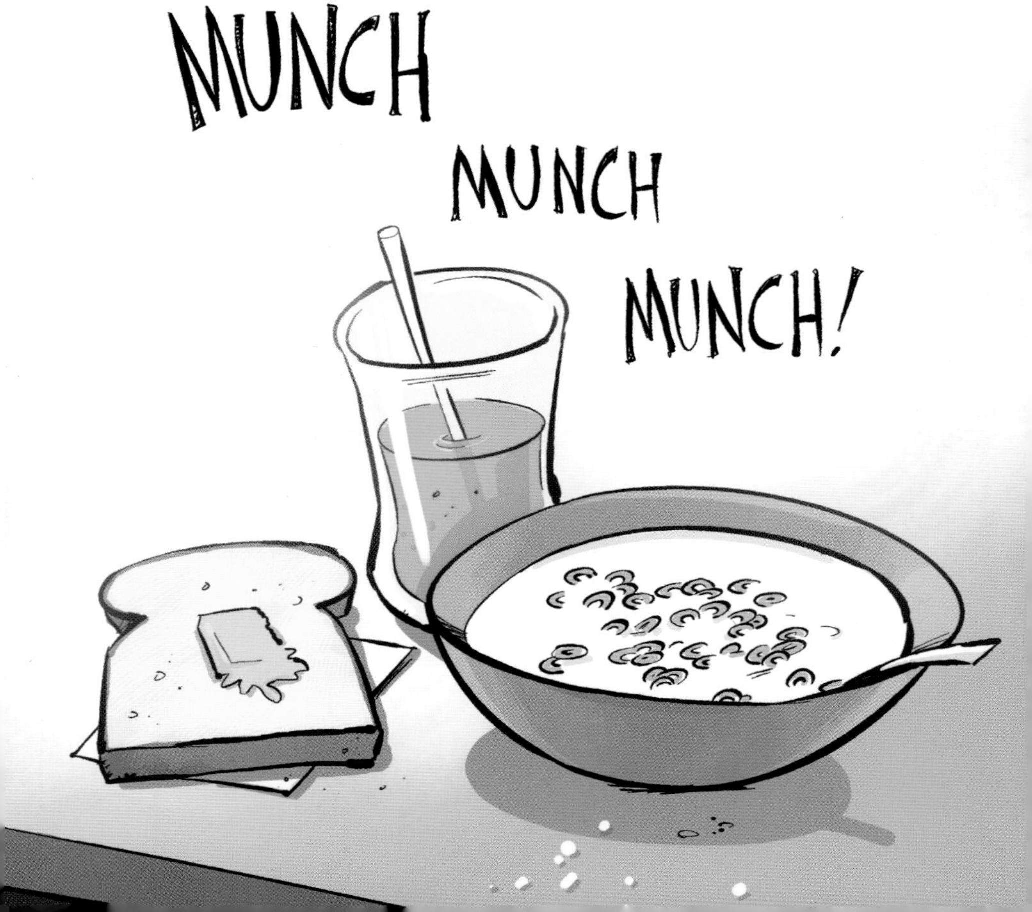
MUNCH
MUNCH
MUNCH!

CHAPTER ONE

I SWEAR THAT THIS IS A TRUE STORY

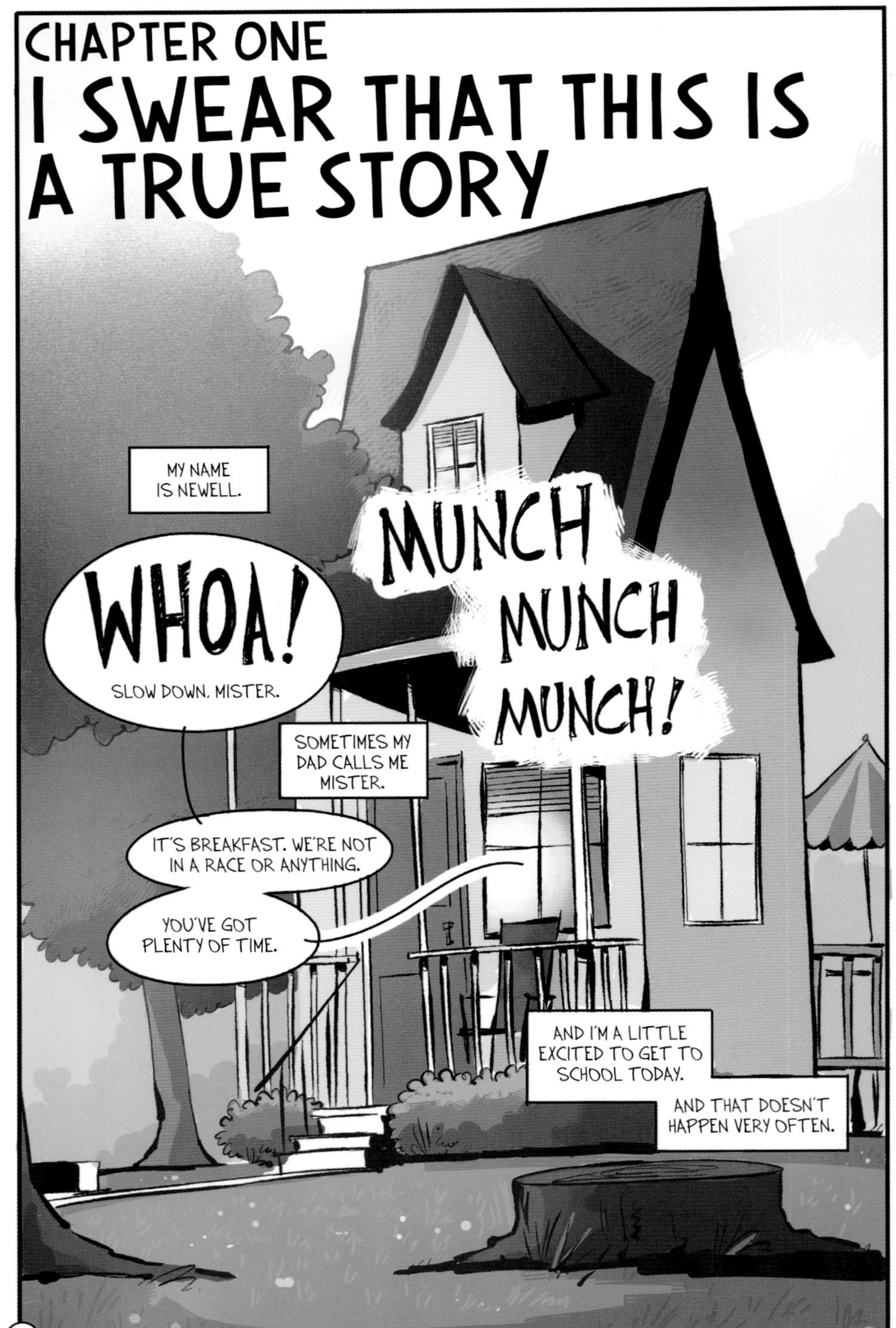
MY NAME IS NEWELL.
MUNCH MUNCH MUNCH!
WHOA!
SLOW DOWN, MISTER.
SOMETIMES MY DAD CALLS ME MISTER.
IT'S BREAKFAST. WE'RE NOT IN A RACE OR ANYTHING.
YOU'VE GOT PLENTY OF TIME.
AND I'M A LITTLE EXCITED TO GET TO SCHOOL TODAY.
AND THAT DOESN'T HAPPEN VERY OFTEN.

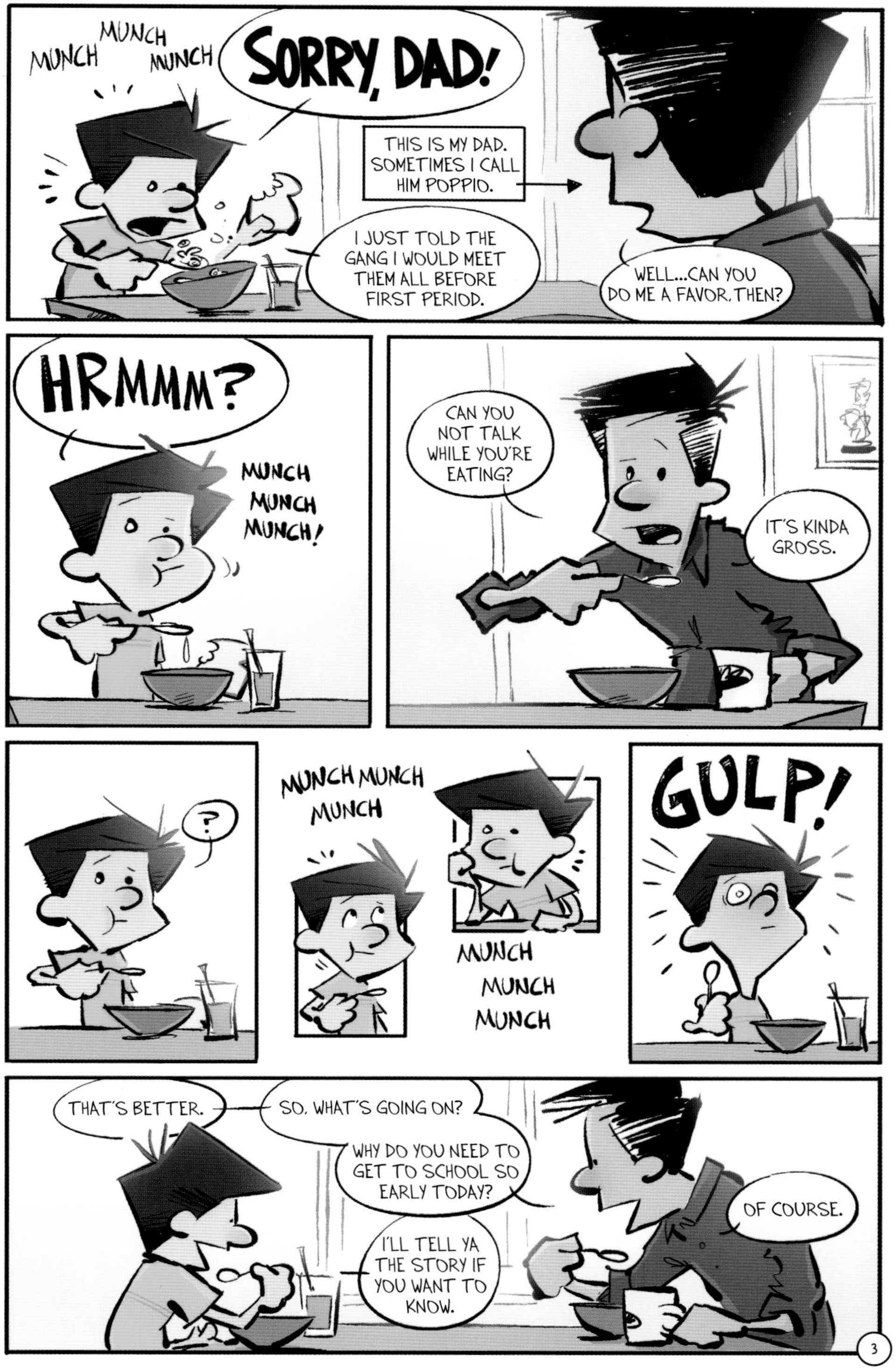
MUNCH MUNCH MUNCH
SORRY, DAD!
THIS IS MY DAD. SOMETIMES I CALL HIM POPPIO.
I JUST TOLD THE GANG I WOULD MEET THEM ALL BEFORE FIRST PERIOD.
WELL...CAN YOU DO ME A FAVOR, THEN?
HRMMM?
MUNCH MUNCH MUNCH!
CAN YOU NOT TALK WHILE YOU'RE EATING?
IT'S KINDA GROSS.
?
MUNCH MUNCH MUNCH
MUNCH MUNCH MUNCH
GULP!
THAT'S BETTER.
SO, WHAT'S GOING ON?
WHY DO YOU NEED TO GET TO SCHOOL SO EARLY TODAY?
I'LL TELL YA THE STORY IF YOU WANT TO KNOW.
OF COURSE.

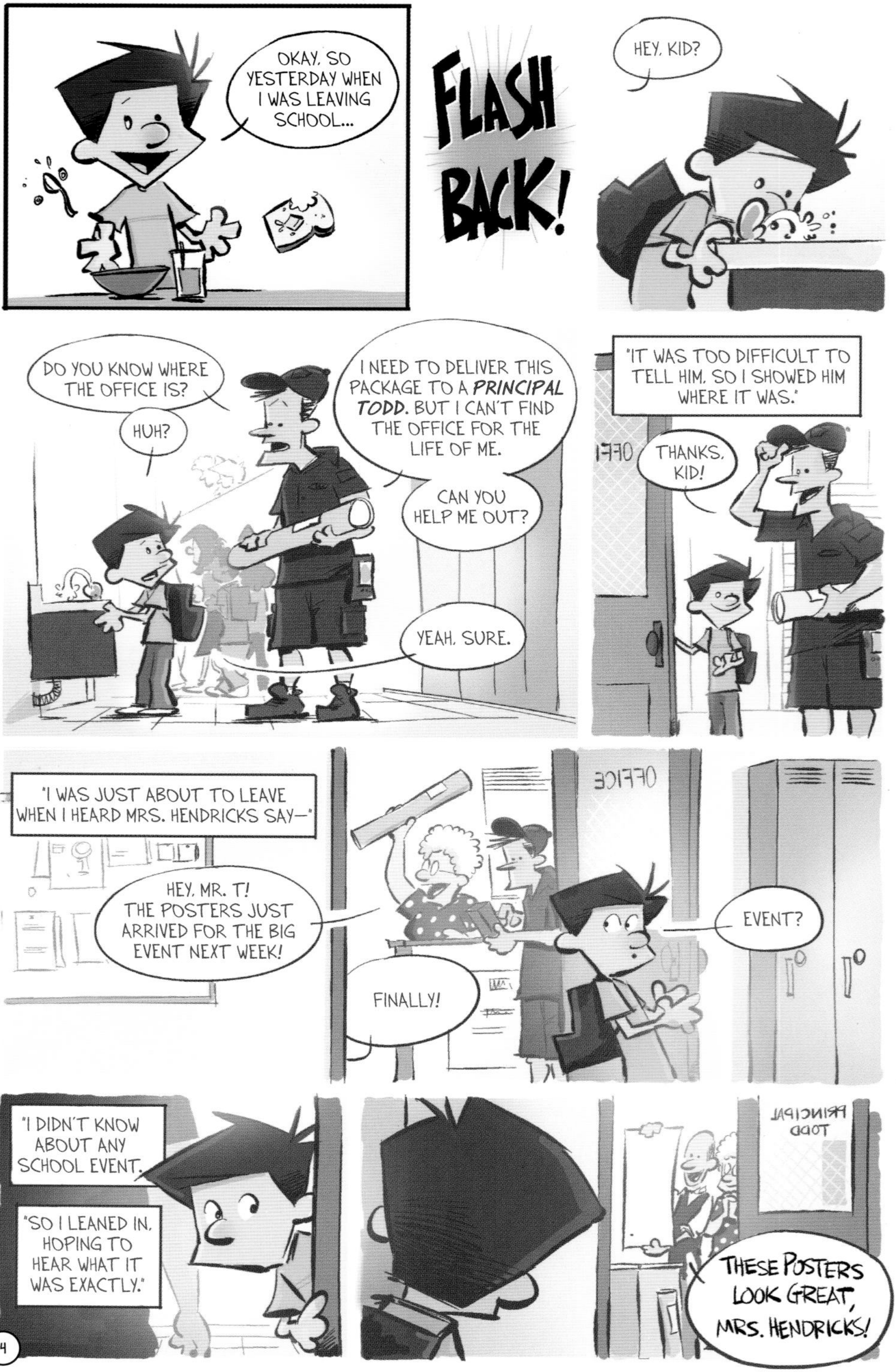

OKAY, SO YESTERDAY WHEN I WAS LEAVING SCHOOL...
FLASH BACK!
HEY, KID?
DO YOU KNOW WHERE THE OFFICE IS?
HUH?
I NEED TO DELIVER THIS PACKAGE TO A **PRINCIPAL TODD.** BUT I CAN'T FIND THE OFFICE FOR THE LIFE OF ME.
CAN YOU HELP ME OUT?
YEAH, SURE.
"IT WAS TOO DIFFICULT TO TELL HIM, SO I SHOWED HIM WHERE IT WAS."
THANKS, KID!
"I WAS JUST ABOUT TO LEAVE WHEN I HEARD MRS. HENDRICKS SAY—"
HEY, MR. T! THE POSTERS JUST ARRIVED FOR THE BIG EVENT NEXT WEEK!
FINALLY!
EVENT?
"I DIDN'T KNOW ABOUT ANY SCHOOL EVENT.
"SO I LEANED IN, HOPING TO HEAR WHAT IT WAS EXACTLY."
THESE POSTERS LOOK GREAT, MRS. HENDRICKS!

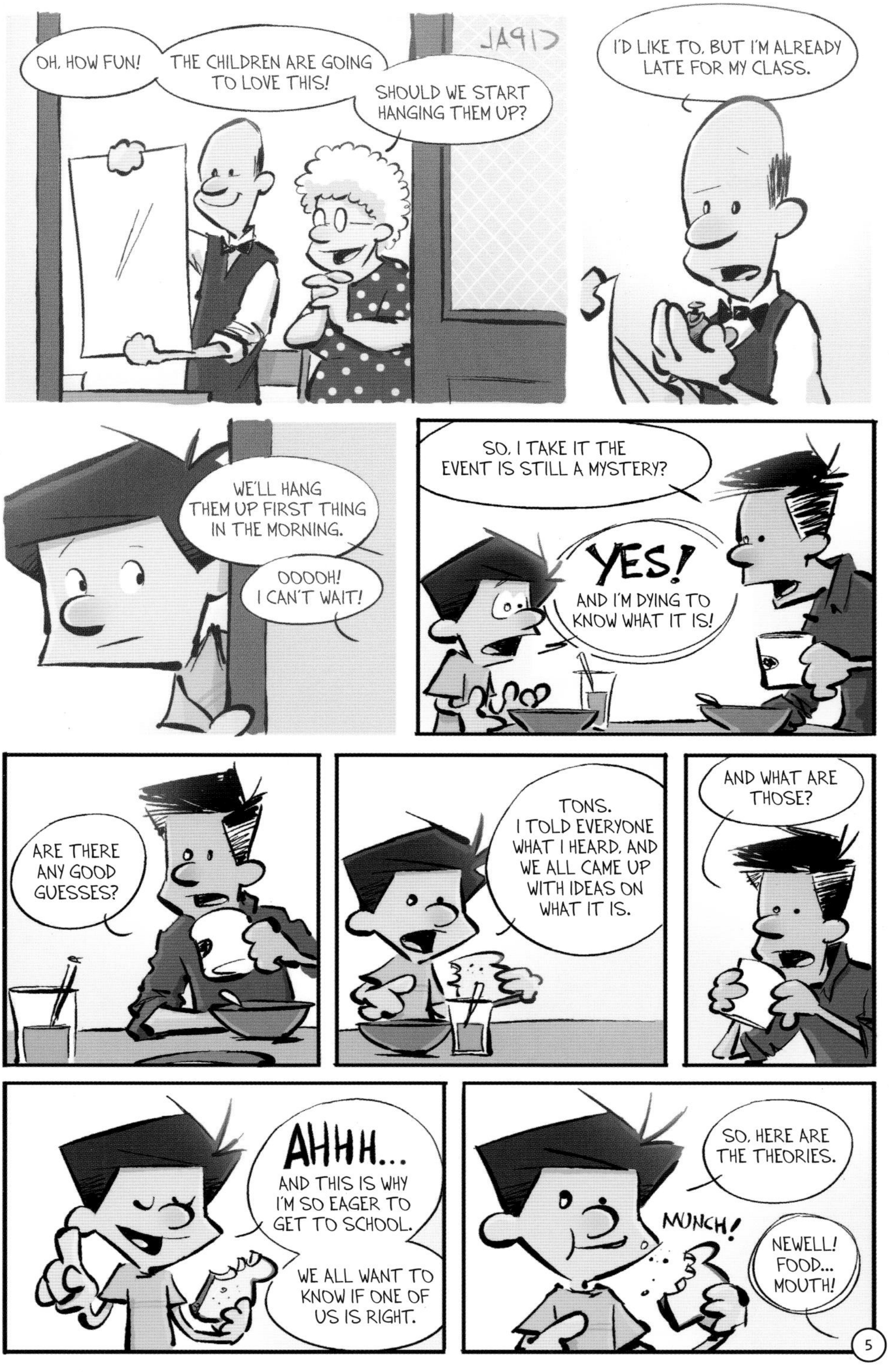

OH, HOW FUN!
THE CHILDREN ARE GOING TO LOVE THIS!
SHOULD WE START HANGING THEM UP?
I'D LIKE TO, BUT I'M ALREADY LATE FOR MY CLASS.
WE'LL HANG THEM UP FIRST THING IN THE MORNING.
OOOOH! I CAN'T WAIT!
SO, I TAKE IT THE EVENT IS STILL A MYSTERY?
YES!
AND I'M DYING TO KNOW WHAT IT IS!
ARE THERE ANY GOOD GUESSES?
TONS. I TOLD EVERYONE WHAT I HEARD, AND WE ALL CAME UP WITH IDEAS ON WHAT IT IS.
AND WHAT ARE THOSE?
AHHH...
AND THIS IS WHY I'M SO EAGER TO GET TO SCHOOL.
WE ALL WANT TO KNOW IF ONE OF US IS RIGHT.
SO, HERE ARE THE THEORIES.
MUNCH!
NEWELL! FOOD... MOUTH!

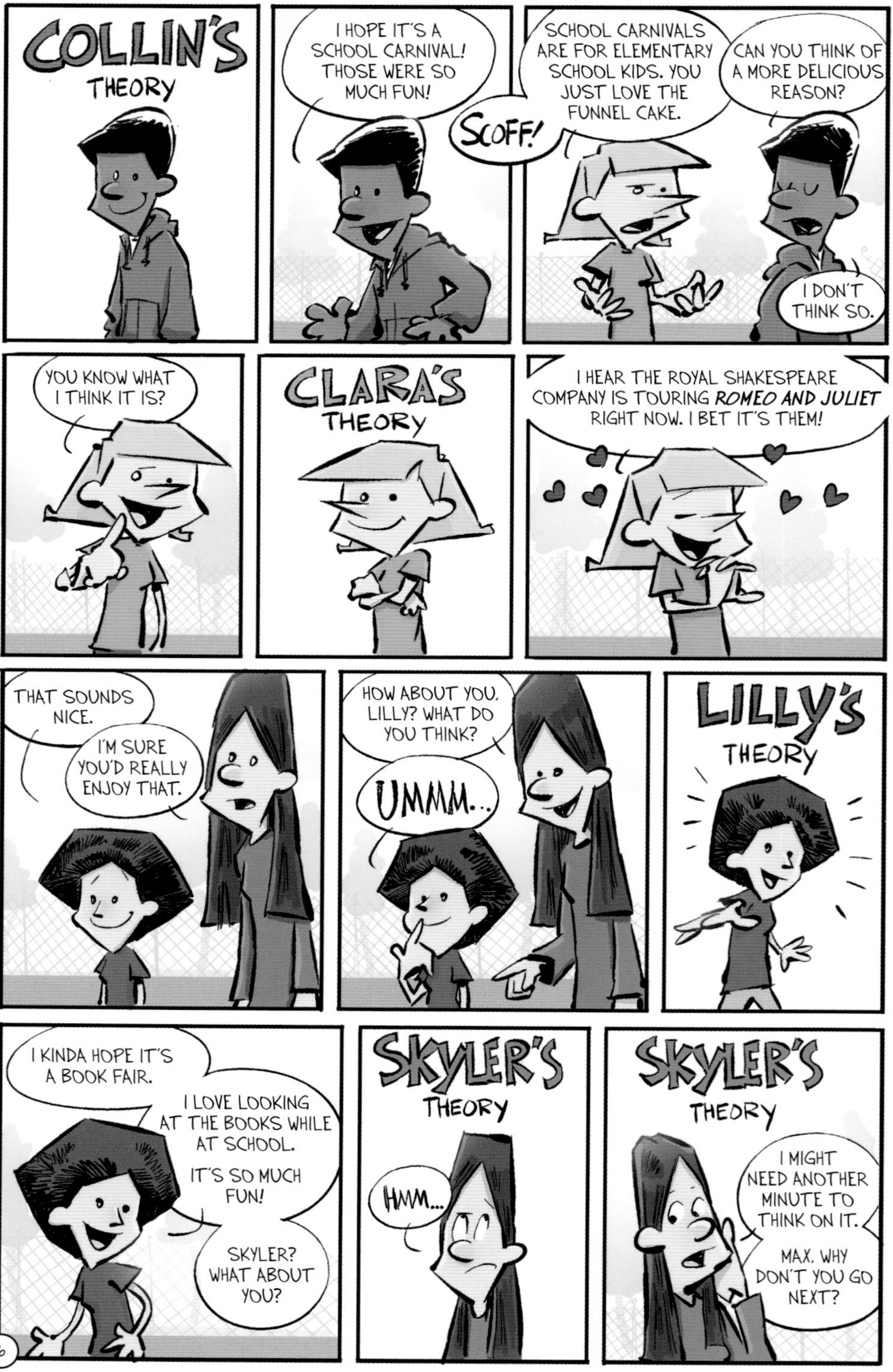
COLLIN'S THEORY
I HOPE IT'S A SCHOOL CARNIVAL! THOSE WERE SO MUCH FUN!
SCOFF!
SCHOOL CARNIVALS ARE FOR ELEMENTARY SCHOOL KIDS. YOU JUST LOVE THE FUNNEL CAKE.
CAN YOU THINK OF A MORE DELICIOUS REASON?
I DON'T THINK SO.
YOU KNOW WHAT I THINK IT IS?
CLARA'S THEORY
I HEAR THE ROYAL SHAKESPEARE COMPANY IS TOURING ROMEO AND JULIET RIGHT NOW. I BET IT'S THEM!
THAT SOUNDS NICE.
I'M SURE YOU'D REALLY ENJOY THAT.
HOW ABOUT YOU, LILLY? WHAT DO YOU THINK?
UMMM...
LILLY'S THEORY
I KINDA HOPE IT'S A BOOK FAIR.
I LOVE LOOKING AT THE BOOKS WHILE AT SCHOOL.
IT'S SO MUCH FUN!
SKYLER? WHAT ABOUT YOU?
SKYLER'S THEORY
HMM...
SKYLER'S THEORY
I MIGHT NEED ANOTHER MINUTE TO THINK ON IT.
MAX, WHY DON'T YOU GO NEXT?

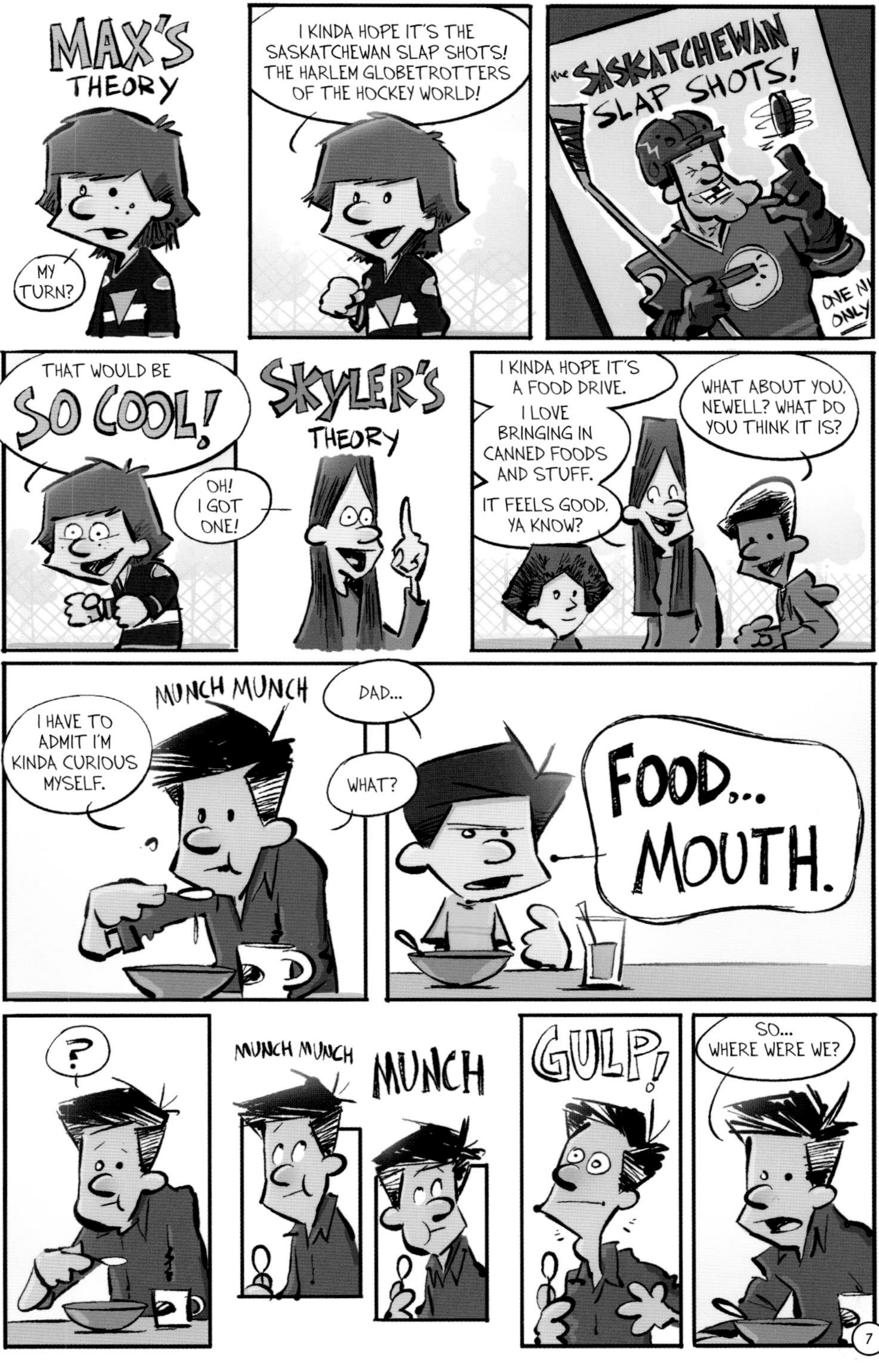
MAX'S THEORY
MY TURN?
I KINDA HOPE IT'S THE SASKATCHEWAN SLAP SHOTS! THE HARLEM GLOBETROTTERS OF THE HOCKEY WORLD!
THE SASKATCHEWAN SLAP SHOTS!
THAT WOULD BE SO COOL!
SKYLER'S THEORY
OH! I GOT ONE!
I KINDA HOPE IT'S A FOOD DRIVE.
I LOVE BRINGING IN CANNED FOODS AND STUFF.
IT FEELS GOOD, YA KNOW?
WHAT ABOUT YOU, NEWELL? WHAT DO YOU THINK IT IS?
I HAVE TO ADMIT I'M KINDA CURIOUS MYSELF.
MUNCH MUNCH
DAD...
WHAT?
FOOD... MOUTH.
?
MUNCH MUNCH
MUNCH
GULP!
SO... WHERE WERE WE?

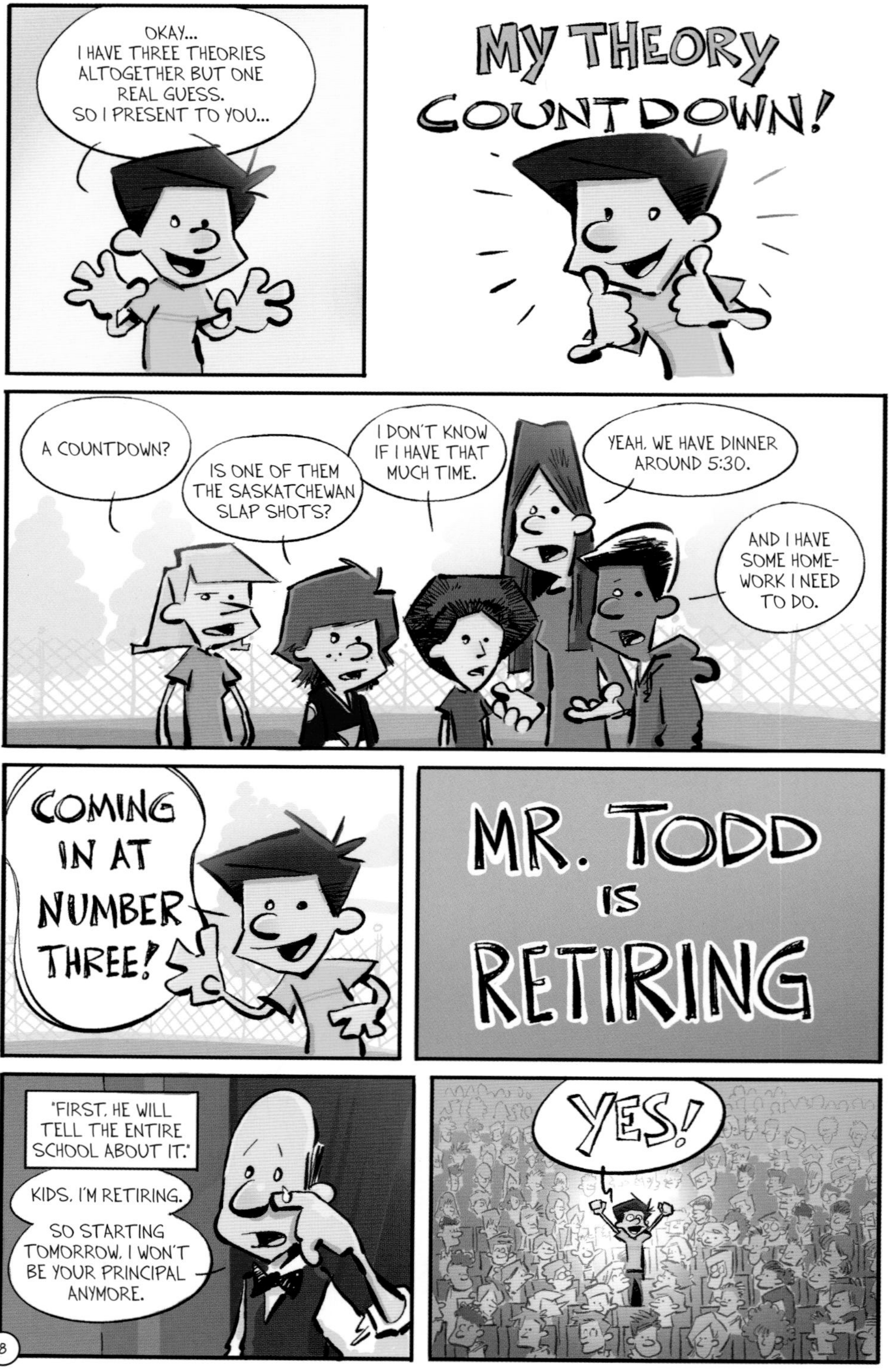
OKAY... I HAVE THREE THEORIES ALTOGETHER BUT ONE REAL GUESS. SO I PRESENT TO YOU...
MY THEORY COUNTDOWN!
A COUNTDOWN?
IS ONE OF THEM THE SASKATCHEWAN SLAP SHOTS?
I DON'T KNOW IF I HAVE THAT MUCH TIME.
YEAH, WE HAVE DINNER AROUND 5:30.
AND I HAVE SOME HOME-WORK I NEED TO DO.
COMING IN AT NUMBER THREE!
MR. TODD IS RETIRING
"FIRST, HE WILL TELL THE ENTIRE SCHOOL ABOUT IT."
KIDS, I'M RETIRING.
SO STARTING TOMORROW, I WON'T BE YOUR PRINCIPAL ANYMORE.
YES!

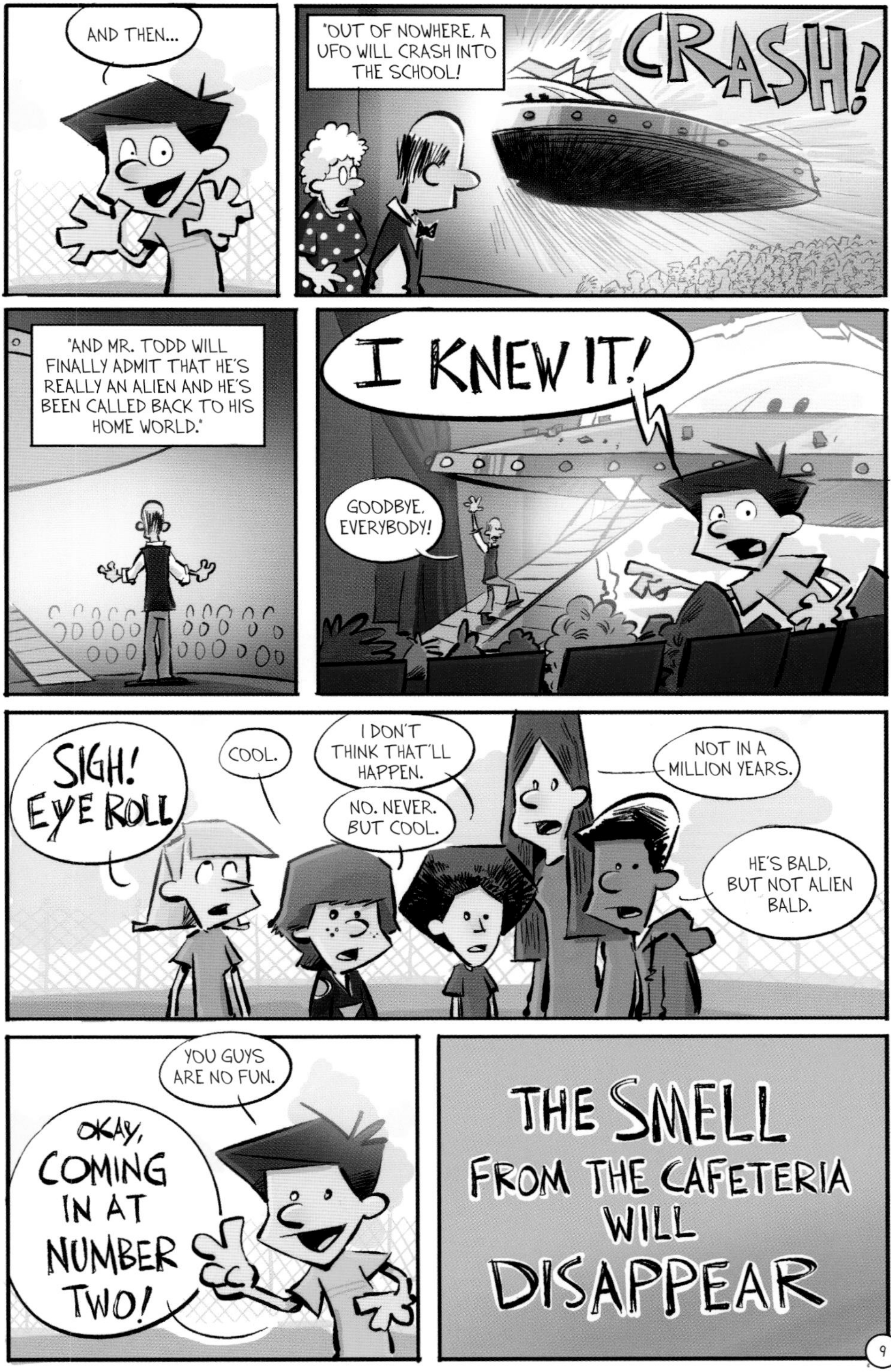
AND THEN...
"OUT OF NOWHERE, A UFO WILL CRASH INTO THE SCHOOL!
CRASH!
"AND MR. TODD WILL FINALLY ADMIT THAT HE'S REALLY AN ALIEN AND HE'S BEEN CALLED BACK TO HIS HOME WORLD."
I KNEW IT!
GOODBYE, EVERYBODY!
SIGH! EYE ROLL
COOL.
I DON'T THINK THAT'LL HAPPEN.
NO. NEVER. BUT COOL.
NOT IN A MILLION YEARS.
HE'S BALD, BUT NOT ALIEN BALD.
YOU GUYS ARE NO FUN.
OKAY, COMING IN AT NUMBER TWO!
THE SMELL FROM THE CAFETERIA WILL DISAPPEAR

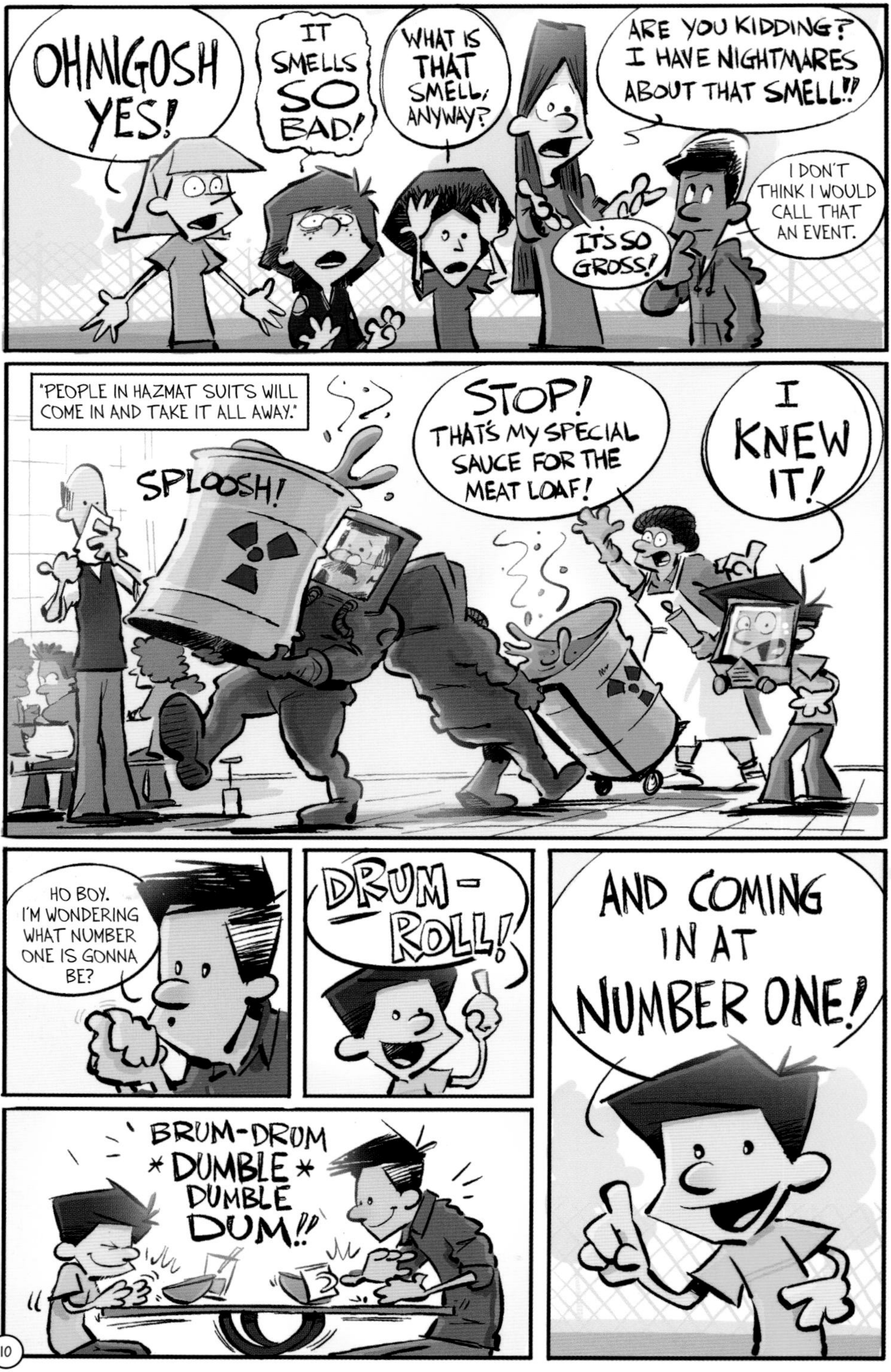
OHMIGOSH YES!
IT SMELLS SO BAD!
WHAT IS THAT SMELL, ANYWAY?
ARE YOU KIDDING? I HAVE NIGHTMARES ABOUT THAT SMELL!!
IT'S SO GROSS!
I DON'T THINK I WOULD CALL THAT AN EVENT.
"PEOPLE IN HAZMAT SUITS WILL COME IN AND TAKE IT ALL AWAY."
SPLOOSH!
STOP! THAT'S MY SPECIAL SAUCE FOR THE MEAT LOAF!
I KNEW IT!
HO BOY. I'M WONDERING WHAT NUMBER ONE IS GONNA BE?
DRUM-ROLL!
AND COMING IN AT NUMBER ONE!
BRUM-DROM *DUMBLE* DUMBLE DUM!!

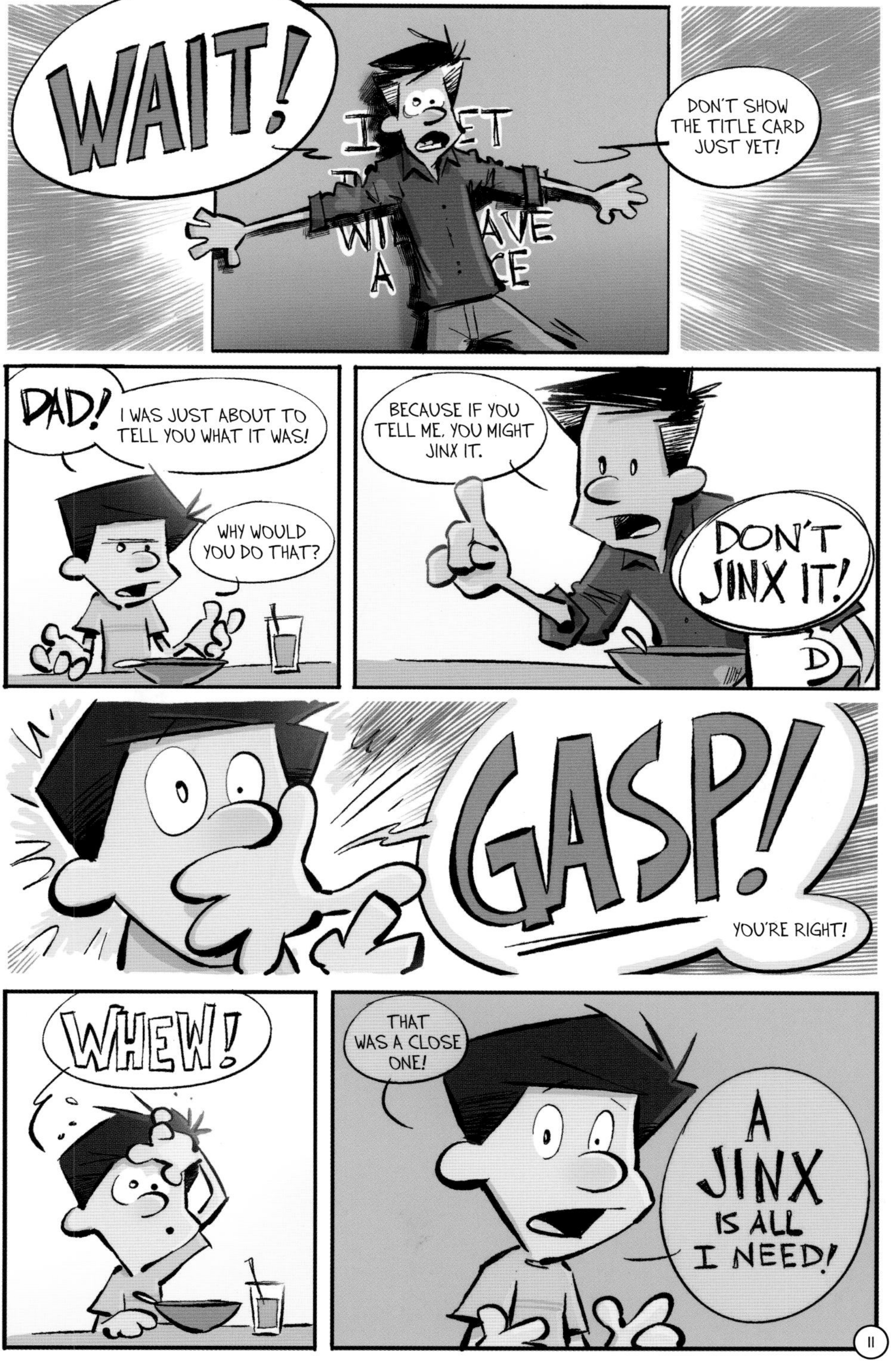
WAIT!
DON'T SHOW THE TITLE CARD JUST YET!
DAD! I WAS JUST ABOUT TO TELL YOU WHAT IT WAS!
WHY WOULD YOU DO THAT?
BECAUSE IF YOU TELL ME, YOU MIGHT JINX IT.
DON'T JINX IT!
GASP!
YOU'RE RIGHT!
WHEW!
THAT WAS A CLOSE ONE!
A JINX IS ALL I NEED!

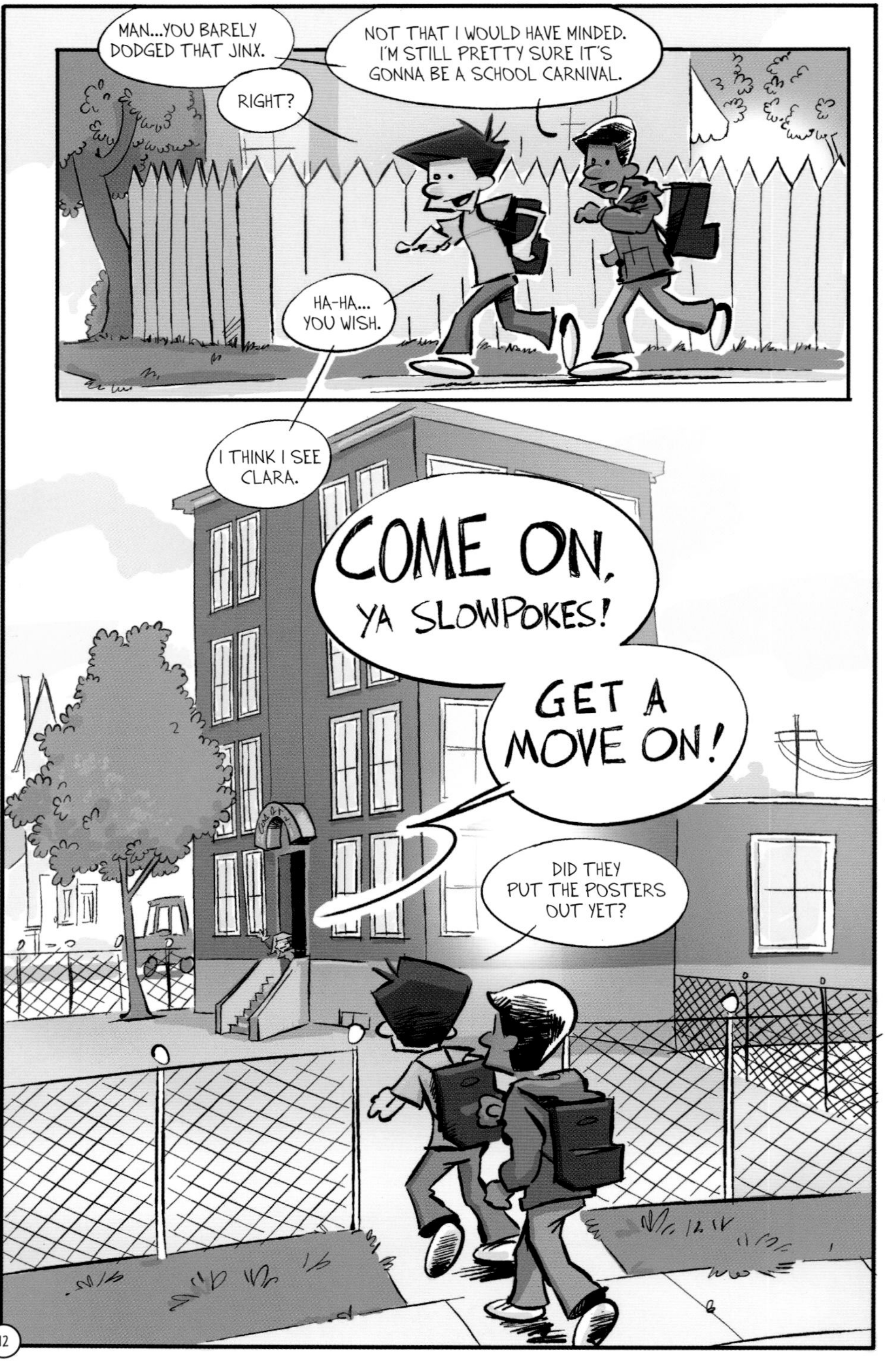
MAN...YOU BARELY DODGED THAT JINX.
NOT THAT I WOULD HAVE MINDED. I'M STILL PRETTY SURE IT'S GONNA BE A SCHOOL CARNIVAL.
RIGHT?
HA-HA... YOU WISH.
I THINK I SEE CLARA.
COME ON, YA SLOWPOKES!
GET A MOVE ON!
DID THEY PUT THE POSTERS OUT YET?

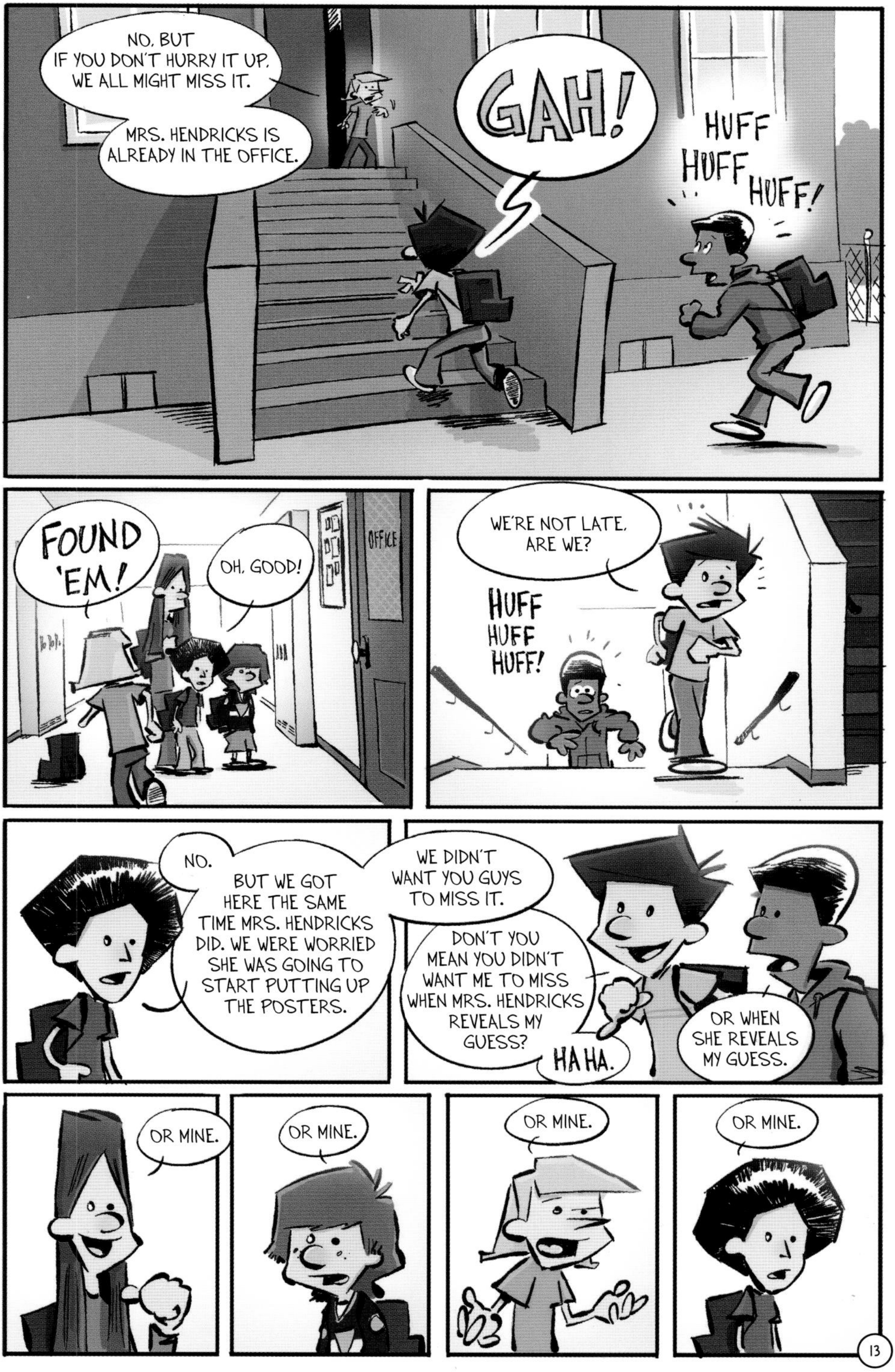

NO, BUT IF YOU DON'T HURRY IT UP, WE ALL MIGHT MISS IT.
MRS. HENDRICKS IS ALREADY IN THE OFFICE.
GAH!
HUFF HUFF HUFF!
FOUND 'EM!
OH, GOOD!
OFFICE
WE'RE NOT LATE, ARE WE?
HUFF HUFF HUFF!
NO.
BUT WE GOT HERE THE SAME TIME MRS. HENDRICKS DID. WE WERE WORRIED SHE WAS GOING TO START PUTTING UP THE POSTERS.
WE DIDN'T WANT YOU GUYS TO MISS IT.
DON'T YOU MEAN YOU DIDN'T WANT ME TO MISS WHEN MRS. HENDRICKS REVEALS MY GUESS?
HA HA.
OR WHEN SHE REVEALS MY GUESS.
OR MINE.
OR MINE.
OR MINE.
OR MINE.

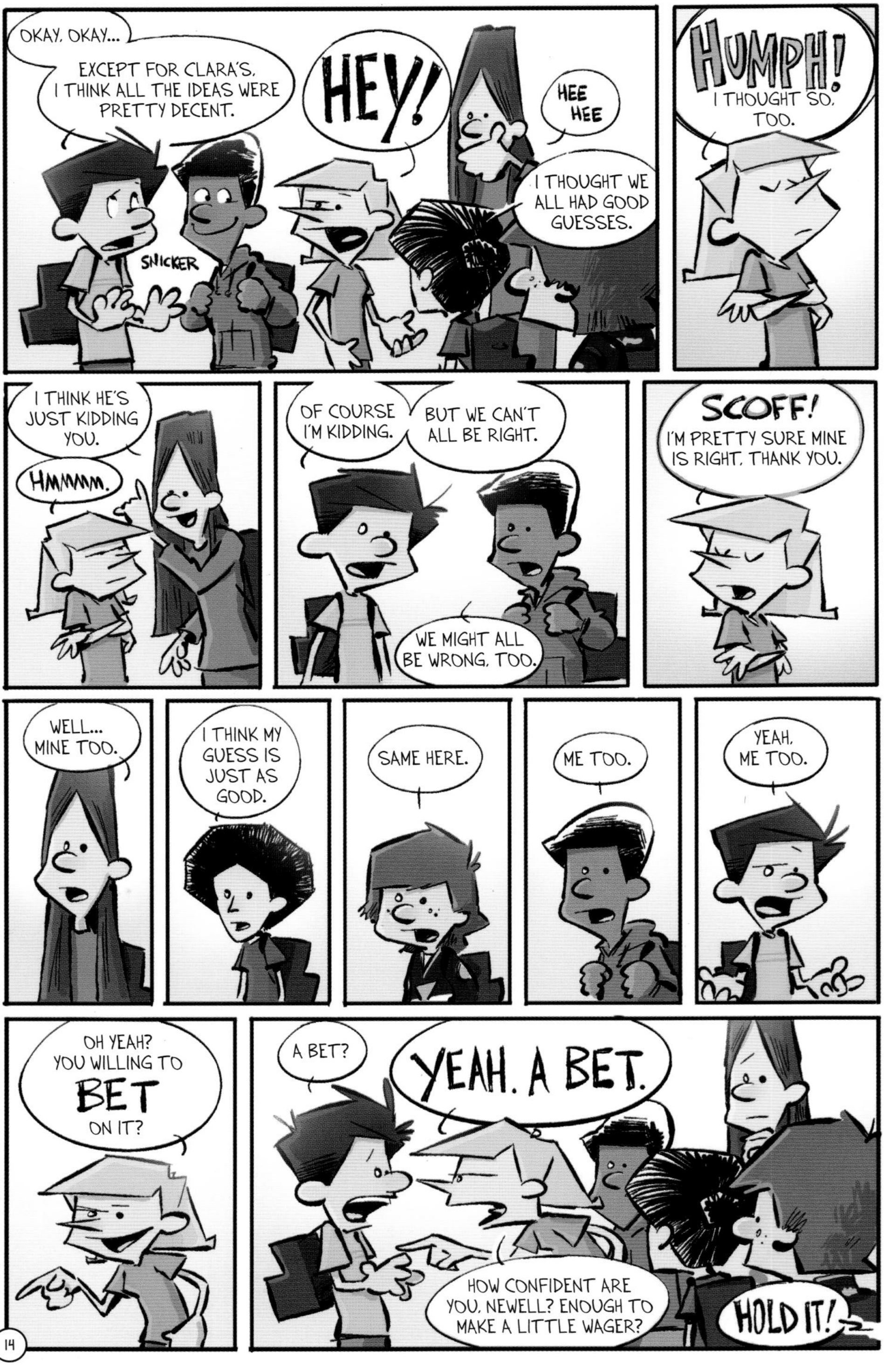
OKAY, OKAY...
EXCEPT FOR CLARA'S, I THINK ALL THE IDEAS WERE PRETTY DECENT.
SNICKER
HEY!
HEE HEE
I THOUGHT WE ALL HAD GOOD GUESSES.
HUMPH!
I THOUGHT SO, TOO.
I THINK HE'S JUST KIDDING YOU.
HMMMM.
OF COURSE I'M KIDDING.
BUT WE CAN'T ALL BE RIGHT.
WE MIGHT ALL BE WRONG, TOO.
SCOFF!
I'M PRETTY SURE MINE IS RIGHT, THANK YOU.
WELL... MINE TOO.
I THINK MY GUESS IS JUST AS GOOD.
SAME HERE.
ME TOO.
YEAH, ME TOO.
OH YEAH? YOU WILLING TO BET ON IT?
A BET?
YEAH. A BET.
HOW CONFIDENT ARE YOU, NEWELL? ENOUGH TO MAKE A LITTLE WAGER?
HOLD IT!

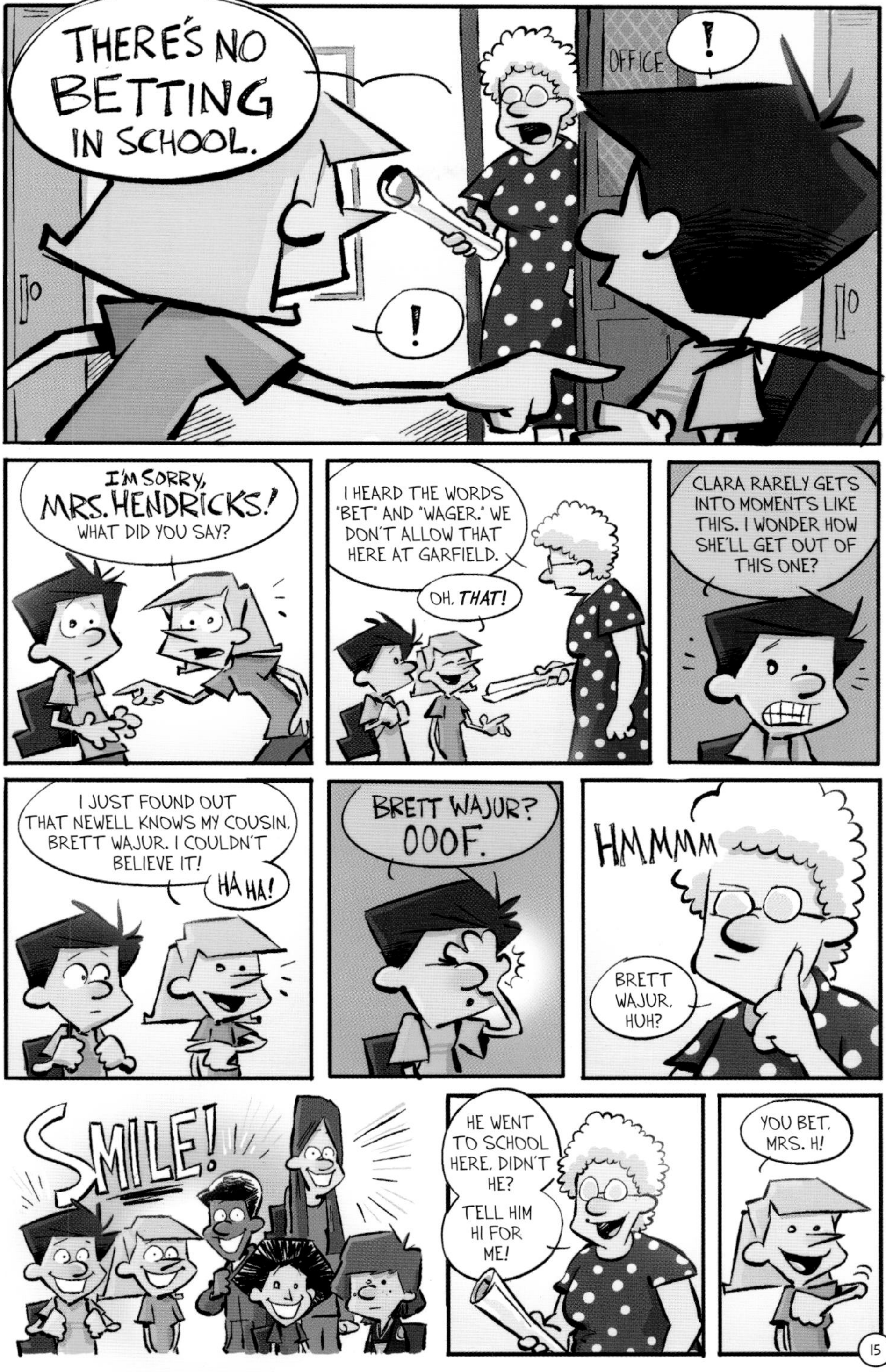
THERE'S NO BETTING IN SCHOOL.
OFFICE
!
!
I'M SORRY, MRS. HENDRICKS! WHAT DID YOU SAY?
I HEARD THE WORDS "BET" AND "WAGER." WE DON'T ALLOW THAT HERE AT GARFIELD.
OH, THAT!
CLARA RARELY GETS INTO MOMENTS LIKE THIS. I WONDER HOW SHE'LL GET OUT OF THIS ONE?
I JUST FOUND OUT THAT NEWELL KNOWS MY COUSIN, BRETT WAJUR. I COULDN'T BELIEVE IT!
HA HA!
BRETT WAJUR? OOOF.
HMMMM
BRETT WAJUR, HUH?
SMILE!
HE WENT TO SCHOOL HERE, DIDN'T HE?
TELL HIM HI FOR ME!
YOU BET, MRS. H!

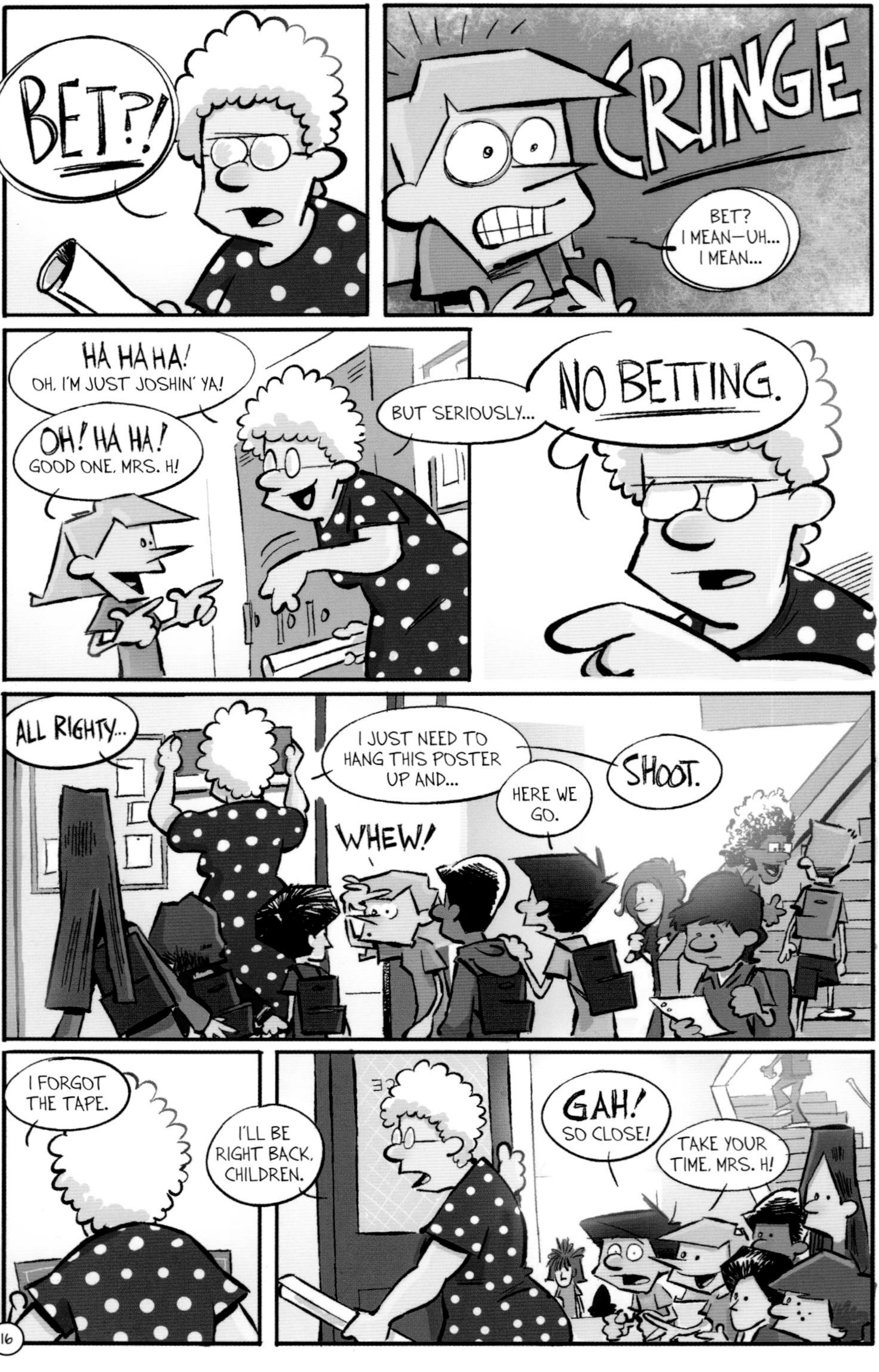
BET?!
CRINGE
BET? I MEAN—UH... I MEAN...
HA HA HA! OH, I'M JUST JOSHIN' YA!
OH! HA HA! GOOD ONE, MRS. H!
BUT SERIOUSLY...
NO BETTING.
ALL RIGHTY...
I JUST NEED TO HANG THIS POSTER UP AND...
SHOOT.
HERE WE GO.
WHEW!
I FORGOT THE TAPE.
I'LL BE RIGHT BACK, CHILDREN.
GAH! SO CLOSE!
TAKE YOUR TIME, MRS. H!

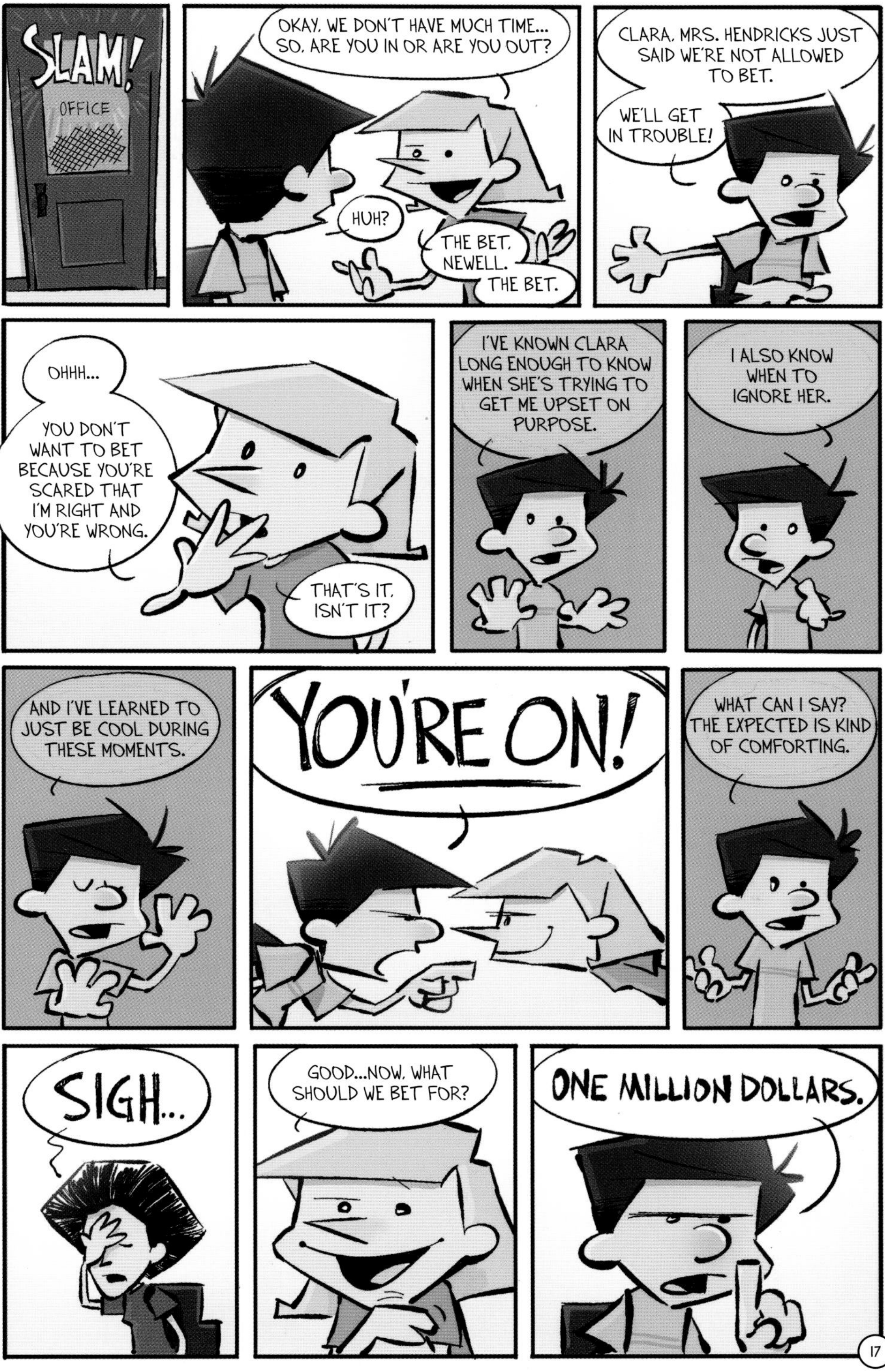
SLAM!
OFFICE
OKAY, WE DON'T HAVE MUCH TIME... SO, ARE YOU IN OR ARE YOU OUT?
HUH?
THE BET, NEWELL.
THE BET.
CLARA, MRS. HENDRICKS JUST SAID WE'RE NOT ALLOWED TO BET.
WE'LL GET IN TROUBLE!
OHHH...
YOU DON'T WANT TO BET BECAUSE YOU'RE SCARED THAT I'M RIGHT AND YOU'RE WRONG.
THAT'S IT, ISN'T IT?
I'VE KNOWN CLARA LONG ENOUGH TO KNOW WHEN SHE'S TRYING TO GET ME UPSET ON PURPOSE.
I ALSO KNOW WHEN TO IGNORE HER.
AND I'VE LEARNED TO JUST BE COOL DURING THESE MOMENTS.
YOU'RE ON!
WHAT CAN I SAY? THE EXPECTED IS KIND OF COMFORTING.
SIGH...
GOOD...NOW, WHAT SHOULD WE BET FOR?
ONE MILLION DOLLARS.

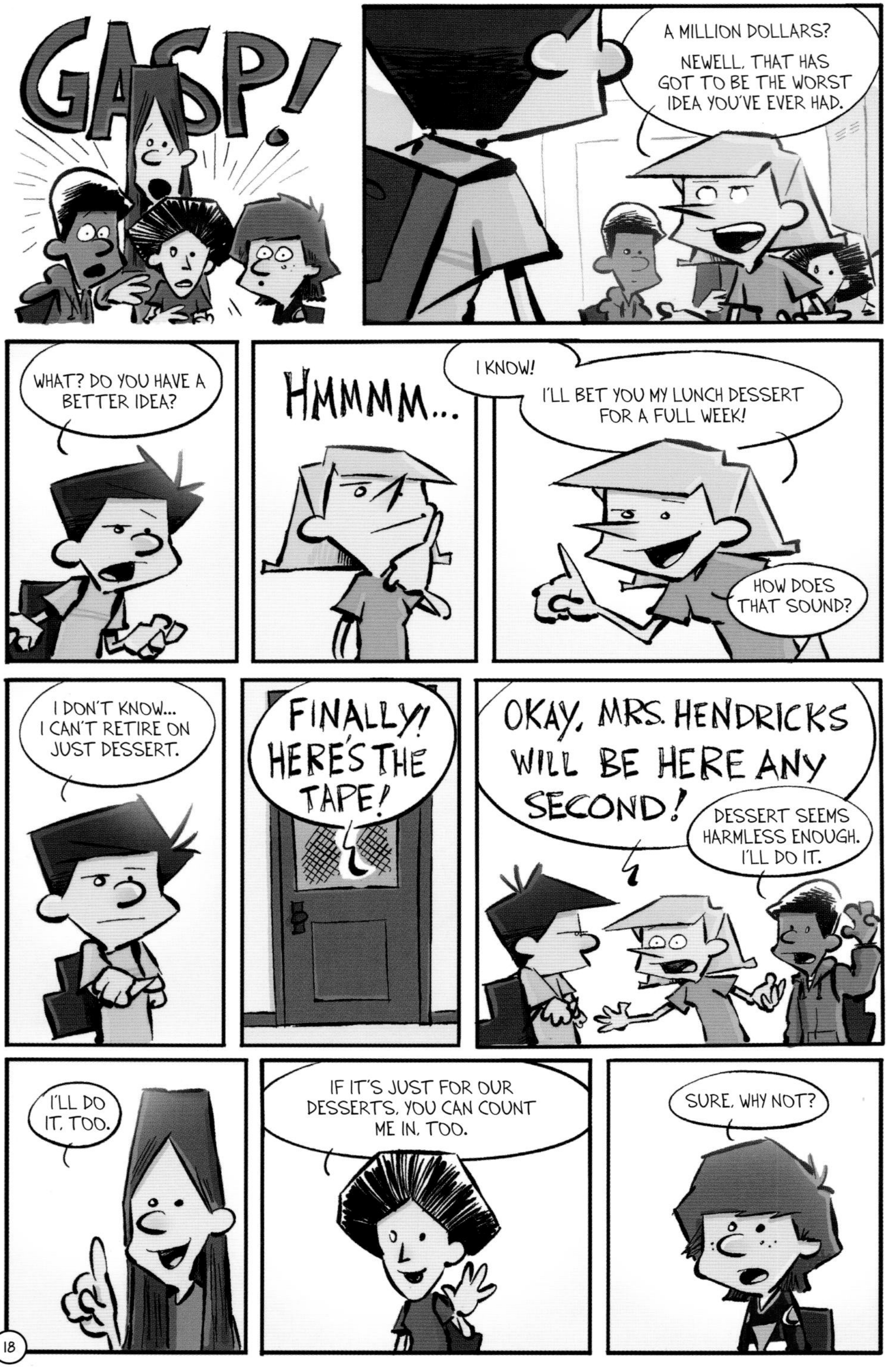
GASP!
A MILLION DOLLARS?
NEWELL, THAT HAS GOT TO BE THE WORST IDEA YOU'VE EVER HAD.
WHAT? DO YOU HAVE A BETTER IDEA?
HMMMM...
I KNOW!
I'LL BET YOU MY LUNCH DESSERT FOR A FULL WEEK!
HOW DOES THAT SOUND?
I DON'T KNOW... I CAN'T RETIRE ON JUST DESSERT.
FINALLY! HERE'S THE TAPE!
OKAY, MRS. HENDRICKS WILL BE HERE ANY SECOND!
DESSERT SEEMS HARMLESS ENOUGH. I'LL DO IT.
I'LL DO IT, TOO.
IF IT'S JUST FOR OUR DESSERTS, YOU CAN COUNT ME IN, TOO.
SURE, WHY NOT?

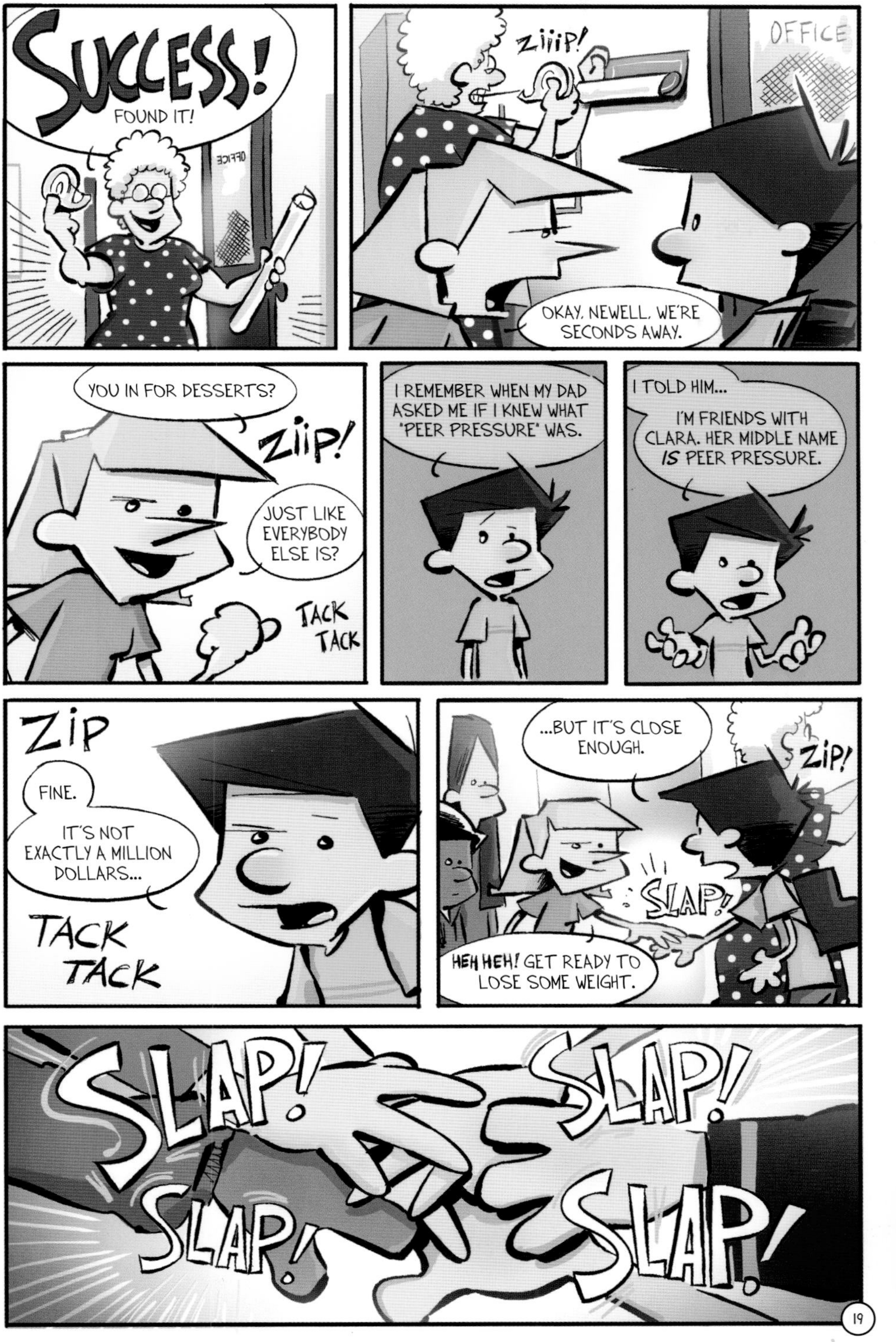
SUCCESS!
FOUND IT!
OFFICE
ZIIIP!
OFFICE
OKAY, NEWELL, WE'RE SECONDS AWAY.
YOU IN FOR DESSERTS?
ZIIP!
JUST LIKE EVERYBODY ELSE IS?
TACK TACK
I REMEMBER WHEN MY DAD ASKED ME IF I KNEW WHAT "PEER PRESSURE" WAS.
I TOLD HIM...
I'M FRIENDS WITH CLARA. HER MIDDLE NAME IS PEER PRESSURE.
ZIP
FINE.
IT'S NOT EXACTLY A MILLION DOLLARS...
TACK TACK
...BUT IT'S CLOSE ENOUGH.
ZIP!
SLAP!
HEH HEH! GET READY TO LOSE SOME WEIGHT.
SLAP!
SLAP!
SLAP!
SLAP!

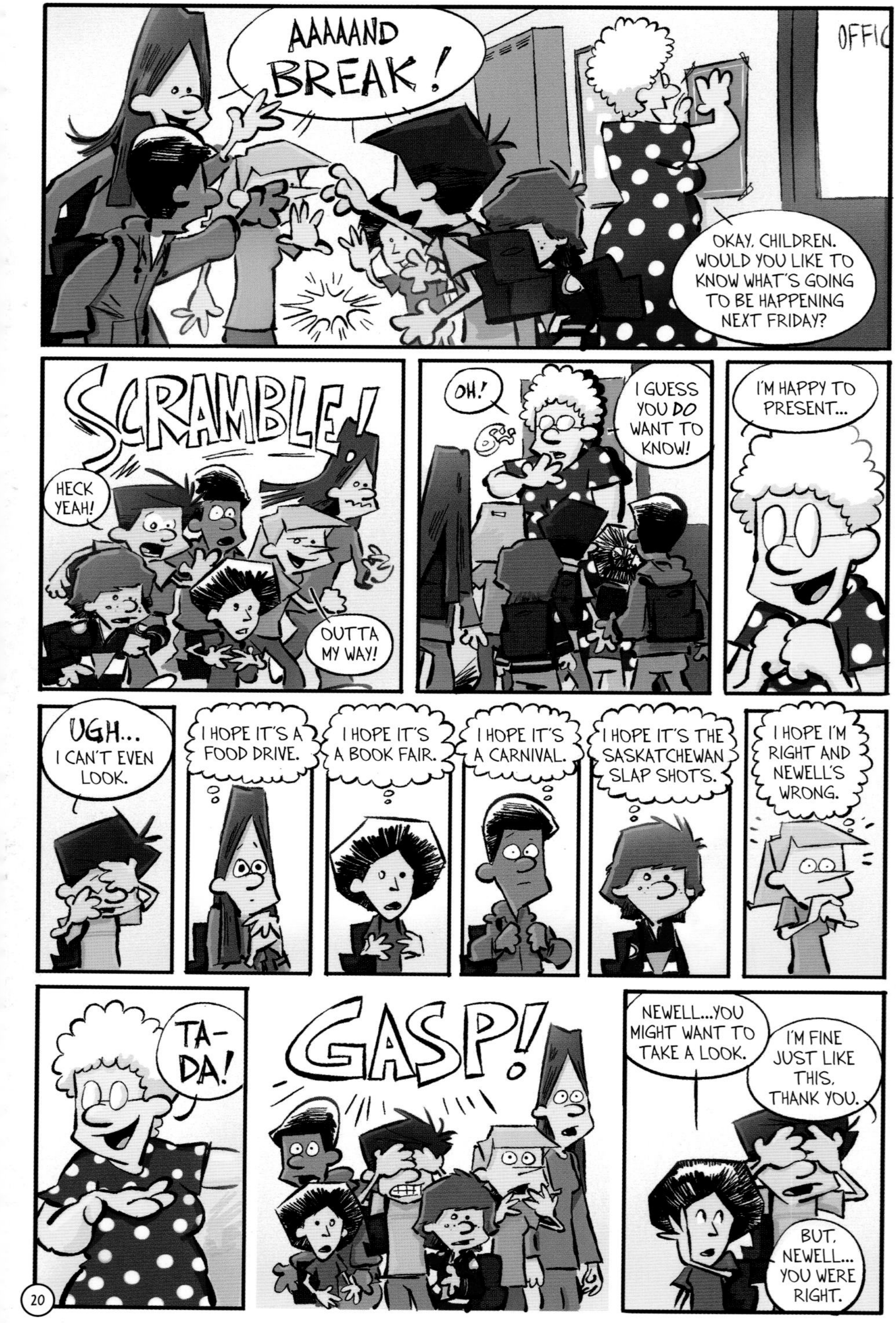
AAAAAND BREAK!
OFFIC
OKAY, CHILDREN. WOULD YOU LIKE TO KNOW WHAT'S GOING TO BE HAPPENING NEXT FRIDAY?
SCRAMBLE!
HECK YEAH!
OUTTA MY WAY!
OH!
I GUESS YOU DO WANT TO KNOW!
I'M HAPPY TO PRESENT...
UGH... I CAN'T EVEN LOOK.
I HOPE IT'S A FOOD DRIVE.
I HOPE IT'S A BOOK FAIR.
I HOPE IT'S A CARNIVAL.
I HOPE IT'S THE SASKATCHEWAN SLAP SHOTS.
I HOPE I'M RIGHT AND NEWELL'S WRONG.
TA-DA!
GASP!
NEWELL...YOU MIGHT WANT TO TAKE A LOOK.
I'M FINE JUST LIKE THIS, THANK YOU.
BUT, NEWELL... YOU WERE RIGHT.

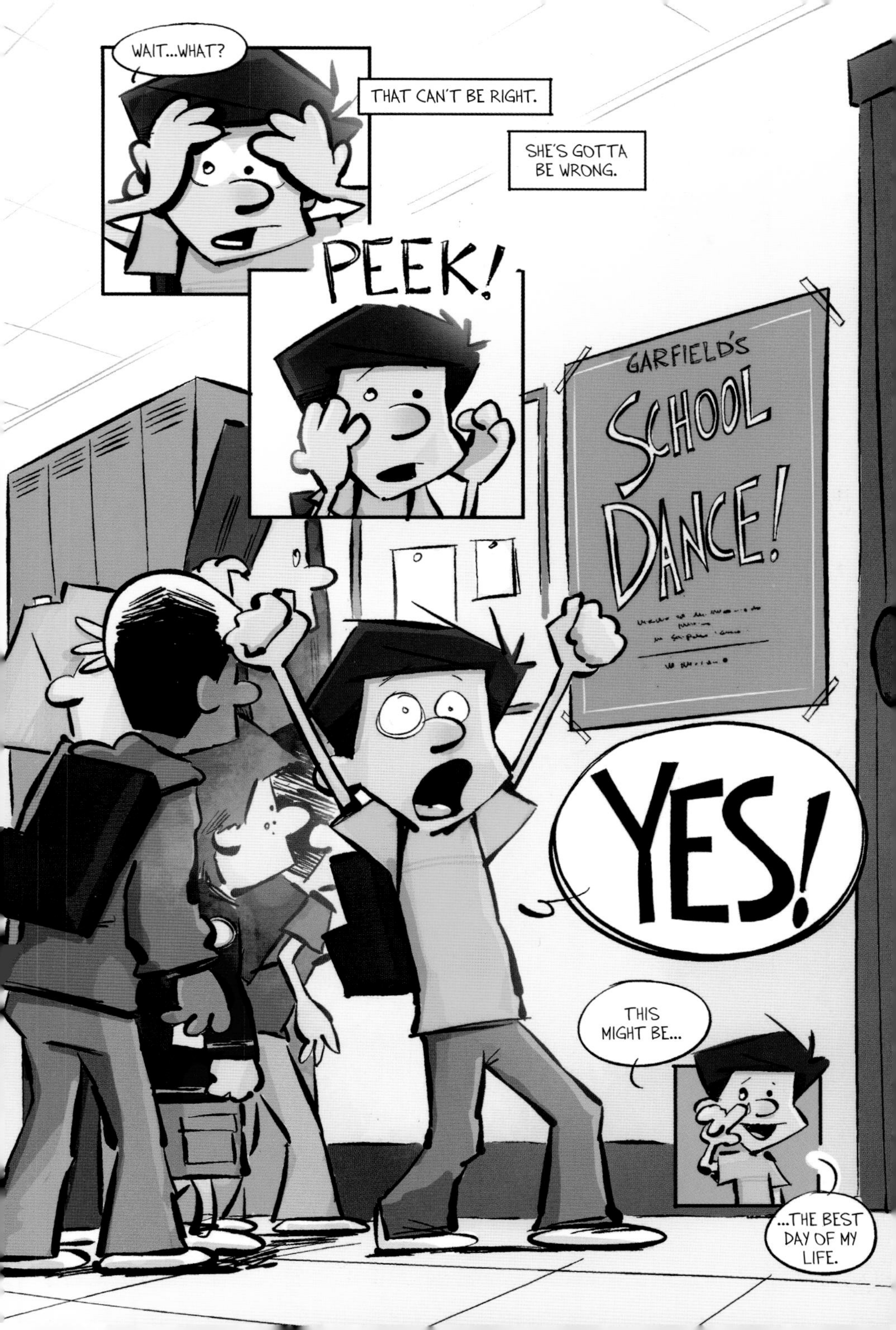
WAIT...WHAT?
THAT CAN'T BE RIGHT.
SHE'S GOTTA BE WRONG.
PEEK!
GARFIELD'S SCHOOL DANCE!
YES!
THIS MIGHT BE...
...THE BEST DAY OF MY LIFE.

CHAPTER TWO
WHAT COULD POSSIBLY GO WRONG?

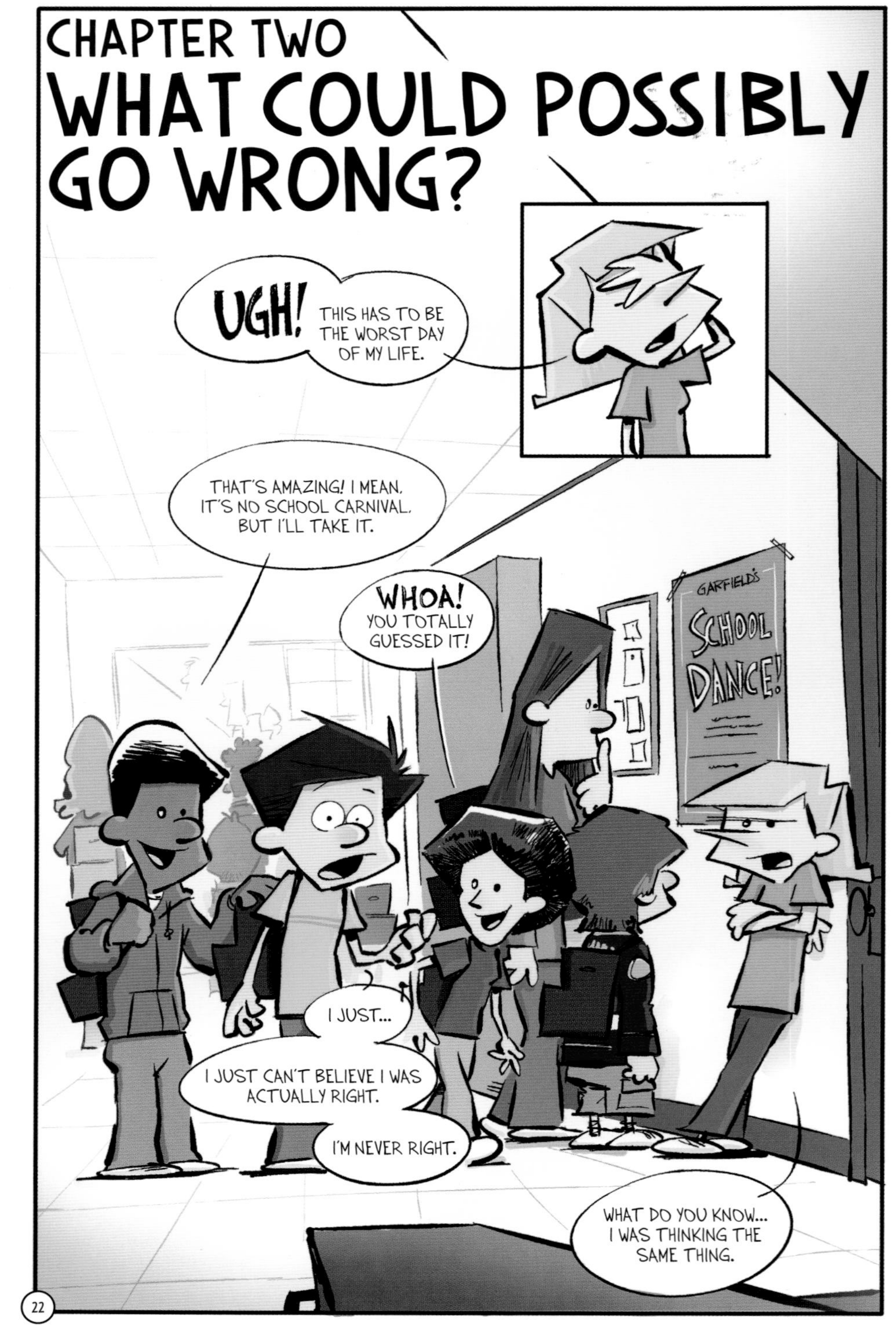

UGH! THIS HAS TO BE THE WORST DAY OF MY LIFE.
THAT'S AMAZING! I MEAN, IT'S NO SCHOOL CARNIVAL, BUT I'LL TAKE IT.
WHOA! YOU TOTALLY GUESSED IT!
GARFIELD'S SCHOOL DANCE!
I JUST...
I JUST CAN'T BELIEVE I WAS ACTUALLY RIGHT.
I'M NEVER RIGHT.
WHAT DO YOU KNOW... I WAS THINKING THE SAME THING.

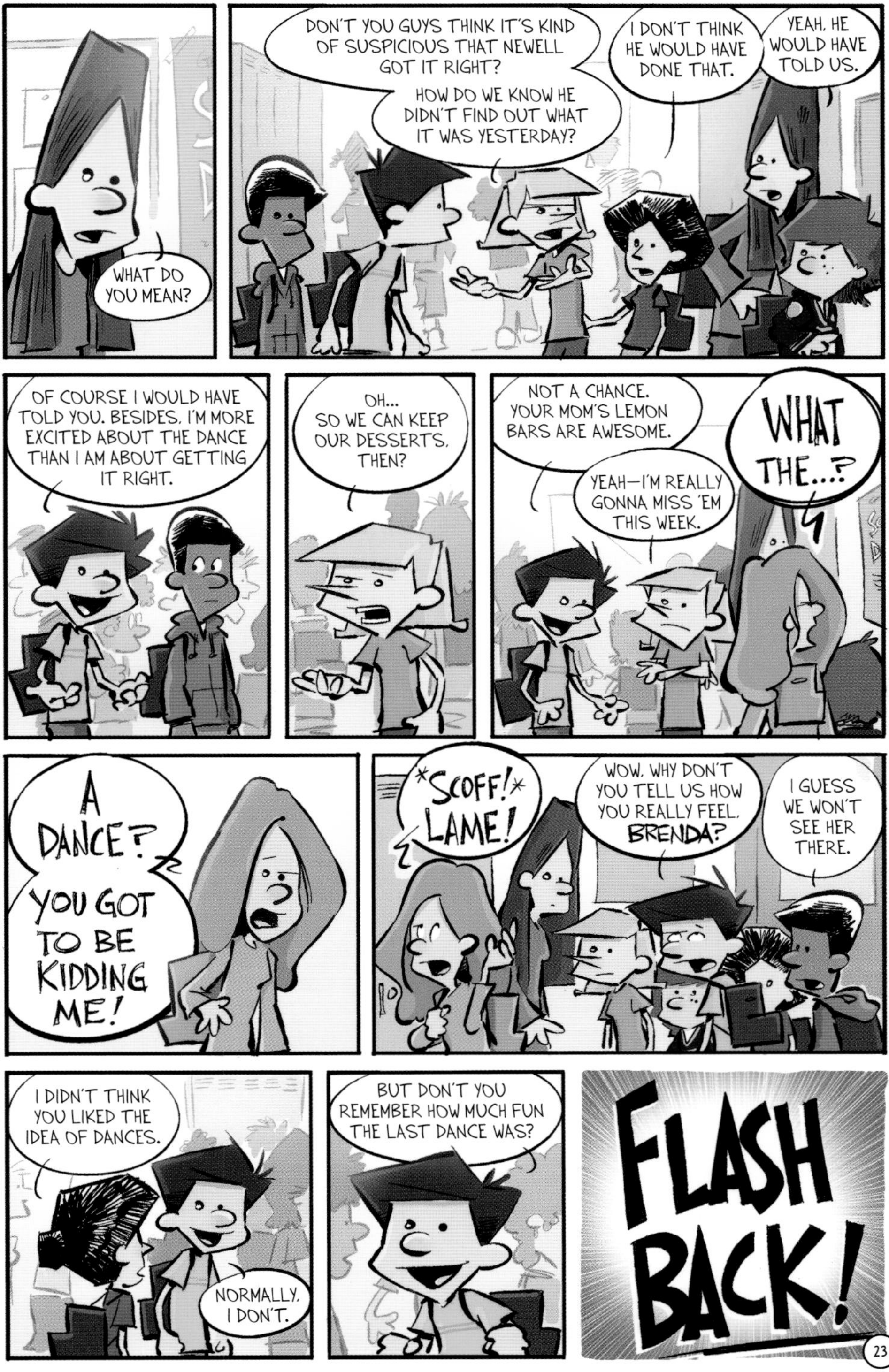
WHAT DO YOU MEAN?
DON'T YOU GUYS THINK IT'S KIND OF SUSPICIOUS THAT NEWELL GOT IT RIGHT?
HOW DO WE KNOW HE DIDN'T FIND OUT WHAT IT WAS YESTERDAY?
I DON'T THINK HE WOULD HAVE DONE THAT.
YEAH, HE WOULD HAVE TOLD US.
OF COURSE I WOULD HAVE TOLD YOU. BESIDES, I'M MORE EXCITED ABOUT THE DANCE THAN I AM ABOUT GETTING IT RIGHT.
OH... SO WE CAN KEEP OUR DESSERTS, THEN?
NOT A CHANCE. YOUR MOM'S LEMON BARS ARE AWESOME.
YEAH—I'M REALLY GONNA MISS 'EM THIS WEEK.
WHAT THE...?
A DANCE?
YOU GOT TO BE KIDDING ME!
SCOFF! LAME!
WOW, WHY DON'T YOU TELL US HOW YOU REALLY FEEL, BRENDA?
I GUESS WE WON'T SEE HER THERE.
I DIDN'T THINK YOU LIKED THE IDEA OF DANCES.
NORMALLY, I DON'T.
BUT DON'T YOU REMEMBER HOW MUCH FUN THE LAST DANCE WAS?
FLASH BACK!

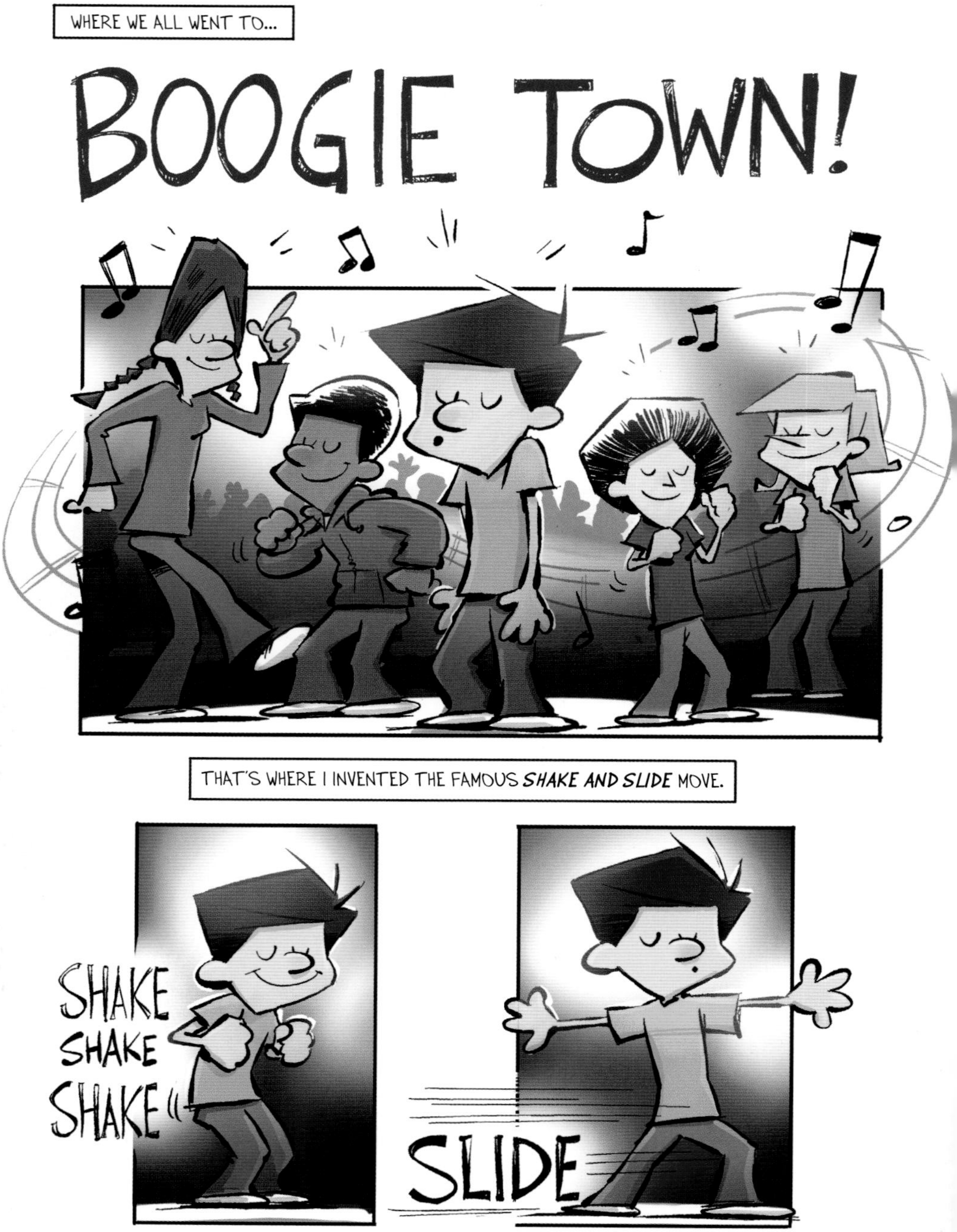
WHERE WE ALL WENT TO...
BOOGIE TOWN!
THAT'S WHERE I INVENTED THE FAMOUS SHAKE AND SLIDE MOVE.
SHAKE
SHAKE
SHAKE
SLIDE
MAN, I WAS SO SMOOTH.

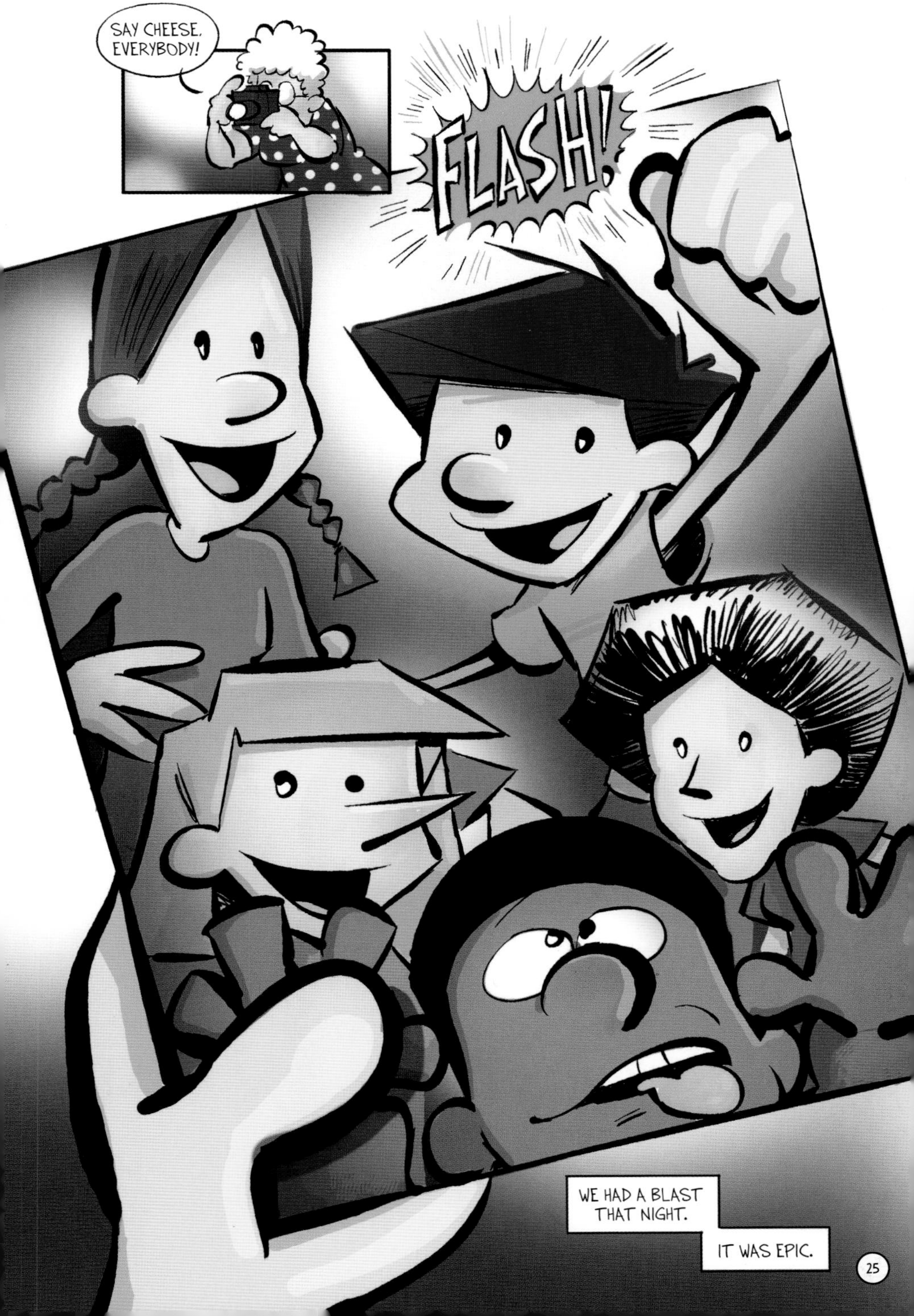
SAY CHEESE, EVERYBODY!
FLASH!
WE HAD A BLAST THAT NIGHT.
IT WAS EPIC.

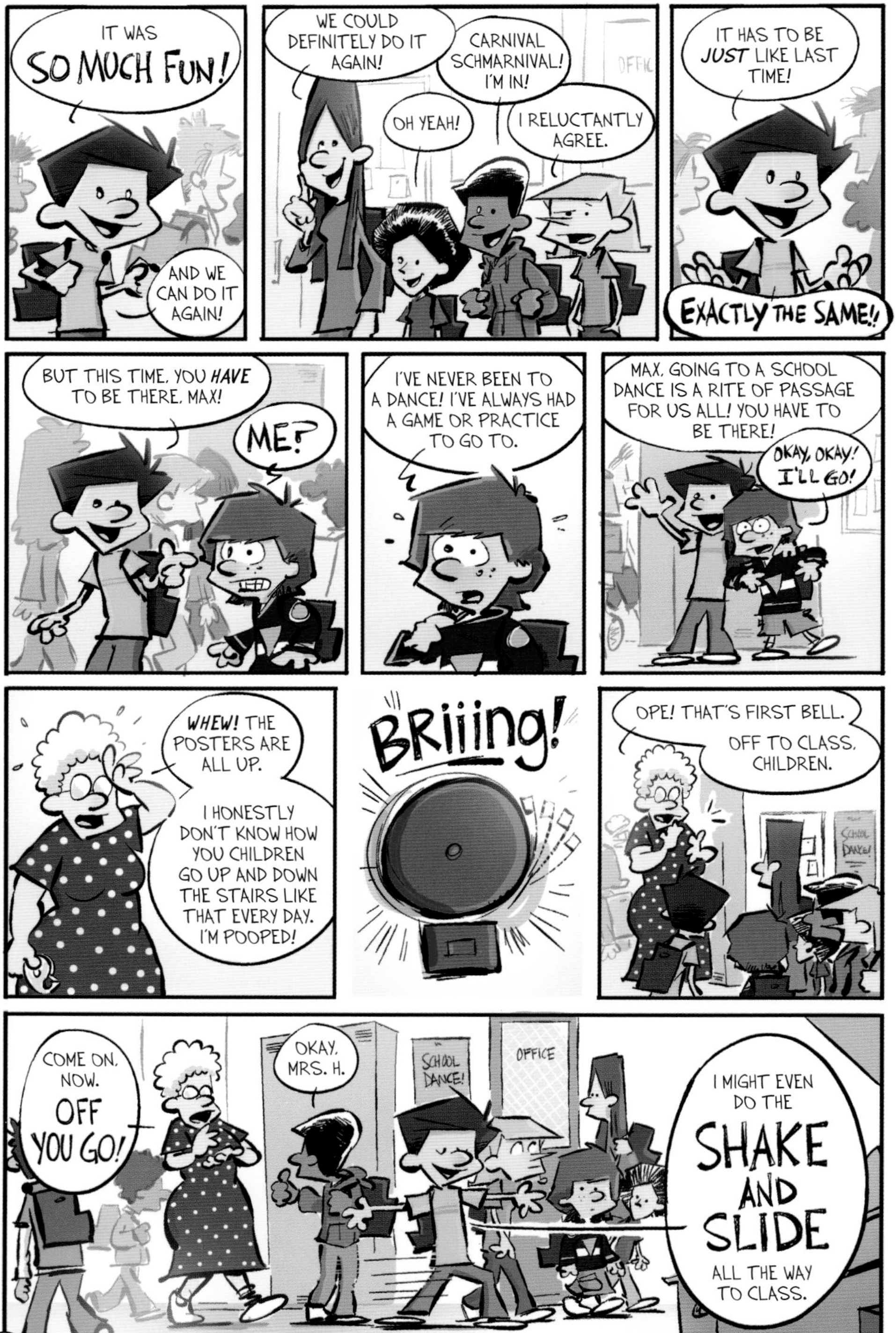
IT WAS SO MUCH FUN!
AND WE CAN DO IT AGAIN!
WE COULD DEFINITELY DO IT AGAIN!
CARNIVAL SCHMARNIVAL! I'M IN!
OH YEAH!
I RELUCTANTLY AGREE.
IT HAS TO BE JUST LIKE LAST TIME!
EXACTLY THE SAME!!
BUT THIS TIME, YOU HAVE TO BE THERE, MAX!
ME?
I'VE NEVER BEEN TO A DANCE! I'VE ALWAYS HAD A GAME OR PRACTICE TO GO TO.
MAX, GOING TO A SCHOOL DANCE IS A RITE OF PASSAGE FOR US ALL! YOU HAVE TO BE THERE!
OKAY, OKAY! I'LL GO!
WHEW! THE POSTERS ARE ALL UP.
I HONESTLY DON'T KNOW HOW YOU CHILDREN GO UP AND DOWN THE STAIRS LIKE THAT EVERY DAY. I'M POOPED!
BRiiing!
OPE! THAT'S FIRST BELL.
OFF TO CLASS, CHILDREN.
COME ON, NOW. OFF YOU GO!
OKAY, MRS. H.
SCHOOL DANCE!
OFFICE
I MIGHT EVEN DO THE SHAKE AND SLIDE ALL THE WAY TO CLASS.

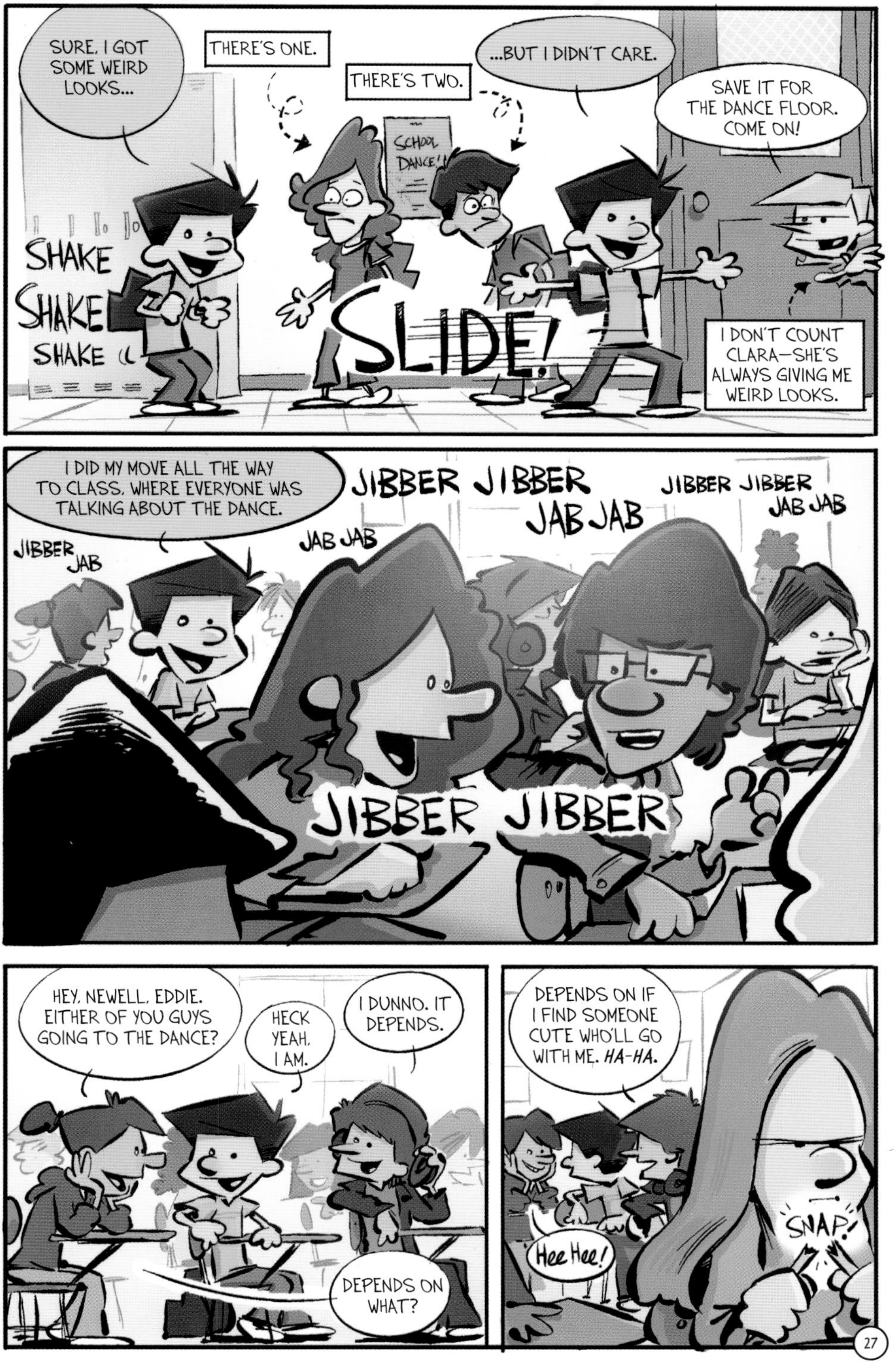
SURE, I GOT SOME WEIRD LOOKS...
THERE'S ONE.
THERE'S TWO.
...BUT I DIDN'T CARE.
SAVE IT FOR THE DANCE FLOOR. COME ON!
SCHOOL DANCE!
SHAKE
SHAKE
SHAKE
SLIDE!
I DON'T COUNT CLARA—SHE'S ALWAYS GIVING ME WEIRD LOOKS.
I DID MY MOVE ALL THE WAY TO CLASS, WHERE EVERYONE WAS TALKING ABOUT THE DANCE.
JIBBER JIBBER JAB JAB
JIBBER JIBBER JAB JAB
JIBBER JAB
JAB JAB
JIBBER JIBBER
HEY, NEWELL, EDDIE. EITHER OF YOU GUYS GOING TO THE DANCE?
HECK YEAH, I AM.
I DUNNO. IT DEPENDS.
DEPENDS ON WHAT?
DEPENDS ON IF I FIND SOMEONE CUTE WHO'LL GO WITH ME. *HA-HA.*
Hee Hee!
SNAP!

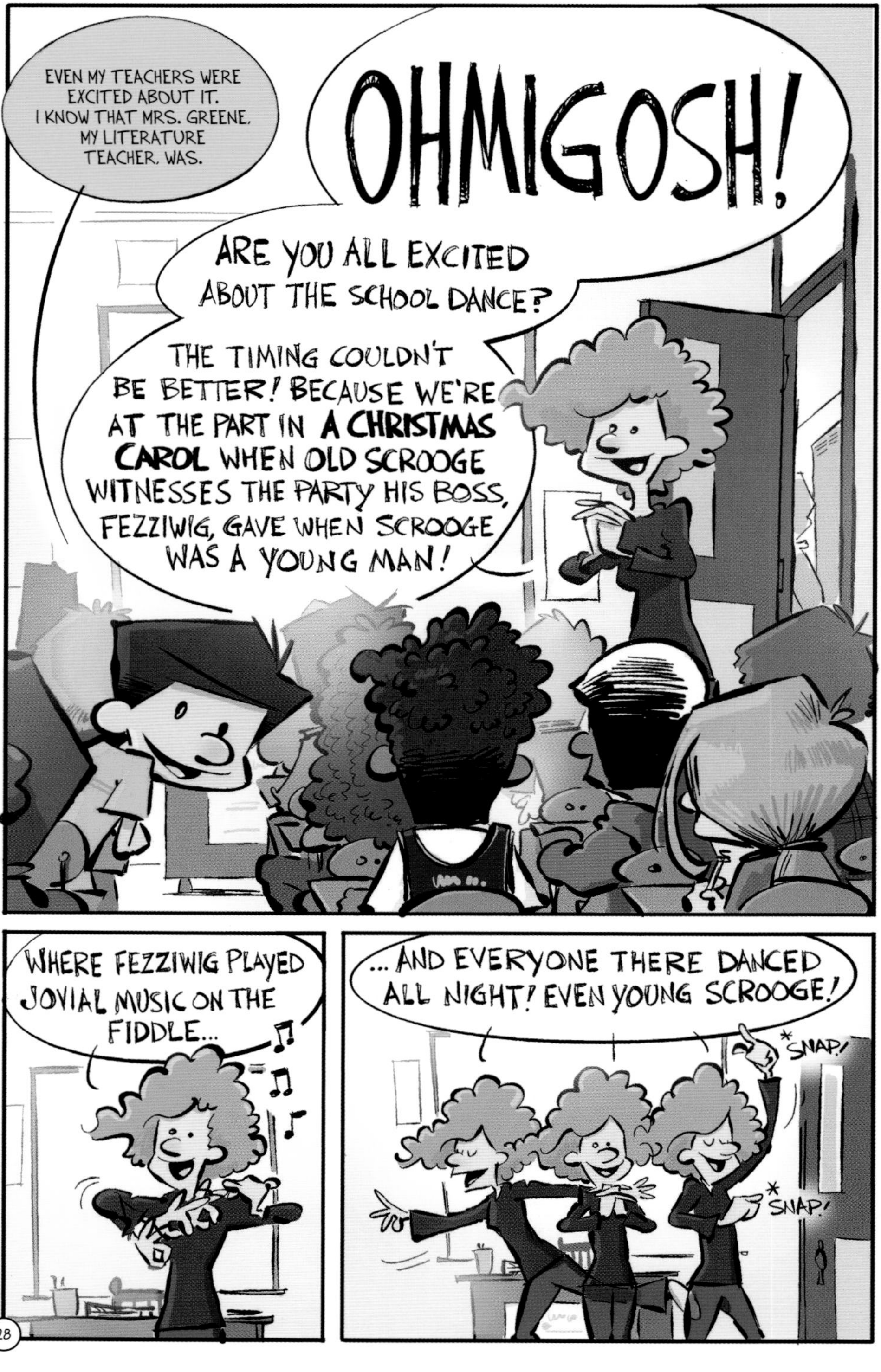
EVEN MY TEACHERS WERE EXCITED ABOUT IT. I KNOW THAT MRS. GREENE, MY LITERATURE TEACHER, WAS.
OHMIGOSH!
ARE YOU ALL EXCITED ABOUT THE SCHOOL DANCE?
THE TIMING COULDN'T BE BETTER! BECAUSE WE'RE AT THE PART IN A CHRISTMAS CAROL WHEN OLD SCROOGE WITNESSES THE PARTY HIS BOSS, FEZZIWIG, GAVE WHEN SCROOGE WAS A YOUNG MAN!
WHERE FEZZIWIG PLAYED JOVIAL MUSIC ON THE FIDDLE...
...AND EVERYONE THERE DANCED ALL NIGHT! EVEN YOUNG SCROOGE!
*SNAP!
*SNAP!

SO MY QUESTION TO YOU IS...

...ARE YOU A *YOUNG* SCROOGE?

OR AN **OLD** SCROOGE?

A YOUNG ONE...

BUT THAT'S NOT ALL.

MISS TANNER, MY MATH TEACHER, WAS EXCITED ABOUT IT, TOO.

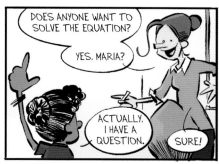

DOES ANYONE WANT TO SOLVE THE EQUATION?

YES, MARIA?

ACTUALLY, I HAVE A QUESTION.

SURE!

I HEARD YOU'RE GOING TO THE DANCE, TOO. IS THAT TRUE?

IT *IS* TRUE. I'VE CHAPERONED EVERY DANCE SINCE I STARTED TEACHING HERE.

WHAT'S A CHAPERONE?

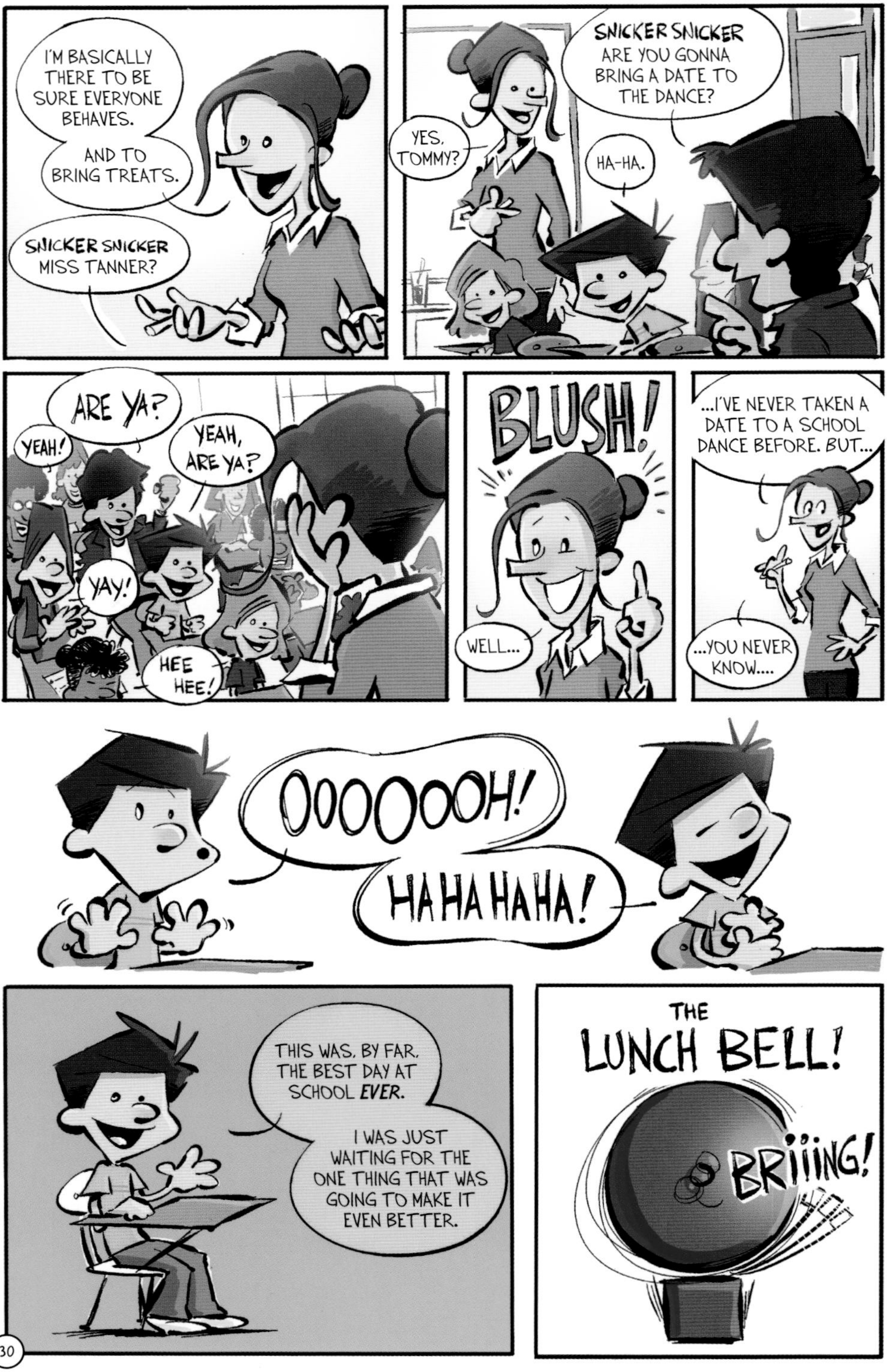

I'M BASICALLY THERE TO BE SURE EVERYONE BEHAVES.
AND TO BRING TREATS.
SNICKER SNICKER MISS TANNER?
YES, TOMMY?
SNICKER SNICKER ARE YOU GONNA BRING A DATE TO THE DANCE?
HA-HA.
ARE YA?
YEAH!
YEAH, ARE YA?
YAY!
HEE HEE!
BLUSH!
WELL...
...I'VE NEVER TAKEN A DATE TO A SCHOOL DANCE BEFORE. BUT...
...YOU NEVER KNOW....
OOOOOOH!
HAHAHAHA!
THIS WAS, BY FAR, THE BEST DAY AT SCHOOL *EVER*.
I WAS JUST WAITING FOR THE ONE THING THAT WAS GOING TO MAKE IT EVEN BETTER.
THE LUNCH BELL!
BRIIING!

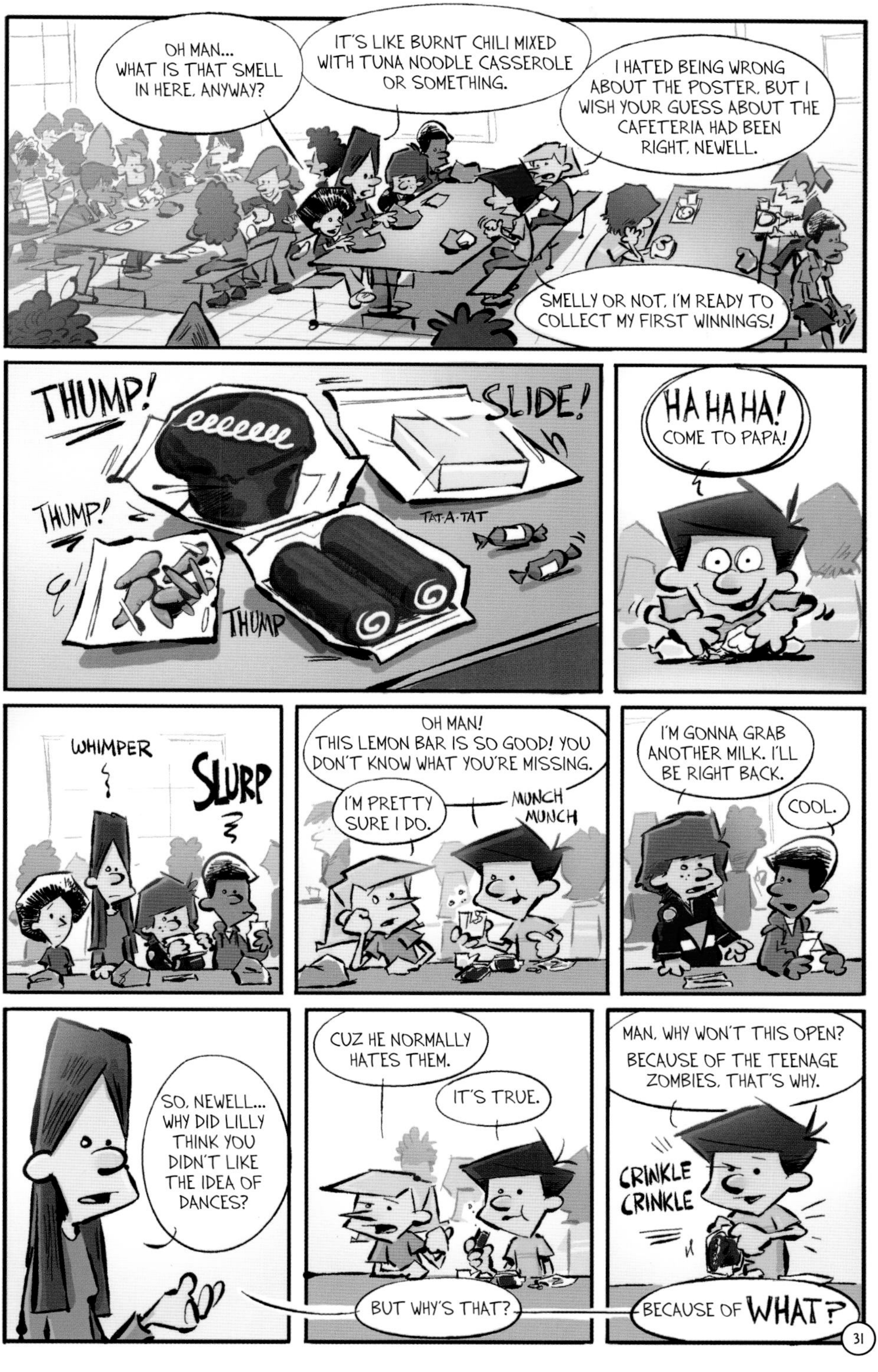
OH MAN... WHAT IS THAT SMELL IN HERE, ANYWAY?
IT'S LIKE BURNT CHILI MIXED WITH TUNA NOODLE CASSEROLE OR SOMETHING.
I HATED BEING WRONG ABOUT THE POSTER, BUT I WISH YOUR GUESS ABOUT THE CAFETERIA HAD BEEN RIGHT, NEWELL.
SMELLY OR NOT, I'M READY TO COLLECT MY FIRST WINNINGS!
THUMP!
SLIDE!
THUMP!
TAT-A-TAT
THUMP
HA HA HA! COME TO PAPA!
WHIMPER
SLURP
OH MAN! THIS LEMON BAR IS SO GOOD! YOU DON'T KNOW WHAT YOU'RE MISSING.
I'M PRETTY SURE I DO.
MUNCH MUNCH
I'M GONNA GRAB ANOTHER MILK. I'LL BE RIGHT BACK.
COOL.
SO, NEWELL... WHY DID LILLY THINK YOU DIDN'T LIKE THE IDEA OF DANCES?
CUZ HE NORMALLY HATES THEM.
IT'S TRUE.
BUT WHY'S THAT?
MAN, WHY WON'T THIS OPEN?
BECAUSE OF THE TEENAGE ZOMBIES, THAT'S WHY.
CRINKLE CRINKLE
BECAUSE OF WHAT?

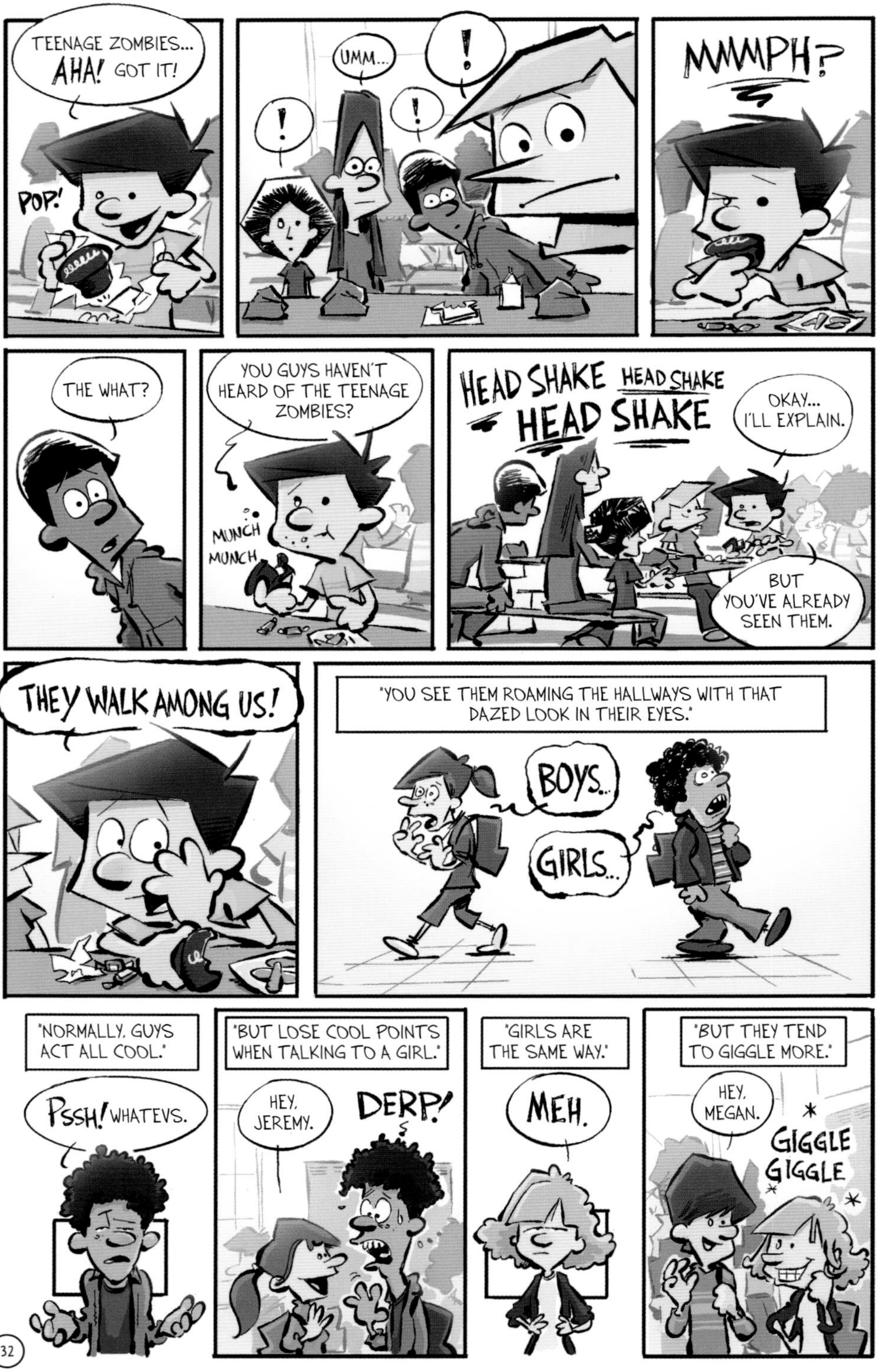

TEENAGE ZOMBIES... AHA! GOT IT!
POP!
UMM...
!
!
!
MMMPH?
THE WHAT?
YOU GUYS HAVEN'T HEARD OF THE TEENAGE ZOMBIES?
MUNCH
MUNCH
HEAD SHAKE HEAD SHAKE
HEAD SHAKE
OKAY... I'LL EXPLAIN.
BUT YOU'VE ALREADY SEEN THEM.
THEY WALK AMONG US!
"YOU SEE THEM ROAMING THE HALLWAYS WITH THAT DAZED LOOK IN THEIR EYES."
BOYS...
GIRLS...
"NORMALLY, GUYS ACT ALL COOL."
PSSH! WHATEVS.
"BUT LOSE COOL POINTS WHEN TALKING TO A GIRL."
HEY, JEREMY.
DERP!
"GIRLS ARE THE SAME WAY."
MEH.
"BUT THEY TEND TO GIGGLE MORE."
HEY, MEGAN.
GIGGLE GIGGLE

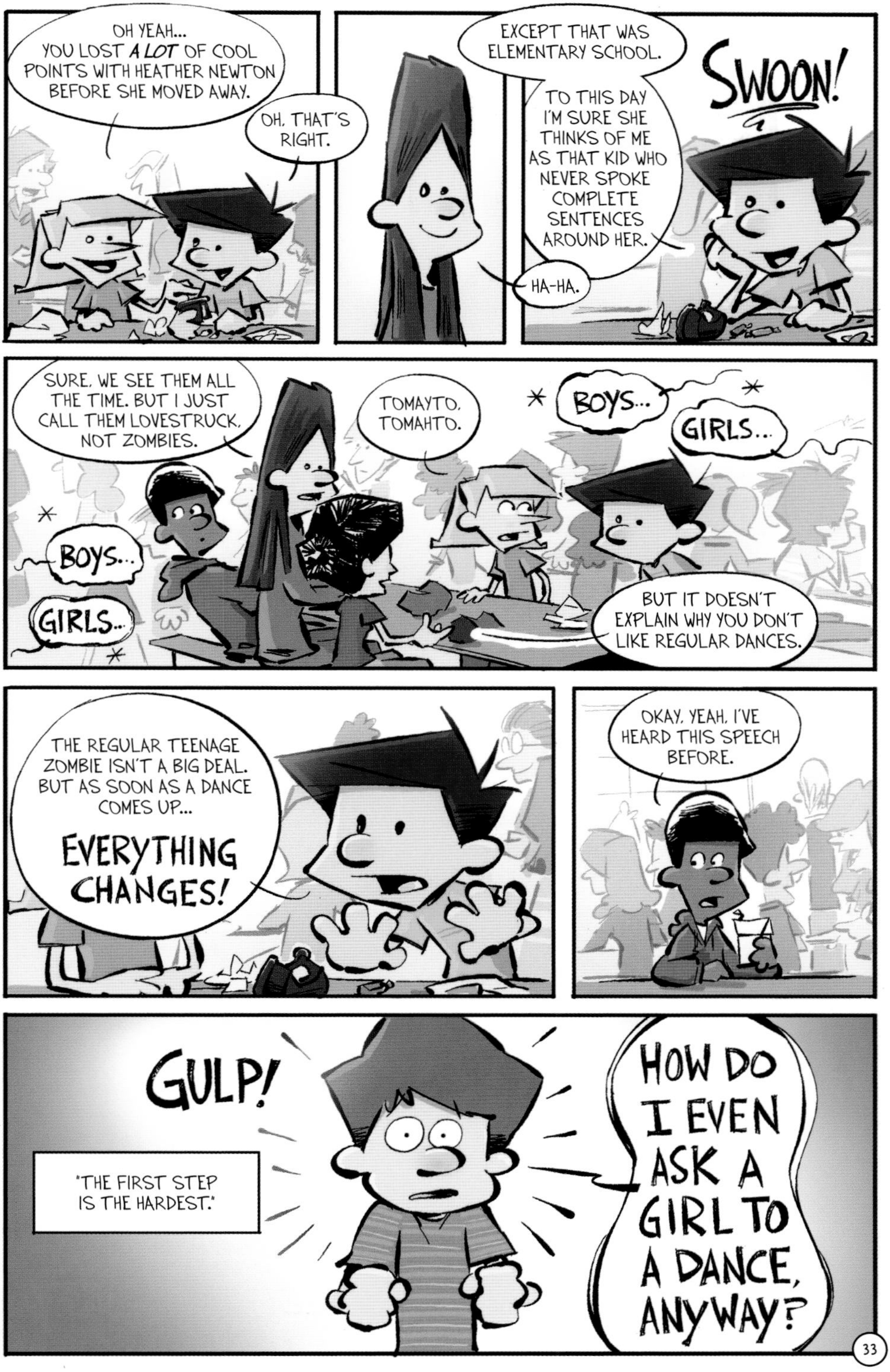

OH YEAH... YOU LOST A LOT OF COOL POINTS WITH HEATHER NEWTON BEFORE SHE MOVED AWAY.
OH, THAT'S RIGHT.
EXCEPT THAT WAS ELEMENTARY SCHOOL.
TO THIS DAY I'M SURE SHE THINKS OF ME AS THAT KID WHO NEVER SPOKE COMPLETE SENTENCES AROUND HER.
HA-HA.
SWOON!
SURE, WE SEE THEM ALL THE TIME. BUT I JUST CALL THEM LOVESTRUCK, NOT ZOMBIES.
TOMAYTO, TOMAHTO.
BOYS...
GIRLS...
BOYS...
GIRLS...
BUT IT DOESN'T EXPLAIN WHY YOU DON'T LIKE REGULAR DANCES.
THE REGULAR TEENAGE ZOMBIE ISN'T A BIG DEAL. BUT AS SOON AS A DANCE COMES UP...
EVERYTHING CHANGES!
OKAY, YEAH, I'VE HEARD THIS SPEECH BEFORE.
GULP!
"THE FIRST STEP IS THE HARDEST."
HOW DO I EVEN ASK A GIRL TO A DANCE, ANYWAY?

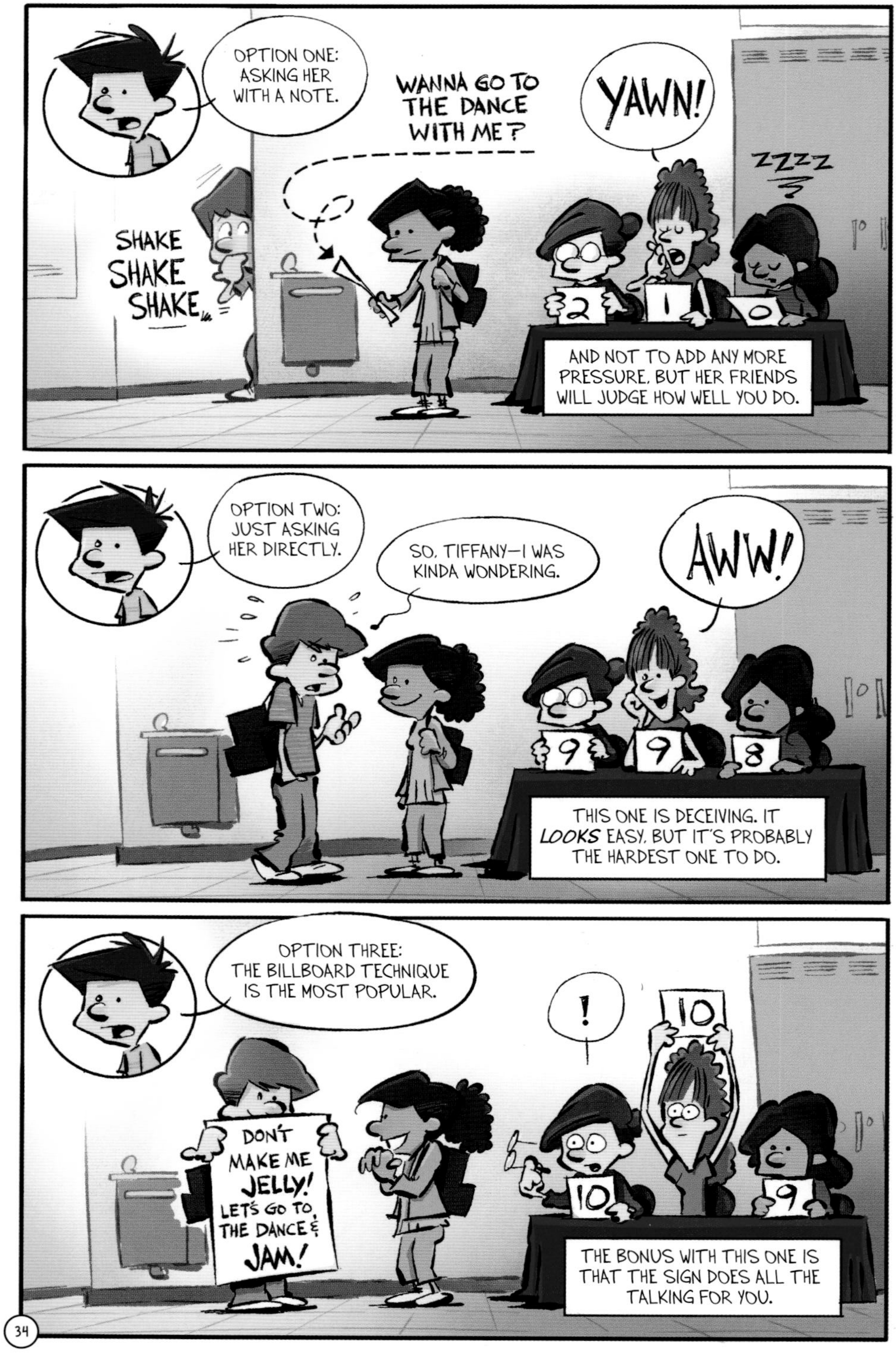
OPTION ONE: ASKING HER WITH A NOTE.
WANNA GO TO THE DANCE WITH ME?
YAWN!
ZZZZ
SHAKE SHAKE SHAKE
2
1
0
AND NOT TO ADD ANY MORE PRESSURE, BUT HER FRIENDS WILL JUDGE HOW WELL YOU DO.
OPTION TWO: JUST ASKING HER DIRECTLY.
SO, TIFFANY—I WAS KINDA WONDERING.
AWW!
9
9
8
THIS ONE IS DECEIVING. IT *LOOKS* EASY, BUT IT'S PROBABLY THE HARDEST ONE TO DO.
OPTION THREE: THE BILLBOARD TECHNIQUE IS THE MOST POPULAR.
!
10
DON'T MAKE ME JELLY! LET'S GO TO THE DANCE & JAM!
10
9
THE BONUS WITH THIS ONE IS THAT THE SIGN DOES ALL THE TALKING FOR YOU.

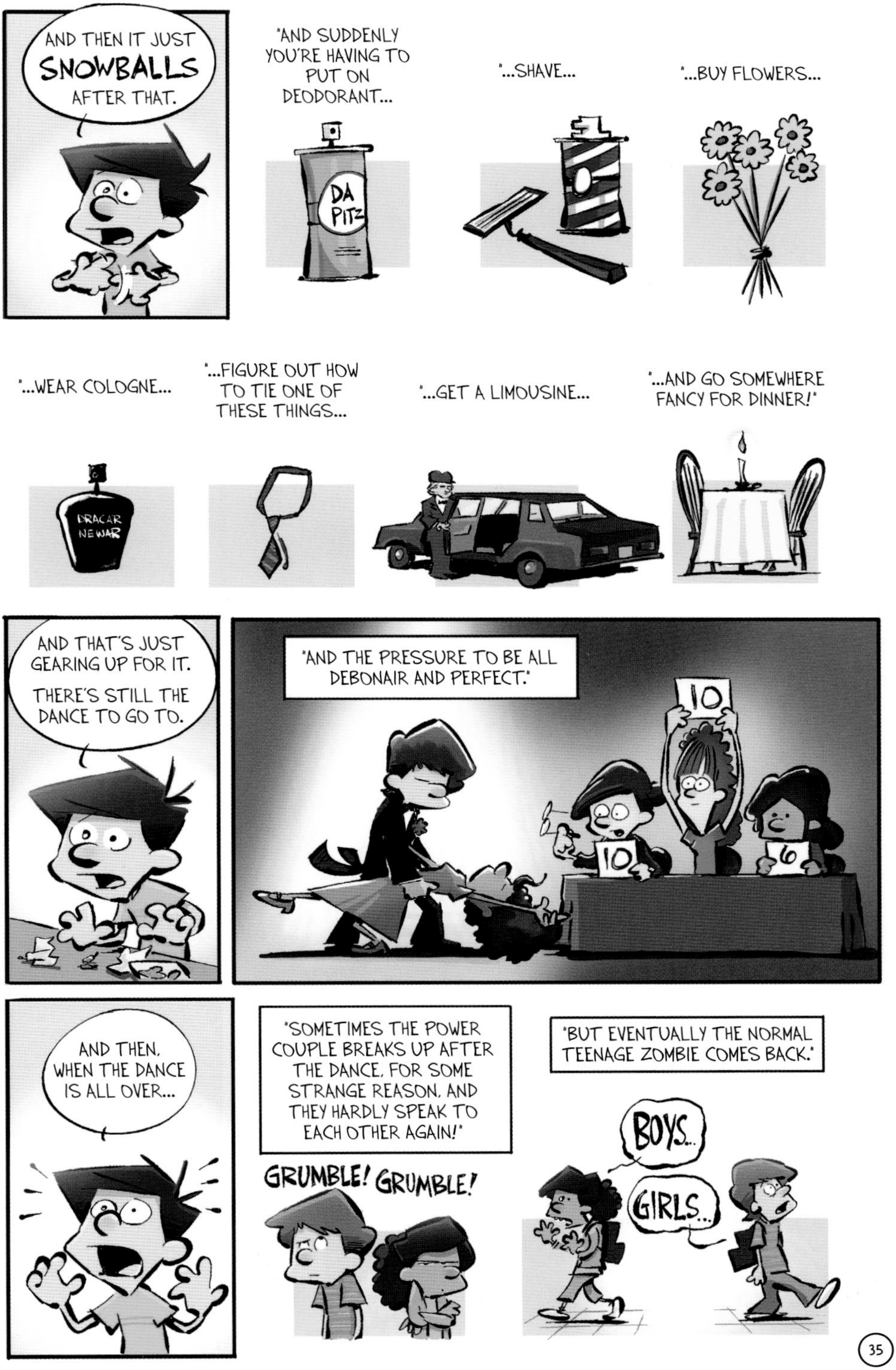

AND THEN IT JUST SNOWBALLS AFTER THAT.
"AND SUDDENLY YOU'RE HAVING TO PUT ON DEODORANT...
DA PITZ
"...SHAVE...
"...BUY FLOWERS...
"...WEAR COLOGNE...
DRACAR NEWAR
"...FIGURE OUT HOW TO TIE ONE OF THESE THINGS...
"...GET A LIMOUSINE...
"...AND GO SOMEWHERE FANCY FOR DINNER!"
AND THAT'S JUST GEARING UP FOR IT.
THERE'S STILL THE DANCE TO GO TO.
"AND THE PRESSURE TO BE ALL DEBONAIR AND PERFECT."
10
10
6
AND THEN, WHEN THE DANCE IS ALL OVER...
"SOMETIMES THE POWER COUPLE BREAKS UP AFTER THE DANCE, FOR SOME STRANGE REASON, AND THEY HARDLY SPEAK TO EACH OTHER AGAIN!"
GRUMBLE! GRUMBLE!
"BUT EVENTUALLY THE NORMAL TEENAGE ZOMBIE COMES BACK."
BOYS...
GIRLS...

ONLY TO START THE PROCESS ALL OVER AGAIN.

SOOO...

POP!

CRINKLE CRINKLE

CHOMP CHOMP CHOMP! THAT'S WHY I DON'T LIKE REGULAR DANCES AND WHY I LOVE OURS.

NO PRESSURE. NO STRESS. JUST PLAIN FUN.

ALL RIGHT, I'M JUST GOING TO POINT OUT THE OBVIOUS.

DEODORANT ISN'T JUST FOR SPECIAL OCCASIONS. YOU CAN WEAR IT EVERY DAY. IN FACT, WE WOULD LIKE IT IF YOU DID.

HA HA.

CRINKLE CRINKLE

OKAY, I GET WHY YOU DON'T LIKE DANCES, BUT—

BUT...?

BUT IF WE'RE GOING BY MOVIES, THEN GIRLS FEEL JUST AS MUCH PRESSURE.

YUP.

SING IT, SISTER.

LIKE HOW?

"FIRST OF ALL, YOU DON'T KNOW IF ANYONE WILL EVEN ASK YOU."

"AND IT'S HARD WHEN THE ONE YOU'RE CRUSHING ON ASKS SOMEONE ELSE."

SIGH

Hee Hee, YES!

I'D RELISH IT IF WE COULD KETCHUP AT THE DANCE!

"EVEN IF SOMEONE DOES ASK YOU, IT DOESN'T MEAN YOU WANT TO GO WITH THEM."

HEY, DARLIN'... WANNA BOOGIE?

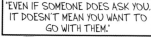

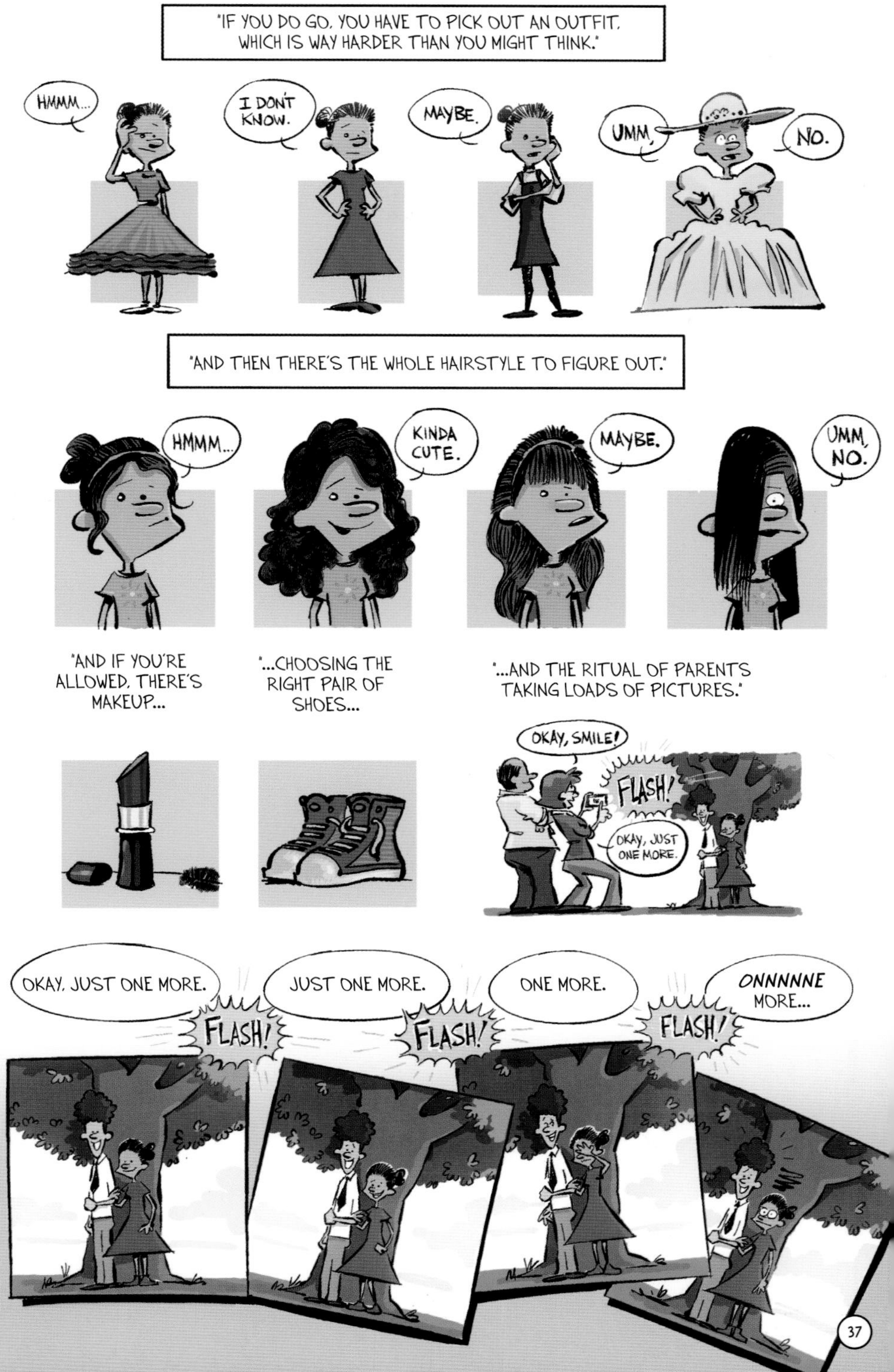
"IF YOU DO GO, YOU HAVE TO PICK OUT AN OUTFIT, WHICH IS WAY HARDER THAN YOU MIGHT THINK."
HMMM...
I DON'T KNOW.
MAYBE.
UMM,
NO.
"AND THEN THERE'S THE WHOLE HAIRSTYLE TO FIGURE OUT."
HMMM...
KINDA CUTE.
MAYBE.
UMM, NO.
"AND IF YOU'RE ALLOWED, THERE'S MAKEUP...
"...CHOOSING THE RIGHT PAIR OF SHOES...
"...AND THE RITUAL OF PARENTS TAKING LOADS OF PICTURES."
OKAY, SMILE!
FLASH!
OKAY, JUST ONE MORE.
OKAY, JUST ONE MORE.
FLASH!
JUST ONE MORE.
FLASH!
ONE MORE.
FLASH!
ONNNNNE MORE...

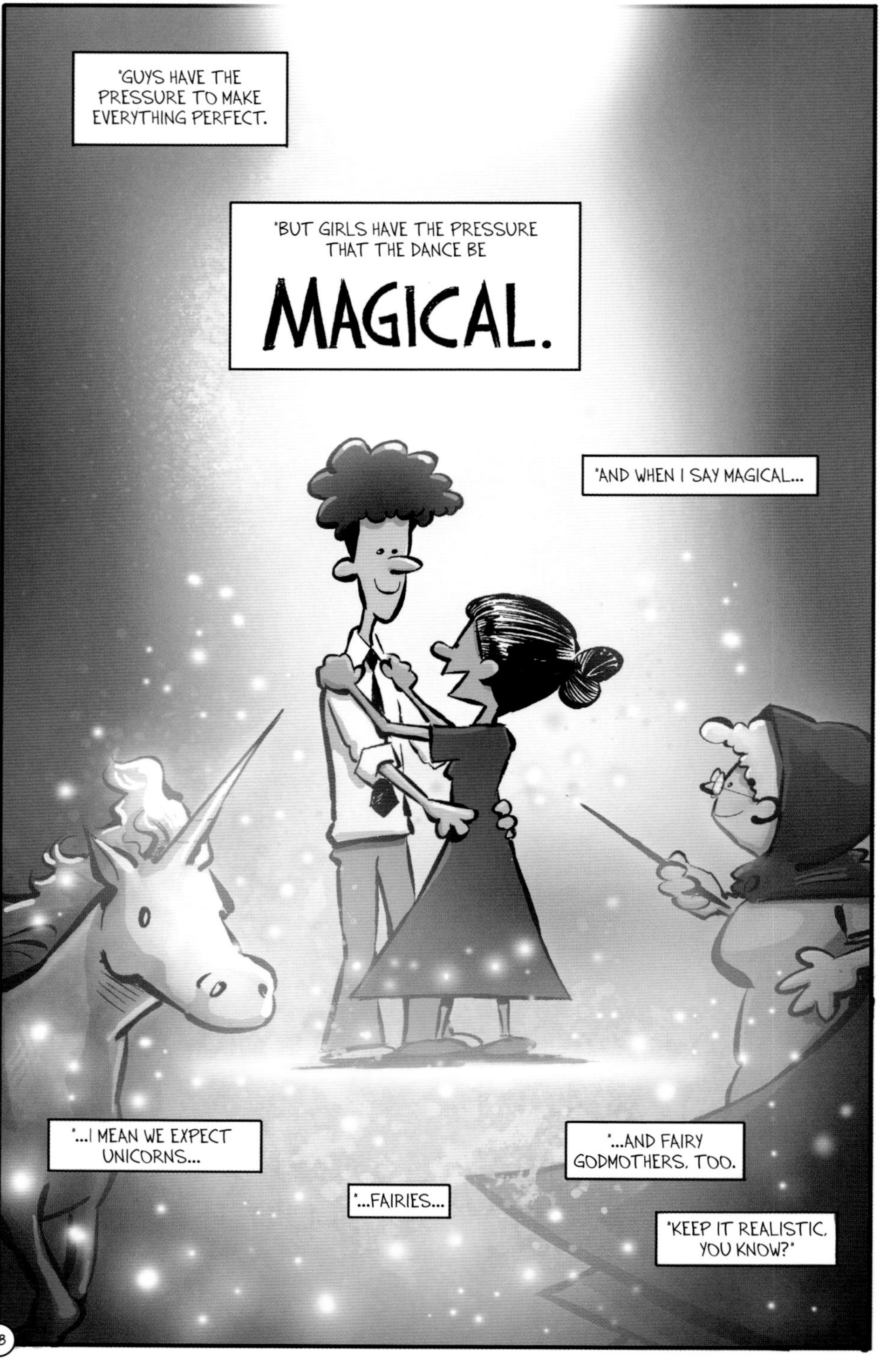
"GUYS HAVE THE PRESSURE TO MAKE EVERYTHING PERFECT.
"BUT GIRLS HAVE THE PRESSURE THAT THE DANCE BE
MAGICAL.
"AND WHEN I SAY MAGICAL...
"...I MEAN WE EXPECT UNICORNS...
"...FAIRIES...
"...AND FAIRY GODMOTHERS, TOO.
"KEEP IT REALISTIC, YOU KNOW?"

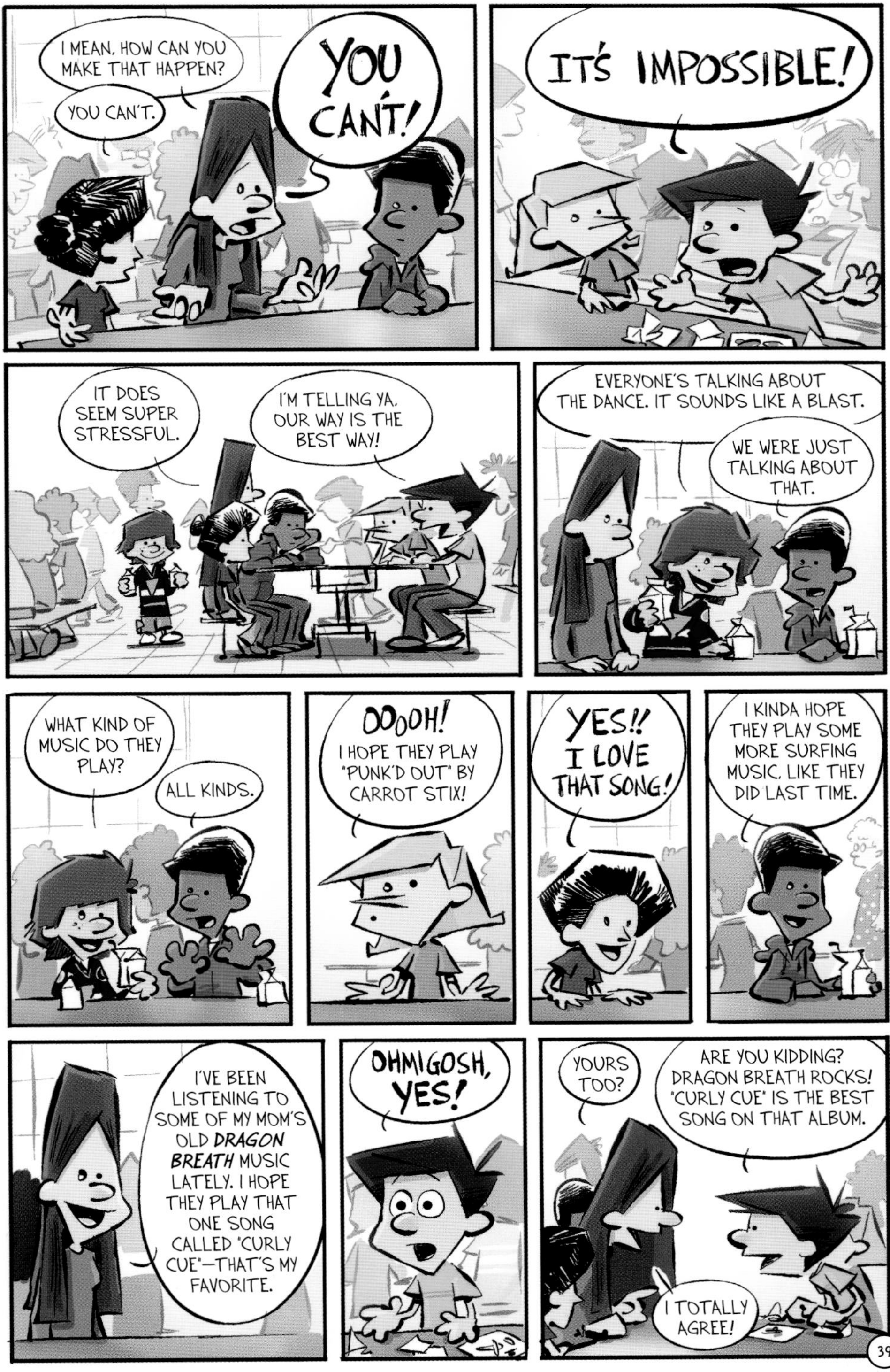
I MEAN, HOW CAN YOU MAKE THAT HAPPEN?
YOU CAN'T.
YOU CAN'T!
IT'S IMPOSSIBLE!
IT DOES SEEM SUPER STRESSFUL.
I'M TELLING YA, OUR WAY IS THE BEST WAY!
EVERYONE'S TALKING ABOUT THE DANCE. IT SOUNDS LIKE A BLAST.
WE WERE JUST TALKING ABOUT THAT.
WHAT KIND OF MUSIC DO THEY PLAY?
ALL KINDS.
OOOOH! I HOPE THEY PLAY "PUNK'D OUT" BY CARROT STIX!
YES!! I LOVE THAT SONG!
I KINDA HOPE THEY PLAY SOME MORE SURFING MUSIC, LIKE THEY DID LAST TIME.
I'VE BEEN LISTENING TO SOME OF MY MOM'S OLD DRAGON BREATH MUSIC LATELY. I HOPE THEY PLAY THAT ONE SONG CALLED "CURLY CUE"—THAT'S MY FAVORITE.
OHMIGOSH, YES!
YOURS TOO?
ARE YOU KIDDING? DRAGON BREATH ROCKS! "CURLY CUE" IS THE BEST SONG ON THAT ALBUM.
I TOTALLY AGREE!

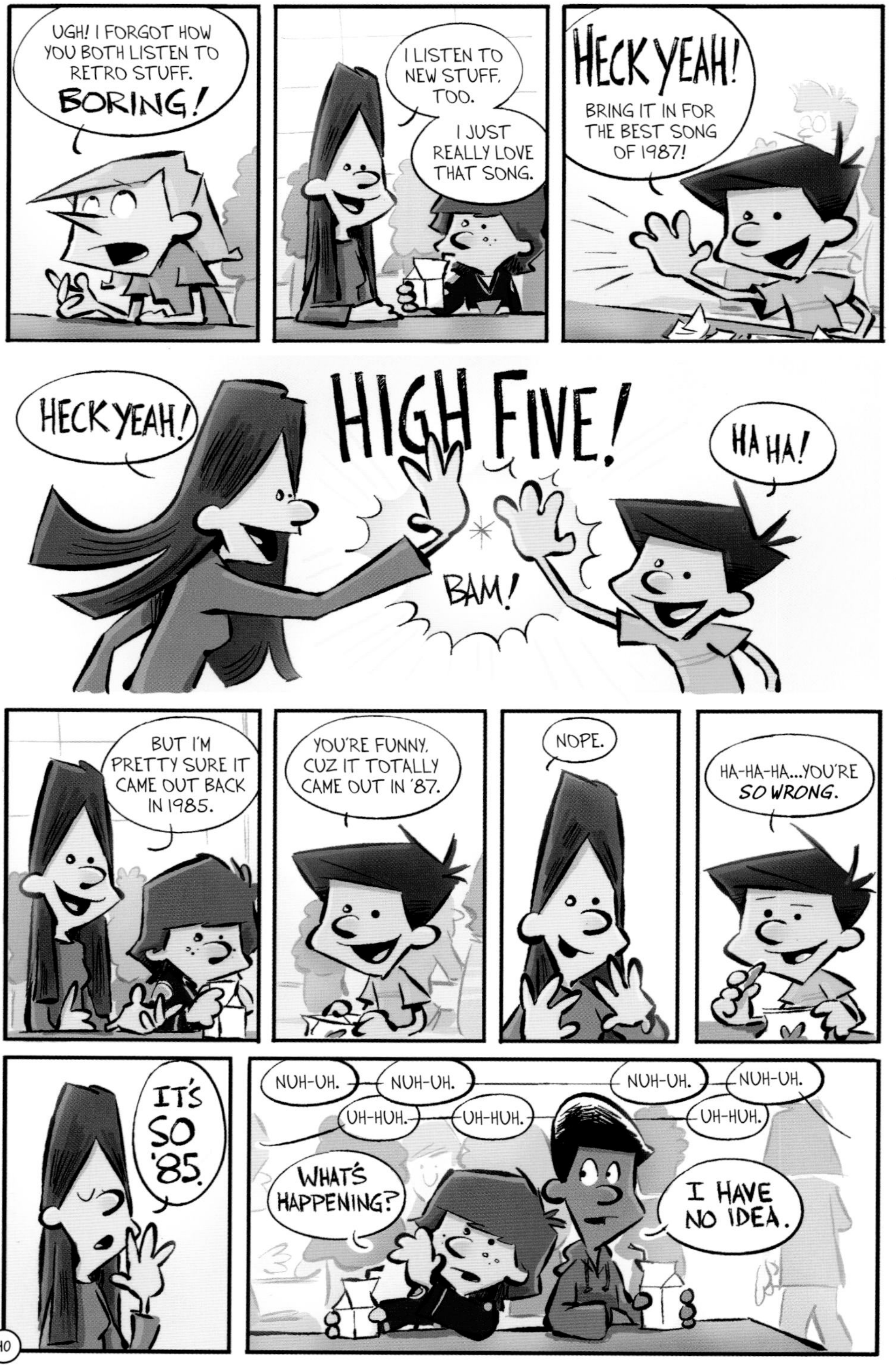
UGH! I FORGOT HOW YOU BOTH LISTEN TO RETRO STUFF. BORING!
I LISTEN TO NEW STUFF, TOO.
I JUST REALLY LOVE THAT SONG.
HECK YEAH!
BRING IT IN FOR THE BEST SONG OF 1987!
HECK YEAH!
HIGH FIVE!
HA HA!
BAM!
BUT I'M PRETTY SURE IT CAME OUT BACK IN 1985.
YOU'RE FUNNY, CUZ IT TOTALLY CAME OUT IN '87.
NOPE.
HA-HA-HA...YOU'RE SO WRONG.
IT'S SO '85.
NUH-UH.
UH-HUH.
NUH-UH.
UH-HUH.
NUH-UH.
UH-HUH.
NUH-UH.
WHAT'S HAPPENING?
I HAVE NO IDEA.

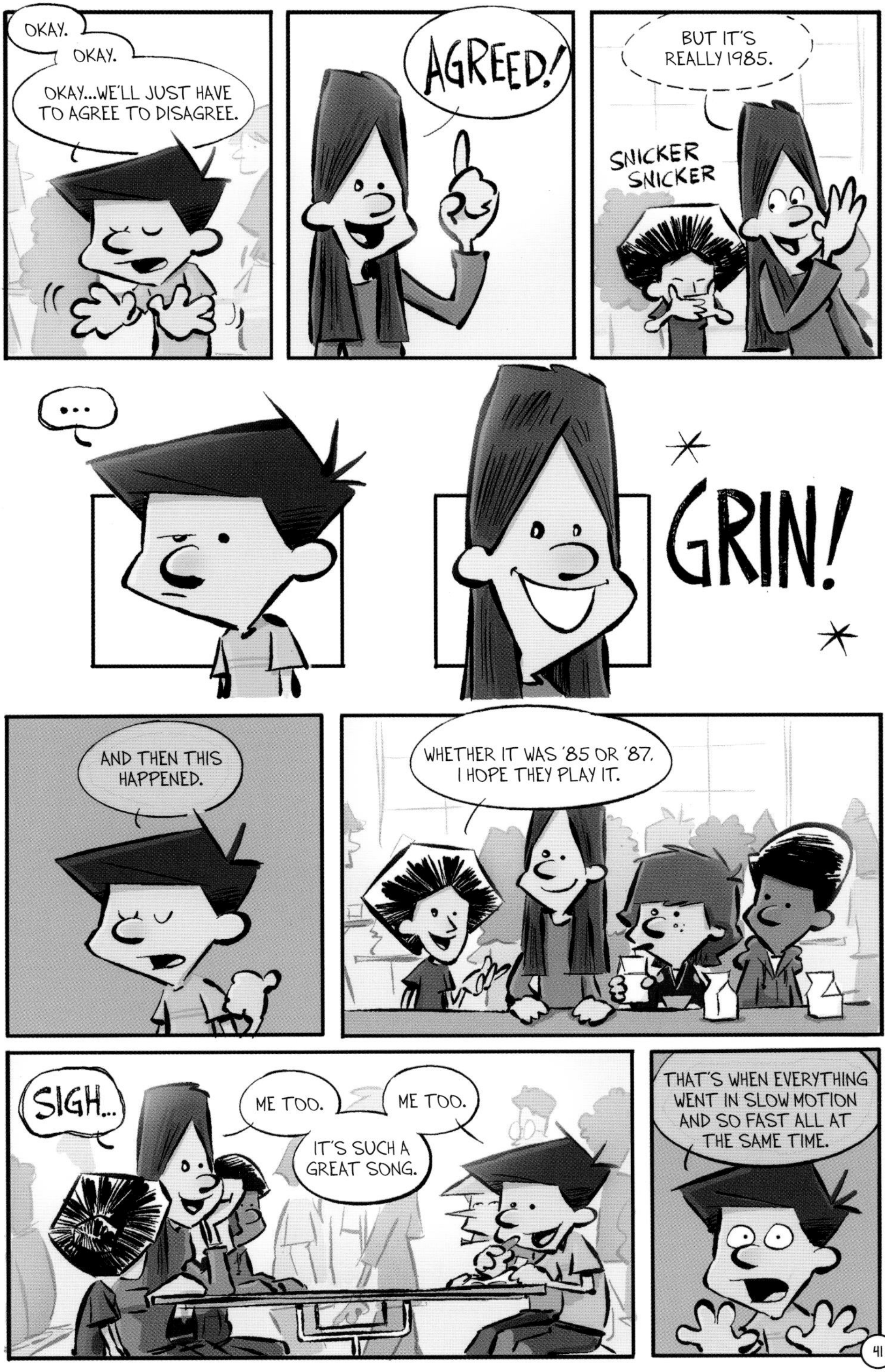
OKAY.
OKAY.
OKAY...WE'LL JUST HAVE TO AGREE TO DISAGREE.
AGREED!
BUT IT'S REALLY 1985.
SNICKER SNICKER
...
GRIN!
AND THEN THIS HAPPENED.
WHETHER IT WAS '85 OR '87, I HOPE THEY PLAY IT.
SIGH...
ME TOO.
ME TOO.
IT'S SUCH A GREAT SONG.
THAT'S WHEN EVERYTHING WENT IN SLOW MOTION AND SO FAST ALL AT THE SAME TIME.

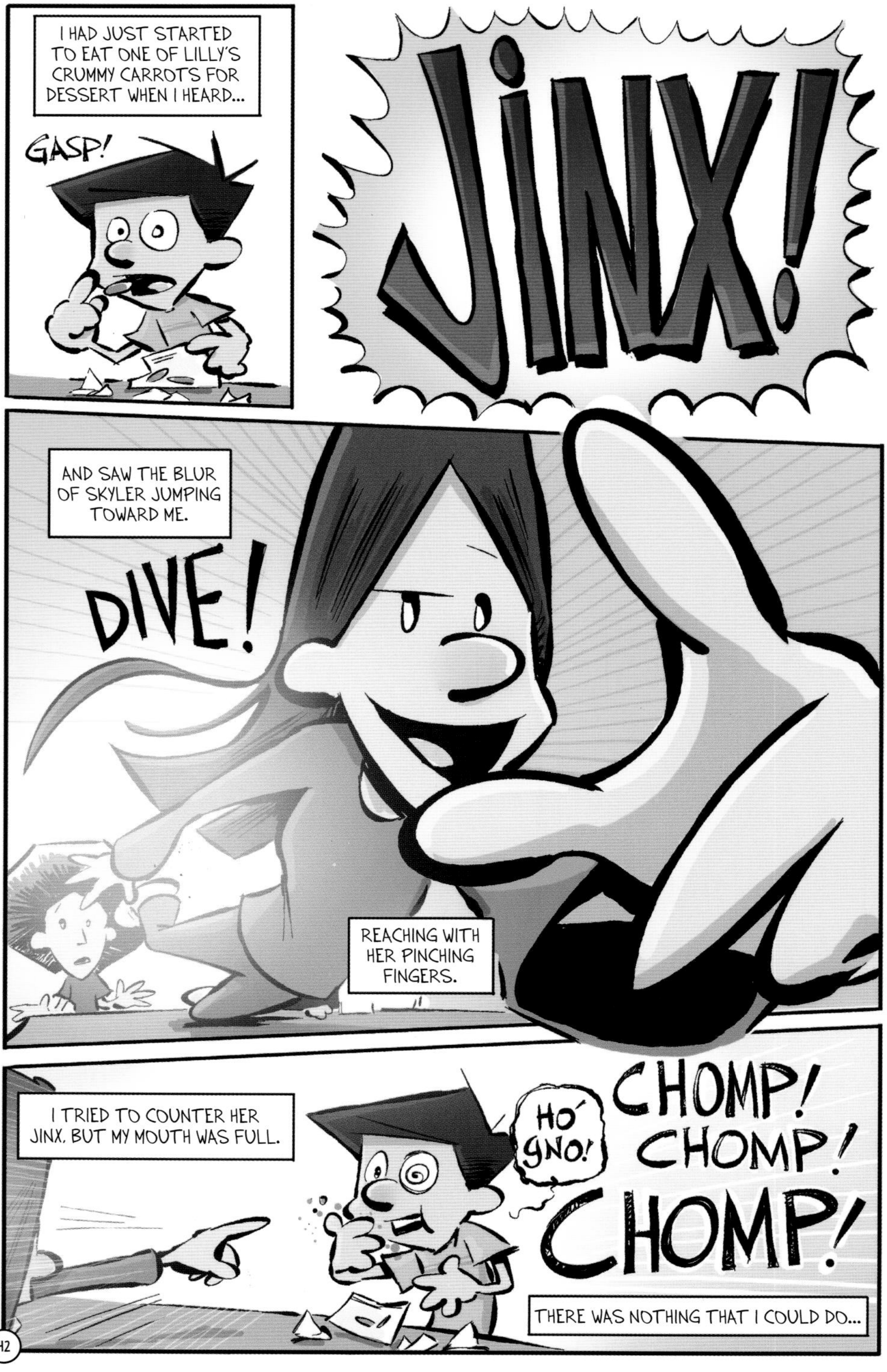

I HAD JUST STARTED TO EAT ONE OF LILLY'S CRUMMY CARROTS FOR DESSERT WHEN I HEARD...
GASP!
JINX!
AND SAW THE BLUR OF SKYLER JUMPING TOWARD ME.
DIVE!
REACHING WITH HER PINCHING FINGERS.
I TRIED TO COUNTER HER JINX, BUT MY MOUTH WAS FULL.
HO' GNO!
CHOMP! CHOMP! CHOMP!
THERE WAS NOTHING THAT I COULD DO...

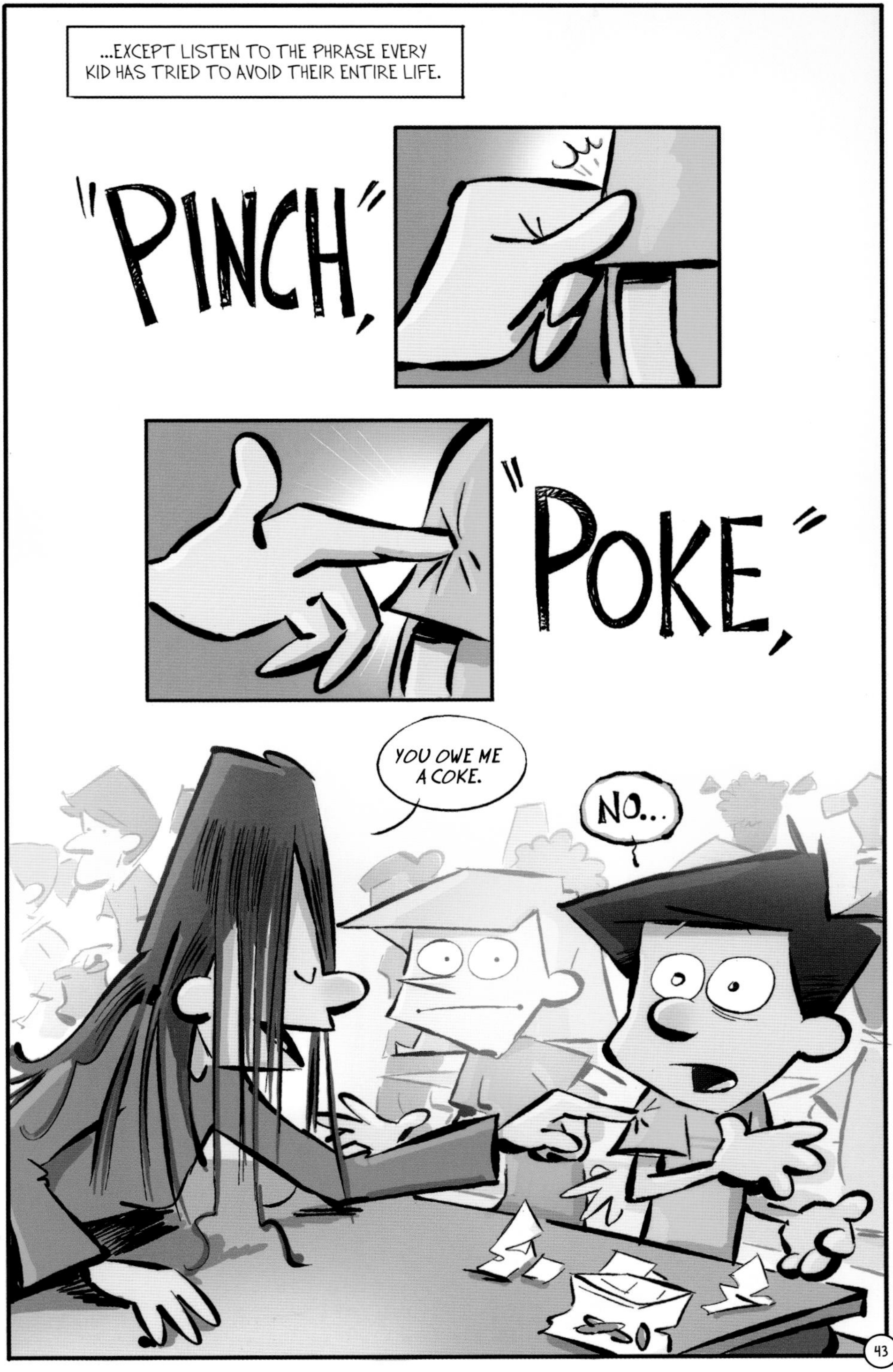
...EXCEPT LISTEN TO THE PHRASE EVERY KID HAS TRIED TO AVOID THEIR ENTIRE LIFE.
"PINCH,"
"POKE,"
YOU OWE ME A COKE.
NO...

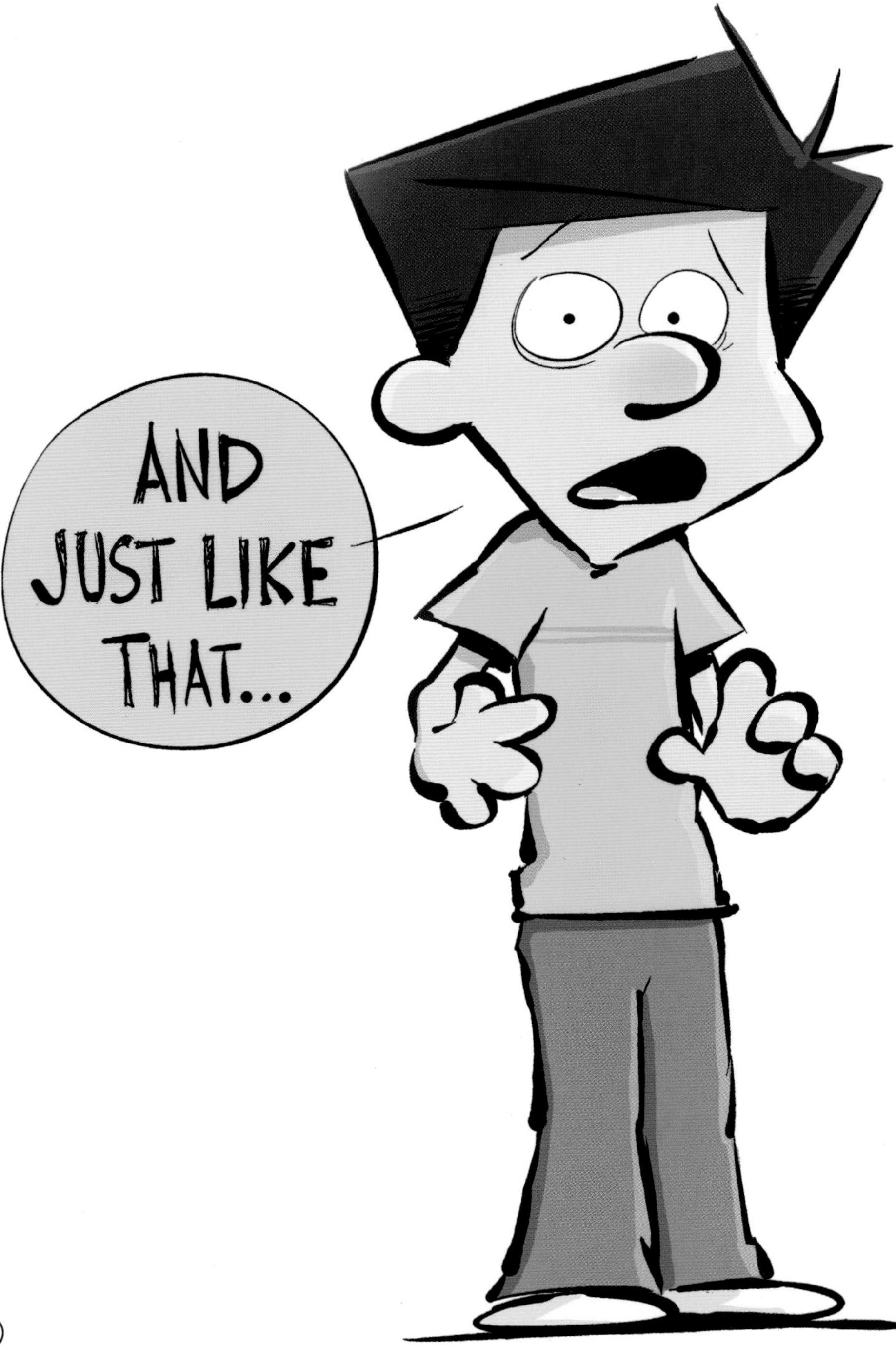
AND JUST LIKE THAT...

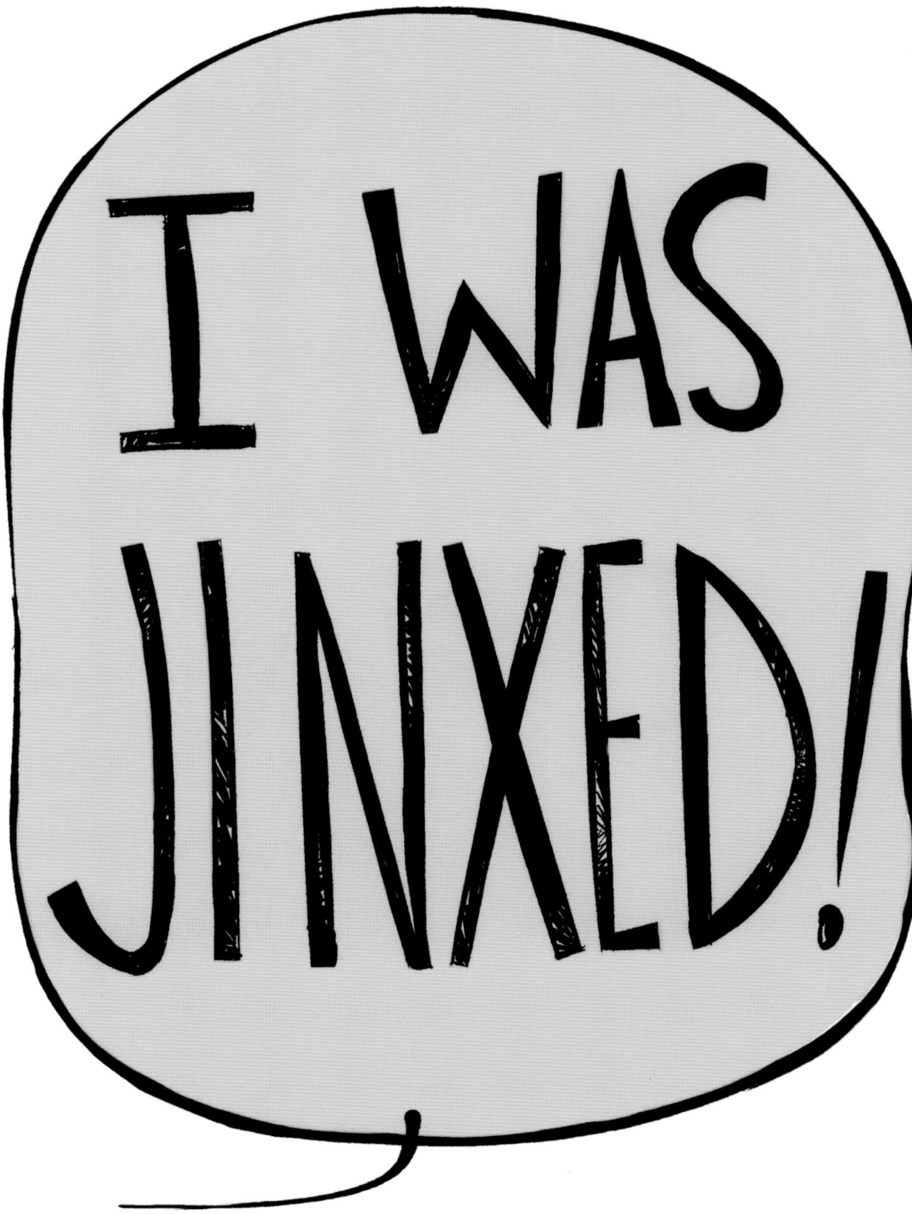
I WAS JINXED!

CHAPTER THREE
JINXED

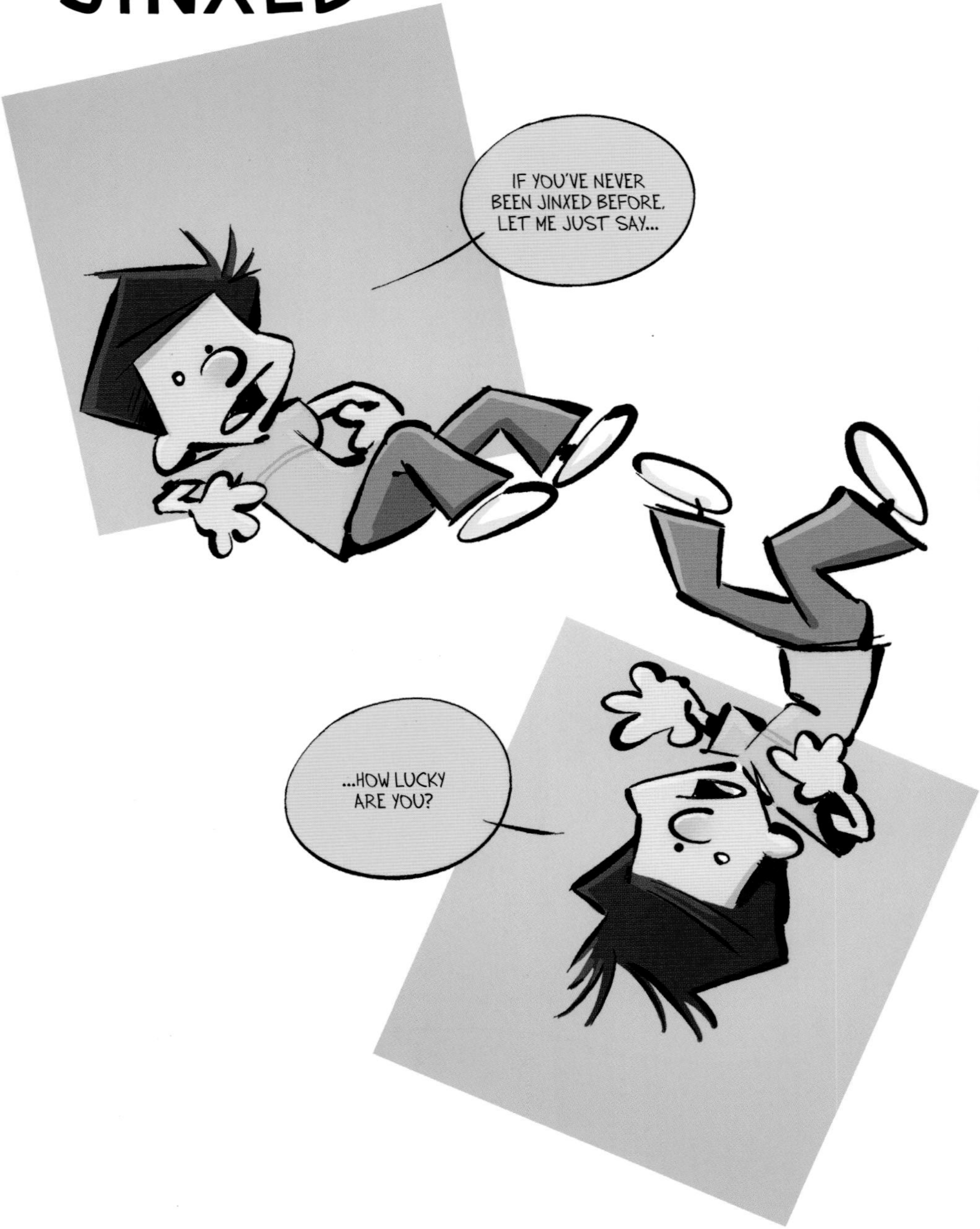
IF YOU'VE NEVER BEEN JINXED BEFORE, LET ME JUST SAY...
...HOW LUCKY ARE YOU?

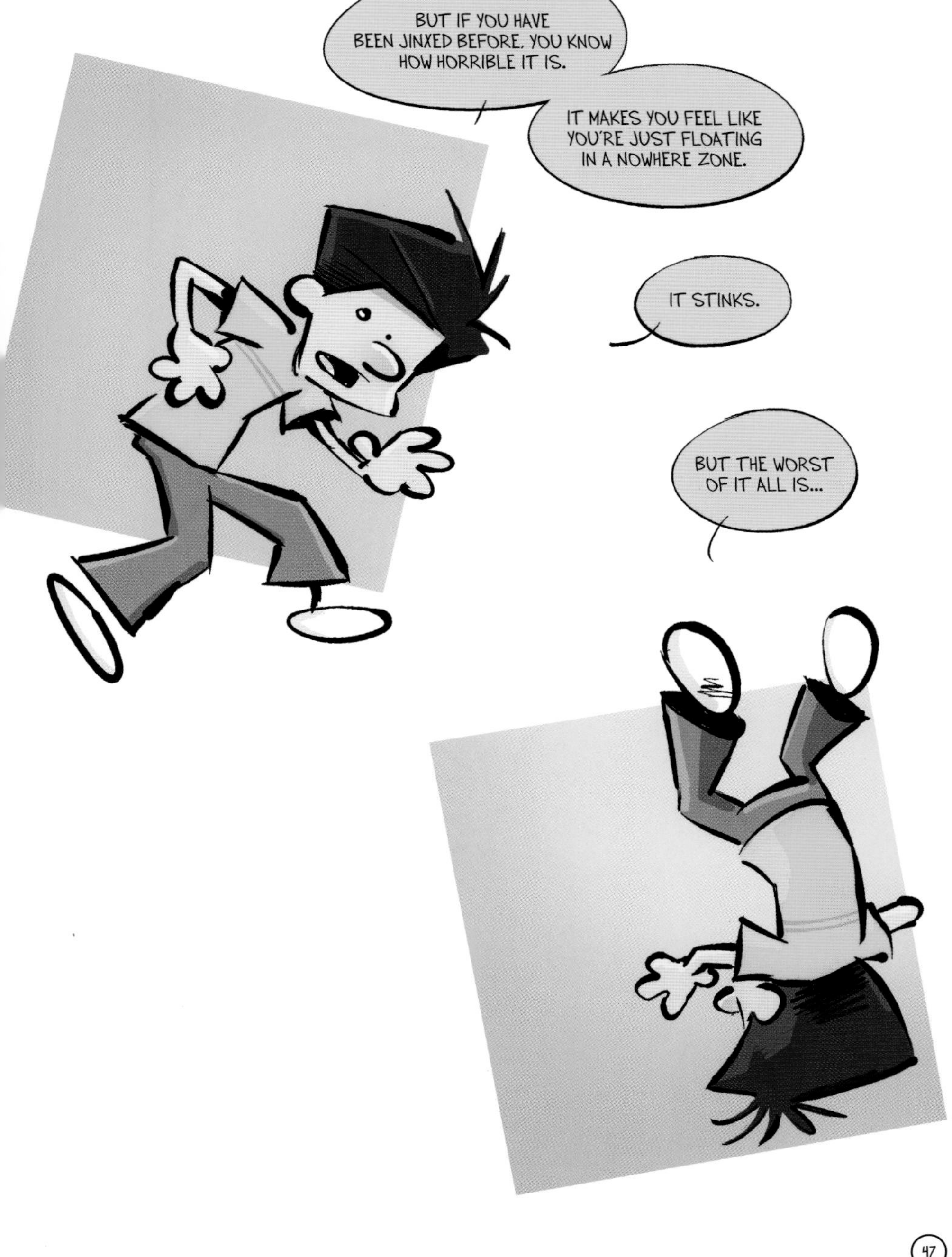
BUT IF YOU HAVE BEEN JINXED BEFORE, YOU KNOW HOW HORRIBLE IT IS.
IT MAKES YOU FEEL LIKE YOU'RE JUST FLOATING IN A NOWHERE ZONE.
IT STINKS.
BUT THE WORST OF IT ALL IS...

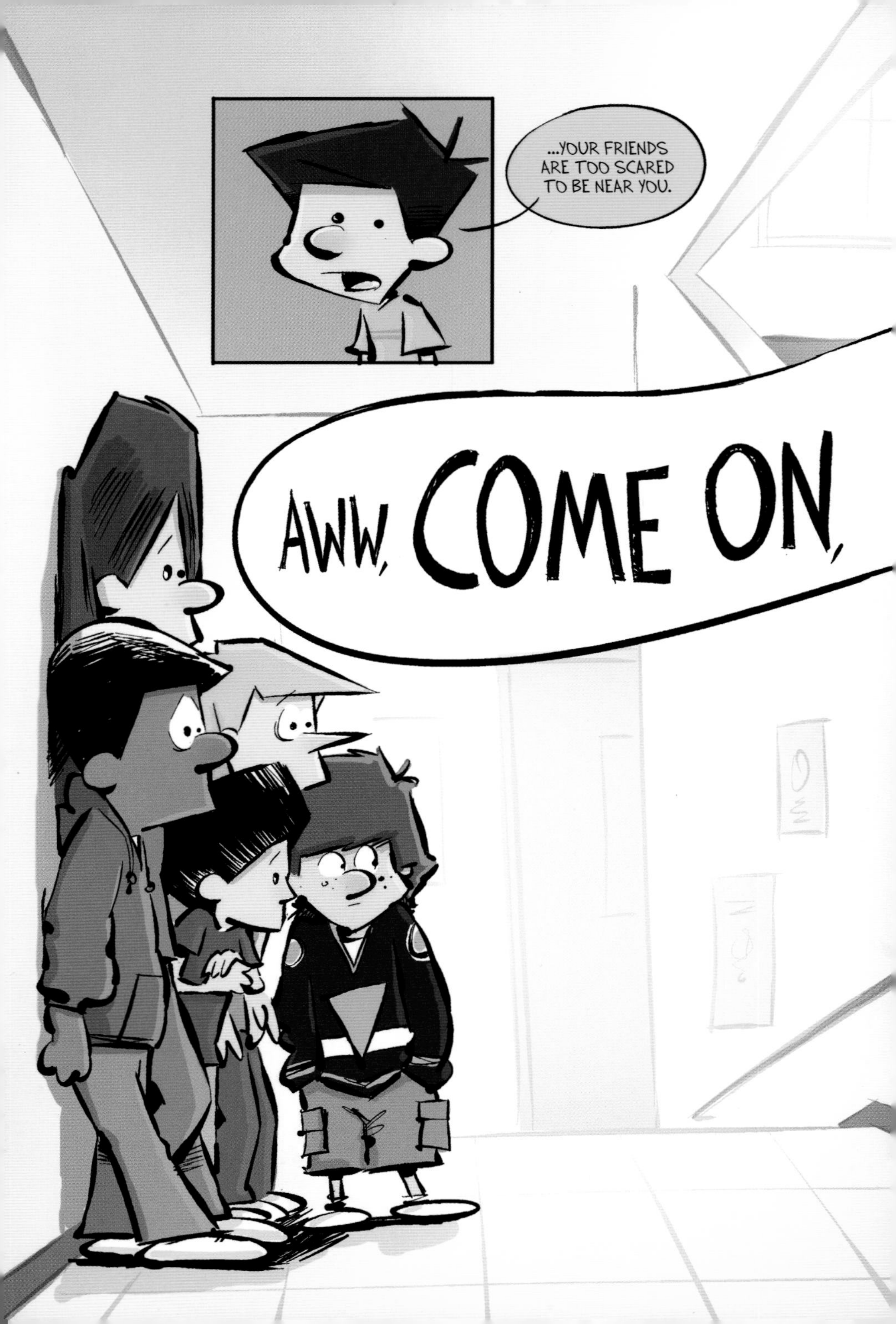
...YOUR FRIENDS ARE TOO SCARED TO BE NEAR YOU.
AWW, COME ON,

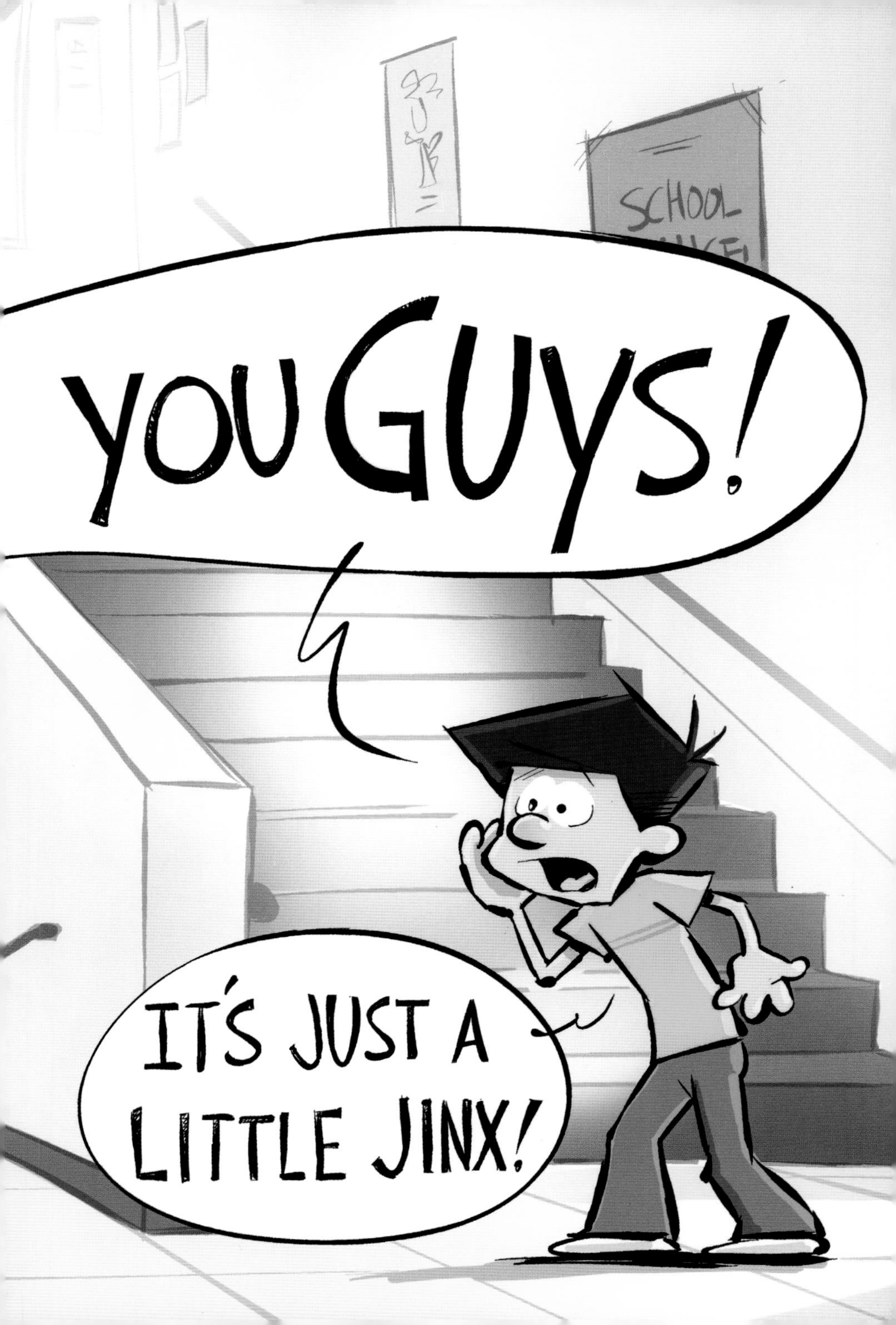
SCHOOL
YOU GUYS!
IT'S JUST A LITTLE JINX!

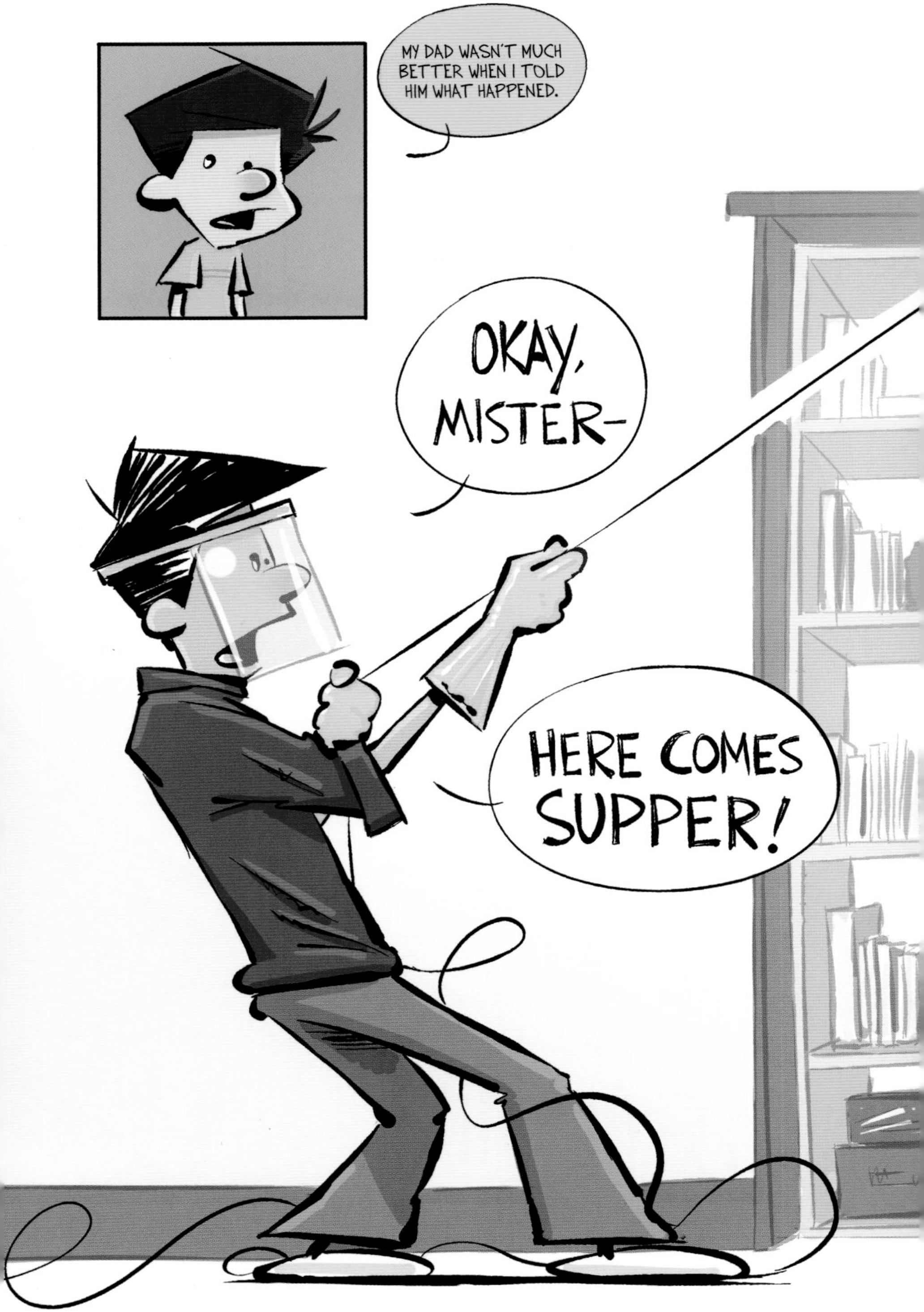
MY DAD WASN'T MUCH BETTER WHEN I TOLD HIM WHAT HAPPENED.
OKAY, MISTER–
HERE COMES SUPPER!

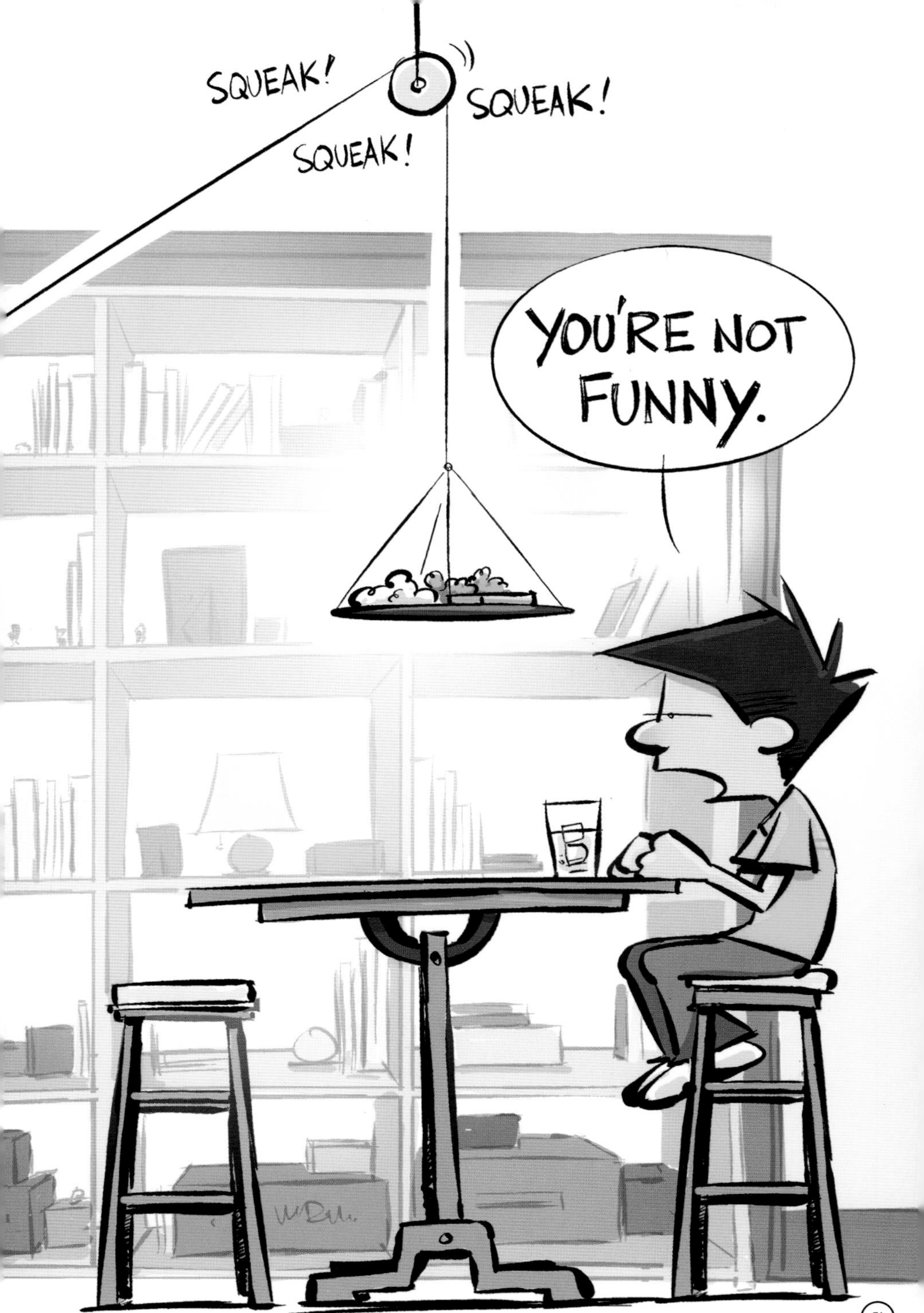
SQUEAK!
SQUEAK!
SQUEAK!
YOU'RE NOT FUNNY.

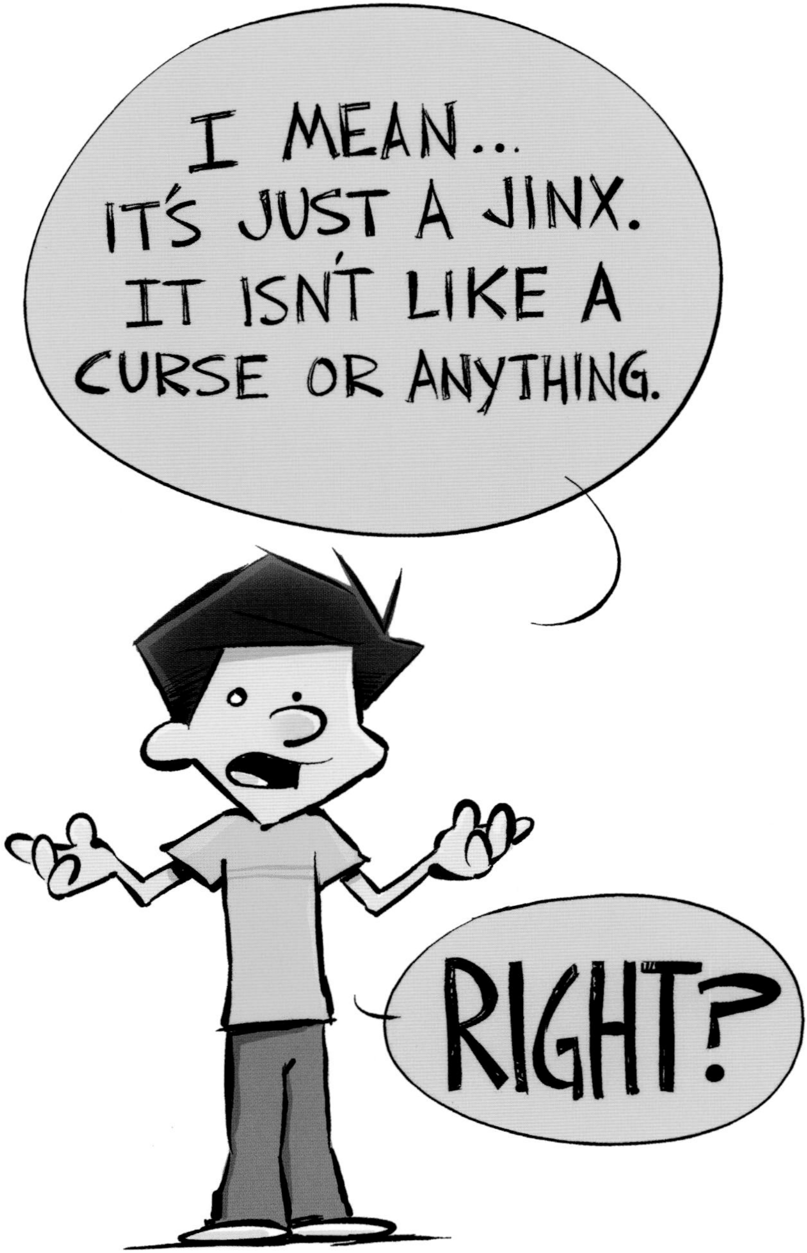
I MEAN...
IT'S JUST A JINX.
IT ISN'T LIKE A
CURSE OR ANYTHING.
RIGHT?

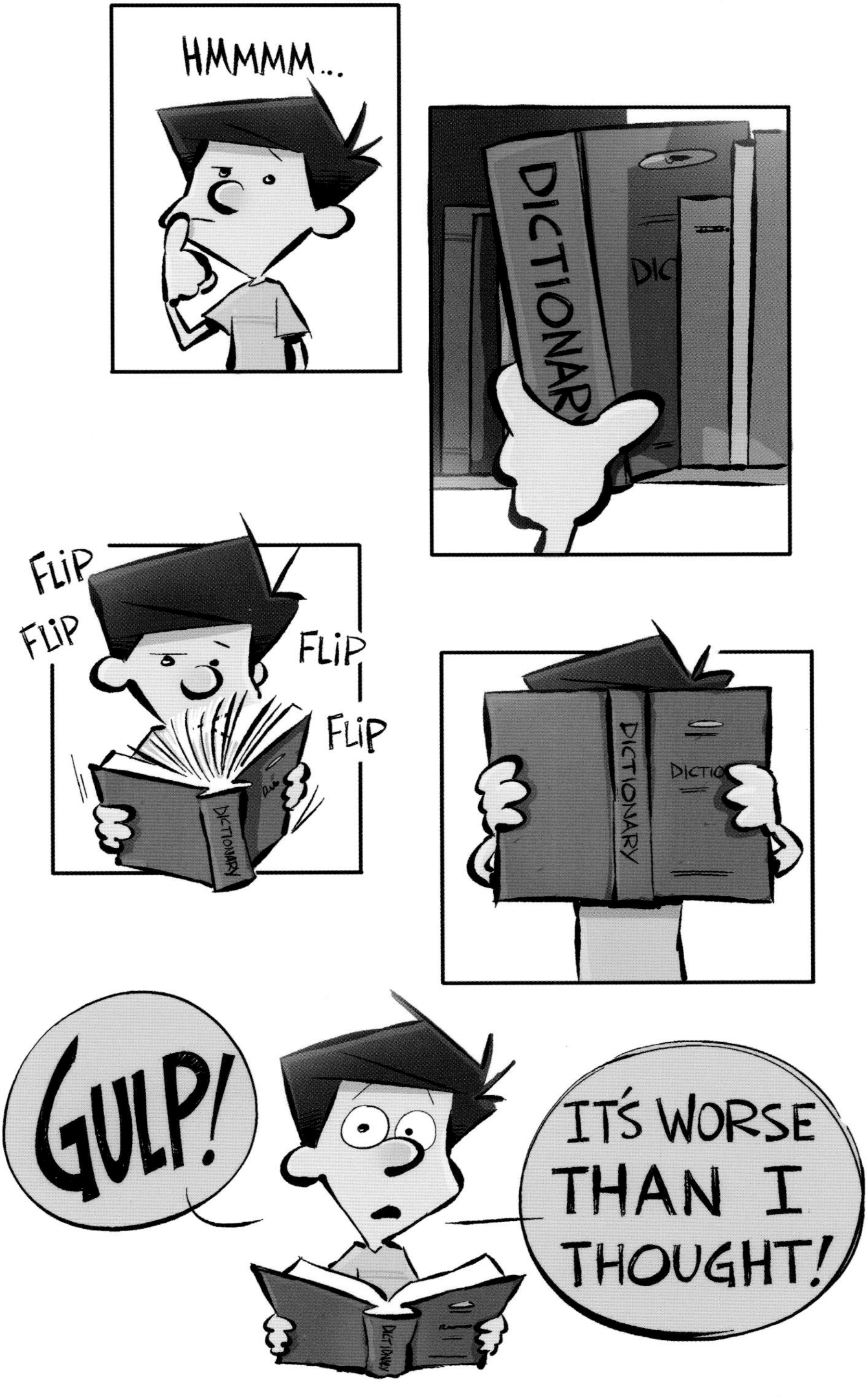
HMMMM...
DICTIONARY
FLIP
FLIP
FLIP
FLIP
DICTIONARY
DICTIONARY
GULP!
IT'S WORSE THAN I THOUGHT!

Jinx \ˈjiŋ(k)s\

(*n*) one that brings bad luck (see photo). (*v*) to foredoom to failure or misfortune; to bring bad luck to.
Synonyms: curse, hex, spell, plague, Newell

EXAMPLE OF ONE WHO IS JINXED →

WARNING! STAY FAR AWAY FROM.

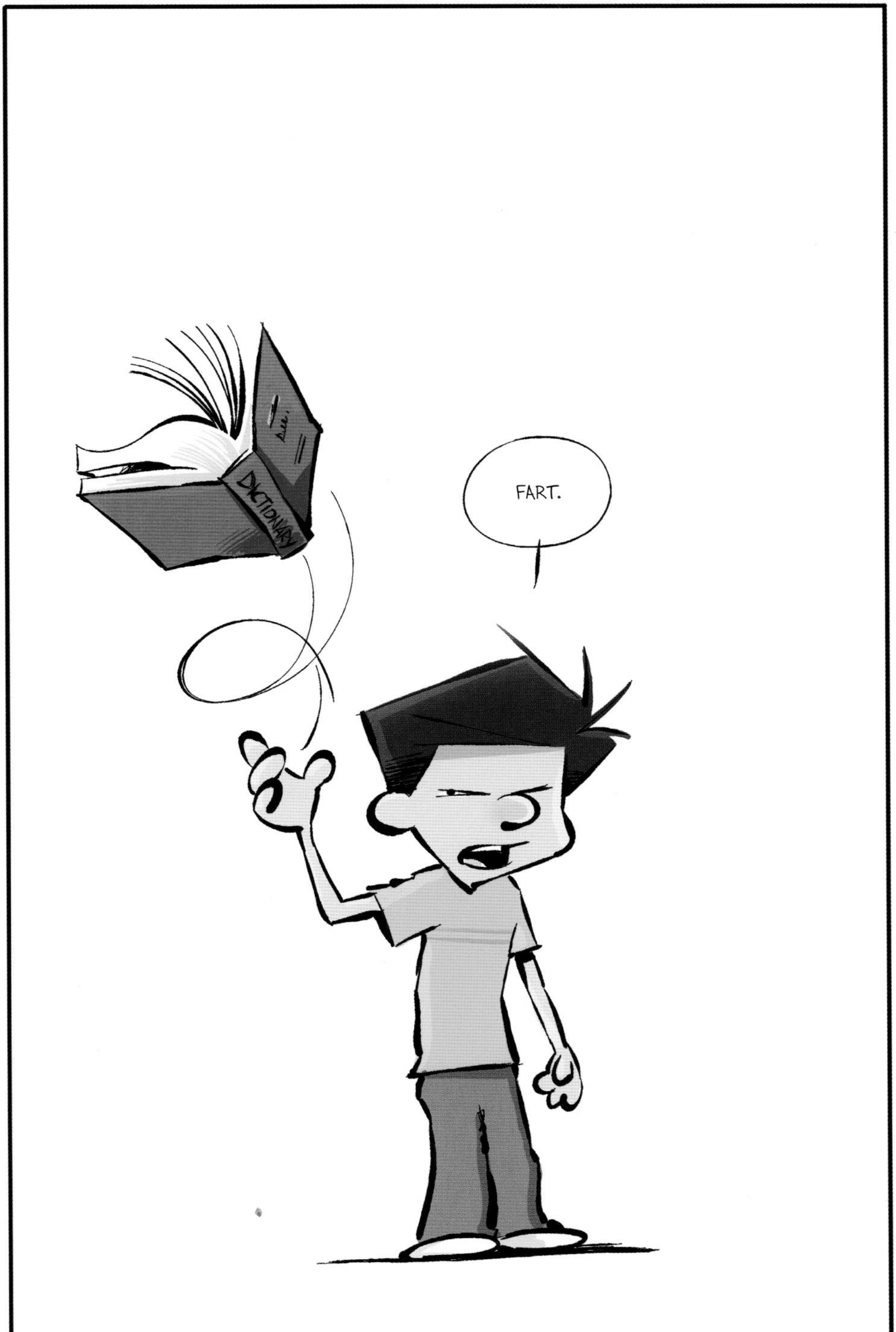
DICTIONARY
FART.

CHAPTER FOUR
IT DOESN'T GET ANY BETTER

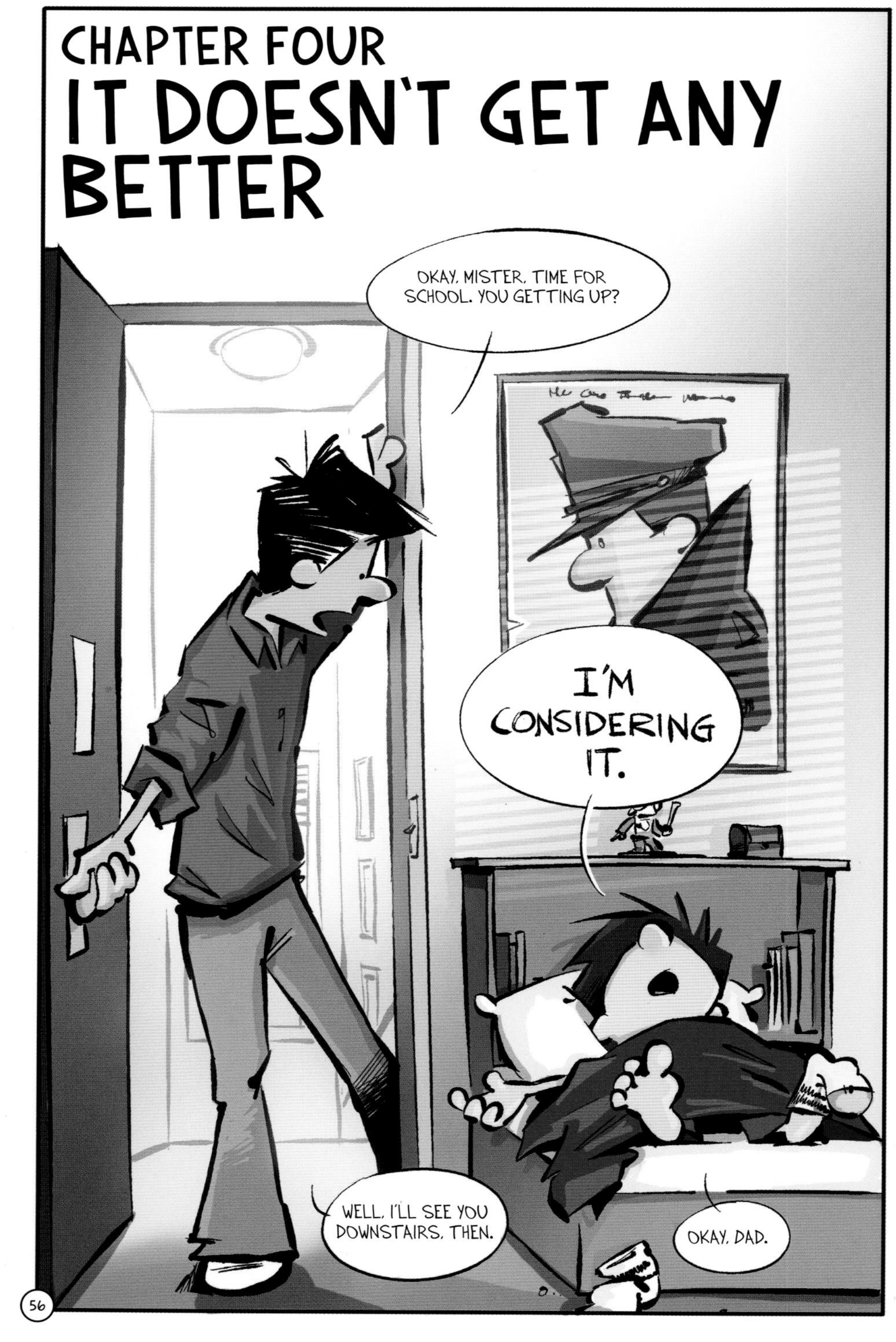
OKAY, MISTER, TIME FOR SCHOOL. YOU GETTING UP?
I'M CONSIDERING IT.
WELL, I'LL SEE YOU DOWNSTAIRS, THEN.
OKAY, DAD.

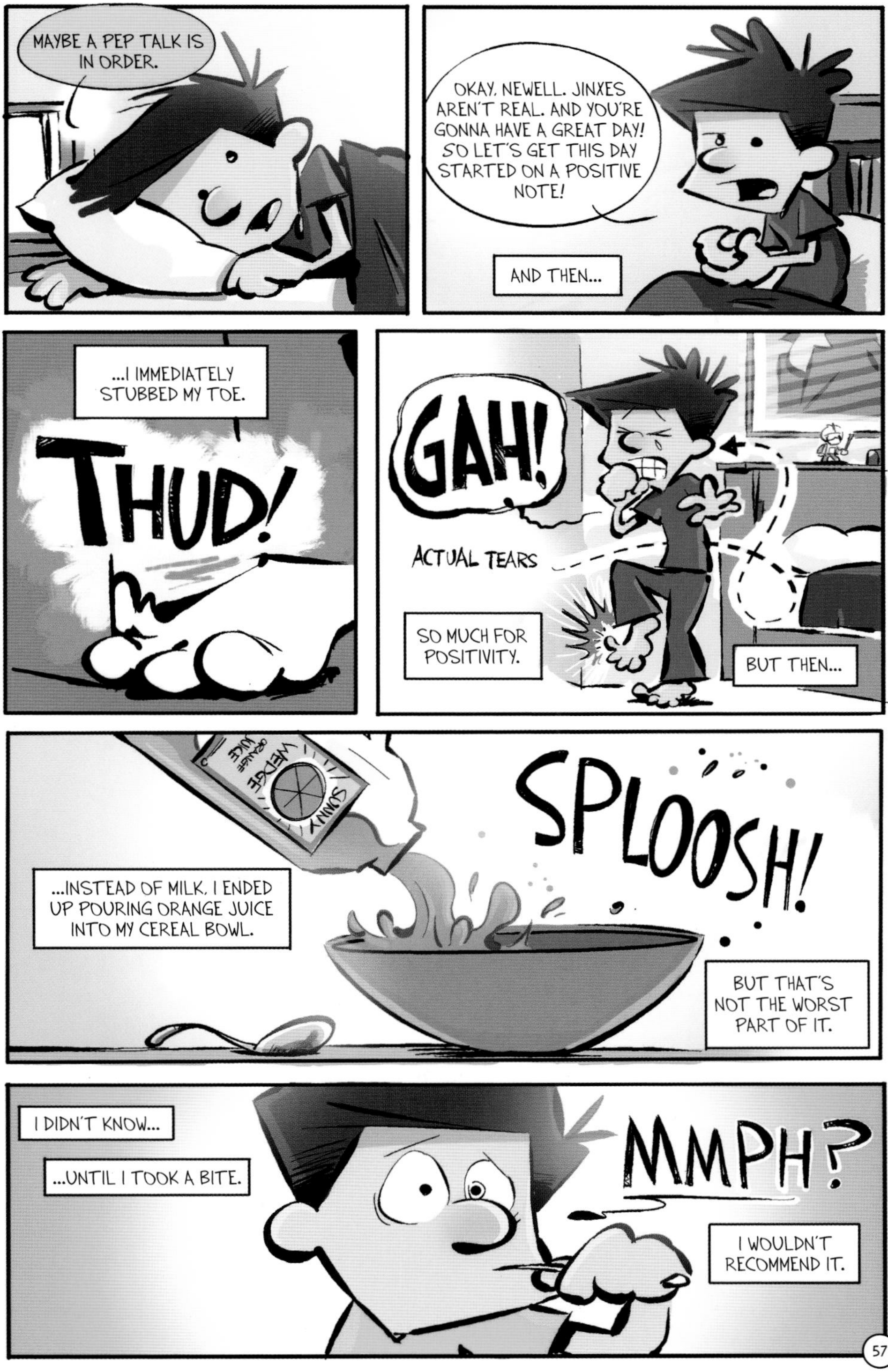

MAYBE A PEP TALK IS IN ORDER.
OKAY, NEWELL. JINXES AREN'T REAL. AND YOU'RE GONNA HAVE A GREAT DAY! SO LET'S GET THIS DAY STARTED ON A POSITIVE NOTE!
AND THEN...
...I IMMEDIATELY STUBBED MY TOE.
THUD!
GAH!
ACTUAL TEARS
SO MUCH FOR POSITIVITY.
BUT THEN...
SONNY WEDGE ORANGE JUICE
SPLOOSH!
...INSTEAD OF MILK, I ENDED UP POURING ORANGE JUICE INTO MY CEREAL BOWL.
BUT THAT'S NOT THE WORST PART OF IT.
I DIDN'T KNOW...
...UNTIL I TOOK A BITE.
MMPH?
I WOULDN'T RECOMMEND IT.

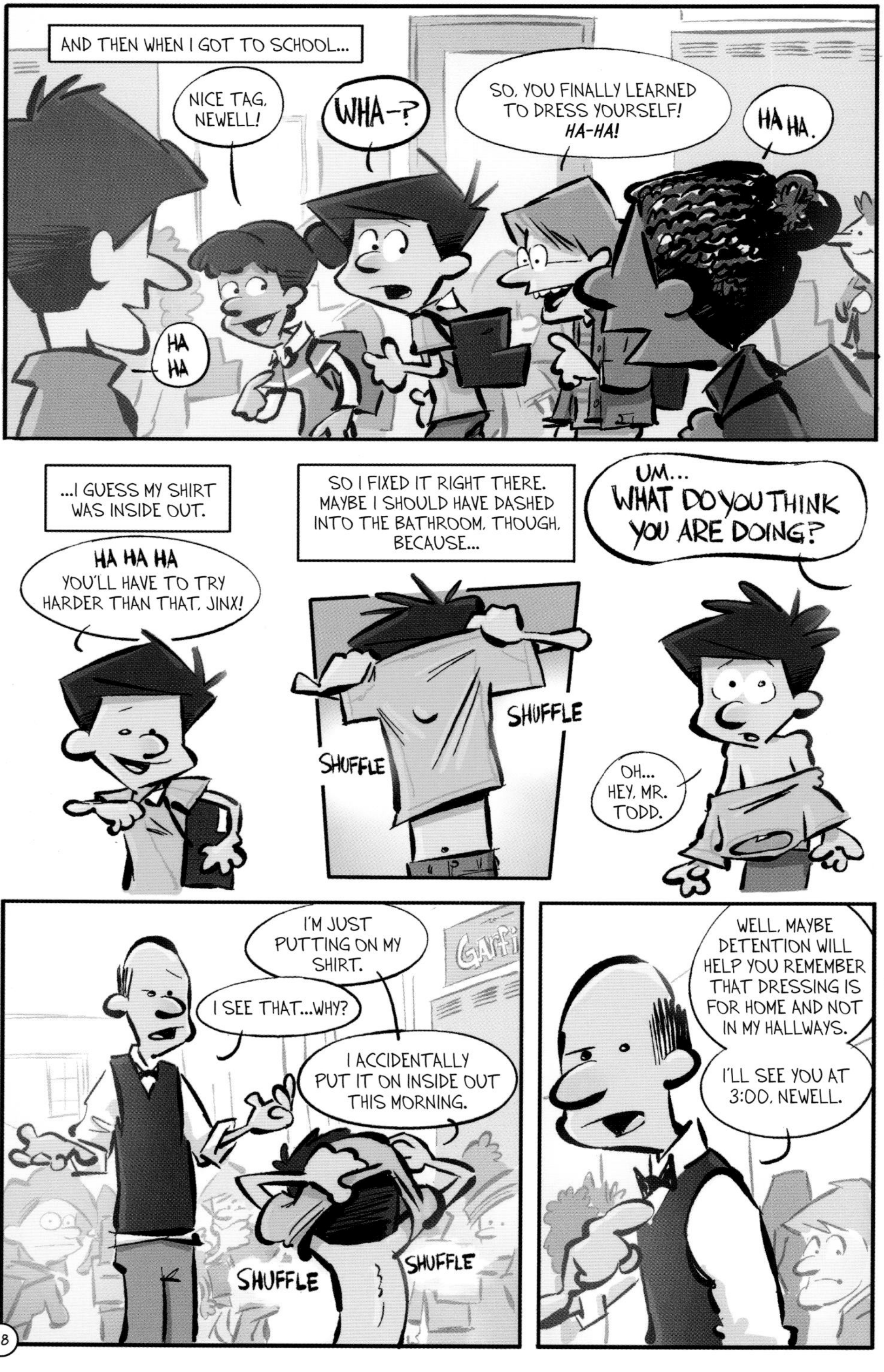
AND THEN WHEN I GOT TO SCHOOL...
NICE TAG, NEWELL!
WHA-?
SO, YOU FINALLY LEARNED TO DRESS YOURSELF! HA-HA!
HA HA.
HA HA
...I GUESS MY SHIRT WAS INSIDE OUT.
HA HA HA YOU'LL HAVE TO TRY HARDER THAN THAT, JINX!
SO I FIXED IT RIGHT THERE. MAYBE I SHOULD HAVE DASHED INTO THE BATHROOM, THOUGH, BECAUSE...
SHUFFLE
SHUFFLE
UM... WHAT DO YOU THINK YOU ARE DOING?
OH... HEY, MR. TODD.
I'M JUST PUTTING ON MY SHIRT.
I SEE THAT...WHY?
I ACCIDENTALLY PUT IT ON INSIDE OUT THIS MORNING.
SHUFFLE
SHUFFLE
WELL, MAYBE DETENTION WILL HELP YOU REMEMBER THAT DRESSING IS FOR HOME AND NOT IN MY HALLWAYS.
I'LL SEE YOU AT 3:00, NEWELL.

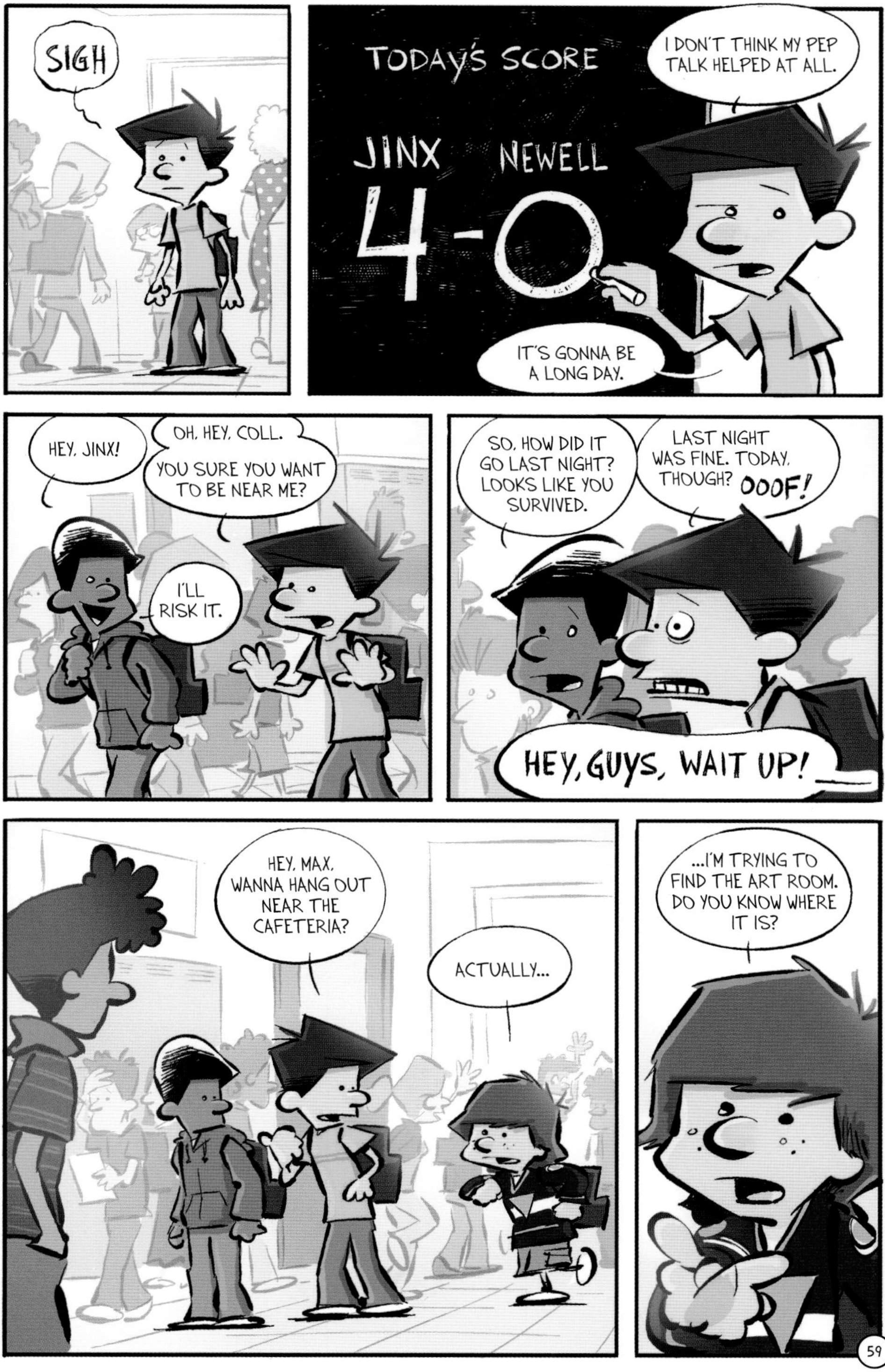
SIGH
TODAY'S SCORE
JINX NEWELL
4-0
I DON'T THINK MY PEP TALK HELPED AT ALL.
IT'S GONNA BE A LONG DAY.
HEY, JINX!
OH, HEY, COLL.
YOU SURE YOU WANT TO BE NEAR ME?
I'LL RISK IT.
SO, HOW DID IT GO LAST NIGHT? LOOKS LIKE YOU SURVIVED.
LAST NIGHT WAS FINE. TODAY, THOUGH? OOOF!
HEY, GUYS, WAIT UP!
HEY, MAX, WANNA HANG OUT NEAR THE CAFETERIA?
ACTUALLY...
...I'M TRYING TO FIND THE ART ROOM. DO YOU KNOW WHERE IT IS?

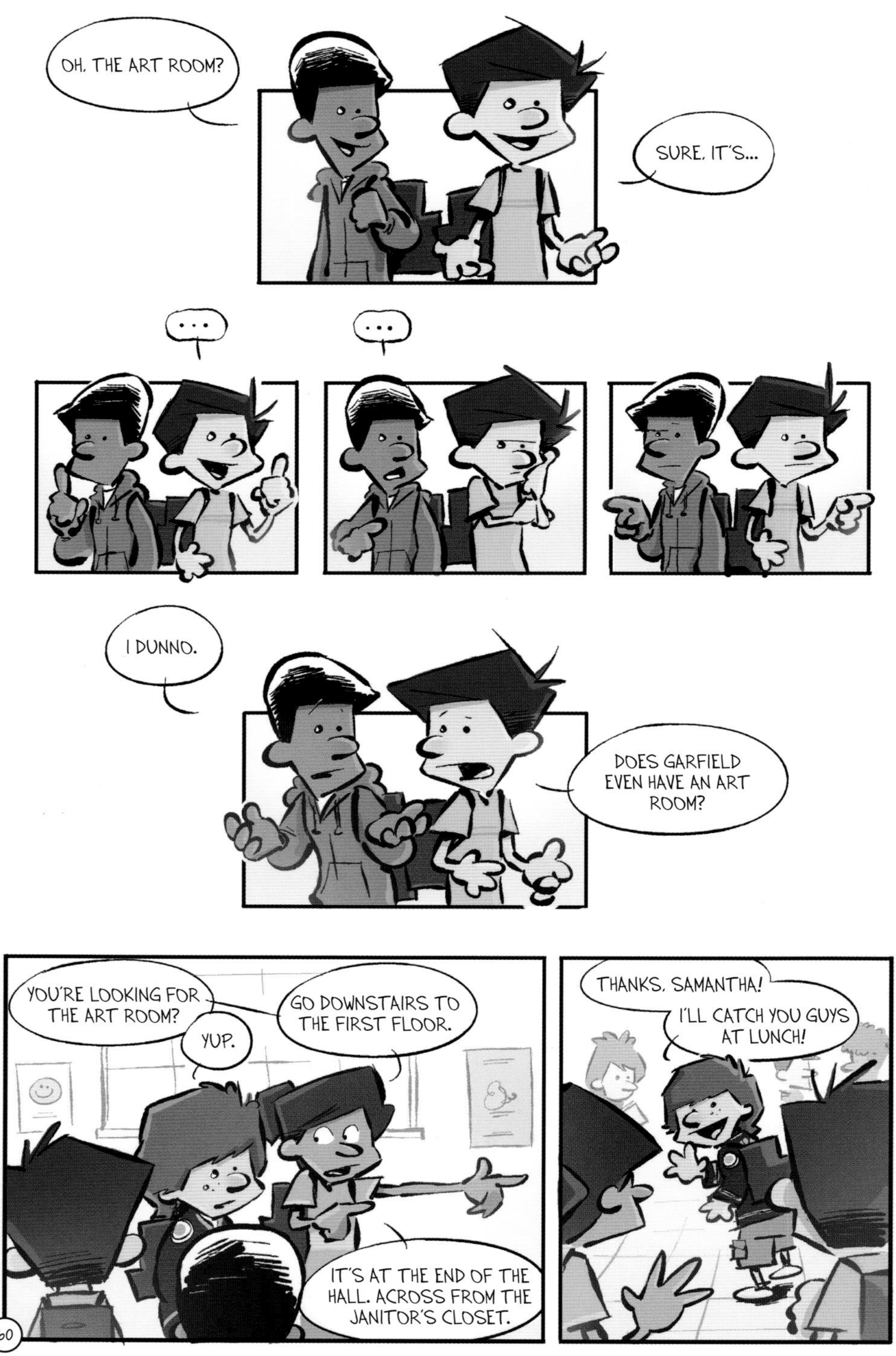
OH, THE ART ROOM?
SURE, IT'S...
...
...
I DUNNO.
DOES GARFIELD EVEN HAVE AN ART ROOM?
YOU'RE LOOKING FOR THE ART ROOM?
YUP.
GO DOWNSTAIRS TO THE FIRST FLOOR.
IT'S AT THE END OF THE HALL. ACROSS FROM THE JANITOR'S CLOSET.
THANKS, SAMANTHA!
I'LL CATCH YOU GUYS AT LUNCH!

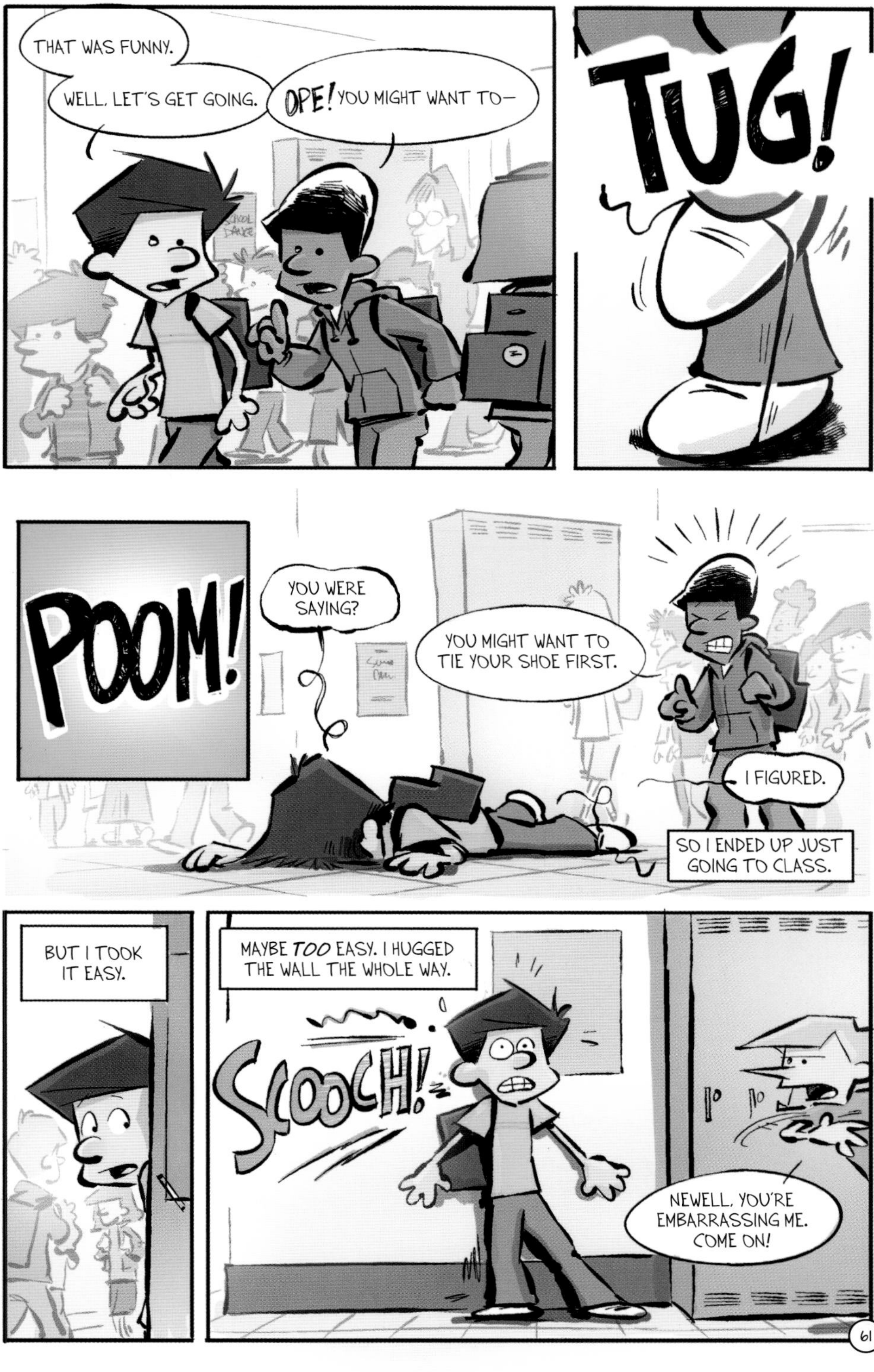
THAT WAS FUNNY.
WELL, LET'S GET GOING.
OPE! YOU MIGHT WANT TO—
TUG!
POOM!
YOU WERE SAYING?
YOU MIGHT WANT TO TIE YOUR SHOE FIRST.
I FIGURED.
SO I ENDED UP JUST GOING TO CLASS.
BUT I TOOK IT EASY.
MAYBE TOO EASY. I HUGGED THE WALL THE WHOLE WAY.
SCOOCH!
NEWELL, YOU'RE EMBARRASSING ME. COME ON!

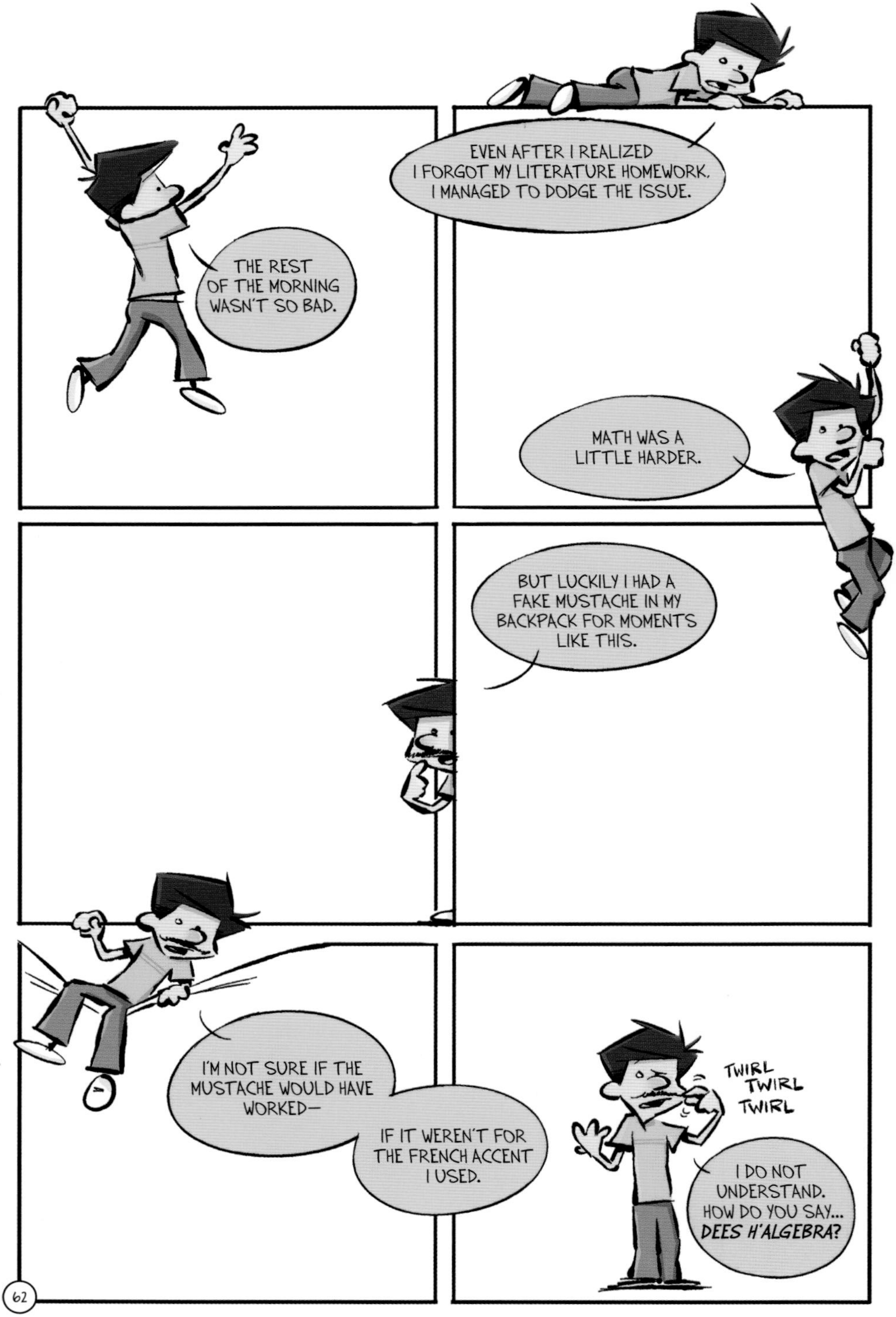
THE REST OF THE MORNING WASN'T SO BAD.
EVEN AFTER I REALIZED I FORGOT MY LITERATURE HOMEWORK, I MANAGED TO DODGE THE ISSUE.
MATH WAS A LITTLE HARDER.
BUT LUCKILY I HAD A FAKE MUSTACHE IN MY BACKPACK FOR MOMENTS LIKE THIS.
I'M NOT SURE IF THE MUSTACHE WOULD HAVE WORKED—
IF IT WEREN'T FOR THE FRENCH ACCENT I USED.
TWIRL TWIRL TWIRL
I DO NOT UNDERSTAND. HOW DO YOU SAY... ***DEES H'ALGEBRA?***

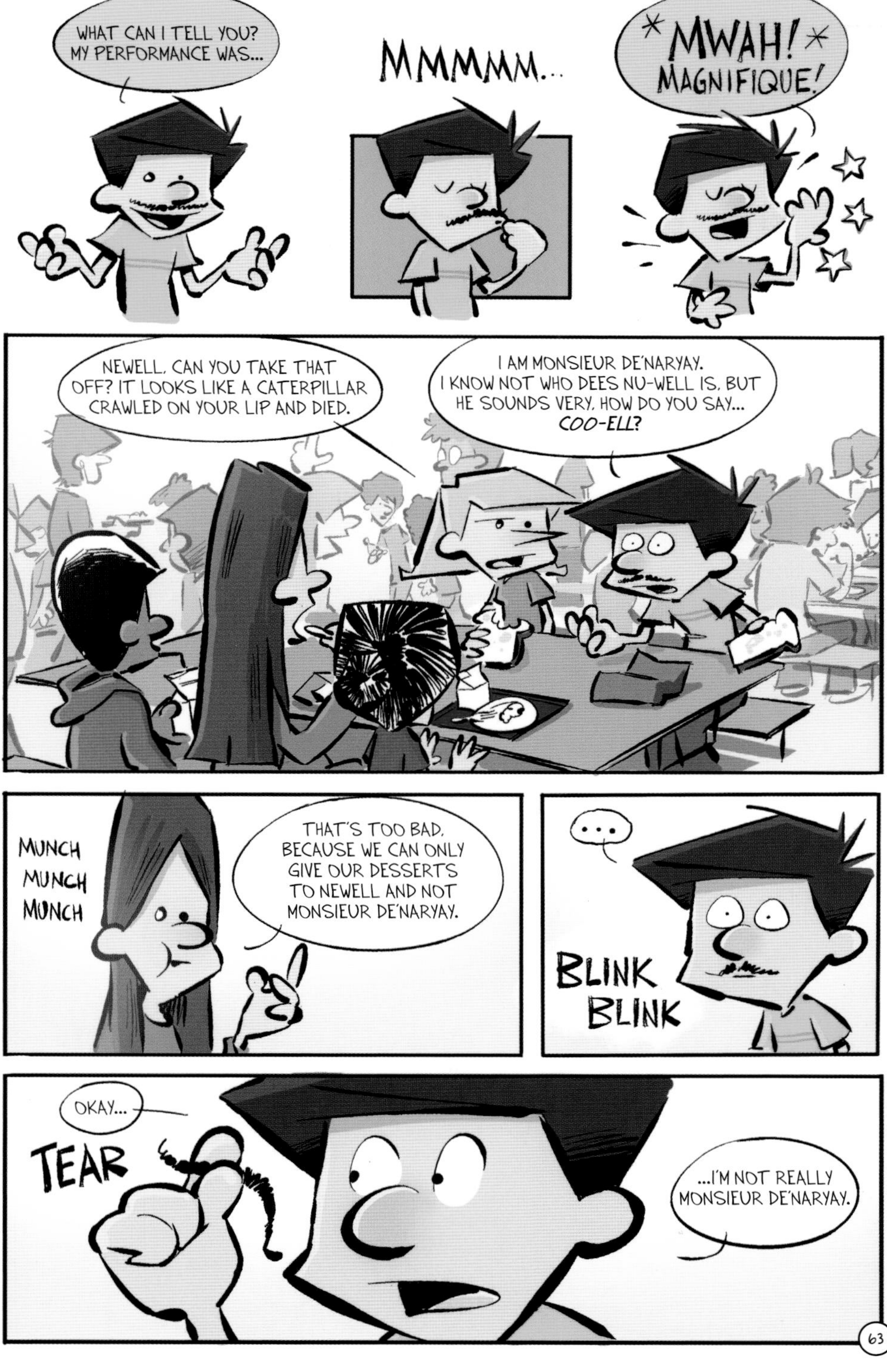
WHAT CAN I TELL YOU? MY PERFORMANCE WAS...
MMMMM...
MWAH! MAGNIFIQUE!
NEWELL, CAN YOU TAKE THAT OFF? IT LOOKS LIKE A CATERPILLAR CRAWLED ON YOUR LIP AND DIED.
I AM MONSIEUR DE'NARYAY. I KNOW NOT WHO DEES NU-WELL IS, BUT HE SOUNDS VERY, HOW DO YOU SAY... COO-ELL?
MUNCH MUNCH MUNCH
THAT'S TOO BAD, BECAUSE WE CAN ONLY GIVE OUR DESSERTS TO NEWELL AND NOT MONSIEUR DE'NARYAY.
...
BLINK BLINK
OKAY...
TEAR
...I'M NOT REALLY MONSIEUR DE'NARYAY.

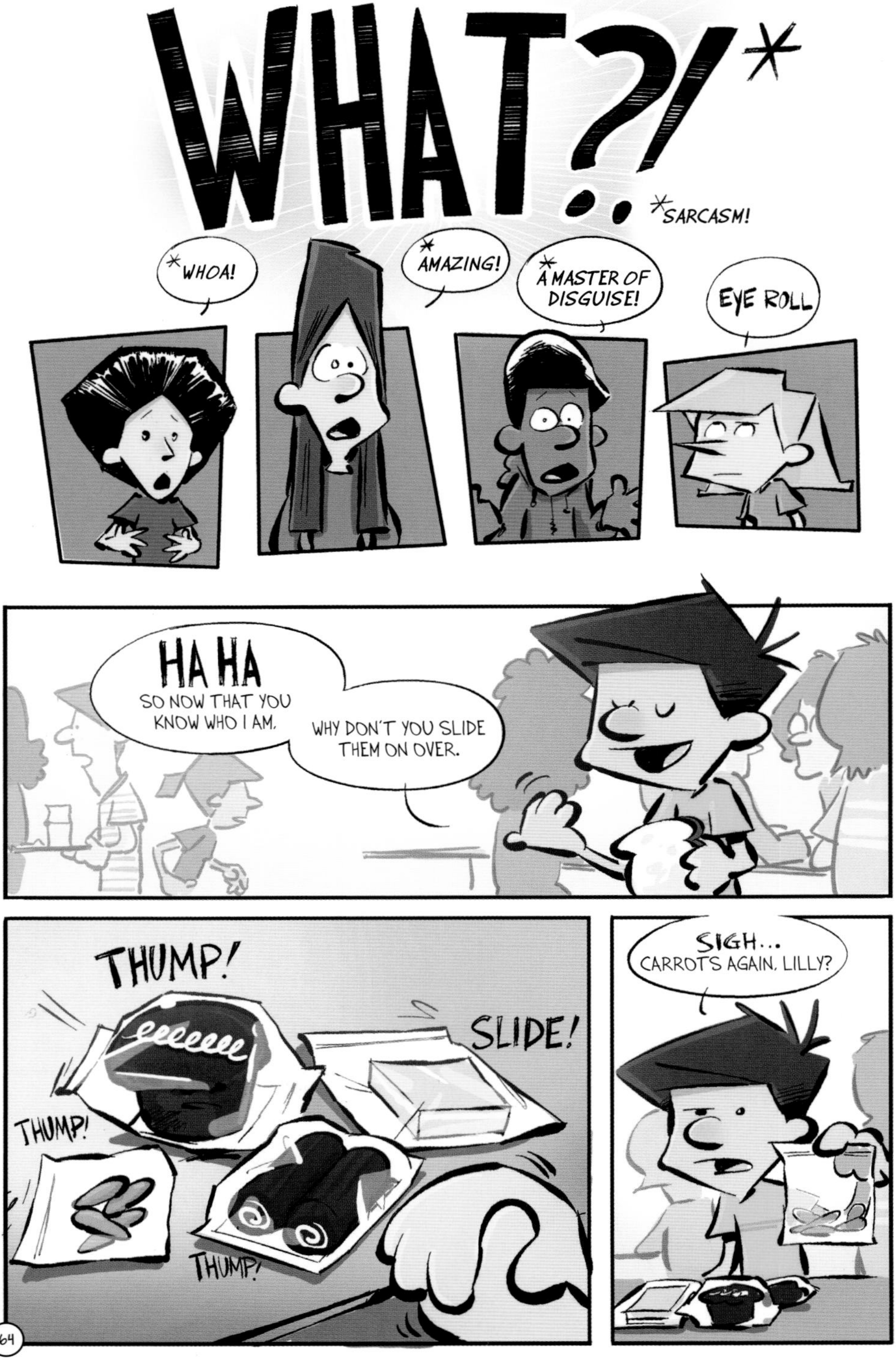
WHAT?!*
*SARCASM!
*WHOA!
*AMAZING!
*A MASTER OF DISGUISE!
EYE ROLL
HA HA SO NOW THAT YOU KNOW WHO I AM,
WHY DON'T YOU SLIDE THEM ON OVER.
THUMP!
SLIDE!
THUMP!
THUMP!
SIGH... CARROTS AGAIN, LILLY?

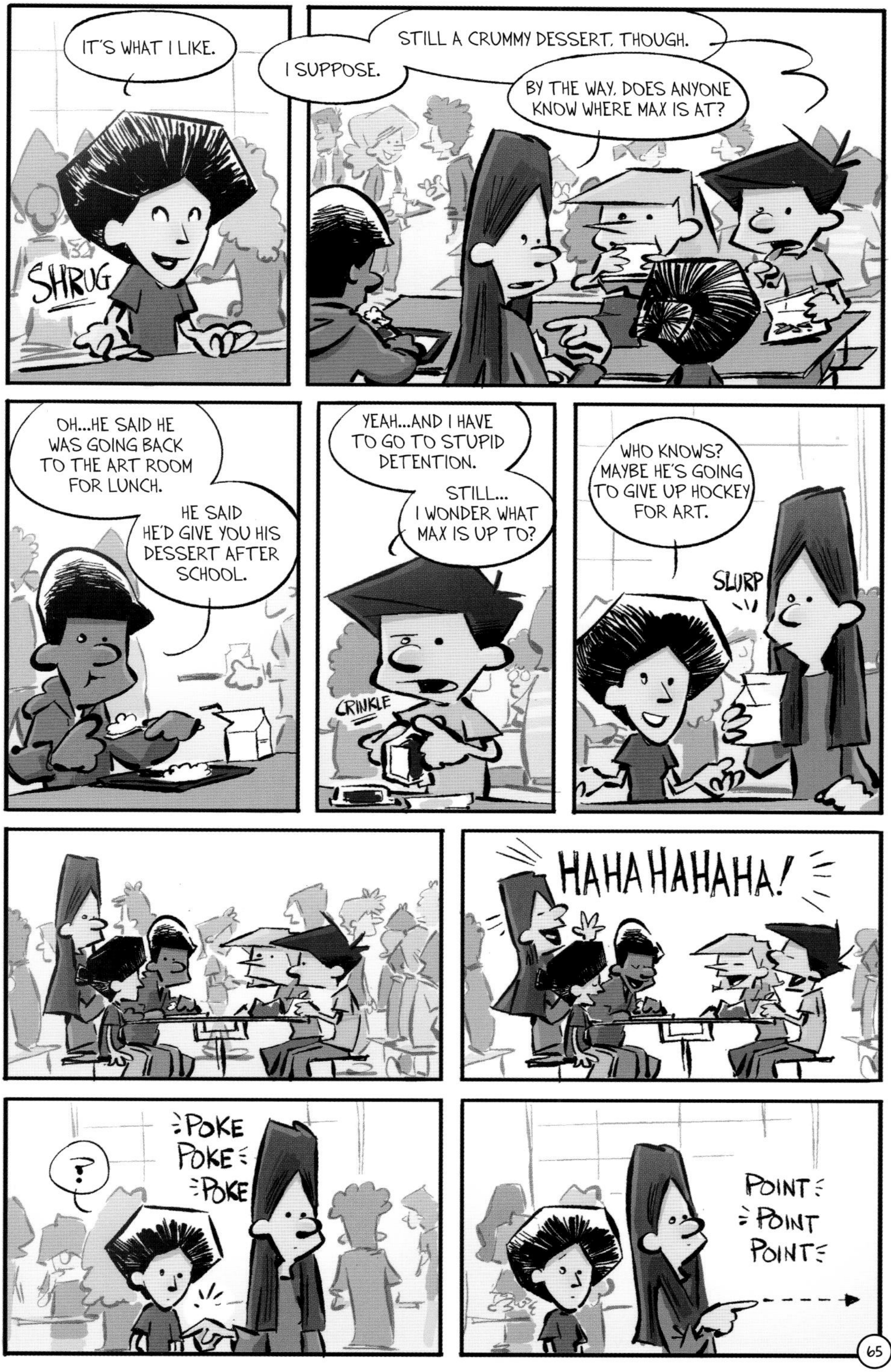
IT'S WHAT I LIKE.
SHRUG
I SUPPOSE.
STILL A CRUMMY DESSERT, THOUGH.
BY THE WAY, DOES ANYONE KNOW WHERE MAX IS AT?
OH...HE SAID HE WAS GOING BACK TO THE ART ROOM FOR LUNCH.
HE SAID HE'D GIVE YOU HIS DESSERT AFTER SCHOOL.
YEAH...AND I HAVE TO GO TO STUPID DETENTION.
STILL... I WONDER WHAT MAX IS UP TO?
CRINKLE
WHO KNOWS? MAYBE HE'S GOING TO GIVE UP HOCKEY FOR ART.
SLURP
HAHAHAHAHA!
?
POKE
POKE
POKE
POINT
POINT
POINT

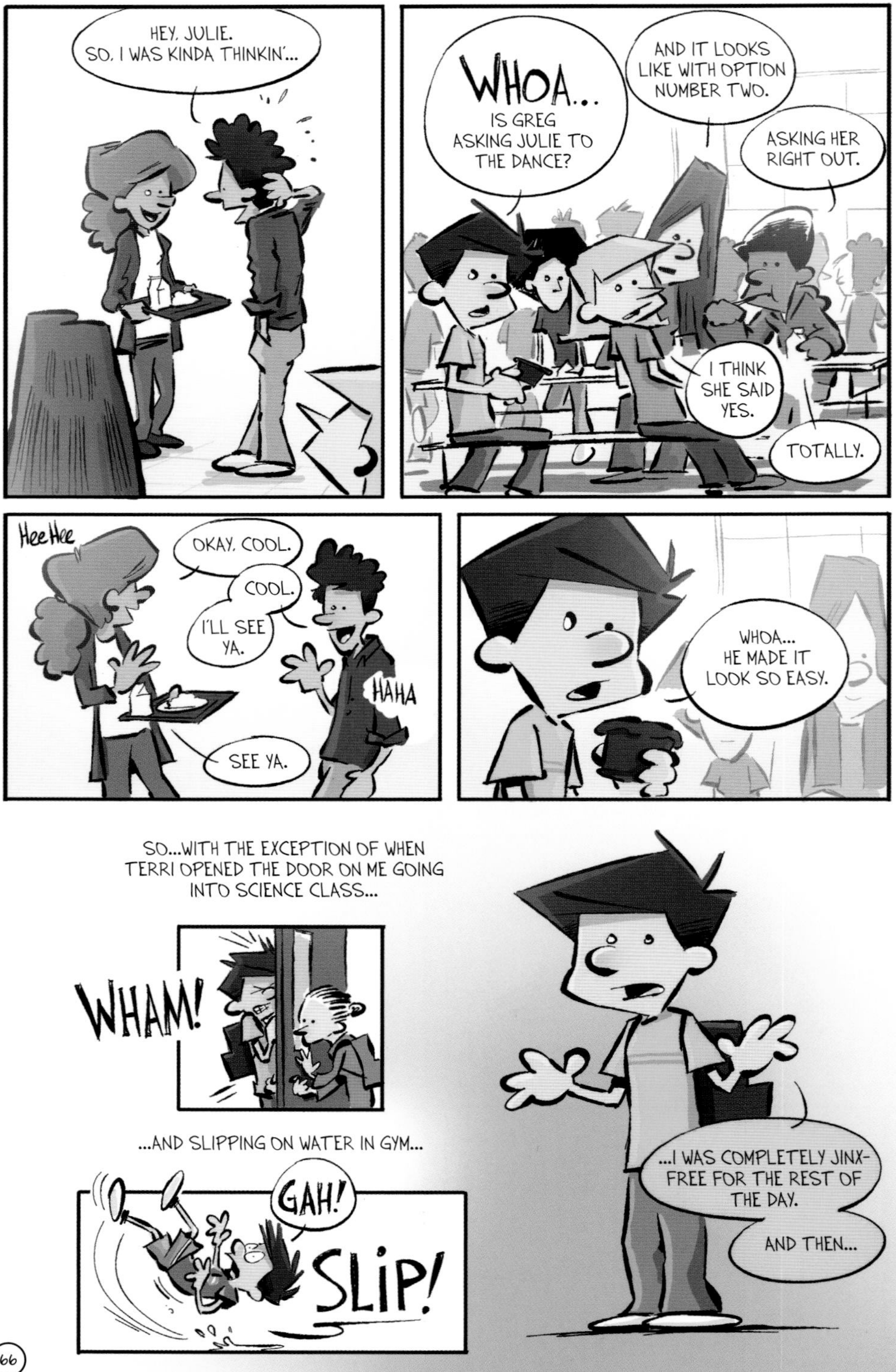
HEY, JULIE.
SO, I WAS KINDA THINKIN'...
WHOA... IS GREG ASKING JULIE TO THE DANCE?
AND IT LOOKS LIKE WITH OPTION NUMBER TWO.
ASKING HER RIGHT OUT.
I THINK SHE SAID YES.
TOTALLY.
Hee Hee
OKAY, COOL.
COOL.
I'LL SEE YA.
HAHA
SEE YA.
WHOA... HE MADE IT LOOK SO EASY.
SO...WITH THE EXCEPTION OF WHEN TERRI OPENED THE DOOR ON ME GOING INTO SCIENCE CLASS...
WHAM!
...AND SLIPPING ON WATER IN GYM...
GAH!
SLIP!
...I WAS COMPLETELY JINX-FREE FOR THE REST OF THE DAY.
AND THEN...

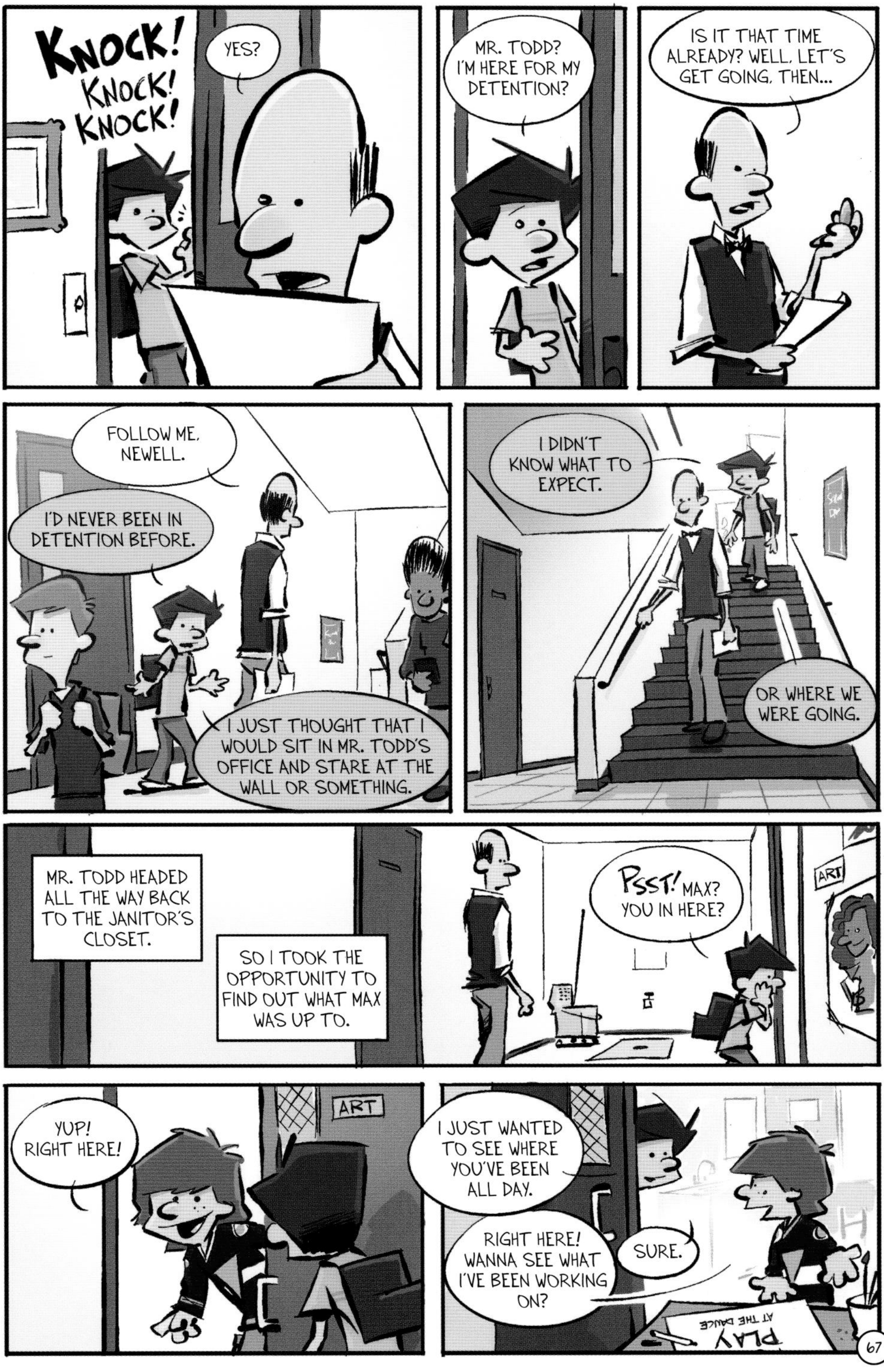
KNOCK!
KNOCK!
KNOCK!
YES?
MR. TODD? I'M HERE FOR MY DETENTION?
IS IT THAT TIME ALREADY? WELL, LET'S GET GOING, THEN...
FOLLOW ME, NEWELL.
I'D NEVER BEEN IN DETENTION BEFORE.
I JUST THOUGHT THAT I WOULD SIT IN MR. TODD'S OFFICE AND STARE AT THE WALL OR SOMETHING.
I DIDN'T KNOW WHAT TO EXPECT.
OR WHERE WE WERE GOING.
MR. TODD HEADED ALL THE WAY BACK TO THE JANITOR'S CLOSET.
SO I TOOK THE OPPORTUNITY TO FIND OUT WHAT MAX WAS UP TO.
ART
PSST! MAX? YOU IN HERE?
ART
YUP! RIGHT HERE!
I JUST WANTED TO SEE WHERE YOU'VE BEEN ALL DAY.
RIGHT HERE! WANNA SEE WHAT I'VE BEEN WORKING ON?
SURE.
PLAY AT THE DANCE

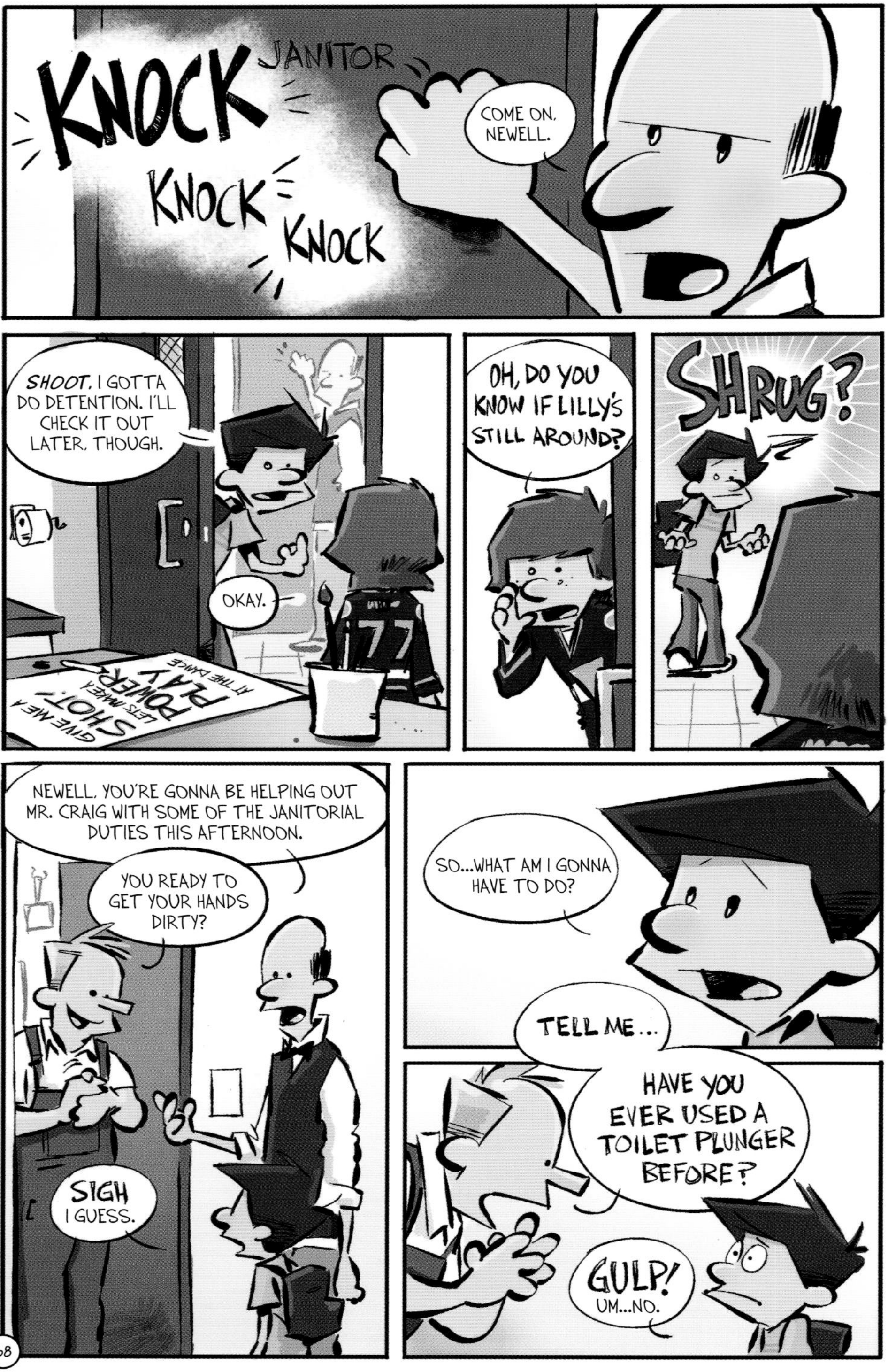
KNOCK
JANITOR
KNOCK
KNOCK
COME ON, NEWELL.
SHOOT. I GOTTA DO DETENTION. I'LL CHECK IT OUT LATER, THOUGH.
OKAY.
GIVE ME A SHOT- LET'S MAKE A POWER PLAY AT THE DANCE
OH, DO YOU KNOW IF LILLY'S STILL AROUND?
SHRUG?
NEWELL, YOU'RE GONNA BE HELPING OUT MR. CRAIG WITH SOME OF THE JANITORIAL DUTIES THIS AFTERNOON.
YOU READY TO GET YOUR HANDS DIRTY?
SIGH
I GUESS.
SO...WHAT AM I GONNA HAVE TO DO?
TELL ME...
HAVE YOU EVER USED A TOILET PLUNGER BEFORE?
GULP!
UM...NO.

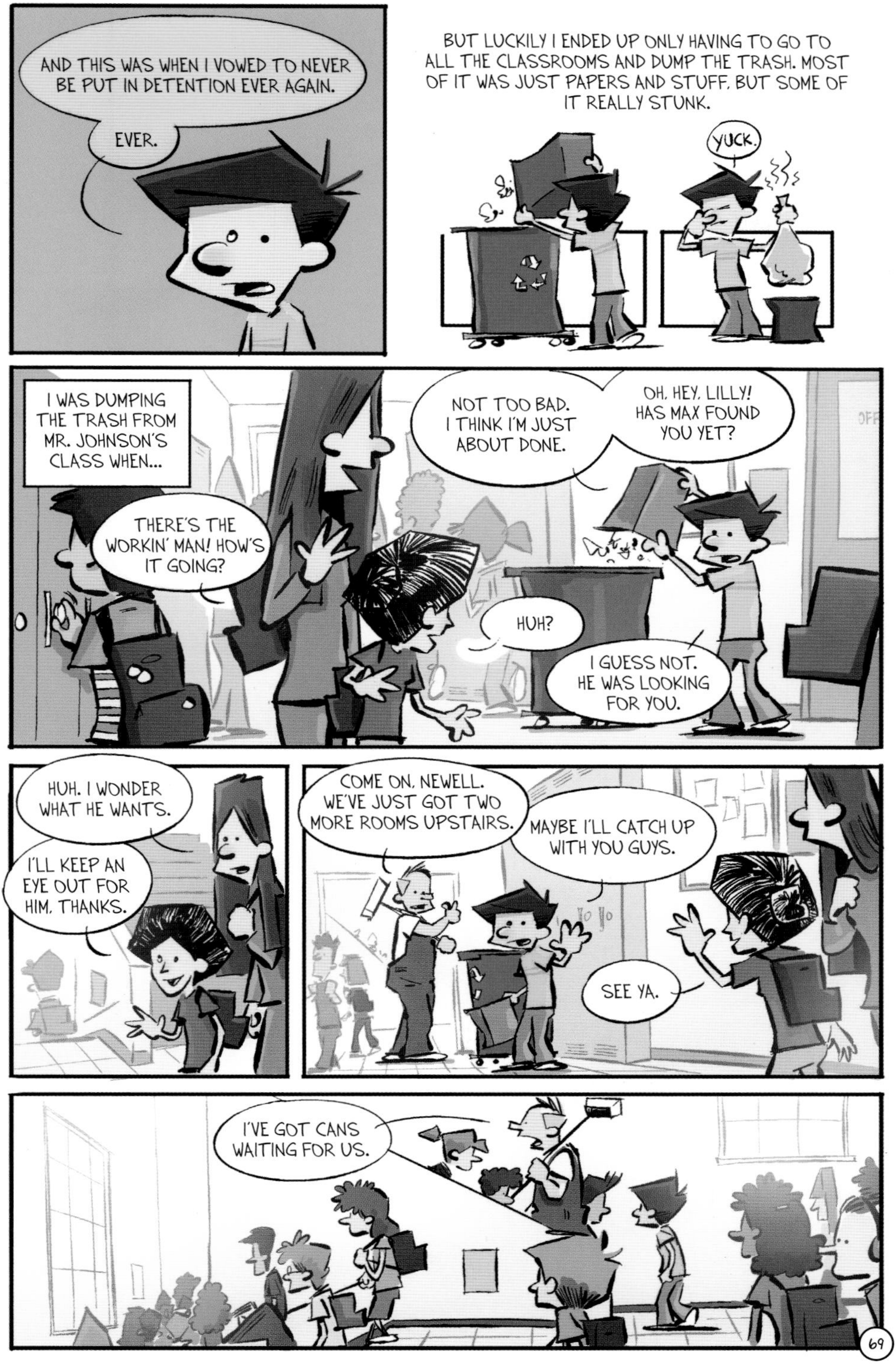

AND THIS WAS WHEN I VOWED TO NEVER BE PUT IN DETENTION EVER AGAIN.
EVER.
BUT LUCKILY I ENDED UP ONLY HAVING TO GO TO ALL THE CLASSROOMS AND DUMP THE TRASH. MOST OF IT WAS JUST PAPERS AND STUFF, BUT SOME OF IT REALLY STUNK.
YUCK.
I WAS DUMPING THE TRASH FROM MR. JOHNSON'S CLASS WHEN...
THERE'S THE WORKIN' MAN! HOW'S IT GOING?
NOT TOO BAD. I THINK I'M JUST ABOUT DONE.
OH, HEY, LILLY! HAS MAX FOUND YOU YET?
HUH?
I GUESS NOT. HE WAS LOOKING FOR YOU.
HUH. I WONDER WHAT HE WANTS.
I'LL KEEP AN EYE OUT FOR HIM. THANKS.
COME ON, NEWELL. WE'VE JUST GOT TWO MORE ROOMS UPSTAIRS.
MAYBE I'LL CATCH UP WITH YOU GUYS.
SEE YA.
I'VE GOT CANS WAITING FOR US.

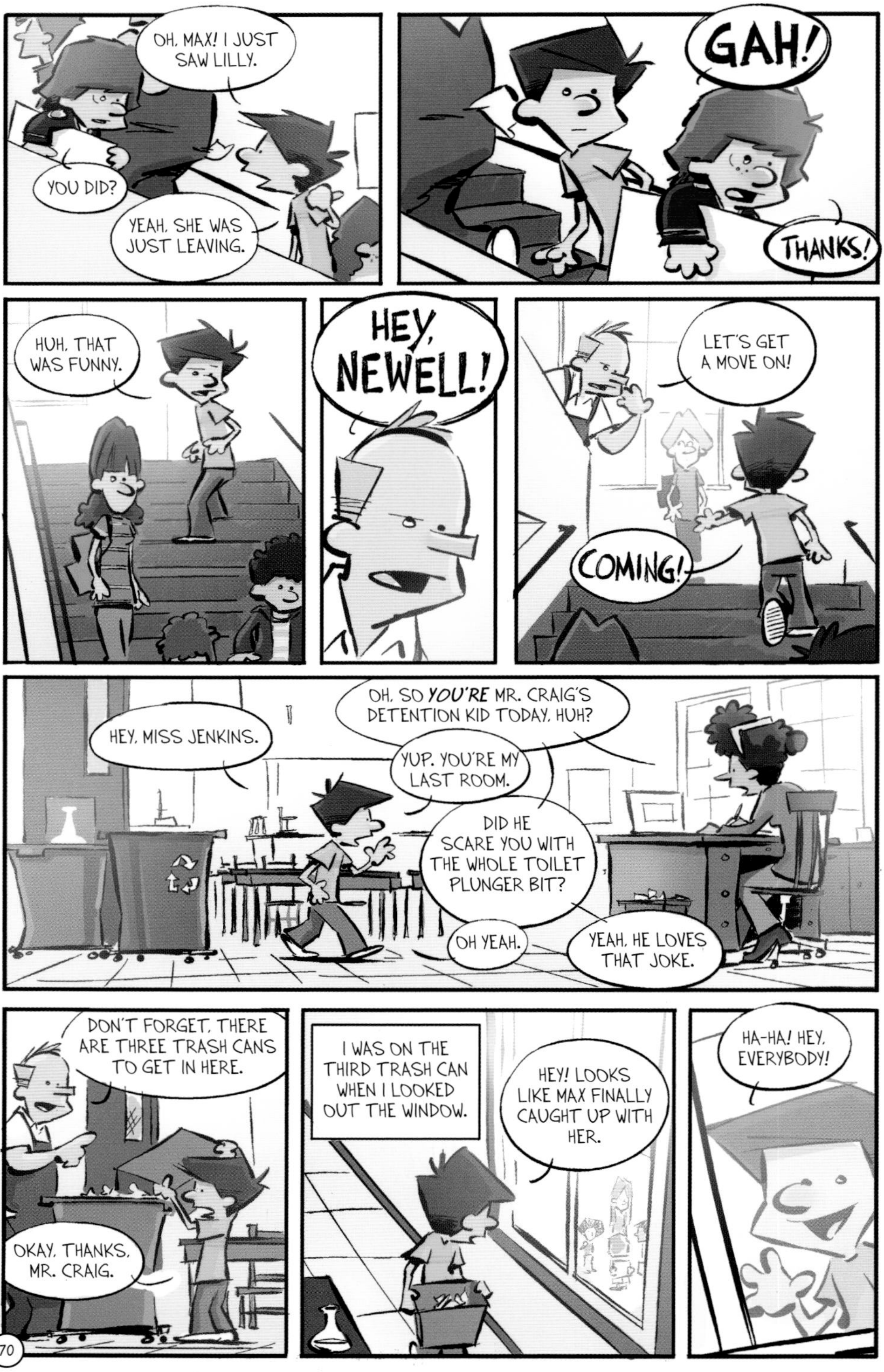
OH, MAX! I JUST SAW LILLY.
YOU DID?
YEAH, SHE WAS JUST LEAVING.
GAH!
THANKS!
HUH, THAT WAS FUNNY.
HEY, NEWELL!
LET'S GET A MOVE ON!
COMING!
HEY, MISS JENKINS.
OH, SO *YOU'RE* MR. CRAIG'S DETENTION KID TODAY, HUH?
YUP. YOU'RE MY LAST ROOM.
DID HE SCARE YOU WITH THE WHOLE TOILET PLUNGER BIT?
OH YEAH.
YEAH, HE LOVES THAT JOKE.
DON'T FORGET, THERE ARE THREE TRASH CANS TO GET IN HERE.
OKAY, THANKS, MR. CRAIG.
I WAS ON THE THIRD TRASH CAN WHEN I LOOKED OUT THE WINDOW.
HEY! LOOKS LIKE MAX FINALLY CAUGHT UP WITH HER.
HA-HA! HEY, EVERYBODY!

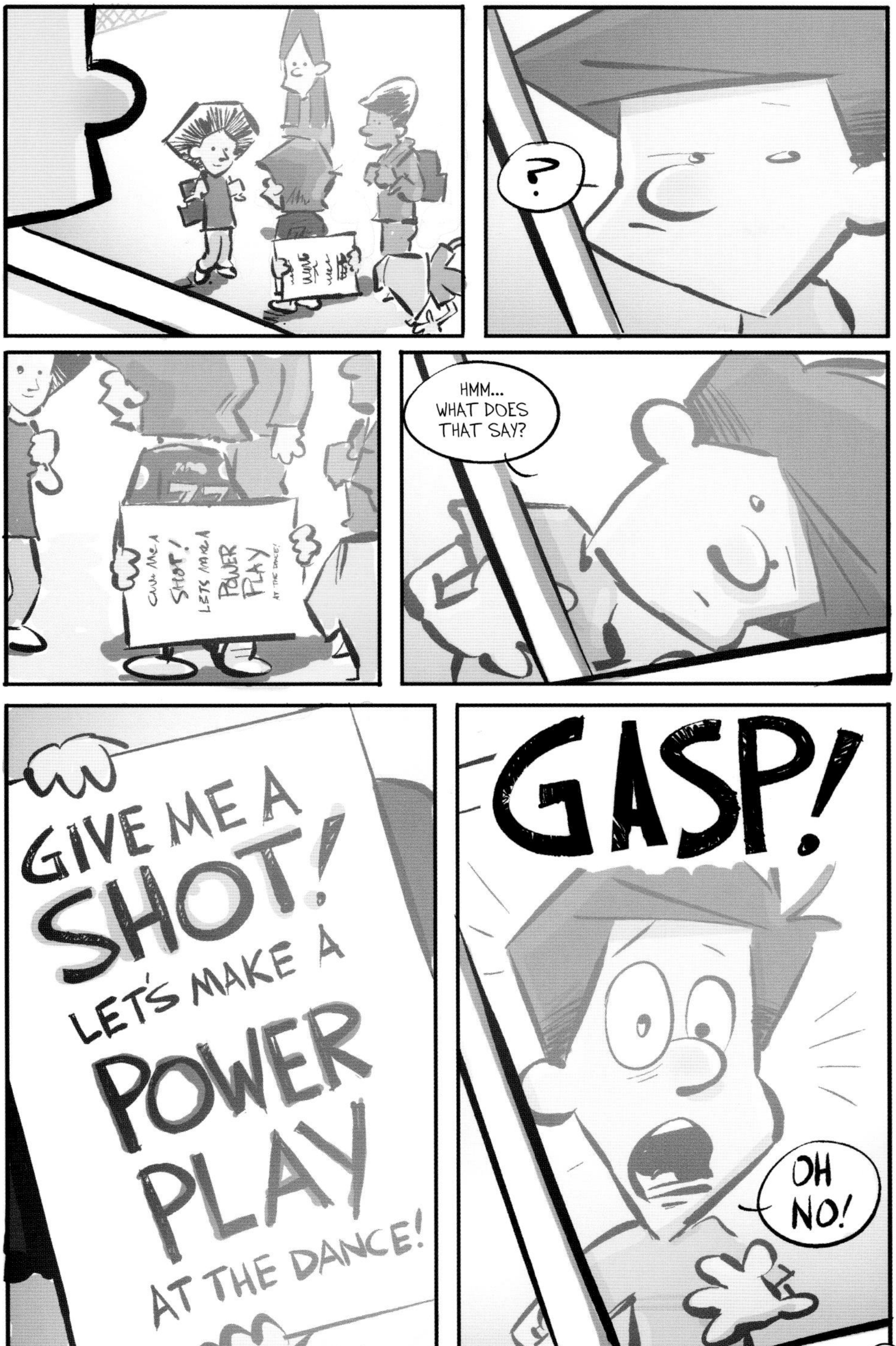
?
HMM... WHAT DOES THAT SAY?
GIVE ME A SHOT! LET'S MAKE A POWER PLAY AT THE DANCE!
GASP!
OH NO!

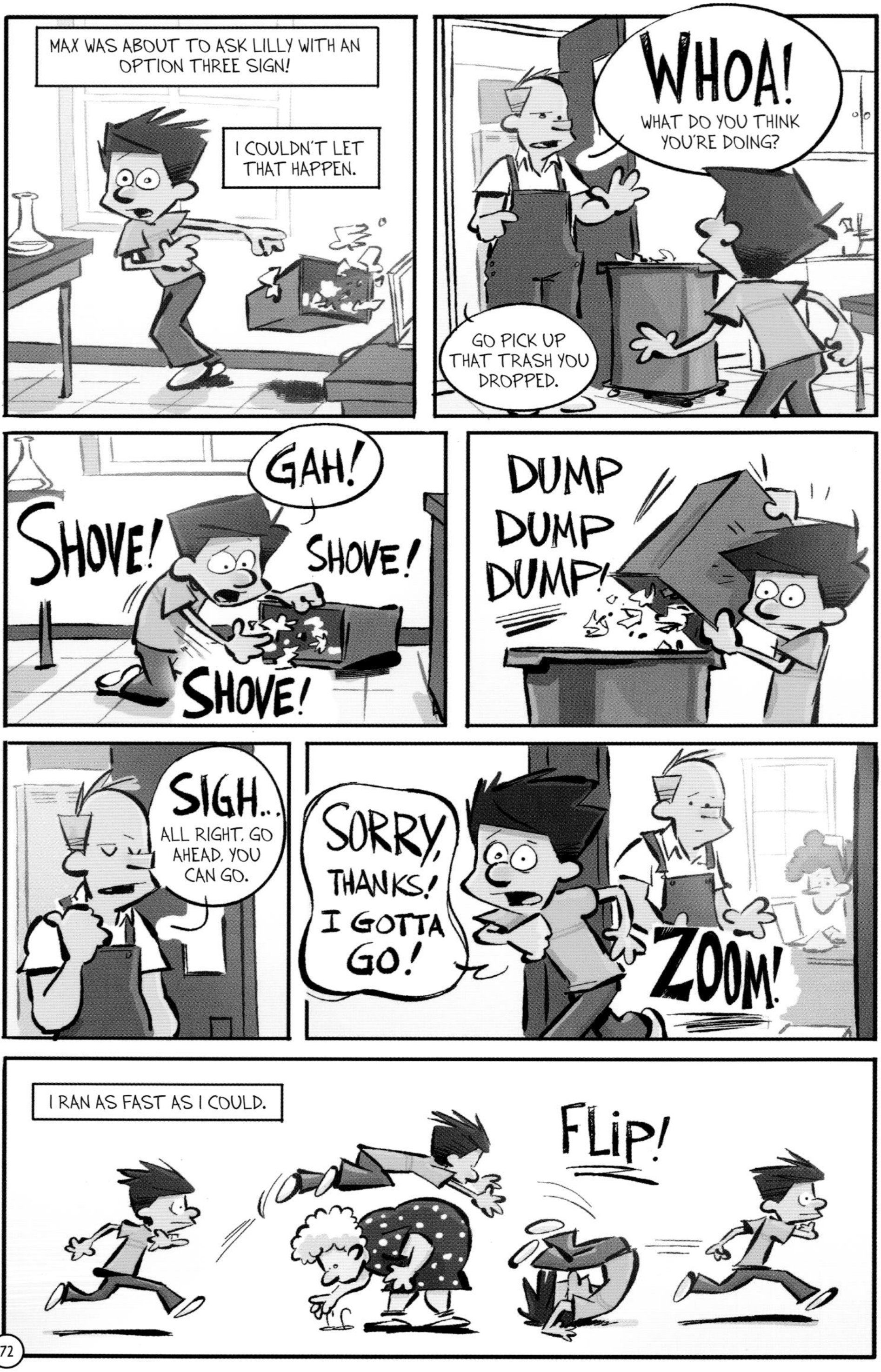
MAX WAS ABOUT TO ASK LILLY WITH AN OPTION THREE SIGN!
I COULDN'T LET THAT HAPPEN.
WHOA!
WHAT DO YOU THINK YOU'RE DOING?
GO PICK UP THAT TRASH YOU DROPPED.
GAH!
SHOVE!
SHOVE!
SHOVE!
DUMP DUMP DUMP!
SIGH...
ALL RIGHT. GO AHEAD. YOU CAN GO.
SORRY, THANKS! I GOTTA GO!
ZOOM!
I RAN AS FAST AS I COULD.
FLIP!

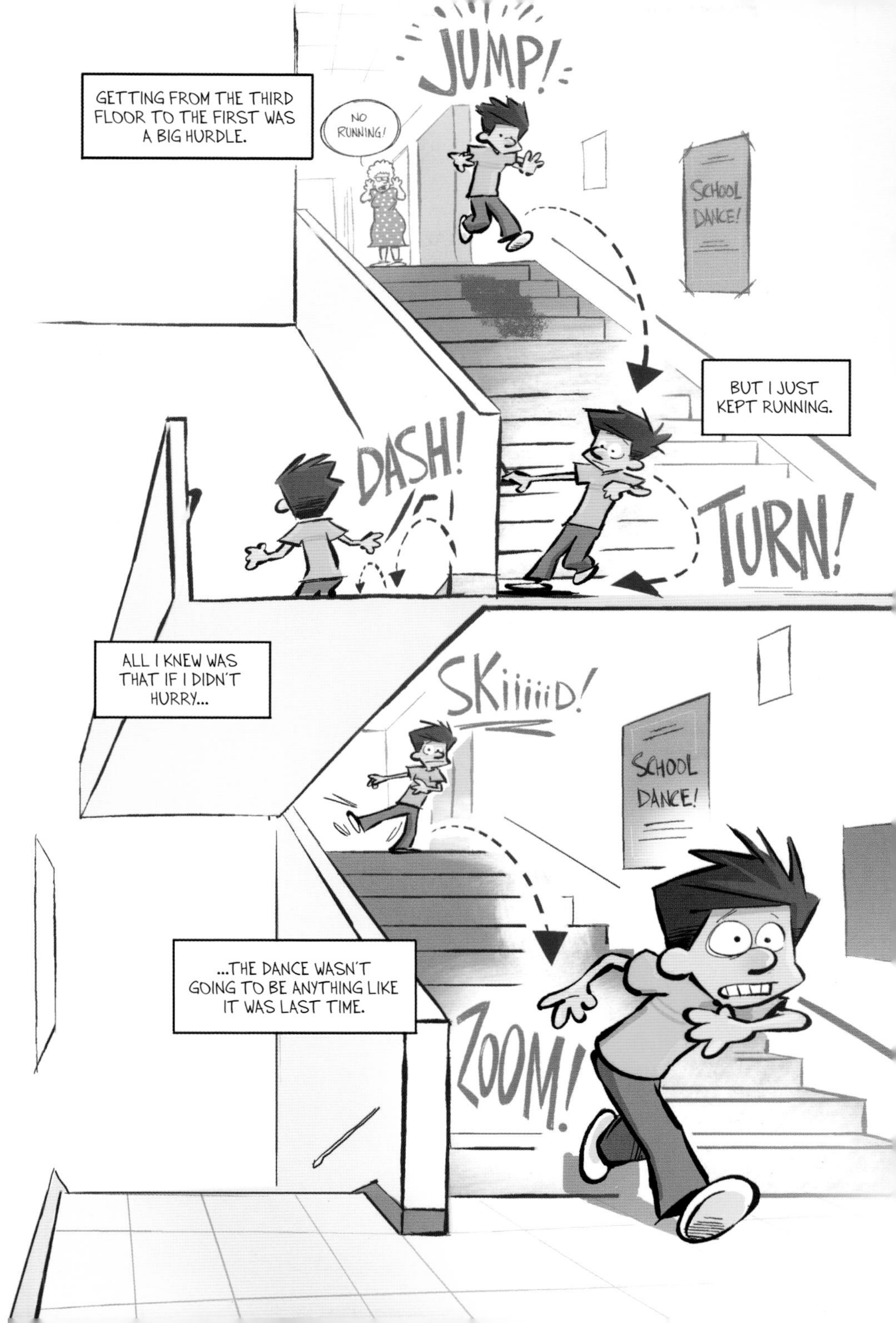
GETTING FROM THE THIRD FLOOR TO THE FIRST WAS A BIG HURDLE.
NO RUNNING!
JUMP!
SCHOOL DANCE!
BUT I JUST KEPT RUNNING.
DASH!
TURN!
ALL I KNEW WAS THAT IF I DIDN'T HURRY...
SKiiiiiD!
SCHOOL DANCE!
...THE DANCE WASN'T GOING TO BE ANYTHING LIKE IT WAS LAST TIME.
ZOOM!

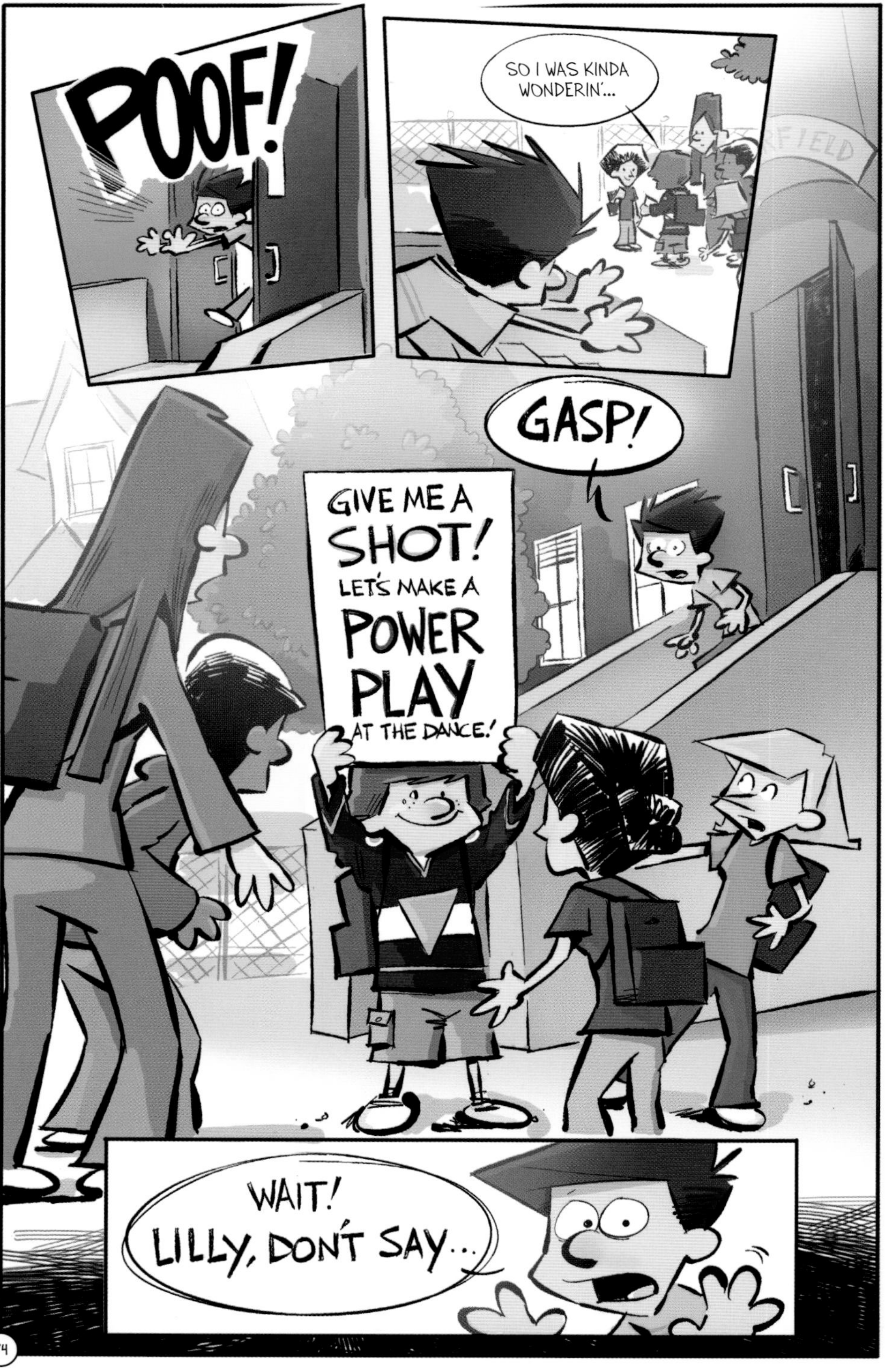

POOF!
SO I WAS KINDA WONDERIN'...
GASP!
GIVE ME A SHOT! LET'S MAKE A POWER PLAY AT THE DANCE!
WAIT! LILLY, DON'T SAY...

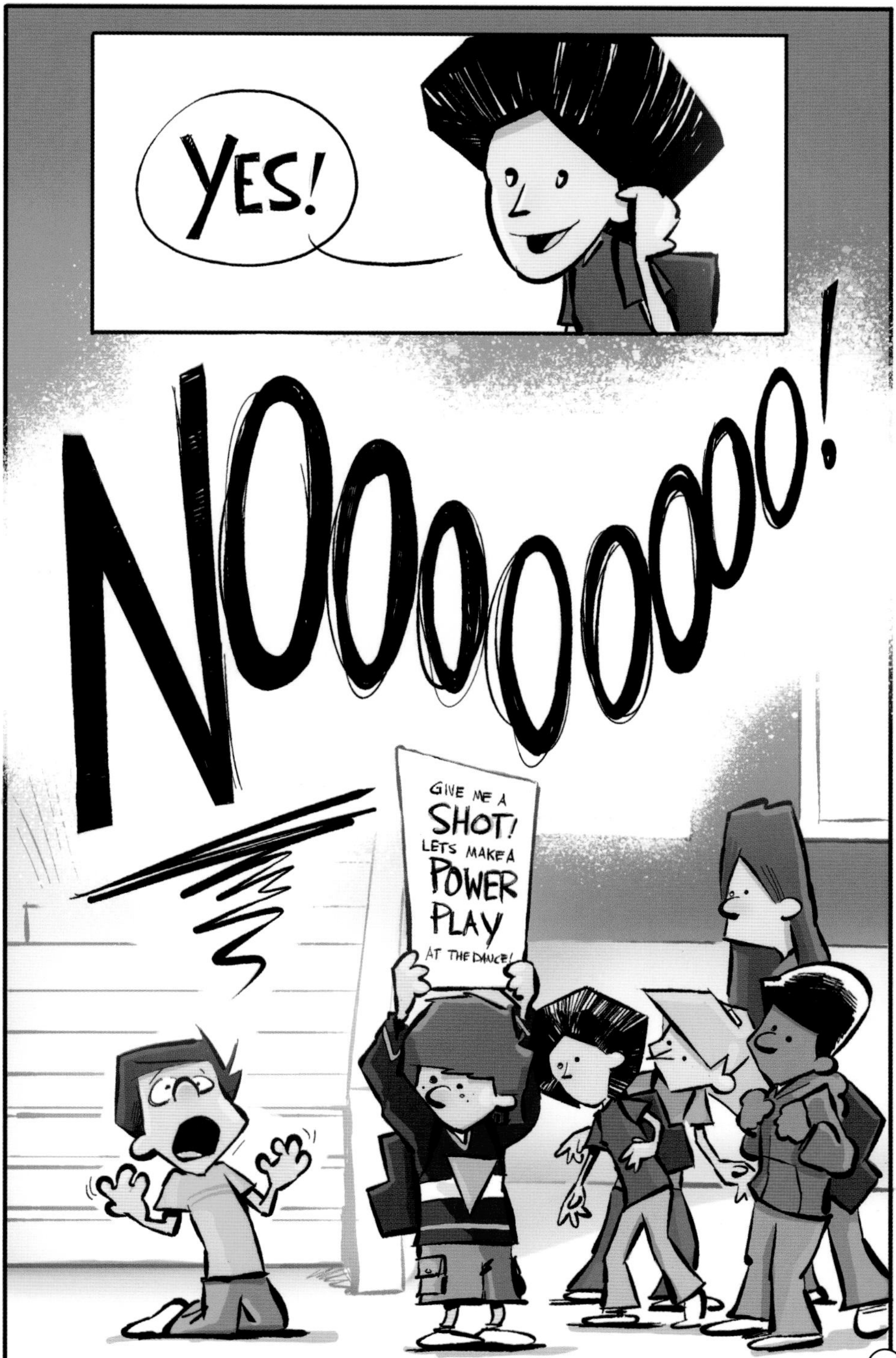
YES!
NOOOOOOOOO!
GIVE ME A SHOT! LETS MAKE A POWER PLAY AT THE DANCE!

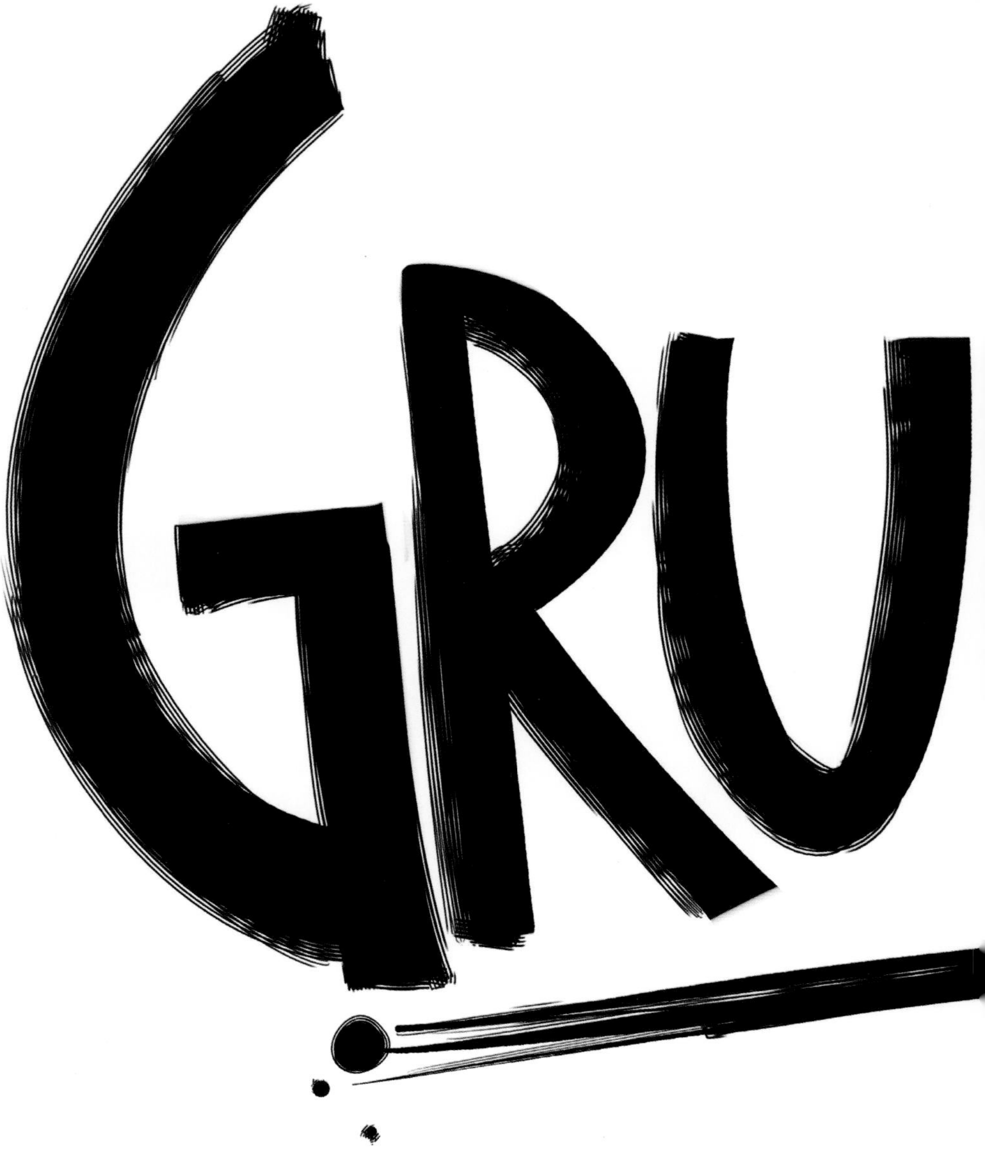
GRU

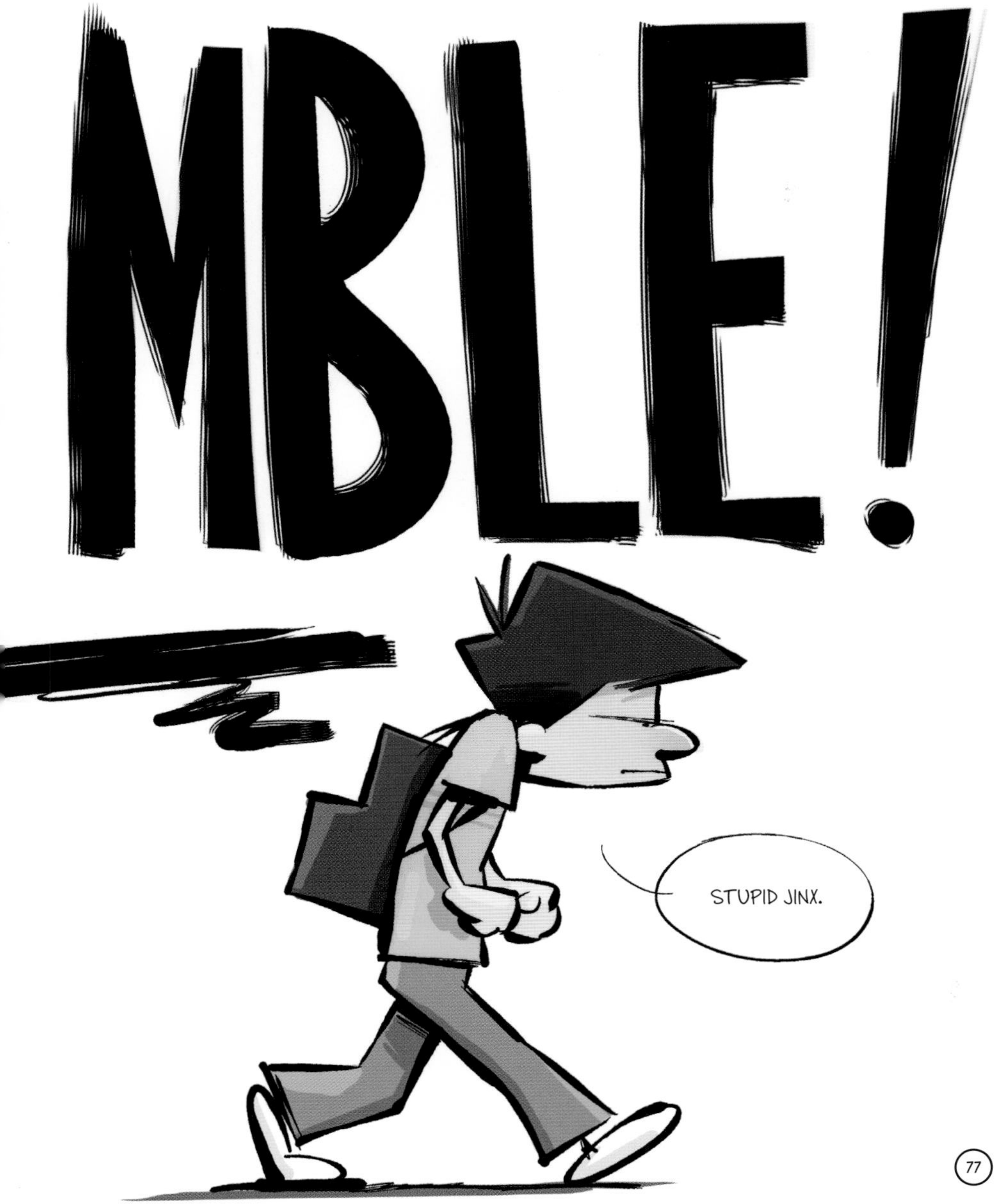

MBLE!
STUPID JINX.

CHAPTER FIVE
THE JINX BREAKER

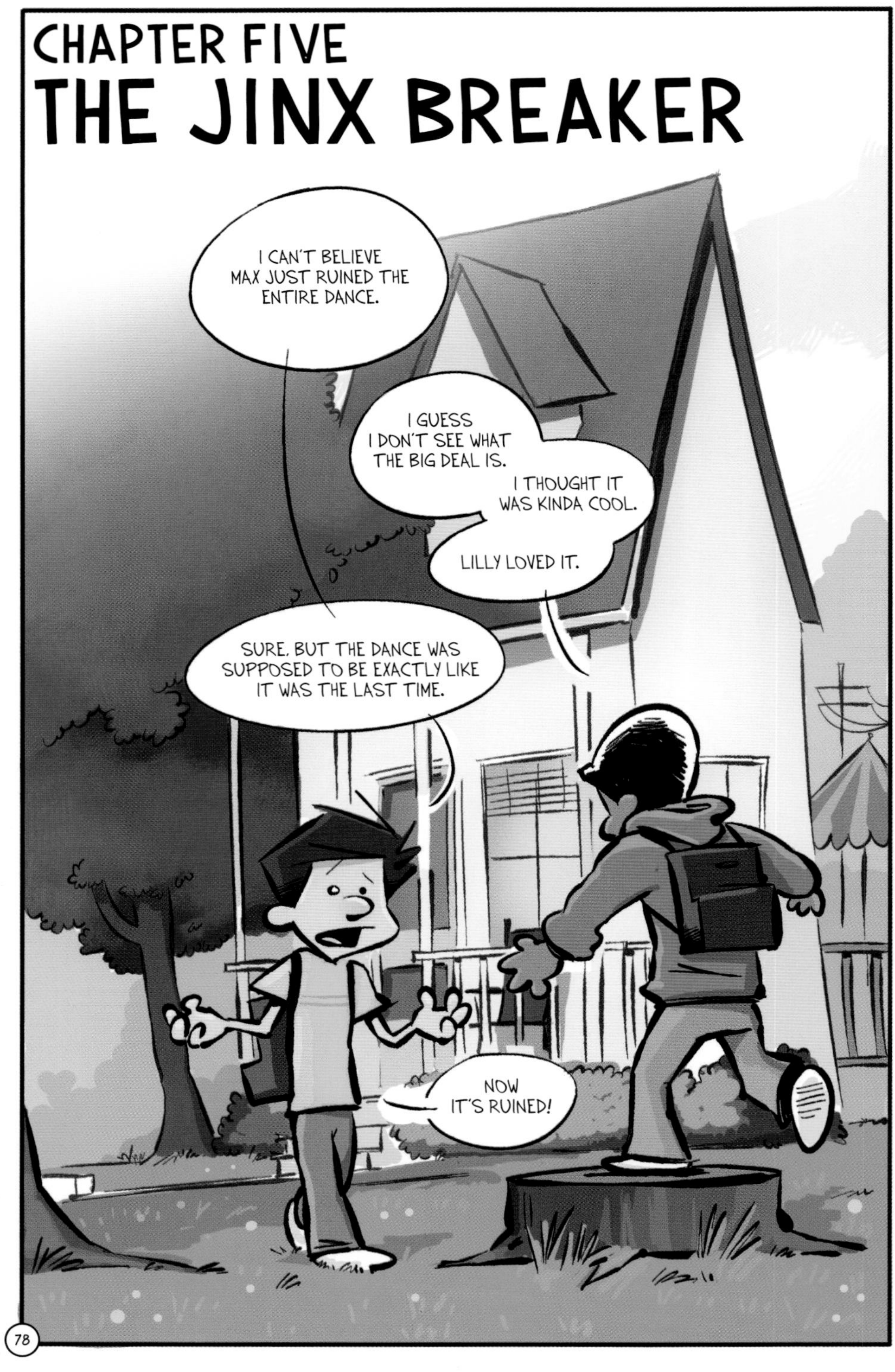
I CAN'T BELIEVE MAX JUST RUINED THE ENTIRE DANCE.
I GUESS I DON'T SEE WHAT THE BIG DEAL IS.
I THOUGHT IT WAS KINDA COOL.
LILLY LOVED IT.
SURE, BUT THE DANCE WAS SUPPOSED TO BE EXACTLY LIKE IT WAS THE LAST TIME.
NOW IT'S RUINED!

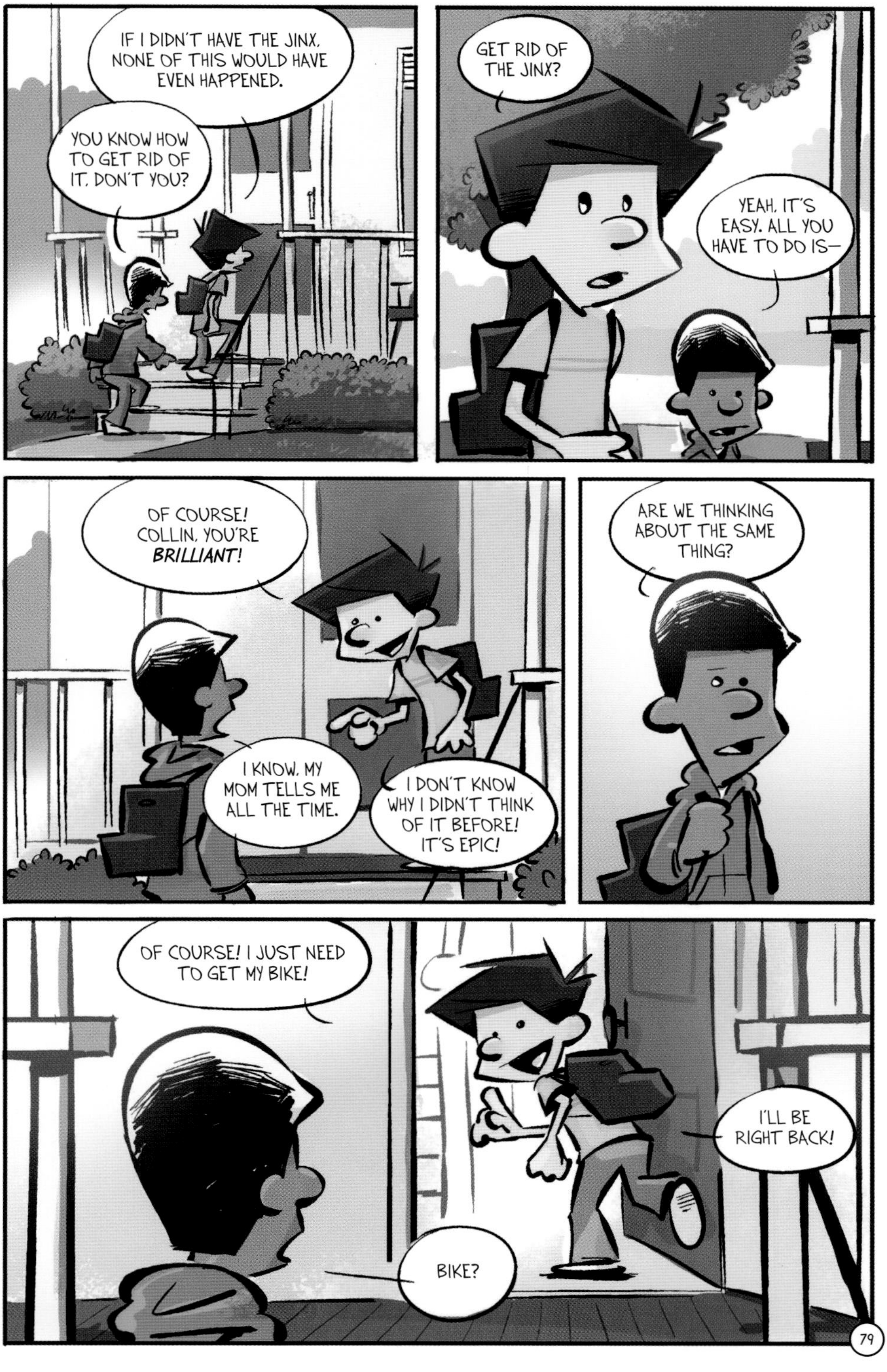
IF I DIDN'T HAVE THE JINX, NONE OF THIS WOULD HAVE EVEN HAPPENED.
YOU KNOW HOW TO GET RID OF IT, DON'T YOU?
GET RID OF THE JINX?
YEAH, IT'S EASY. ALL YOU HAVE TO DO IS—
OF COURSE! COLLIN, YOU'RE **BRILLIANT!**
I KNOW. MY MOM TELLS ME ALL THE TIME.
I DON'T KNOW WHY I DIDN'T THINK OF IT BEFORE! IT'S EPIC!
ARE WE THINKING ABOUT THE SAME THING?
OF COURSE! I JUST NEED TO GET MY BIKE!
I'LL BE RIGHT BACK!
BIKE?

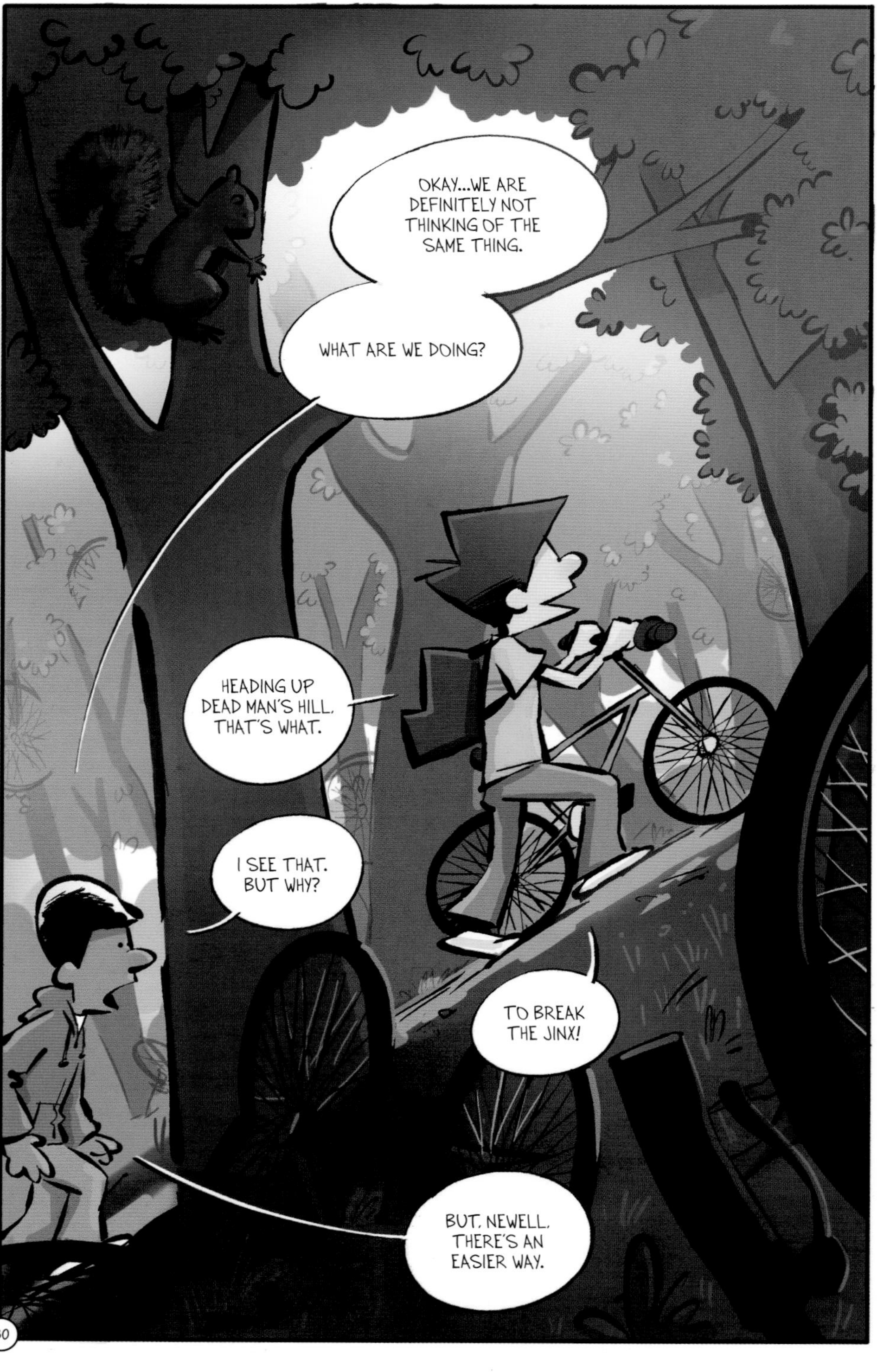

OKAY...WE ARE DEFINITELY NOT THINKING OF THE SAME THING.
WHAT ARE WE DOING?
HEADING UP DEAD MAN'S HILL. THAT'S WHAT.
I SEE THAT. BUT WHY?
TO BREAK THE JINX!
BUT, NEWELL, THERE'S AN EASIER WAY.

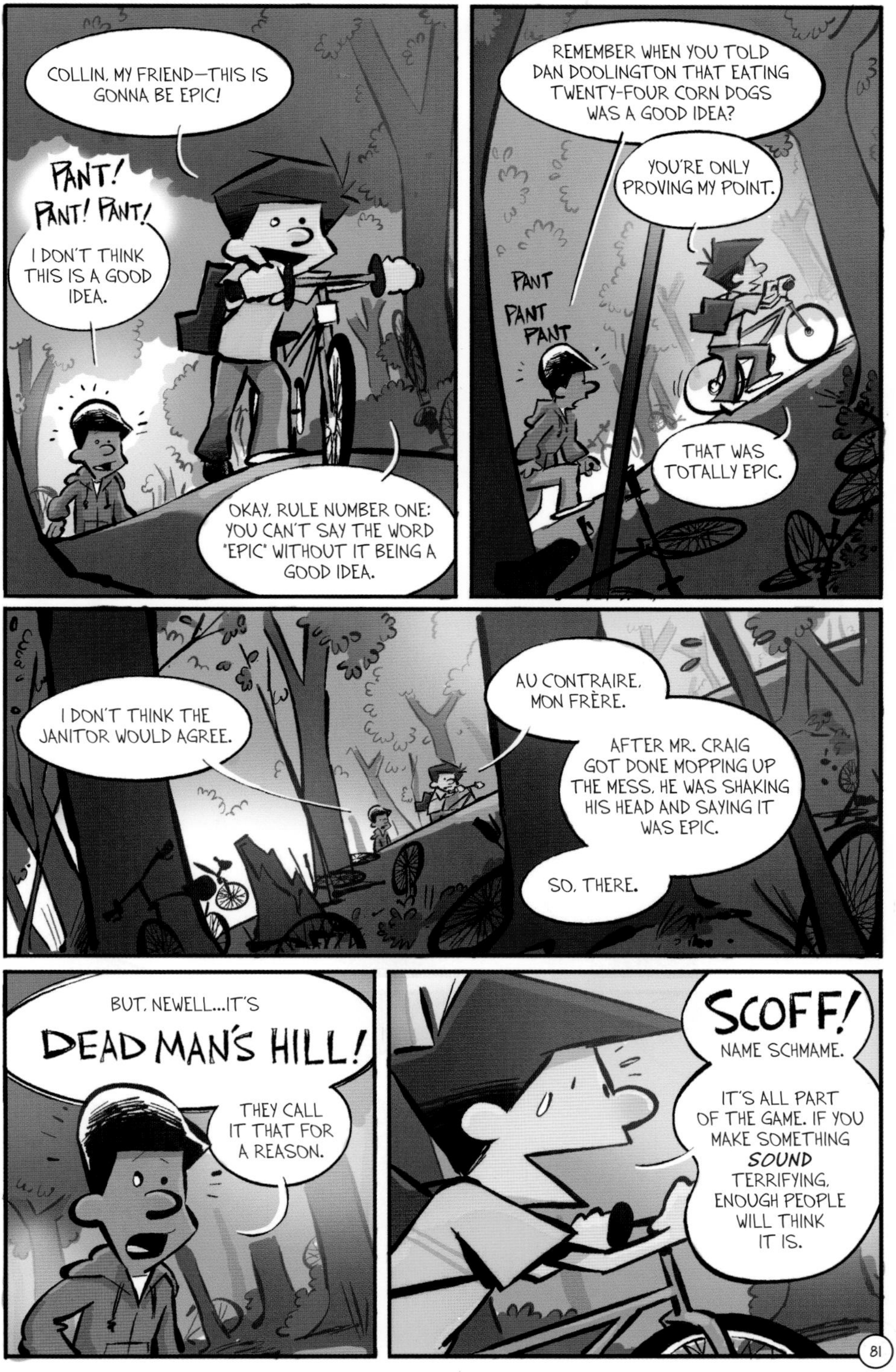
COLLIN, MY FRIEND—THIS IS GONNA BE EPIC!
PANT! PANT! PANT!
I DON'T THINK THIS IS A GOOD IDEA.
OKAY, RULE NUMBER ONE: YOU CAN'T SAY THE WORD "EPIC" WITHOUT IT BEING A GOOD IDEA.
REMEMBER WHEN YOU TOLD DAN DOOLINGTON THAT EATING TWENTY-FOUR CORN DOGS WAS A GOOD IDEA?
YOU'RE ONLY PROVING MY POINT.
PANT PANT PANT
THAT WAS TOTALLY EPIC.
I DON'T THINK THE JANITOR WOULD AGREE.
AU CONTRAIRE, MON FRÈRE.
AFTER MR. CRAIG GOT DONE MOPPING UP THE MESS, HE WAS SHAKING HIS HEAD AND SAYING IT WAS EPIC.
SO, THERE.
BUT, NEWELL...IT'S DEAD MAN'S HILL!
THEY CALL IT THAT FOR A REASON.
SCOFF! NAME SCHMAME.
IT'S ALL PART OF THE GAME. IF YOU MAKE SOMETHING SOUND TERRIFYING, ENOUGH PEOPLE WILL THINK IT IS.

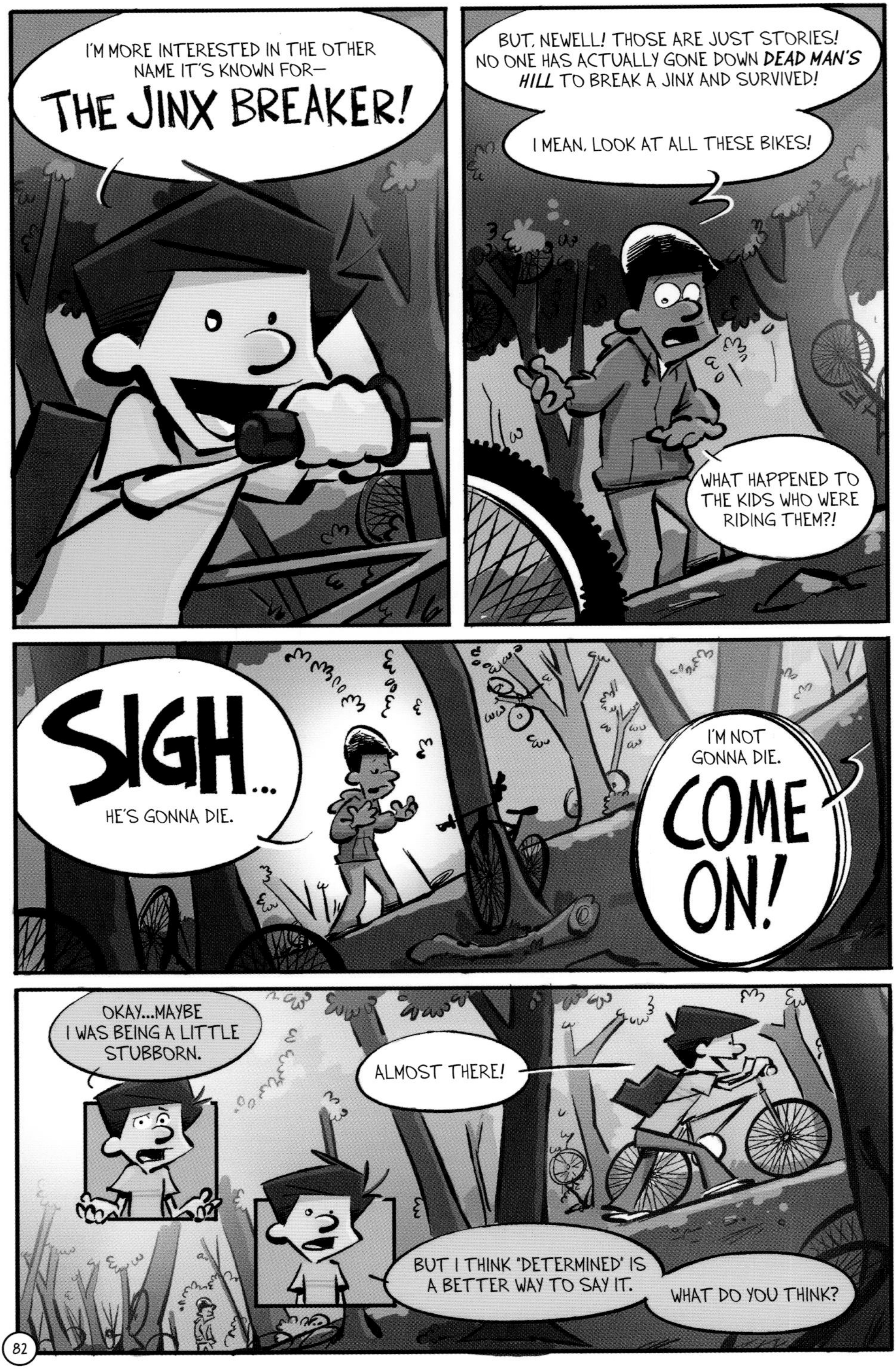

I'M MORE INTERESTED IN THE OTHER NAME IT'S KNOWN FOR— THE JINX BREAKER!
BUT, NEWELL! THOSE ARE JUST STORIES! NO ONE HAS ACTUALLY GONE DOWN DEAD MAN'S HILL TO BREAK A JINX AND SURVIVED!
I MEAN, LOOK AT ALL THESE BIKES!
WHAT HAPPENED TO THE KIDS WHO WERE RIDING THEM?!
SIGH... HE'S GONNA DIE.
I'M NOT GONNA DIE. COME ON!
OKAY...MAYBE I WAS BEING A LITTLE STUBBORN.
ALMOST THERE!
BUT I THINK "DETERMINED" IS A BETTER WAY TO SAY IT.
WHAT DO YOU THINK?

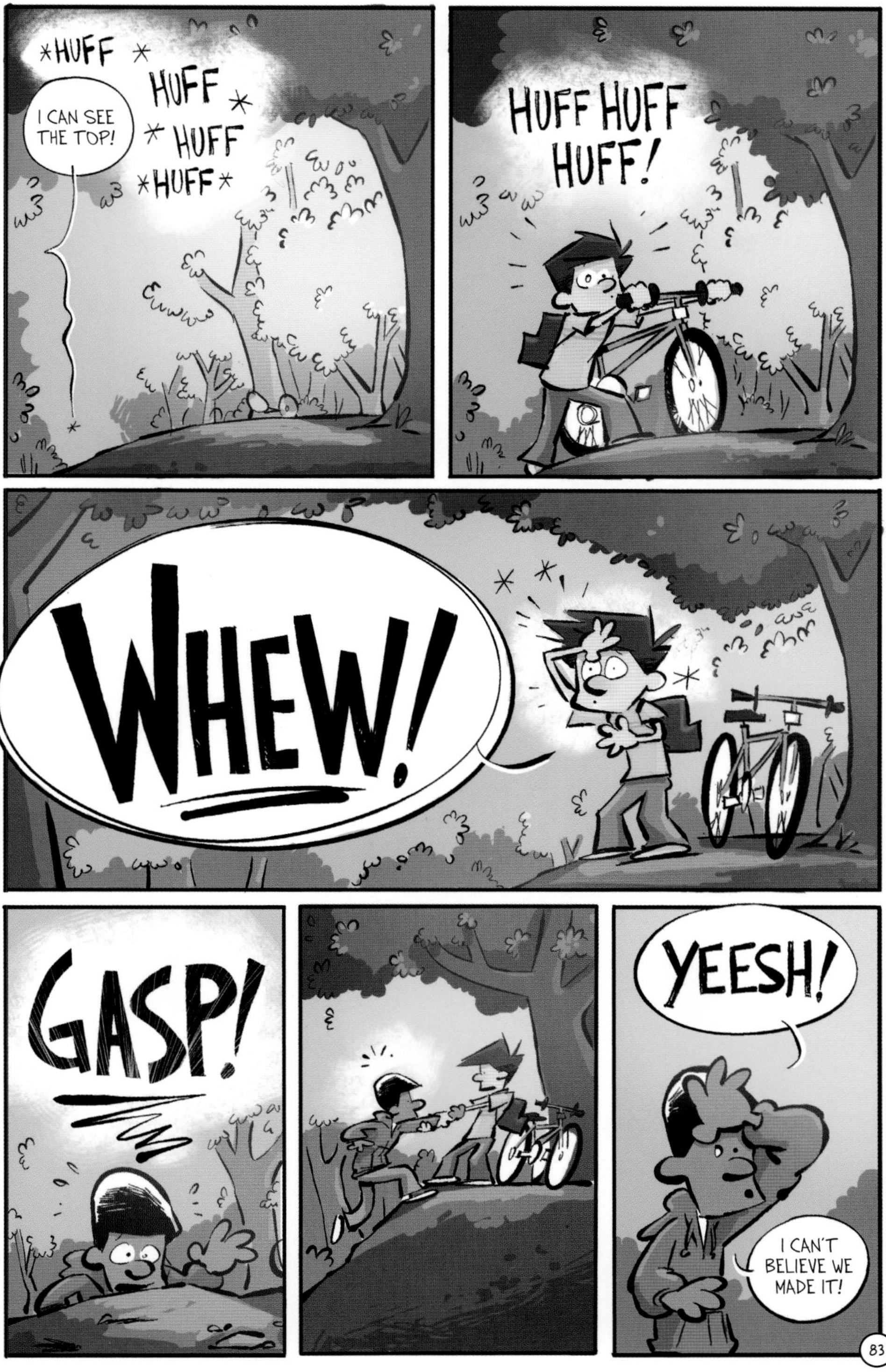
*HUFF *
I CAN SEE THE TOP!
HUFF *
* HUFF
HUFF
HUFF HUFF HUFF!
WHEW!
GASP!
YEESH!
I CAN'T BELIEVE WE MADE IT!

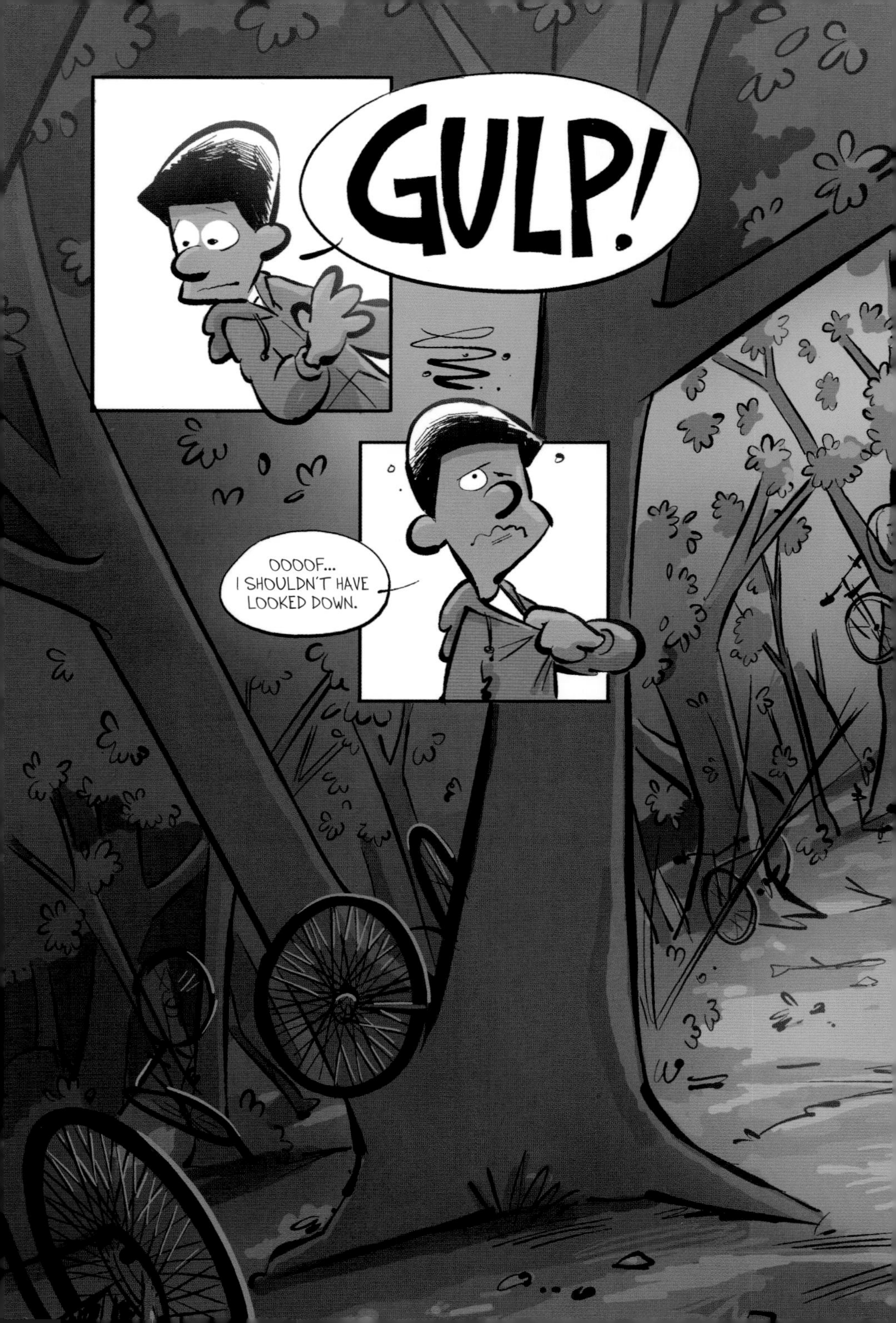
GULP!
OOOOF... I SHOULDN'T HAVE LOOKED DOWN.

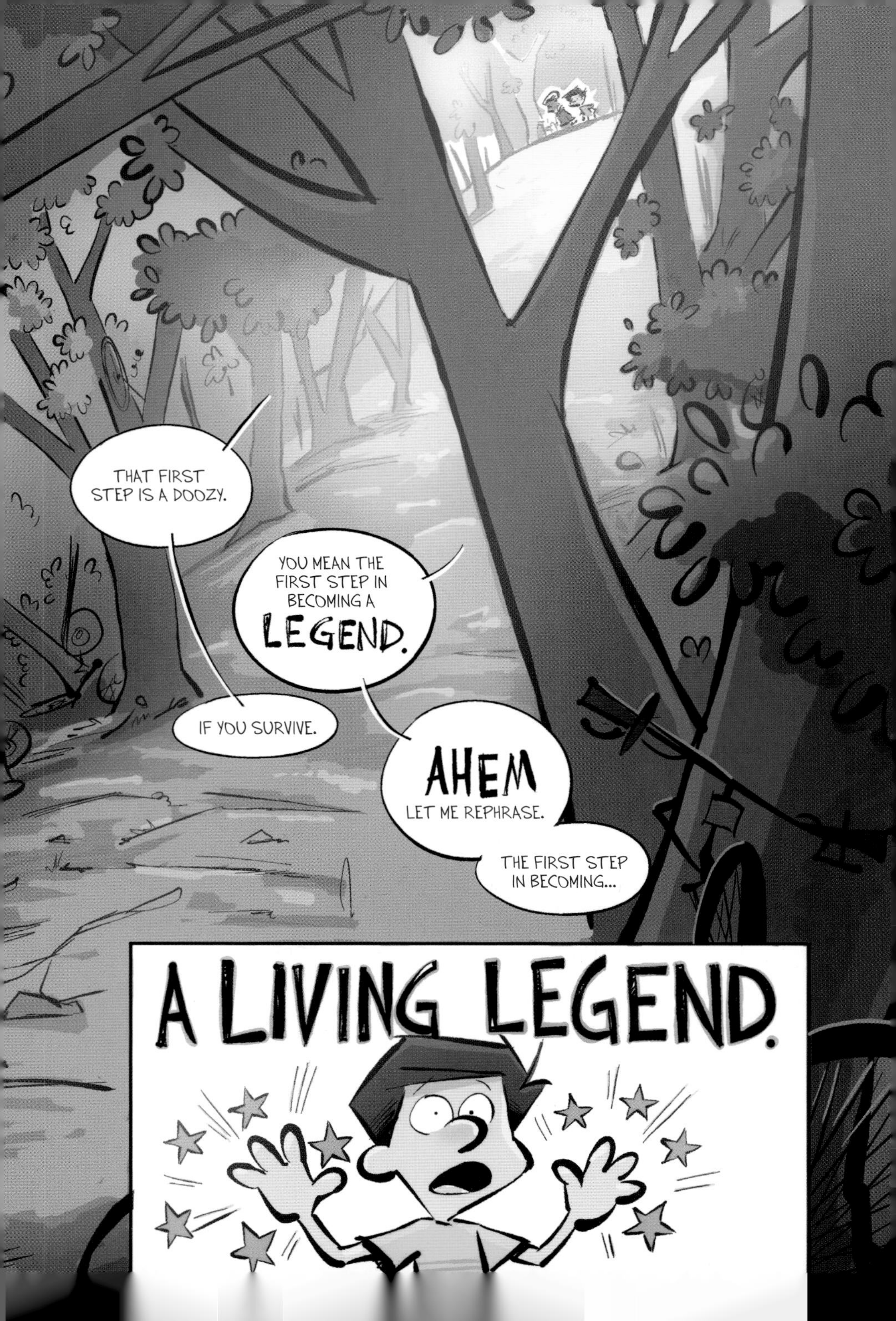
THAT FIRST STEP IS A DOOZY.
YOU MEAN THE FIRST STEP IN BECOMING A LEGEND.
IF YOU SURVIVE.
AHEM
LET ME REPHRASE.
THE FIRST STEP IN BECOMING...
A LIVING LEGEND.

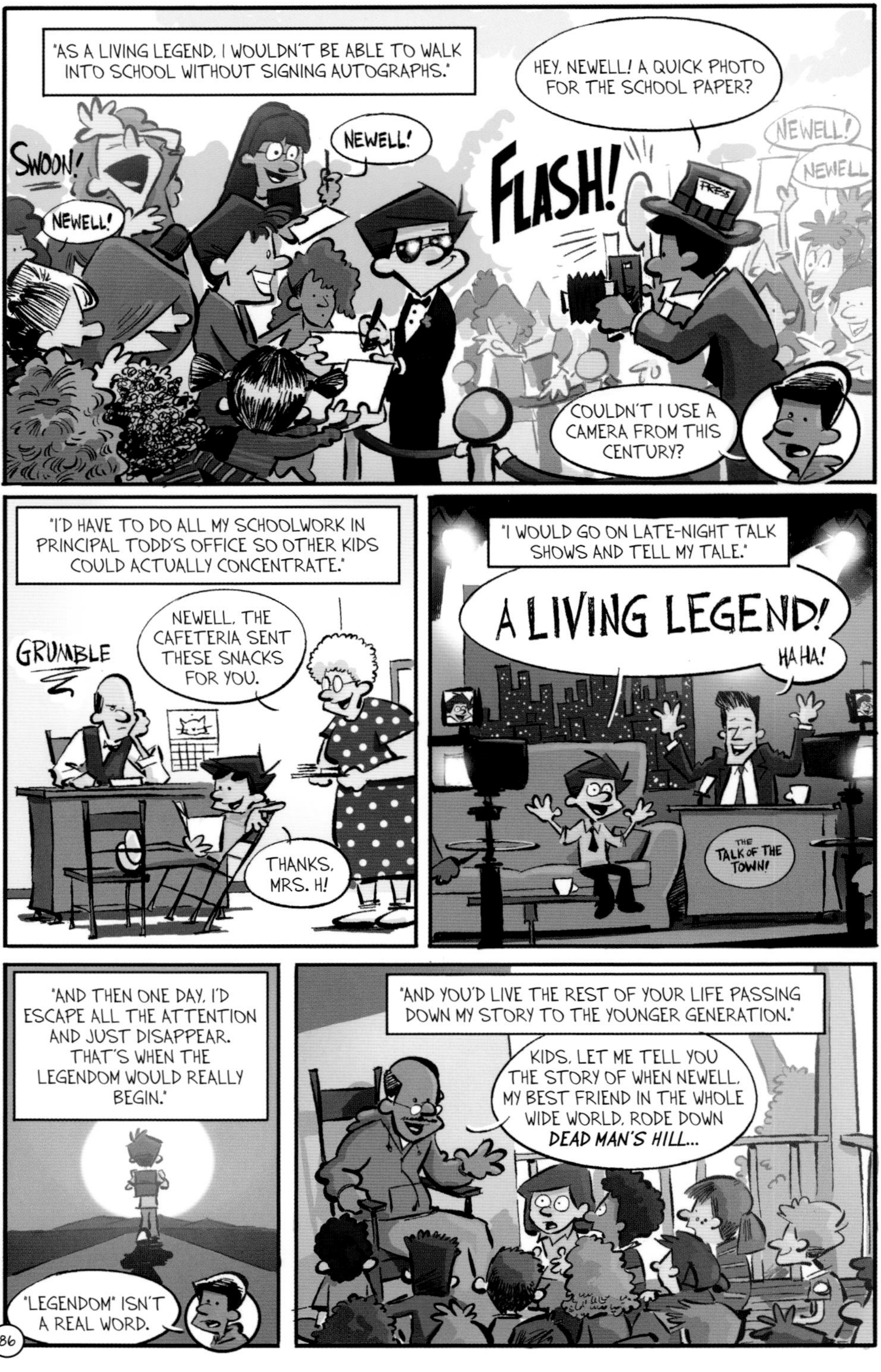

"AS A LIVING LEGEND, I WOULDN'T BE ABLE TO WALK INTO SCHOOL WITHOUT SIGNING AUTOGRAPHS."
SWOON!
NEWELL!
NEWELL!
FLASH!
HEY, NEWELL! A QUICK PHOTO FOR THE SCHOOL PAPER?
NEWELL!
NEWELL
PRESS
COULDN'T I USE A CAMERA FROM THIS CENTURY?
"I'D HAVE TO DO ALL MY SCHOOLWORK IN PRINCIPAL TODD'S OFFICE SO OTHER KIDS COULD ACTUALLY CONCENTRATE."
GRUMBLE
NEWELL, THE CAFETERIA SENT THESE SNACKS FOR YOU.
THANKS, MRS. H!
"I WOULD GO ON LATE-NIGHT TALK SHOWS AND TELL MY TALE."
A LIVING LEGEND!
HA HA!
THE TALK OF THE TOWN!
"AND THEN ONE DAY, I'D ESCAPE ALL THE ATTENTION AND JUST DISAPPEAR. THAT'S WHEN THE LEGENDOM WOULD REALLY BEGIN."
"LEGENDOM" ISN'T A REAL WORD.
"AND YOU'D LIVE THE REST OF YOUR LIFE PASSING DOWN MY STORY TO THE YOUNGER GENERATION."
KIDS, LET ME TELL YOU THE STORY OF WHEN NEWELL, MY BEST FRIEND IN THE WHOLE WIDE WORLD, RODE DOWN ***DEAD MAN'S HILL...***

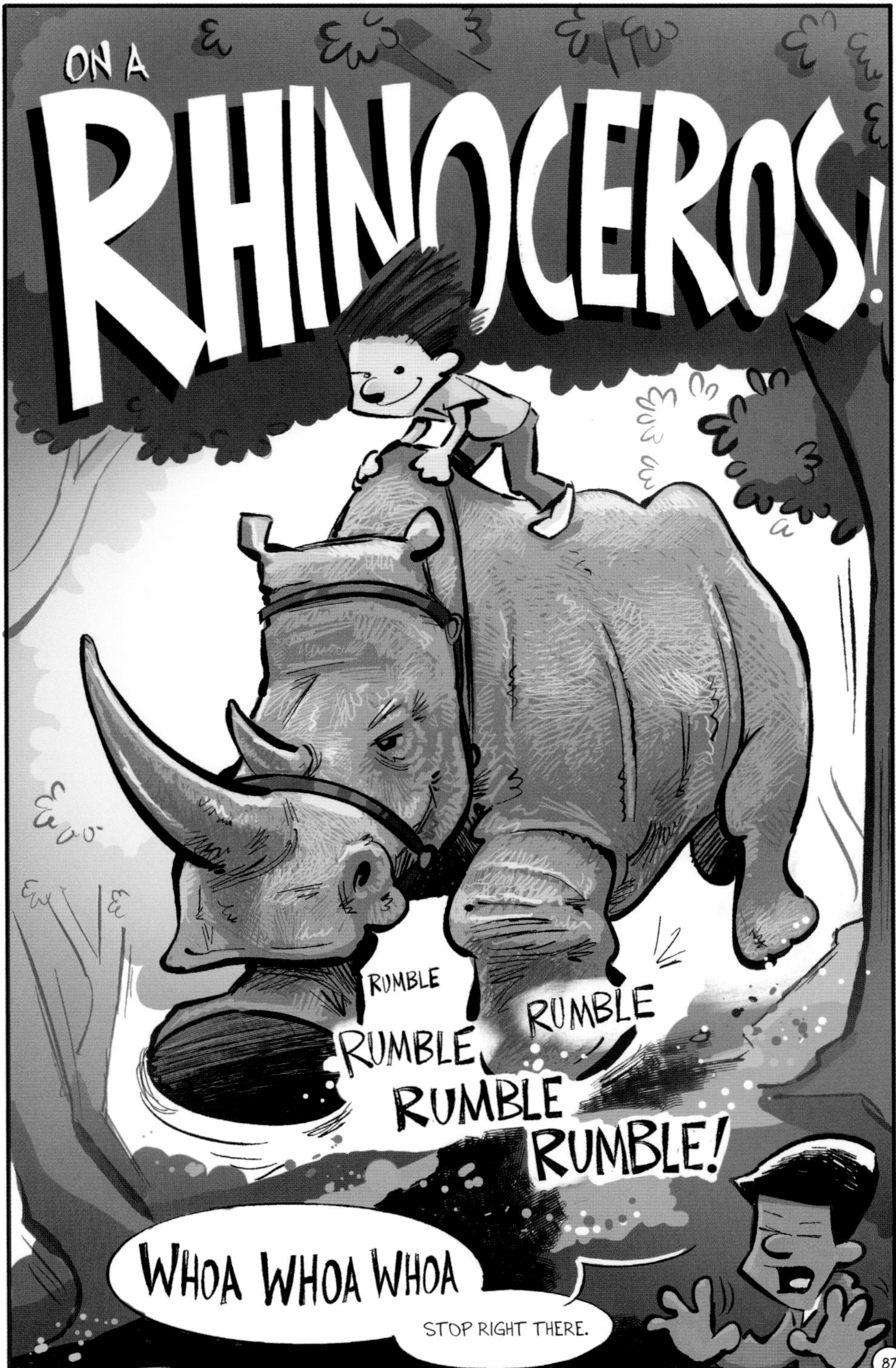
ON A
RHINOCEROS!
RUMBLE
RUMBLE
RUMBLE
RUMBLE
RUMBLE!
WHOA WHOA WHOA
STOP RIGHT THERE.

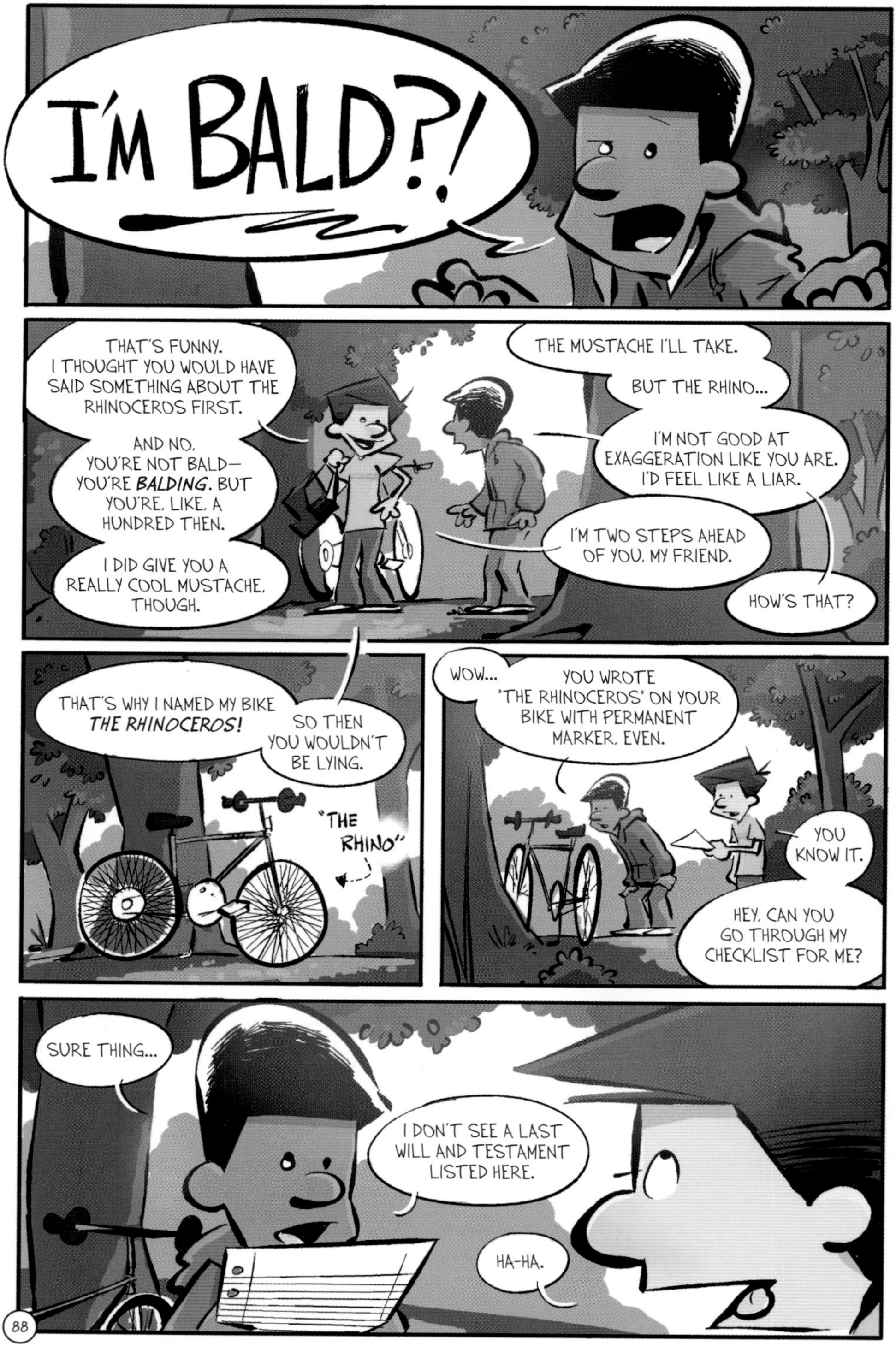
I'M BALD?!
THAT'S FUNNY. I THOUGHT YOU WOULD HAVE SAID SOMETHING ABOUT THE RHINOCEROS FIRST.
AND NO, YOU'RE NOT BALD— YOU'RE **BALDING**. BUT YOU'RE, LIKE, A HUNDRED THEN.
I DID GIVE YOU A REALLY COOL MUSTACHE, THOUGH.
THE MUSTACHE I'LL TAKE.
BUT THE RHINO...
I'M NOT GOOD AT EXAGGERATION LIKE YOU ARE. I'D FEEL LIKE A LIAR.
I'M TWO STEPS AHEAD OF YOU, MY FRIEND.
HOW'S THAT?
THAT'S WHY I NAMED MY BIKE ***THE RHINOCEROS!***
SO THEN YOU WOULDN'T BE LYING.
"THE RHINO"
WOW...
YOU WROTE "THE RHINOCEROS" ON YOUR BIKE WITH PERMANENT MARKER, EVEN.
YOU KNOW IT.
HEY, CAN YOU GO THROUGH MY CHECKLIST FOR ME?
SURE THING...
I DON'T SEE A LAST WILL AND TESTAMENT LISTED HERE.
HA-HA.

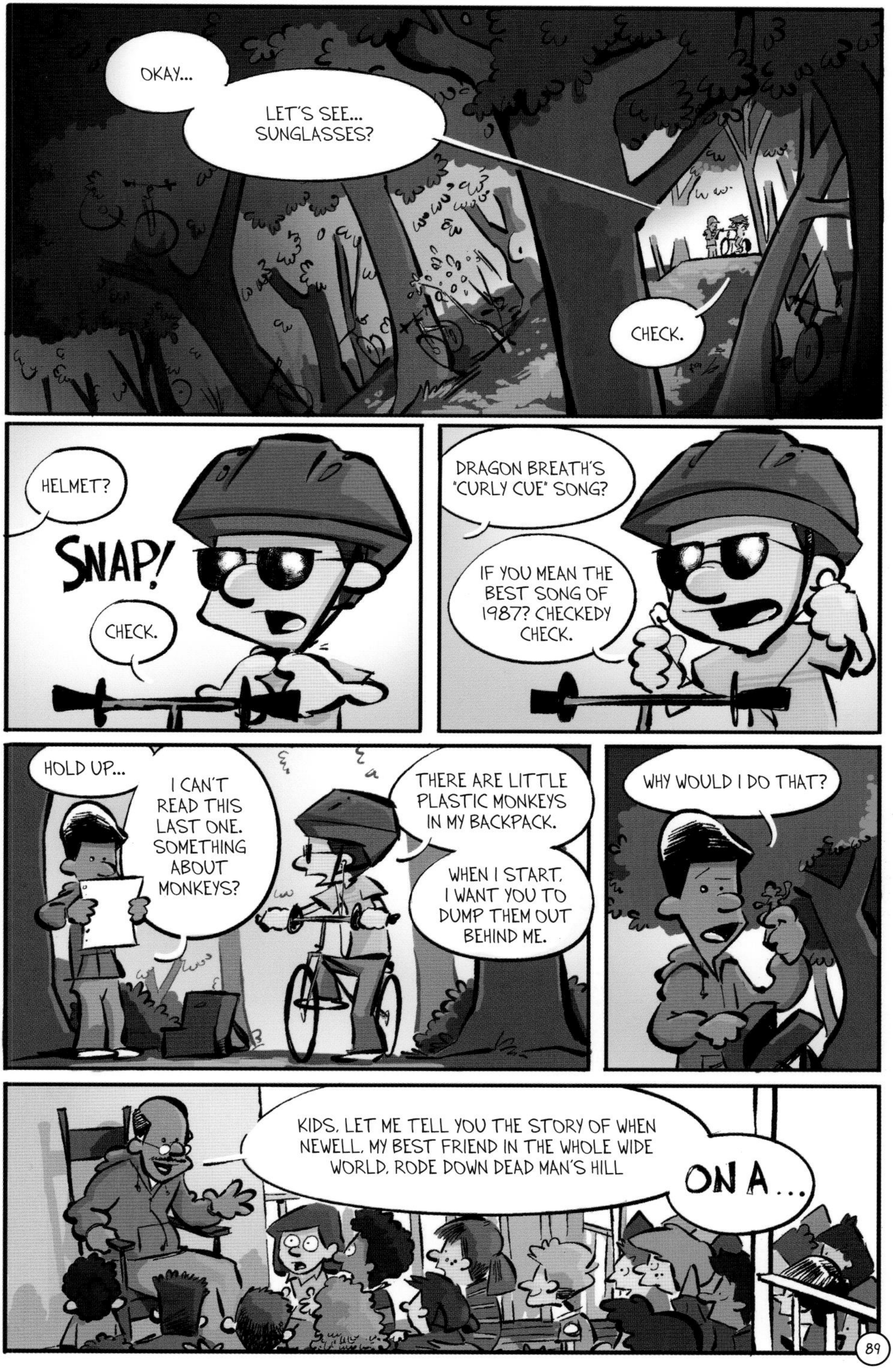
OKAY...
LET'S SEE... SUNGLASSES?
CHECK.
HELMET?
SNAP!
CHECK.
DRAGON BREATH'S "CURLY CUE" SONG?
IF YOU MEAN THE BEST SONG OF 1987? CHECKEDY CHECK.
HOLD UP...
I CAN'T READ THIS LAST ONE. SOMETHING ABOUT MONKEYS?
THERE ARE LITTLE PLASTIC MONKEYS IN MY BACKPACK.
WHEN I START, I WANT YOU TO DUMP THEM OUT BEHIND ME.
WHY WOULD I DO THAT?
KIDS, LET ME TELL YOU THE STORY OF WHEN NEWELL, MY BEST FRIEND IN THE WHOLE WIDE WORLD, RODE DOWN DEAD MAN'S HILL
ON A...

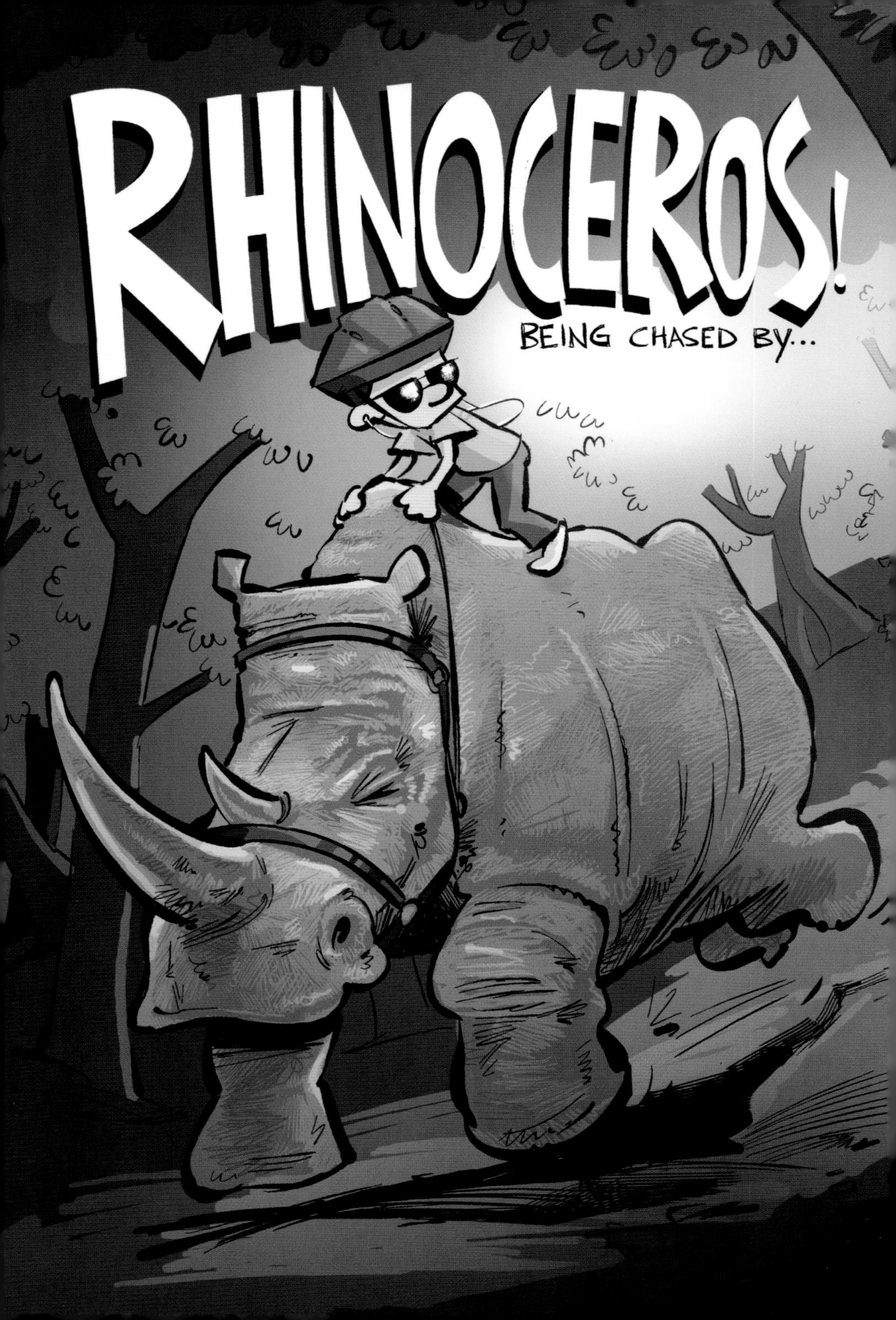
RHINOCEROS!
BEING CHASED BY...

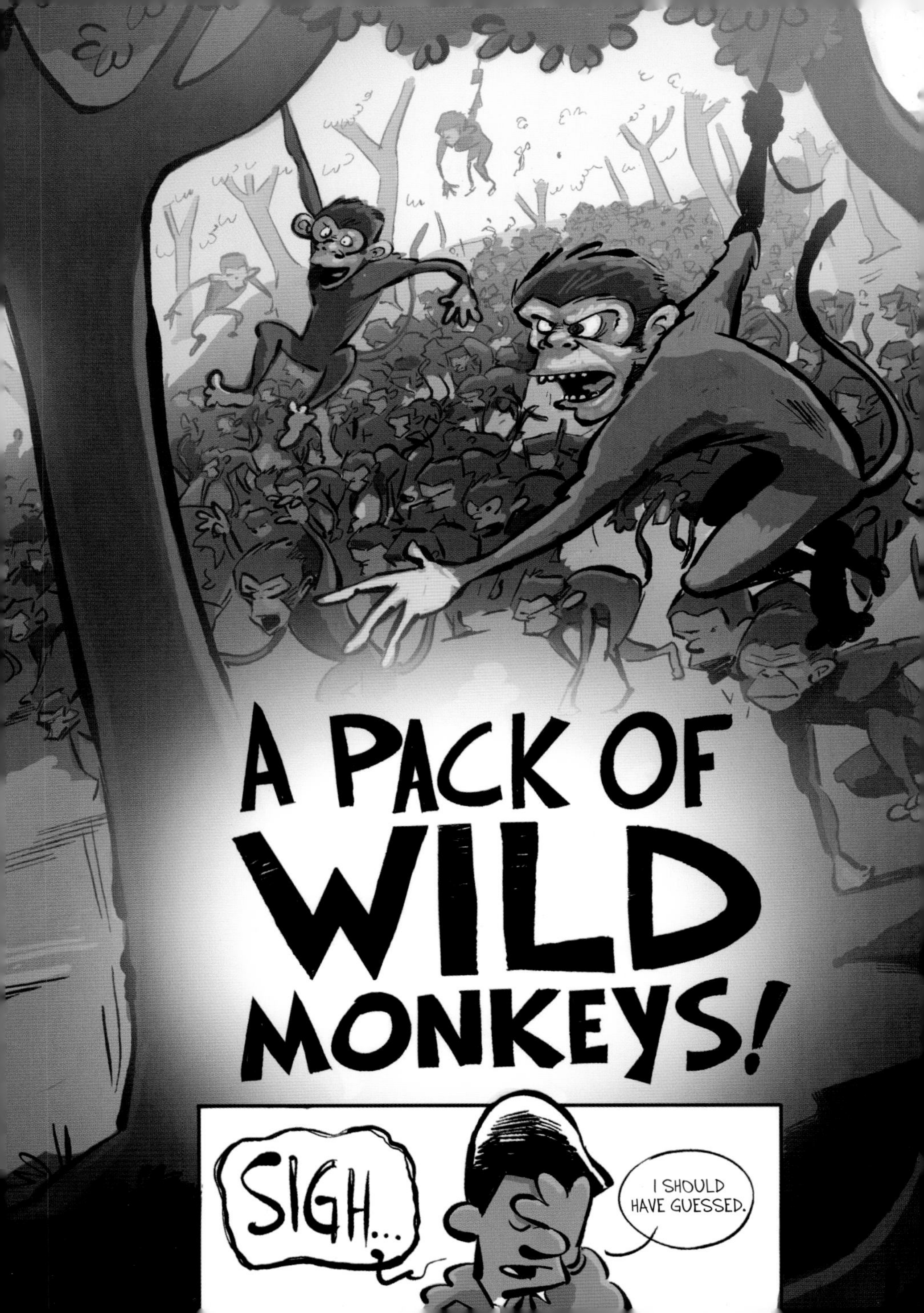
A PACK OF WILD MONKEYS!
SIGH...
I SHOULD HAVE GUESSED.

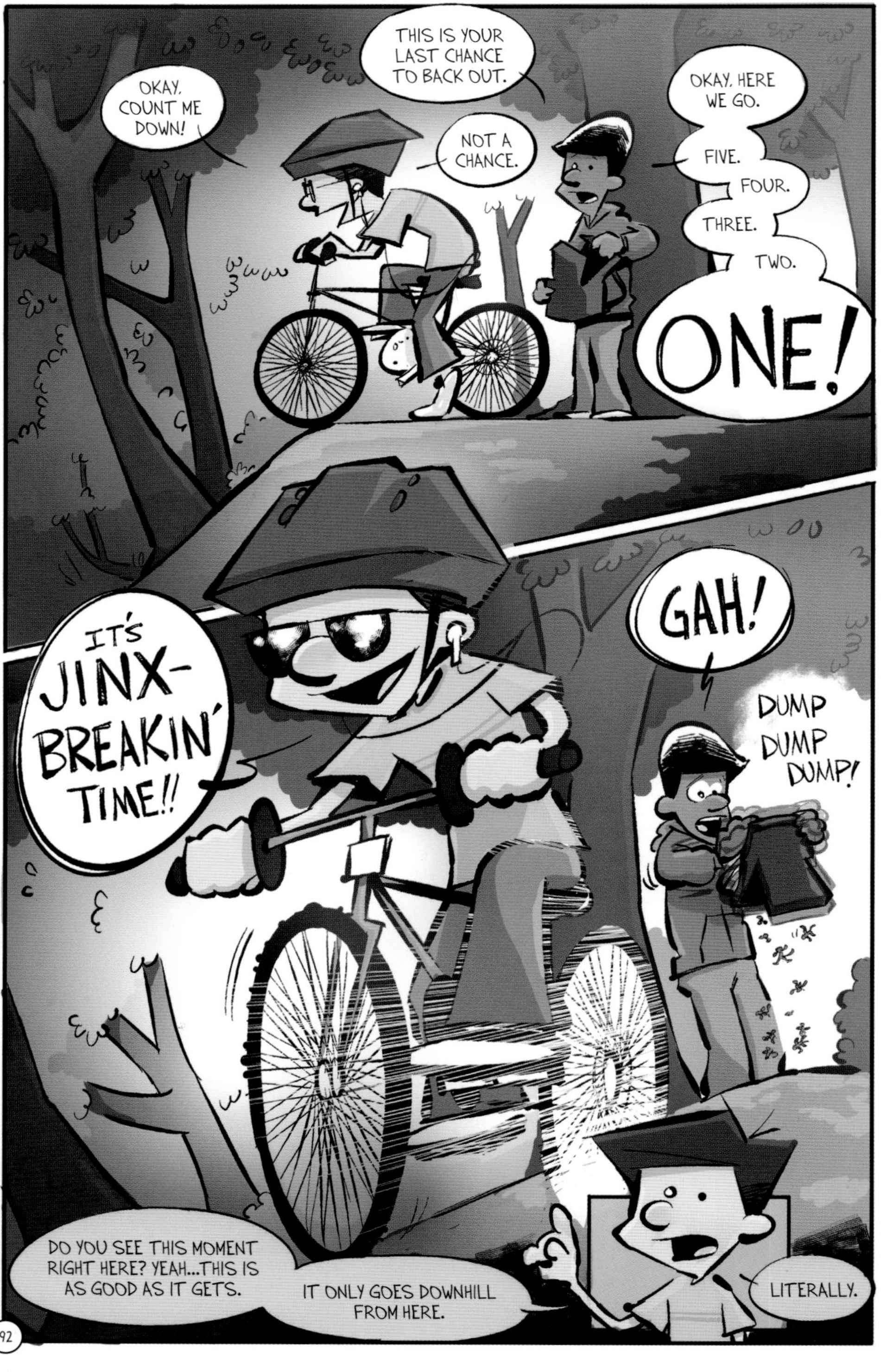
OKAY, COUNT ME DOWN!
THIS IS YOUR LAST CHANCE TO BACK OUT.
NOT A CHANCE.
OKAY, HERE WE GO.
FIVE.
FOUR.
THREE.
TWO.
ONE!
IT'S JINX-BREAKIN' TIME!!
GAH!
DUMP DUMP DUMP!
DO YOU SEE THIS MOMENT RIGHT HERE? YEAH...THIS IS AS GOOD AS IT GETS.
IT ONLY GOES DOWNHILL FROM HERE.
LITERALLY.

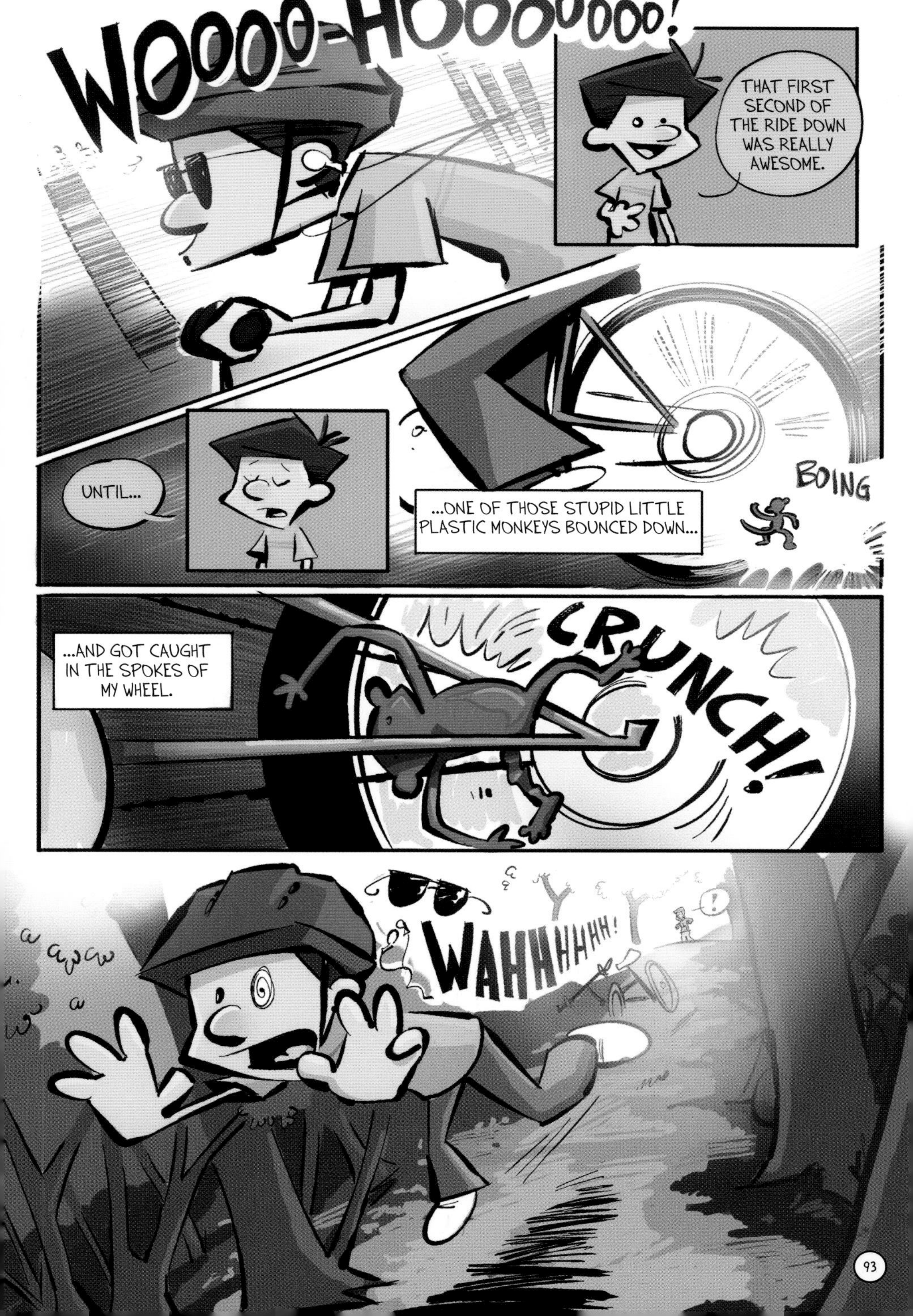
WOOOO-HOOOOOOO!
THAT FIRST SECOND OF THE RIDE DOWN WAS REALLY AWESOME.
UNTIL...
...ONE OF THOSE STUPID LITTLE PLASTIC MONKEYS BOUNCED DOWN...
BOING
...AND GOT CAUGHT IN THE SPOKES OF MY WHEEL.
CRUNCH!
WAHHHHHH!

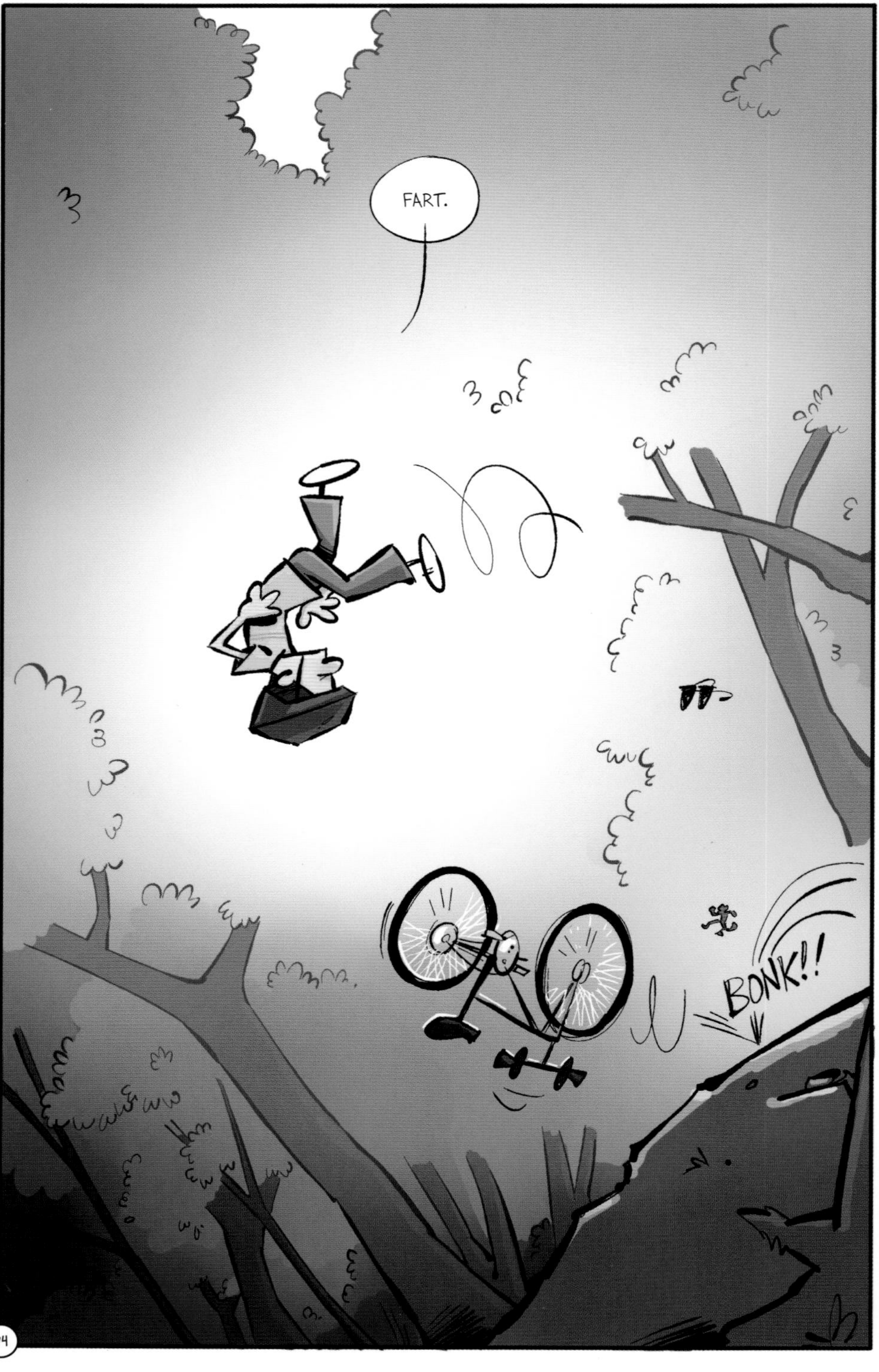
FART.
BONK!!

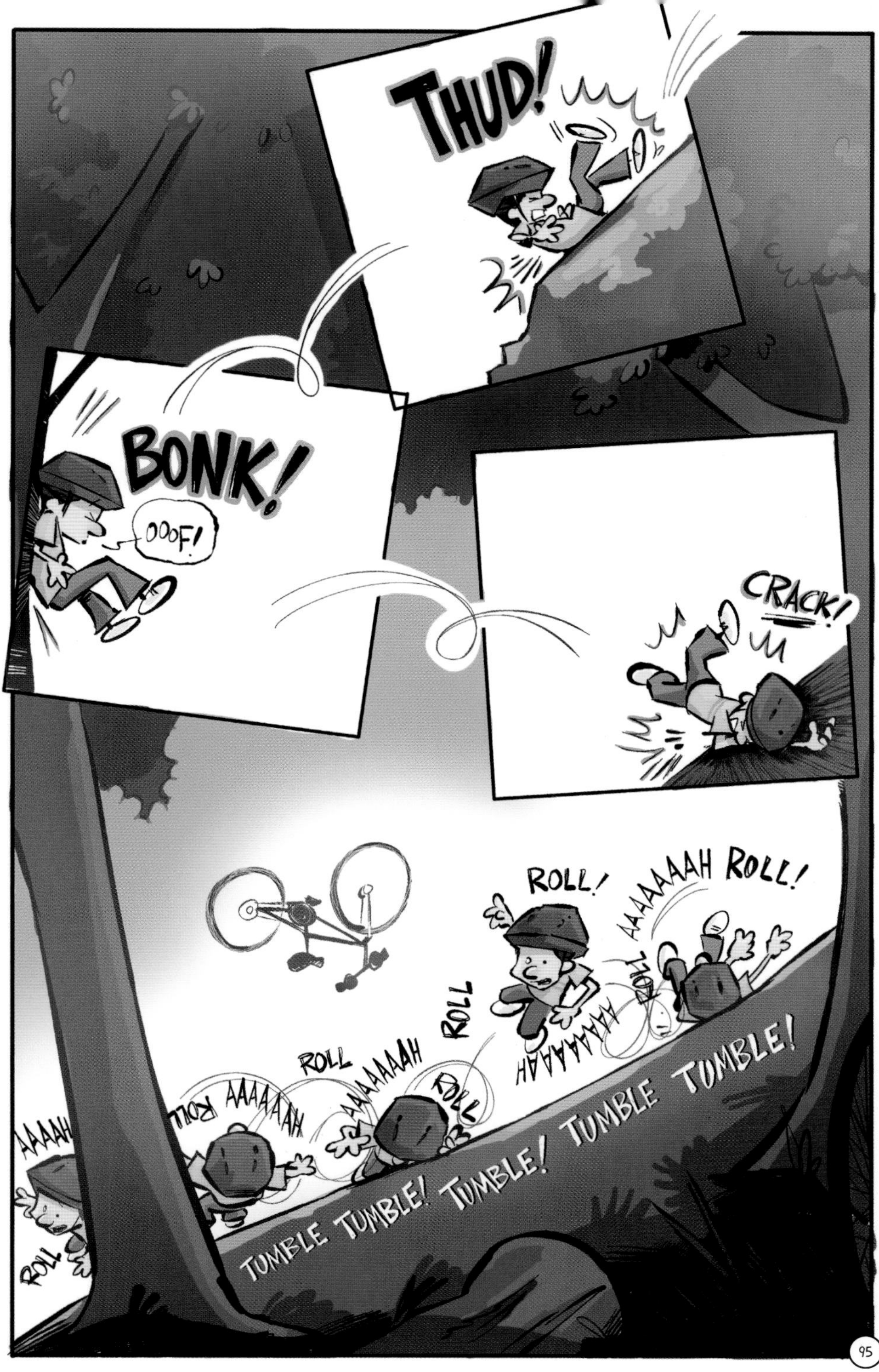
THUD!
BONK!
OOOF!
CRACK!
ROLL!
AAAAAAAH ROLL!
ROLL
AAAAAAAH
ROLL
AAAAAAAH
ROLL
AAAAAAAH
ROLL
AAAAAAAH
ROLL
AAAAH
ROLL
TUMBLE TUMBLE! TUMBLE! TUMBLE TUMBLE!

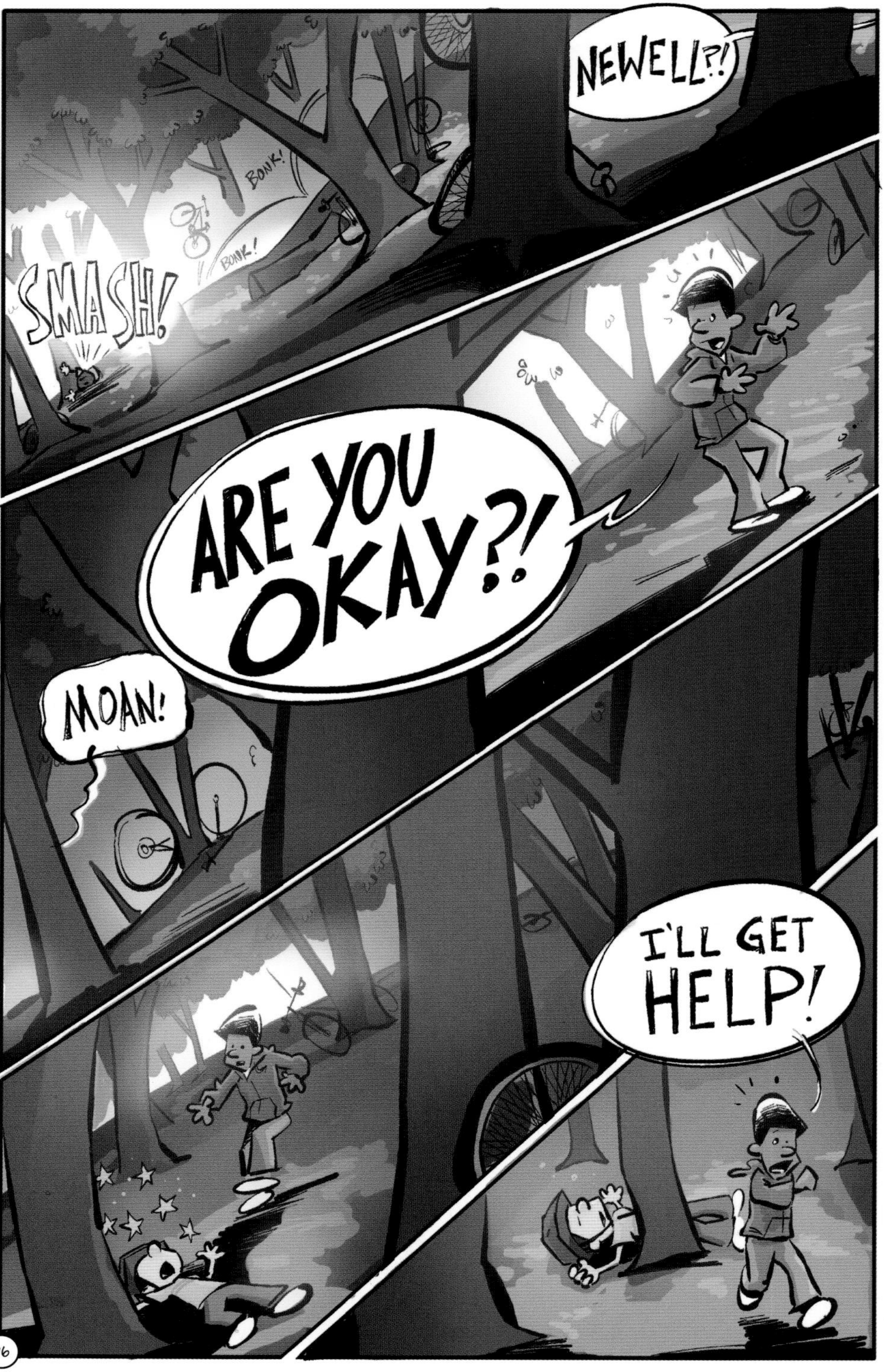
NEWELL?!
BONK!
BONK!
SMASH!
ARE YOU OKAY?!
MOAN!
I'LL GET HELP!

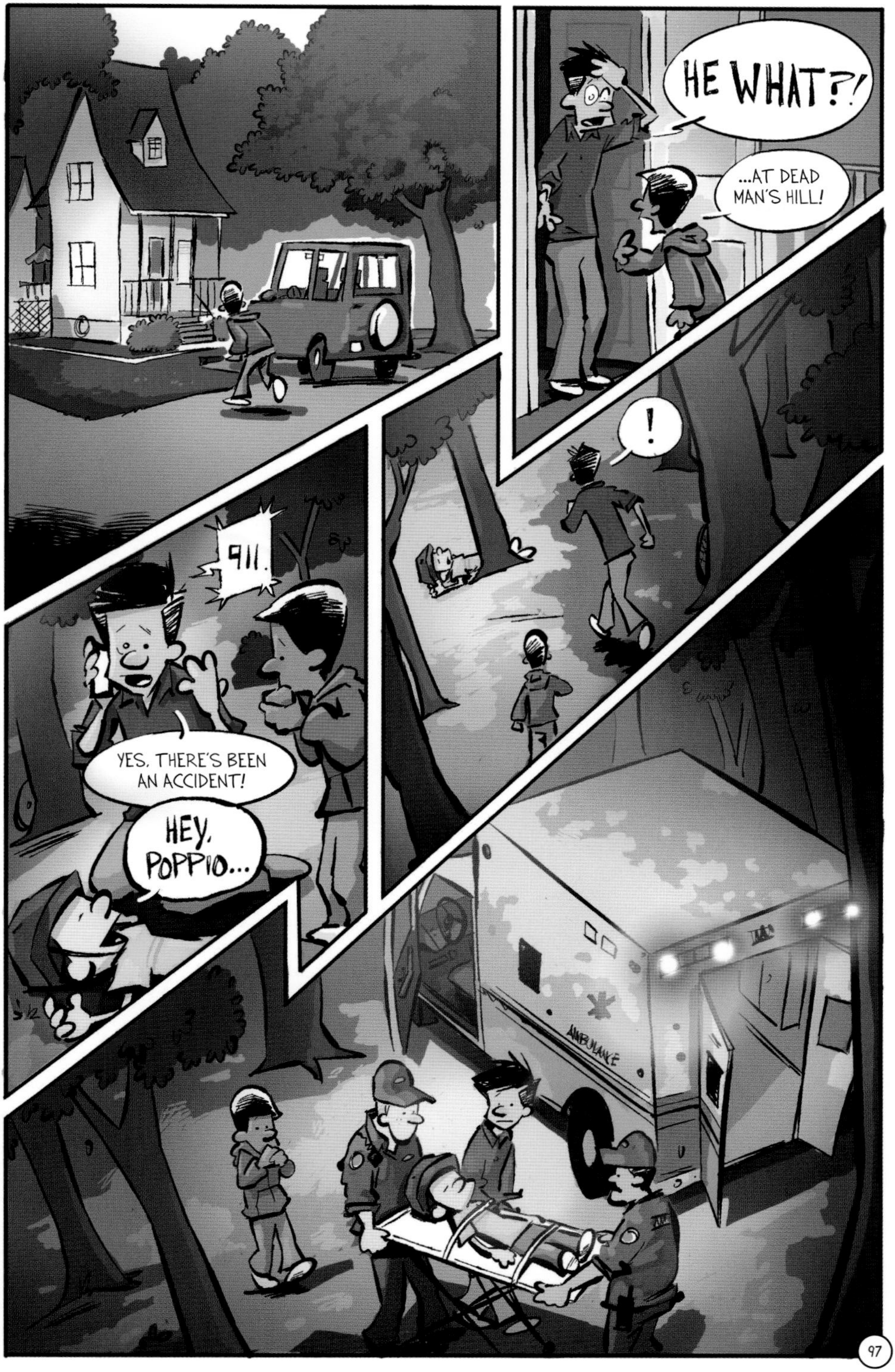
HE WHAT?!
...AT DEAD MAN'S HILL!
!
911.
YES, THERE'S BEEN AN ACCIDENT!
HEY, POPPIO...
AMBULANCE

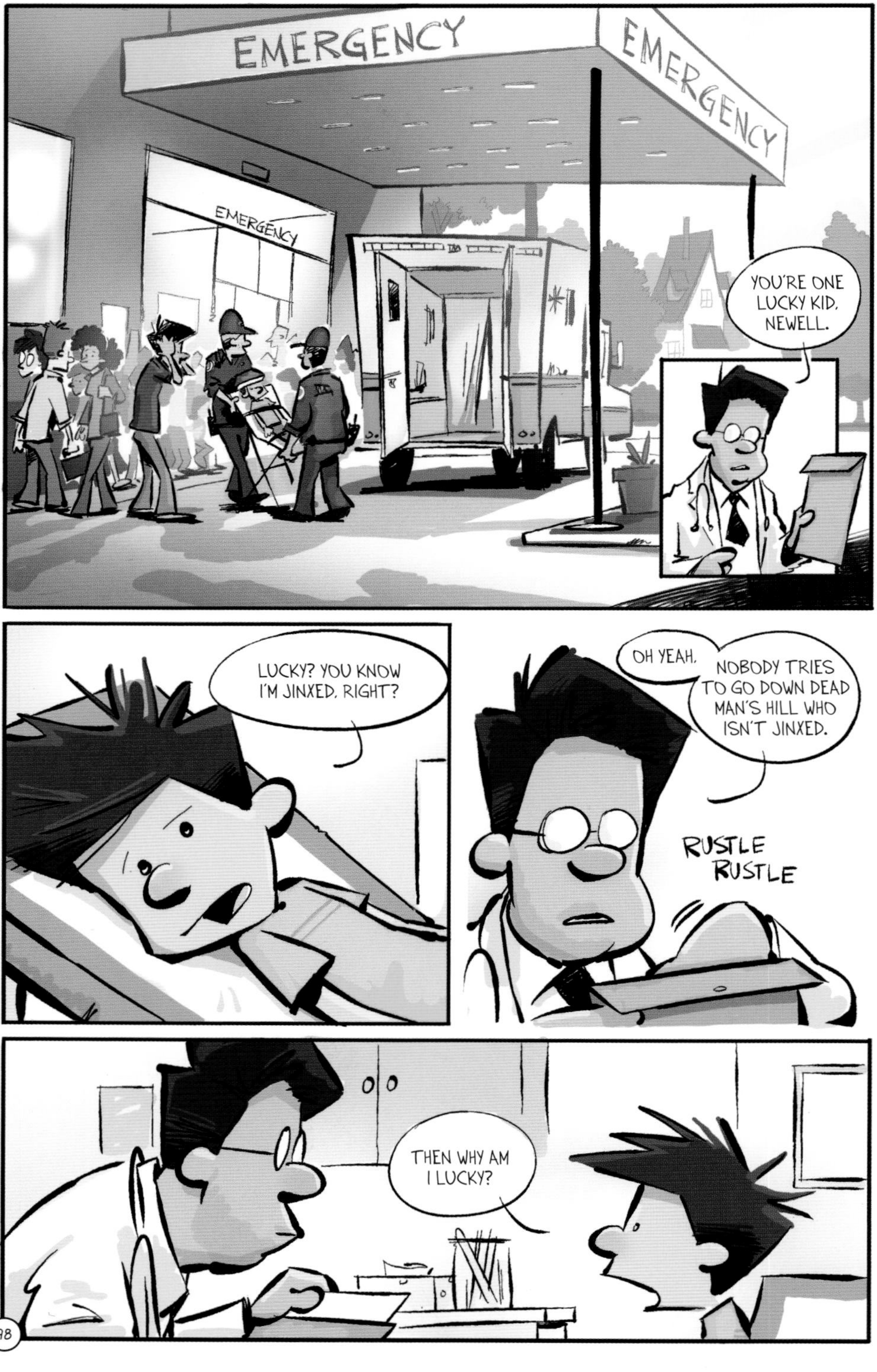
EMERGENCY
EMERGENCY
EMERGENCY
YOU'RE ONE LUCKY KID, NEWELL.
LUCKY? YOU KNOW I'M JINXED, RIGHT?
OH YEAH.
NOBODY TRIES TO GO DOWN DEAD MAN'S HILL WHO ISN'T JINXED.
RUSTLE RUSTLE
THEN WHY AM I LUCKY?

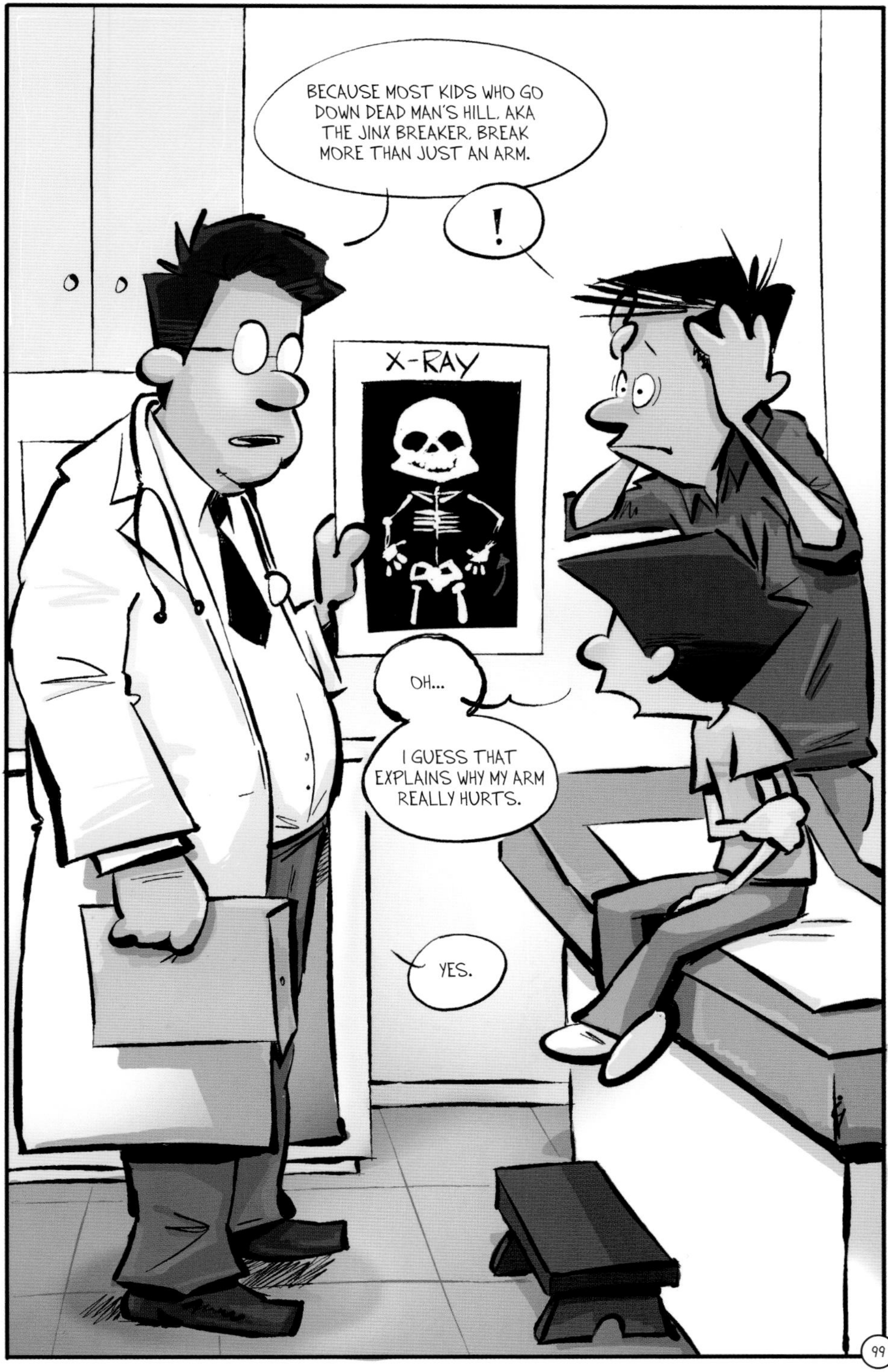
BECAUSE MOST KIDS WHO GO DOWN DEAD MAN'S HILL, AKA THE JINX BREAKER, BREAK MORE THAN JUST AN ARM.
!
X-RAY
OH...
I GUESS THAT EXPLAINS WHY MY ARM REALLY HURTS.
YES.

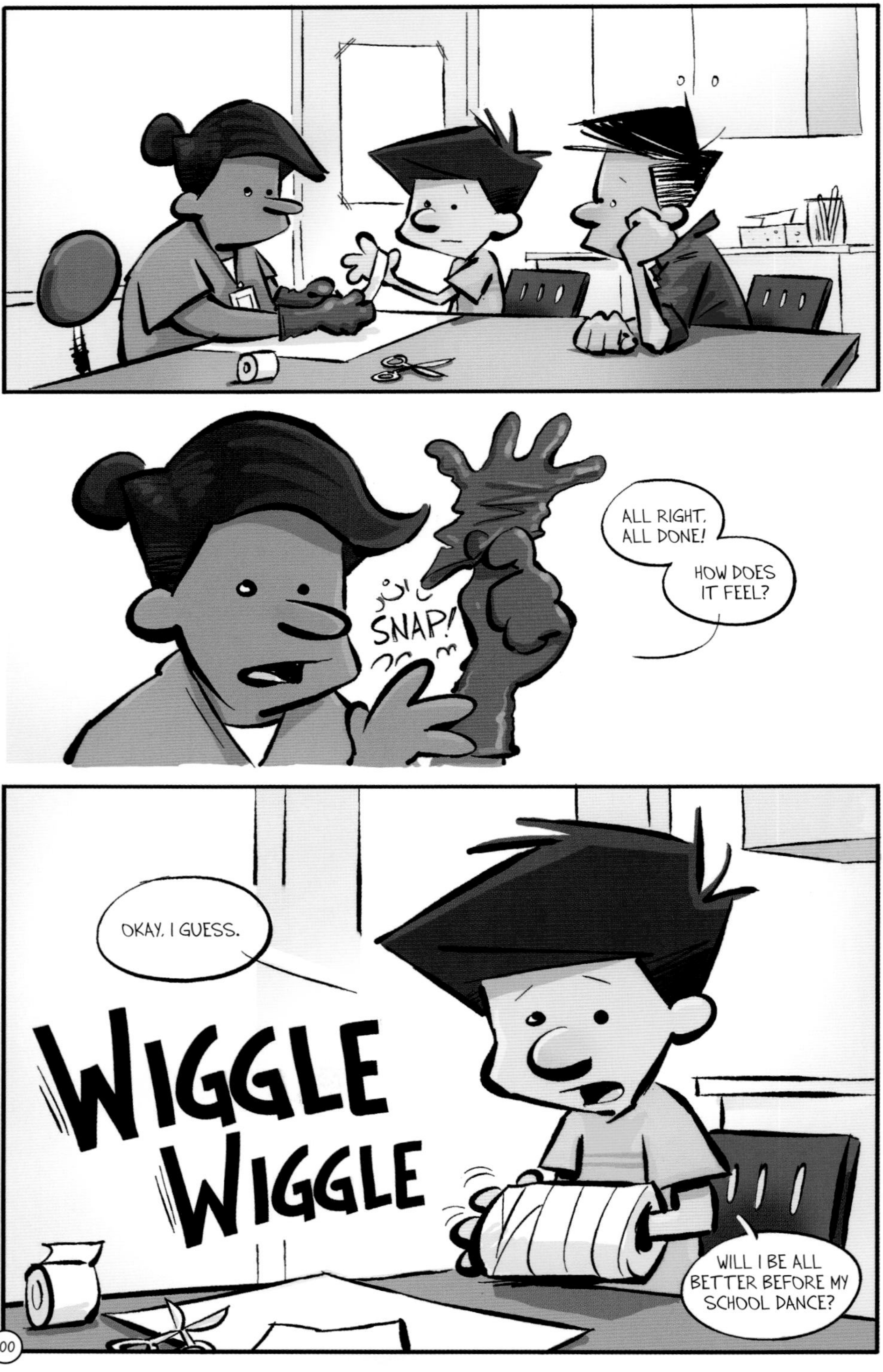
ALL RIGHT, ALL DONE!
HOW DOES IT FEEL?
SNAP!
OKAY, I GUESS.
WIGGLE WIGGLE
WILL I BE ALL BETTER BEFORE MY SCHOOL DANCE?

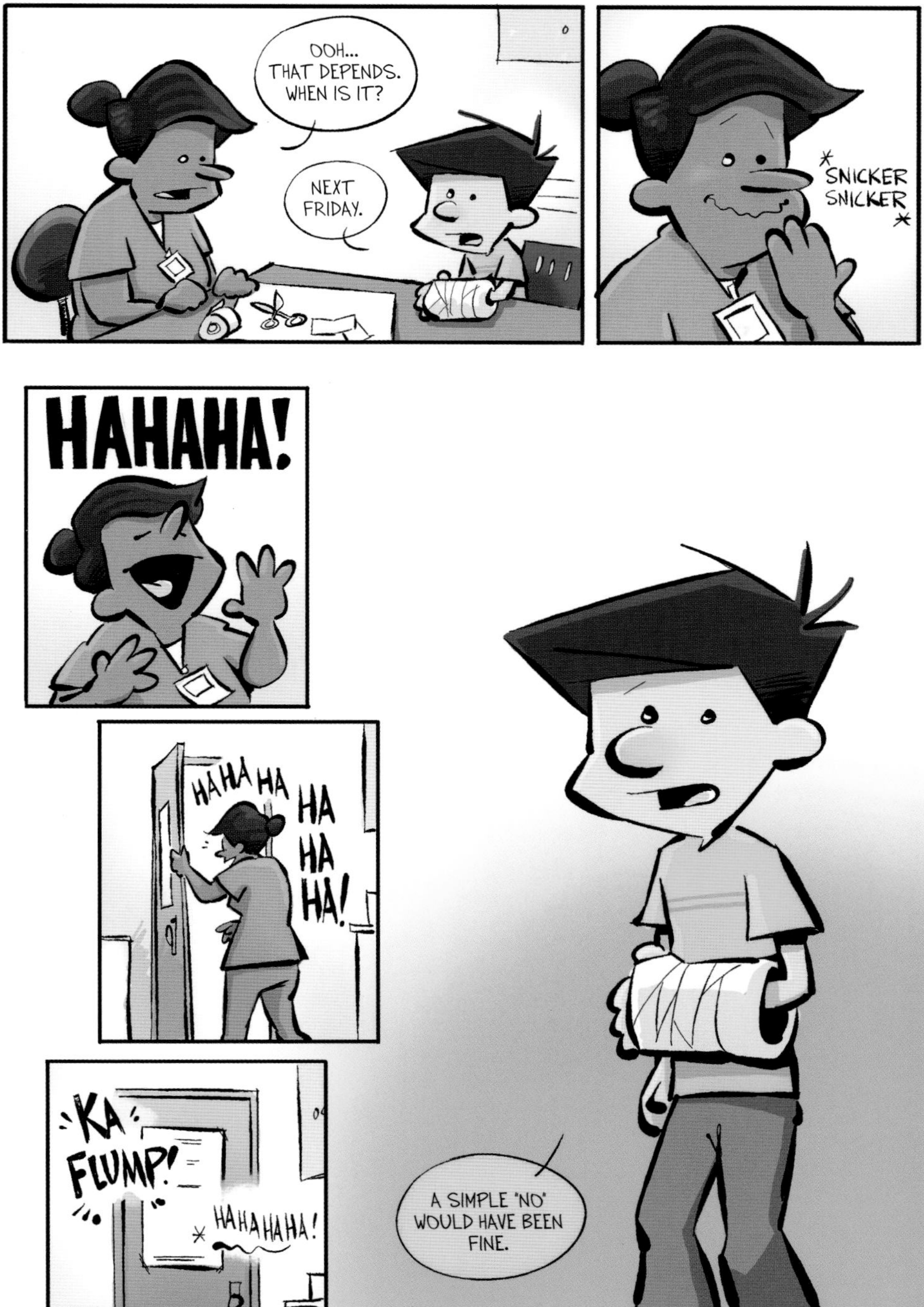

OOH... THAT DEPENDS. WHEN IS IT?
NEXT FRIDAY.
SNICKER SNICKER
HAHAHA!
HA HA HA HA HA HA!
KA FLUMP!
*HAHAHAHA!
A SIMPLE "NO" WOULD HAVE BEEN FINE.

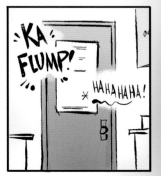

CHAPTER SIX
BROKEN

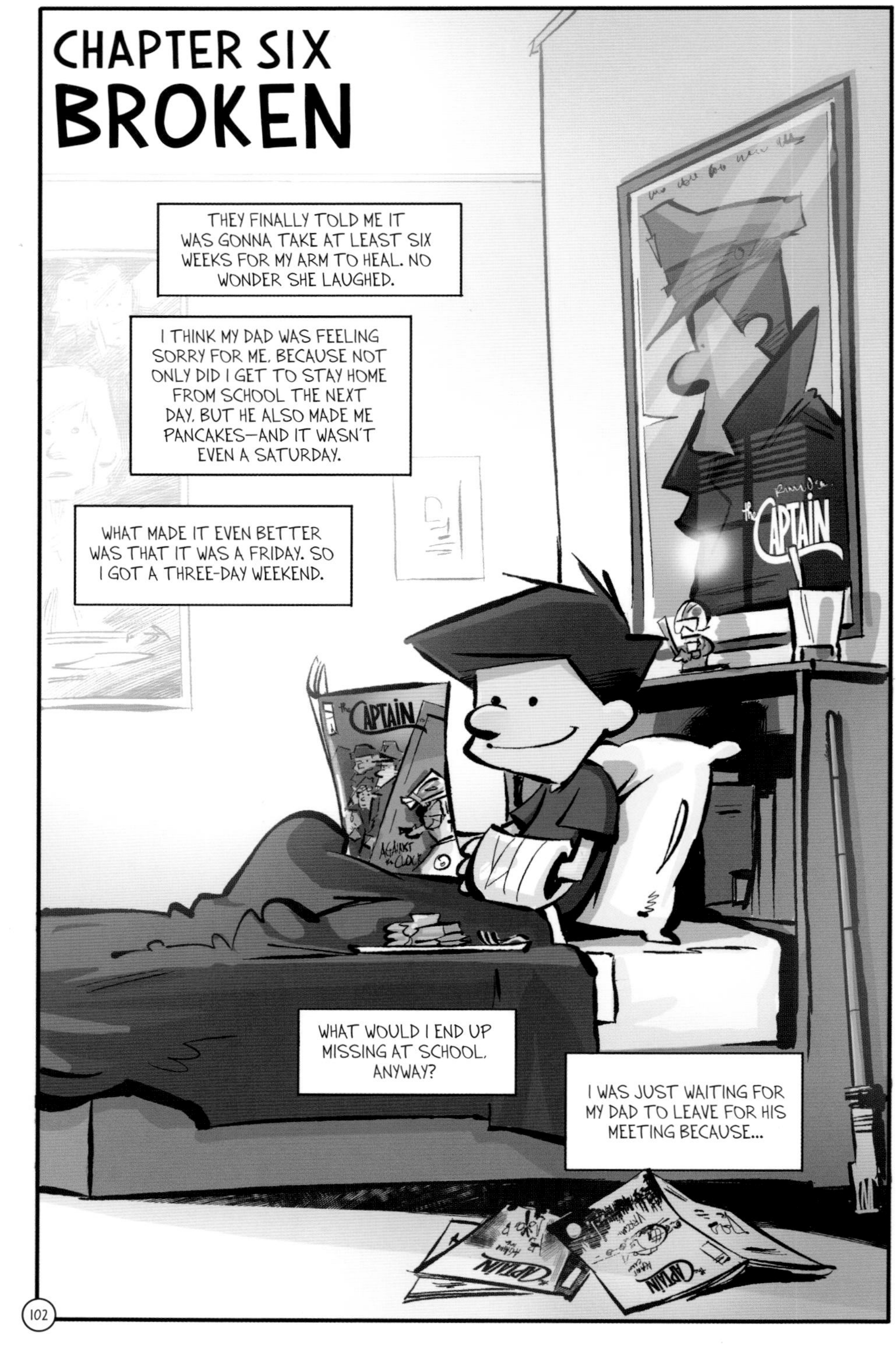
THEY FINALLY TOLD ME IT WAS GONNA TAKE AT LEAST SIX WEEKS FOR MY ARM TO HEAL. NO WONDER SHE LAUGHED.
I THINK MY DAD WAS FEELING SORRY FOR ME, BECAUSE NOT ONLY DID I GET TO STAY HOME FROM SCHOOL THE NEXT DAY, BUT HE ALSO MADE ME PANCAKES—AND IT WASN'T EVEN A SATURDAY.
WHAT MADE IT EVEN BETTER WAS THAT IT WAS A FRIDAY. SO I GOT A THREE-DAY WEEKEND.
WHAT WOULD I END UP MISSING AT SCHOOL, ANYWAY?
I WAS JUST WAITING FOR MY DAD TO LEAVE FOR HIS MEETING BECAUSE...

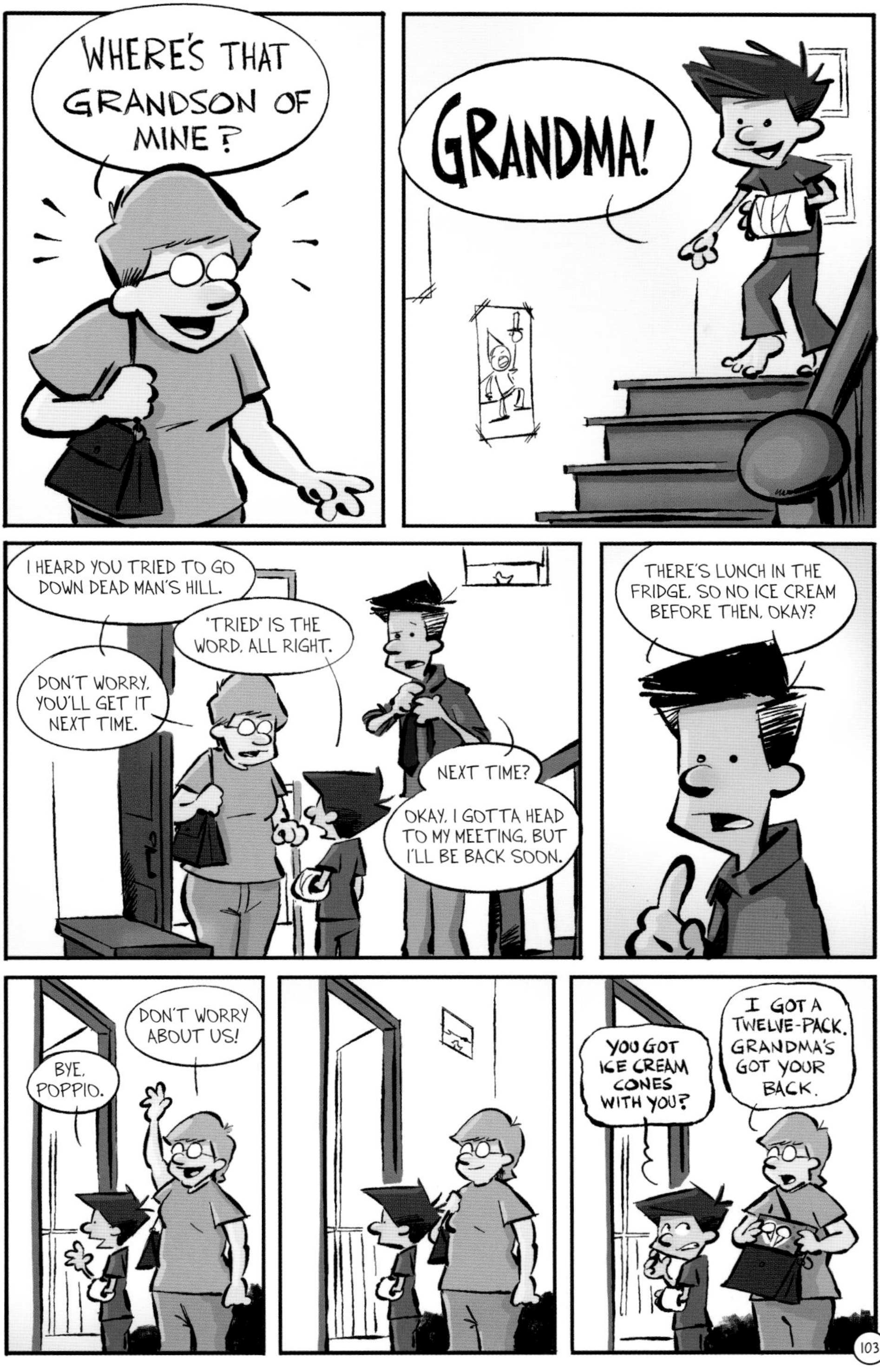
WHERE'S THAT GRANDSON OF MINE?
GRANDMA!
I HEARD YOU TRIED TO GO DOWN DEAD MAN'S HILL.
"TRIED" IS THE WORD, ALL RIGHT.
DON'T WORRY, YOU'LL GET IT NEXT TIME.
NEXT TIME?
OKAY, I GOTTA HEAD TO MY MEETING, BUT I'LL BE BACK SOON.
THERE'S LUNCH IN THE FRIDGE, SO NO ICE CREAM BEFORE THEN, OKAY?
BYE, POPPIO.
DON'T WORRY ABOUT US!
YOU GOT ICE CREAM CONES WITH YOU?
I GOT A TWELVE-PACK. GRANDMA'S GOT YOUR BACK.

TWO MINUTES LATER.

AFTER DAD GOT BACK AND GRANDMA WENT HOME, I TRIED PLAYING SOME GAMES.

TAP!
TAP!
TAP!

BUT HOLDING THE CONTROLLER WITH MY CAST WAS HARDER THAN I THOUGHT.

FUMBLE

FUMBLE

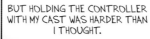

CRACK!

FART.

I EVEN TRIED TAKING A NAP. BUT I COULDN'T SLEEP.

SIGH...

IT WAS THEN THAT A WEIRD THOUGHT CAME TO MIND...

I KINDA WISH I WERE IN SCHOOL RIGHT NOW.

CRINGE!

I HOPE THIS DOESN'T MEAN THAT I'M SICKER THAN THE DOCTORS THOUGHT!

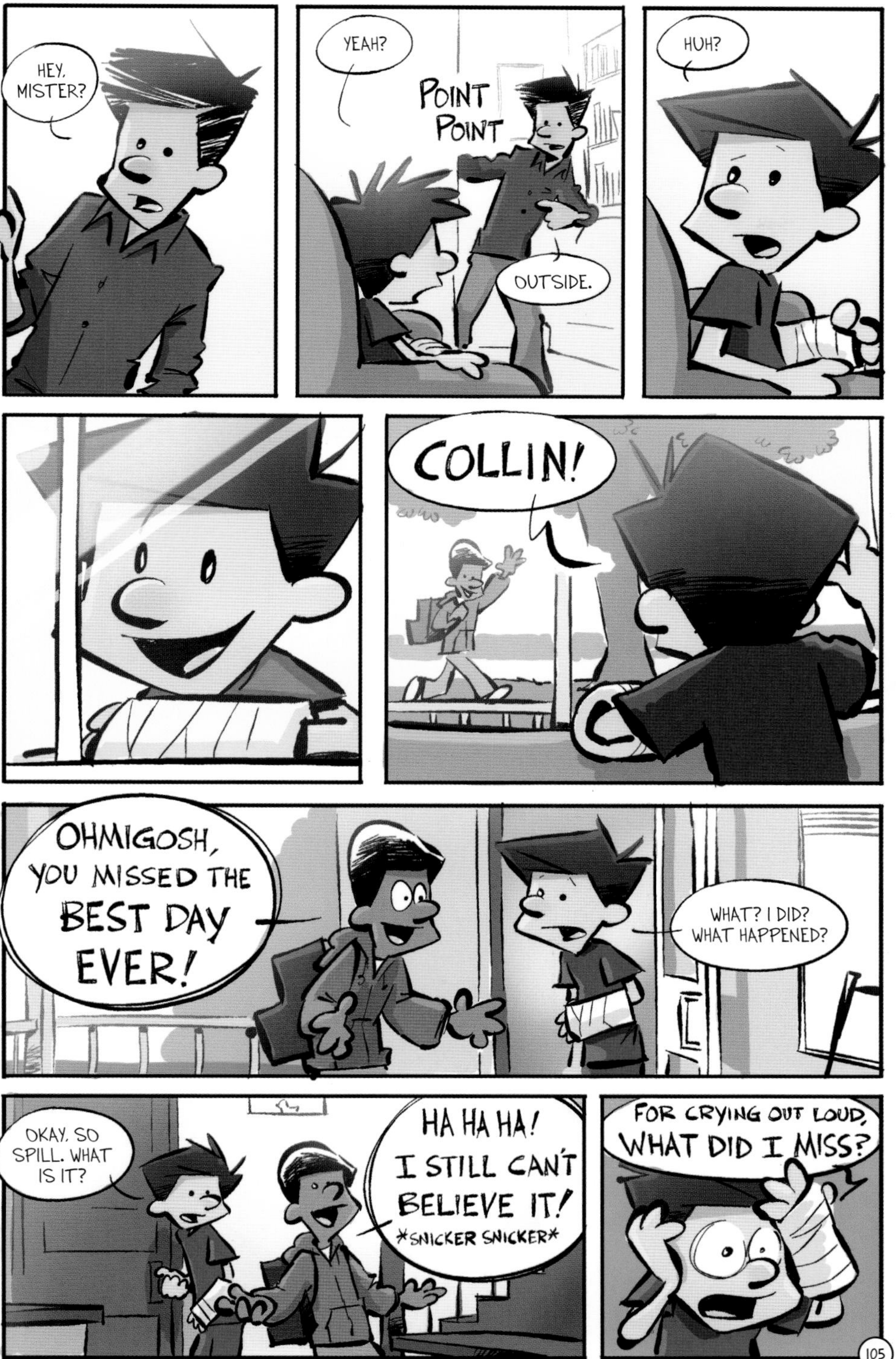
HEY, MISTER?
YEAH?
POINT POINT
OUTSIDE.
HUH?
COLLIN!
OHMIGOSH, YOU MISSED THE BEST DAY EVER!
WHAT? I DID? WHAT HAPPENED?
OKAY, SO SPILL. WHAT IS IT?
HA HA HA! I STILL CAN'T BELIEVE IT!
SNICKER SNICKER
FOR CRYING OUT LOUD, WHAT DID I MISS?

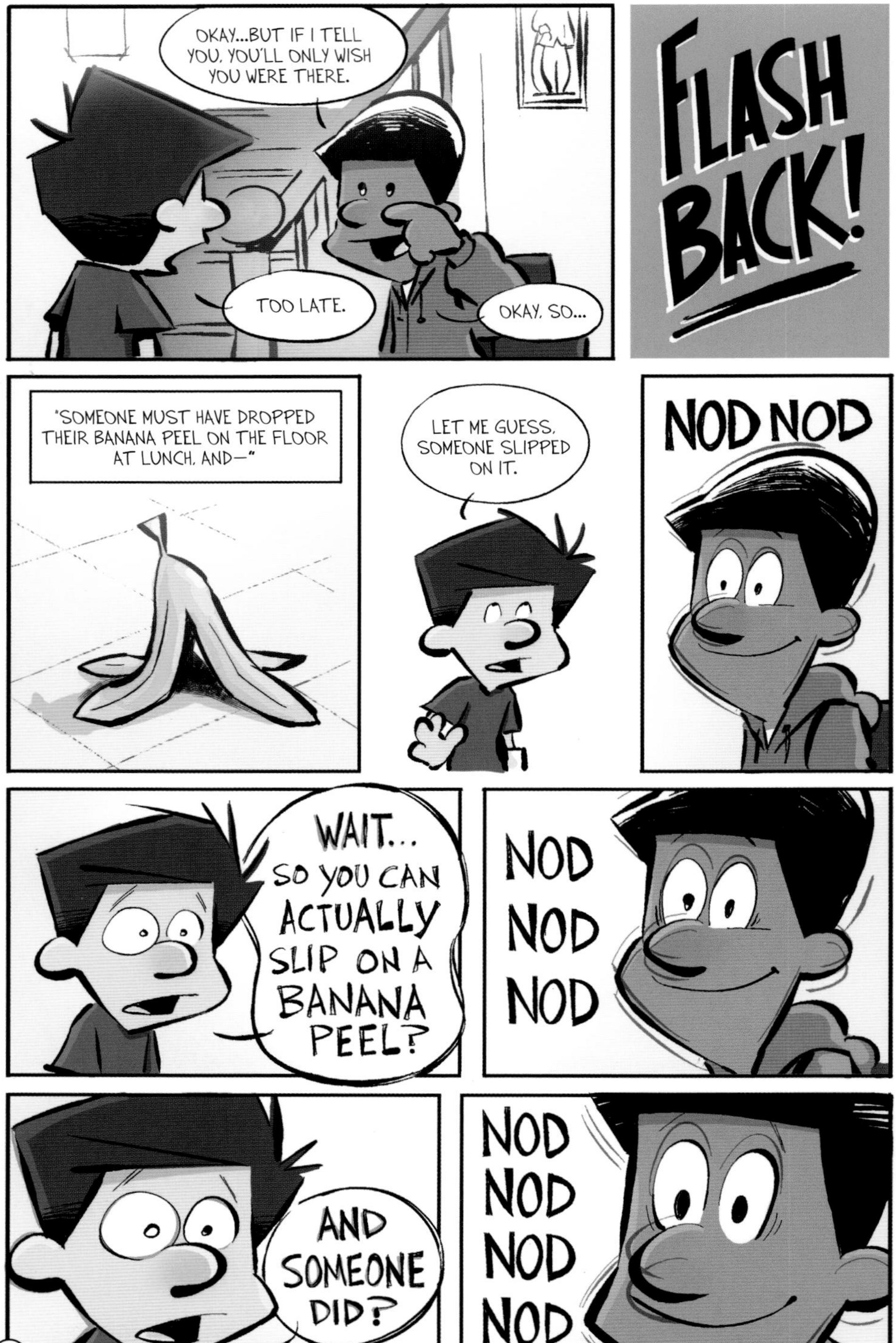
OKAY...BUT IF I TELL YOU, YOU'LL ONLY WISH YOU WERE THERE.
TOO LATE.
OKAY, SO...
FLASH BACK!
"SOMEONE MUST HAVE DROPPED THEIR BANANA PEEL ON THE FLOOR AT LUNCH, AND—"
LET ME GUESS, SOMEONE SLIPPED ON IT.
NOD NOD
WAIT... SO YOU CAN ACTUALLY SLIP ON A BANANA PEEL?
NOD NOD NOD
AND SOMEONE DID?
NOD NOD NOD NOD

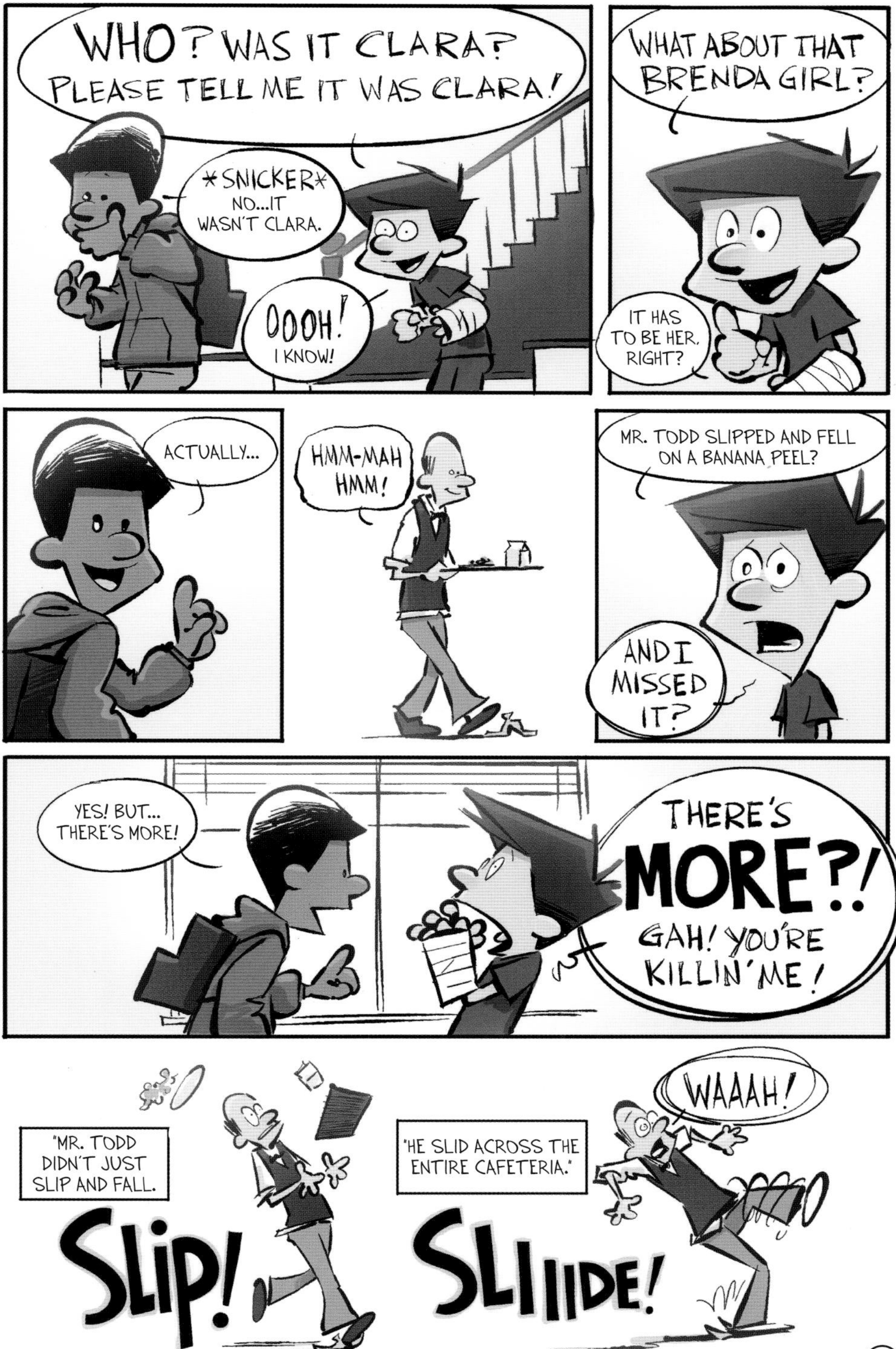

WHO? WAS IT CLARA? PLEASE TELL ME IT WAS CLARA!
SNICKER NO...IT WASN'T CLARA.
OOOH! I KNOW!
WHAT ABOUT THAT BRENDA GIRL?
IT HAS TO BE HER, RIGHT?
ACTUALLY...
HMM-MAH HMM!
MR. TODD SLIPPED AND FELL ON A BANANA PEEL?
AND I MISSED IT?
YES! BUT... THERE'S MORE!
THERE'S MORE?! GAH! YOU'RE KILLIN' ME!
"MR. TODD DIDN'T JUST SLIP AND FALL.
SLIP!
"HE SLID ACROSS THE ENTIRE CAFETERIA."
WAAAH!
SLIIIIDE!

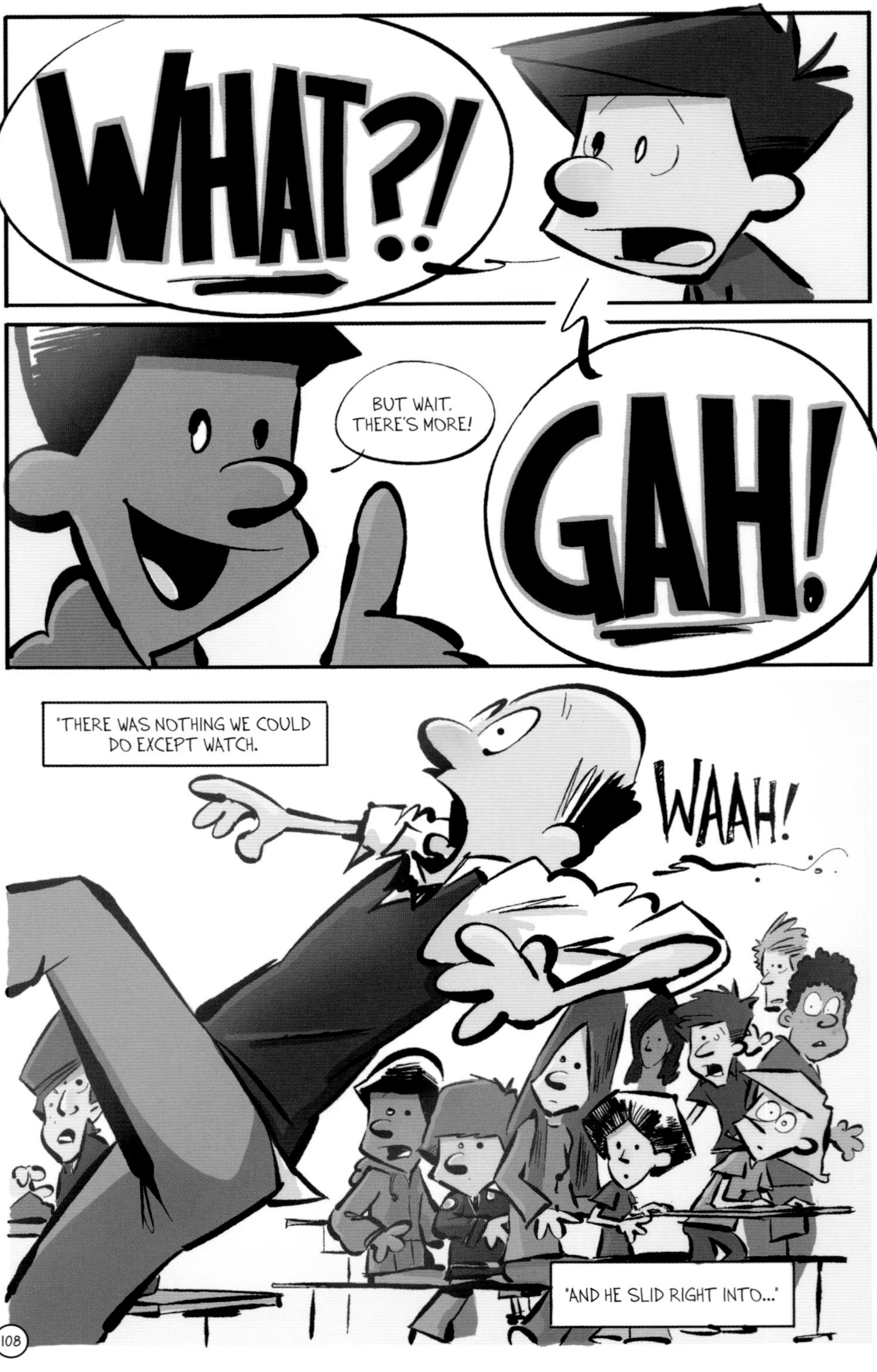
WHAT?!
BUT WAIT. THERE'S MORE!
GAH!
"THERE WAS NOTHING WE COULD DO EXCEPT WATCH.
WAAH!
"AND HE SLID RIGHT INTO..."

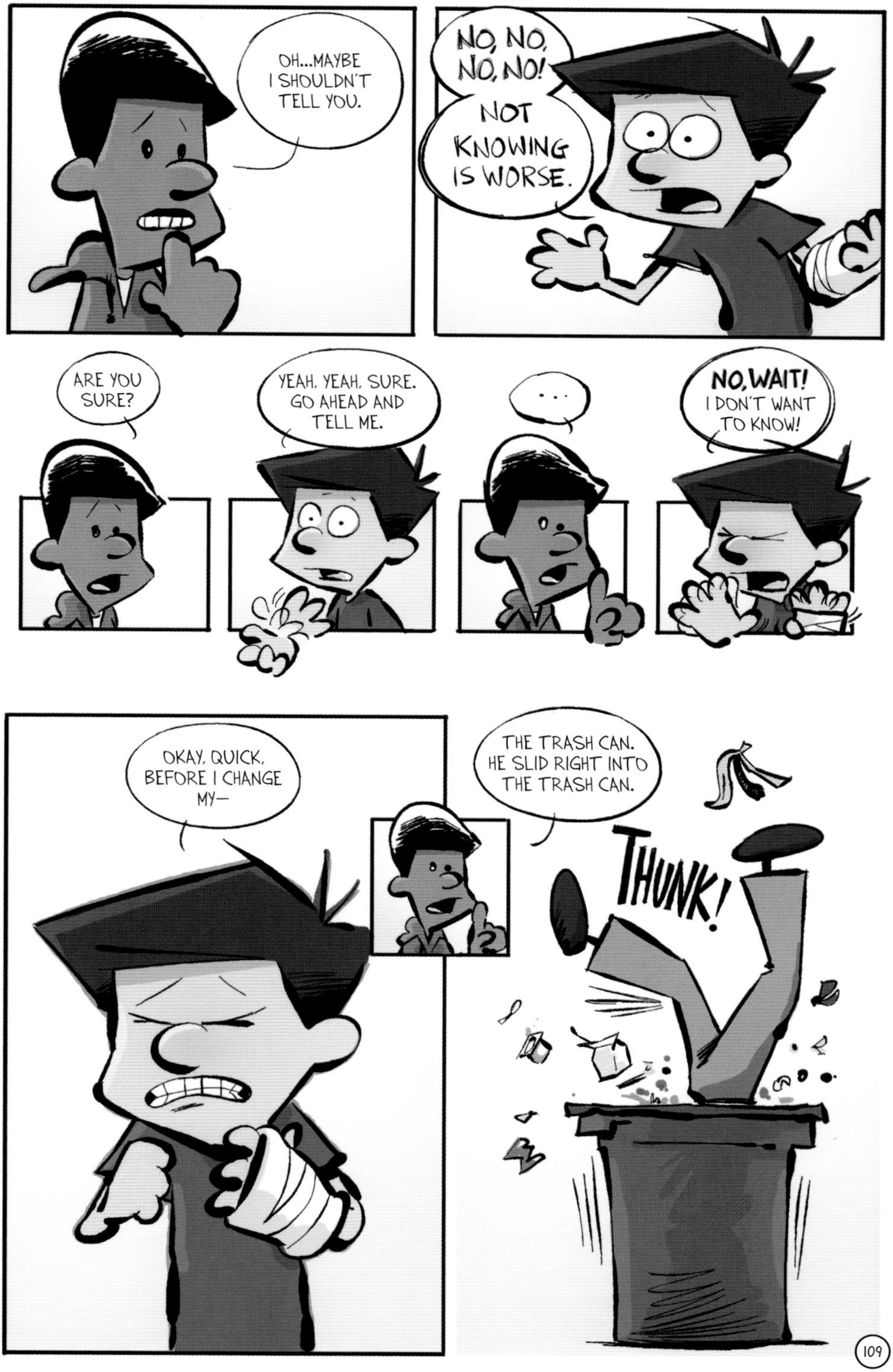

OH...MAYBE I SHOULDN'T TELL YOU.
NO, NO, NO, NO!
NOT KNOWING IS WORSE.
ARE YOU SURE?
YEAH, YEAH, SURE. GO AHEAD AND TELL ME.
. . .
NO, WAIT! I DON'T WANT TO KNOW!
OKAY, QUICK, BEFORE I CHANGE MY—
THE TRASH CAN. HE SLID RIGHT INTO THE TRASH CAN.
THUNK!

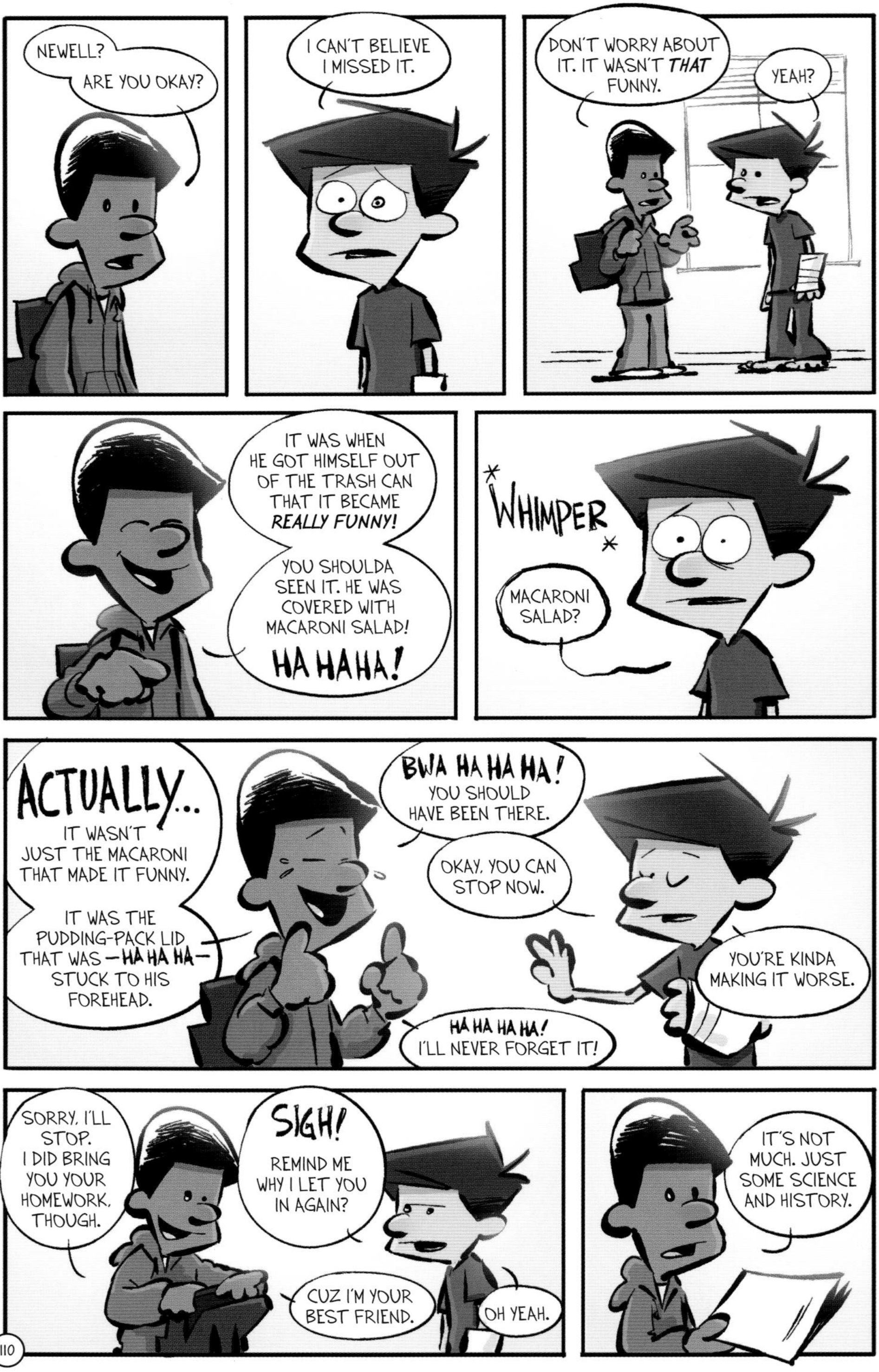
NEWELL?
ARE YOU OKAY?
I CAN'T BELIEVE I MISSED IT.
DON'T WORRY ABOUT IT. IT WASN'T THAT FUNNY.
YEAH?
IT WAS WHEN HE GOT HIMSELF OUT OF THE TRASH CAN THAT IT BECAME REALLY FUNNY!
YOU SHOULDA SEEN IT. HE WAS COVERED WITH MACARONI SALAD!
HA HAHA!
WHIMPER
MACARONI SALAD?
ACTUALLY...
IT WASN'T JUST THE MACARONI THAT MADE IT FUNNY.
IT WAS THE PUDDING-PACK LID THAT WAS —HA HA HA— STUCK TO HIS FOREHEAD.
BWA HA HA HA! YOU SHOULD HAVE BEEN THERE.
OKAY, YOU CAN STOP NOW.
YOU'RE KINDA MAKING IT WORSE.
HA HA HA HA! I'LL NEVER FORGET IT!
SORRY, I'LL STOP. I DID BRING YOU YOUR HOMEWORK, THOUGH.
SIGH!
REMIND ME WHY I LET YOU IN AGAIN?
CUZ I'M YOUR BEST FRIEND.
OH YEAH.
IT'S NOT MUCH. JUST SOME SCIENCE AND HISTORY.

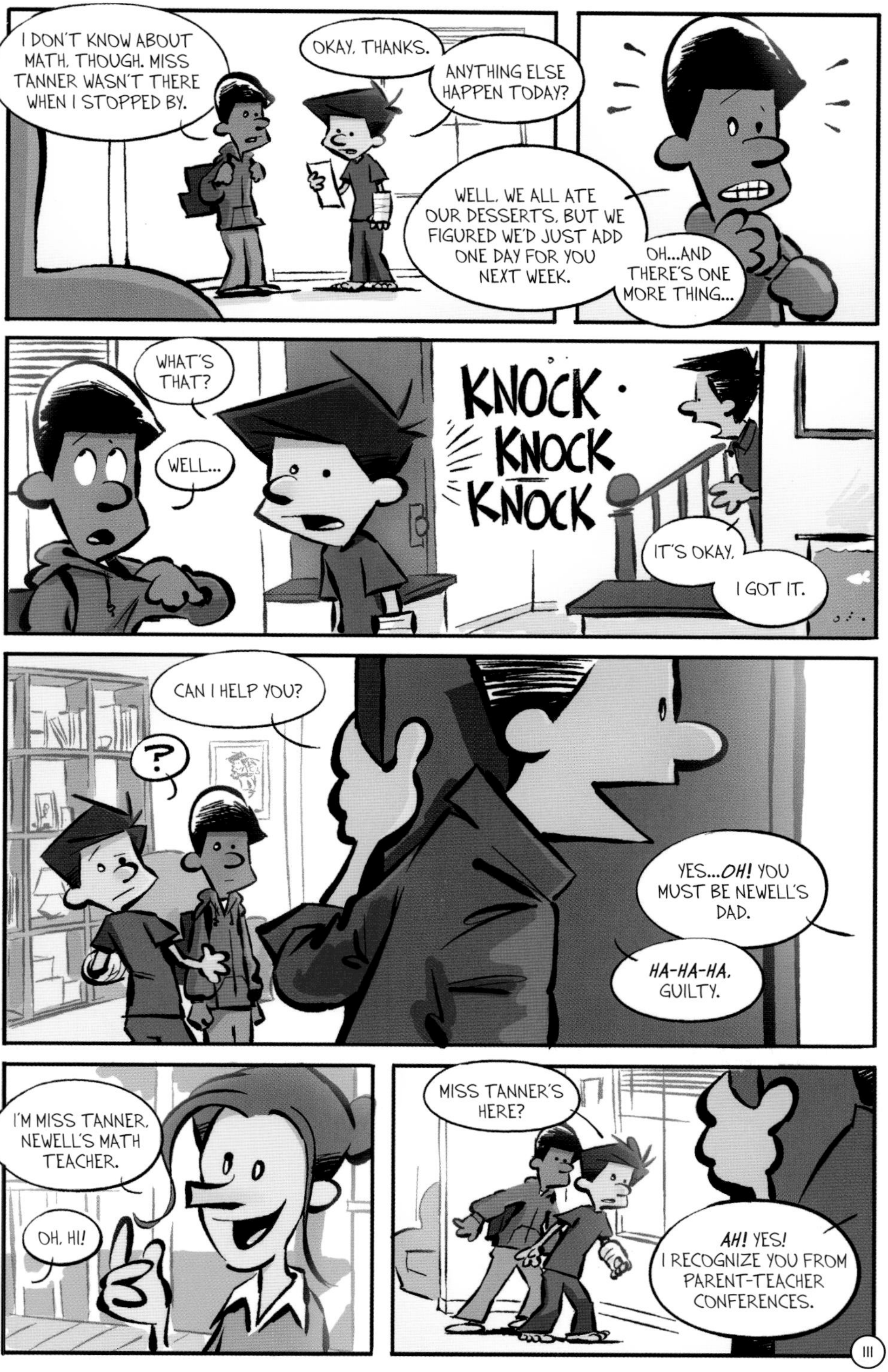
I DON'T KNOW ABOUT MATH, THOUGH. MISS TANNER WASN'T THERE WHEN I STOPPED BY.
OKAY, THANKS.
ANYTHING ELSE HAPPEN TODAY?
WELL, WE ALL ATE OUR DESSERTS, BUT WE FIGURED WE'D JUST ADD ONE DAY FOR YOU NEXT WEEK.
OH...AND THERE'S ONE MORE THING...
WHAT'S THAT?
WELL...
KNOCK KNOCK KNOCK
IT'S OKAY,
I GOT IT.
CAN I HELP YOU?
?
YES...OH! YOU MUST BE NEWELL'S DAD.
HA-HA-HA, GUILTY.
I'M MISS TANNER, NEWELL'S MATH TEACHER.
OH, HI!
MISS TANNER'S HERE?
AH! YES! I RECOGNIZE YOU FROM PARENT-TEACHER CONFERENCES.

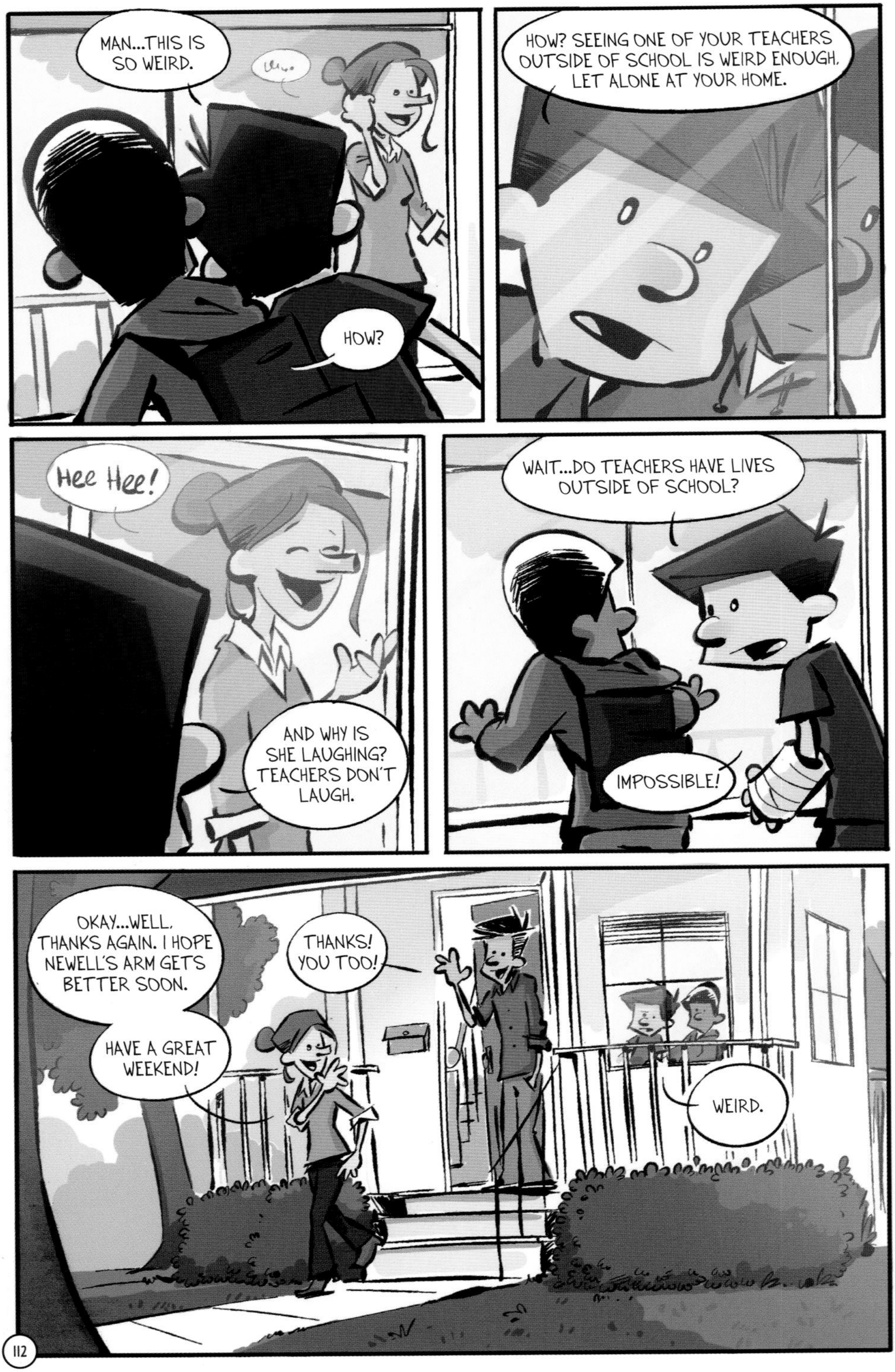
MAN...THIS IS SO WEIRD.
HOW?
HOW? SEEING ONE OF YOUR TEACHERS OUTSIDE OF SCHOOL IS WEIRD ENOUGH, LET ALONE AT YOUR HOME.
Hee Hee!
AND WHY IS SHE LAUGHING? TEACHERS DON'T LAUGH.
WAIT...DO TEACHERS HAVE LIVES OUTSIDE OF SCHOOL?
IMPOSSIBLE!
OKAY...WELL, THANKS AGAIN. I HOPE NEWELL'S ARM GETS BETTER SOON.
HAVE A GREAT WEEKEND!
THANKS! YOU TOO!
WEIRD.

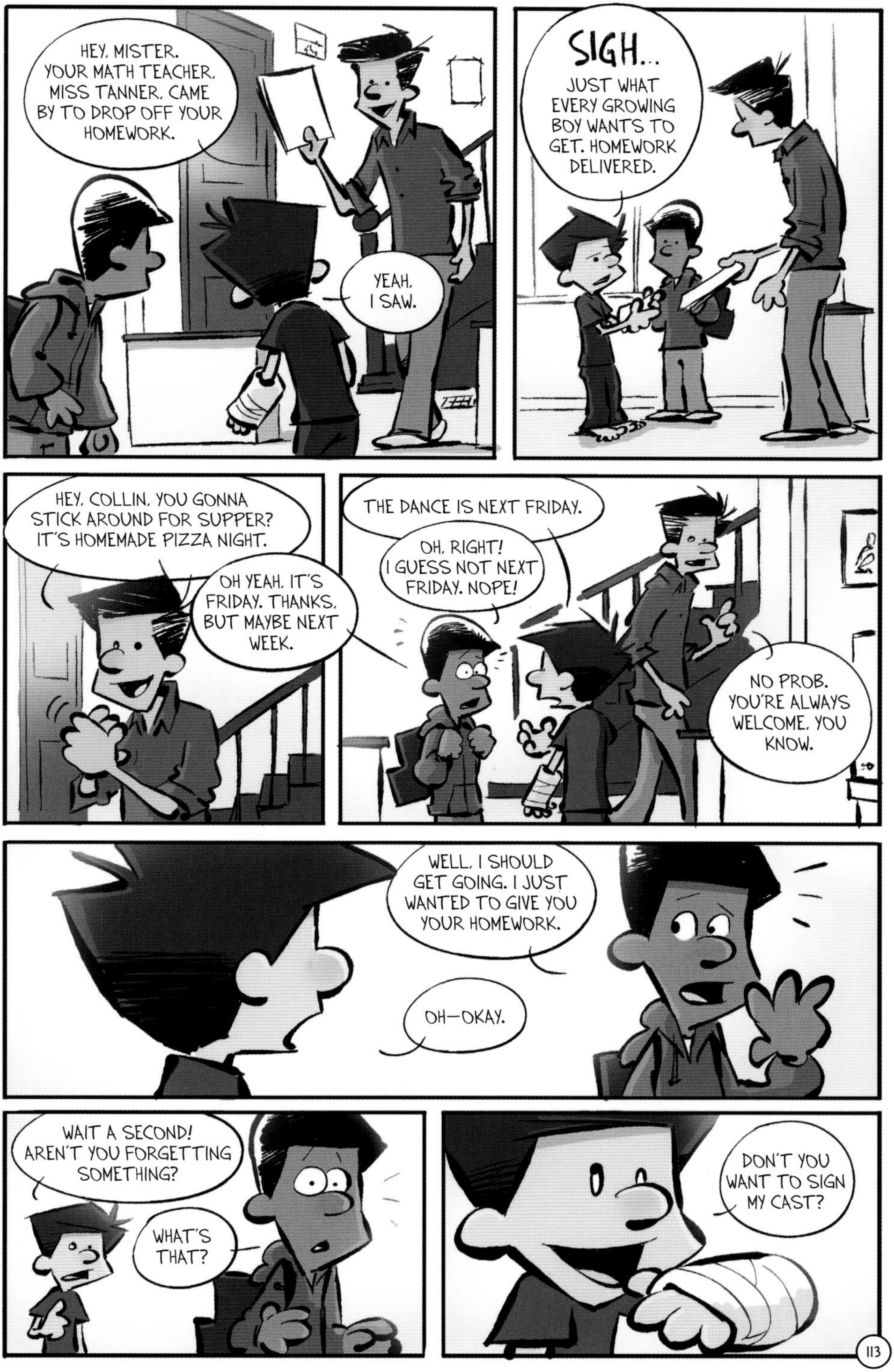
HEY, MISTER. YOUR MATH TEACHER, MISS TANNER, CAME BY TO DROP OFF YOUR HOMEWORK.
YEAH, I SAW.
SIGH...
JUST WHAT EVERY GROWING BOY WANTS TO GET. HOMEWORK DELIVERED.
HEY, COLLIN, YOU GONNA STICK AROUND FOR SUPPER? IT'S HOMEMADE PIZZA NIGHT.
OH YEAH, IT'S FRIDAY. THANKS, BUT MAYBE NEXT WEEK.
THE DANCE IS NEXT FRIDAY.
OH, RIGHT! I GUESS NOT NEXT FRIDAY. NOPE!
NO PROB. YOU'RE ALWAYS WELCOME, YOU KNOW.
WELL, I SHOULD GET GOING. I JUST WANTED TO GIVE YOU YOUR HOMEWORK.
OH—OKAY.
WAIT A SECOND! AREN'T YOU FORGETTING SOMETHING?
WHAT'S THAT?
DON'T YOU WANT TO SIGN MY CAST?

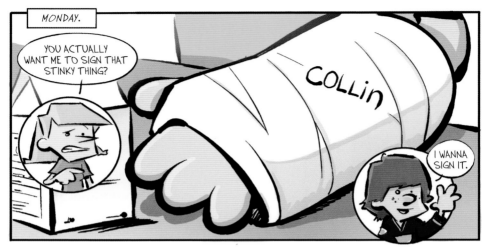

MONDAY.

YOU ACTUALLY WANT ME TO SIGN THAT STINKY THING?

COLLIN

I WANNA SIGN IT.

I DON'T KNOW, MAX. ASKING LILLY TO THE DANCE MESSED EVERYTHING UP.

YOU'RE STILL MAD ABOUT THAT?

SIGH!

FINE... YES, YOU CAN SIGN IT.

I WANNA SIGN IT, TOO.

IF IT WEREN'T FOR YOUR JINX, I WOULDN'T HAVE GONE DOWN DEAD MAN'S HILL IN THE FIRST PLACE.

MILK

COLLIN

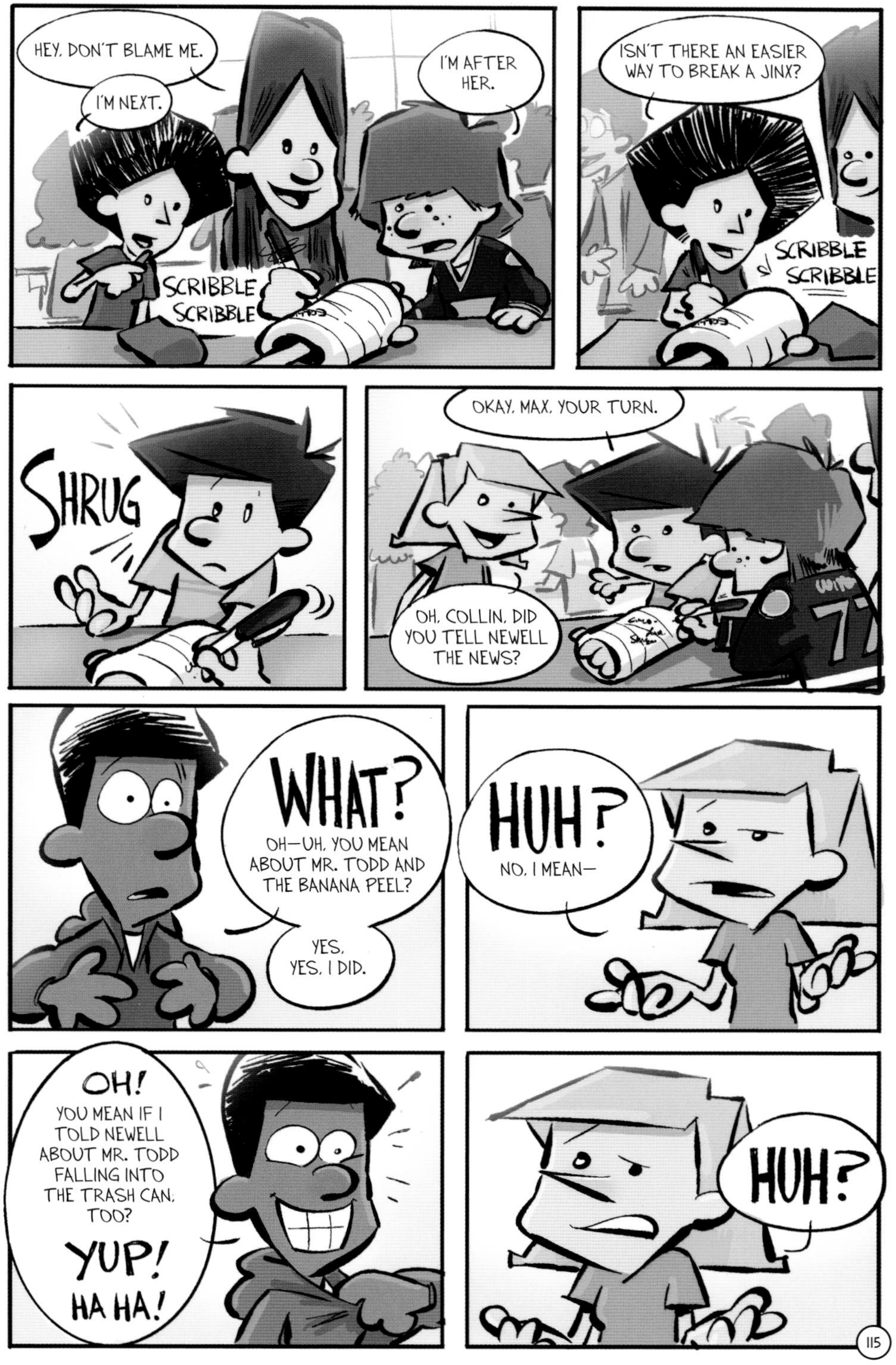
HEY, DON'T BLAME ME.
I'M NEXT.
I'M AFTER HER.
SCRIBBLE SCRIBBLE
ISN'T THERE AN EASIER WAY TO BREAK A JINX?
SCRIBBLE SCRIBBLE
SHRUG
OKAY, MAX, YOUR TURN.
OH, COLLIN, DID YOU TELL NEWELL THE NEWS?
WHAT?
OH—UH, YOU MEAN ABOUT MR. TODD AND THE BANANA PEEL?
YES, YES, I DID.
HUH?
NO, I MEAN—
OH!
YOU MEAN IF I TOLD NEWELL ABOUT MR. TODD FALLING INTO THE TRASH CAN, TOO?
YUP!
HA HA!
HUH?

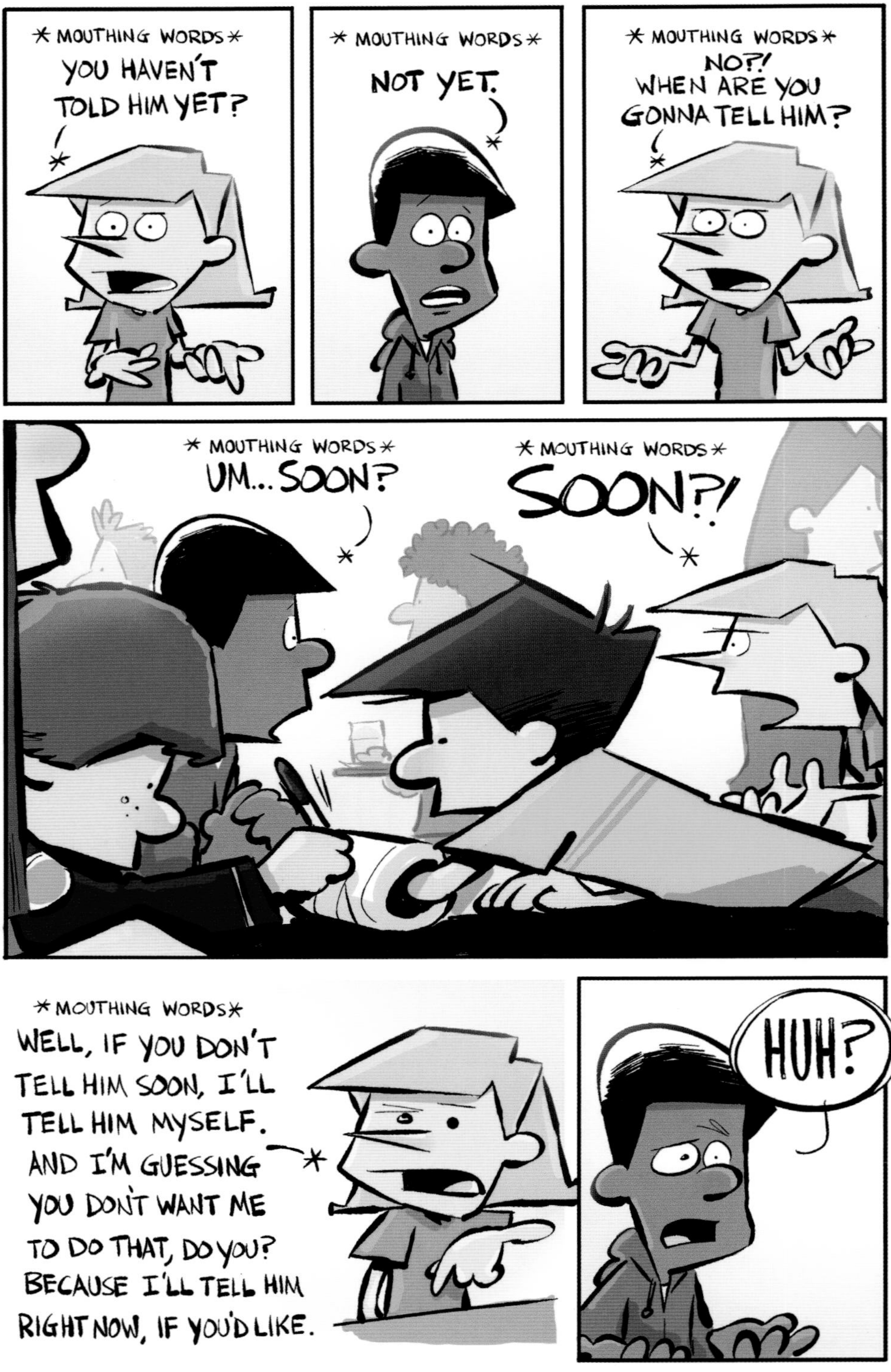
MOUTHING WORDS
YOU HAVEN'T TOLD HIM YET?
MOUTHING WORDS
NOT YET.
MOUTHING WORDS
NO?! WHEN ARE YOU GONNA TELL HIM?
MOUTHING WORDS
UM... SOON?
MOUTHING WORDS
SOON?!
MOUTHING WORDS
WELL, IF YOU DON'T TELL HIM SOON, I'LL TELL HIM MYSELF. AND I'M GUESSING YOU DON'T WANT ME TO DO THAT, DO YOU? BECAUSE I'LL TELL HIM RIGHT NOW, IF YOU'D LIKE.
HUH?

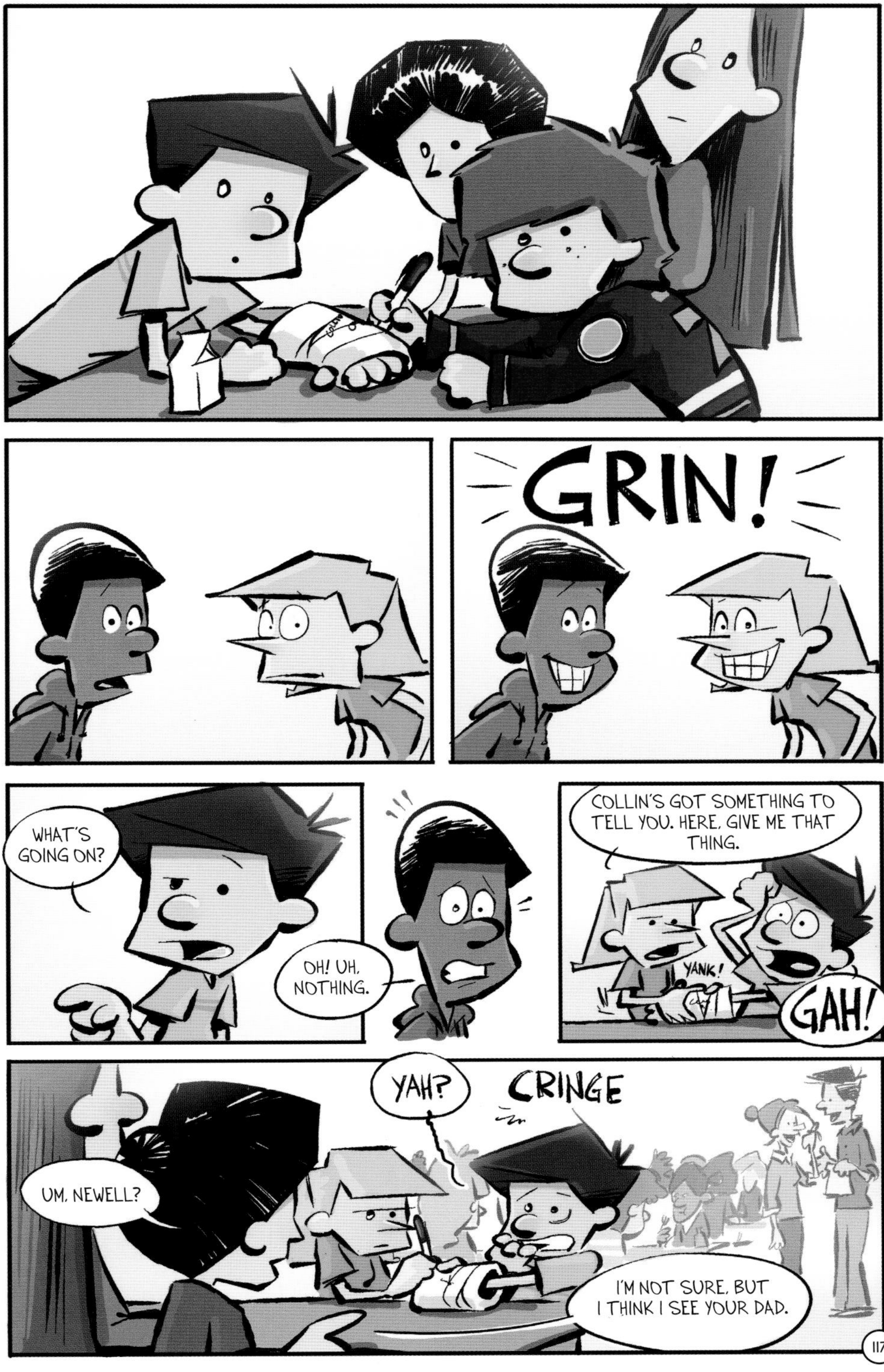
GRIN!
WHAT'S GOING ON?
OH! UH, NOTHING.
COLLIN'S GOT SOMETHING TO TELL YOU. HERE, GIVE ME THAT THING.
YANK!
GAH!
YAH?
CRINGE
UM, NEWELL?
I'M NOT SURE, BUT I THINK I SEE YOUR DAD.

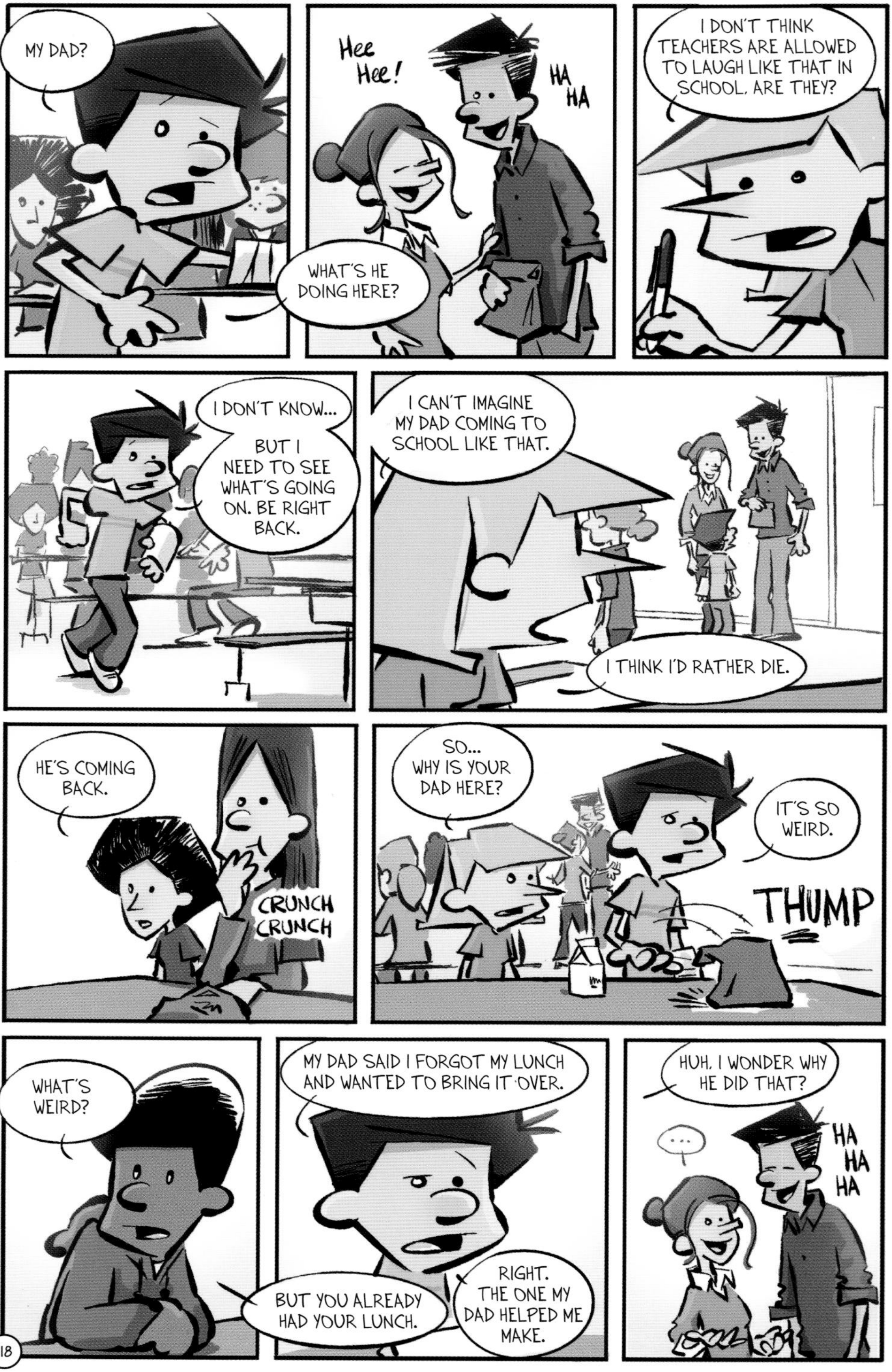
MY DAD?
Hee Hee!
HA HA
WHAT'S HE DOING HERE?
I DON'T THINK TEACHERS ARE ALLOWED TO LAUGH LIKE THAT IN SCHOOL, ARE THEY?
I DON'T KNOW...
BUT I NEED TO SEE WHAT'S GOING ON. BE RIGHT BACK.
I CAN'T IMAGINE MY DAD COMING TO SCHOOL LIKE THAT.
I THINK I'D RATHER DIE.
HE'S COMING BACK.
CRUNCH CRUNCH
SO... WHY IS YOUR DAD HERE?
IT'S SO WEIRD.
THUMP
WHAT'S WEIRD?
MY DAD SAID I FORGOT MY LUNCH AND WANTED TO BRING IT OVER.
BUT YOU ALREADY HAD YOUR LUNCH.
RIGHT. THE ONE MY DAD HELPED ME MAKE.
HUH. I WONDER WHY HE DID THAT?
...
HA HA HA

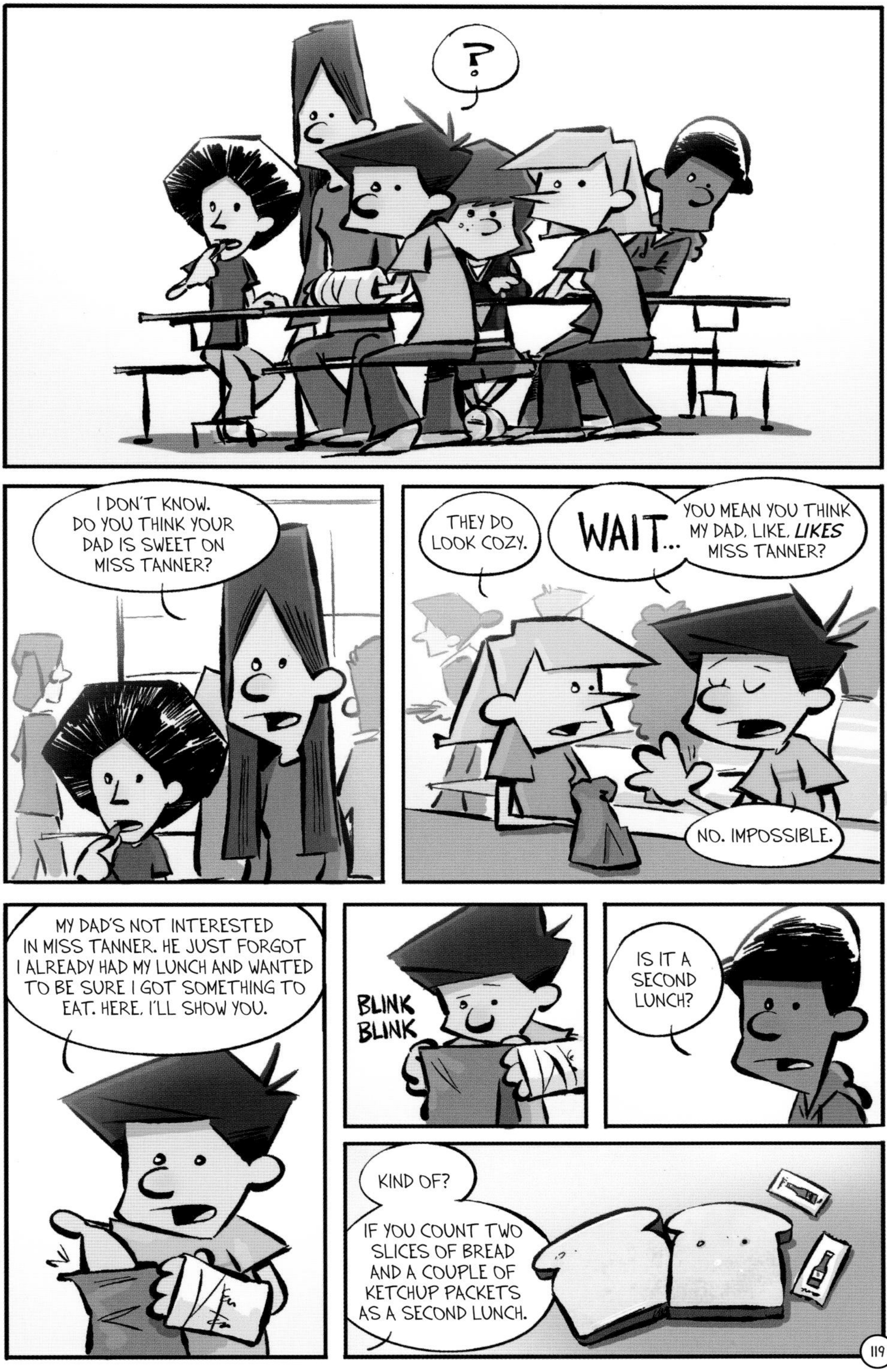

?
I DON'T KNOW. DO YOU THINK YOUR DAD IS SWEET ON MISS TANNER?
THEY DO LOOK COZY.
WAIT...
YOU MEAN YOU THINK MY DAD, LIKE, *LIKES* MISS TANNER?
NO. IMPOSSIBLE.
MY DAD'S NOT INTERESTED IN MISS TANNER. HE JUST FORGOT I ALREADY HAD MY LUNCH AND WANTED TO BE SURE I GOT SOMETHING TO EAT. HERE, I'LL SHOW YOU.
BLINK BLINK
IS IT A SECOND LUNCH?
KIND OF?
IF YOU COUNT TWO SLICES OF BREAD AND A COUPLE OF KETCHUP PACKETS AS A SECOND LUNCH.

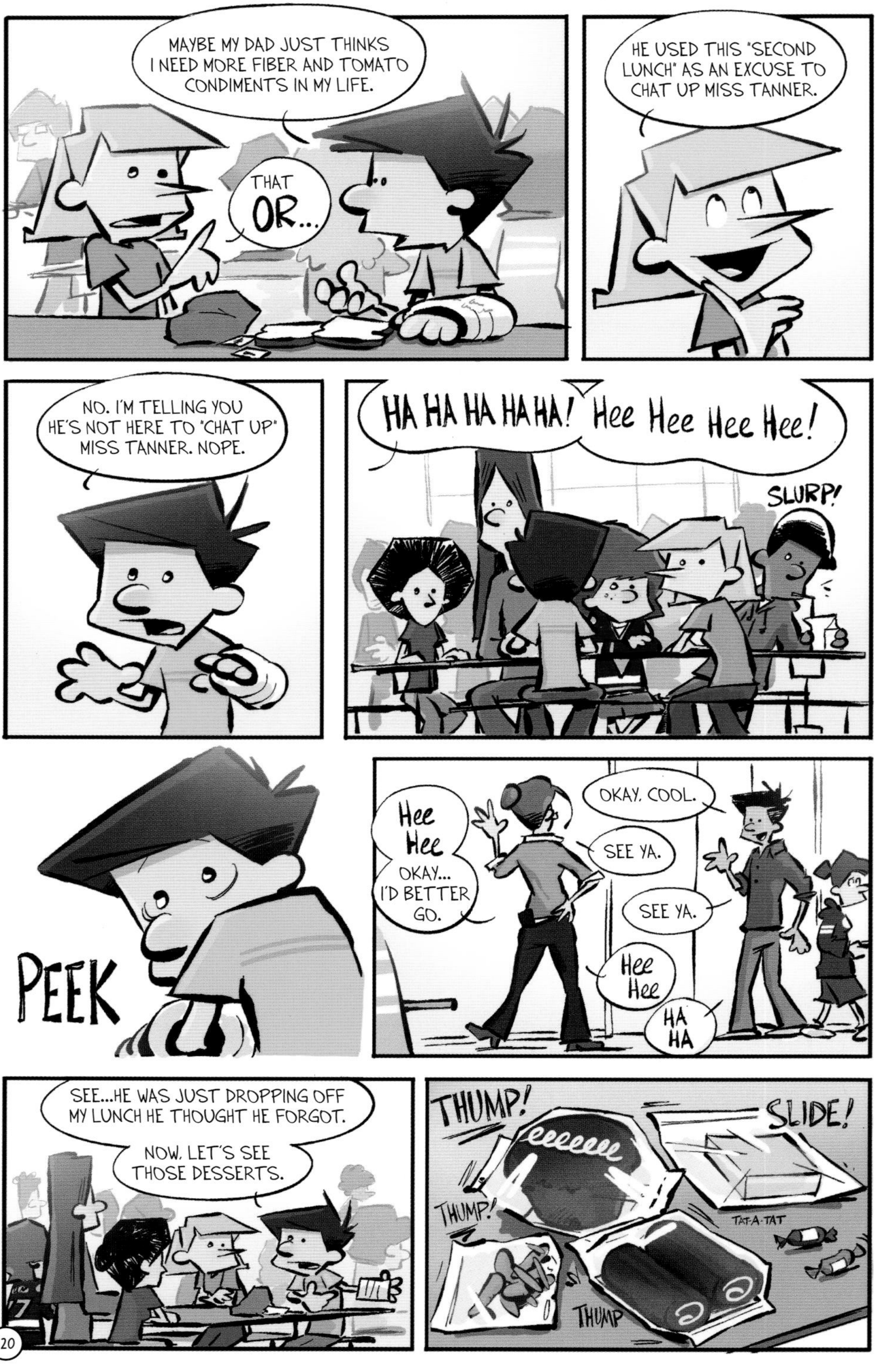
MAYBE MY DAD JUST THINKS I NEED MORE FIBER AND TOMATO CONDIMENTS IN MY LIFE.
THAT OR...
HE USED THIS "SECOND LUNCH" AS AN EXCUSE TO CHAT UP MISS TANNER.
NO. I'M TELLING YOU HE'S NOT HERE TO "CHAT UP" MISS TANNER. NOPE.
HA HA HA HA HA!
Hee Hee Hee Hee!
SLURP!
PEEK
Hee Hee
OKAY... I'D BETTER GO.
OKAY, COOL.
SEE YA.
SEE YA.
Hee Hee
HA HA
SEE...HE WAS JUST DROPPING OFF MY LUNCH HE THOUGHT HE FORGOT.
NOW, LET'S SEE THOSE DESSERTS.
THUMP!
SLIDE!
THUMP!
TAT-A-TAT
THUMP

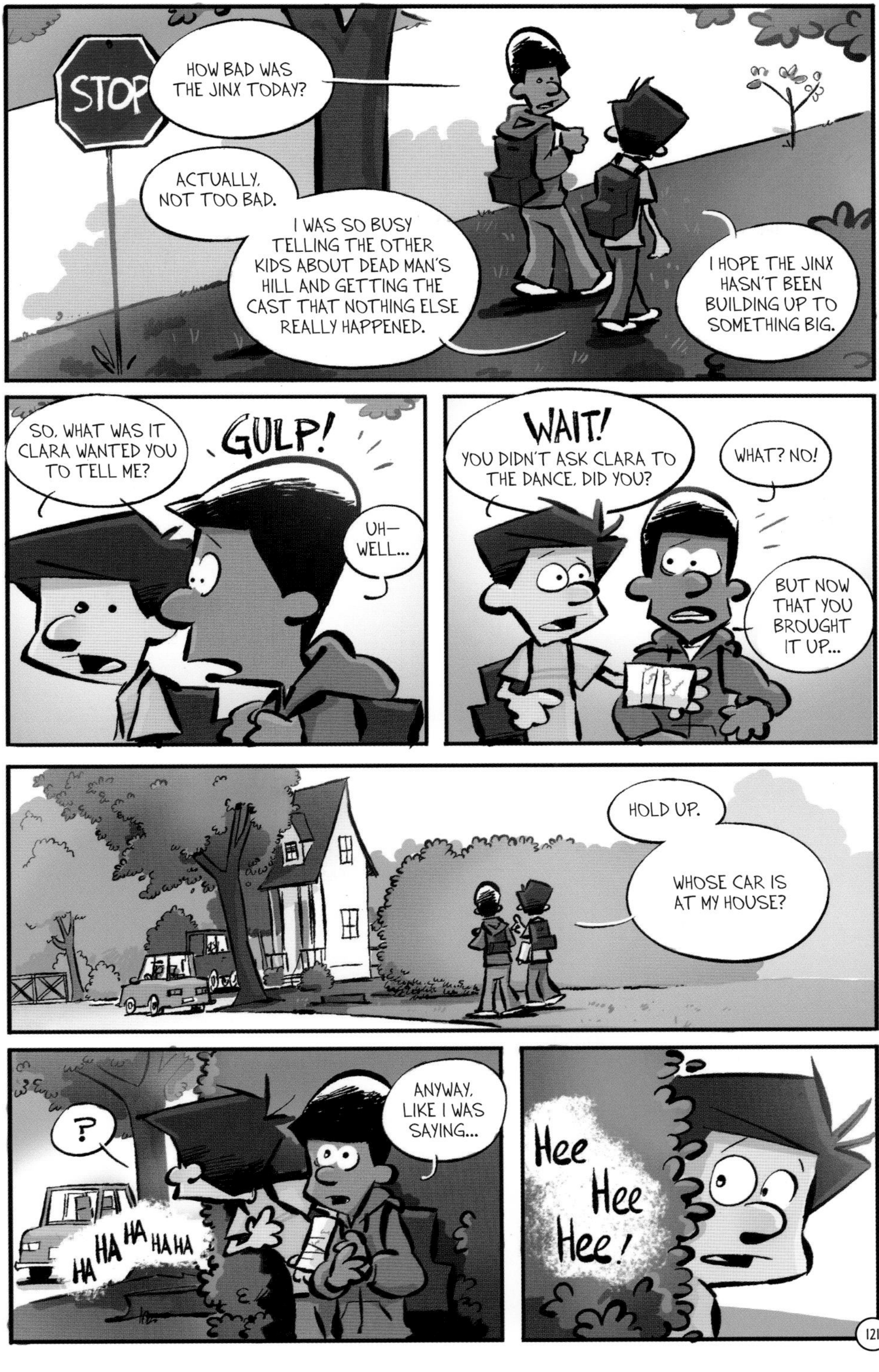
STOP
HOW BAD WAS THE JINX TODAY?
ACTUALLY, NOT TOO BAD.
I WAS SO BUSY TELLING THE OTHER KIDS ABOUT DEAD MAN'S HILL AND GETTING THE CAST THAT NOTHING ELSE REALLY HAPPENED.
I HOPE THE JINX HASN'T BEEN BUILDING UP TO SOMETHING BIG.
SO, WHAT WAS IT CLARA WANTED YOU TO TELL ME?
GULP!
UH— WELL...
WAIT! YOU DIDN'T ASK CLARA TO THE DANCE, DID YOU?
WHAT? NO!
BUT NOW THAT YOU BROUGHT IT UP...
HOLD UP.
WHOSE CAR IS AT MY HOUSE?
?
HA HA HA HA HA
ANYWAY, LIKE I WAS SAYING...
Hee Hee Hee!

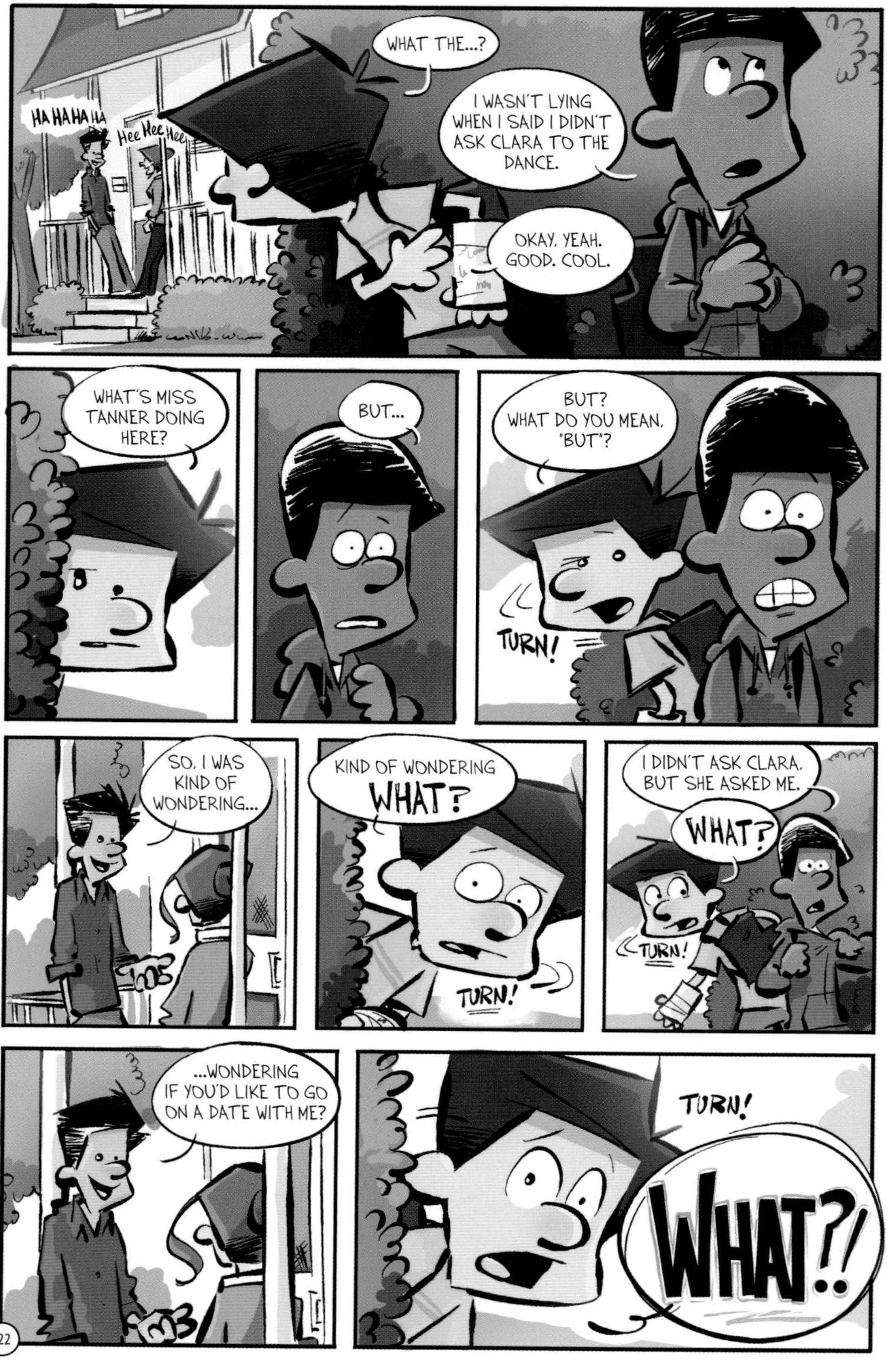
WHAT THE...?
HA HA HA HA HA
Hee Hee Hee Hee
I WASN'T LYING WHEN I SAID I DIDN'T ASK CLARA TO THE DANCE.
OKAY, YEAH. GOOD. COOL.
WHAT'S MISS TANNER DOING HERE?
BUT...
BUT? WHAT DO YOU MEAN, "BUT"?
TURN!
SO, I WAS KIND OF WONDERING...
KIND OF WONDERING WHAT?
TURN!
I DIDN'T ASK CLARA, BUT SHE ASKED ME.
WHAT?
TURN!
...WONDERING IF YOU'D LIKE TO GO ON A DATE WITH ME?
TURN!
WHAT?!

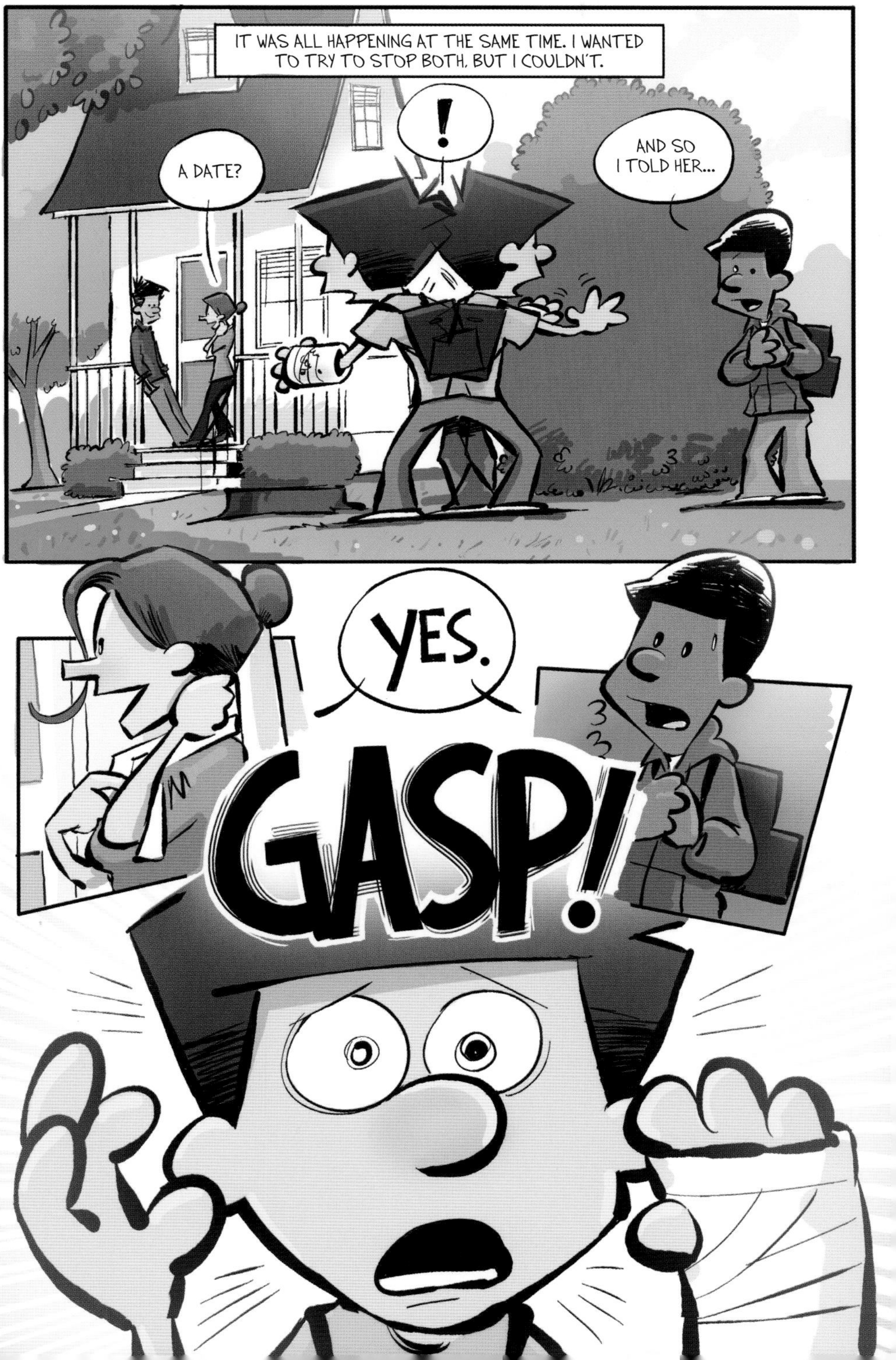
IT WAS ALL HAPPENING AT THE SAME TIME. I WANTED TO TRY TO STOP BOTH, BUT I COULDN'T.
A DATE?
!
AND SO I TOLD HER...
YES.
GASP!

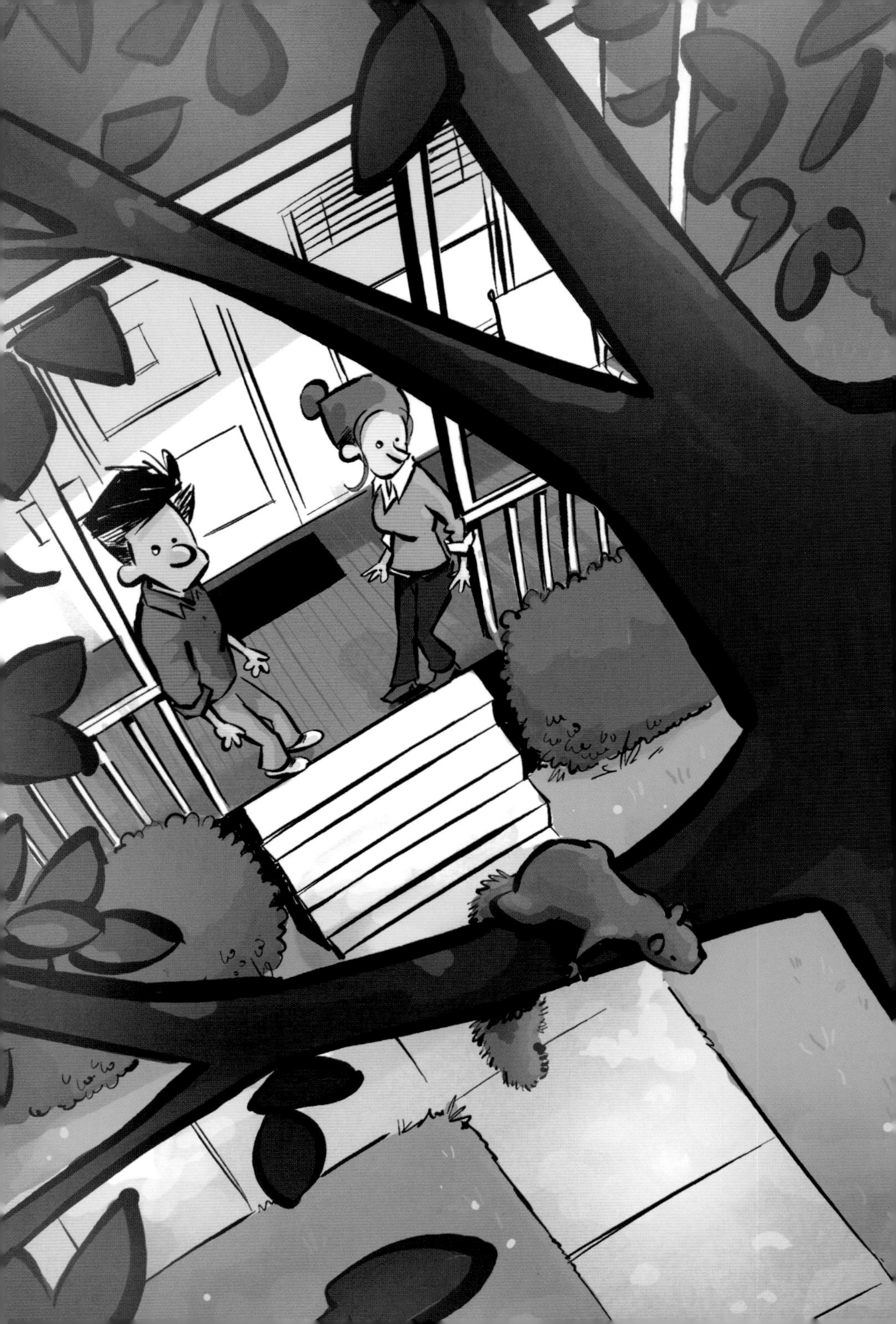

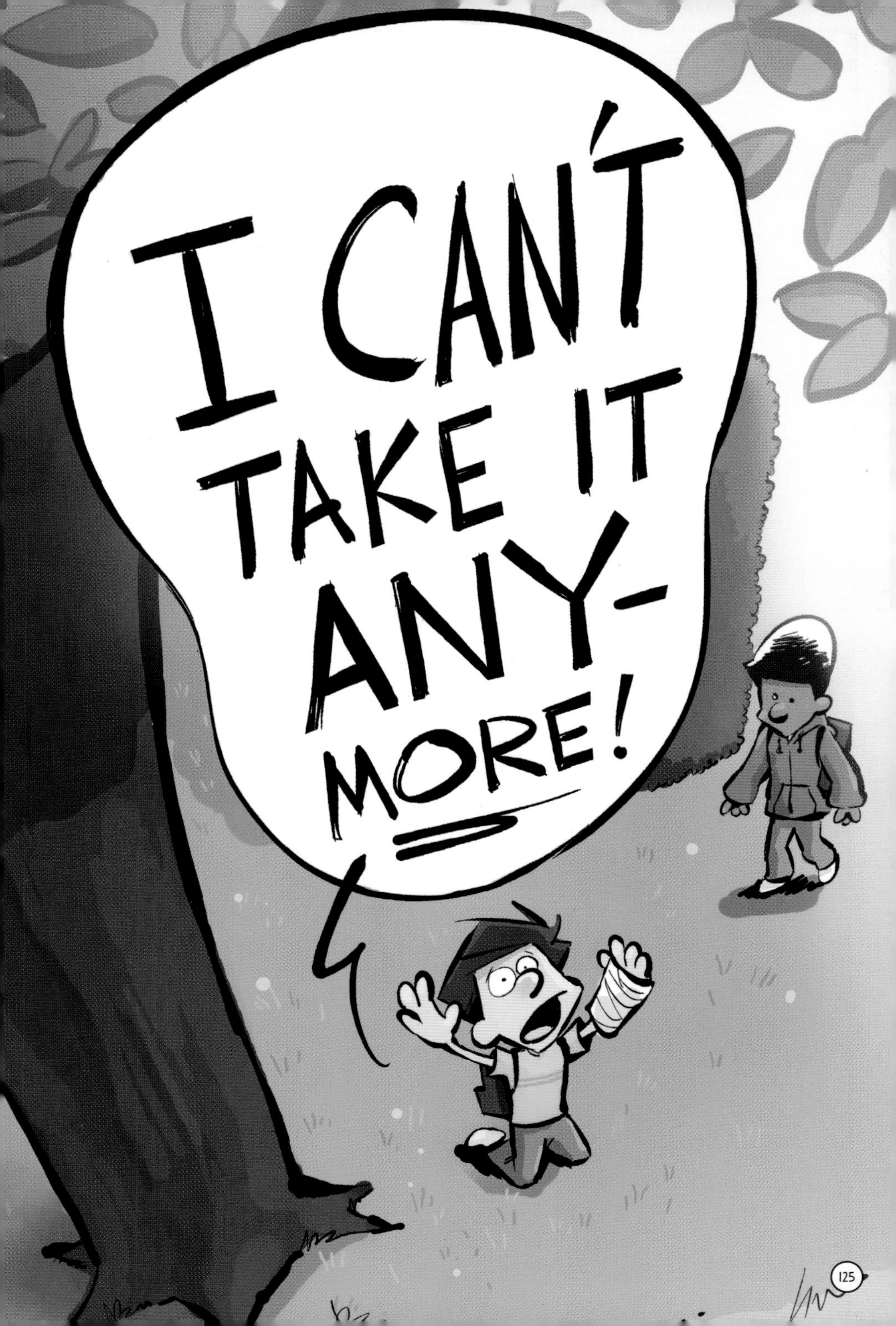
I CAN'T TAKE IT ANY-MORE!

CHAPTER SEVEN
NOTHING IS THE SAME

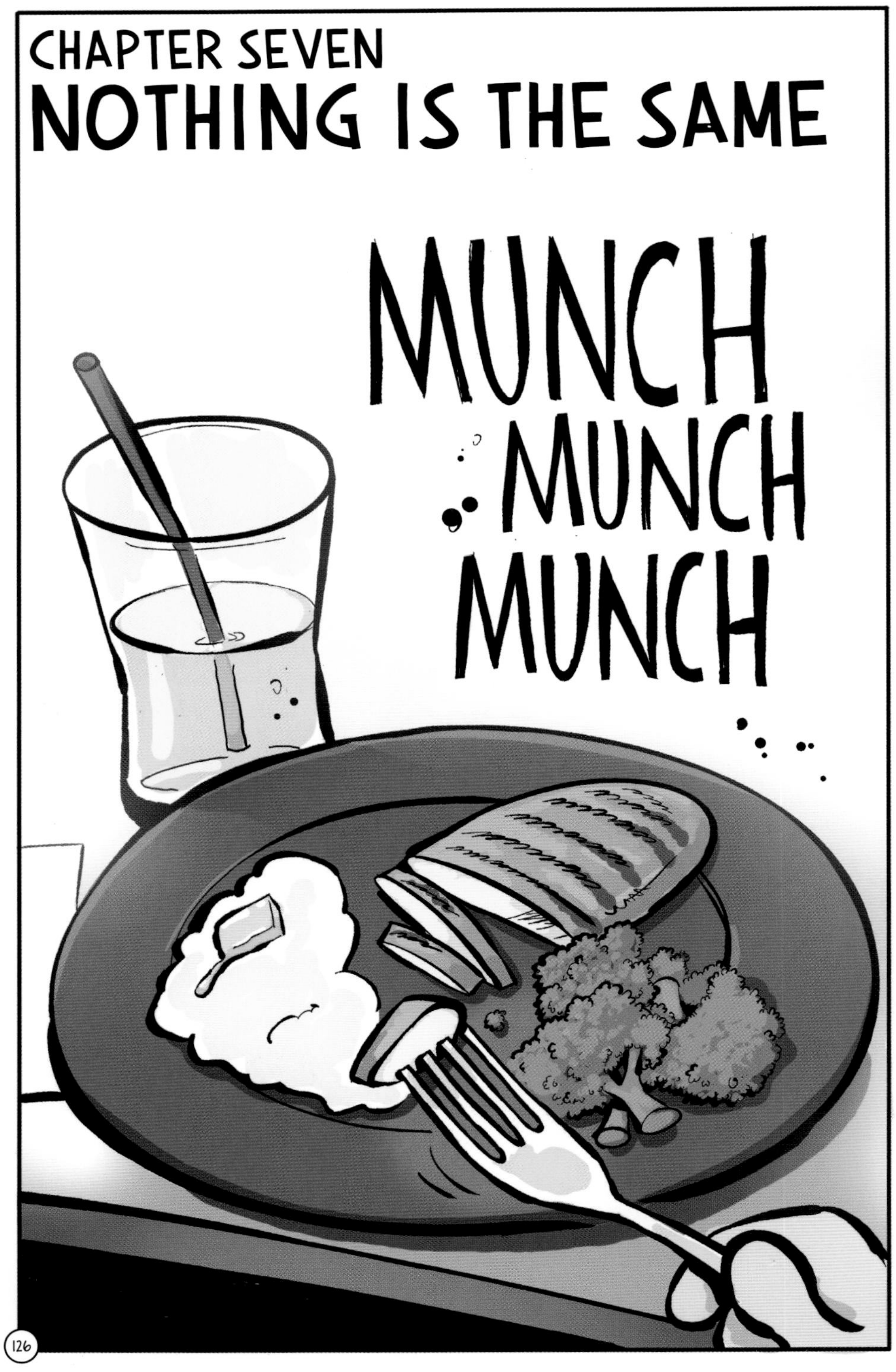
MUNCH
MUNCH
MUNCH

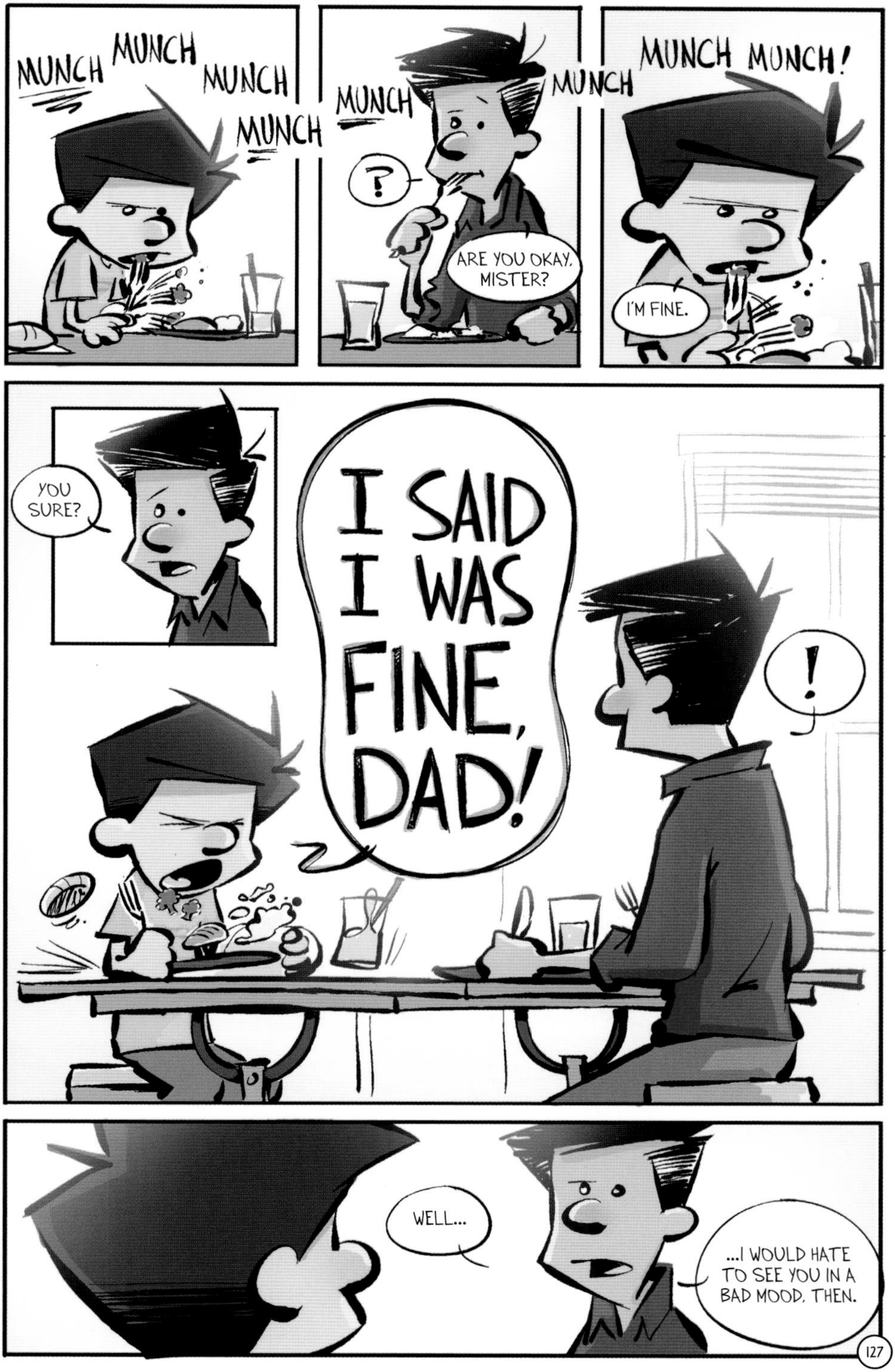
MUNCH MUNCH MUNCH
MUNCH MUNCH
?
ARE YOU OKAY, MISTER?
MUNCH MUNCH MUNCH!
I'M FINE.
YOU SURE?
I SAID I WAS FINE, DAD!
!
WELL...
...I WOULD HATE TO SEE YOU IN A BAD MOOD, THEN.

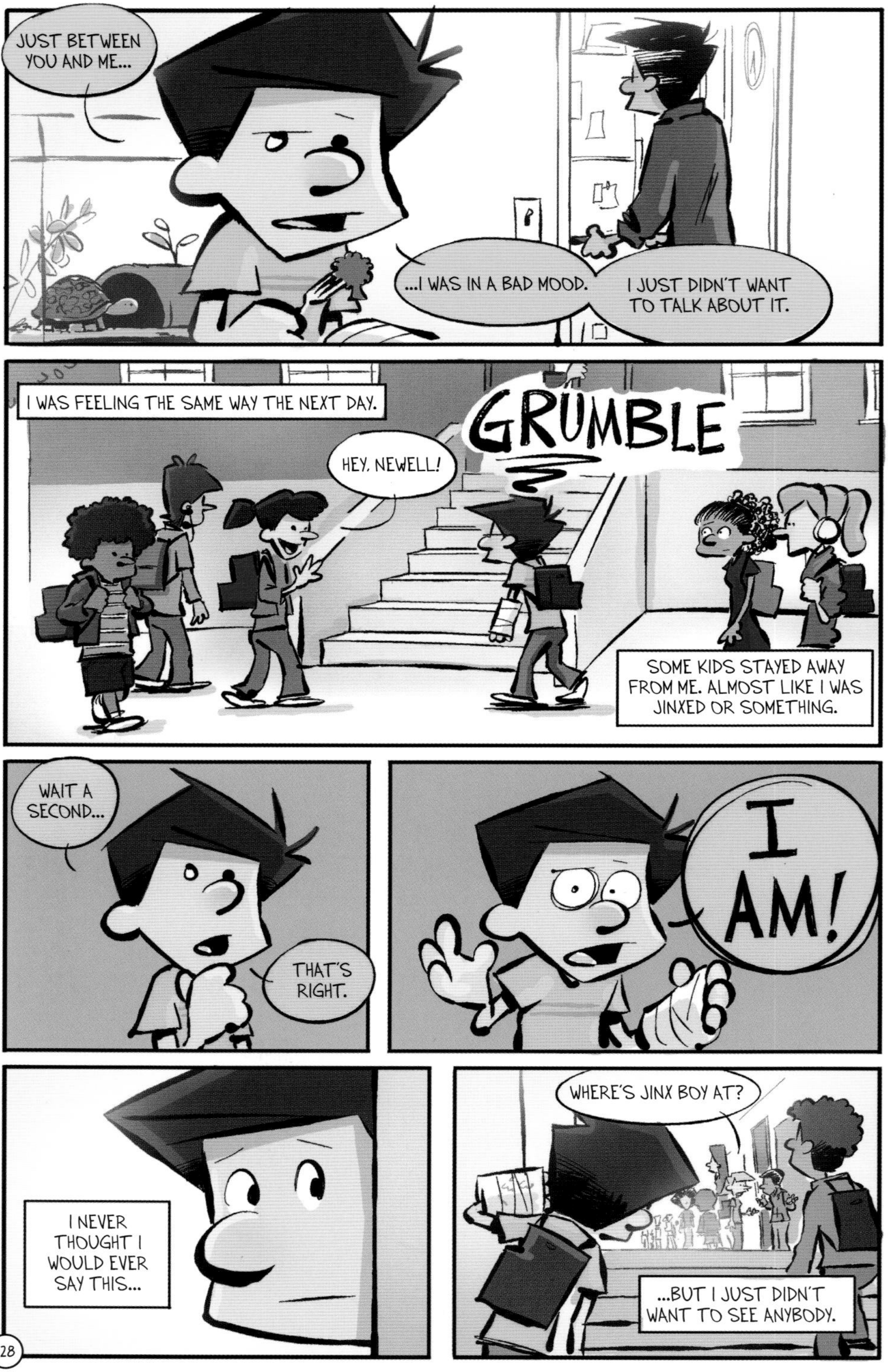
JUST BETWEEN YOU AND ME...
...I WAS IN A BAD MOOD.
I JUST DIDN'T WANT TO TALK ABOUT IT.
I WAS FEELING THE SAME WAY THE NEXT DAY.
HEY, NEWELL!
GRUMBLE
SOME KIDS STAYED AWAY FROM ME. ALMOST LIKE I WAS JINXED OR SOMETHING.
WAIT A SECOND...
THAT'S RIGHT.
I AM!
I NEVER THOUGHT I WOULD EVER SAY THIS...
WHERE'S JINX BOY AT?
...BUT I JUST DIDN'T WANT TO SEE ANYBODY.

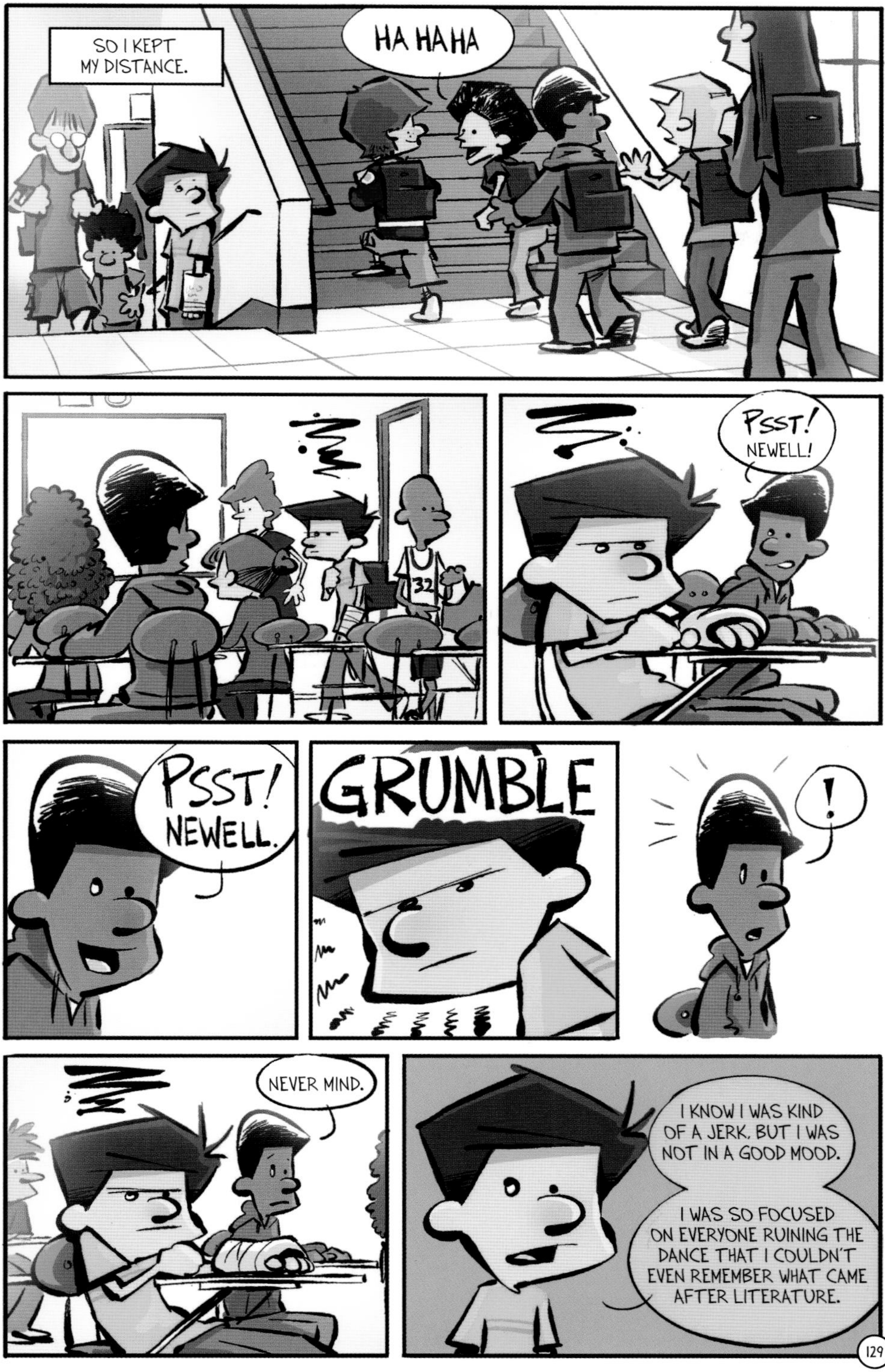
SO I KEPT MY DISTANCE.
HA HA HA
PSST! NEWELL!
PSST! NEWELL.
GRUMBLE
!
NEVER MIND.
I KNOW I WAS KIND OF A JERK, BUT I WAS NOT IN A GOOD MOOD.
I WAS SO FOCUSED ON EVERYONE RUINING THE DANCE THAT I COULDN'T EVEN REMEMBER WHAT CAME AFTER LITERATURE.

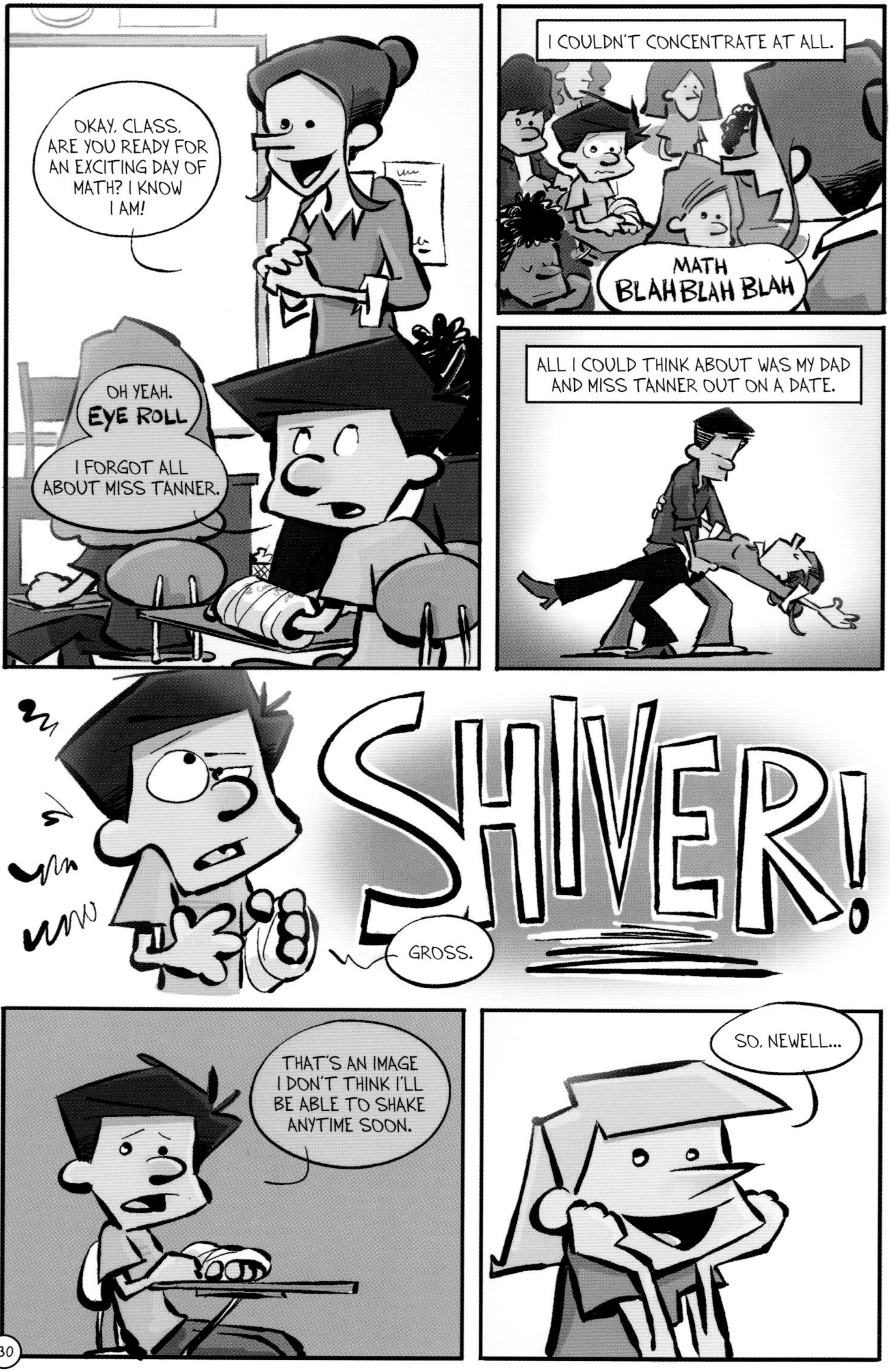
OKAY, CLASS, ARE YOU READY FOR AN EXCITING DAY OF MATH? I KNOW I AM!
OH YEAH. EYE ROLL
I FORGOT ALL ABOUT MISS TANNER.
I COULDN'T CONCENTRATE AT ALL.
MATH BLAH BLAH BLAH
ALL I COULD THINK ABOUT WAS MY DAD AND MISS TANNER OUT ON A DATE.
SHIVER!
GROSS.
THAT'S AN IMAGE I DON'T THINK I'LL BE ABLE TO SHAKE ANYTIME SOON.
SO, NEWELL...

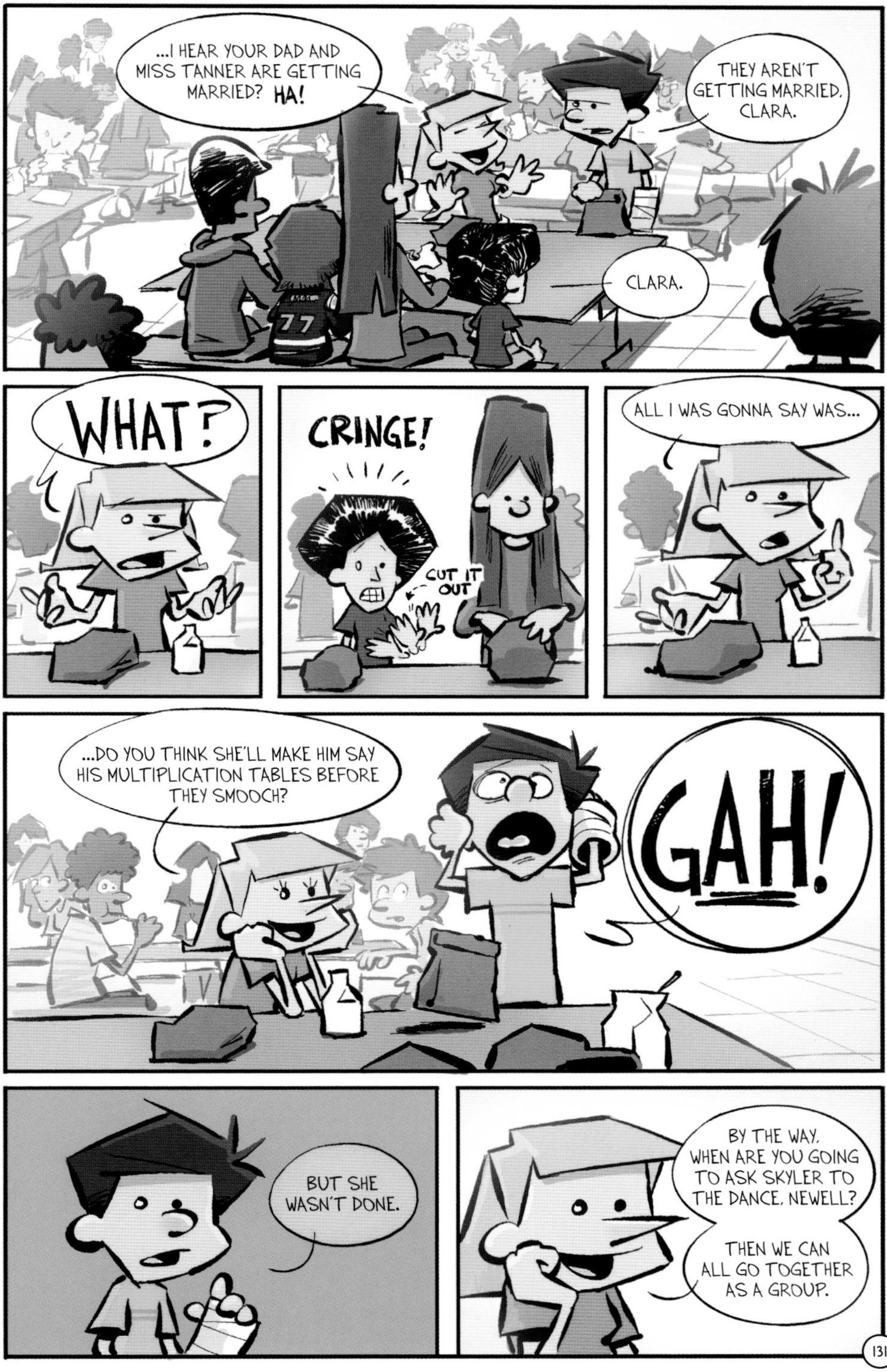
...I HEAR YOUR DAD AND MISS TANNER ARE GETTING MARRIED? HA!
THEY AREN'T GETTING MARRIED, CLARA.
CLARA.
WHAT?
CRINGE!
CUT IT OUT
ALL I WAS GONNA SAY WAS...
...DO YOU THINK SHE'LL MAKE HIM SAY HIS MULTIPLICATION TABLES BEFORE THEY SMOOCH?
GAH!
BUT SHE WASN'T DONE.
BY THE WAY, WHEN ARE YOU GOING TO ASK SKYLER TO THE DANCE, NEWELL?
THEN WE CAN ALL GO TOGETHER AS A GROUP.

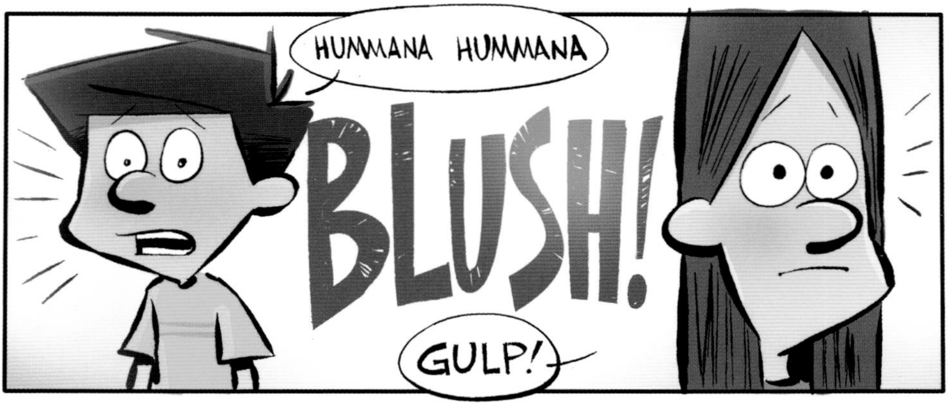
HUMMANA HUMMANA
BLUSH!
GULP!

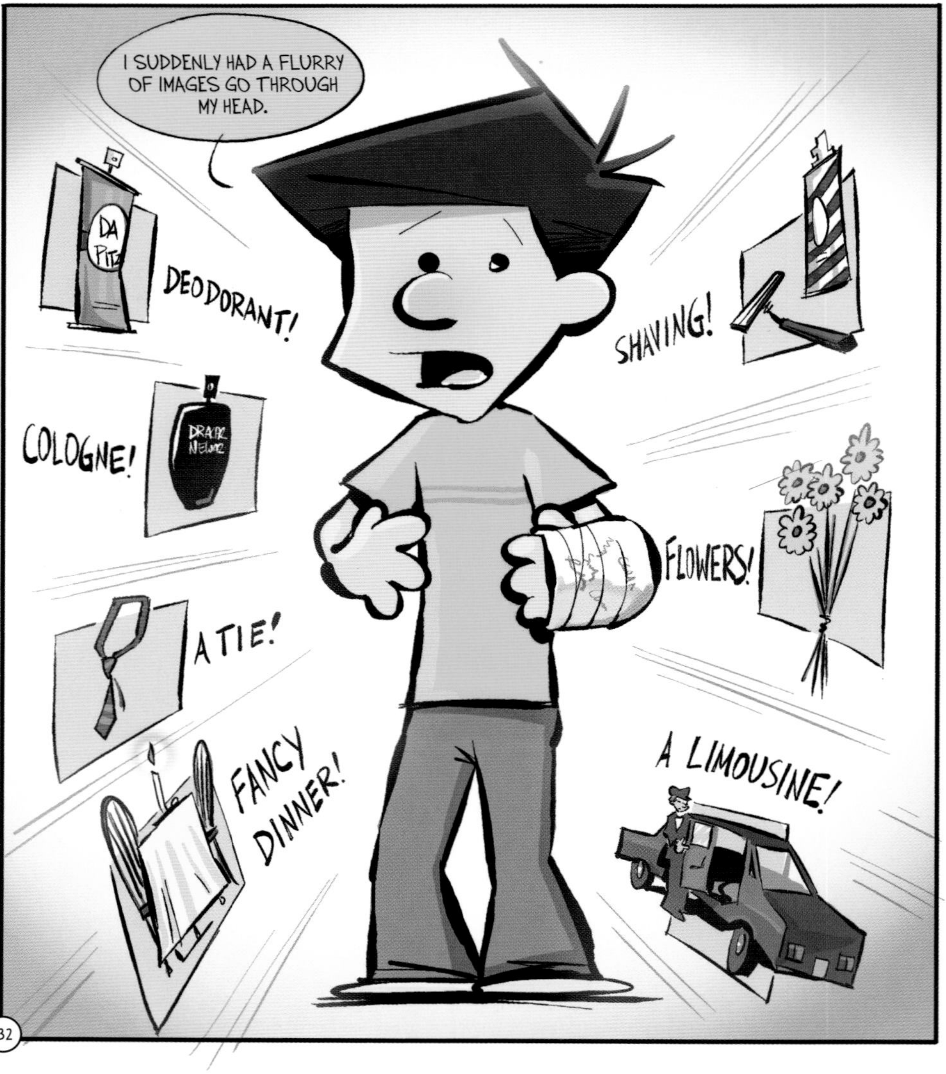
I SUDDENLY HAD A FLURRY OF IMAGES GO THROUGH MY HEAD.
DA PITZ
DEODORANT!
SHAVING!
COLOGNE!
FLOWERS!
A TIE!
FANCY DINNER!
A LIMOUSINE!

AND THAT WAS THE EASY PART!

HOW IN THE WORLD WAS I SUPPOSED TO WRANGLE UP...

...A UNICORN?

...FAIRIES?

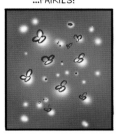

...OR A FAIRY GODMOTHER?!

I MEAN...CAN YOU RENT THEM OUT OR SOMETHING?

BUT THAT WAS NOTHING COMPARED WITH WHAT I WAS REALLY WORRIED ABOUT.

"WHAT IF SKYLER AND I WENT TO THE DANCE...

GRUMBLE!

HUMPH!

"...AND WE STOPPED BEING FRIENDS?"

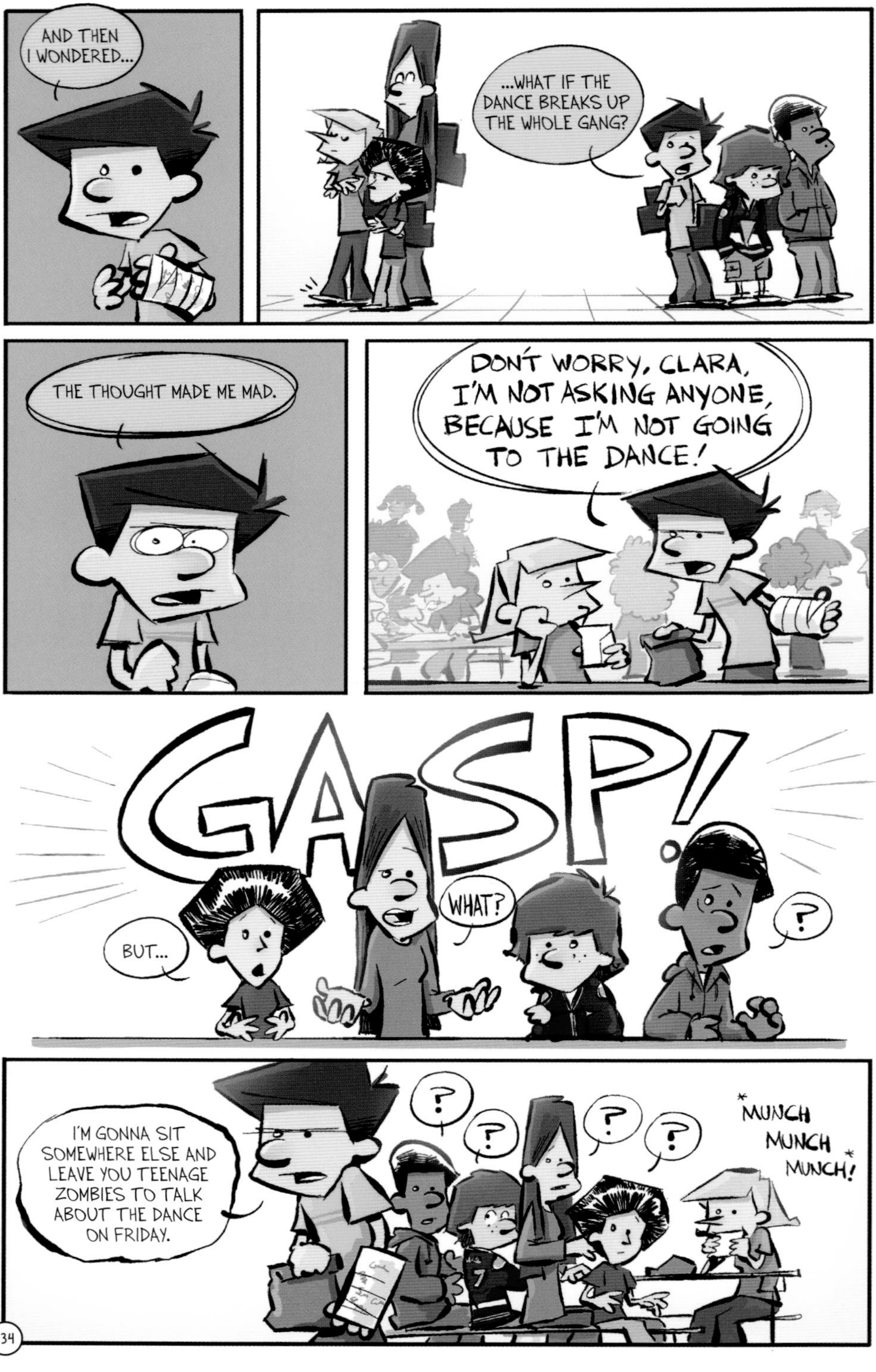
AND THEN I WONDERED...
...WHAT IF THE DANCE BREAKS UP THE WHOLE GANG?
THE THOUGHT MADE ME MAD.
DON'T WORRY, CLARA, I'M NOT ASKING ANYONE, BECAUSE I'M NOT GOING TO THE DANCE!
GASP!
BUT...
WHAT?
?
I'M GONNA SIT SOMEWHERE ELSE AND LEAVE YOU TEENAGE ZOMBIES TO TALK ABOUT THE DANCE ON FRIDAY.
?
?
?
?
MUNCH MUNCH MUNCH!

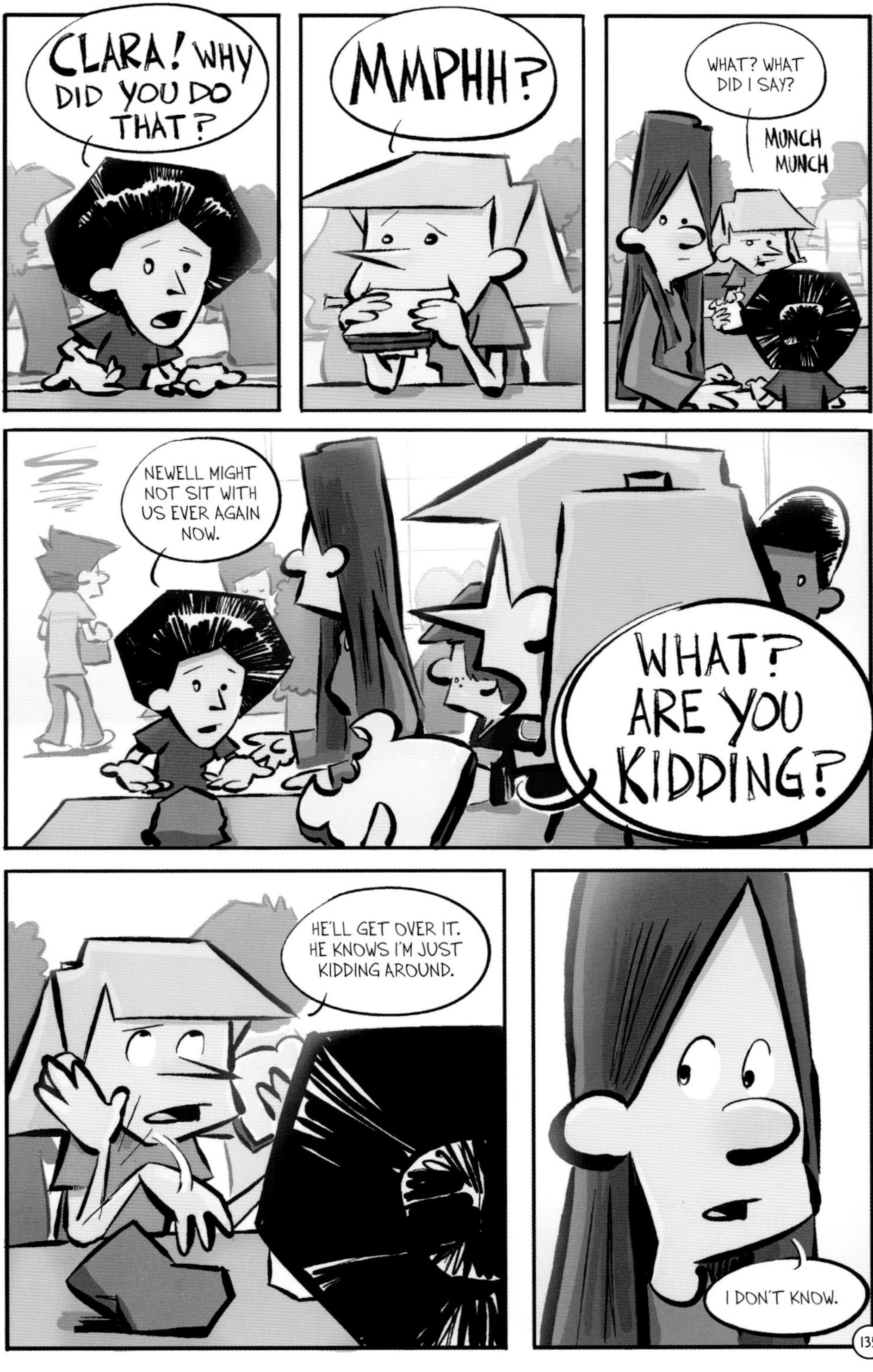
CLARA! WHY DID YOU DO THAT?
MMPHH?
WHAT? WHAT DID I SAY?
MUNCH MUNCH
NEWELL MIGHT NOT SIT WITH US EVER AGAIN NOW.
WHAT? ARE YOU KIDDING?
HE'LL GET OVER IT. HE KNOWS I'M JUST KIDDING AROUND.
I DON'T KNOW.

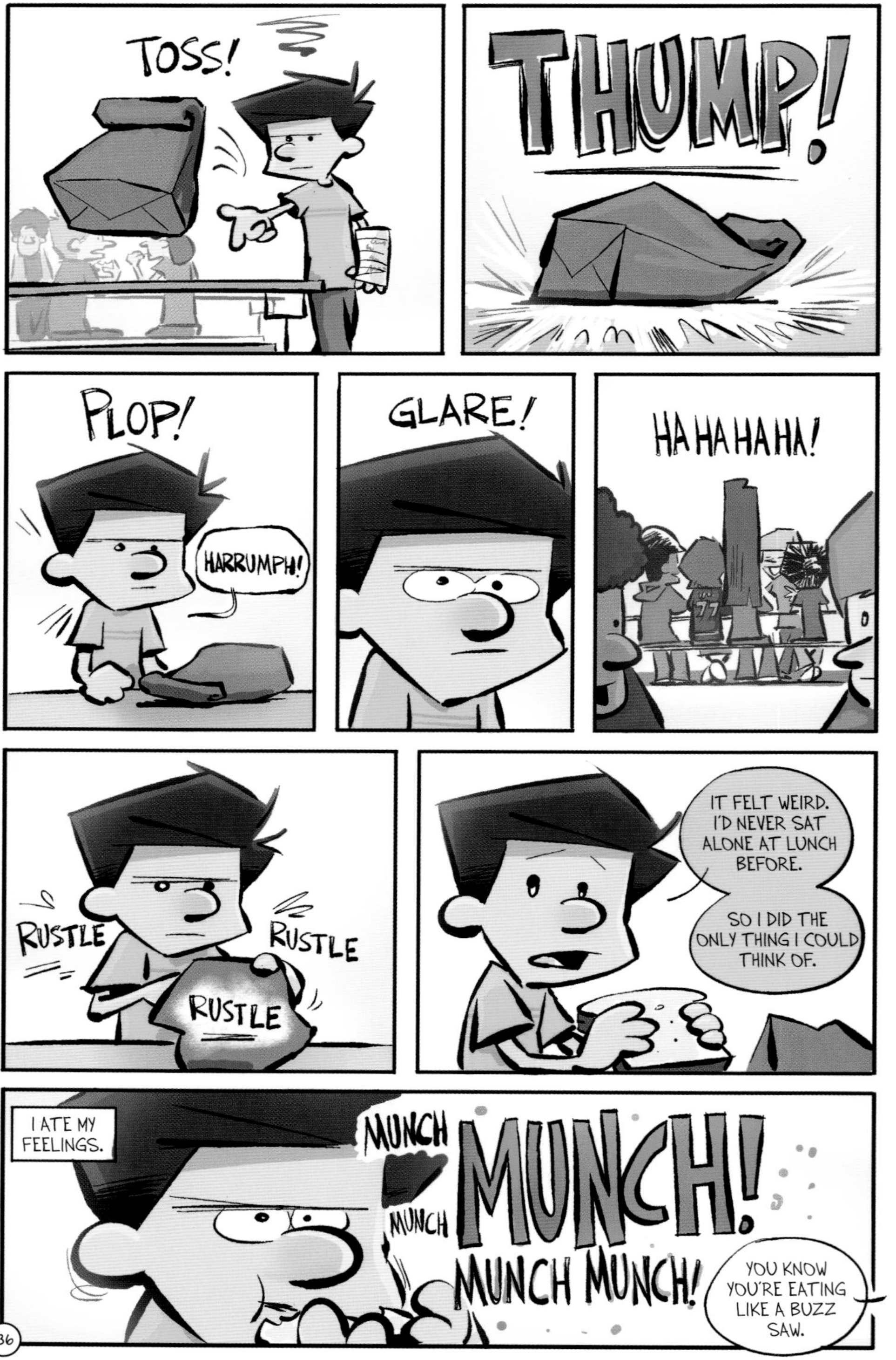
TOSS!
THUMP!
PLOP!
HARRUMPH!
GLARE!
HA HA HA HA!
RUSTLE
RUSTLE
RUSTLE
IT FELT WEIRD. I'D NEVER SAT ALONE AT LUNCH BEFORE.
SO I DID THE ONLY THING I COULD THINK OF.
I ATE MY FEELINGS.
MUNCH
MUNCH!
MUNCH
MUNCH MUNCH!
YOU KNOW YOU'RE EATING LIKE A BUZZ SAW.

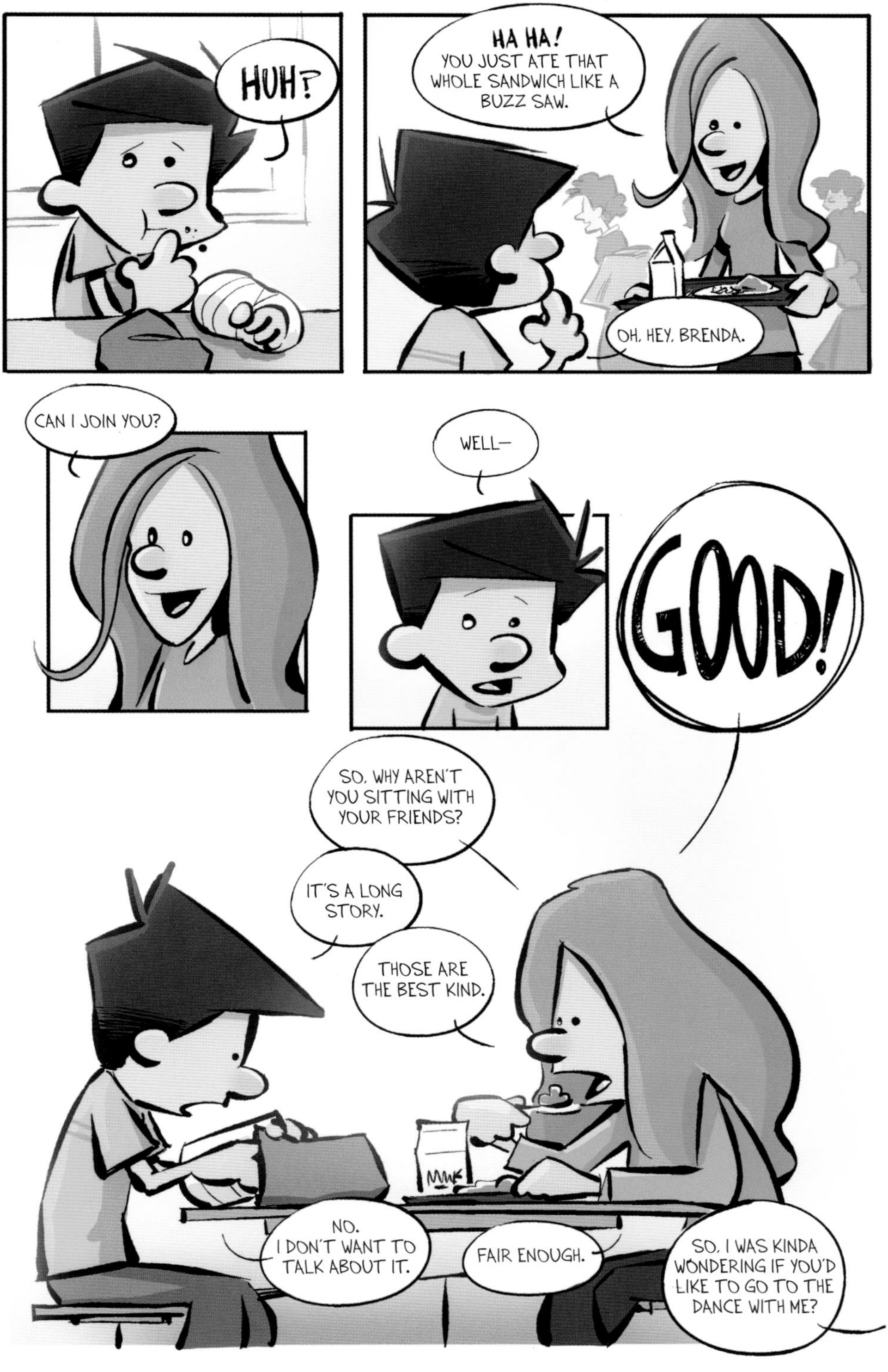
HUH?
HA HA! YOU JUST ATE THAT WHOLE SANDWICH LIKE A BUZZ SAW.
OH, HEY, BRENDA.
CAN I JOIN YOU?
WELL—
GOOD!
SO, WHY AREN'T YOU SITTING WITH YOUR FRIENDS?
IT'S A LONG STORY.
THOSE ARE THE BEST KIND.
NO. I DON'T WANT TO TALK ABOUT IT.
FAIR ENOUGH.
SO, I WAS KINDA WONDERING IF YOU'D LIKE TO GO TO THE DANCE WITH ME?
MILK

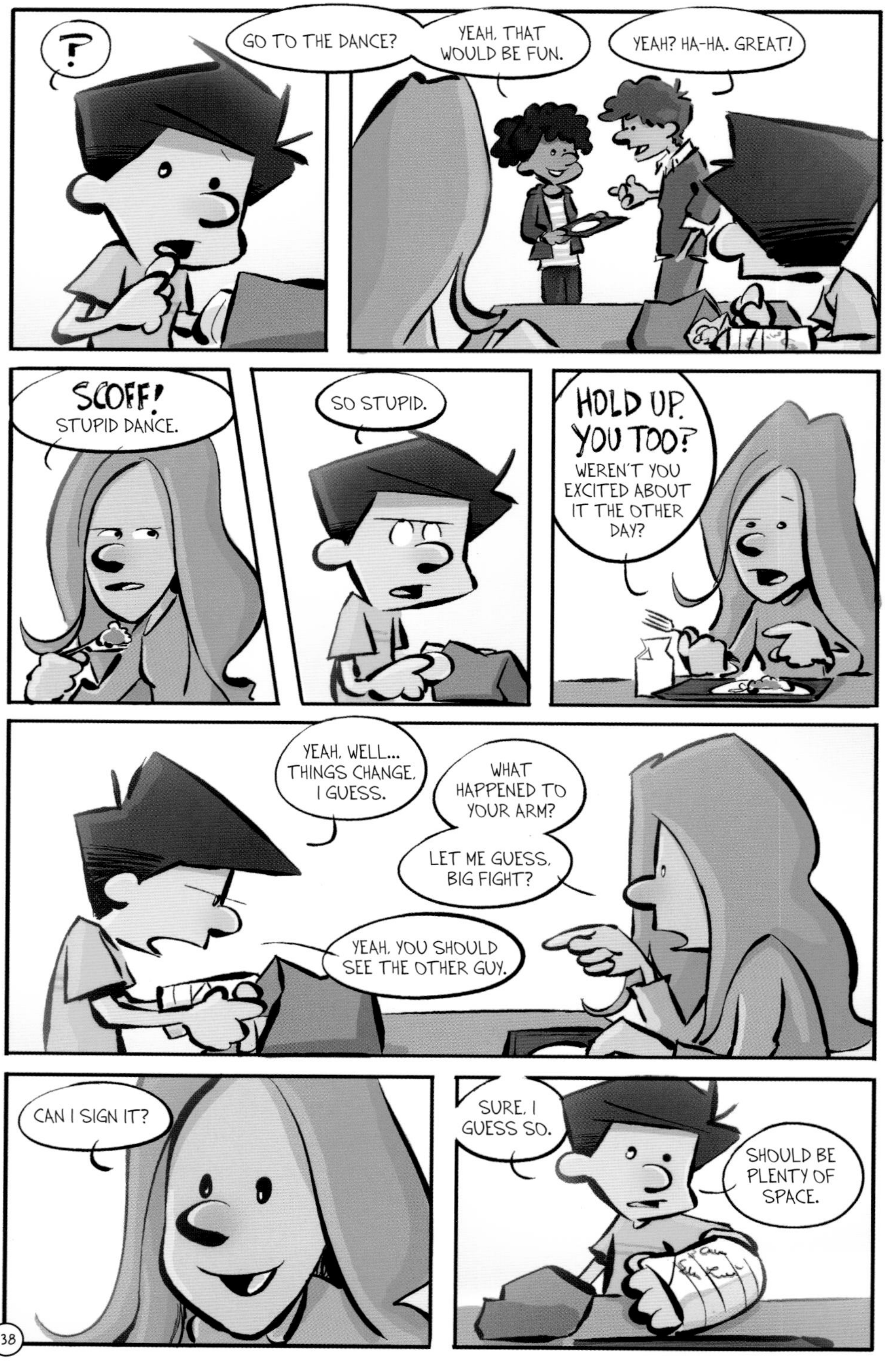
?
GO TO THE DANCE?
YEAH, THAT WOULD BE FUN.
YEAH? HA-HA. GREAT!
SCOFF! STUPID DANCE.
SO STUPID.
HOLD UP. YOU TOO?
WEREN'T YOU EXCITED ABOUT IT THE OTHER DAY?
YEAH, WELL... THINGS CHANGE, I GUESS.
WHAT HAPPENED TO YOUR ARM?
LET ME GUESS, BIG FIGHT?
YEAH, YOU SHOULD SEE THE OTHER GUY.
CAN I SIGN IT?
SURE, I GUESS SO.
SHOULD BE PLENTY OF SPACE.

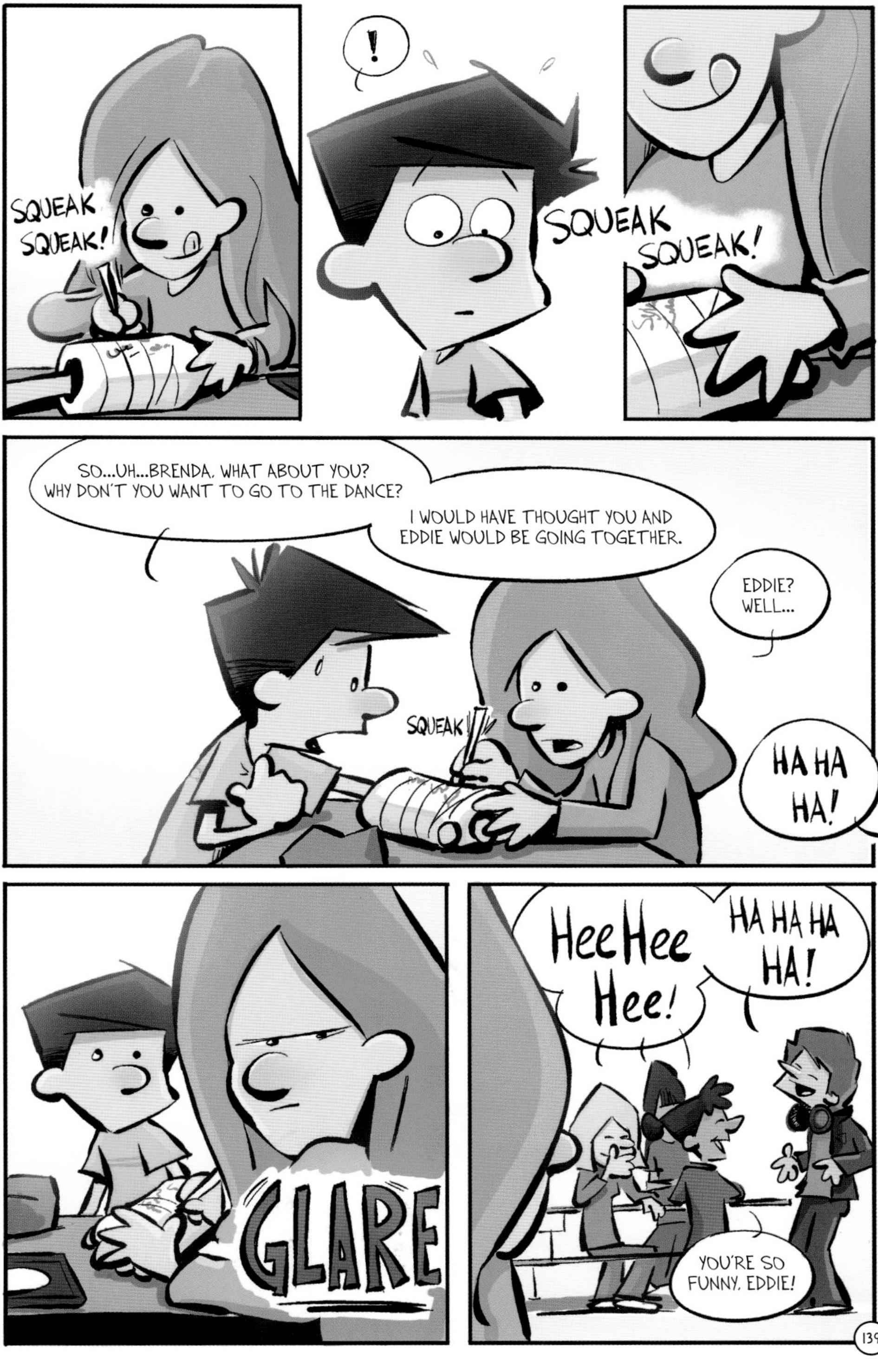

SQUEAK SQUEAK!
!
SQUEAK SQUEAK!
SO...UH...BRENDA, WHAT ABOUT YOU? WHY DON'T YOU WANT TO GO TO THE DANCE?
I WOULD HAVE THOUGHT YOU AND EDDIE WOULD BE GOING TOGETHER.
EDDIE? WELL...
SQUEAK
HA HA HA!
GLARE
HeeHee Hee!
HA HA HA HA!
YOU'RE SO FUNNY, EDDIE!

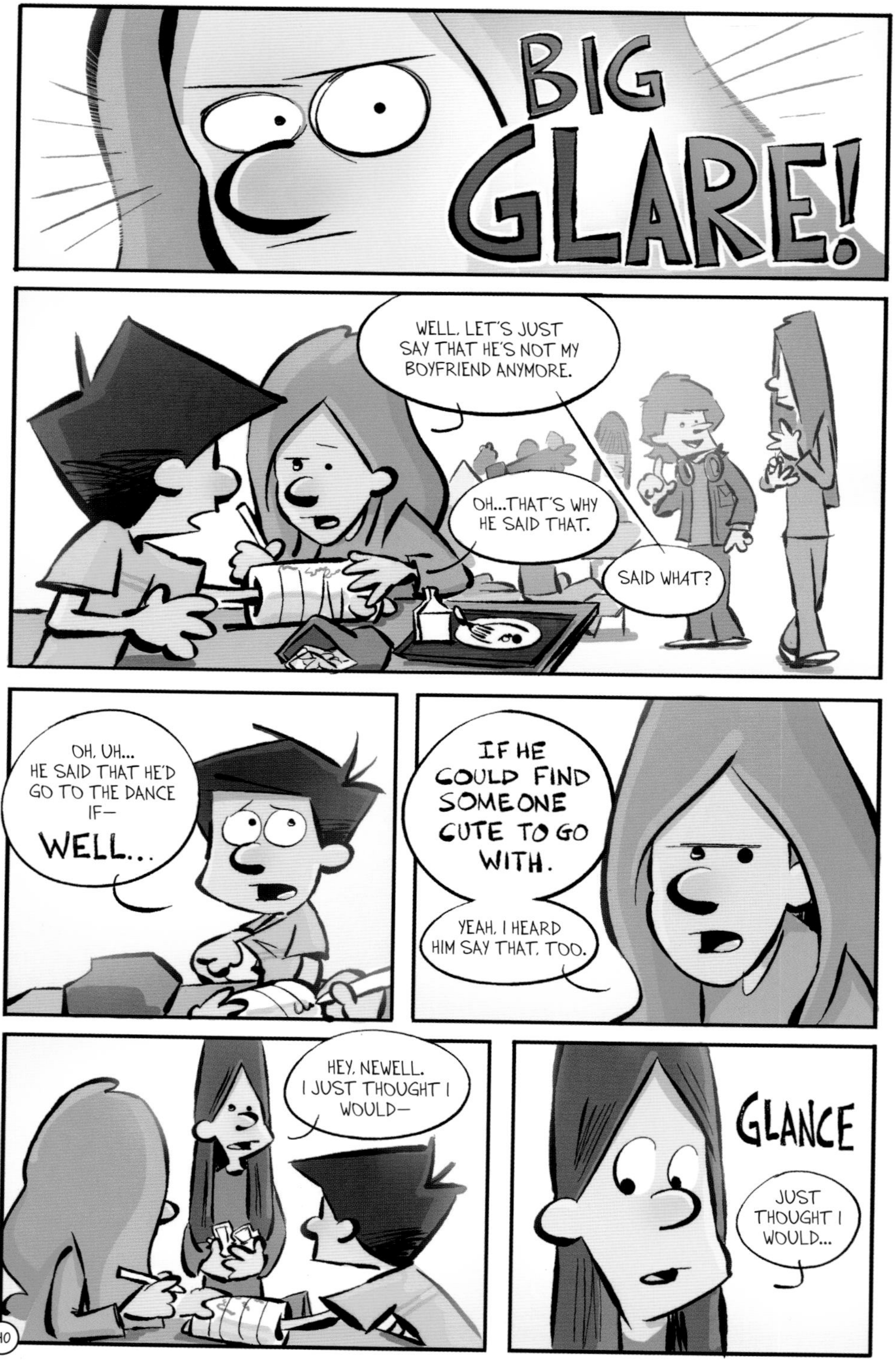
BIG GLARE!
WELL, LET'S JUST SAY THAT HE'S NOT MY BOYFRIEND ANYMORE.
OH...THAT'S WHY HE SAID THAT.
SAID WHAT?
OH, UH... HE SAID THAT HE'D GO TO THE DANCE IF— WELL...
IF HE COULD FIND SOMEONE CUTE TO GO WITH.
YEAH, I HEARD HIM SAY THAT, TOO.
HEY, NEWELL. I JUST THOUGHT I WOULD—
GLANCE
JUST THOUGHT I WOULD...

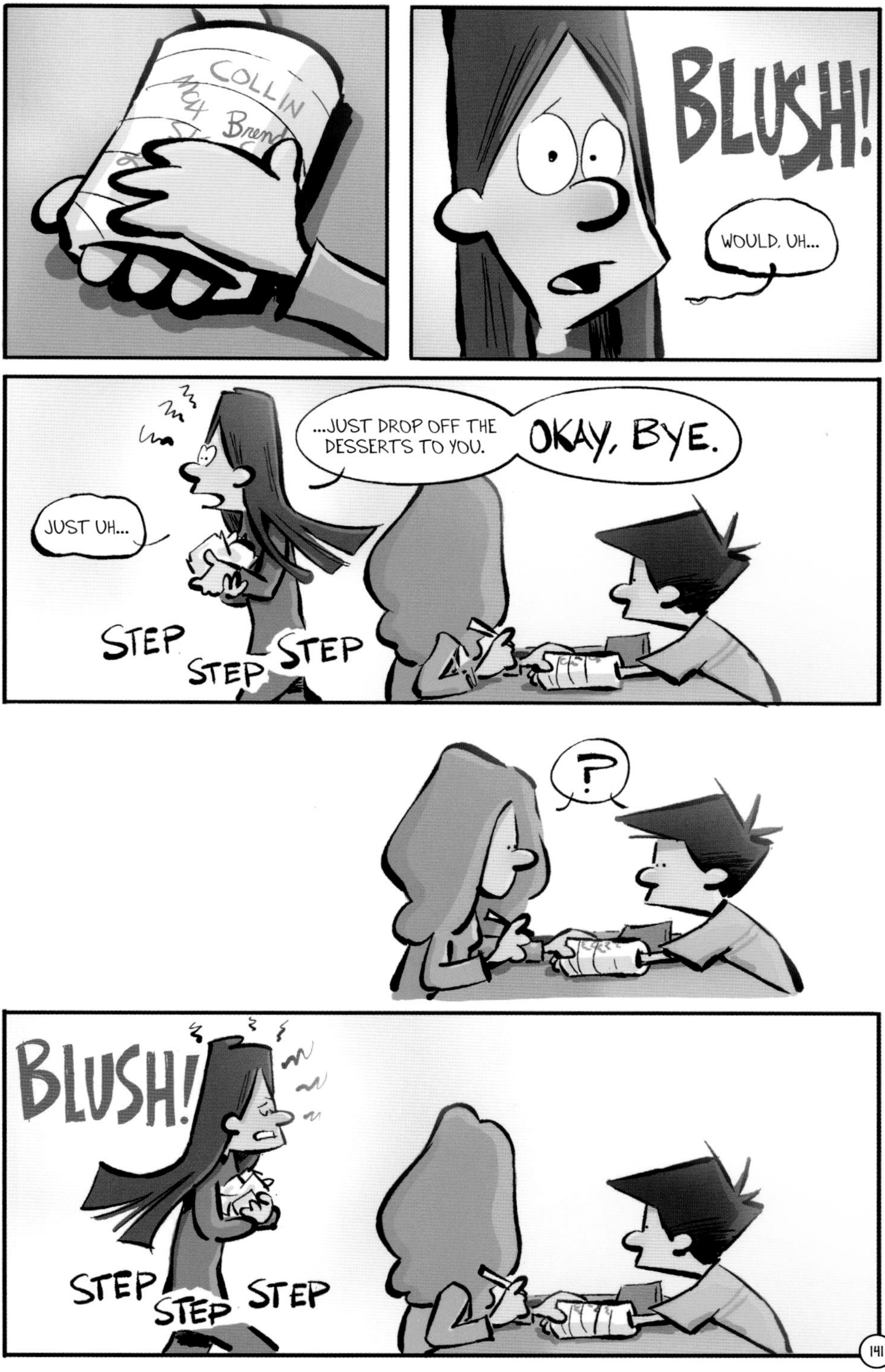
COLLIN
Brend
BLUSH!
WOULD, UH...
JUST UH...
...JUST DROP OFF THE DESSERTS TO YOU.
OKAY, BYE.
STEP
STEP
STEP
?
BLUSH!
STEP
STEP
STEP

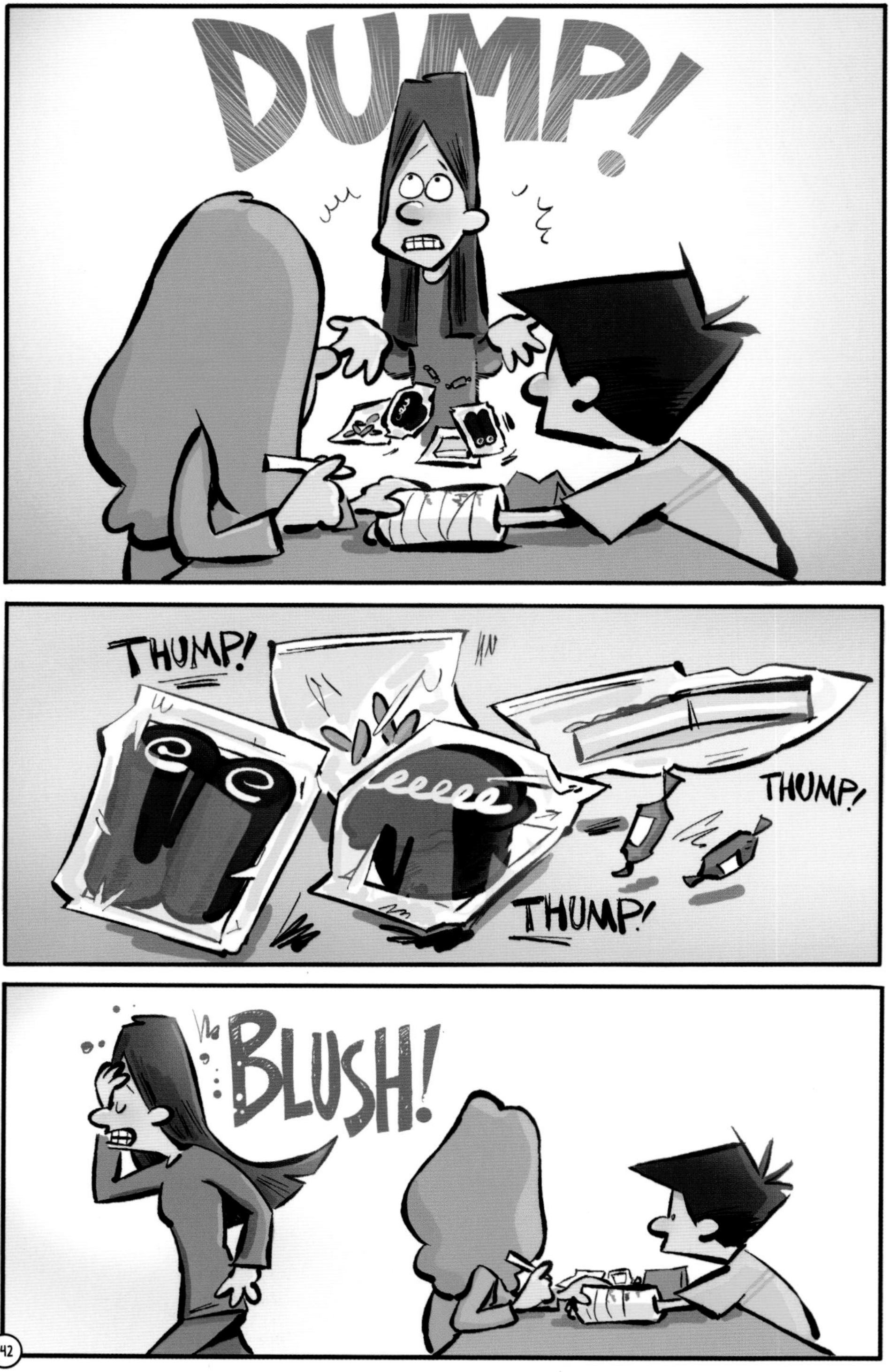
DUMP!
THUMP!
THUMP!
THUMP!
BLUSH!

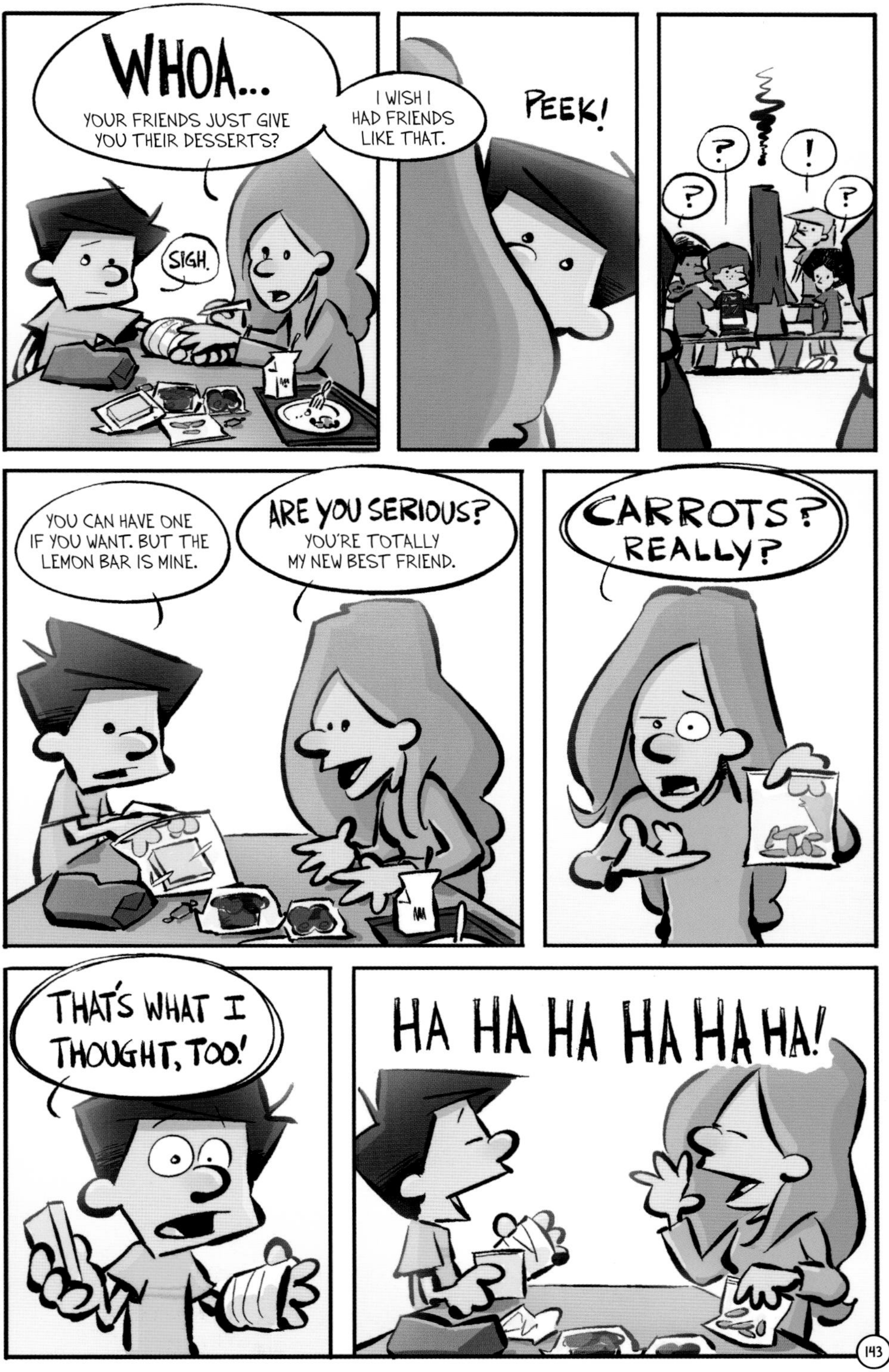
WHOA...
YOUR FRIENDS JUST GIVE YOU THEIR DESSERTS?
I WISH I HAD FRIENDS LIKE THAT.
SIGH.
PEEK!
?
?
!
?
YOU CAN HAVE ONE IF YOU WANT. BUT THE LEMON BAR IS MINE.
ARE YOU SERIOUS?
YOU'RE TOTALLY MY NEW BEST FRIEND.
CARROTS? REALLY?
THAT'S WHAT I THOUGHT, TOO!
HA HA HA HA HA HA!

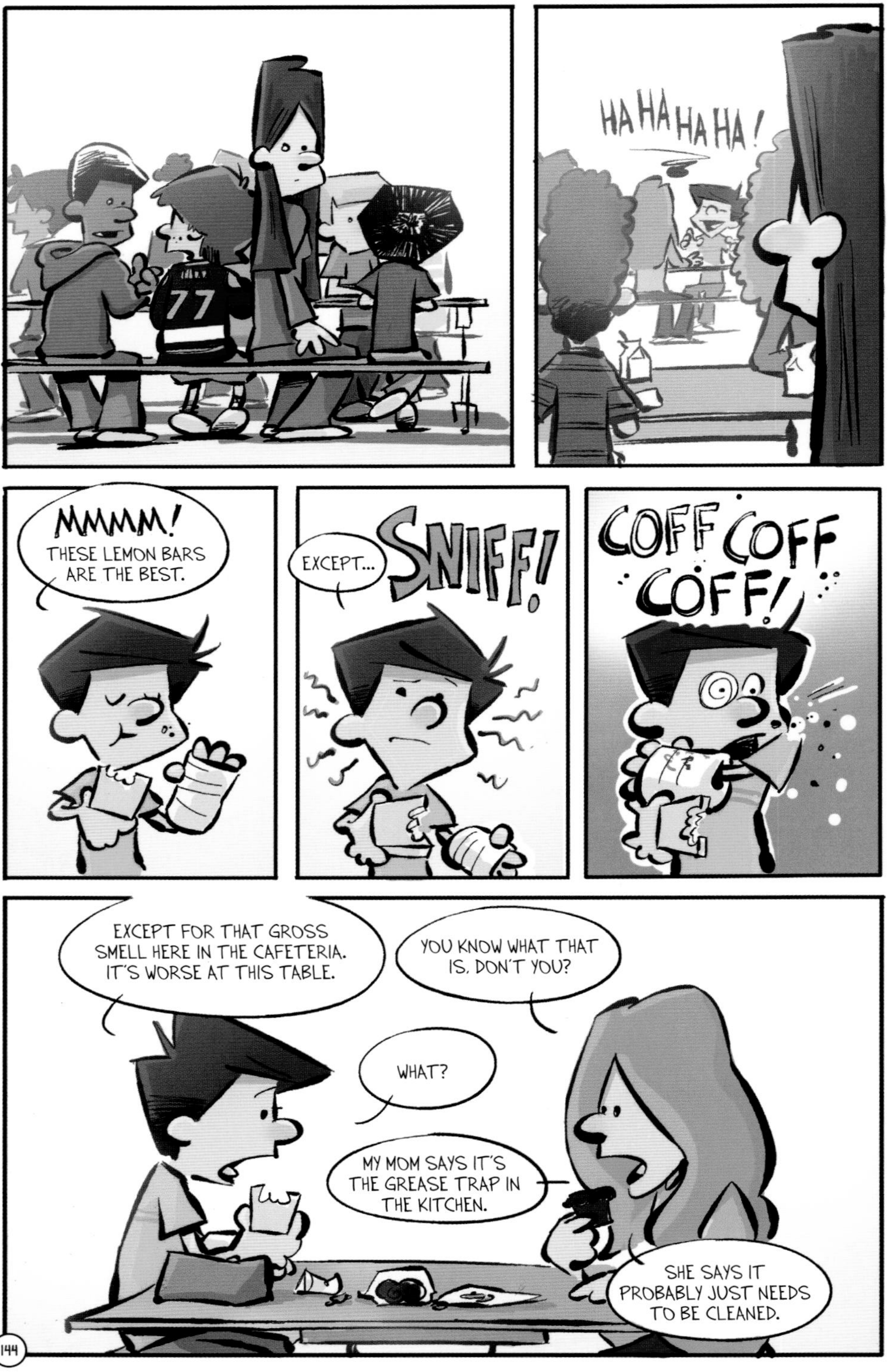

HA HA HA HA!
MMMM! THESE LEMON BARS ARE THE BEST.
EXCEPT...
SNIFF!
COFF COFF COFF!
EXCEPT FOR THAT GROSS SMELL HERE IN THE CAFETERIA. IT'S WORSE AT THIS TABLE.
YOU KNOW WHAT THAT IS, DON'T YOU?
WHAT?
MY MOM SAYS IT'S THE GREASE TRAP IN THE KITCHEN.
SHE SAYS IT PROBABLY JUST NEEDS TO BE CLEANED.

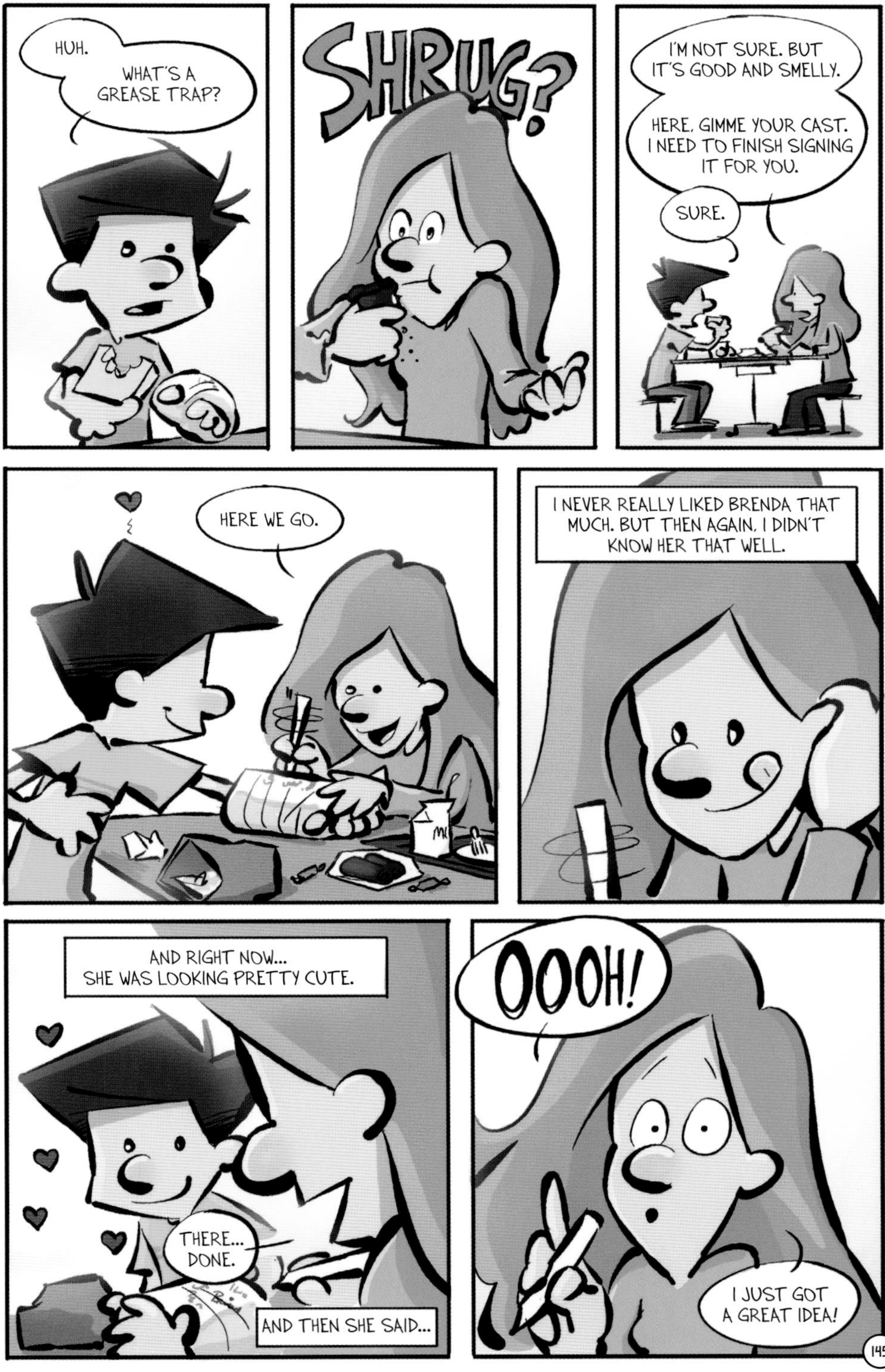
HUH.
WHAT'S A GREASE TRAP?
SHRUG?
I'M NOT SURE. BUT IT'S GOOD AND SMELLY.
HERE, GIMME YOUR CAST. I NEED TO FINISH SIGNING IT FOR YOU.
SURE.
HERE WE GO.
I NEVER REALLY LIKED BRENDA THAT MUCH. BUT THEN AGAIN, I DIDN'T KNOW HER THAT WELL.
AND RIGHT NOW... SHE WAS LOOKING PRETTY CUTE.
THERE... DONE.
AND THEN SHE SAID...
OOOH!
I JUST GOT A GREAT IDEA!

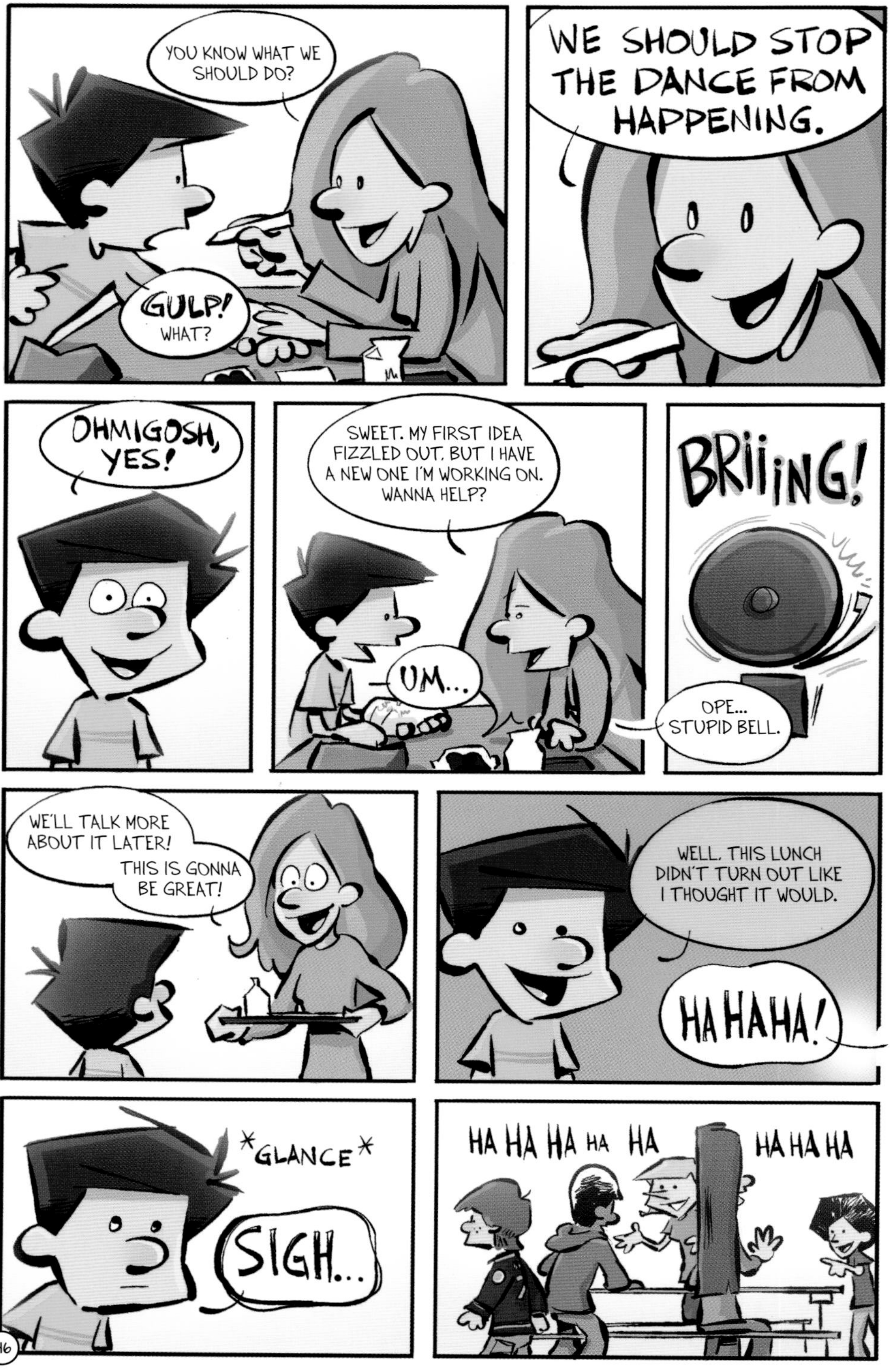
YOU KNOW WHAT WE SHOULD DO?
GULP! WHAT?
WE SHOULD STOP THE DANCE FROM HAPPENING.
OHMIGOSH, YES!
SWEET. MY FIRST IDEA FIZZLED OUT, BUT I HAVE A NEW ONE I'M WORKING ON. WANNA HELP?
UM...
BRIIING!
OPE... STUPID BELL.
WE'LL TALK MORE ABOUT IT LATER!
THIS IS GONNA BE GREAT!
WELL, THIS LUNCH DIDN'T TURN OUT LIKE I THOUGHT IT WOULD.
HAHAHA!
GLANCE
SIGH...
HA HA HA HA HA HA HA HA

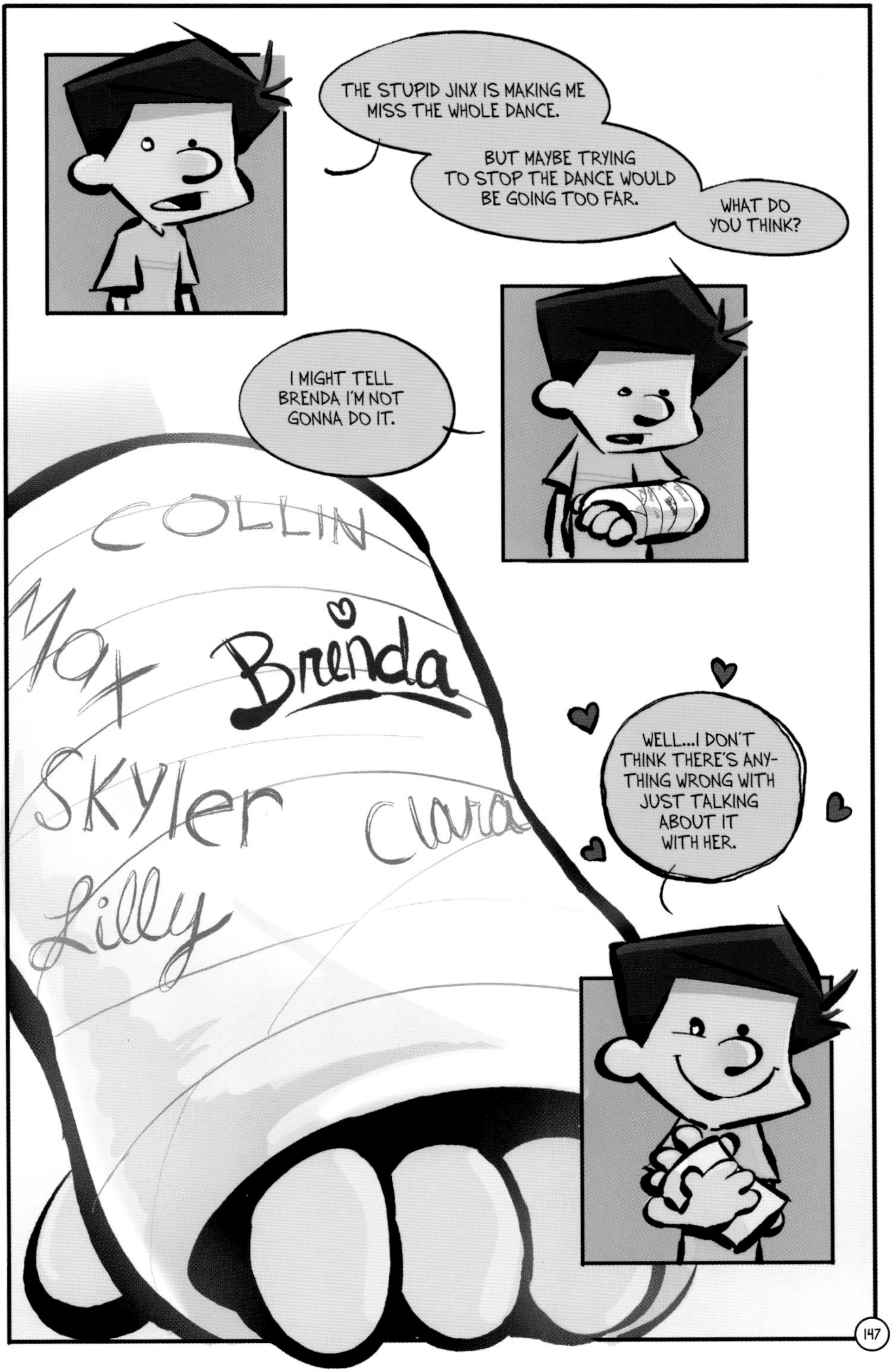
THE STUPID JINX IS MAKING ME MISS THE WHOLE DANCE.
BUT MAYBE TRYING TO STOP THE DANCE WOULD BE GOING TOO FAR.
WHAT DO YOU THINK?
I MIGHT TELL BRENDA I'M NOT GONNA DO IT.
COLLIN
Max
Brenda
Skyler
Clara
Lilly
WELL...I DON'T THINK THERE'S ANY-THING WRONG WITH JUST TALKING ABOUT IT WITH HER.

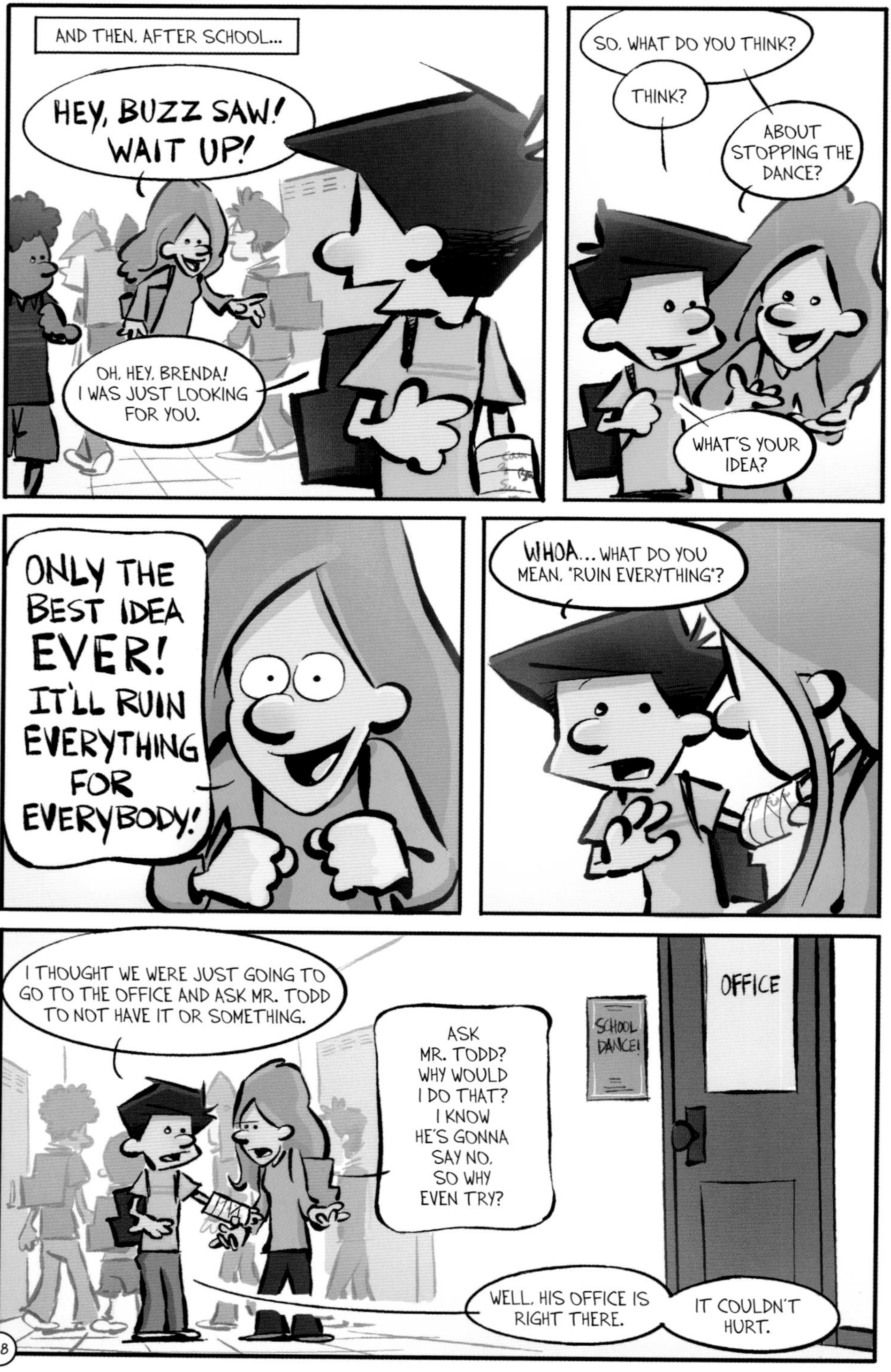
AND THEN, AFTER SCHOOL...
HEY, BUZZ SAW! WAIT UP!
OH, HEY, BRENDA! I WAS JUST LOOKING FOR YOU.
SO, WHAT DO YOU THINK?
THINK?
ABOUT STOPPING THE DANCE?
WHAT'S YOUR IDEA?
ONLY THE BEST IDEA EVER! IT'LL RUIN EVERYTHING FOR EVERYBODY!
WHOA... WHAT DO YOU MEAN, "RUIN EVERYTHING"?
I THOUGHT WE WERE JUST GOING TO GO TO THE OFFICE AND ASK MR. TODD TO NOT HAVE IT OR SOMETHING.
ASK MR. TODD? WHY WOULD I DO THAT? I KNOW HE'S GONNA SAY NO, SO WHY EVEN TRY?
OFFICE
SCHOOL DANCE!
WELL, HIS OFFICE IS RIGHT THERE.
IT COULDN'T HURT.

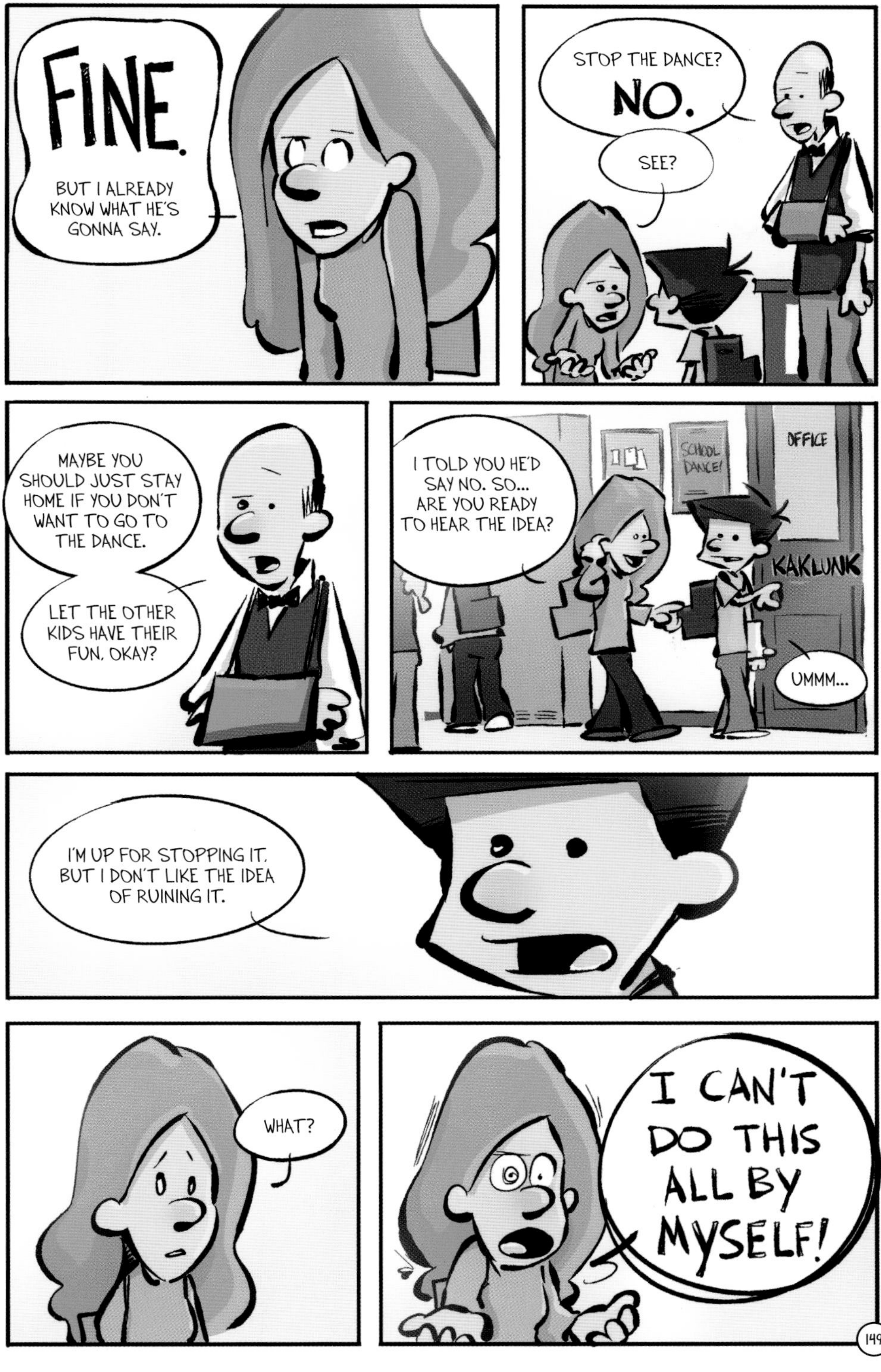
FINE.
BUT I ALREADY KNOW WHAT HE'S GONNA SAY.
STOP THE DANCE? NO.
SEE?
MAYBE YOU SHOULD JUST STAY HOME IF YOU DON'T WANT TO GO TO THE DANCE.
LET THE OTHER KIDS HAVE THEIR FUN, OKAY?
SCHOOL DANCE!
OFFICE
I TOLD YOU HE'D SAY NO. SO... ARE YOU READY TO HEAR THE IDEA?
KAKLUNK
UMMM...
I'M UP FOR STOPPING IT, BUT I DON'T LIKE THE IDEA OF RUINING IT.
WHAT?
I CAN'T DO THIS ALL BY MYSELF!

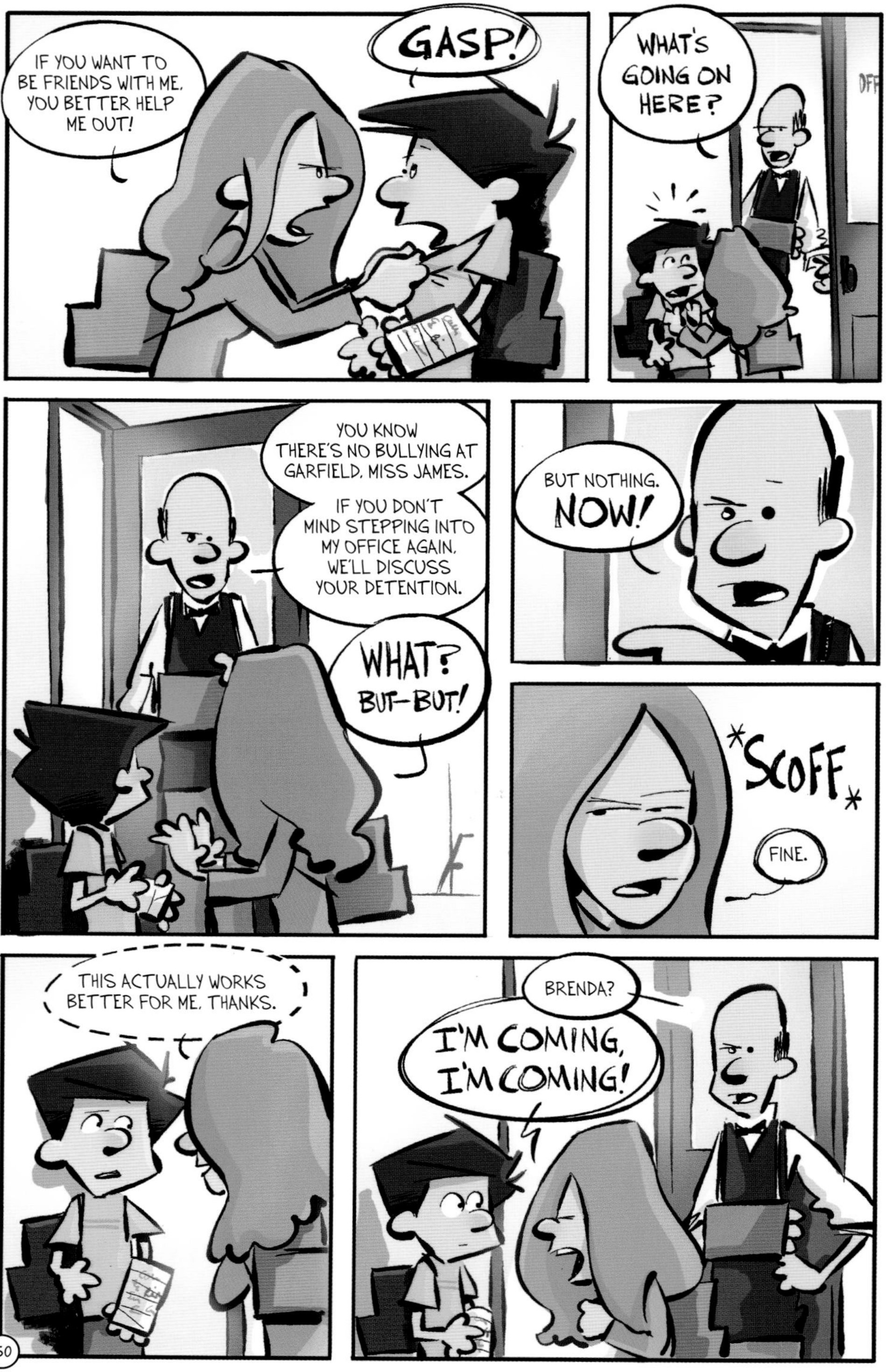

IF YOU WANT TO BE FRIENDS WITH ME, YOU BETTER HELP ME OUT!
GASP!
WHAT'S GOING ON HERE?
YOU KNOW THERE'S NO BULLYING AT GARFIELD, MISS JAMES.
IF YOU DON'T MIND STEPPING INTO MY OFFICE AGAIN, WE'LL DISCUSS YOUR DETENTION.
WHAT? BUT-BUT!
BUT NOTHING. NOW!
SCOFF
FINE.
THIS ACTUALLY WORKS BETTER FOR ME, THANKS.
BRENDA?
I'M COMING, I'M COMING!

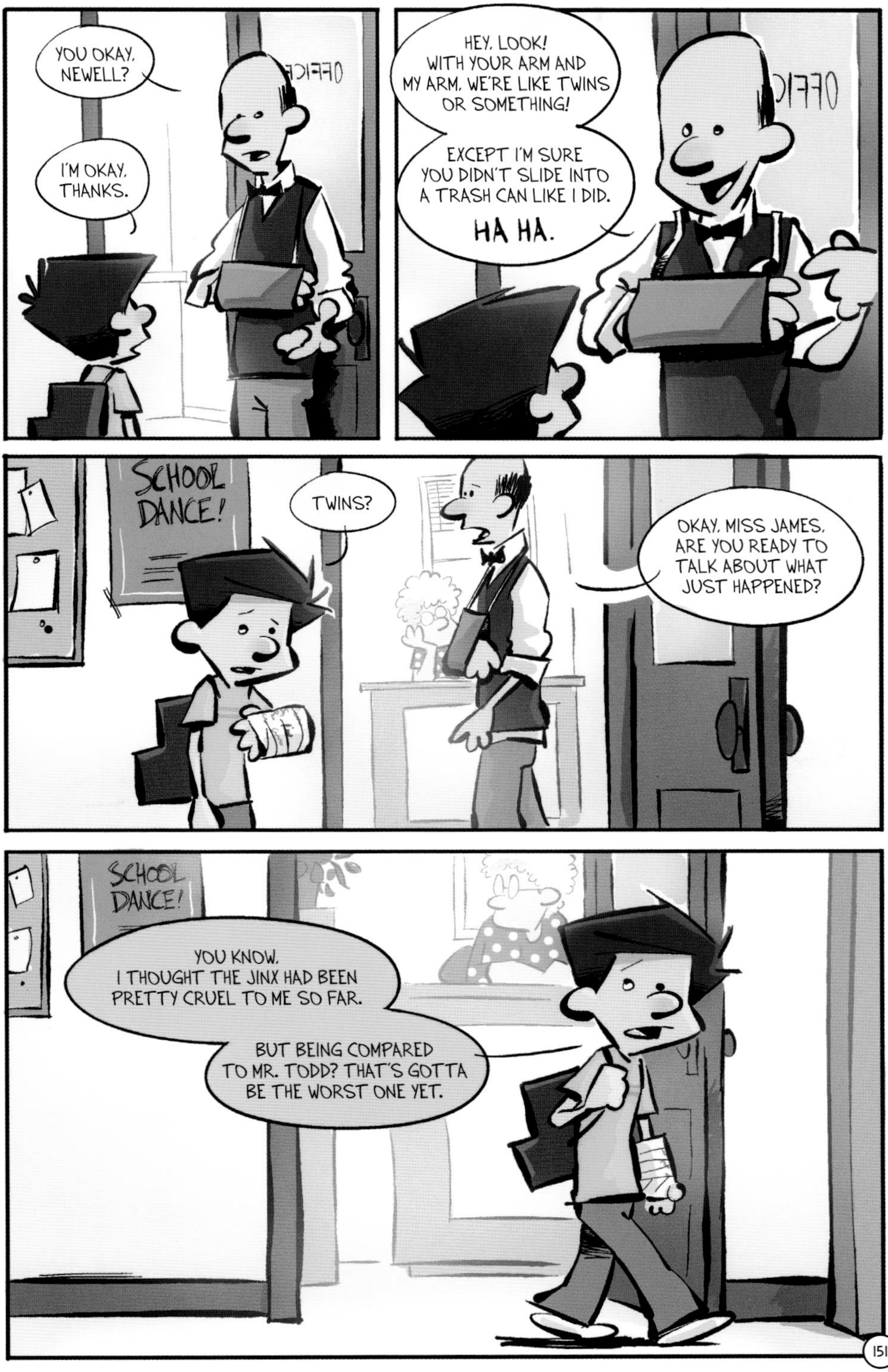

OFFICE
YOU OKAY, NEWELL?
I'M OKAY, THANKS.
HEY, LOOK! WITH YOUR ARM AND MY ARM, WE'RE LIKE TWINS OR SOMETHING!
EXCEPT I'M SURE YOU DIDN'T SLIDE INTO A TRASH CAN LIKE I DID.
HA HA.
SCHOOL DANCE!
TWINS?
OKAY, MISS JAMES, ARE YOU READY TO TALK ABOUT WHAT JUST HAPPENED?
SCHOOL DANCE!
YOU KNOW, I THOUGHT THE JINX HAD BEEN PRETTY CRUEL TO ME SO FAR.
BUT BEING COMPARED TO MR. TODD? THAT'S GOTTA BE THE WORST ONE YET.

CHAPTER EIGHT
MY WORLD KEEPS CRUMBLING

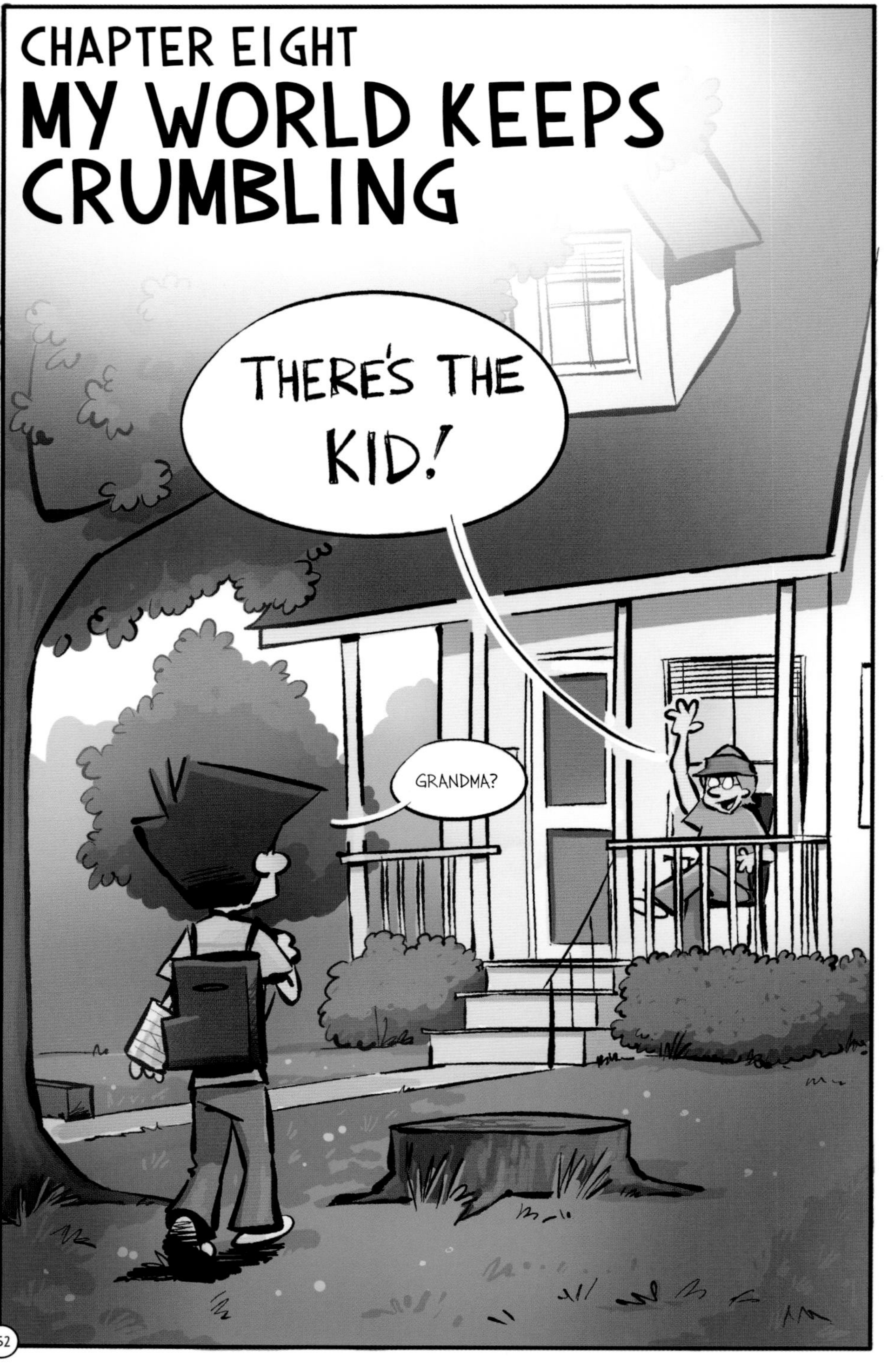
THERE'S THE KID!
GRANDMA?

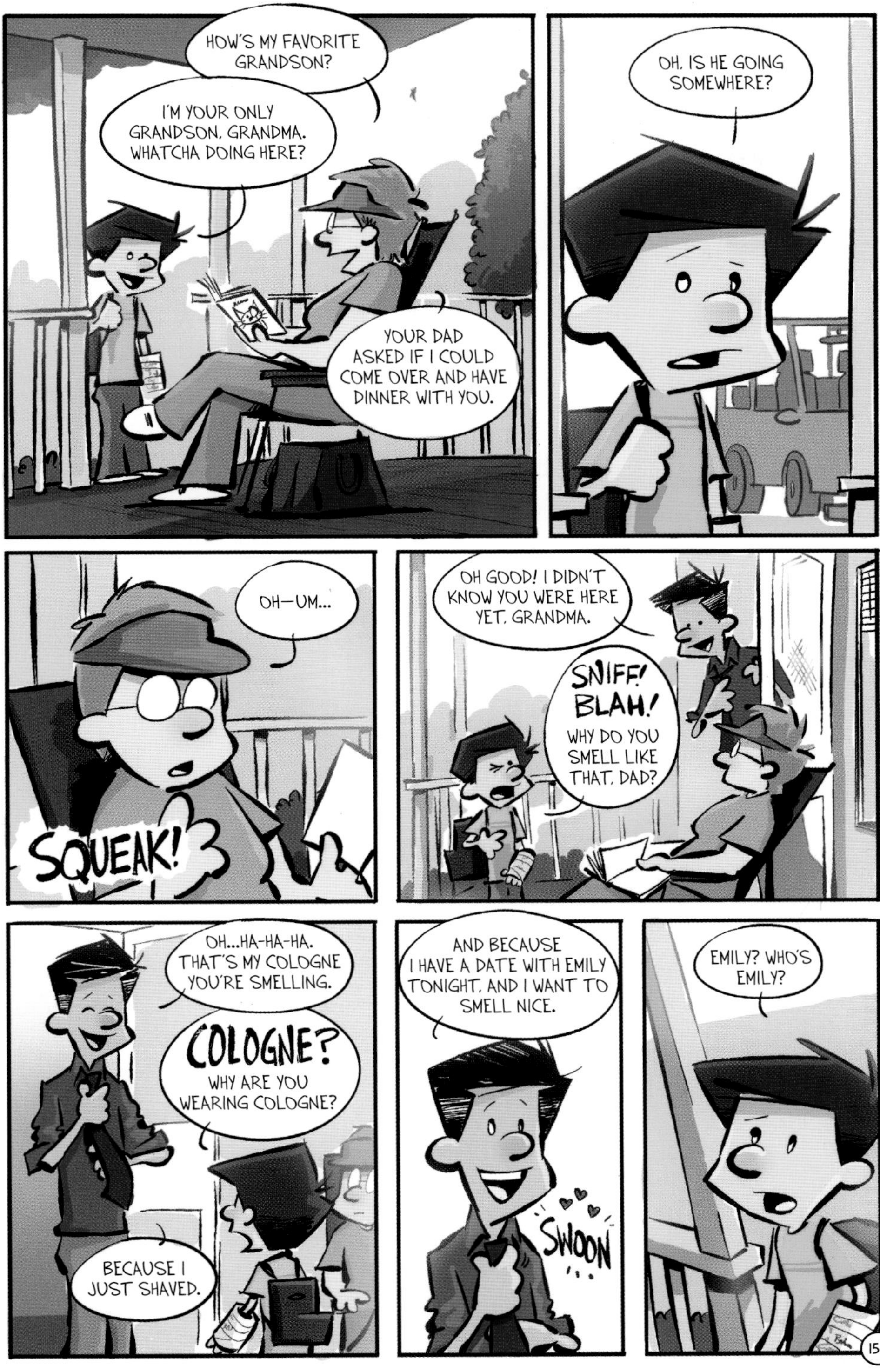
HOW'S MY FAVORITE GRANDSON?
I'M YOUR ONLY GRANDSON, GRANDMA. WHATCHA DOING HERE?
YOUR DAD ASKED IF I COULD COME OVER AND HAVE DINNER WITH YOU.
OH, IS HE GOING SOMEWHERE?
OH—UM...
SQUEAK!
OH GOOD! I DIDN'T KNOW YOU WERE HERE YET, GRANDMA.
SNIFF! BLAH! WHY DO YOU SMELL LIKE THAT, DAD?
OH...HA-HA-HA. THAT'S MY COLOGNE YOU'RE SMELLING.
COLOGNE? WHY ARE YOU WEARING COLOGNE?
BECAUSE I JUST SHAVED.
AND BECAUSE I HAVE A DATE WITH EMILY TONIGHT, AND I WANT TO SMELL NICE.
SWOON
EMILY? WHO'S EMILY?

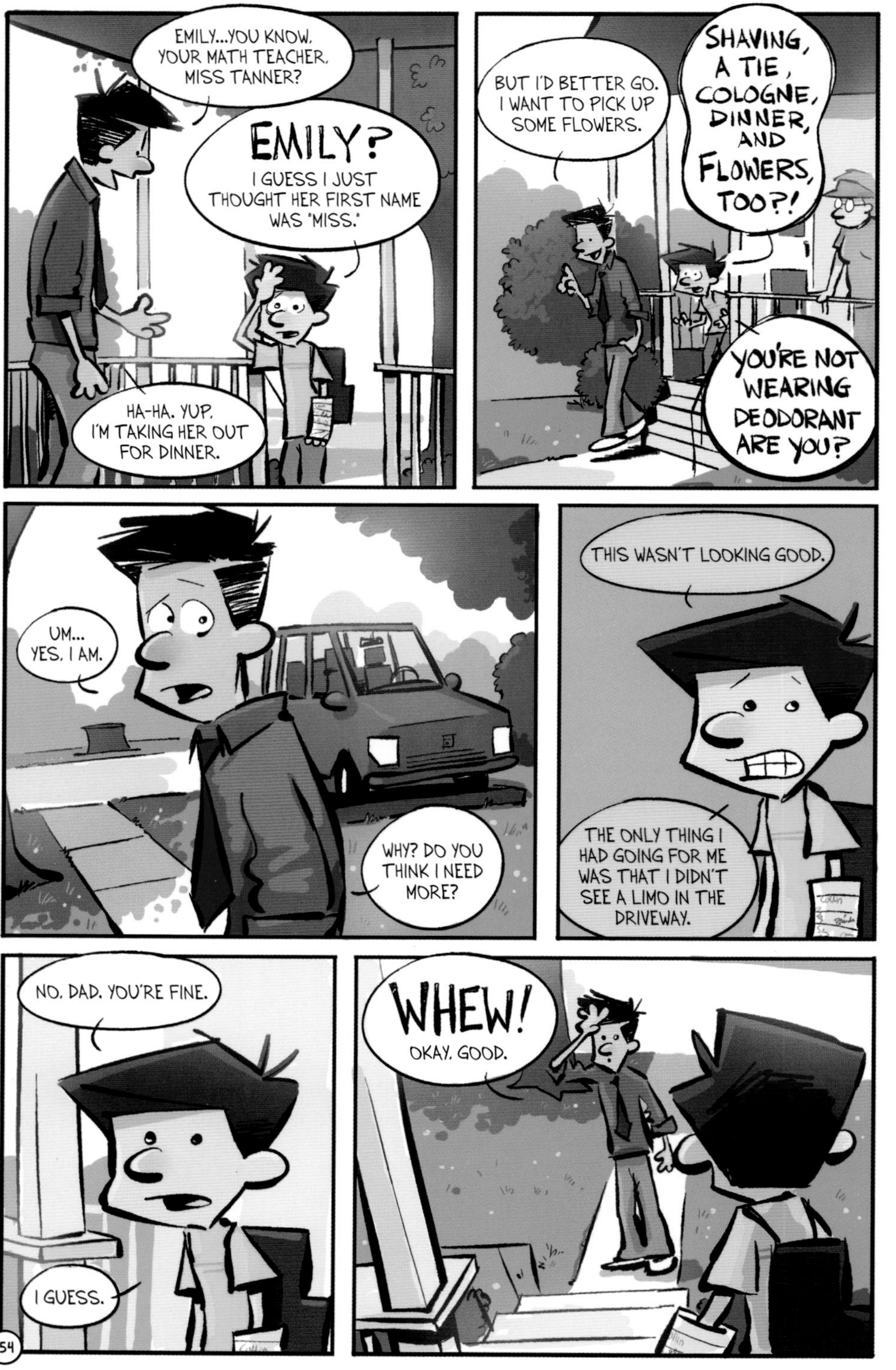
EMILY...YOU KNOW, YOUR MATH TEACHER, MISS TANNER?
EMILY? I GUESS I JUST THOUGHT HER FIRST NAME WAS "MISS."
HA-HA. YUP, I'M TAKING HER OUT FOR DINNER.
BUT I'D BETTER GO. I WANT TO PICK UP SOME FLOWERS.
SHAVING, A TIE, COLOGNE, DINNER, AND FLOWERS, TOO?!
YOU'RE NOT WEARING DEODORANT ARE YOU?
UM... YES, I AM.
WHY? DO YOU THINK I NEED MORE?
THIS WASN'T LOOKING GOOD.
THE ONLY THING I HAD GOING FOR ME WAS THAT I DIDN'T SEE A LIMO IN THE DRIVEWAY.
NO, DAD. YOU'RE FINE.
I GUESS.
WHEW! OKAY, GOOD.

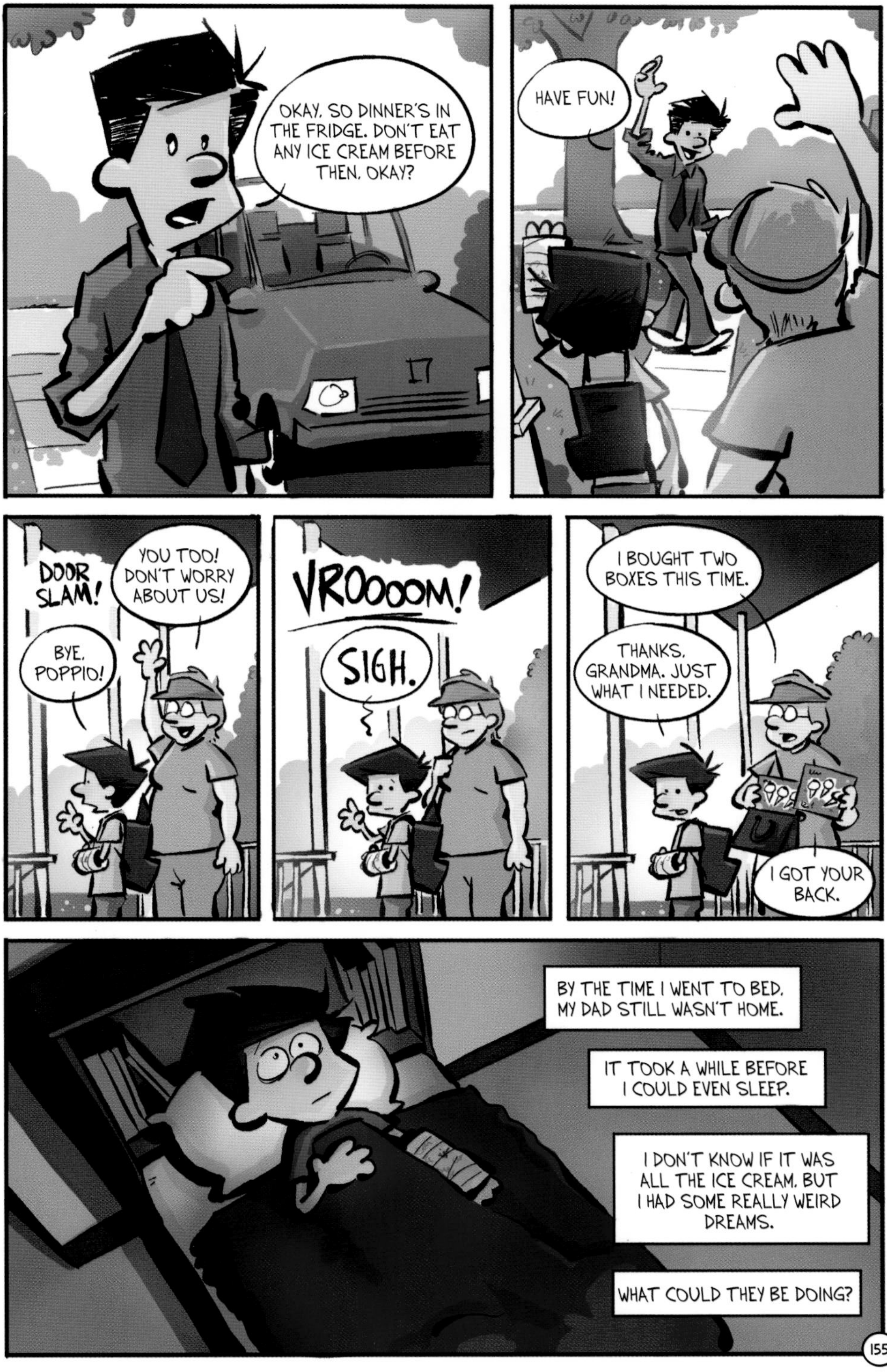
OKAY. SO DINNER'S IN THE FRIDGE. DON'T EAT ANY ICE CREAM BEFORE THEN. OKAY?
HAVE FUN!
DOOR SLAM!
YOU TOO! DON'T WORRY ABOUT US!
BYE. POPPIO!
VROOOOM!
SIGH.
I BOUGHT TWO BOXES THIS TIME.
THANKS. GRANDMA. JUST WHAT I NEEDED.
I GOT YOUR BACK.
BY THE TIME I WENT TO BED. MY DAD STILL WASN'T HOME.
IT TOOK A WHILE BEFORE I COULD EVEN SLEEP.
I DON'T KNOW IF IT WAS ALL THE ICE CREAM. BUT I HAD SOME REALLY WEIRD DREAMS.
WHAT COULD THEY BE DOING?

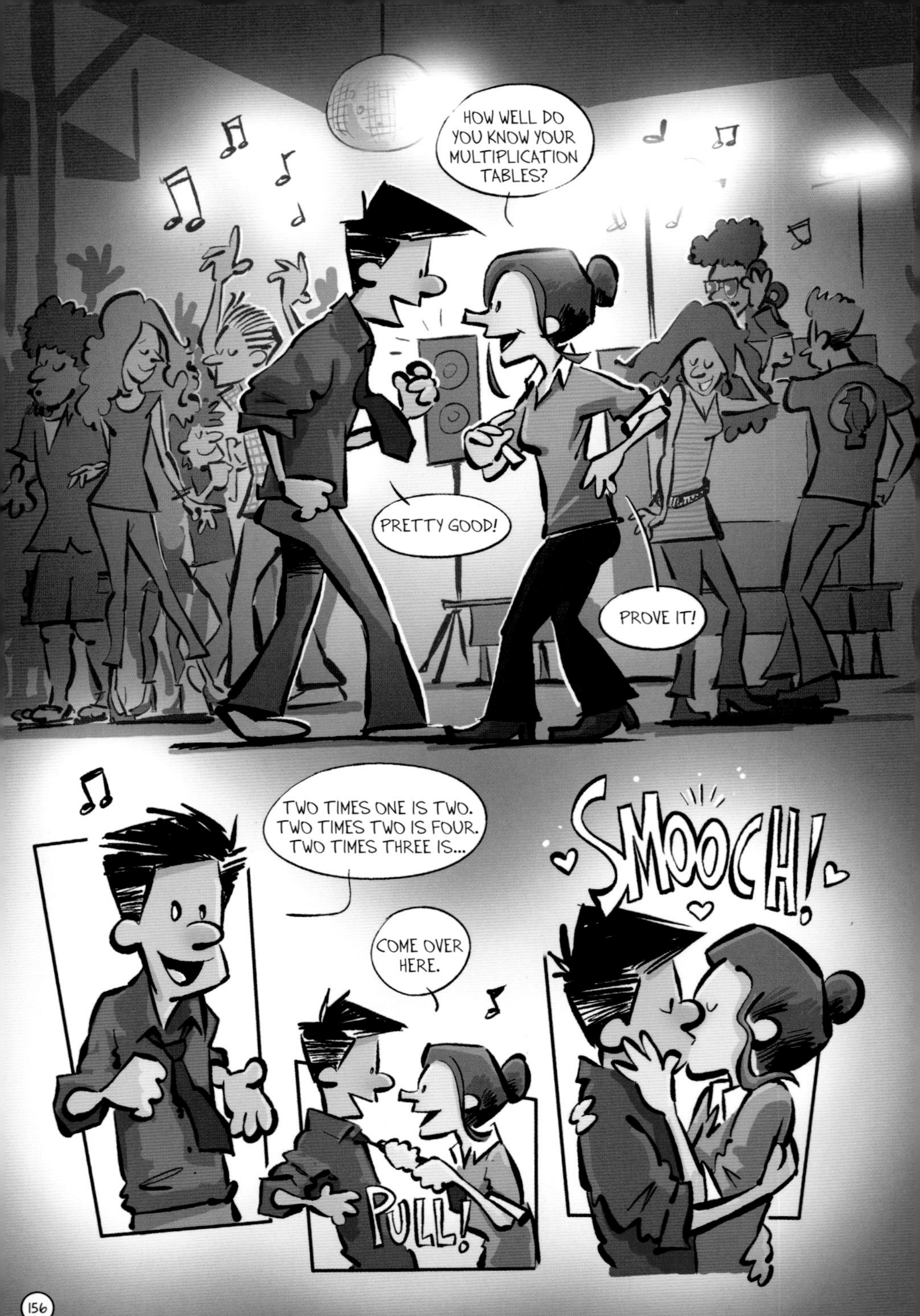
HOW WELL DO YOU KNOW YOUR MULTIPLICATION TABLES?
PRETTY GOOD!
PROVE IT!
TWO TIMES ONE IS TWO. TWO TIMES TWO IS FOUR. TWO TIMES THREE IS...
COME OVER HERE.
PULL!
SMOOCH!

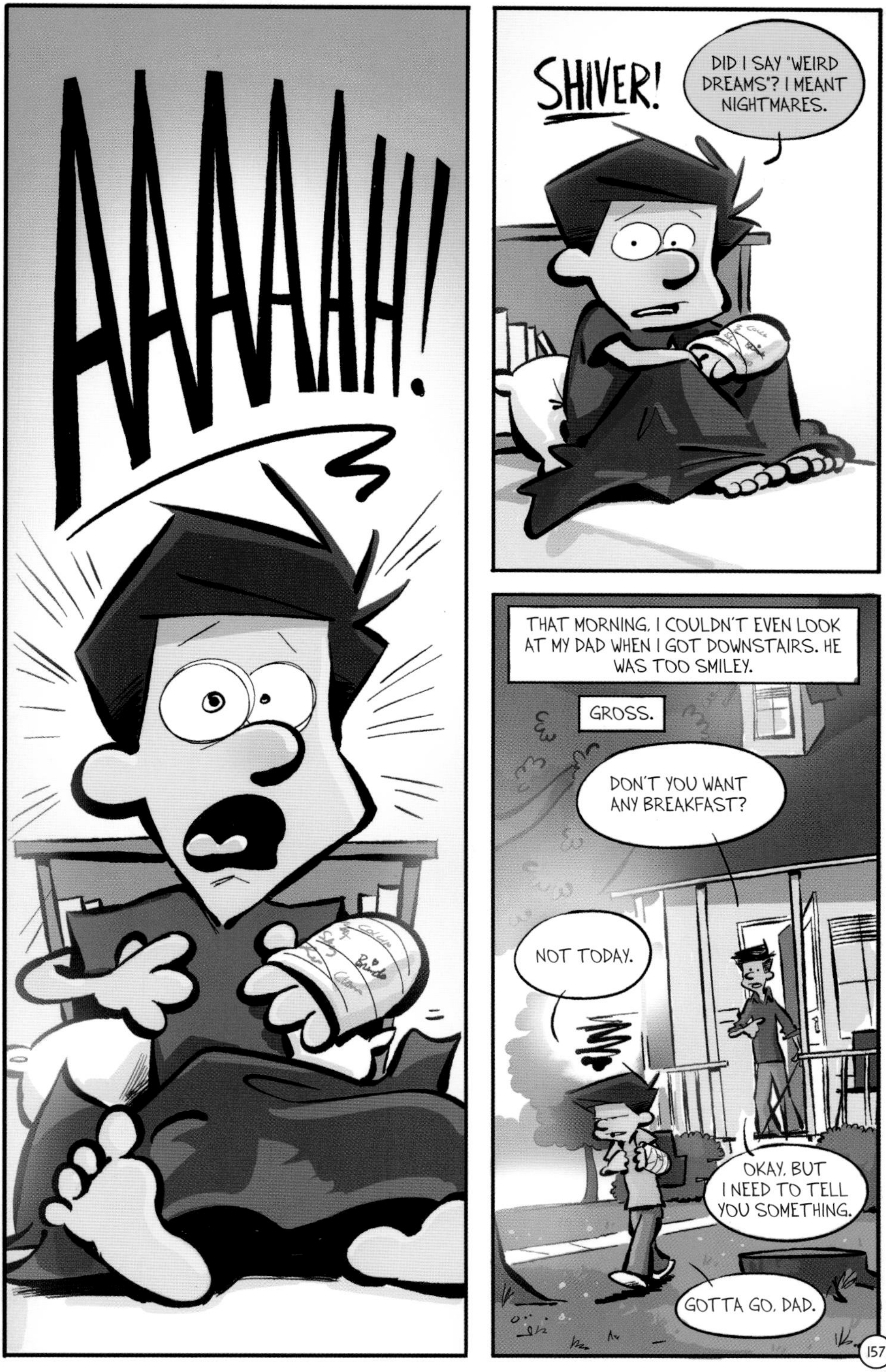
AAAAAH!
SHIVER!
DID I SAY "WEIRD DREAMS"? I MEANT NIGHTMARES.
THAT MORNING, I COULDN'T EVEN LOOK AT MY DAD WHEN I GOT DOWNSTAIRS. HE WAS TOO SMILEY.
GROSS.
DON'T YOU WANT ANY BREAKFAST?
NOT TODAY.
OKAY, BUT I NEED TO TELL YOU SOMETHING.
GOTTA GO, DAD.

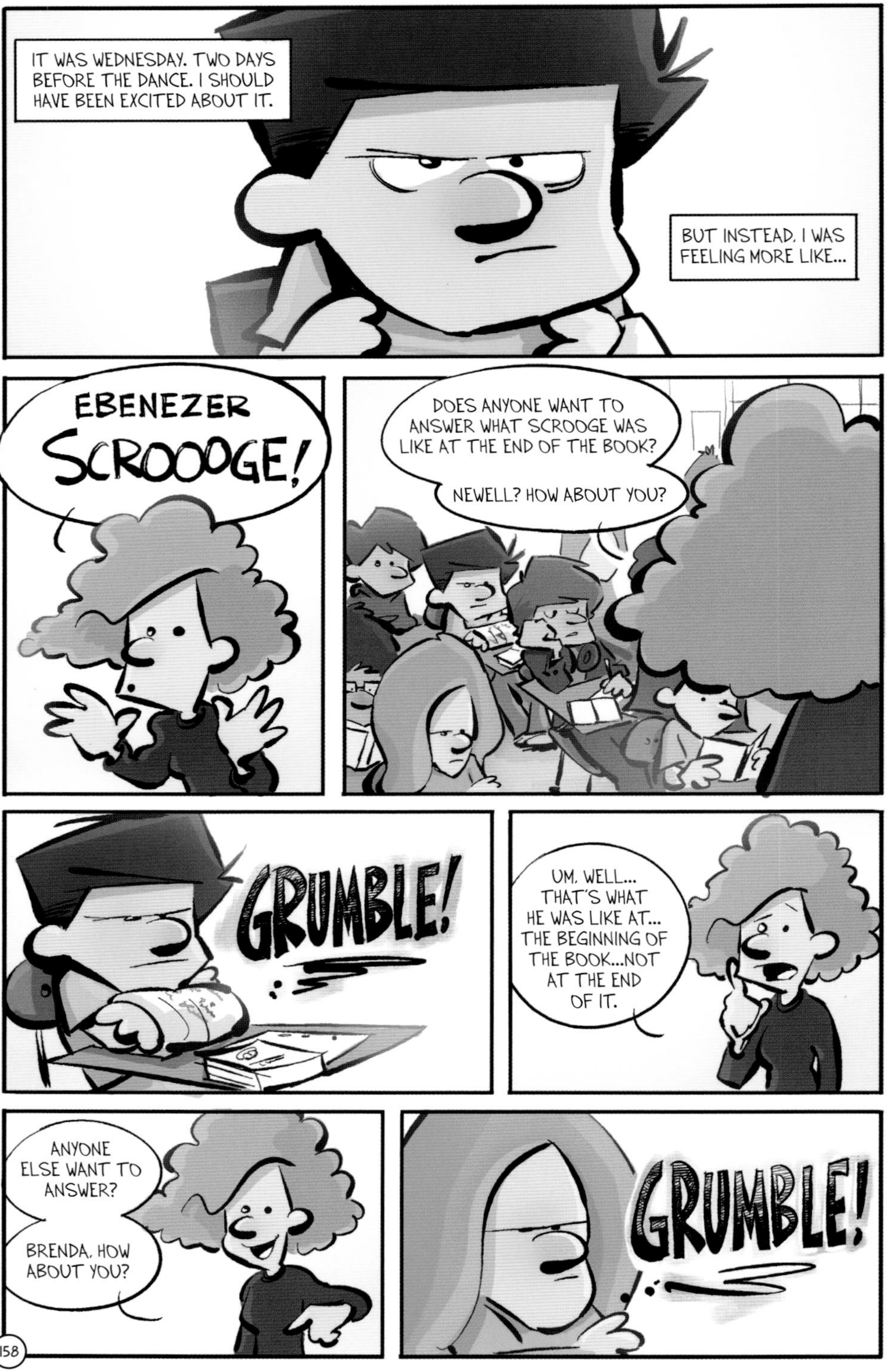

IT WAS WEDNESDAY. TWO DAYS BEFORE THE DANCE. I SHOULD HAVE BEEN EXCITED ABOUT IT.
BUT INSTEAD, I WAS FEELING MORE LIKE...
EBENEZER SCROOOGE!
DOES ANYONE WANT TO ANSWER WHAT SCROOGE WAS LIKE AT THE END OF THE BOOK?
NEWELL? HOW ABOUT YOU?
GRUMBLE!
UM, WELL... THAT'S WHAT HE WAS LIKE AT... THE BEGINNING OF THE BOOK...NOT AT THE END OF IT.
ANYONE ELSE WANT TO ANSWER?
BRENDA, HOW ABOUT YOU?
GRUMBLE!

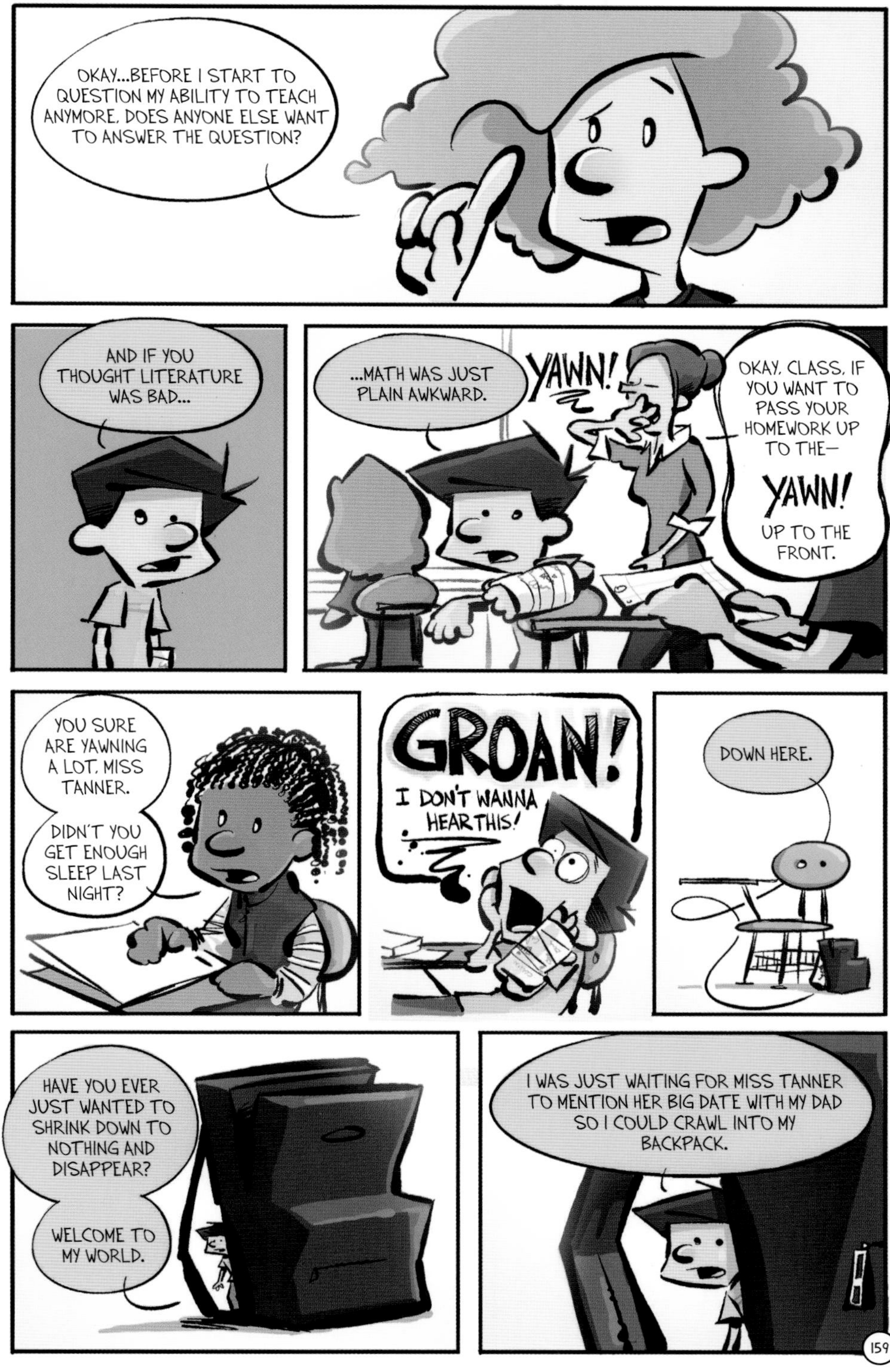
OKAY...BEFORE I START TO QUESTION MY ABILITY TO TEACH ANYMORE, DOES ANYONE ELSE WANT TO ANSWER THE QUESTION?
AND IF YOU THOUGHT LITERATURE WAS BAD...
...MATH WAS JUST PLAIN AWKWARD.
YAWN!
OKAY, CLASS, IF YOU WANT TO PASS YOUR HOMEWORK UP TO THE—
YAWN!
UP TO THE FRONT.
YOU SURE ARE YAWNING A LOT, MISS TANNER.
DIDN'T YOU GET ENOUGH SLEEP LAST NIGHT?
GROAN!
I DON'T WANNA HEAR THIS!
DOWN HERE.
HAVE YOU EVER JUST WANTED TO SHRINK DOWN TO NOTHING AND DISAPPEAR?
WELCOME TO MY WORLD.
I WAS JUST WAITING FOR MISS TANNER TO MENTION HER BIG DATE WITH MY DAD SO I COULD CRAWL INTO MY BACKPACK.

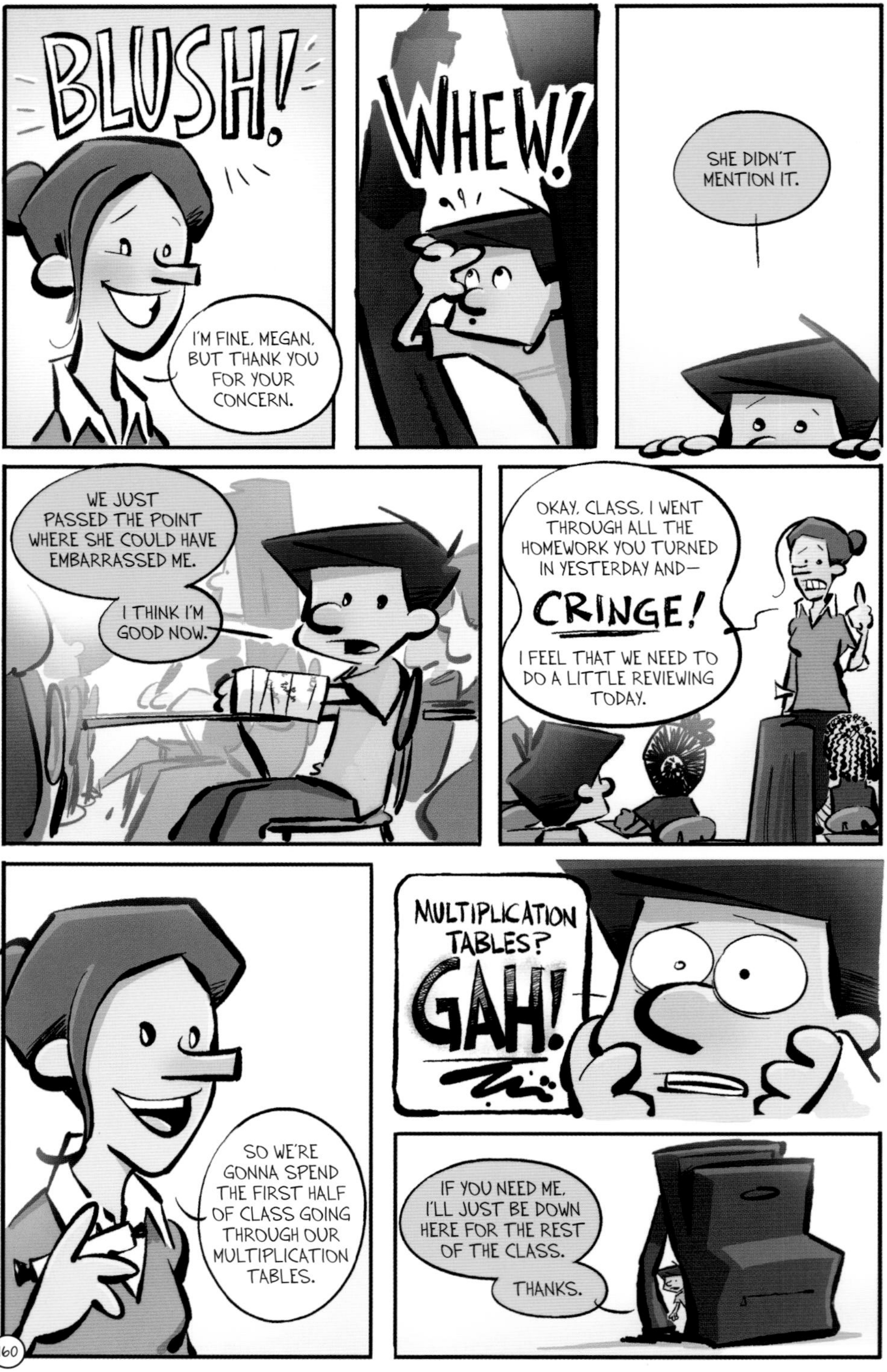
BLUSH!
I'M FINE, MEGAN, BUT THANK YOU FOR YOUR CONCERN.
WHEW!
SHE DIDN'T MENTION IT.
WE JUST PASSED THE POINT WHERE SHE COULD HAVE EMBARRASSED ME.
I THINK I'M GOOD NOW.
OKAY, CLASS, I WENT THROUGH ALL THE HOMEWORK YOU TURNED IN YESTERDAY AND—
CRINGE!
I FEEL THAT WE NEED TO DO A LITTLE REVIEWING TODAY.
SO WE'RE GONNA SPEND THE FIRST HALF OF CLASS GOING THROUGH OUR MULTIPLICATION TABLES.
MULTIPLICATION TABLES?
GAH!
IF YOU NEED ME, I'LL JUST BE DOWN HERE FOR THE REST OF THE CLASS.
THANKS.

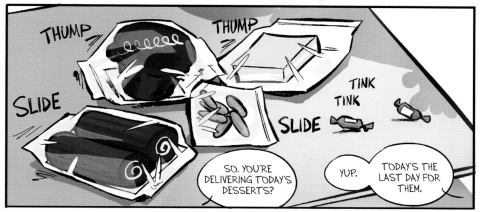

THUMP THUMP SLIDE TINK TINK SLIDE

SO, YOU'RE DELIVERING TODAY'S DESSERTS?

YUP.

TODAY'S THE LAST DAY FOR THEM.

YEAH...*SIGH*. THAT WEEK WENT BY FAST.

CAN I SIT WITH YOU A MOMENT, OR IS BRENDA SITTING HERE?

SURE, IT'S A FREE COUNTRY.

BUT BRENDA? I DON'T THINK WE'RE GONNA BE FRIENDS.

SPEAKING OF... LOOK.

HUH, WHAT'S SHE DOING WITH MS. FERNAND?

IT'S PROBABLY THE DETENTION SHE GOT YESTERDAY.

RASPBERRY *THBBFT!*

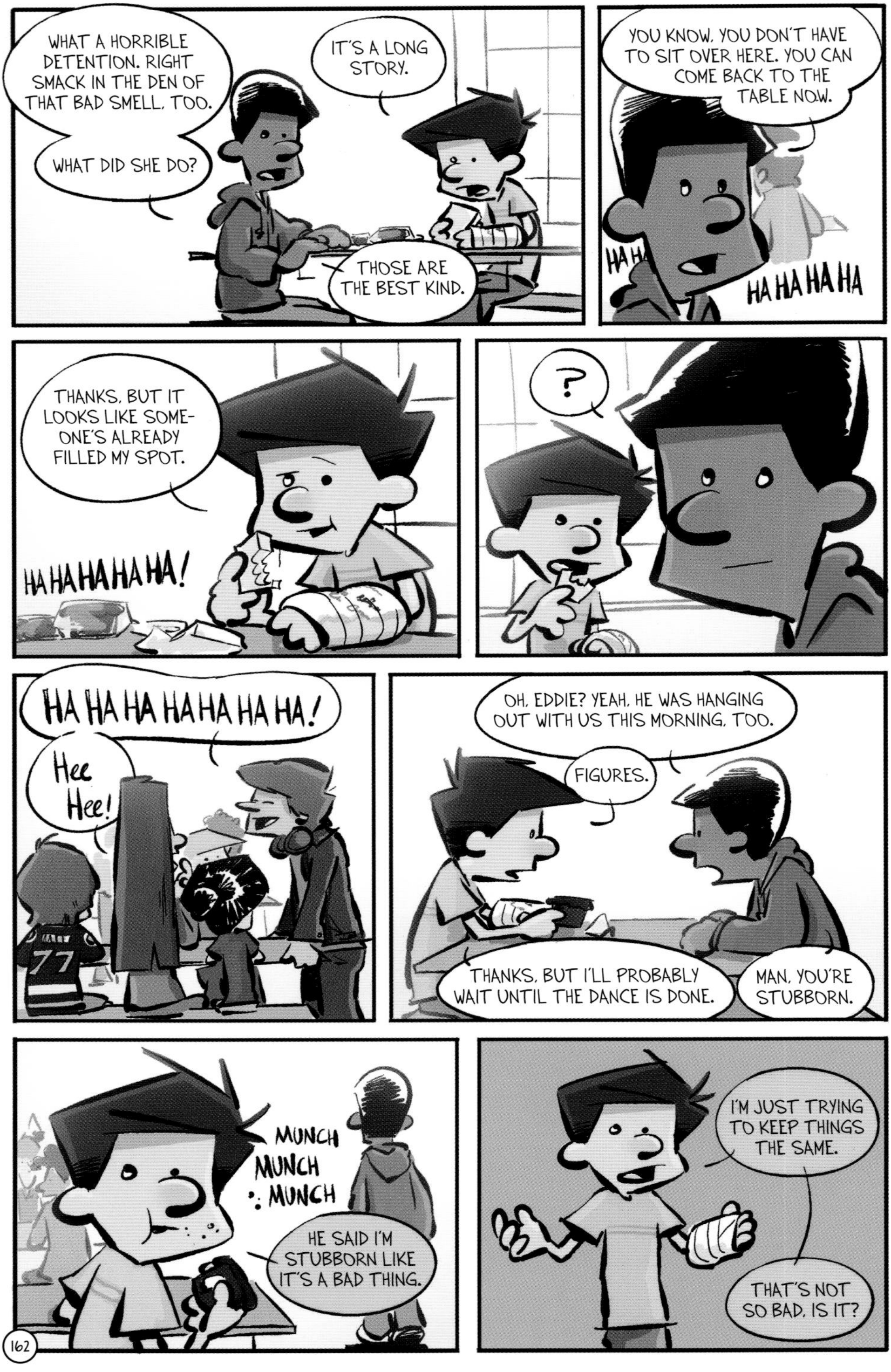

WHAT A HORRIBLE DETENTION. RIGHT SMACK IN THE DEN OF THAT BAD SMELL, TOO.
WHAT DID SHE DO?
IT'S A LONG STORY.
THOSE ARE THE BEST KIND.
YOU KNOW, YOU DON'T HAVE TO SIT OVER HERE. YOU CAN COME BACK TO THE TABLE NOW.
HA HA
HA HA HA HA
THANKS, BUT IT LOOKS LIKE SOME-ONE'S ALREADY FILLED MY SPOT.
HA HA HA HA HA!
?
HA HA HA HA HA HA HA!
Hee Hee!
77
OH, EDDIE? YEAH, HE WAS HANGING OUT WITH US THIS MORNING, TOO.
FIGURES.
THANKS, BUT I'LL PROBABLY WAIT UNTIL THE DANCE IS DONE.
MAN, YOU'RE STUBBORN.
MUNCH
MUNCH
MUNCH
HE SAID I'M STUBBORN LIKE IT'S A BAD THING.
I'M JUST TRYING TO KEEP THINGS THE SAME.
THAT'S NOT SO BAD, IS IT?

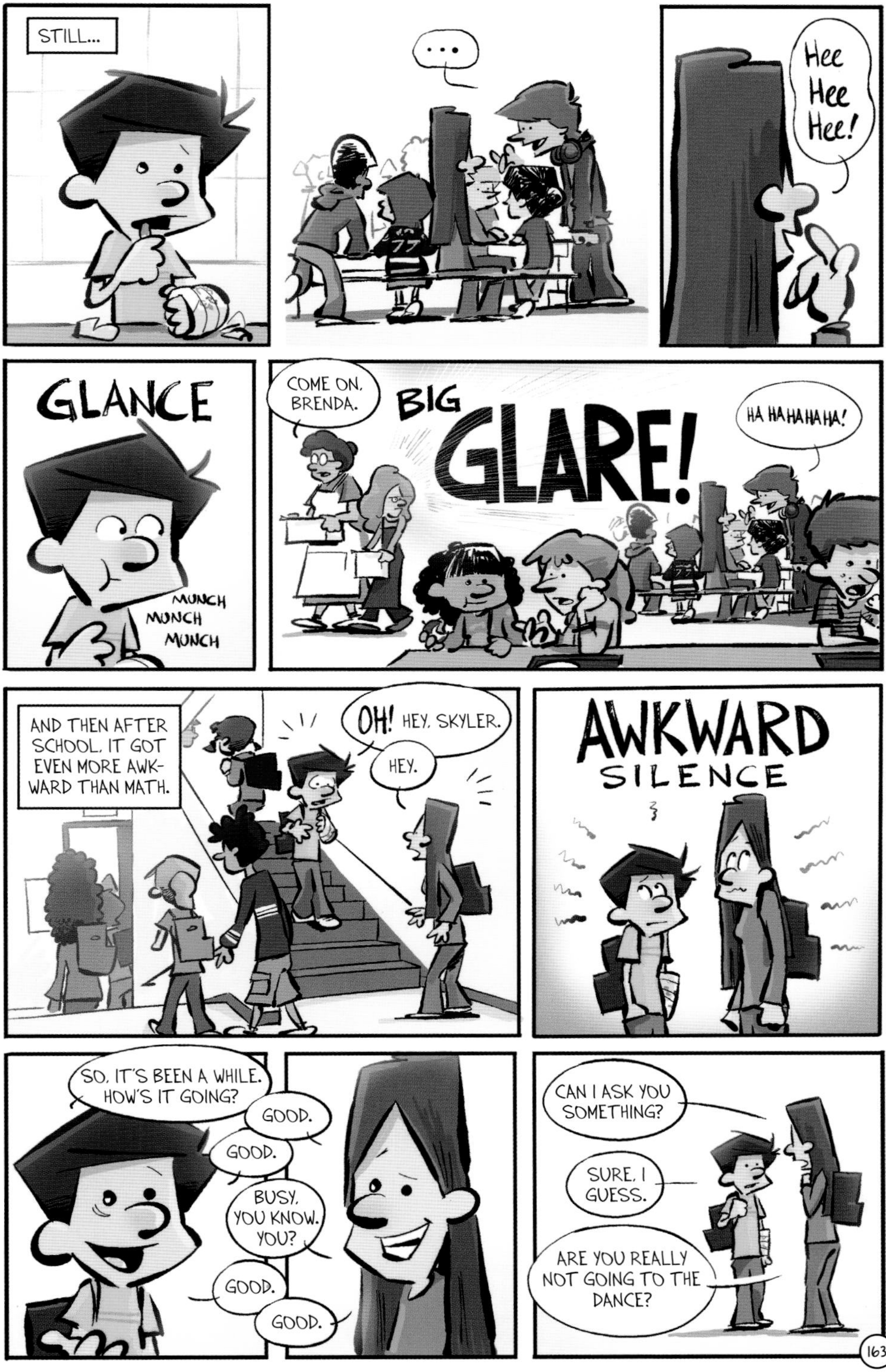
STILL...
...
Hee Hee Hee!
GLANCE
MUNCH MUNCH MUNCH
COME ON, BRENDA.
BIG GLARE!
HA HA HA HA HA HA!
AND THEN AFTER SCHOOL, IT GOT EVEN MORE AWK-WARD THAN MATH.
OH! HEY, SKYLER.
HEY.
AWKWARD SILENCE
SO, IT'S BEEN A WHILE. HOW'S IT GOING?
GOOD.
GOOD.
BUSY, YOU KNOW. YOU?
GOOD.
GOOD.
CAN I ASK YOU SOMETHING?
SURE, I GUESS.
ARE YOU REALLY NOT GOING TO THE DANCE?

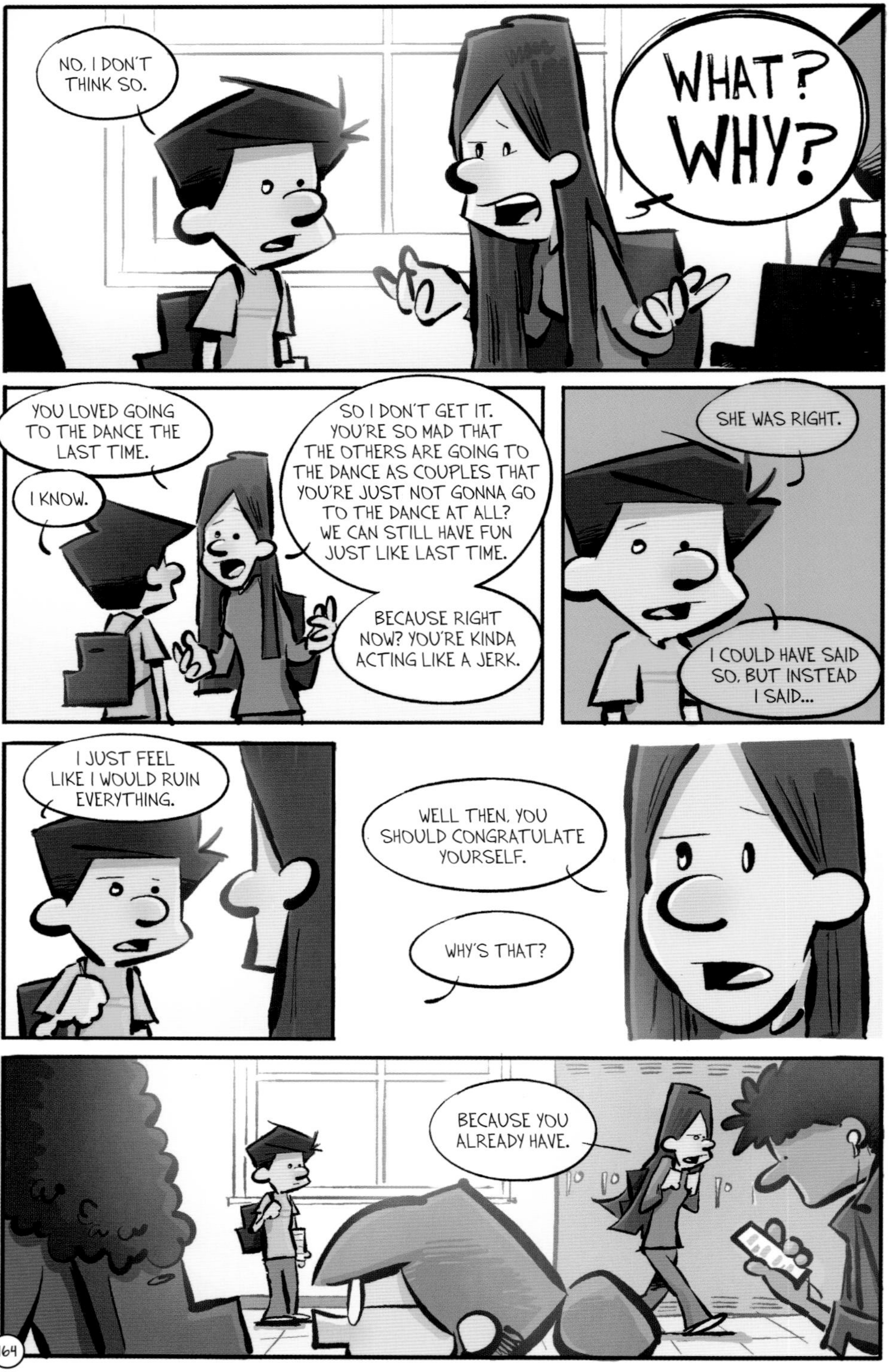
NO, I DON'T THINK SO.
WHAT? WHY?
YOU LOVED GOING TO THE DANCE THE LAST TIME.
I KNOW.
SO I DON'T GET IT. YOU'RE SO MAD THAT THE OTHERS ARE GOING TO THE DANCE AS COUPLES THAT YOU'RE JUST NOT GONNA GO TO THE DANCE AT ALL? WE CAN STILL HAVE FUN JUST LIKE LAST TIME.
BECAUSE RIGHT NOW? YOU'RE KINDA ACTING LIKE A JERK.
SHE WAS RIGHT.
I COULD HAVE SAID SO, BUT INSTEAD I SAID...
I JUST FEEL LIKE I WOULD RUIN EVERYTHING.
WELL THEN, YOU SHOULD CONGRATULATE YOURSELF.
WHY'S THAT?
BECAUSE YOU ALREADY HAVE.

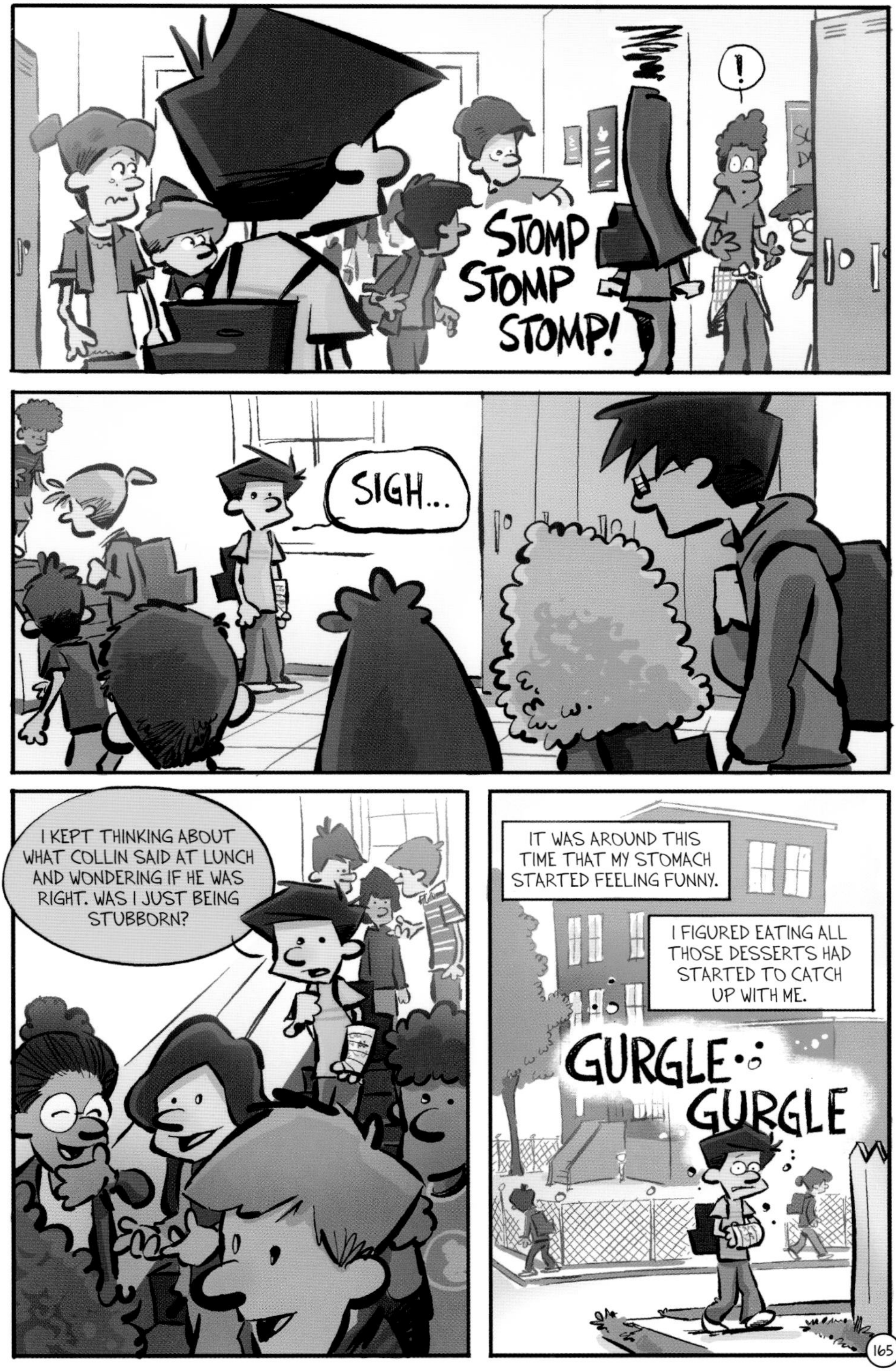

!
STOMP
STOMP
STOMP!
SIGH...
I KEPT THINKING ABOUT WHAT COLLIN SAID AT LUNCH AND WONDERING IF HE WAS RIGHT. WAS I JUST BEING STUBBORN?
IT WAS AROUND THIS TIME THAT MY STOMACH STARTED FEELING FUNNY.
I FIGURED EATING ALL THOSE DESSERTS HAD STARTED TO CATCH UP WITH ME.
GURGLE
GURGLE

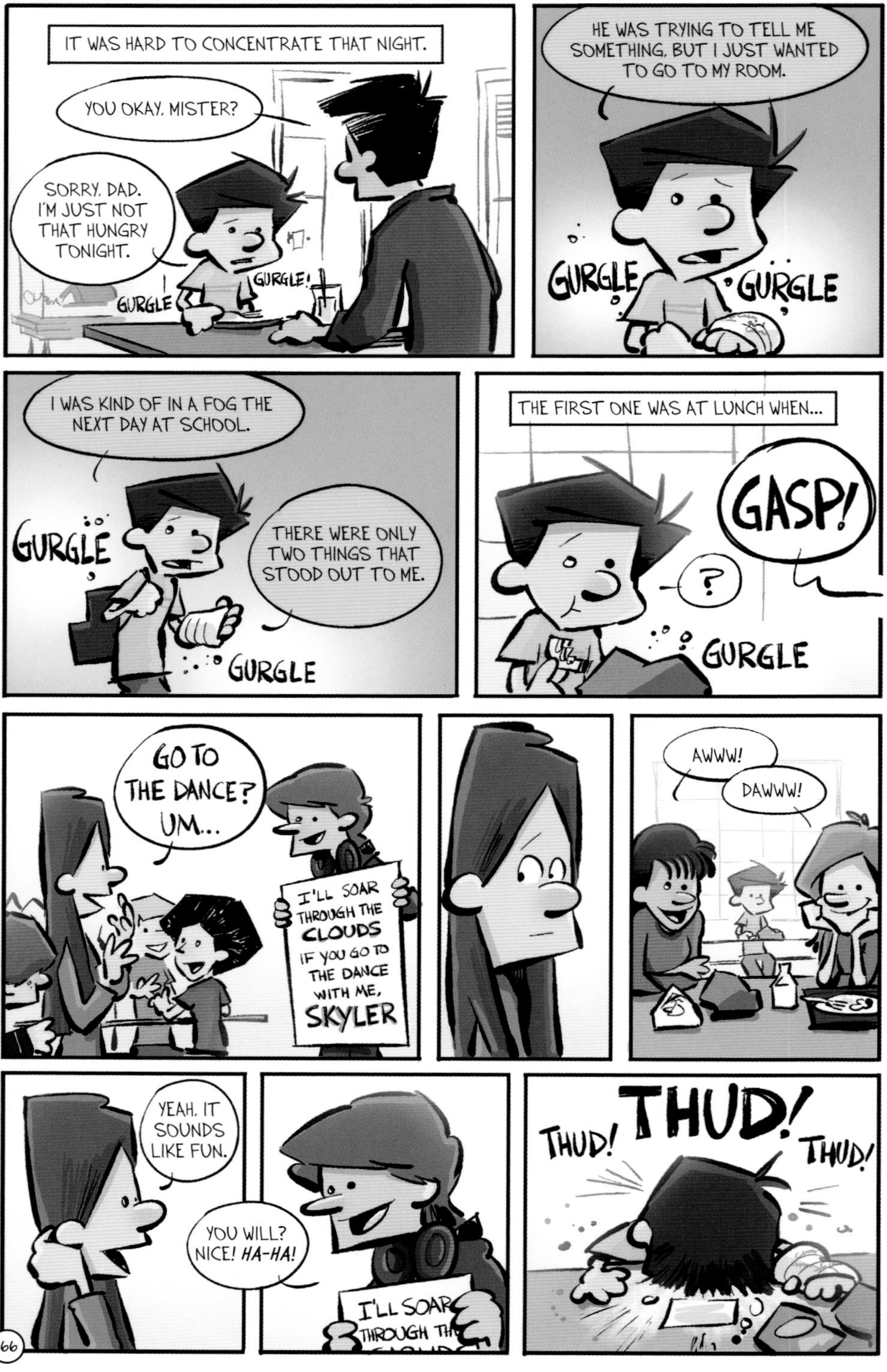
IT WAS HARD TO CONCENTRATE THAT NIGHT.
YOU OKAY, MISTER?
SORRY, DAD. I'M JUST NOT THAT HUNGRY TONIGHT.
GURGLE
GURGLE!
HE WAS TRYING TO TELL ME SOMETHING, BUT I JUST WANTED TO GO TO MY ROOM.
GURGLE
GURGLE
I WAS KIND OF IN A FOG THE NEXT DAY AT SCHOOL.
GURGLE
THERE WERE ONLY TWO THINGS THAT STOOD OUT TO ME.
GURGLE
THE FIRST ONE WAS AT LUNCH WHEN...
GASP!
?
GURGLE
GO TO THE DANCE? UM...
I'LL SOAR THROUGH THE CLOUDS IF YOU GO TO THE DANCE WITH ME, SKYLER
AWWW!
DAWWW!
YEAH, IT SOUNDS LIKE FUN.
YOU WILL? NICE! HA-HA!
THUD!
THUD!
THUD!

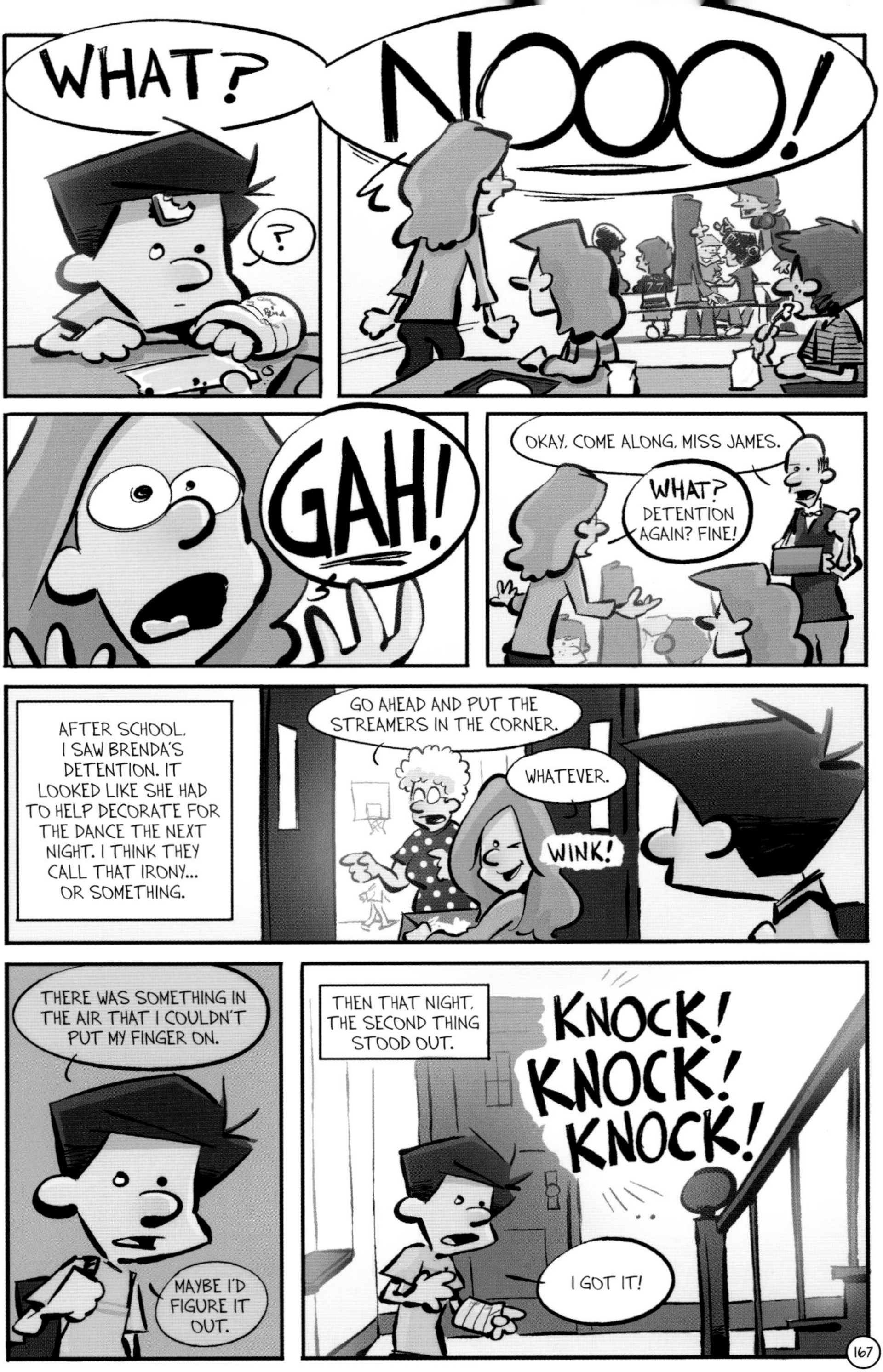
WHAT?
?
NOOO!
GAH!
OKAY, COME ALONG, MISS JAMES.
WHAT? DETENTION AGAIN? FINE!
AFTER SCHOOL, I SAW BRENDA'S DETENTION. IT LOOKED LIKE SHE HAD TO HELP DECORATE FOR THE DANCE THE NEXT NIGHT. I THINK THEY CALL THAT IRONY... OR SOMETHING.
GO AHEAD AND PUT THE STREAMERS IN THE CORNER.
WHATEVER.
WINK!
THERE WAS SOMETHING IN THE AIR THAT I COULDN'T PUT MY FINGER ON.
MAYBE I'D FIGURE IT OUT.
THEN THAT NIGHT, THE SECOND THING STOOD OUT.
KNOCK! KNOCK! KNOCK!
I GOT IT!

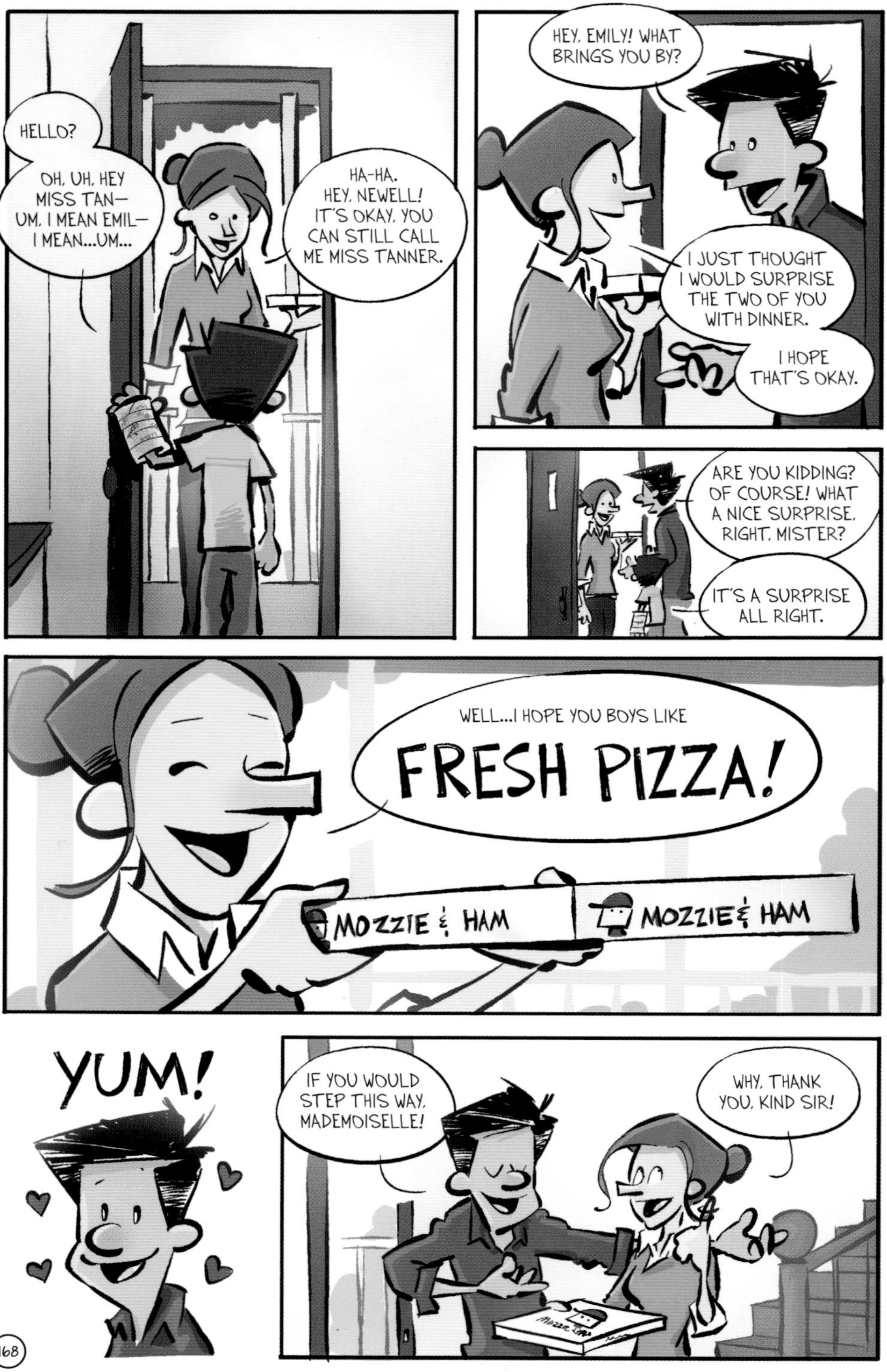
HELLO?
OH, UH, HEY MISS TAN— UM, I MEAN EMIL— I MEAN...UM...
HA-HA. HEY, NEWELL! IT'S OKAY, YOU CAN STILL CALL ME MISS TANNER.
HEY, EMILY! WHAT BRINGS YOU BY?
I JUST THOUGHT I WOULD SURPRISE THE TWO OF YOU WITH DINNER.
I HOPE THAT'S OKAY.
ARE YOU KIDDING? OF COURSE! WHAT A NICE SURPRISE, RIGHT, MISTER?
IT'S A SURPRISE ALL RIGHT.
WELL...I HOPE YOU BOYS LIKE
FRESH PIZZA!
MOZZIE & HAM
MOZZIE & HAM
YUM!
IF YOU WOULD STEP THIS WAY, MADEMOISELLE!
WHY, THANK YOU, KIND SIR!

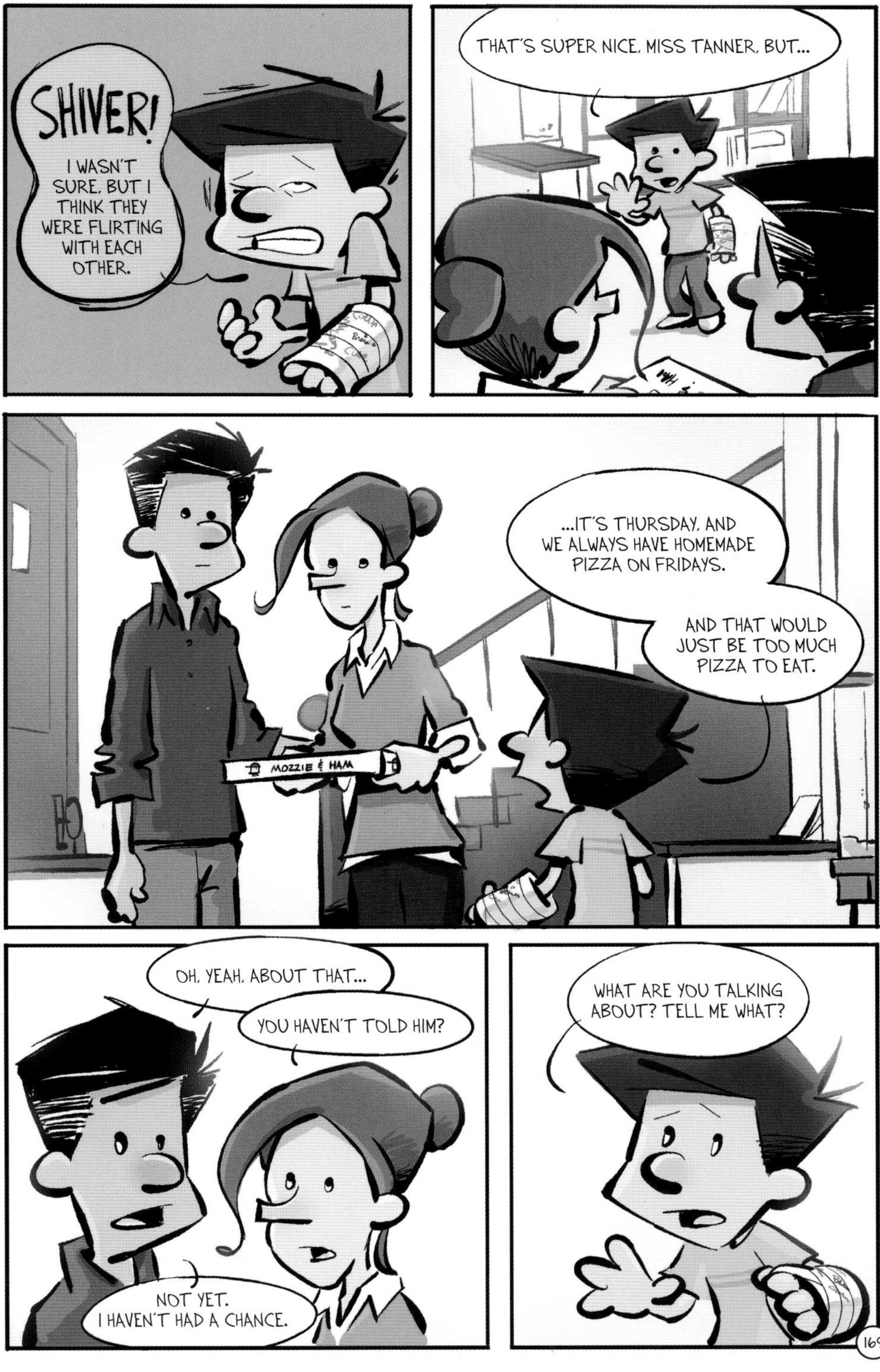
SHIVER!
I WASN'T SURE, BUT I THINK THEY WERE FLIRTING WITH EACH OTHER.
THAT'S SUPER NICE, MISS TANNER, BUT...
...IT'S THURSDAY, AND WE ALWAYS HAVE HOMEMADE PIZZA ON FRIDAYS.
AND THAT WOULD JUST BE TOO MUCH PIZZA TO EAT.
MOZZIE & HAM
OH, YEAH, ABOUT THAT...
YOU HAVEN'T TOLD HIM?
NOT YET. I HAVEN'T HAD A CHANCE.
WHAT ARE YOU TALKING ABOUT? TELL ME WHAT?

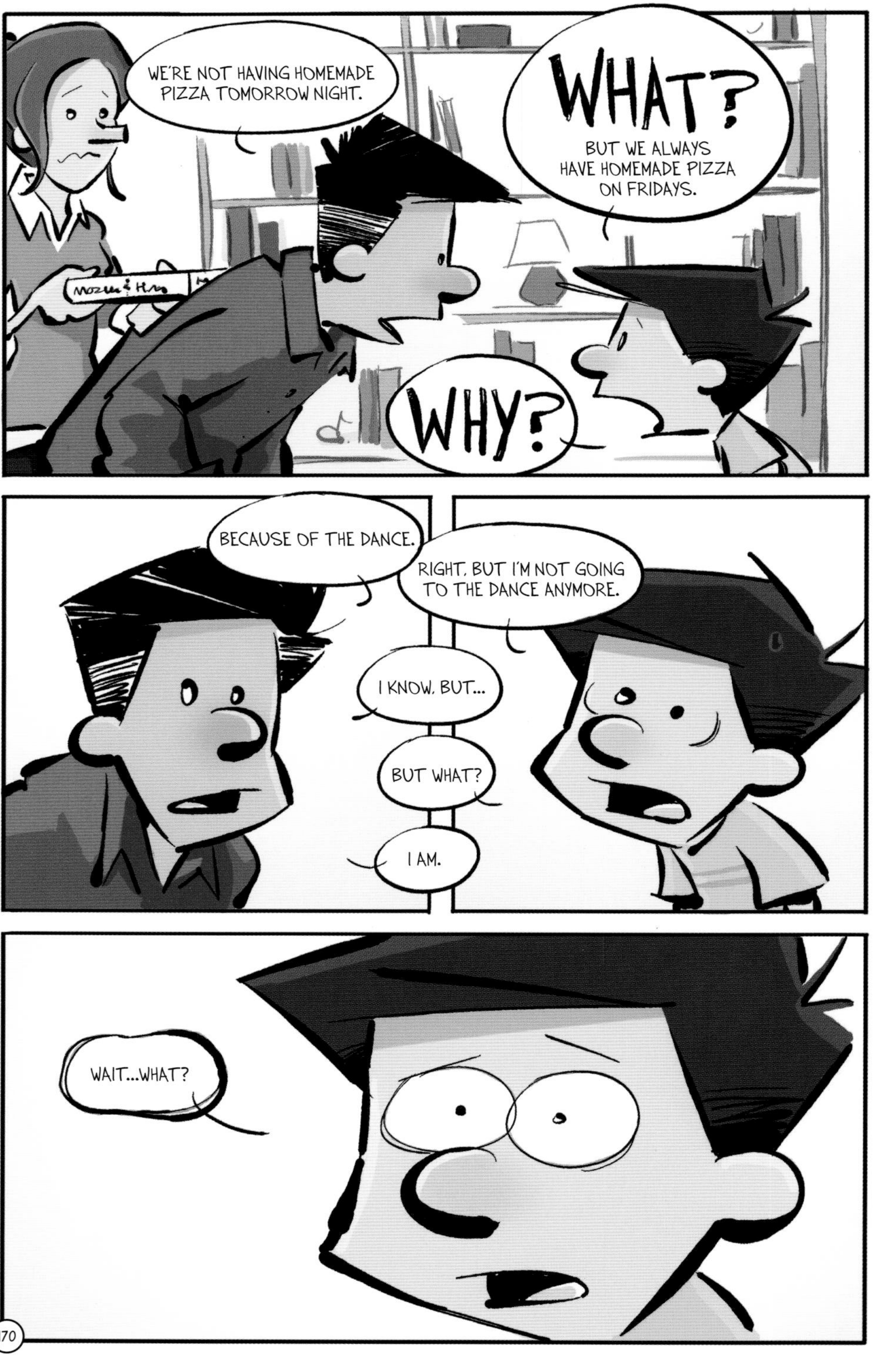
WE'RE NOT HAVING HOMEMADE PIZZA TOMORROW NIGHT.
WHAT?
BUT WE ALWAYS HAVE HOMEMADE PIZZA ON FRIDAYS.
WHY?
BECAUSE OF THE DANCE.
RIGHT, BUT I'M NOT GOING TO THE DANCE ANYMORE.
I KNOW, BUT...
BUT WHAT?
I AM.
WAIT...WHAT?

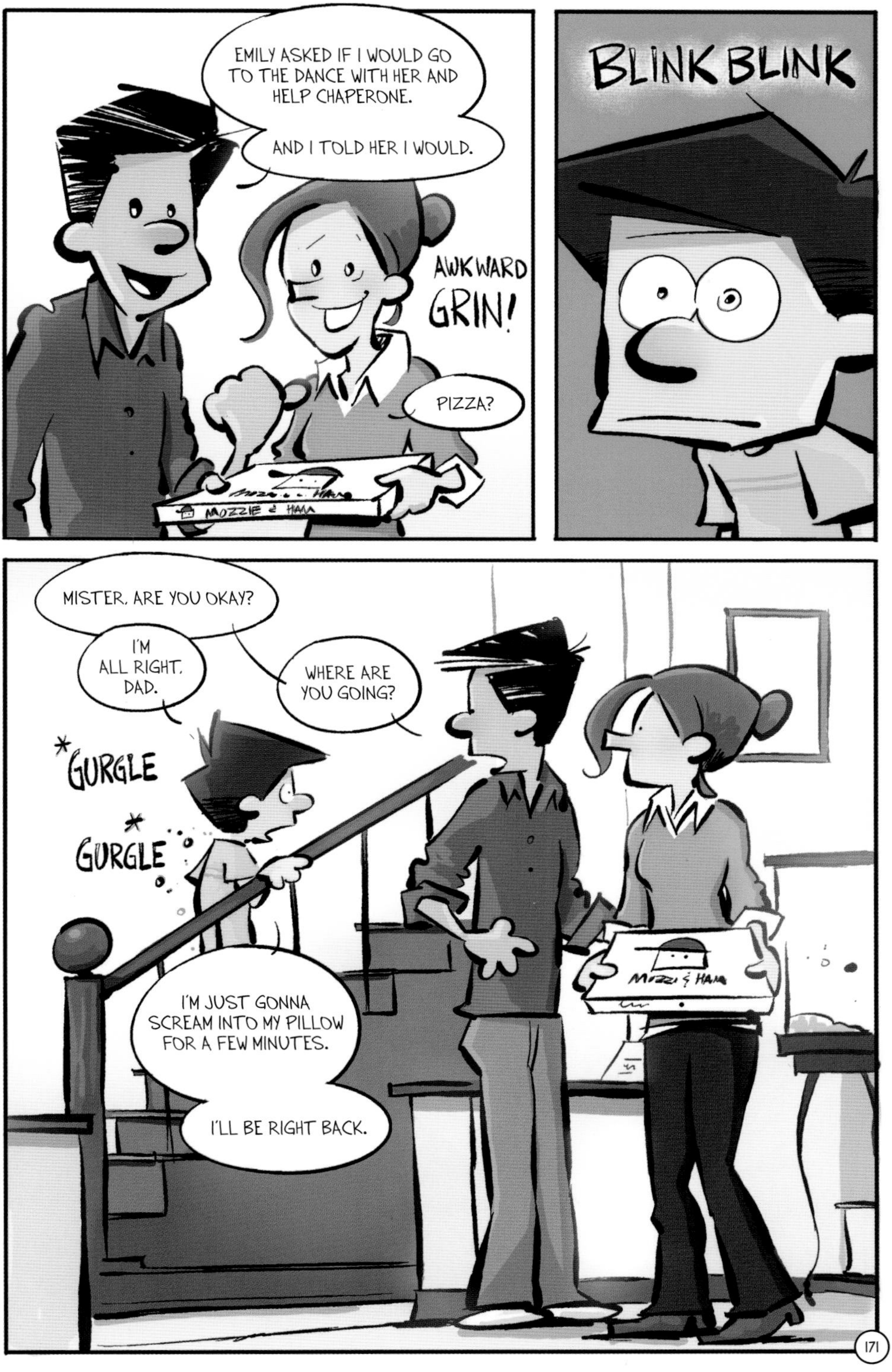
EMILY ASKED IF I WOULD GO TO THE DANCE WITH HER AND HELP CHAPERONE.
AND I TOLD HER I WOULD.
AWKWARD GRIN!
PIZZA?
MOZZIE & HAM
BLINK BLINK
MISTER, ARE YOU OKAY?
I'M ALL RIGHT, DAD.
WHERE ARE YOU GOING?
*GURGLE
*GURGLE
I'M JUST GONNA SCREAM INTO MY PILLOW FOR A FEW MINUTES.
I'LL BE RIGHT BACK.

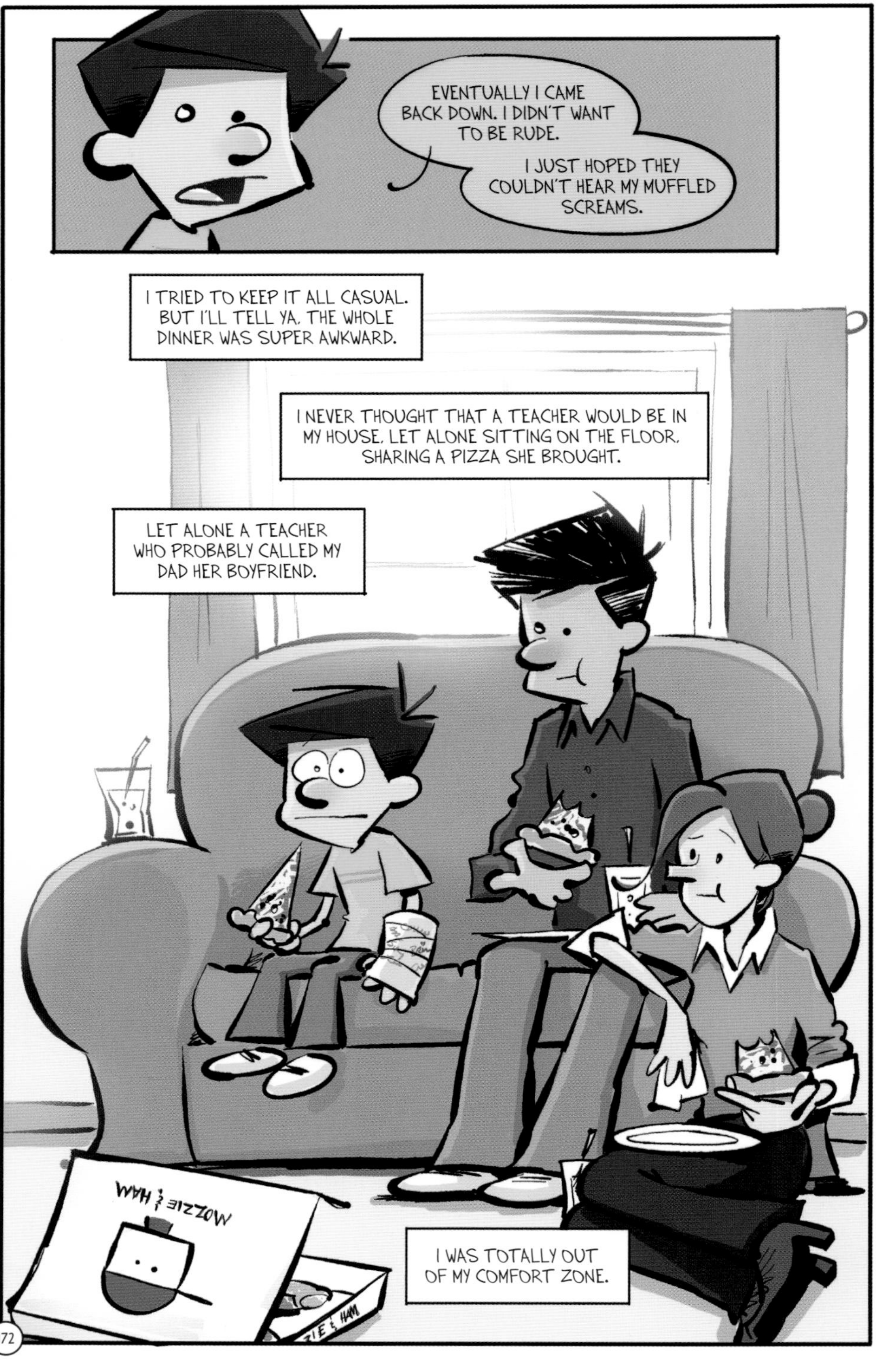
EVENTUALLY I CAME BACK DOWN. I DIDN'T WANT TO BE RUDE.
I JUST HOPED THEY COULDN'T HEAR MY MUFFLED SCREAMS.
I TRIED TO KEEP IT ALL CASUAL. BUT I'LL TELL YA, THE WHOLE DINNER WAS SUPER AWKWARD.
I NEVER THOUGHT THAT A TEACHER WOULD BE IN MY HOUSE, LET ALONE SITTING ON THE FLOOR, SHARING A PIZZA SHE BROUGHT.
LET ALONE A TEACHER WHO PROBABLY CALLED MY DAD HER BOYFRIEND.
I WAS TOTALLY OUT OF MY COMFORT ZONE.

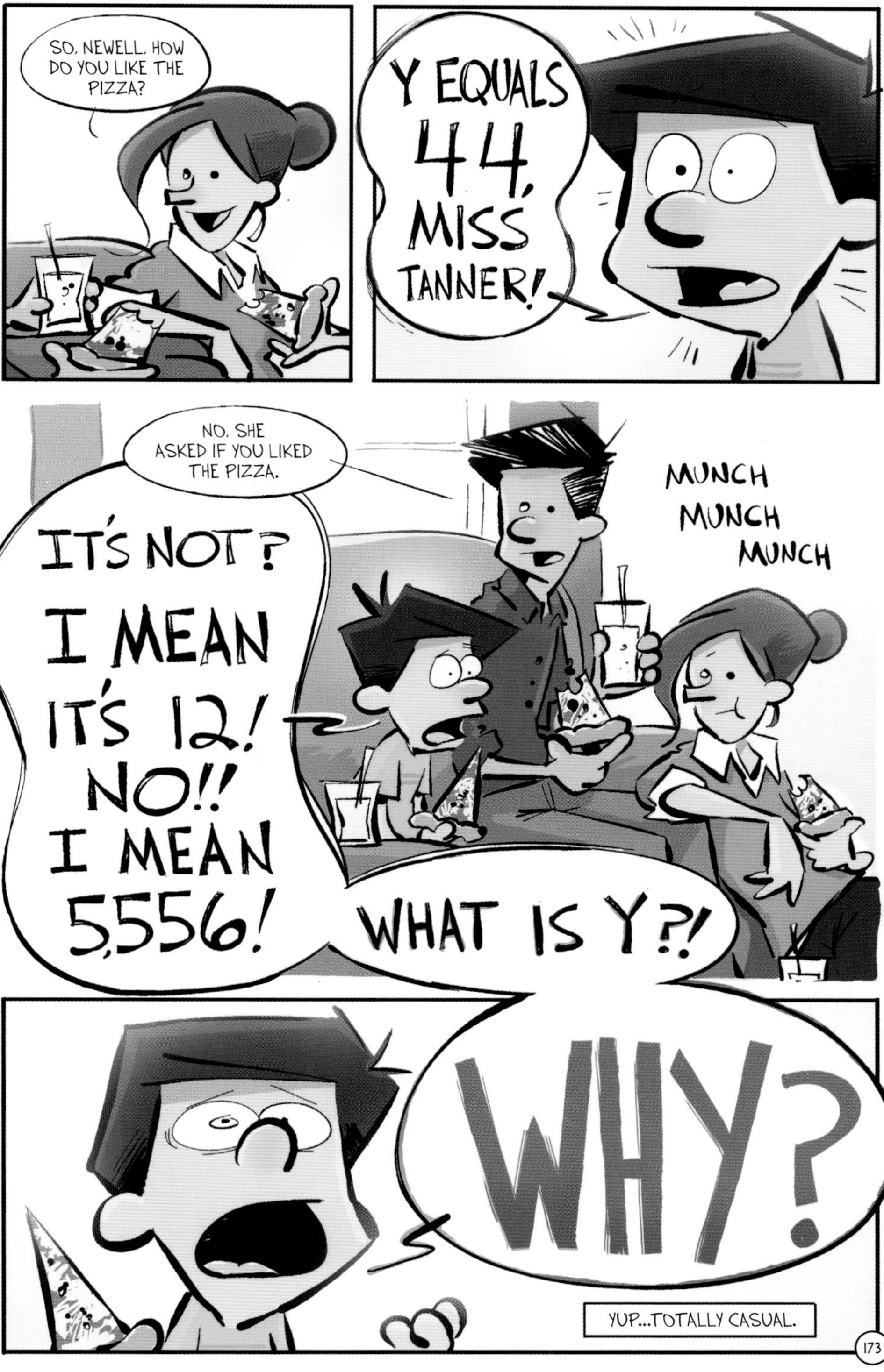
SO, NEWELL, HOW DO YOU LIKE THE PIZZA?
Y EQUALS 44, MISS TANNER!
NO, SHE ASKED IF YOU LIKED THE PIZZA.
MUNCH MUNCH MUNCH
IT'S NOT? I MEAN IT'S 12! NO!! I MEAN 5,556!
WHAT IS Y?!
WHY?
YUP...TOTALLY CASUAL.

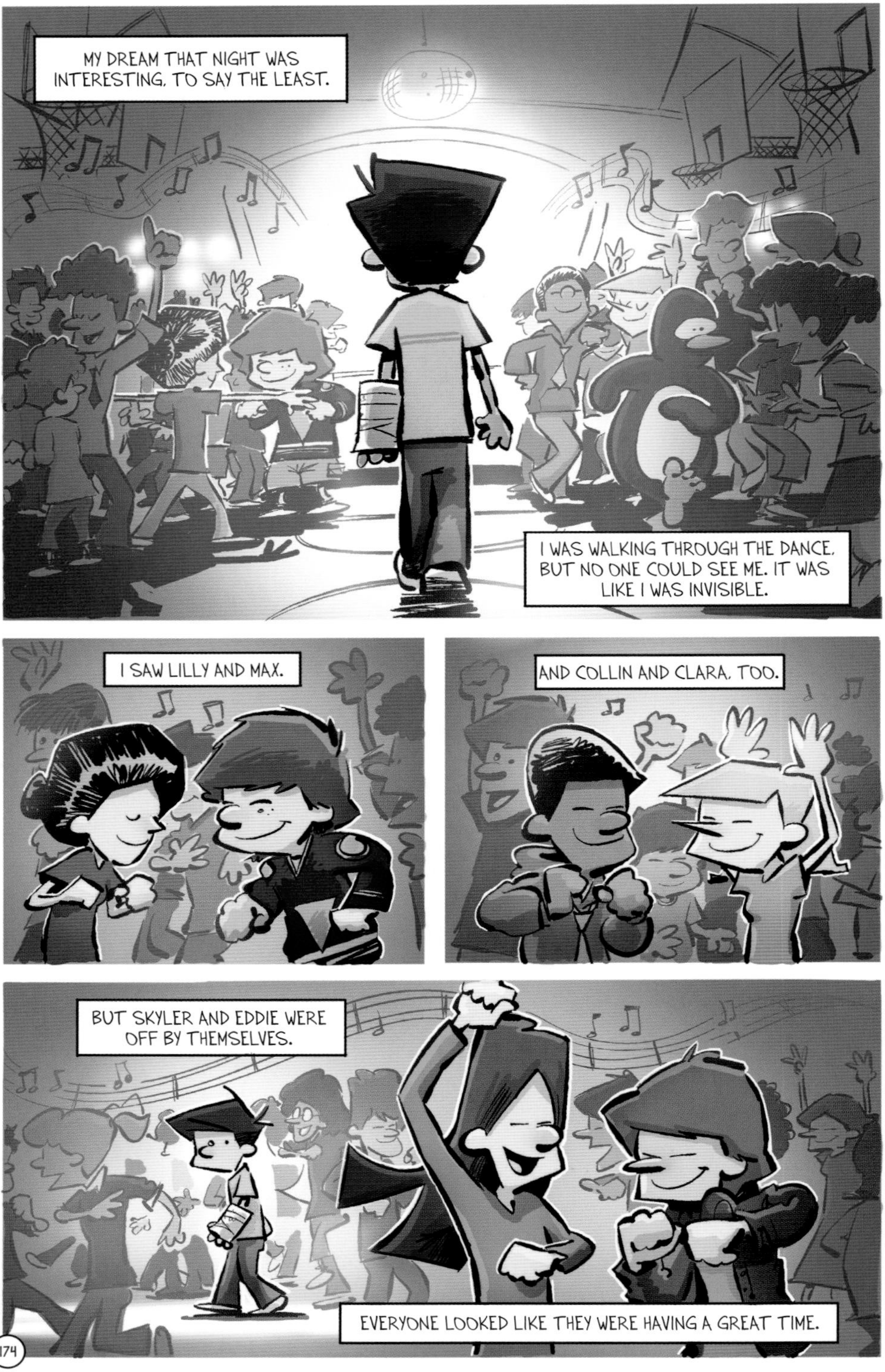
MY DREAM THAT NIGHT WAS INTERESTING, TO SAY THE LEAST.
I WAS WALKING THROUGH THE DANCE, BUT NO ONE COULD SEE ME. IT WAS LIKE I WAS INVISIBLE.
I SAW LILLY AND MAX.
AND COLLIN AND CLARA, TOO.
BUT SKYLER AND EDDIE WERE OFF BY THEMSELVES.
EVERYONE LOOKED LIKE THEY WERE HAVING A GREAT TIME.

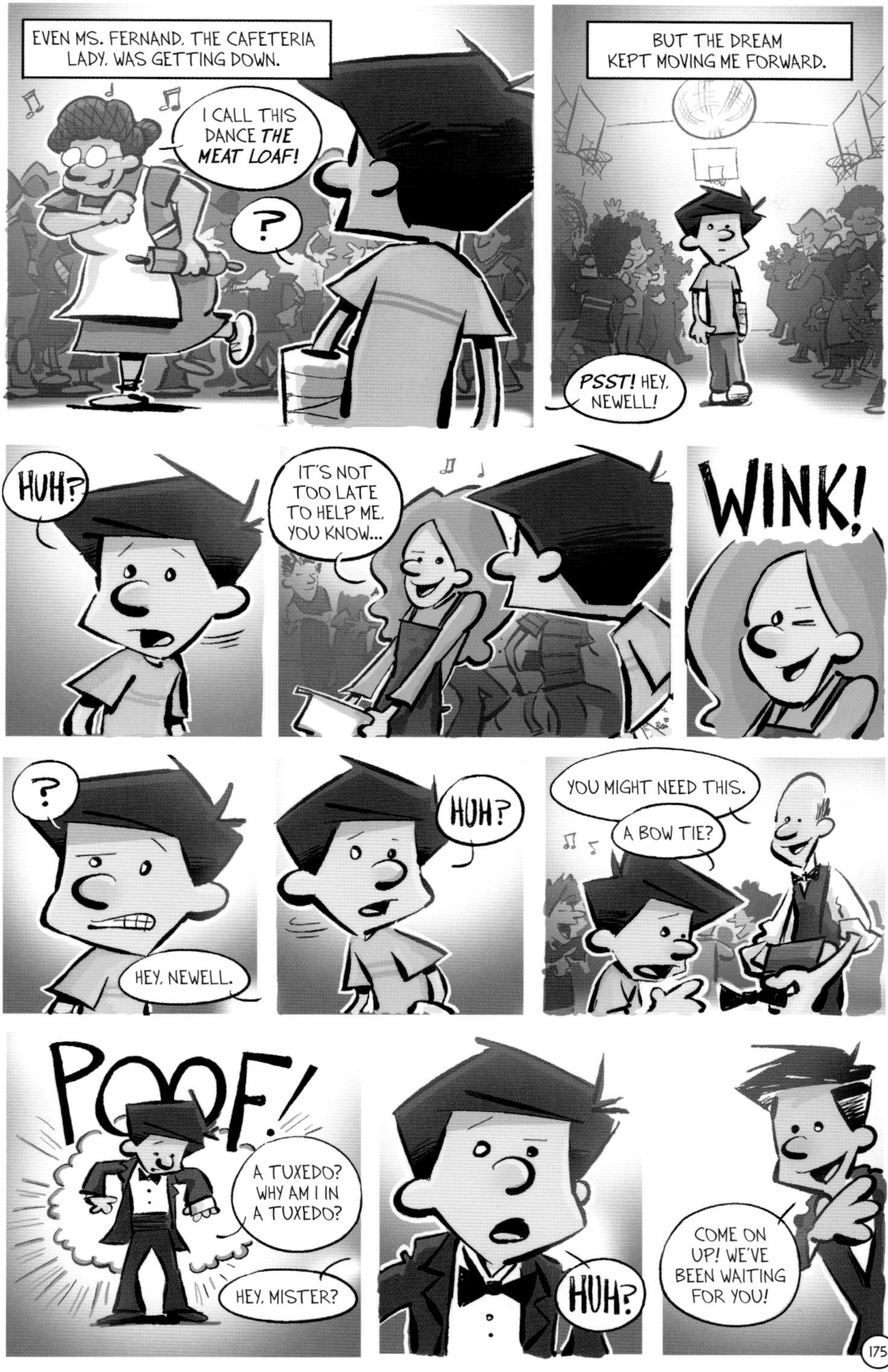
EVEN MS. FERNAND, THE CAFETERIA LADY, WAS GETTING DOWN.
I CALL THIS DANCE ***THE MEAT LOAF!***
?
BUT THE DREAM KEPT MOVING ME FORWARD.
PSST! HEY, NEWELL!
HUH?
IT'S NOT TOO LATE TO HELP ME, YOU KNOW...
WINK!
?
HEY, NEWELL.
HUH?
YOU MIGHT NEED THIS.
A BOW TIE?
POOF!
A TUXEDO? WHY AM I IN A TUXEDO?
HEY, MISTER?
HUH?
COME ON UP! WE'VE BEEN WAITING FOR YOU!

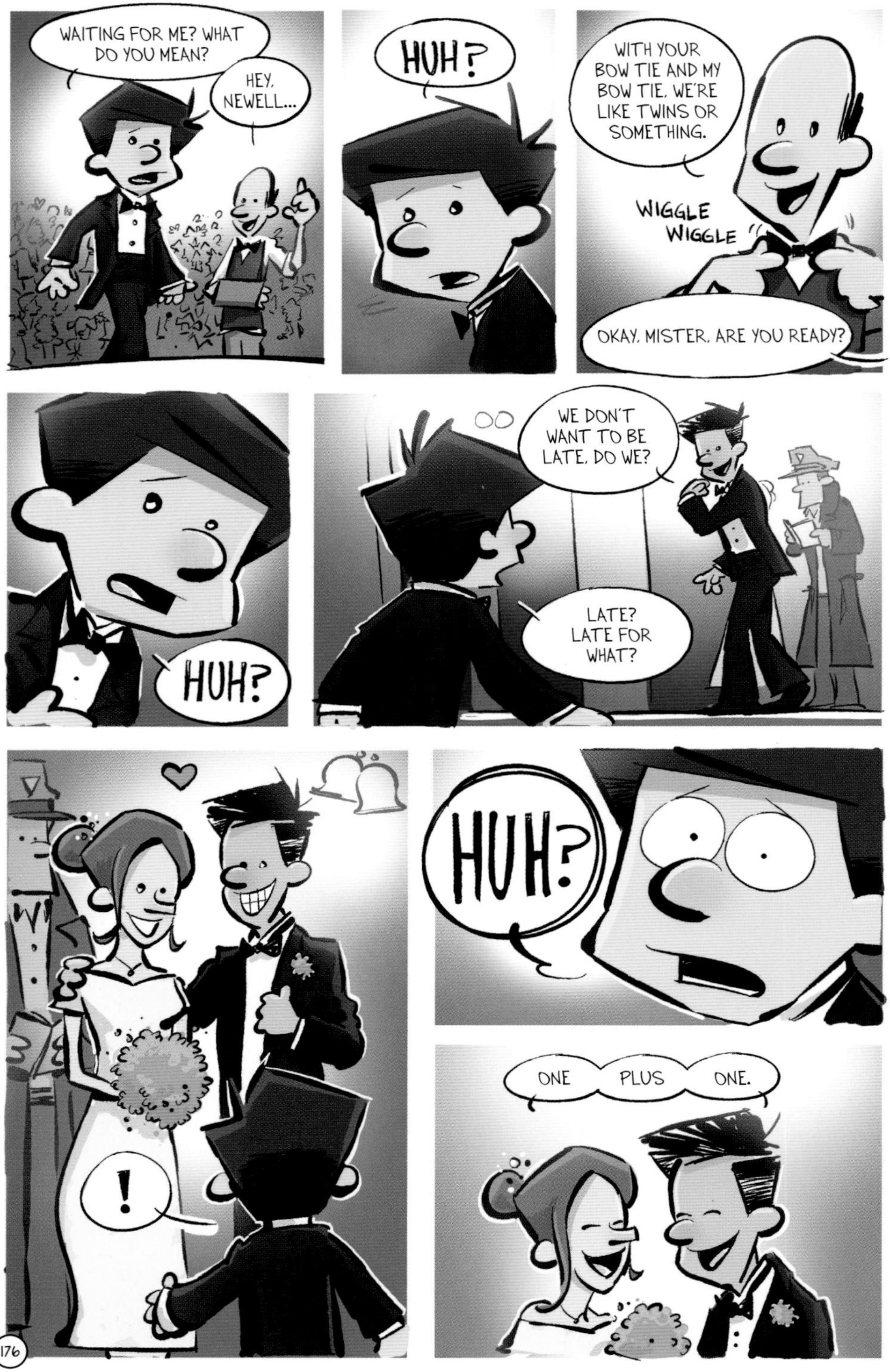

WAITING FOR ME? WHAT DO YOU MEAN?
HEY, NEWELL...
HUH?
WITH YOUR BOW TIE AND MY BOW TIE, WE'RE LIKE TWINS OR SOMETHING.
WIGGLE WIGGLE
OKAY, MISTER, ARE YOU READY?
HUH?
WE DON'T WANT TO BE LATE, DO WE?
LATE? LATE FOR WHAT?
!
HUH?
ONE
PLUS
ONE.

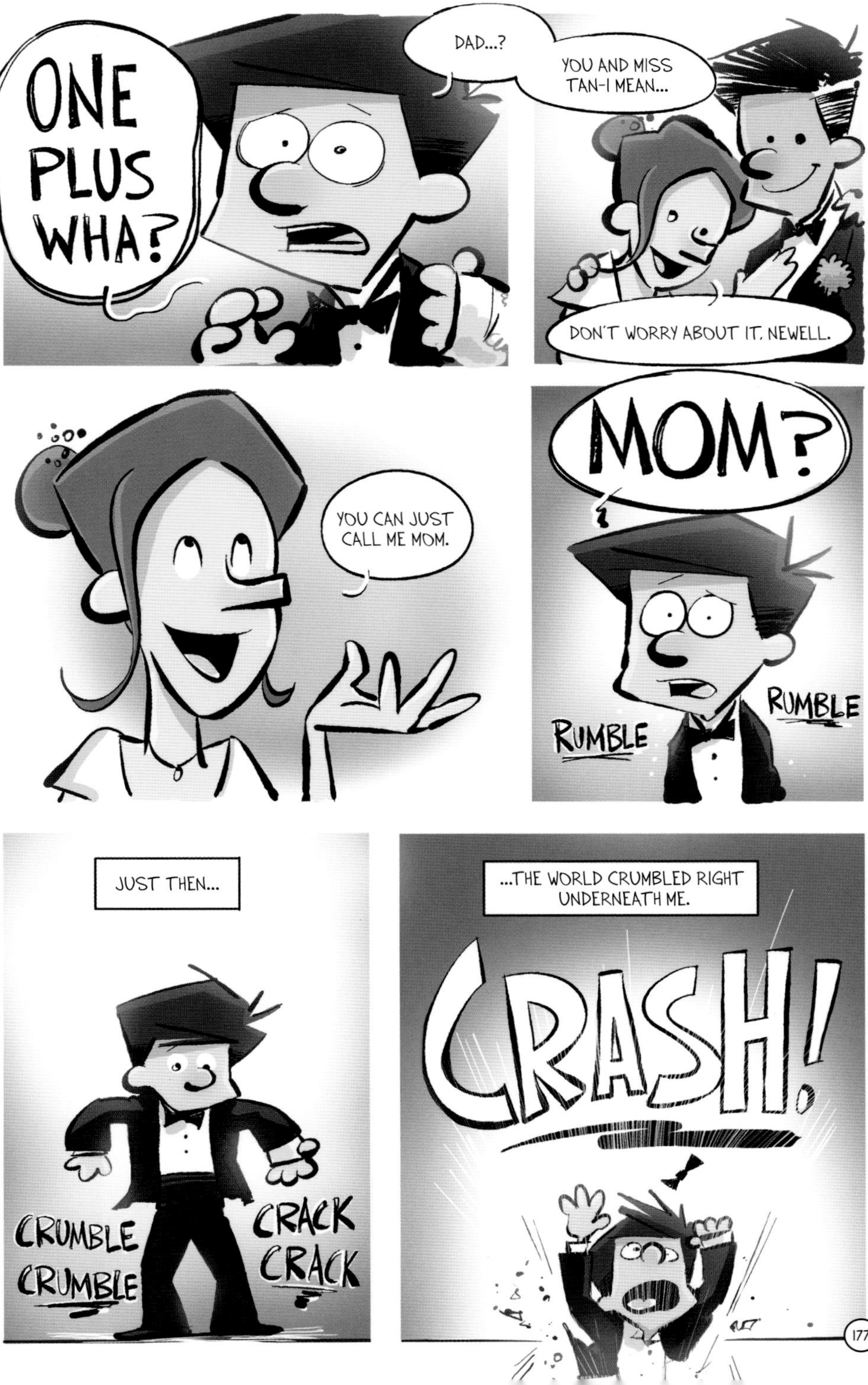
ONE PLUS WHA?
DAD...?
YOU AND MISS TAN-I MEAN...
DON'T WORRY ABOUT IT, NEWELL.
YOU CAN JUST CALL ME MOM.
MOM?
RUMBLE
RUMBLE
JUST THEN...
CRUMBLE
CRUMBLE
CRACK
CRACK
...THE WORLD CRUMBLED RIGHT UNDERNEATH ME.
CRASH!

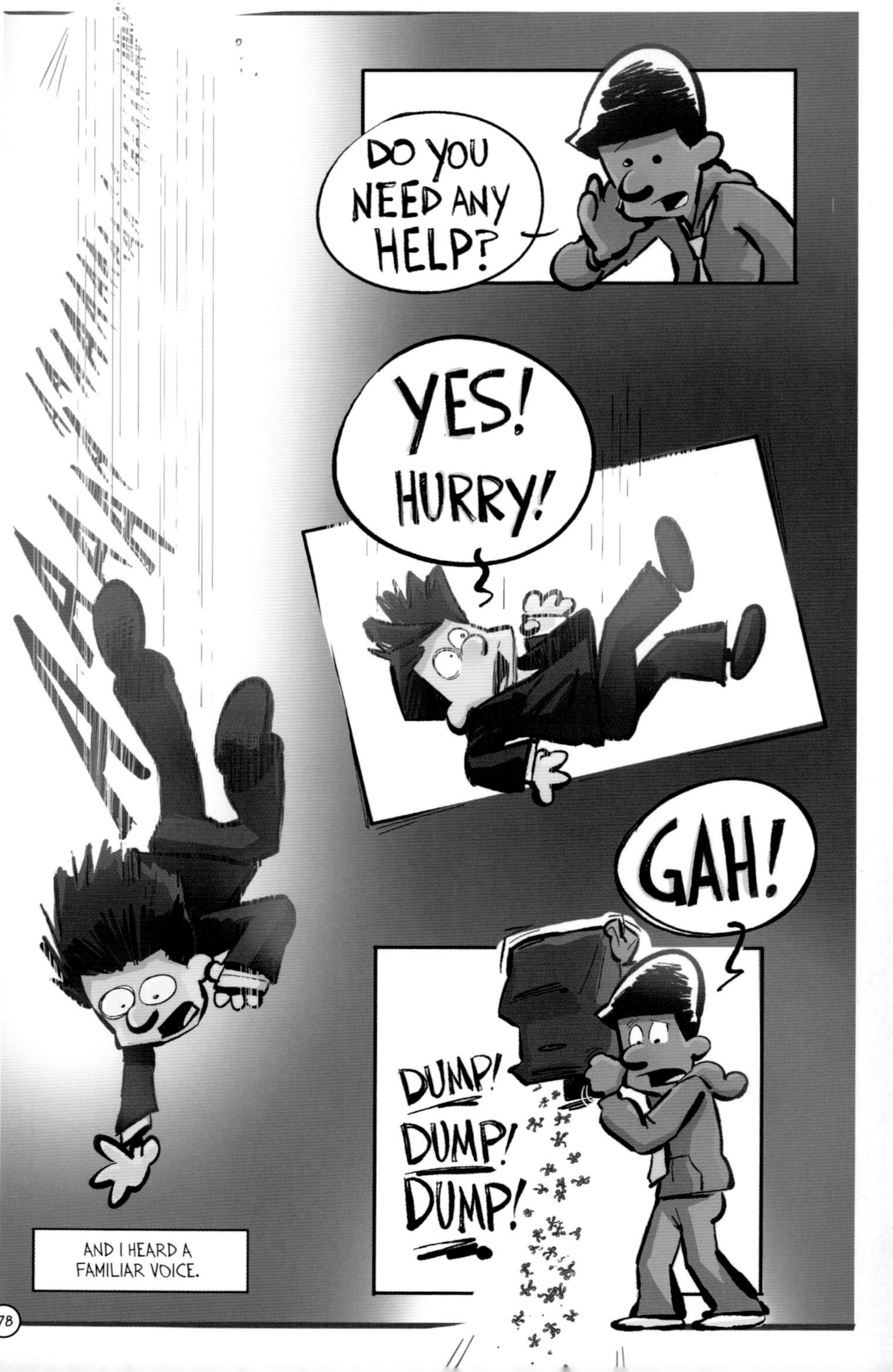
DO YOU NEED ANY HELP?
YES! HURRY!
GAH!
DUMP! DUMP! DUMP!
AND I HEARD A FAMILIAR VOICE.

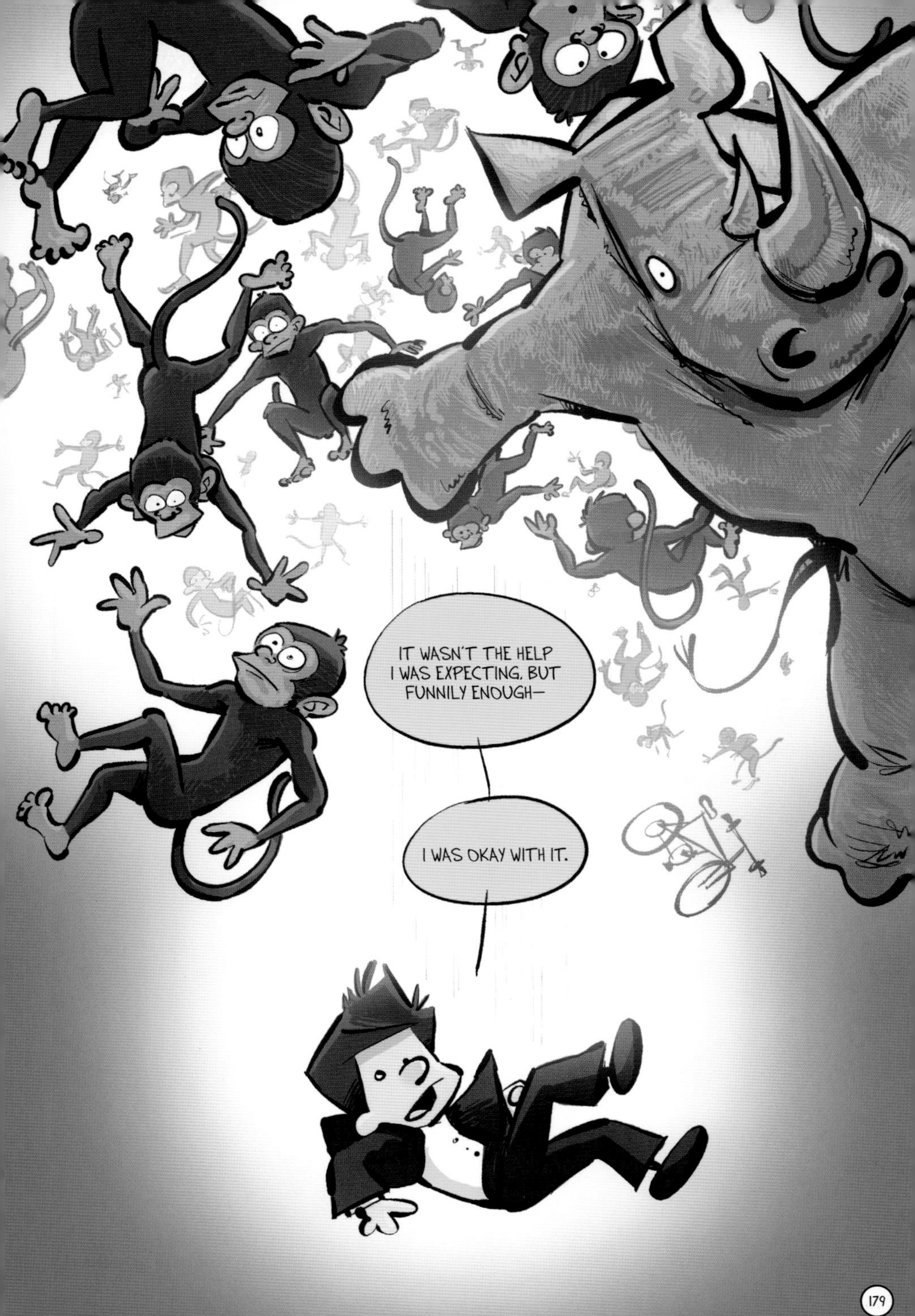
IT WASN'T THE HELP I WAS EXPECTING, BUT FUNNILY ENOUGH—
I WAS OKAY WITH IT.

CHAPTER NINE
THE DAY OF THE DANCE

I COULDN'T BELIEVE IT WAS TONIGHT.

IT SEEMED LIKE THIS POSTER HAD BEEN PUT UP TEN YEARS AGO.

GARFIELD'S
SCHOOL
DANCE!

I'D BEEN SO EXCITED ABOUT IT.

AND NOW, NOTHING WAS THE SAME.

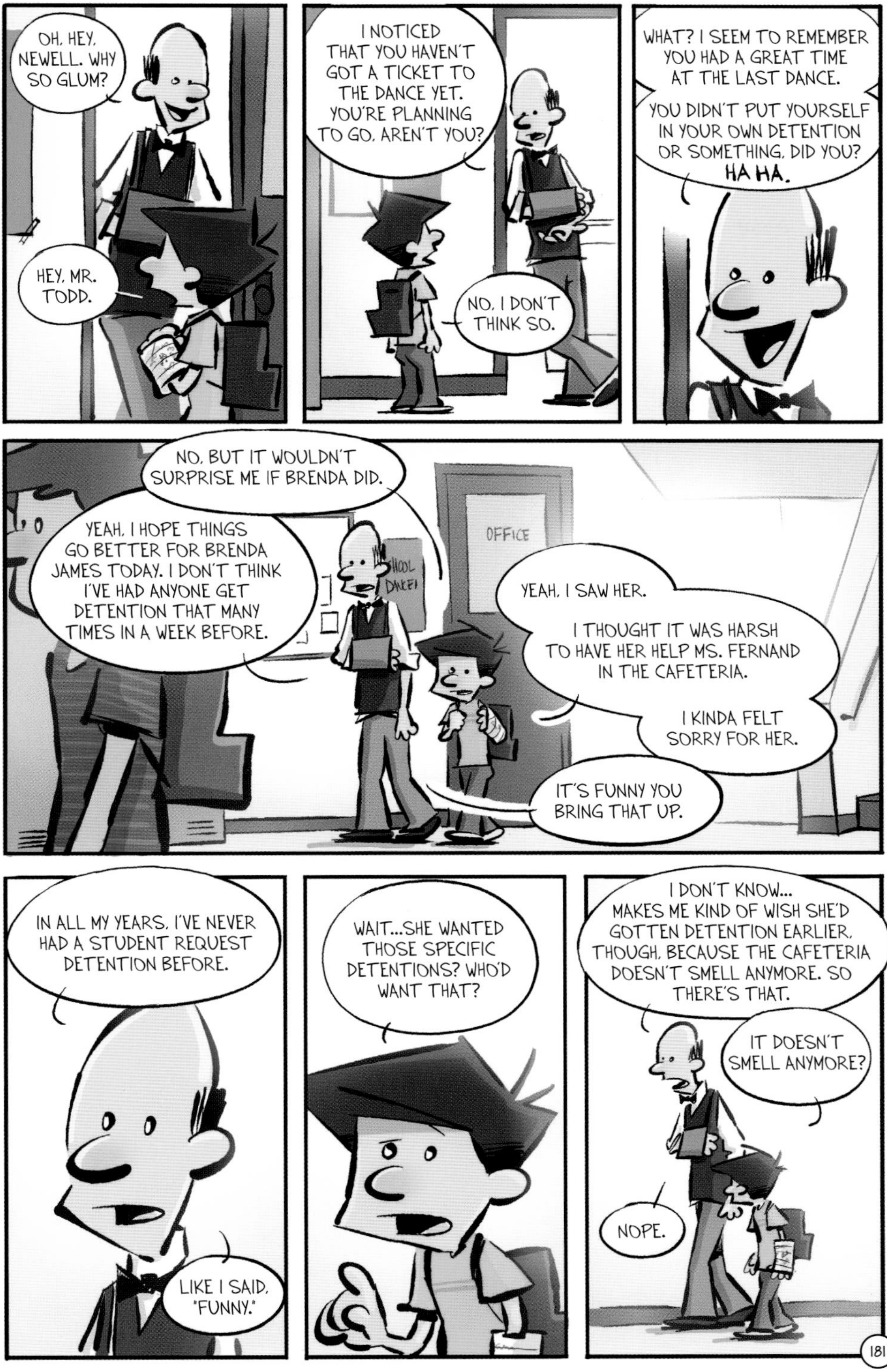
OH, HEY, NEWELL. WHY SO GLUM?
HEY, MR. TODD.
I NOTICED THAT YOU HAVEN'T GOT A TICKET TO THE DANCE YET. YOU'RE PLANNING TO GO, AREN'T YOU?
NO, I DON'T THINK SO.
WHAT? I SEEM TO REMEMBER YOU HAD A GREAT TIME AT THE LAST DANCE.
YOU DIDN'T PUT YOURSELF IN YOUR OWN DETENTION OR SOMETHING, DID YOU? HA HA.
NO, BUT IT WOULDN'T SURPRISE ME IF BRENDA DID.
YEAH, I HOPE THINGS GO BETTER FOR BRENDA JAMES TODAY. I DON'T THINK I'VE HAD ANYONE GET DETENTION THAT MANY TIMES IN A WEEK BEFORE.
OFFICE
YEAH, I SAW HER.
I THOUGHT IT WAS HARSH TO HAVE HER HELP MS. FERNAND IN THE CAFETERIA.
I KINDA FELT SORRY FOR HER.
IT'S FUNNY YOU BRING THAT UP.
IN ALL MY YEARS, I'VE NEVER HAD A STUDENT REQUEST DETENTION BEFORE.
LIKE I SAID, "FUNNY."
WAIT...SHE WANTED THOSE SPECIFIC DETENTIONS? WHO'D WANT THAT?
I DON'T KNOW... MAKES ME KIND OF WISH SHE'D GOTTEN DETENTION EARLIER, THOUGH, BECAUSE THE CAFETERIA DOESN'T SMELL ANYMORE. SO THERE'S THAT.
IT DOESN'T SMELL ANYMORE?
NOPE.

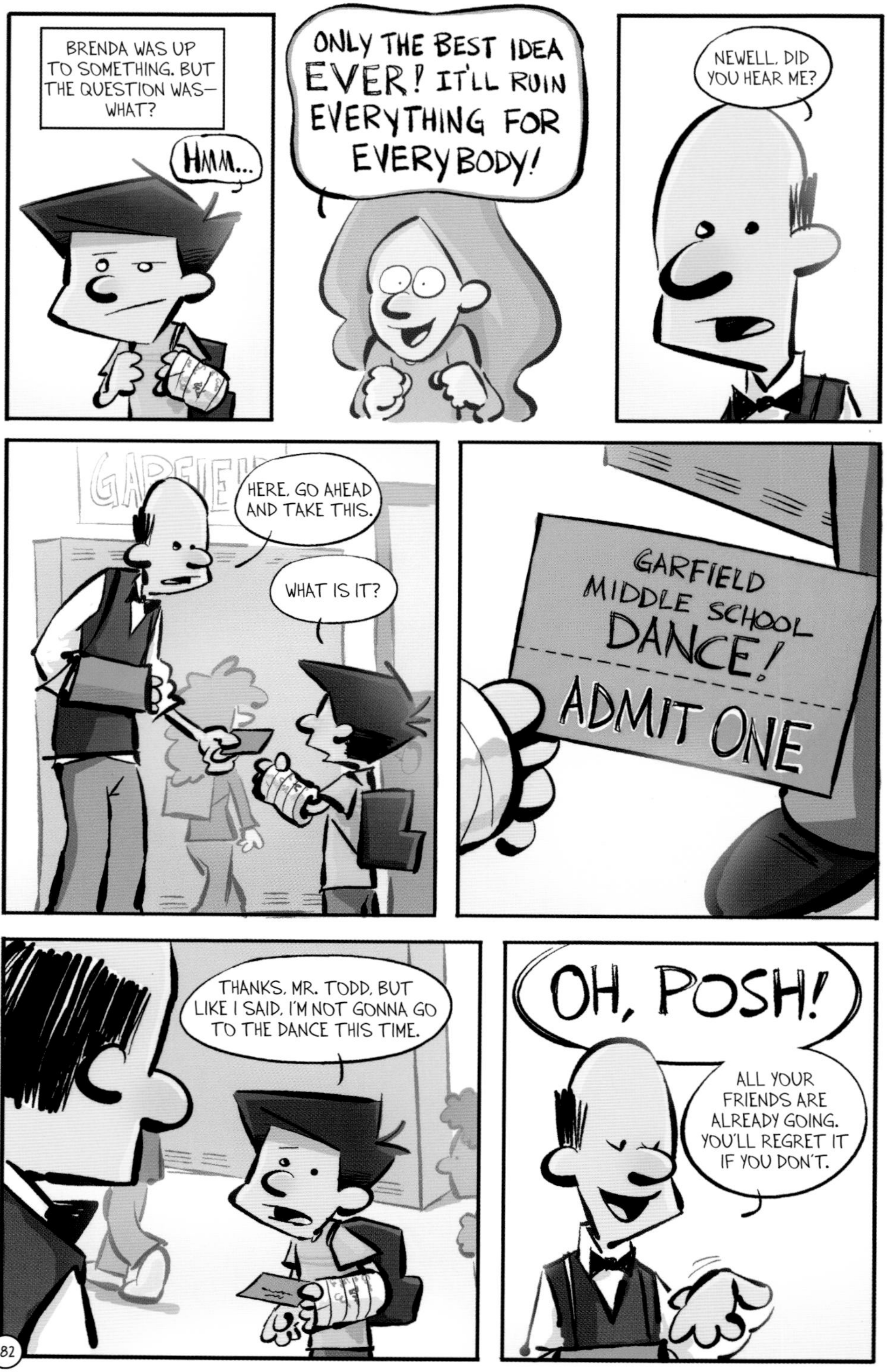
BRENDA WAS UP TO SOMETHING. BUT THE QUESTION WAS— WHAT?
HMM...
ONLY THE BEST IDEA EVER! IT'LL RUIN EVERYTHING FOR EVERYBODY!
NEWELL, DID YOU HEAR ME?
HERE, GO AHEAD AND TAKE THIS.
WHAT IS IT?
GARFIELD MIDDLE SCHOOL DANCE!
ADMIT ONE
THANKS, MR. TODD, BUT LIKE I SAID, I'M NOT GONNA GO TO THE DANCE THIS TIME.
OH, POSH!
ALL YOUR FRIENDS ARE ALREADY GOING. YOU'LL REGRET IT IF YOU DON'T.

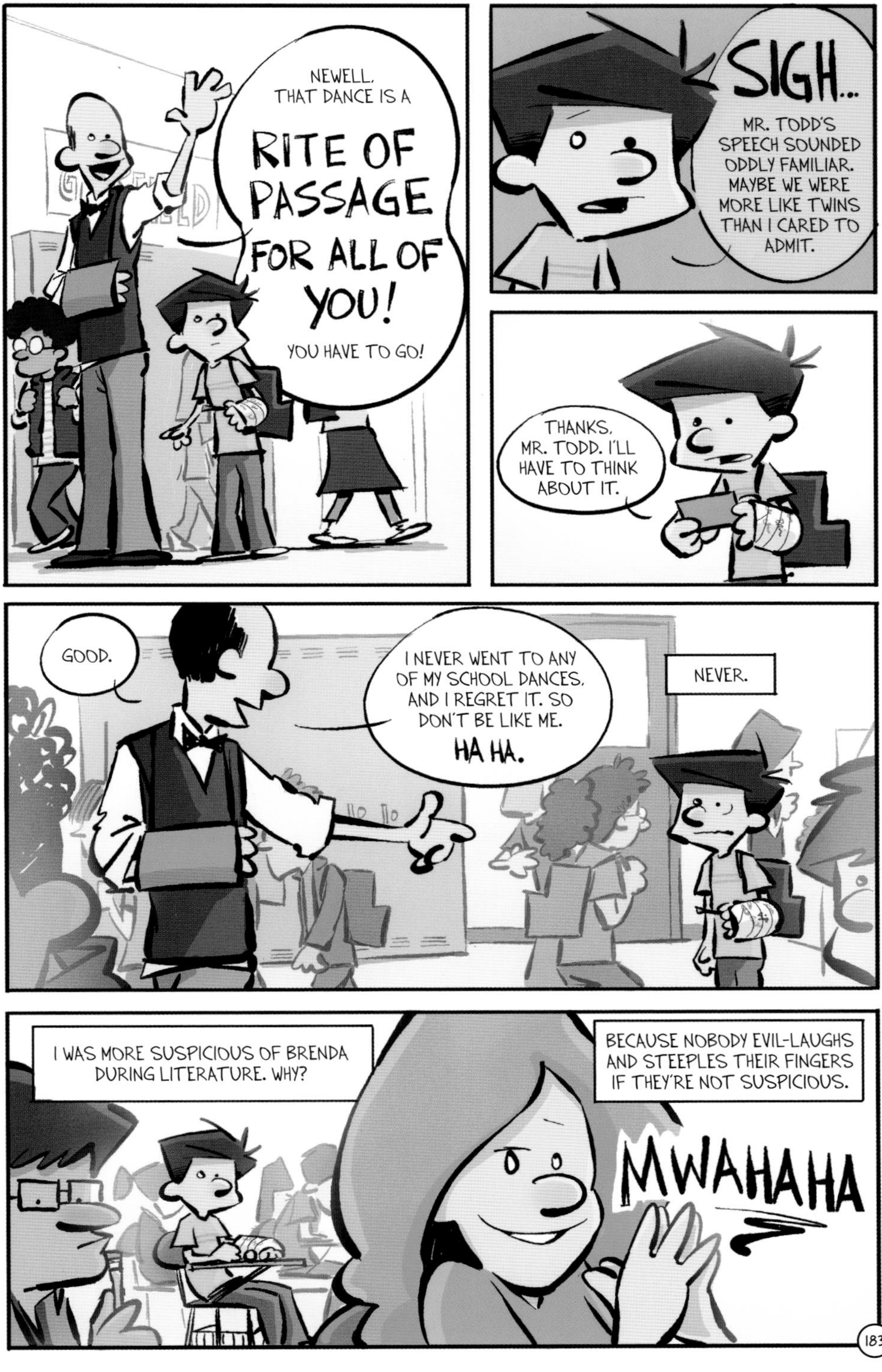

NEWELL, THAT DANCE IS A RITE OF PASSAGE FOR ALL OF YOU! YOU HAVE TO GO!
SIGH...
MR. TODD'S SPEECH SOUNDED ODDLY FAMILIAR. MAYBE WE WERE MORE LIKE TWINS THAN I CARED TO ADMIT.
THANKS, MR. TODD. I'LL HAVE TO THINK ABOUT IT.
GOOD.
I NEVER WENT TO ANY OF MY SCHOOL DANCES, AND I REGRET IT. SO DON'T BE LIKE ME. HA HA.
NEVER.
I WAS MORE SUSPICIOUS OF BRENDA DURING LITERATURE. WHY?
BECAUSE NOBODY EVIL-LAUGHS AND STEEPLES THEIR FINGERS IF THEY'RE NOT SUSPICIOUS.
MWAHAHA

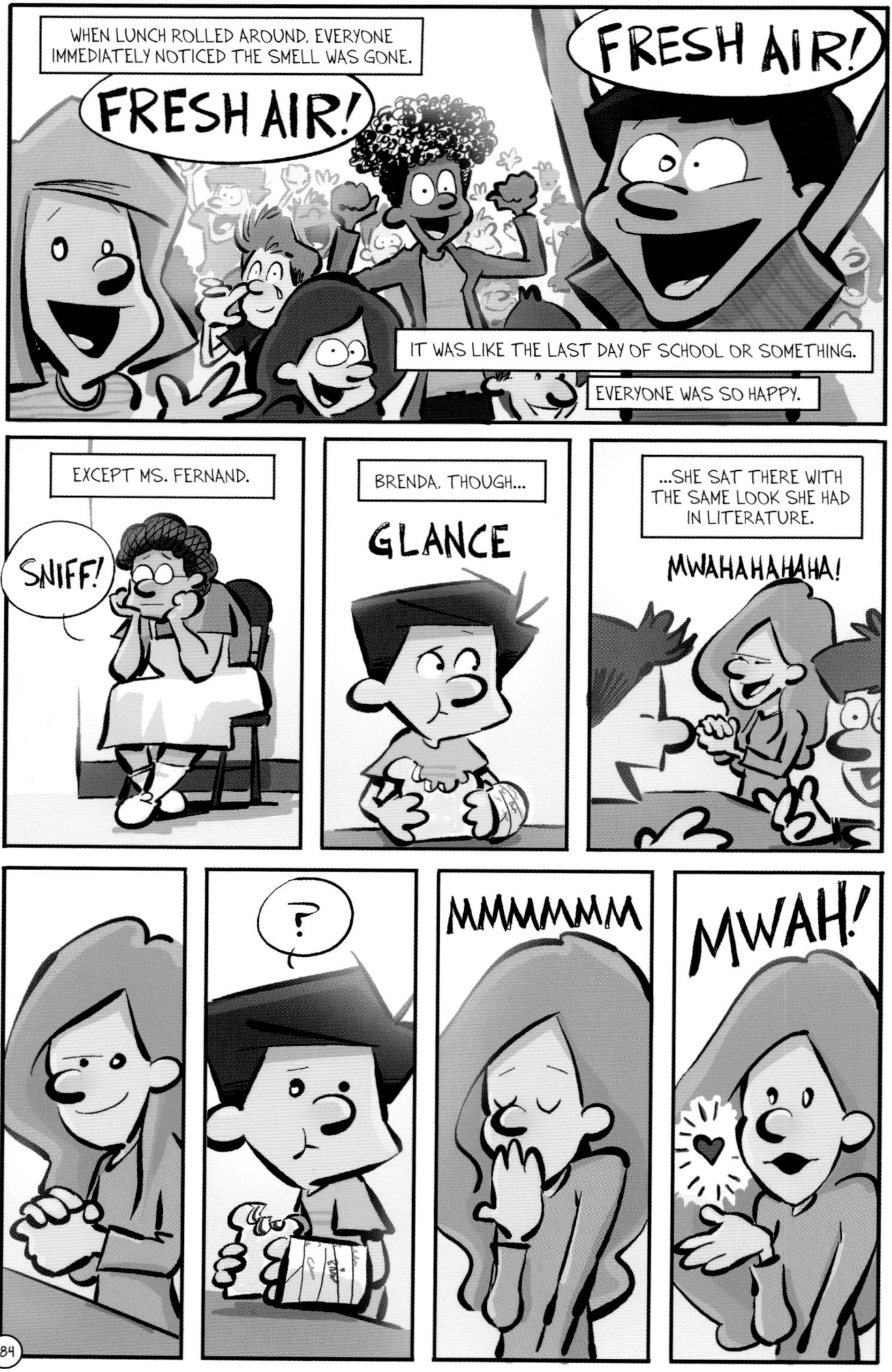
WHEN LUNCH ROLLED AROUND, EVERYONE IMMEDIATELY NOTICED THE SMELL WAS GONE.
FRESH AIR!
FRESH AIR!
IT WAS LIKE THE LAST DAY OF SCHOOL OR SOMETHING.
EVERYONE WAS SO HAPPY.
EXCEPT MS. FERNAND.
SNIFF!
BRENDA, THOUGH...
GLANCE
...SHE SAT THERE WITH THE SAME LOOK SHE HAD IN LITERATURE.
MWAHAHAHAHA!
?
MMMMMM
MWAH!

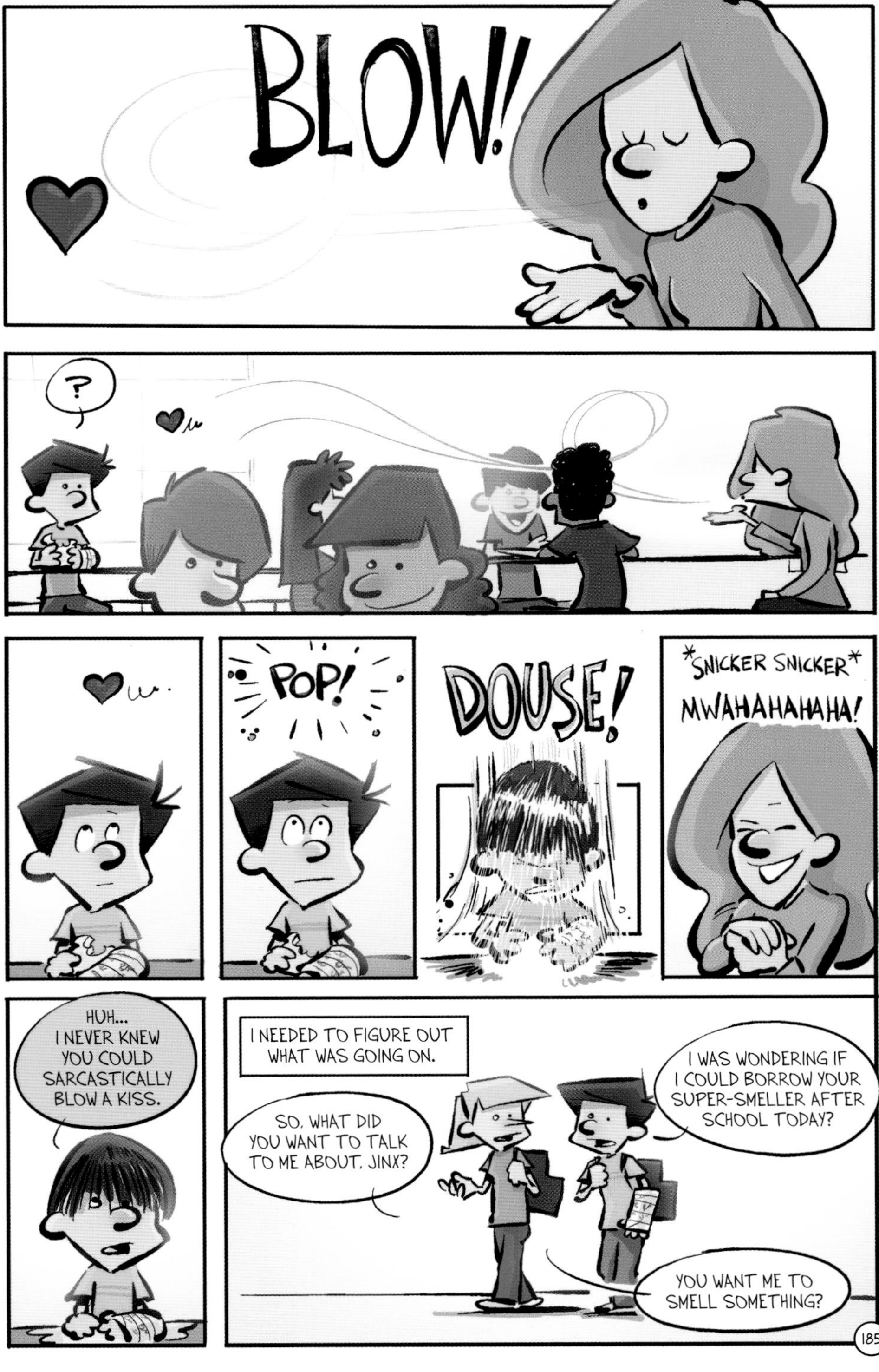
BLOW!
?
POP!
DOUSE!
SNICKER SNICKER
MWAHAHAHAHA!
HUH... I NEVER KNEW YOU COULD SARCASTICALLY BLOW A KISS.
I NEEDED TO FIGURE OUT WHAT WAS GOING ON.
SO, WHAT DID YOU WANT TO TALK TO ME ABOUT, JINX?
I WAS WONDERING IF I COULD BORROW YOUR SUPER-SMELLER AFTER SCHOOL TODAY?
YOU WANT ME TO SMELL SOMETHING?

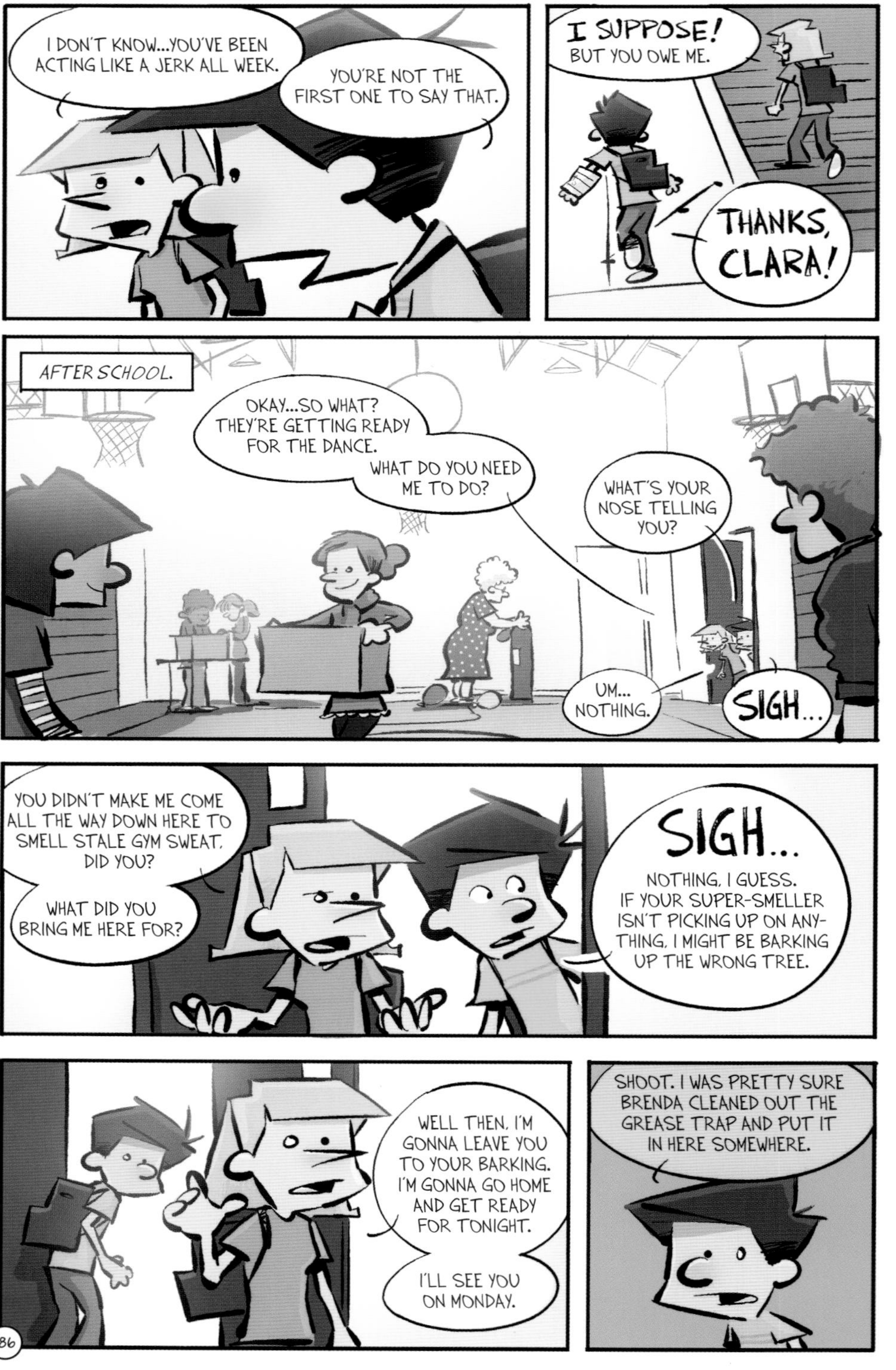
I DON'T KNOW...YOU'VE BEEN ACTING LIKE A JERK ALL WEEK.
YOU'RE NOT THE FIRST ONE TO SAY THAT.
I SUPPOSE! BUT YOU OWE ME.
THANKS, CLARA!
AFTER SCHOOL.
OKAY...SO WHAT? THEY'RE GETTING READY FOR THE DANCE.
WHAT DO YOU NEED ME TO DO?
WHAT'S YOUR NOSE TELLING YOU?
UM... NOTHING.
SIGH...
YOU DIDN'T MAKE ME COME ALL THE WAY DOWN HERE TO SMELL STALE GYM SWEAT, DID YOU?
WHAT DID YOU BRING ME HERE FOR?
SIGH...
NOTHING, I GUESS. IF YOUR SUPER-SMELLER ISN'T PICKING UP ON ANYTHING, I MIGHT BE BARKING UP THE WRONG TREE.
WELL THEN, I'M GONNA LEAVE YOU TO YOUR BARKING. I'M GONNA GO HOME AND GET READY FOR TONIGHT.
I'LL SEE YOU ON MONDAY.
SHOOT. I WAS PRETTY SURE BRENDA CLEANED OUT THE GREASE TRAP AND PUT IT IN HERE SOMEWHERE.

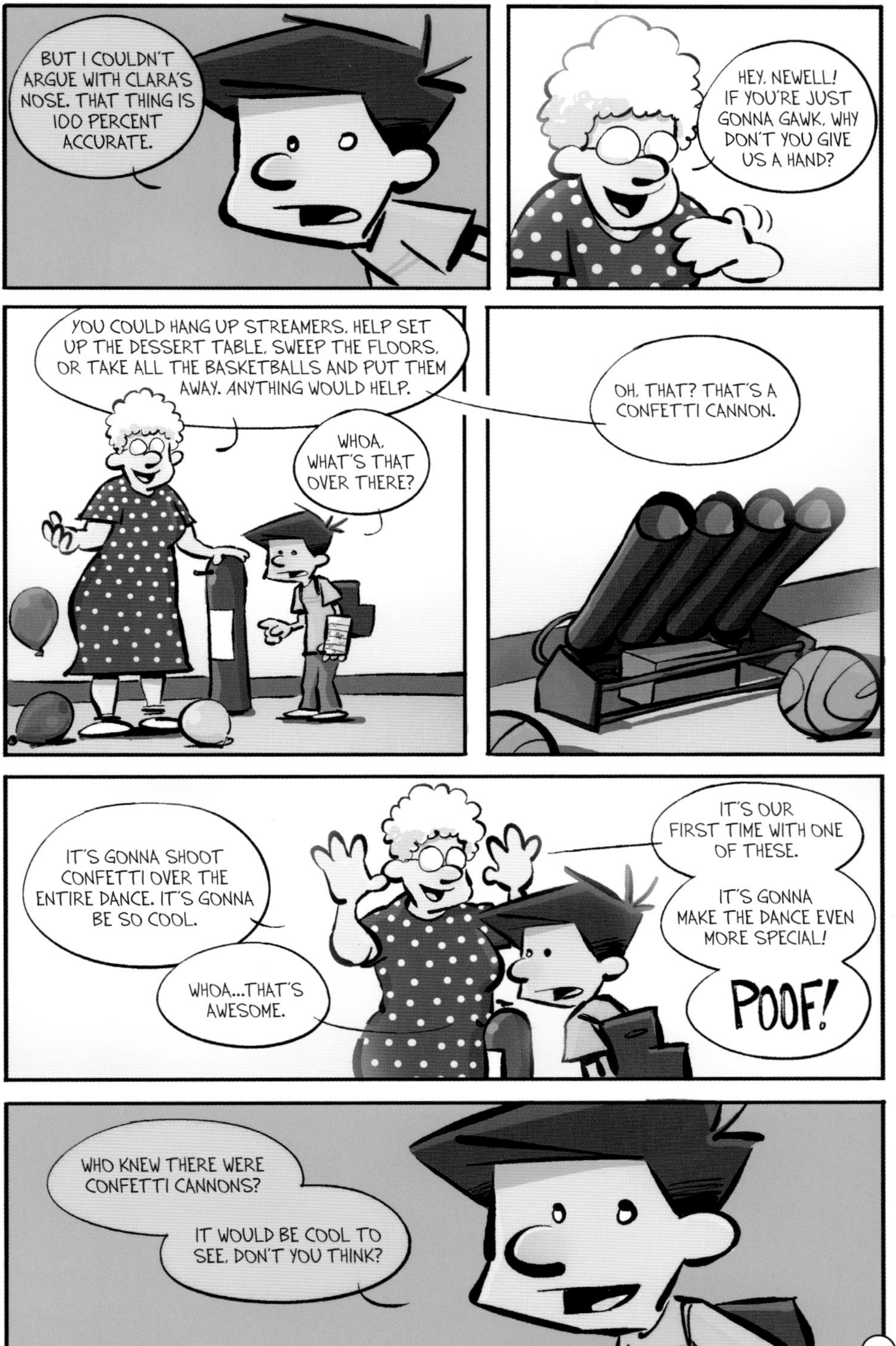

BUT I COULDN'T ARGUE WITH CLARA'S NOSE. THAT THING IS 100 PERCENT ACCURATE.
HEY, NEWELL! IF YOU'RE JUST GONNA GAWK, WHY DON'T YOU GIVE US A HAND?
YOU COULD HANG UP STREAMERS, HELP SET UP THE DESSERT TABLE, SWEEP THE FLOORS, OR TAKE ALL THE BASKETBALLS AND PUT THEM AWAY. ANYTHING WOULD HELP.
WHOA, WHAT'S THAT OVER THERE?
OH, THAT? THAT'S A CONFETTI CANNON.
IT'S GONNA SHOOT CONFETTI OVER THE ENTIRE DANCE. IT'S GONNA BE SO COOL.
WHOA...THAT'S AWESOME.
IT'S OUR FIRST TIME WITH ONE OF THESE.
IT'S GONNA MAKE THE DANCE EVEN MORE SPECIAL!
POOF!
WHO KNEW THERE WERE CONFETTI CANNONS?
IT WOULD BE COOL TO SEE, DON'T YOU THINK?

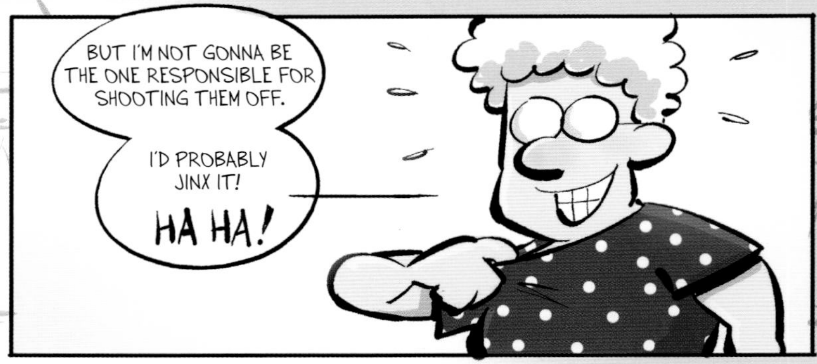
BUT I'M NOT GONNA BE THE ONE RESPONSIBLE FOR SHOOTING THEM OFF.
I'D PROBABLY JINX IT!
HA HA!

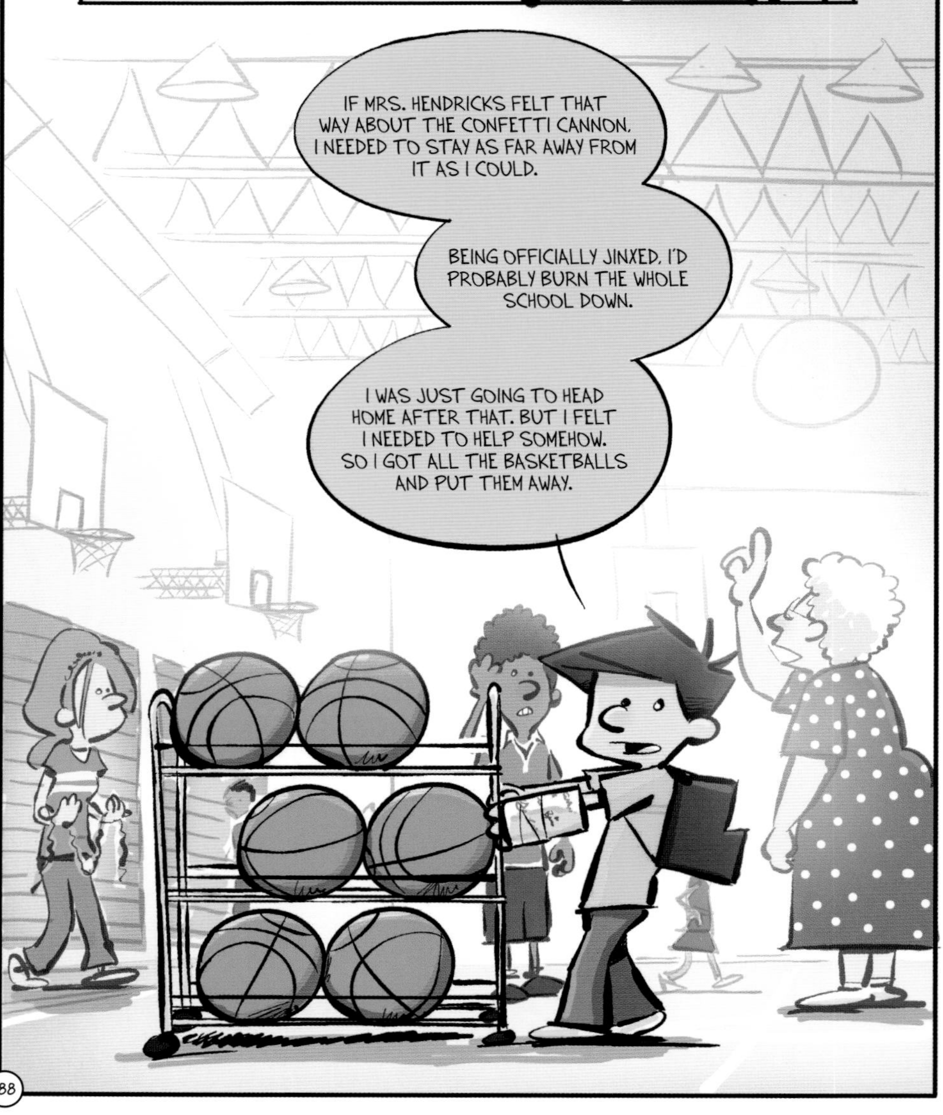
IF MRS. HENDRICKS FELT THAT WAY ABOUT THE CONFETTI CANNON, I NEEDED TO STAY AS FAR AWAY FROM IT AS I COULD.
BEING OFFICIALLY JINXED, I'D PROBABLY BURN THE WHOLE SCHOOL DOWN.
I WAS JUST GOING TO HEAD HOME AFTER THAT. BUT I FELT I NEEDED TO HELP SOMEHOW. SO I GOT ALL THE BASKETBALLS AND PUT THEM AWAY.

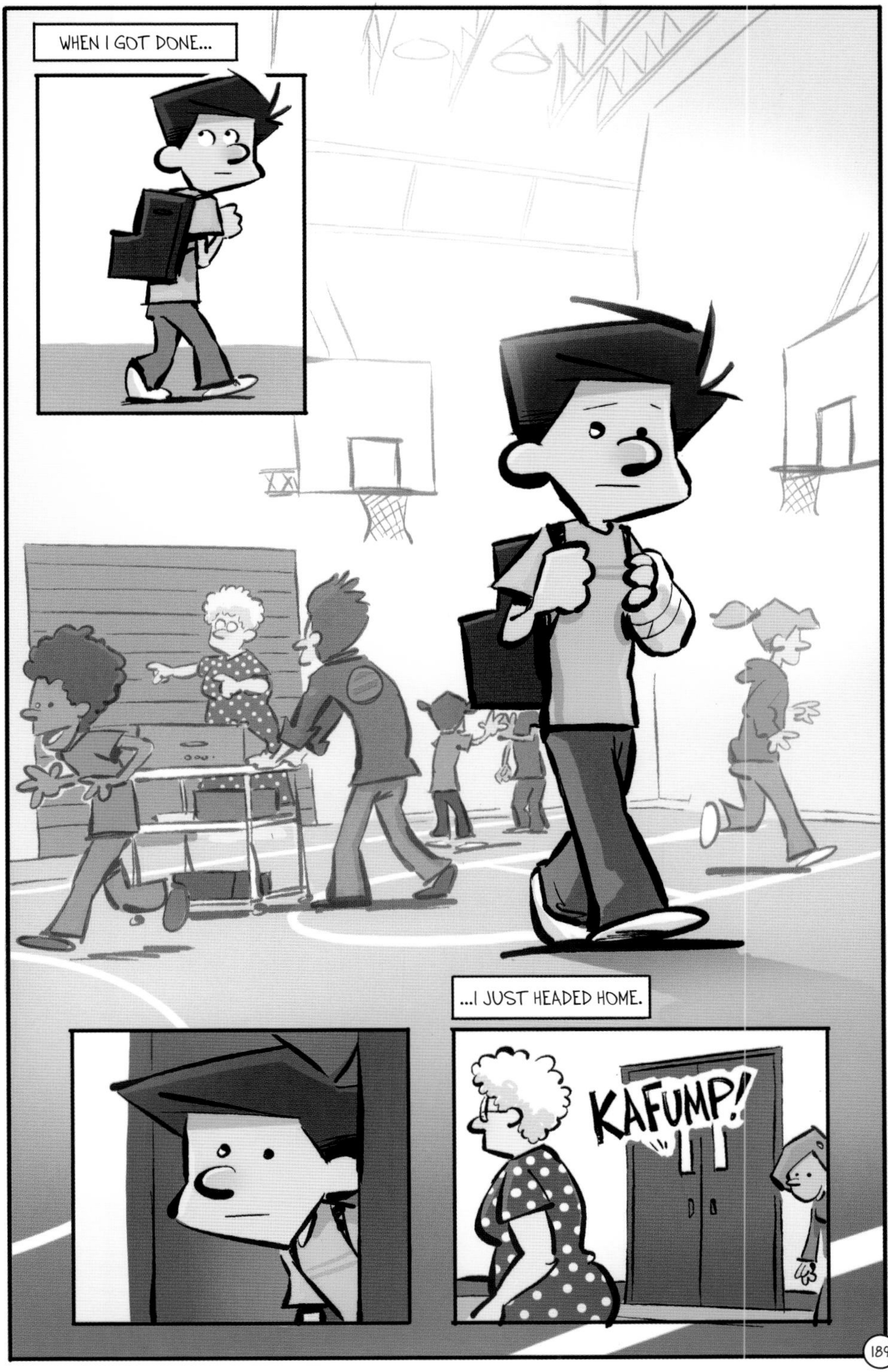
WHEN I GOT DONE...
...I JUST HEADED HOME.
KAFUMP!

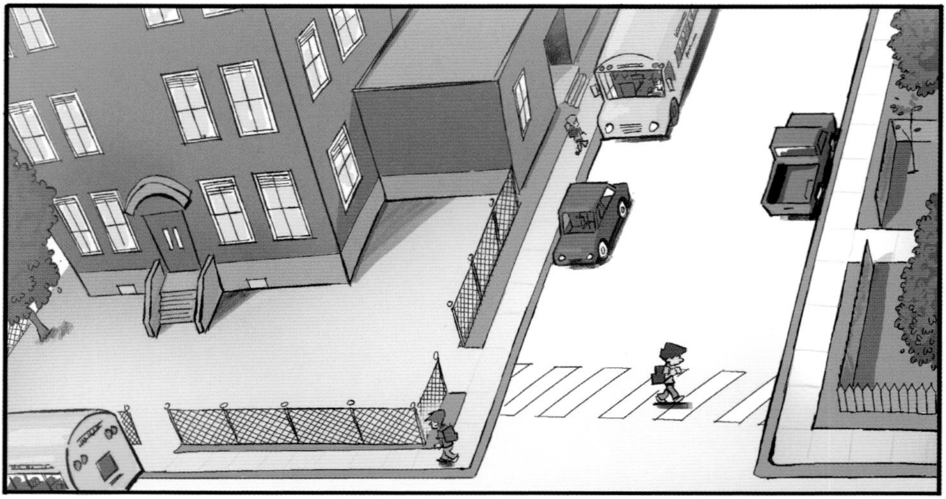

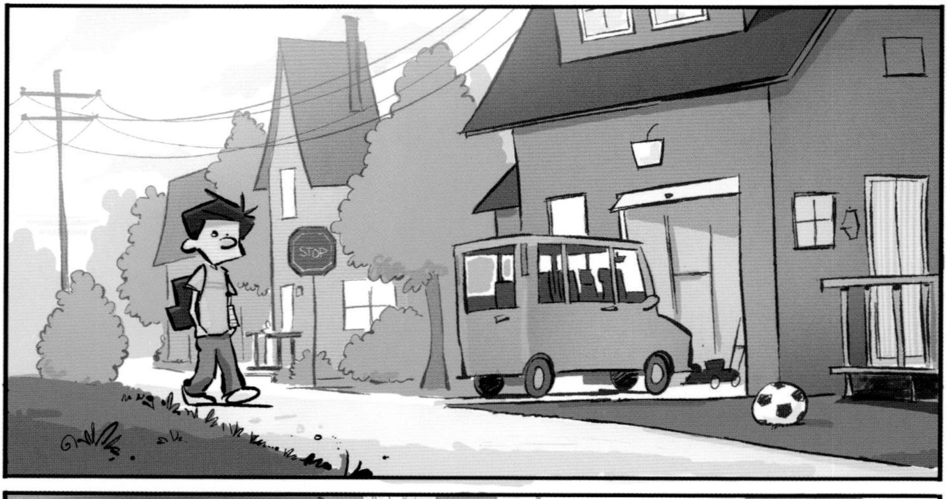
STOP

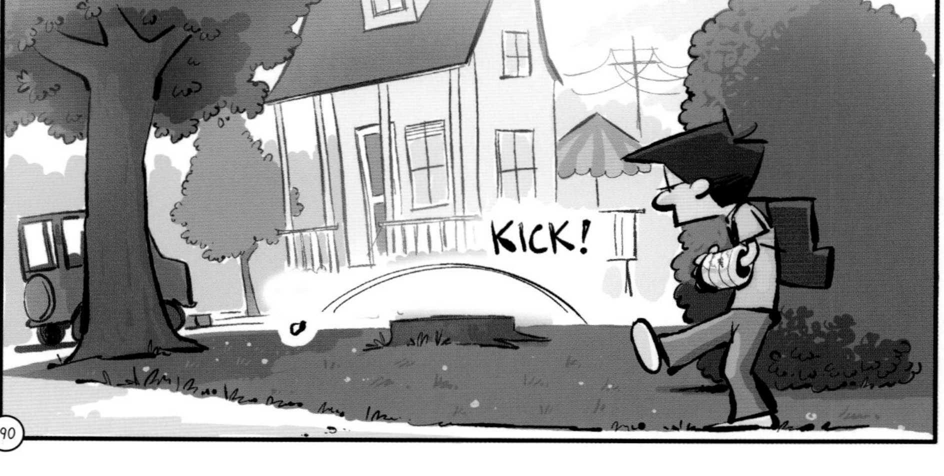
KICK!

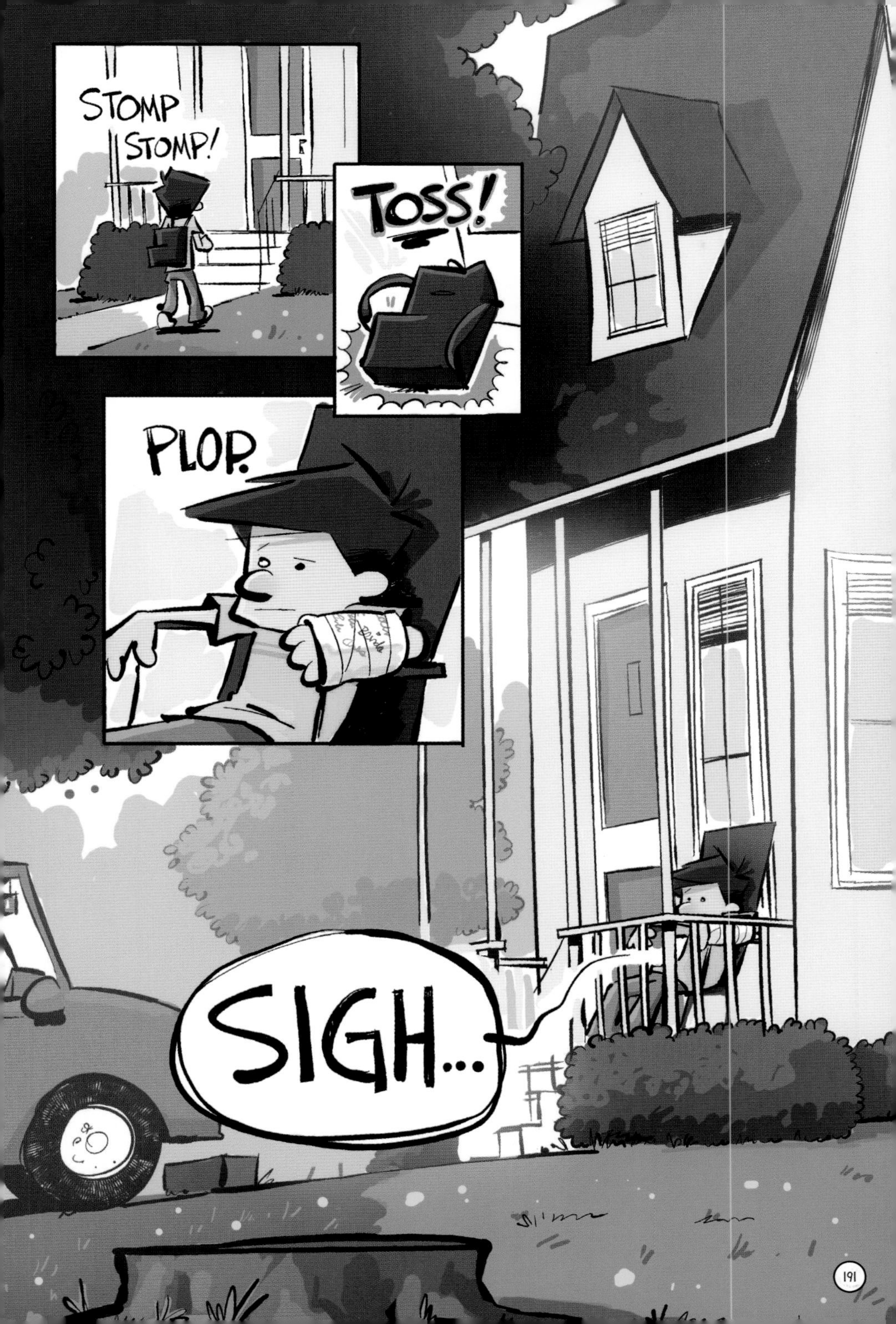
STOMP
STOMP!
TOSS!
PLOP.
SIGH...

CHAPTER TEN
A MESSY REALIZATION

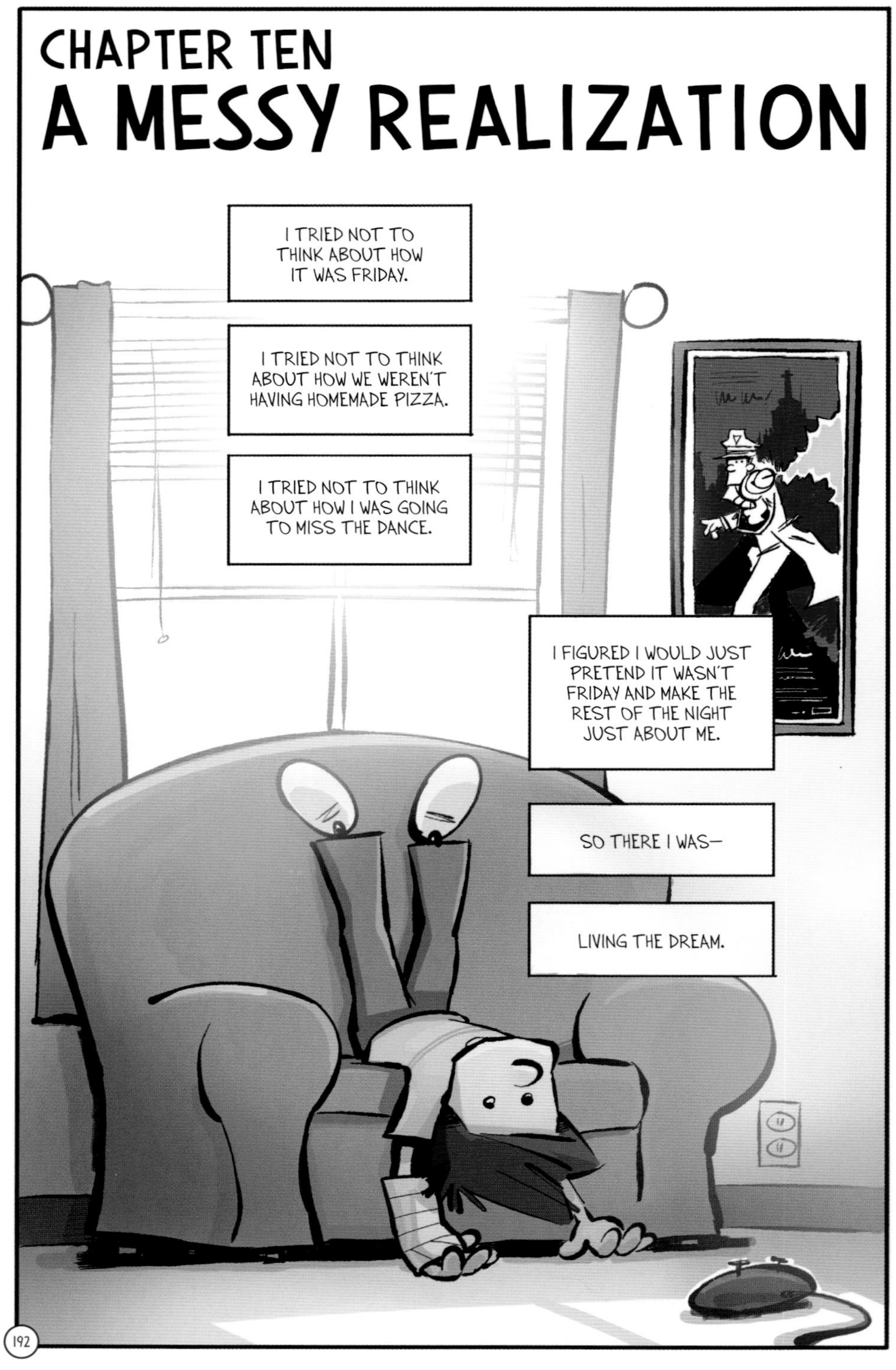
I TRIED NOT TO THINK ABOUT HOW IT WAS FRIDAY.
I TRIED NOT TO THINK ABOUT HOW WE WEREN'T HAVING HOMEMADE PIZZA.
I TRIED NOT TO THINK ABOUT HOW I WAS GOING TO MISS THE DANCE.
I FIGURED I WOULD JUST PRETEND IT WASN'T FRIDAY AND MAKE THE REST OF THE NIGHT JUST ABOUT ME.
SO THERE I WAS—
LIVING THE DREAM.

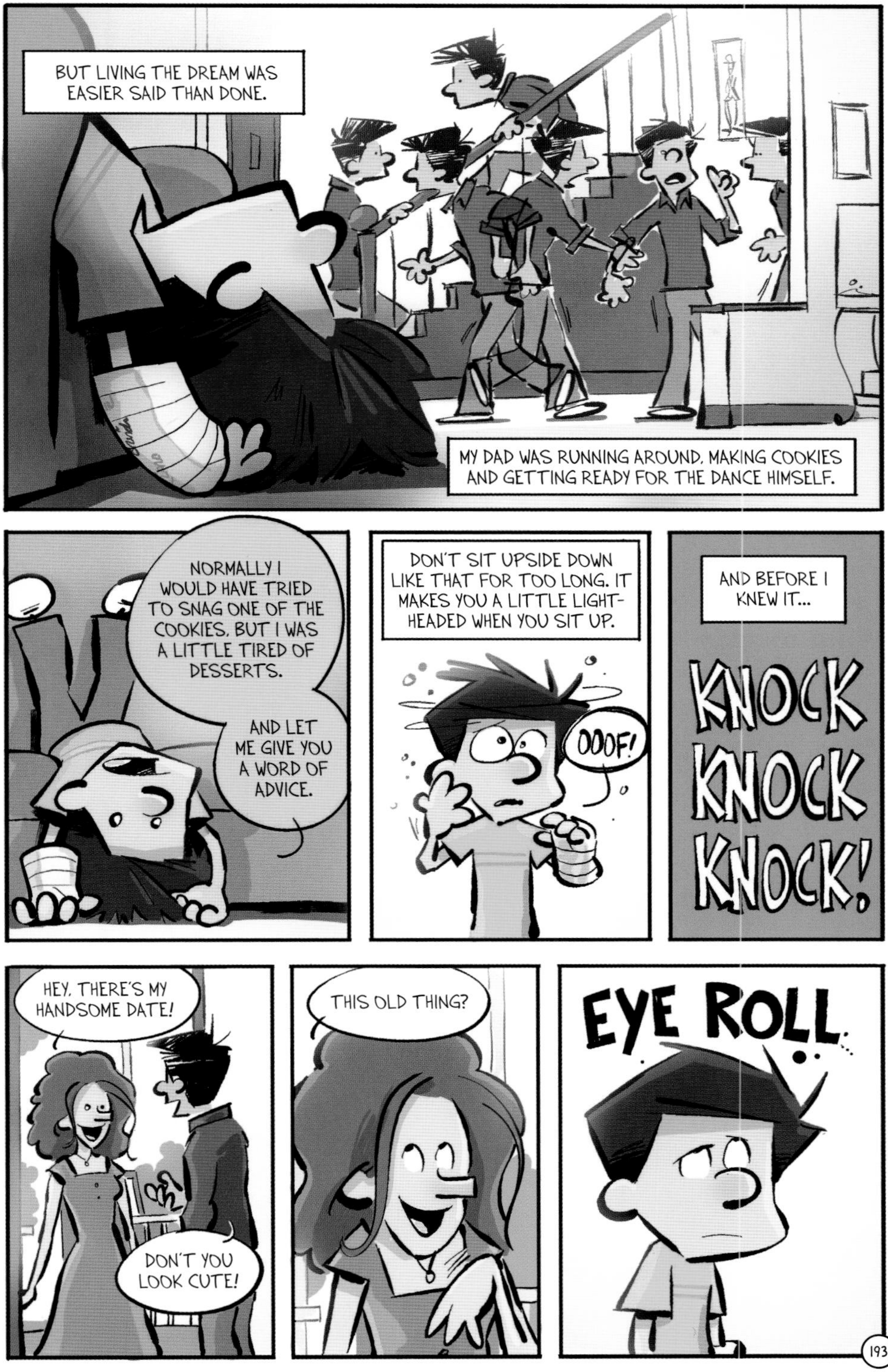

BUT LIVING THE DREAM WAS EASIER SAID THAN DONE.
MY DAD WAS RUNNING AROUND, MAKING COOKIES AND GETTING READY FOR THE DANCE HIMSELF.
NORMALLY I WOULD HAVE TRIED TO SNAG ONE OF THE COOKIES, BUT I WAS A LITTLE TIRED OF DESSERTS.
AND LET ME GIVE YOU A WORD OF ADVICE.
DON'T SIT UPSIDE DOWN LIKE THAT FOR TOO LONG. IT MAKES YOU A LITTLE LIGHT-HEADED WHEN YOU SIT UP.
OOOF!
AND BEFORE I KNEW IT...
KNOCK KNOCK KNOCK!
HEY, THERE'S MY HANDSOME DATE!
DON'T YOU LOOK CUTE!
THIS OLD THING?
EYE ROLL

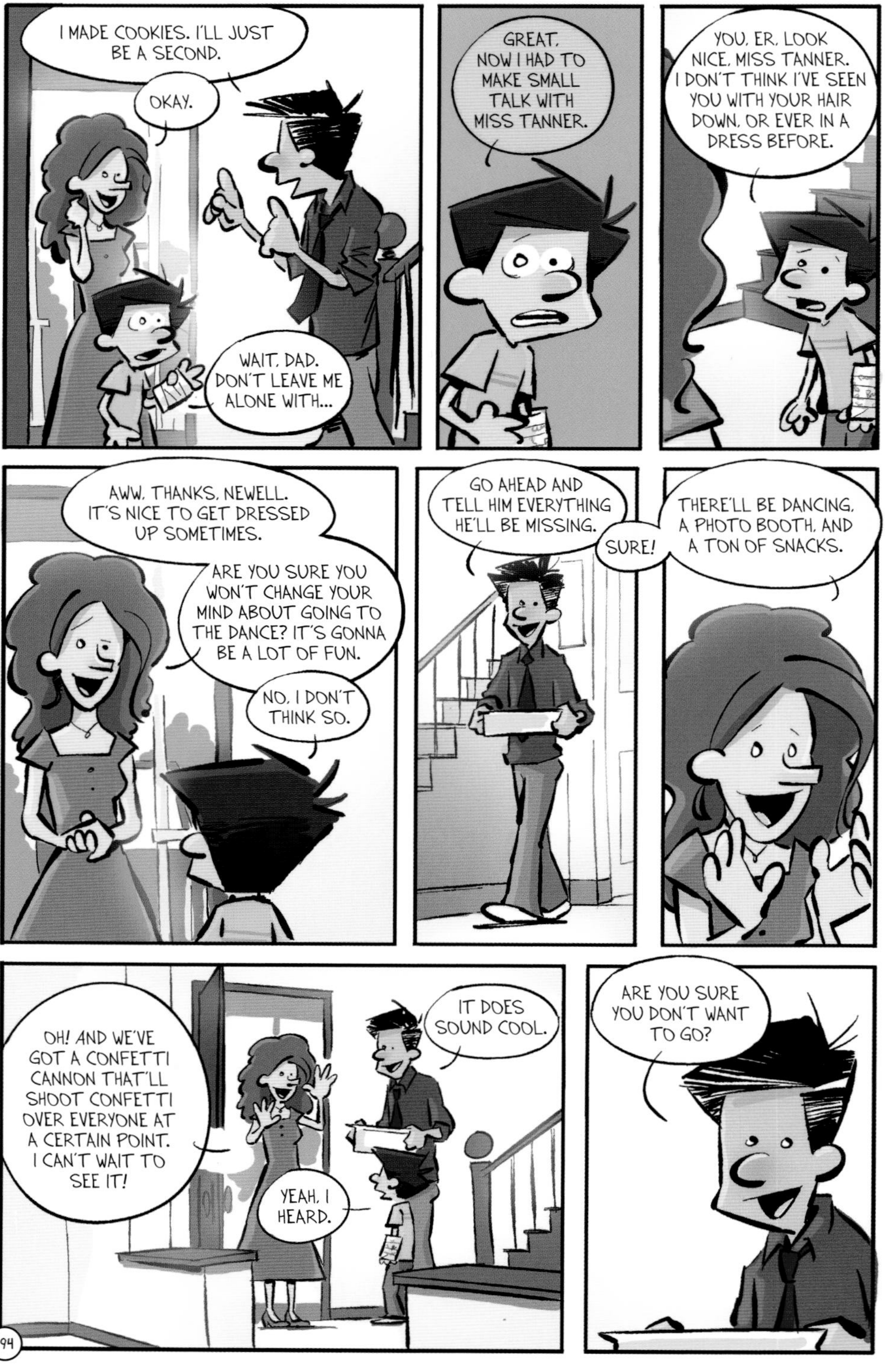
I MADE COOKIES. I'LL JUST BE A SECOND.
OKAY.
WAIT, DAD. DON'T LEAVE ME ALONE WITH...
GREAT, NOW I HAD TO MAKE SMALL TALK WITH MISS TANNER.
YOU, ER, LOOK NICE, MISS TANNER. I DON'T THINK I'VE SEEN YOU WITH YOUR HAIR DOWN, OR EVER IN A DRESS BEFORE.
AWW, THANKS, NEWELL. IT'S NICE TO GET DRESSED UP SOMETIMES.
ARE YOU SURE YOU WON'T CHANGE YOUR MIND ABOUT GOING TO THE DANCE? IT'S GONNA BE A LOT OF FUN.
NO, I DON'T THINK SO.
GO AHEAD AND TELL HIM EVERYTHING HE'LL BE MISSING.
SURE!
THERE'LL BE DANCING, A PHOTO BOOTH, AND A TON OF SNACKS.
OH! AND WE'VE GOT A CONFETTI CANNON THAT'LL SHOOT CONFETTI OVER EVERYONE AT A CERTAIN POINT. I CAN'T WAIT TO SEE IT!
IT DOES SOUND COOL.
YEAH, I HEARD.
ARE YOU SURE YOU DON'T WANT TO GO?

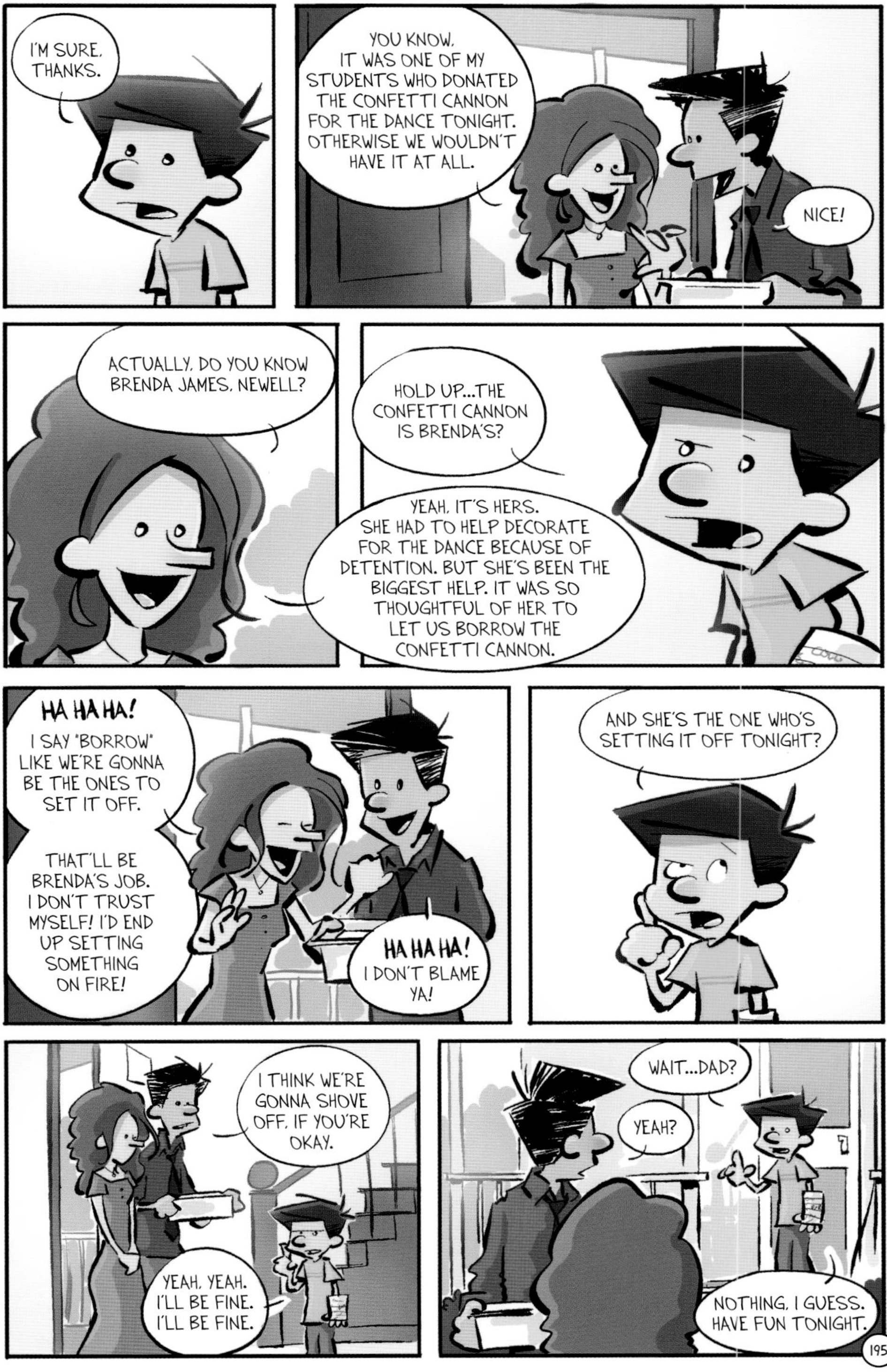
I'M SURE. THANKS.
YOU KNOW, IT WAS ONE OF MY STUDENTS WHO DONATED THE CONFETTI CANNON FOR THE DANCE TONIGHT. OTHERWISE WE WOULDN'T HAVE IT AT ALL.
NICE!
ACTUALLY, DO YOU KNOW BRENDA JAMES, NEWELL?
HOLD UP...THE CONFETTI CANNON IS BRENDA'S?
YEAH, IT'S HERS. SHE HAD TO HELP DECORATE FOR THE DANCE BECAUSE OF DETENTION. BUT SHE'S BEEN THE BIGGEST HELP. IT WAS SO THOUGHTFUL OF HER TO LET US BORROW THE CONFETTI CANNON.
HA HA HA! I SAY "BORROW" LIKE WE'RE GONNA BE THE ONES TO SET IT OFF.
THAT'LL BE BRENDA'S JOB. I DON'T TRUST MYSELF! I'D END UP SETTING SOMETHING ON FIRE!
HA HA HA! I DON'T BLAME YA!
AND SHE'S THE ONE WHO'S SETTING IT OFF TONIGHT?
I THINK WE'RE GONNA SHOVE OFF, IF YOU'RE OKAY.
YEAH, YEAH. I'LL BE FINE. I'LL BE FINE.
WAIT...DAD?
YEAH?
NOTHING, I GUESS. HAVE FUN TONIGHT.

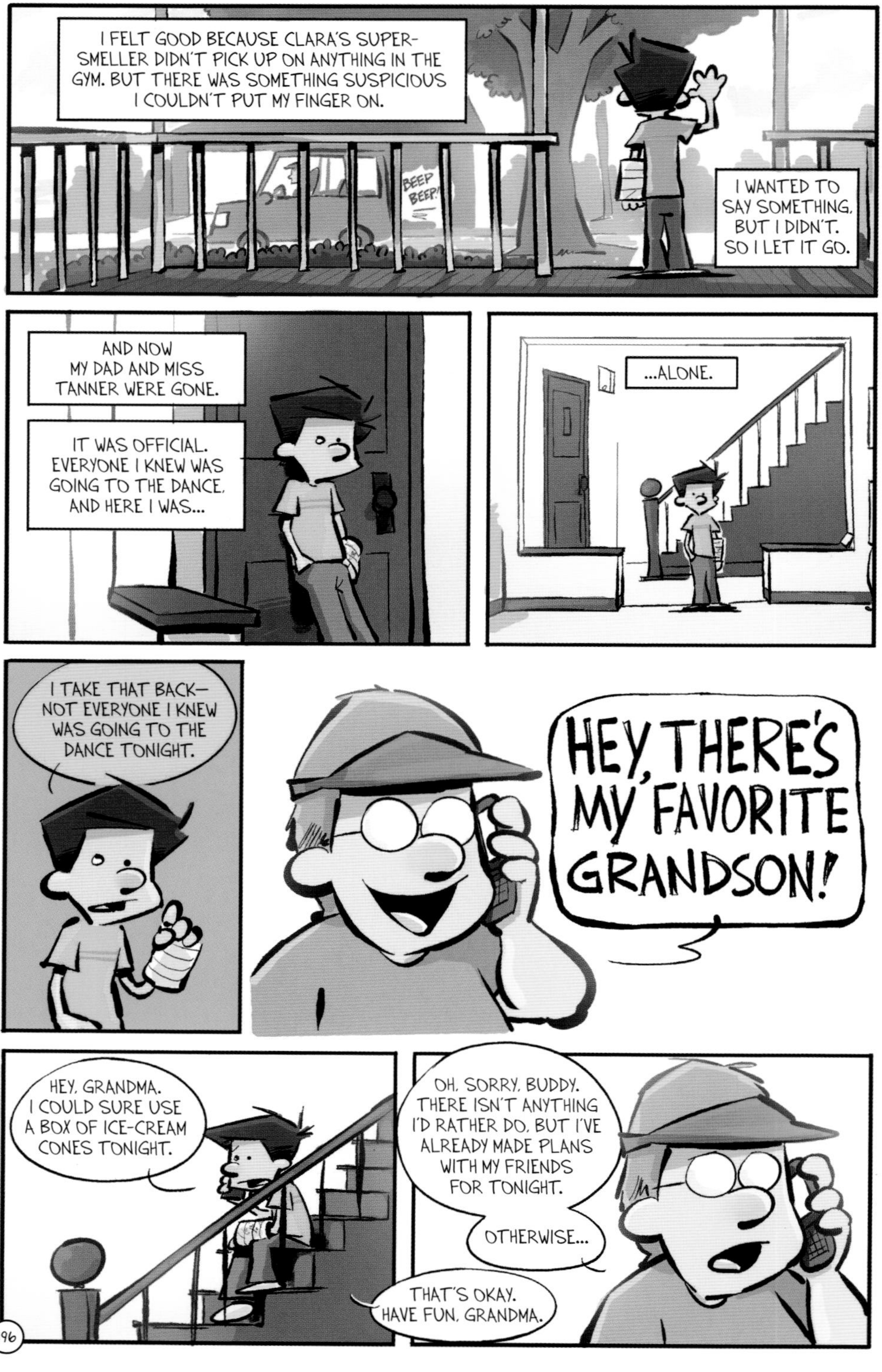
I FELT GOOD BECAUSE CLARA'S SUPER-SMELLER DIDN'T PICK UP ON ANYTHING IN THE GYM. BUT THERE WAS SOMETHING SUSPICIOUS I COULDN'T PUT MY FINGER ON.
BEEP BEEP!
I WANTED TO SAY SOMETHING, BUT I DIDN'T. SO I LET IT GO.
AND NOW MY DAD AND MISS TANNER WERE GONE.
IT WAS OFFICIAL. EVERYONE I KNEW WAS GOING TO THE DANCE, AND HERE I WAS...
...ALONE.
I TAKE THAT BACK— NOT EVERYONE I KNEW WAS GOING TO THE DANCE TONIGHT.
HEY, THERE'S MY FAVORITE GRANDSON!
HEY, GRANDMA. I COULD SURE USE A BOX OF ICE-CREAM CONES TONIGHT.
OH, SORRY, BUDDY. THERE ISN'T ANYTHING I'D RATHER DO, BUT I'VE ALREADY MADE PLANS WITH MY FRIENDS FOR TONIGHT.
OTHERWISE...
THAT'S OKAY. HAVE FUN, GRANDMA.

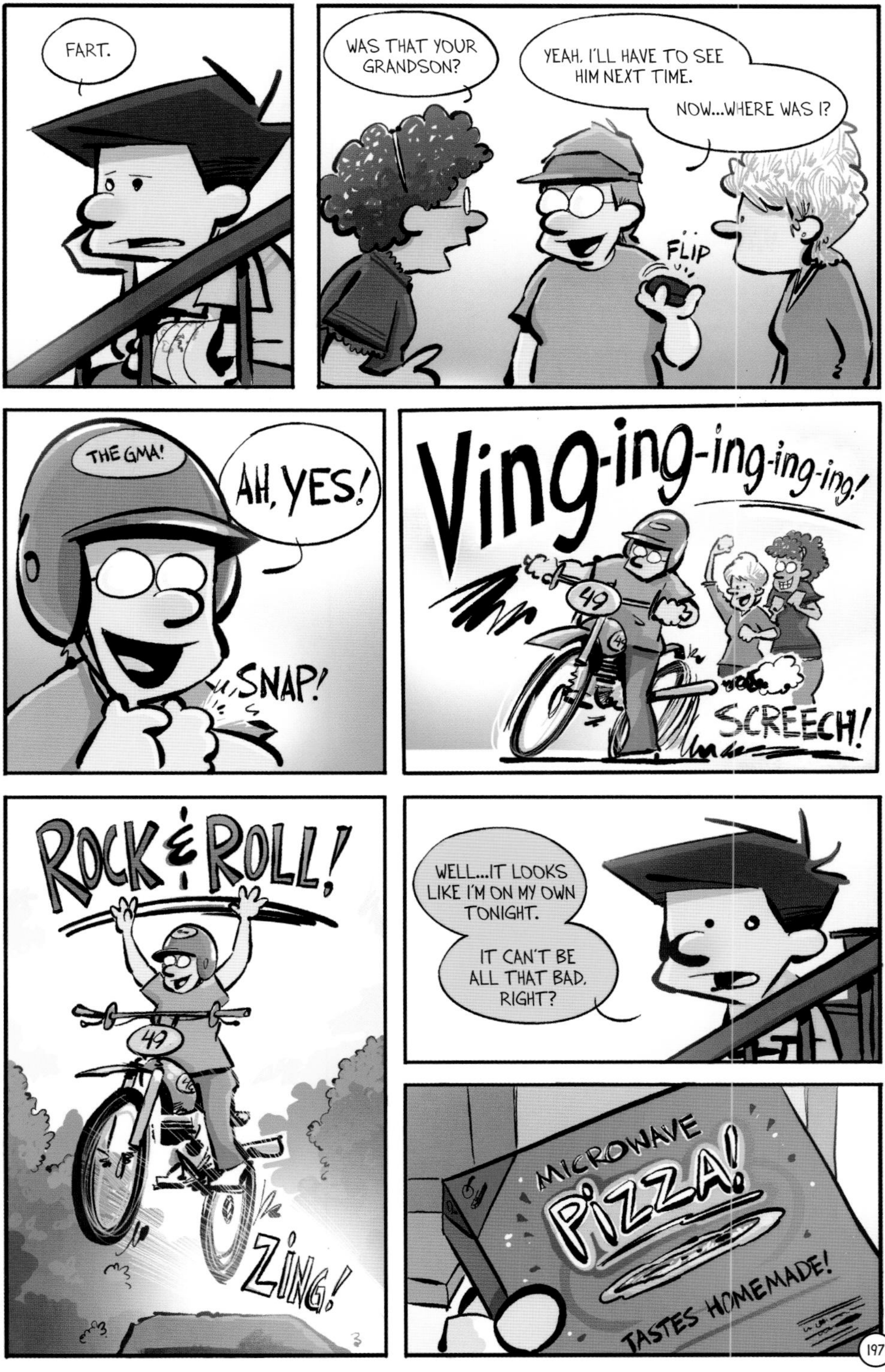
FART.
WAS THAT YOUR GRANDSON?
YEAH, I'LL HAVE TO SEE HIM NEXT TIME.
NOW...WHERE WAS I?
FLIP
THE GMA!
AH, YES!
SNAP!
Ving-ing-ing-ing-ing!
SCREECH!
ROCK & ROLL!
ZING!
WELL...IT LOOKS LIKE I'M ON MY OWN TONIGHT.
IT CAN'T BE ALL THAT BAD, RIGHT?
MICROWAVE PIZZA!
TASTES HOMEMADE!

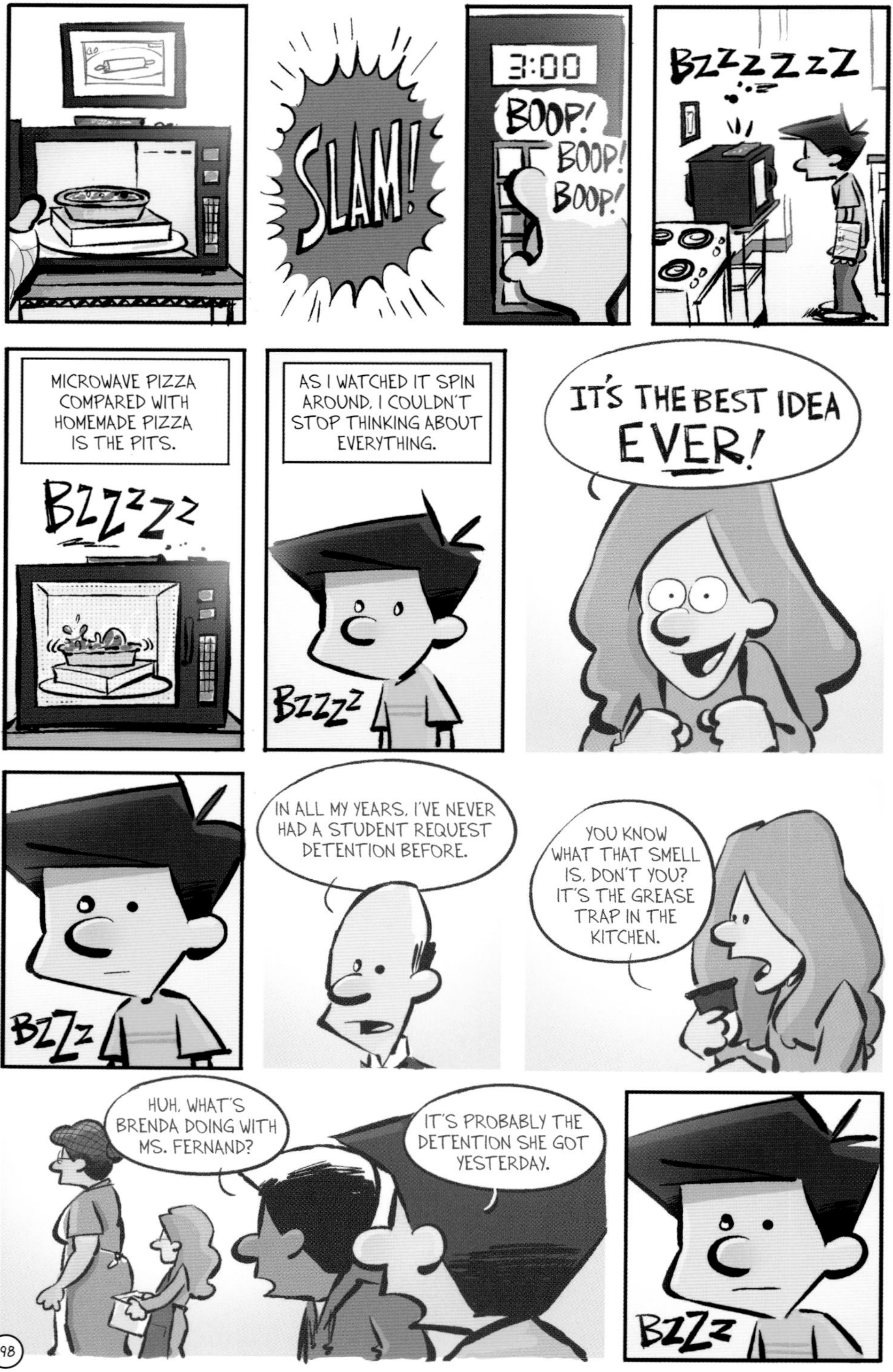
SLAM!
3:00
BOOP!
BOOP!
BOOP!
BZZZZZZ
MICROWAVE PIZZA COMPARED WITH HOMEMADE PIZZA IS THE PITS.
BZZZZZ
AS I WATCHED IT SPIN AROUND, I COULDN'T STOP THINKING ABOUT EVERYTHING.
BZZZZ
IT'S THE BEST IDEA EVER!
BZZZ
IN ALL MY YEARS, I'VE NEVER HAD A STUDENT REQUEST DETENTION BEFORE.
YOU KNOW WHAT THAT SMELL IS, DON'T YOU? IT'S THE GREASE TRAP IN THE KITCHEN.
HUH, WHAT'S BRENDA DOING WITH MS. FERNAND?
IT'S PROBABLY THE DETENTION SHE GOT YESTERDAY.
BZZZ

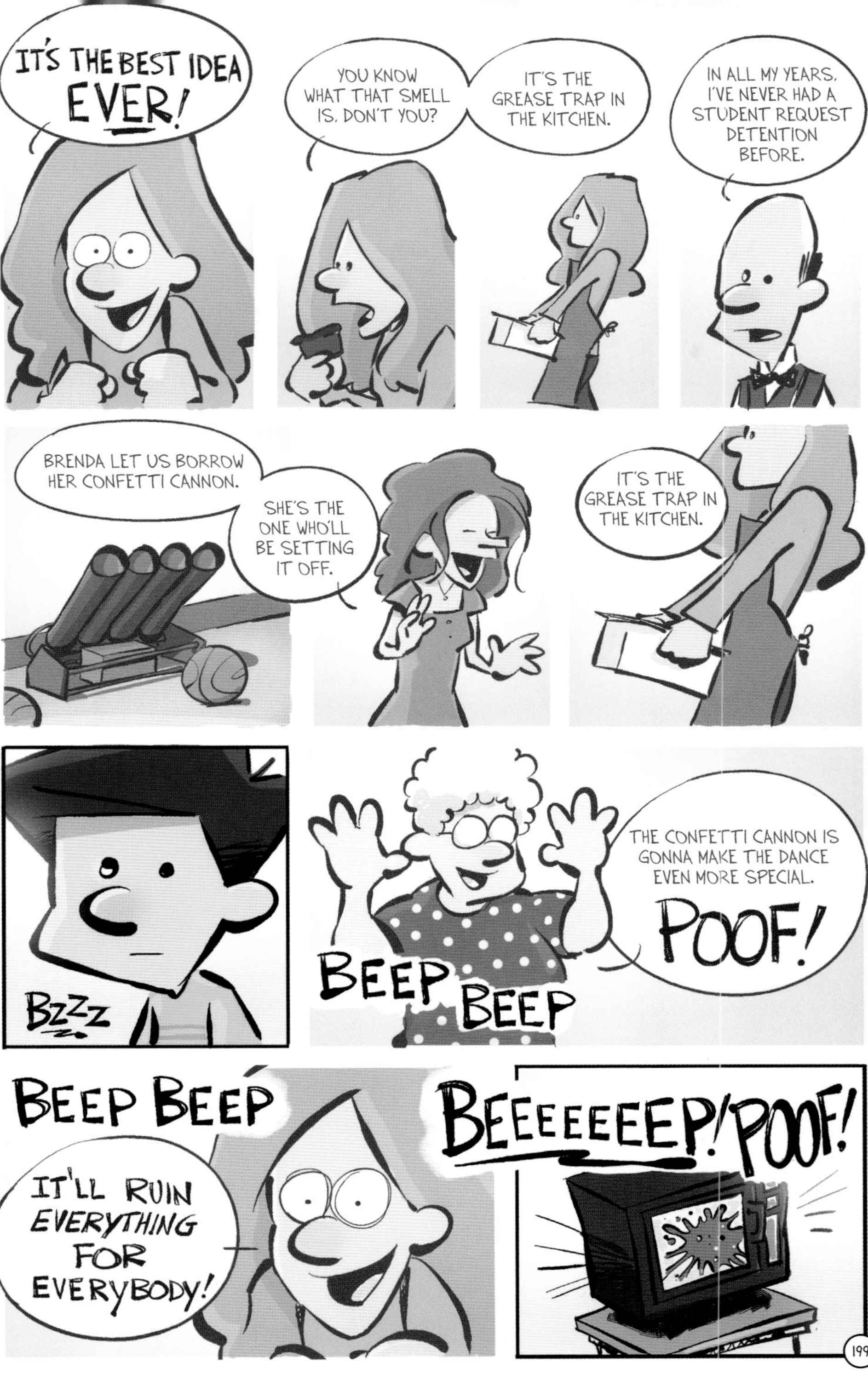

IT'S THE BEST IDEA EVER!
YOU KNOW WHAT THAT SMELL IS, DON'T YOU?
IT'S THE GREASE TRAP IN THE KITCHEN.
IN ALL MY YEARS, I'VE NEVER HAD A STUDENT REQUEST DETENTION BEFORE.
BRENDA LET US BORROW HER CONFETTI CANNON.
SHE'S THE ONE WHO'LL BE SETTING IT OFF.
IT'S THE GREASE TRAP IN THE KITCHEN.
BZZZ
BEEP BEEP
THE CONFETTI CANNON IS GONNA MAKE THE DANCE EVEN MORE SPECIAL.
POOF!
BEEP BEEP
IT'LL RUIN EVERYTHING FOR EVERYBODY!
BEEEEEEEEP! POOF!

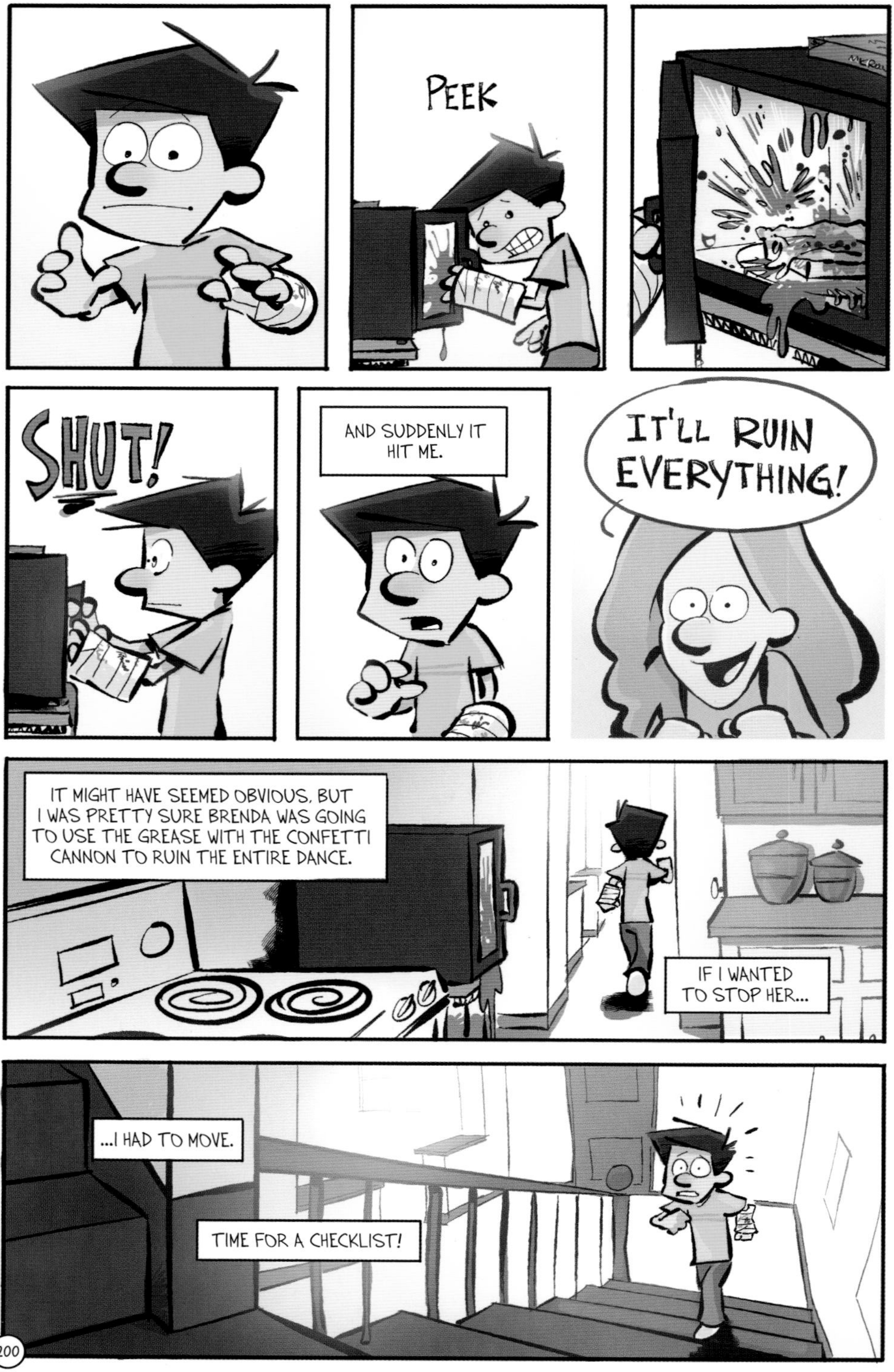
PEEK
SHUT!
AND SUDDENLY IT HIT ME.
IT'LL RUIN EVERYTHING!
IT MIGHT HAVE SEEMED OBVIOUS, BUT I WAS PRETTY SURE BRENDA WAS GOING TO USE THE GREASE WITH THE CONFETTI CANNON TO RUIN THE ENTIRE DANCE.
IF I WANTED TO STOP HER...
...I HAD TO MOVE.
TIME FOR A CHECKLIST!

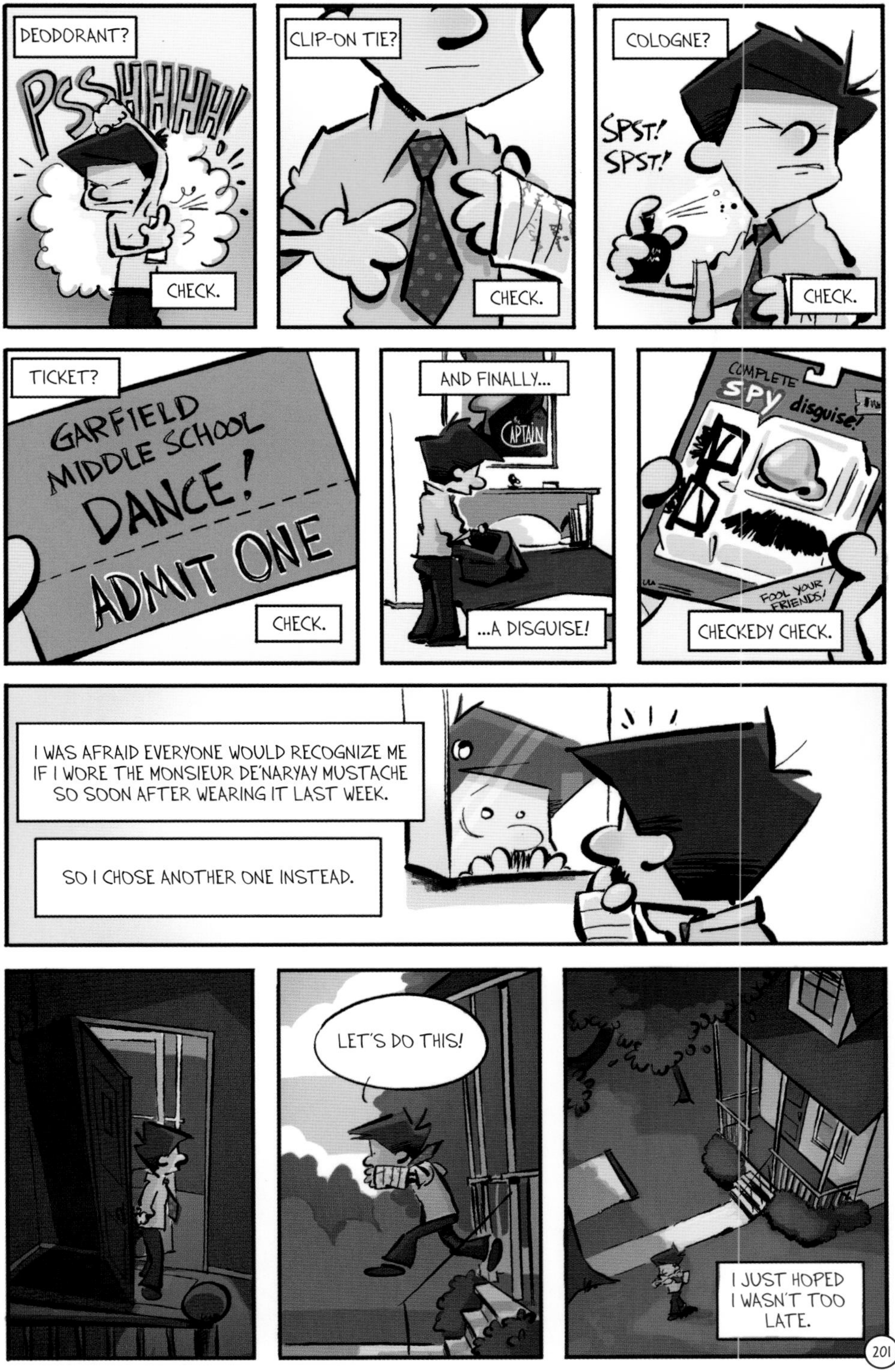
DEODORANT?
PSSHHHH!
CHECK.
CLIP-ON TIE?
CHECK.
COLOGNE?
SPST! SPST!
CHECK.
TICKET?
GARFIELD MIDDLE SCHOOL DANCE!
ADMIT ONE
CHECK.
AND FINALLY...
CAPTAIN
...A DISGUISE!
COMPLETE SPY disguise!
FOOL YOUR FRIENDS!
CHECKEDY CHECK.
I WAS AFRAID EVERYONE WOULD RECOGNIZE ME IF I WORE THE MONSIEUR DE'NARYAY MUSTACHE SO SOON AFTER WEARING IT LAST WEEK.
SO I CHOSE ANOTHER ONE INSTEAD.
LET'S DO THIS!
I JUST HOPED I WASN'T TOO LATE.

CHAPTER ELEVEN
THE DANCE

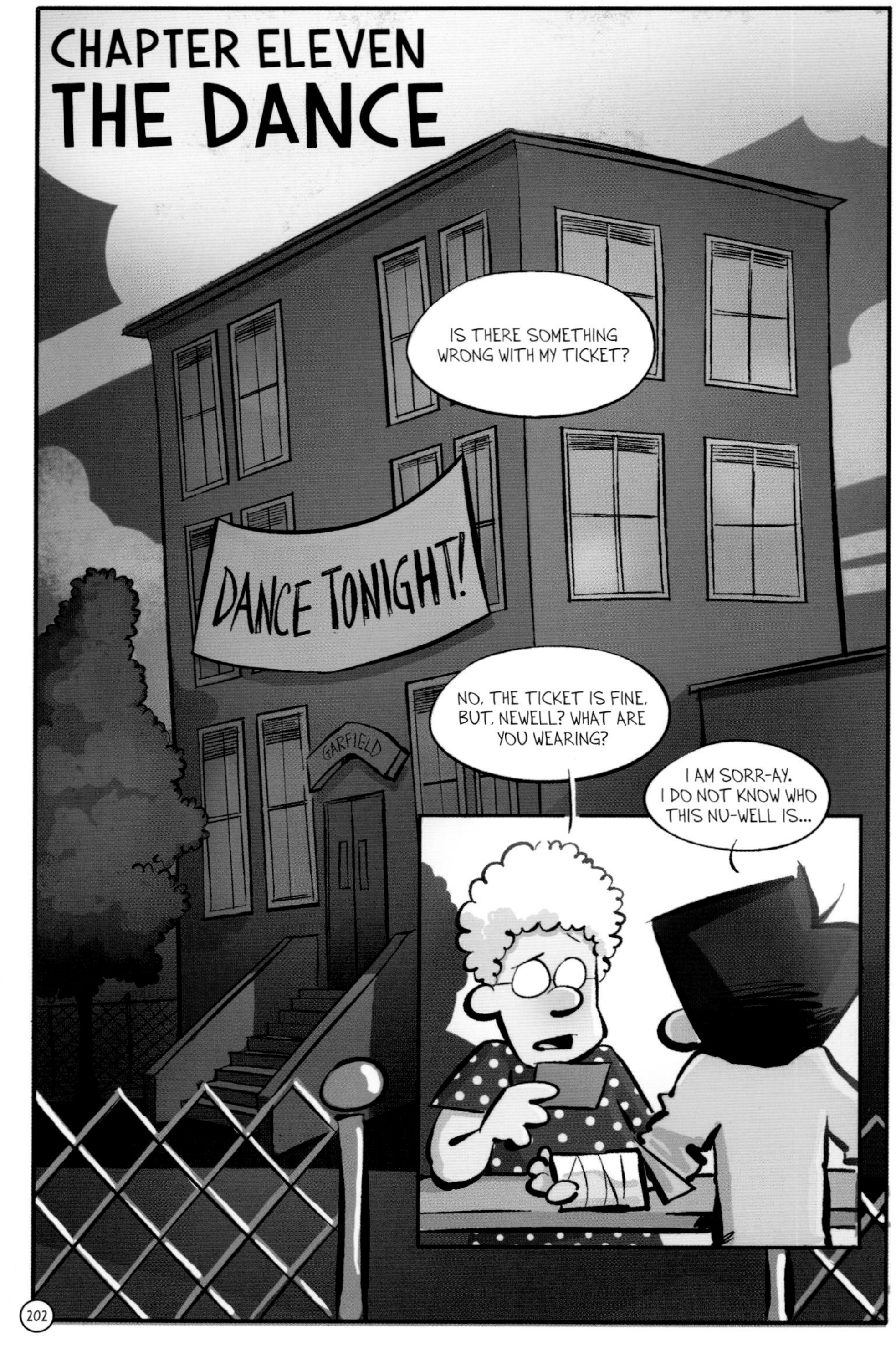
IS THERE SOMETHING WRONG WITH MY TICKET?
DANCE TONIGHT!
GARFIELD
NO, THE TICKET IS FINE, BUT, NEWELL? WHAT ARE YOU WEARING?
I AM SORR-AY. I DO NOT KNOW WHO THIS NU-WELL IS...

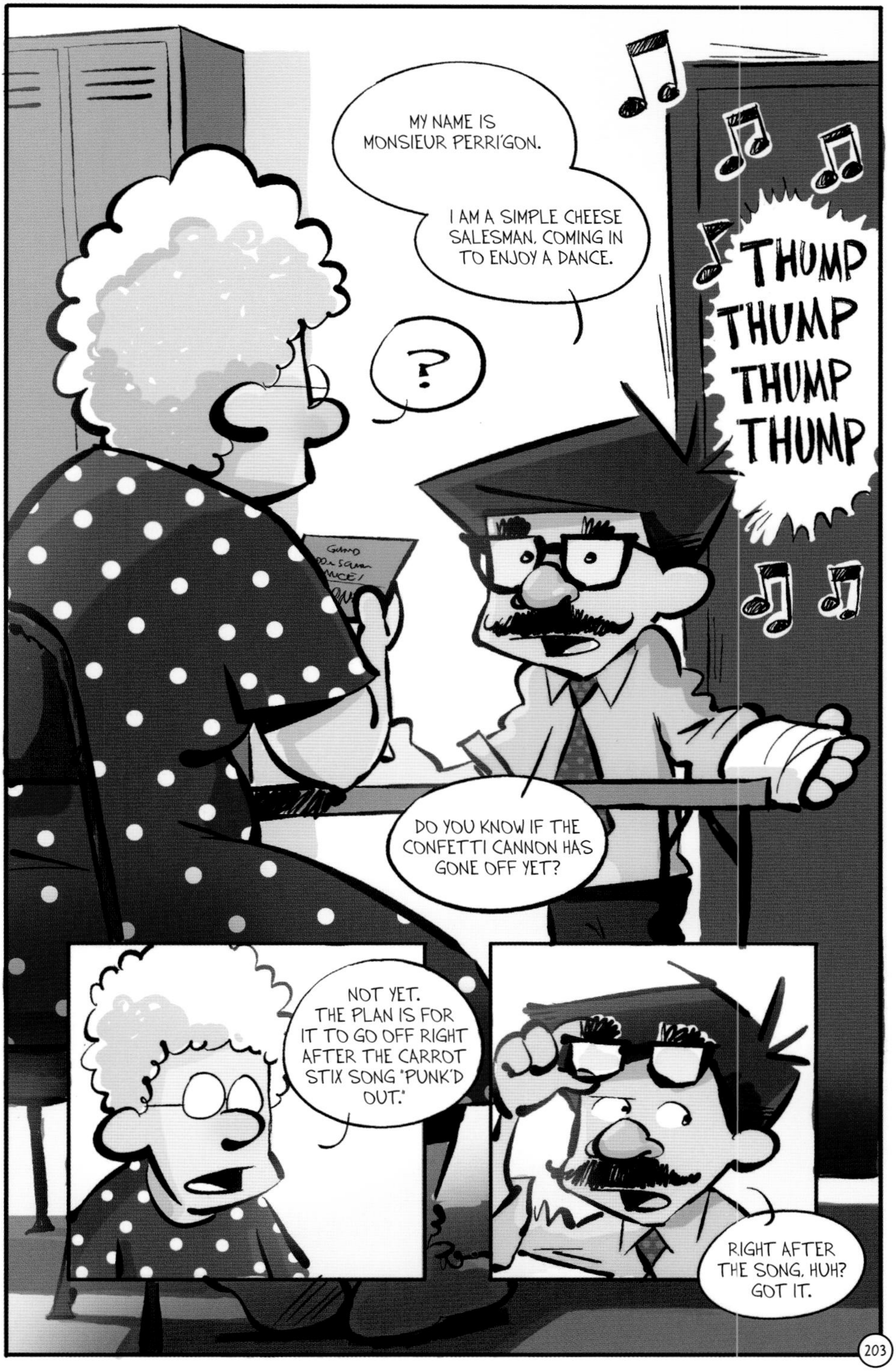
MY NAME IS MONSIEUR PERRI'GON.
I AM A SIMPLE CHEESE SALESMAN, COMING IN TO ENJOY A DANCE.
?
THUMP THUMP THUMP THUMP
DO YOU KNOW IF THE CONFETTI CANNON HAS GONE OFF YET?
NOT YET. THE PLAN IS FOR IT TO GO OFF RIGHT AFTER THE CARROT STIX SONG "PUNK'D OUT."
RIGHT AFTER THE SONG, HUH? GOT IT.

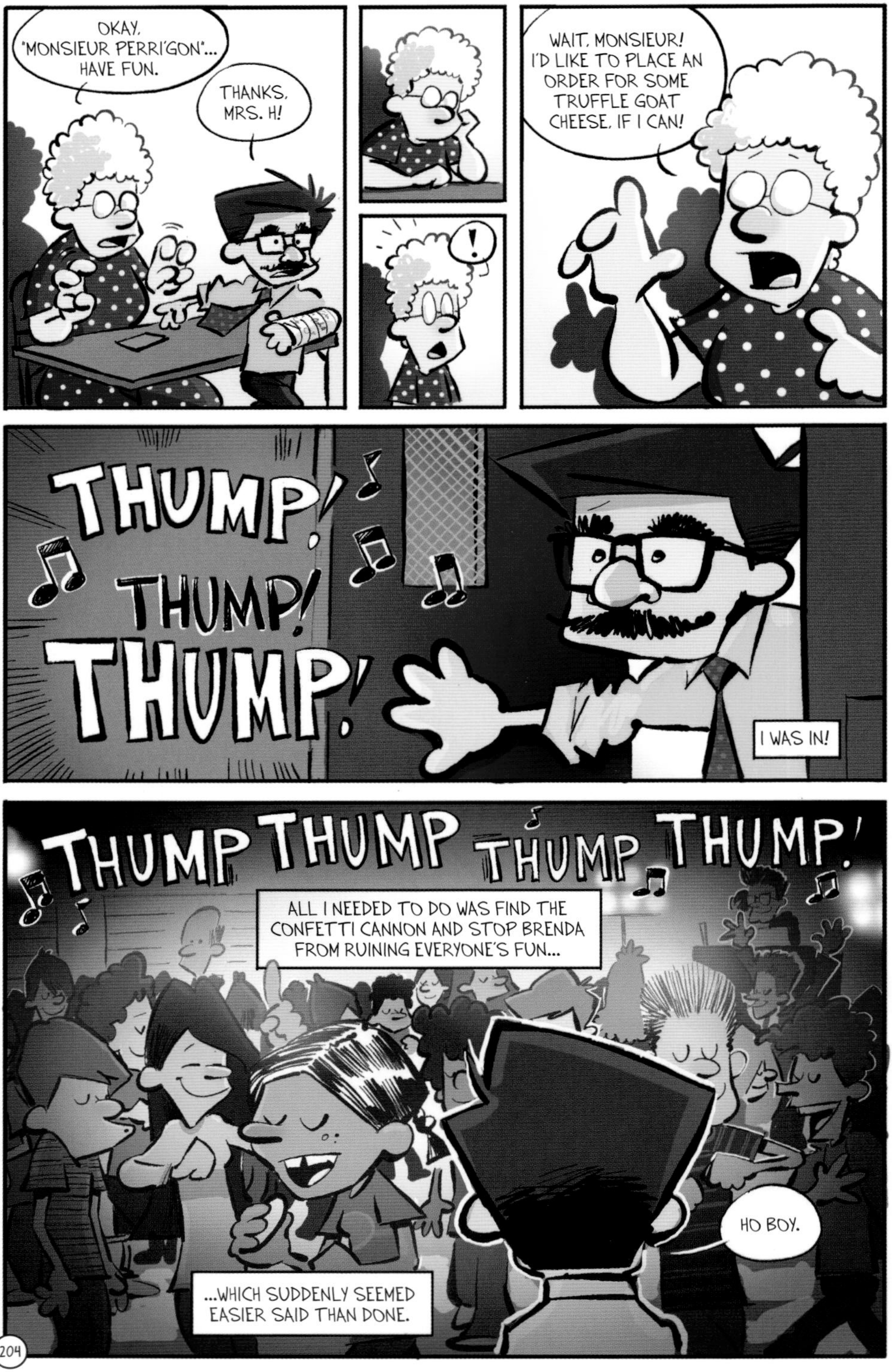
OKAY, "MONSIEUR PERRI'GON"... HAVE FUN.
THANKS, MRS. H!
!
WAIT, MONSIEUR! I'D LIKE TO PLACE AN ORDER FOR SOME TRUFFLE GOAT CHEESE, IF I CAN!
THUMP! THUMP! THUMP!
I WAS IN!
THUMP THUMP THUMP THUMP!
ALL I NEEDED TO DO WAS FIND THE CONFETTI CANNON AND STOP BRENDA FROM RUINING EVERYONE'S FUN...
HO BOY.
...WHICH SUDDENLY SEEMED EASIER SAID THAN DONE.

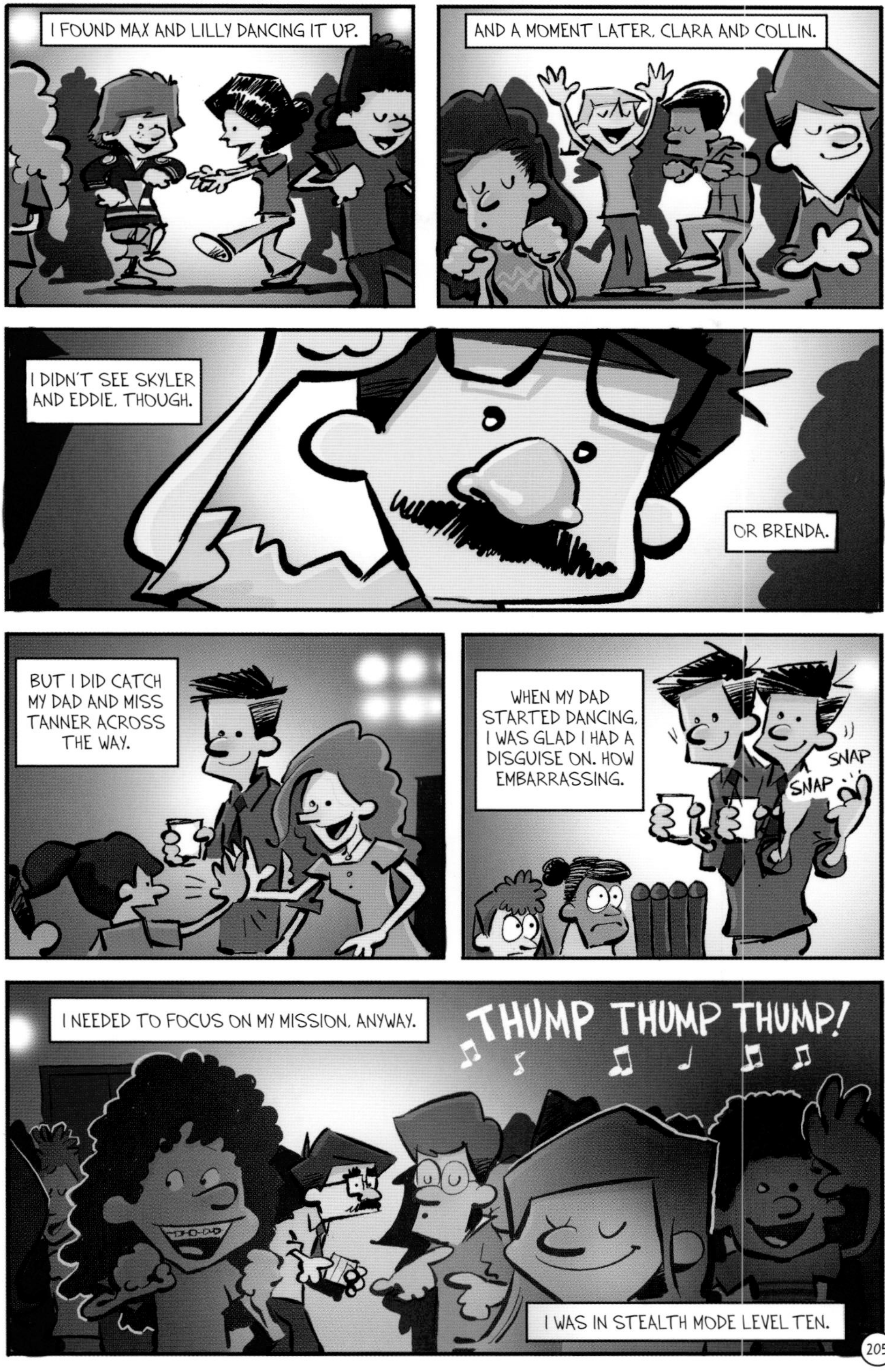
I FOUND MAX AND LILLY DANCING IT UP.
AND A MOMENT LATER, CLARA AND COLLIN.
I DIDN'T SEE SKYLER AND EDDIE, THOUGH.
OR BRENDA.
BUT I DID CATCH MY DAD AND MISS TANNER ACROSS THE WAY.
WHEN MY DAD STARTED DANCING, I WAS GLAD I HAD A DISGUISE ON. HOW EMBARRASSING.
SNAP
SNAP
I NEEDED TO FOCUS ON MY MISSION, ANYWAY.
THUMP THUMP THUMP!
I WAS IN STEALTH MODE LEVEL TEN.

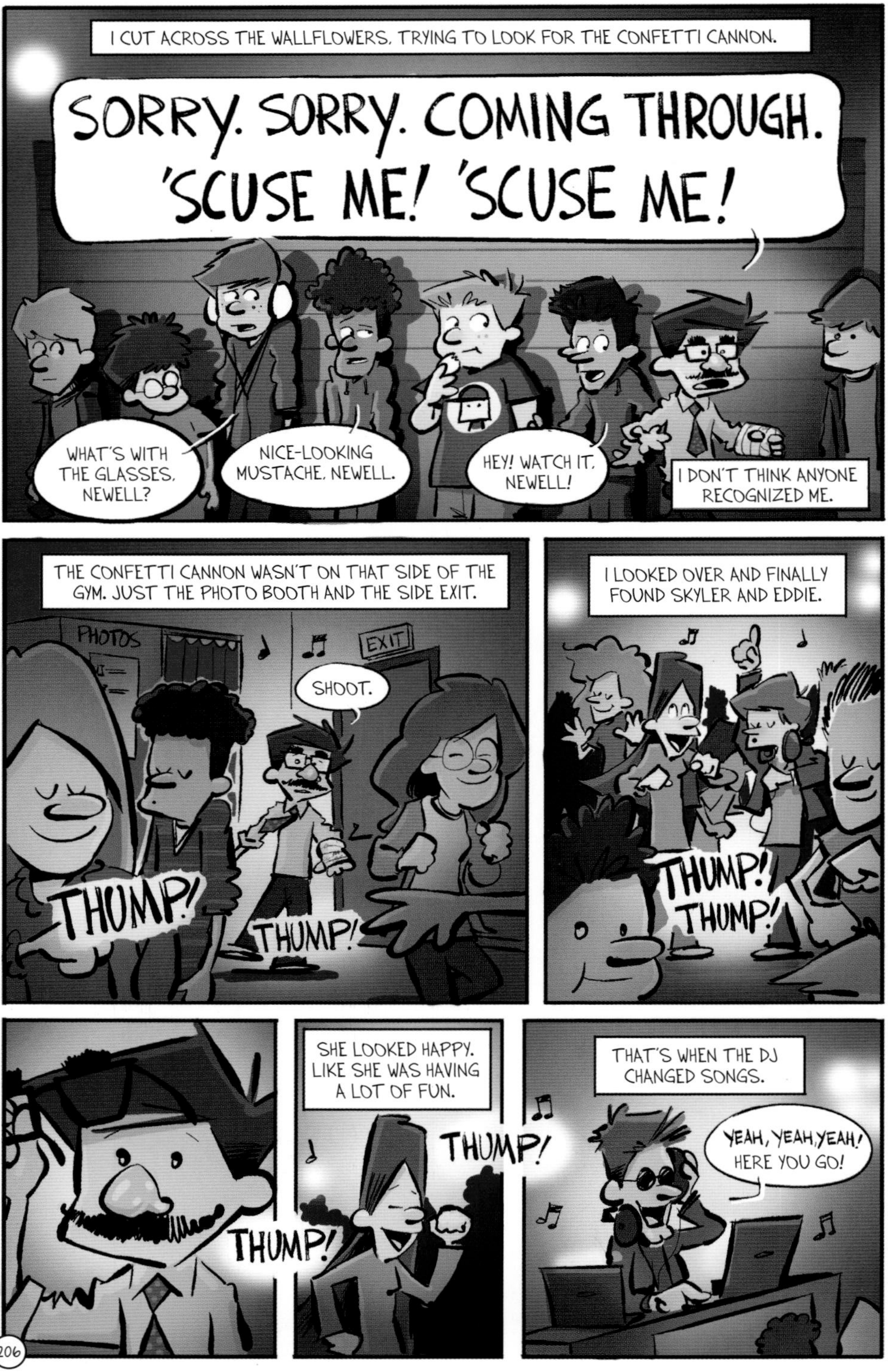

I CUT ACROSS THE WALLFLOWERS, TRYING TO LOOK FOR THE CONFETTI CANNON.
SORRY. SORRY. COMING THROUGH. 'SCUSE ME! 'SCUSE ME!
WHAT'S WITH THE GLASSES, NEWELL?
NICE-LOOKING MUSTACHE, NEWELL.
HEY! WATCH IT, NEWELL!
I DON'T THINK ANYONE RECOGNIZED ME.
THE CONFETTI CANNON WASN'T ON THAT SIDE OF THE GYM. JUST THE PHOTO BOOTH AND THE SIDE EXIT.
PHOTOS
EXIT
SHOOT.
THUMP!
THUMP!
I LOOKED OVER AND FINALLY FOUND SKYLER AND EDDIE.
THUMP! THUMP!
SHE LOOKED HAPPY. LIKE SHE WAS HAVING A LOT OF FUN.
THUMP!
THUMP!
THAT'S WHEN THE DJ CHANGED SONGS.
YEAH, YEAH, YEAH! HERE YOU GO!

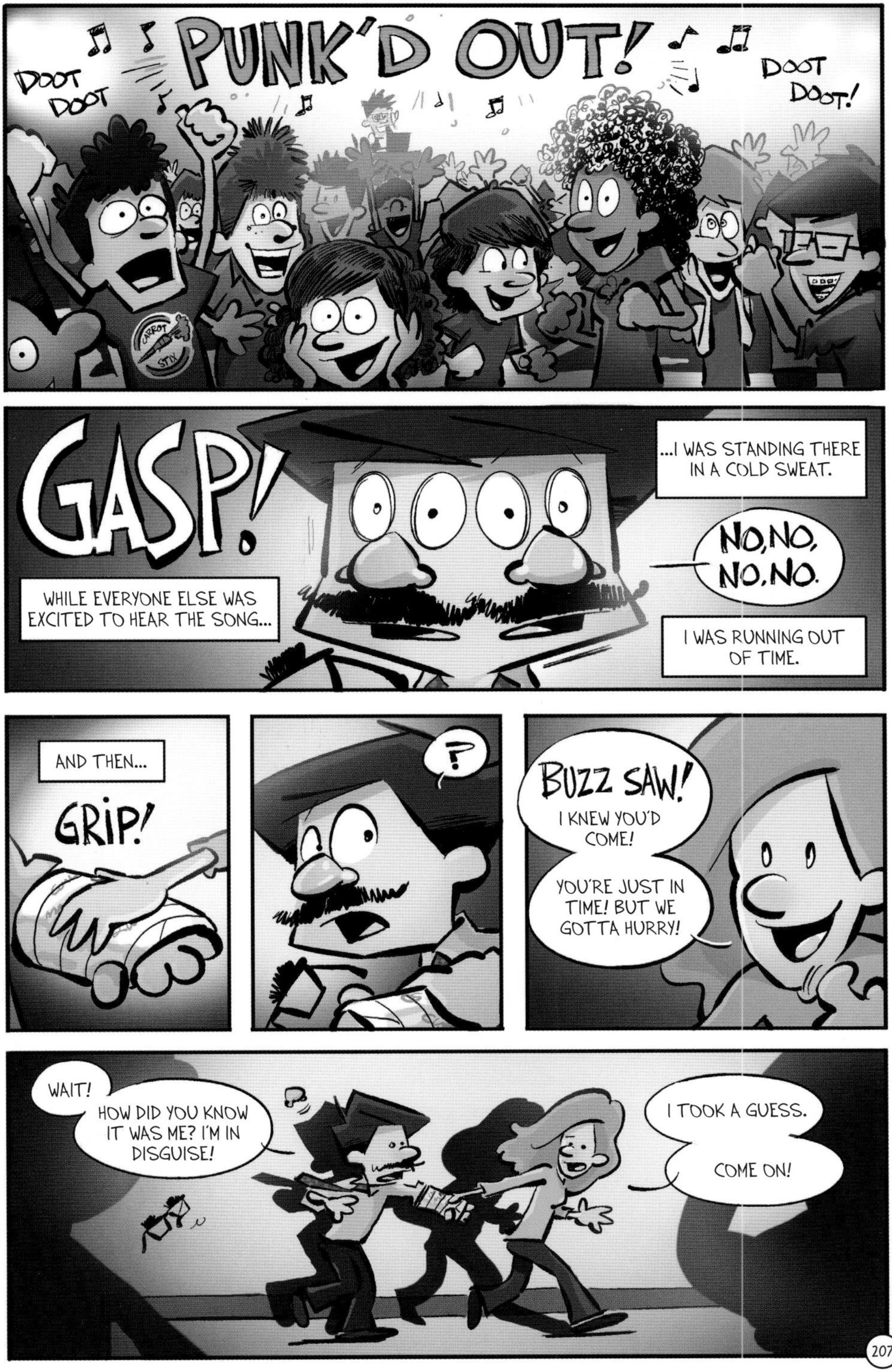
DOOT DOOT
PUNK'D OUT!
DOOT DOOT!
CARROT STIX
GASP!
WHILE EVERYONE ELSE WAS EXCITED TO HEAR THE SONG...
...I WAS STANDING THERE IN A COLD SWEAT.
NO, NO, NO, NO.
I WAS RUNNING OUT OF TIME.
AND THEN...
GRIP!
?
BUZZ SAW! I KNEW YOU'D COME!
YOU'RE JUST IN TIME! BUT WE GOTTA HURRY!
WAIT! HOW DID YOU KNOW IT WAS ME? I'M IN DISGUISE!
I TOOK A GUESS.
COME ON!

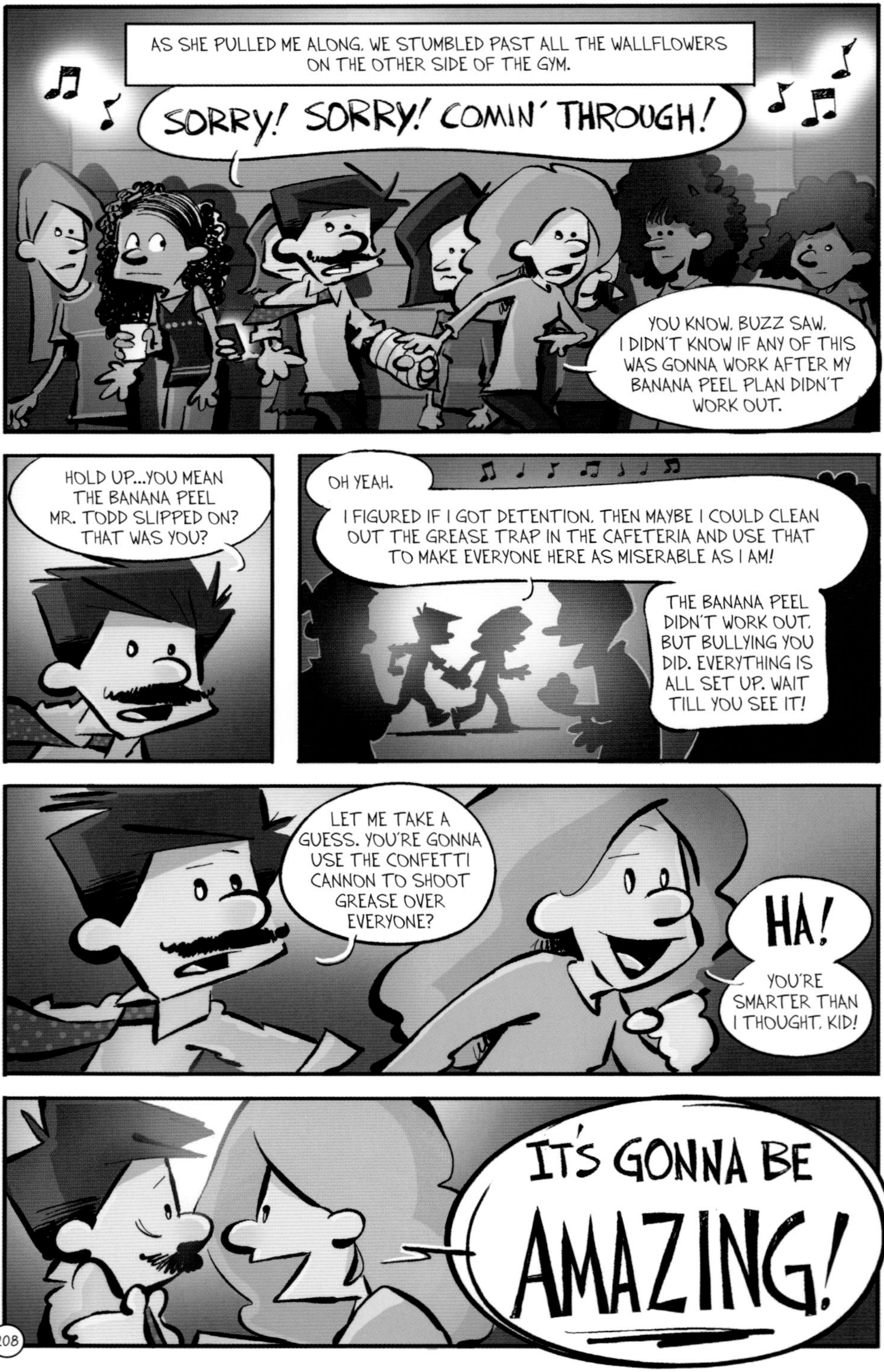
AS SHE PULLED ME ALONG, WE STUMBLED PAST ALL THE WALLFLOWERS ON THE OTHER SIDE OF THE GYM.
SORRY! SORRY! COMIN' THROUGH!
YOU KNOW, BUZZ SAW, I DIDN'T KNOW IF ANY OF THIS WAS GONNA WORK AFTER MY BANANA PEEL PLAN DIDN'T WORK OUT.
HOLD UP...YOU MEAN THE BANANA PEEL MR. TODD SLIPPED ON? THAT WAS YOU?
OH YEAH.
I FIGURED IF I GOT DETENTION, THEN MAYBE I COULD CLEAN OUT THE GREASE TRAP IN THE CAFETERIA AND USE THAT TO MAKE EVERYONE HERE AS MISERABLE AS I AM!
THE BANANA PEEL DIDN'T WORK OUT, BUT BULLYING YOU DID. EVERYTHING IS ALL SET UP. WAIT TILL YOU SEE IT!
LET ME TAKE A GUESS. YOU'RE GONNA USE THE CONFETTI CANNON TO SHOOT GREASE OVER EVERYONE?
HA!
YOU'RE SMARTER THAN I THOUGHT, KID!
IT'S GONNA BE AMAZING!

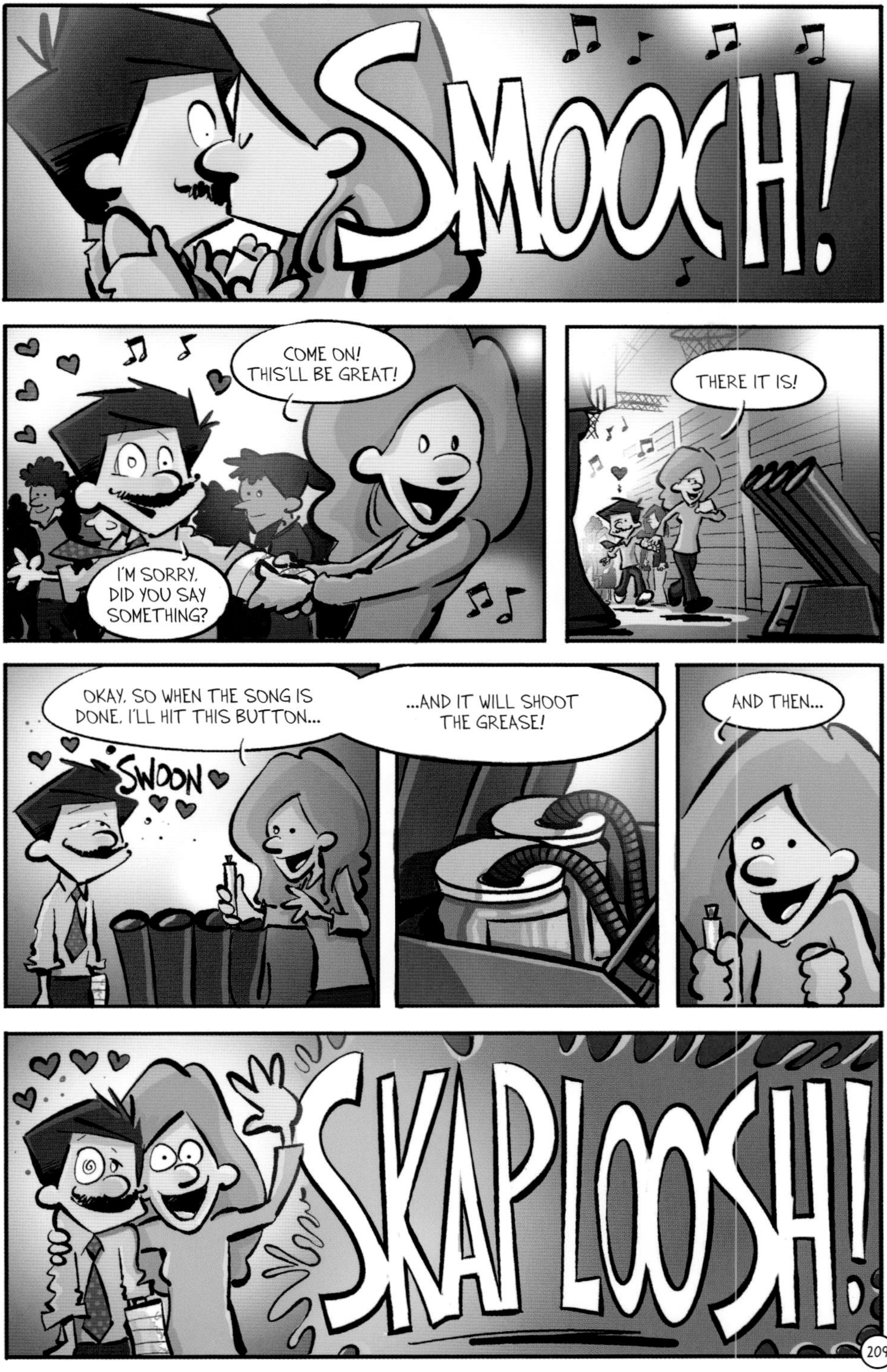
SMOOCH!
COME ON! THIS'LL BE GREAT!
I'M SORRY, DID YOU SAY SOMETHING?
THERE IT IS!
OKAY, SO WHEN THE SONG IS DONE, I'LL HIT THIS BUTTON...
SWOON
...AND IT WILL SHOOT THE GREASE!
AND THEN...
SKAPLOOSH!

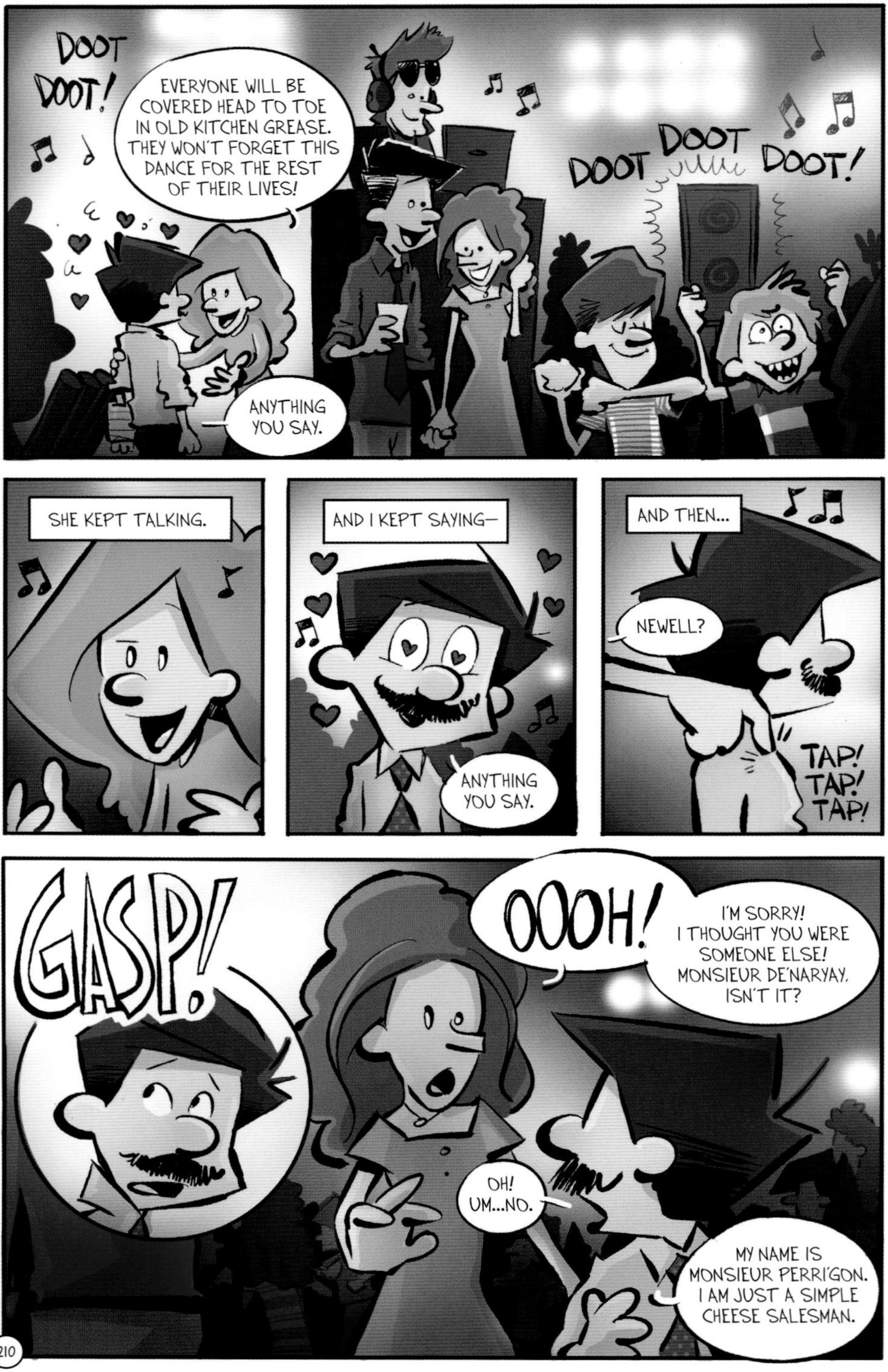
DOOT DOOT!
EVERYONE WILL BE COVERED HEAD TO TOE IN OLD KITCHEN GREASE. THEY WON'T FORGET THIS DANCE FOR THE REST OF THEIR LIVES!
DOOT DOOT DOOT!
ANYTHING YOU SAY.
SHE KEPT TALKING.
AND I KEPT SAYING—
ANYTHING YOU SAY.
AND THEN...
NEWELL?
TAP! TAP! TAP!
GASP!
OOOH!
I'M SORRY! I THOUGHT YOU WERE SOMEONE ELSE! MONSIEUR DE'NARYAY, ISN'T IT?
OH! UM...NO.
MY NAME IS MONSIEUR PERRI'GON. I AM JUST A SIMPLE CHEESE SALESMAN.

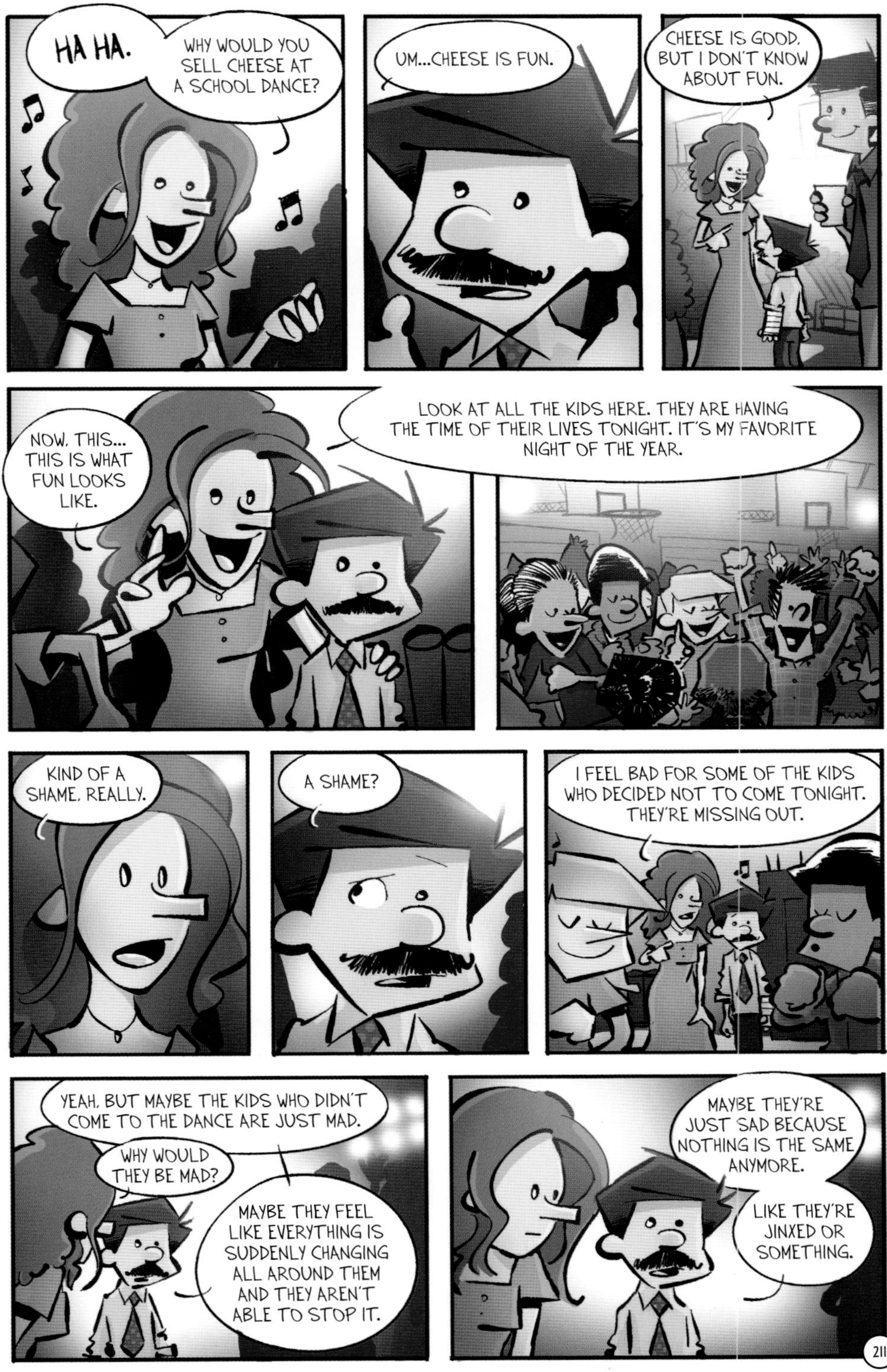
HA HA.
WHY WOULD YOU SELL CHEESE AT A SCHOOL DANCE?
UM...CHEESE IS FUN.
CHEESE IS GOOD, BUT I DON'T KNOW ABOUT FUN.
NOW, THIS... THIS IS WHAT FUN LOOKS LIKE.
LOOK AT ALL THE KIDS HERE. THEY ARE HAVING THE TIME OF THEIR LIVES TONIGHT. IT'S MY FAVORITE NIGHT OF THE YEAR.
KIND OF A SHAME, REALLY.
A SHAME?
I FEEL BAD FOR SOME OF THE KIDS WHO DECIDED NOT TO COME TONIGHT. THEY'RE MISSING OUT.
YEAH, BUT MAYBE THE KIDS WHO DIDN'T COME TO THE DANCE ARE JUST MAD.
WHY WOULD THEY BE MAD?
MAYBE THEY FEEL LIKE EVERYTHING IS SUDDENLY CHANGING ALL AROUND THEM AND THEY AREN'T ABLE TO STOP IT.
MAYBE THEY'RE JUST SAD BECAUSE NOTHING IS THE SAME ANYMORE.
LIKE THEY'RE JINXED OR SOMETHING.

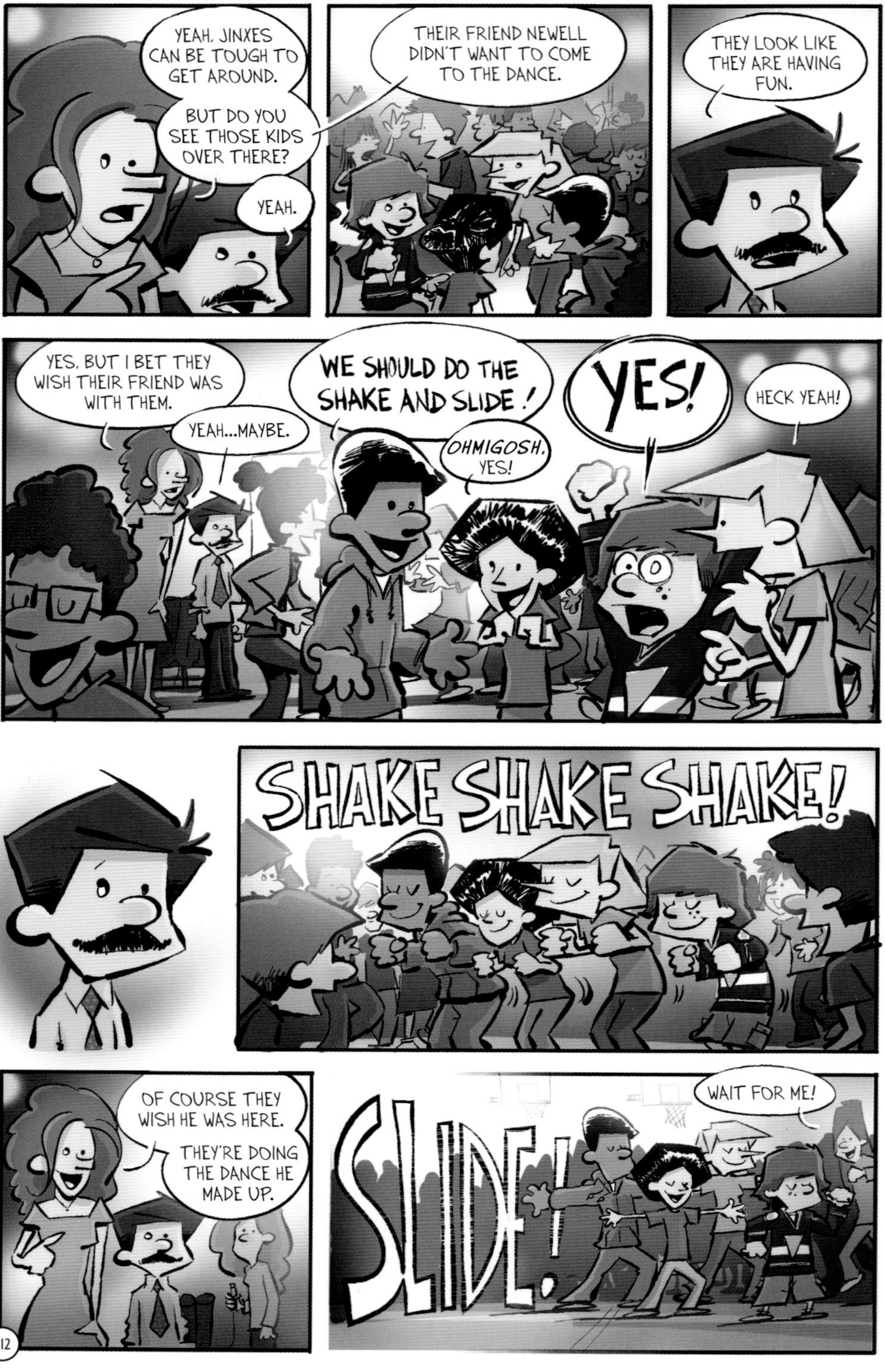
YEAH, JINXES CAN BE TOUGH TO GET AROUND.
BUT DO YOU SEE THOSE KIDS OVER THERE?
YEAH.
THEIR FRIEND NEWELL DIDN'T WANT TO COME TO THE DANCE.
THEY LOOK LIKE THEY ARE HAVING FUN.
YES, BUT I BET THEY WISH THEIR FRIEND WAS WITH THEM.
YEAH...MAYBE.
WE SHOULD DO THE SHAKE AND SLIDE!
OHMIGOSH, YES!
YES!
HECK YEAH!
SHAKE SHAKE SHAKE!
OF COURSE THEY WISH HE WAS HERE.
THEY'RE DOING THE DANCE HE MADE UP.
SLIDE!
WAIT FOR ME!

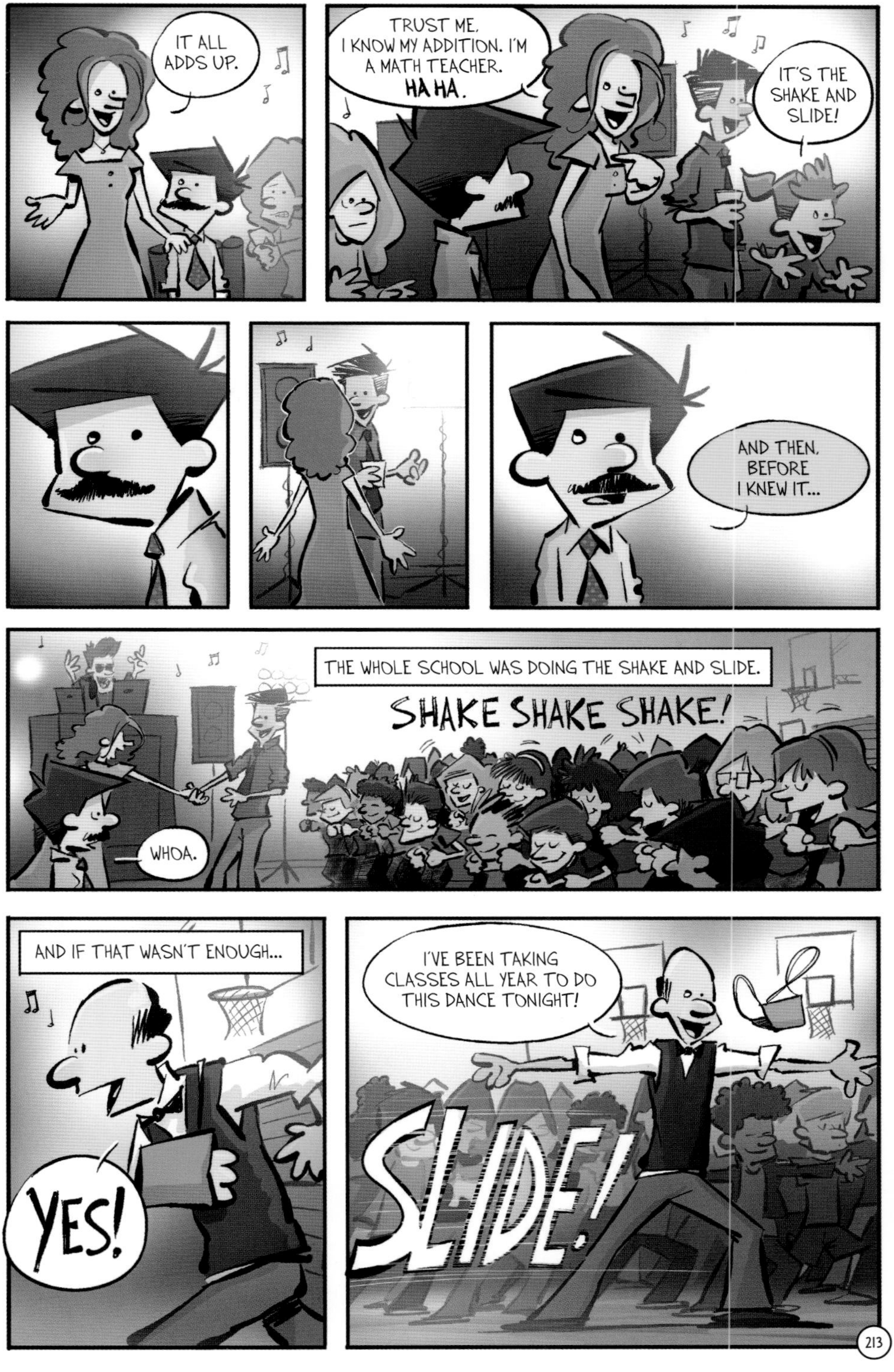
IT ALL ADDS UP.
TRUST ME, I KNOW MY ADDITION. I'M A MATH TEACHER. HA HA.
IT'S THE SHAKE AND SLIDE!
AND THEN, BEFORE I KNEW IT...
THE WHOLE SCHOOL WAS DOING THE SHAKE AND SLIDE.
SHAKE SHAKE SHAKE!
WHOA.
AND IF THAT WASN'T ENOUGH...
YES!
I'VE BEEN TAKING CLASSES ALL YEAR TO DO THIS DANCE TONIGHT!
SLIDE!

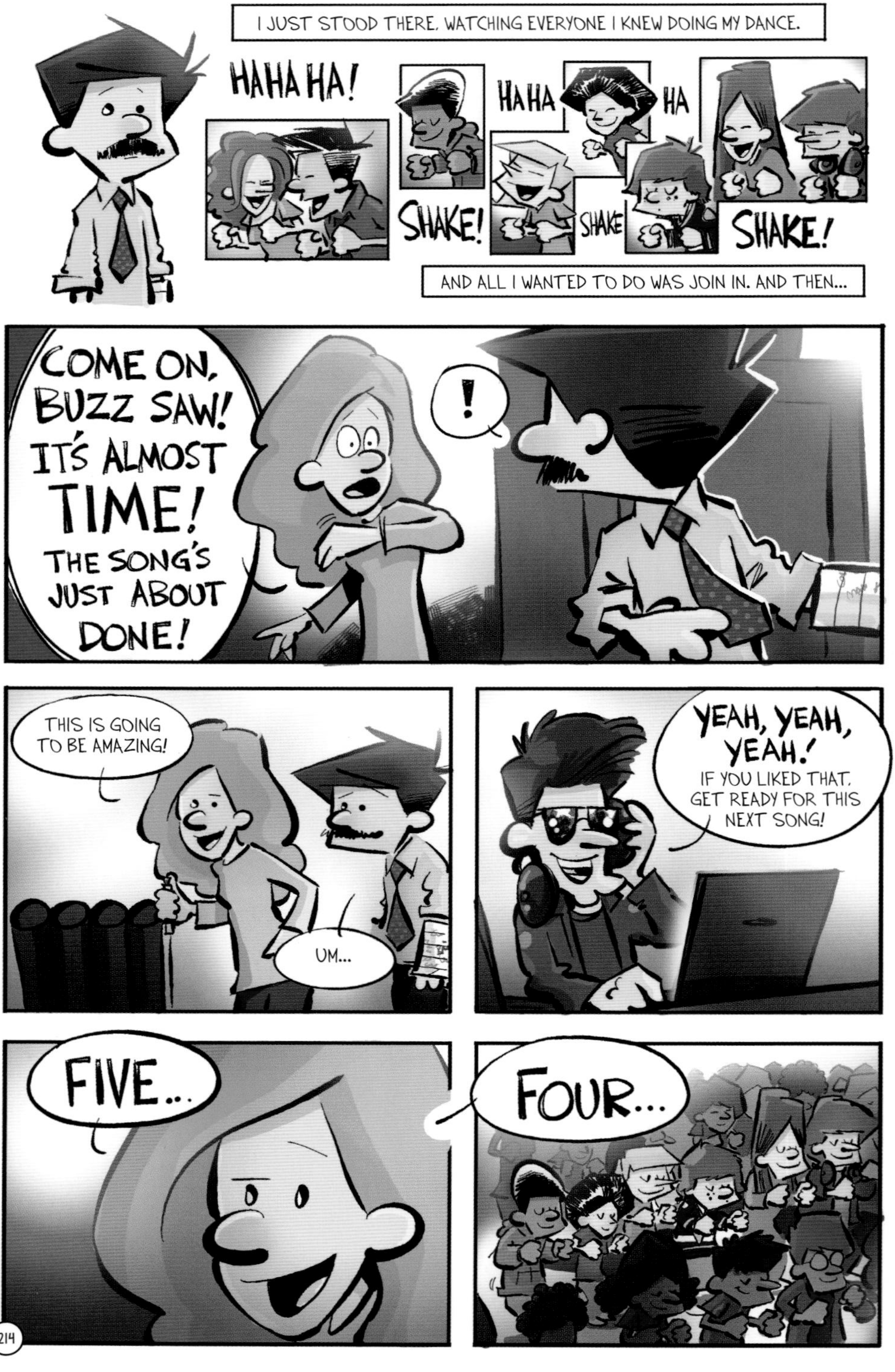
I JUST STOOD THERE, WATCHING EVERYONE I KNEW DOING MY DANCE.
HAHAHA!
HAHA
HA
SHAKE!
SHAKE
SHAKE!
AND ALL I WANTED TO DO WAS JOIN IN. AND THEN...
COME ON, BUZZ SAW! IT'S ALMOST TIME! THE SONG'S JUST ABOUT DONE!
!
THIS IS GOING TO BE AMAZING!
UM...
YEAH, YEAH, YEAH! IF YOU LIKED THAT, GET READY FOR THIS NEXT SONG!
FIVE...
FOUR...

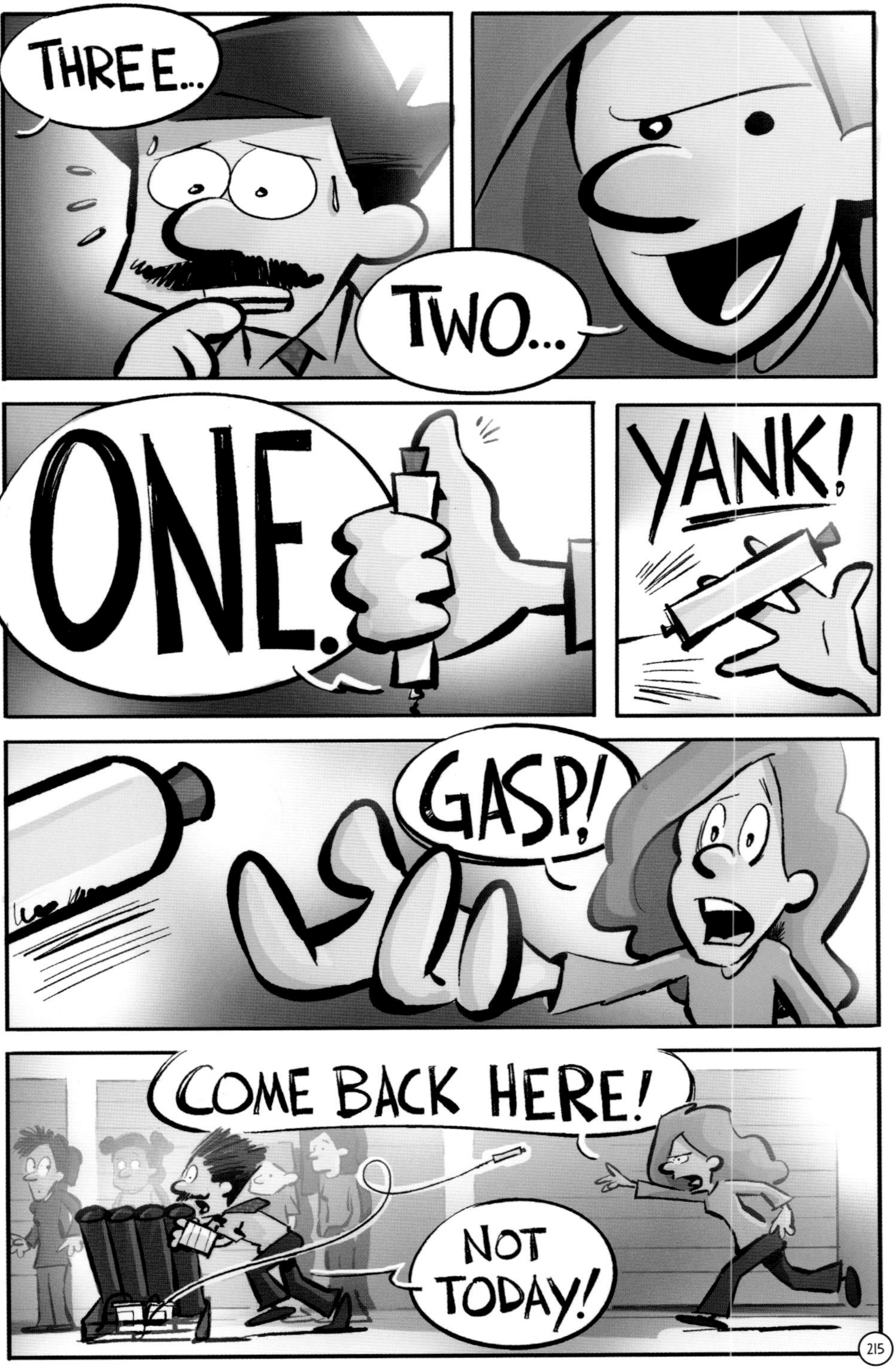
THREE...
TWO...
ONE.
YANK!
GASP!
COME BACK HERE!
NOT TODAY!

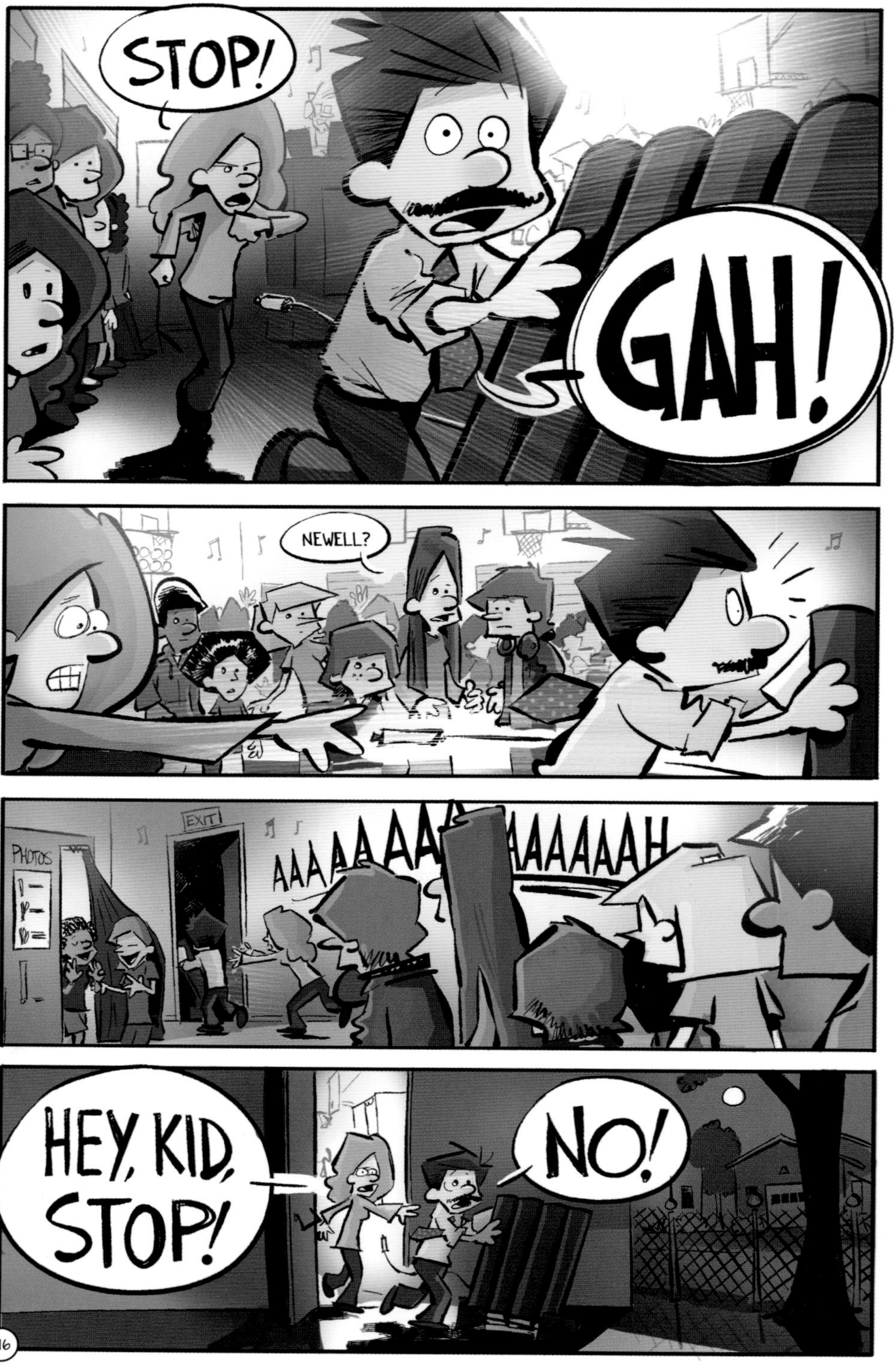
STOP!
GAH!
NEWELL?
AAAAAAAAAAAAAAAAH
PHOTOS
EXIT
HEY, KID, STOP!
NO!

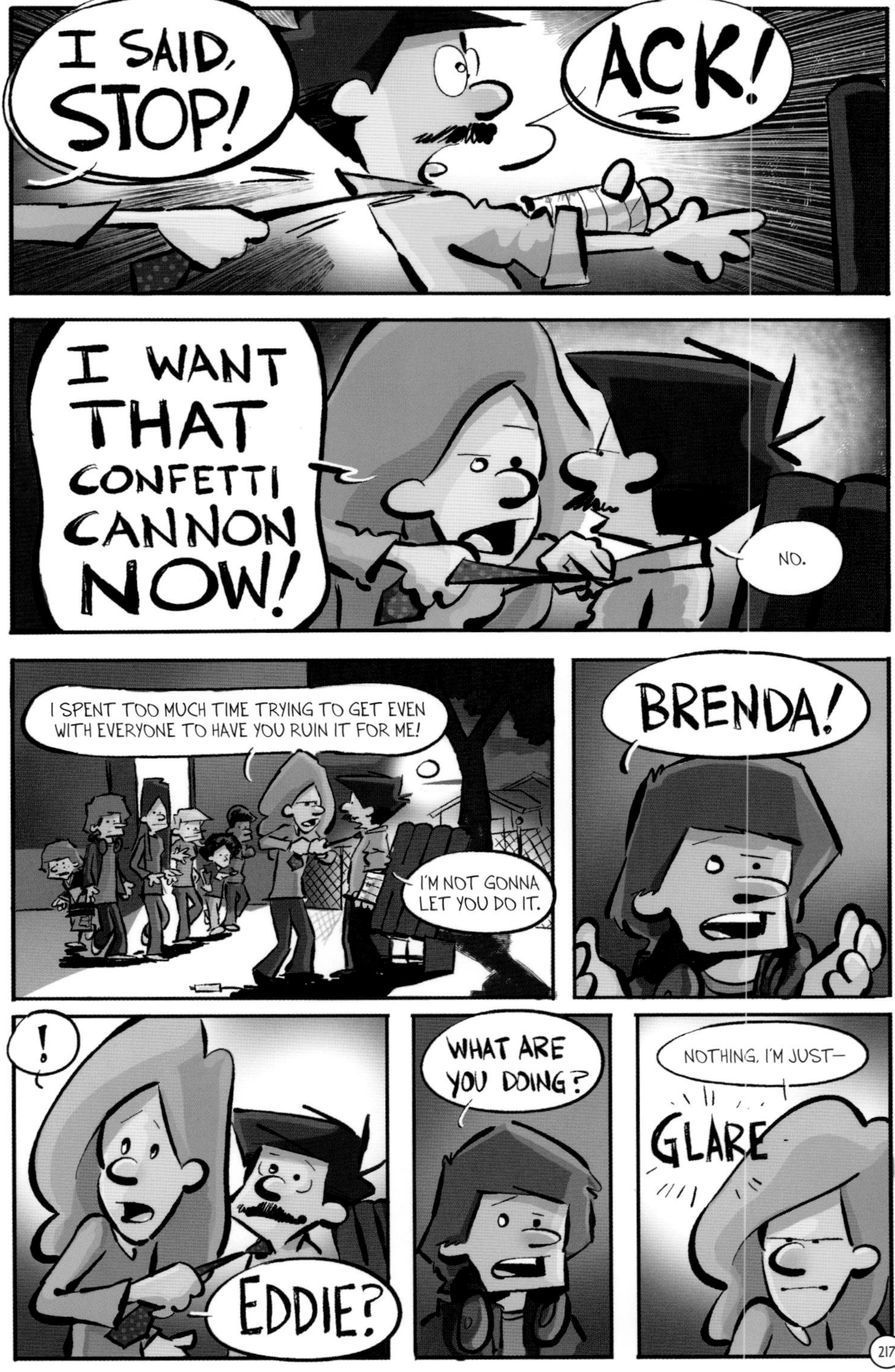

I SAID, STOP!
ACK!
I WANT THAT CONFETTI CANNON NOW!
NO.
I SPENT TOO MUCH TIME TRYING TO GET EVEN WITH EVERYONE TO HAVE YOU RUIN IT FOR ME!
I'M NOT GONNA LET YOU DO IT.
BRENDA!
!
EDDIE?
WHAT ARE YOU DOING?
NOTHING, I'M JUST—
GLARE

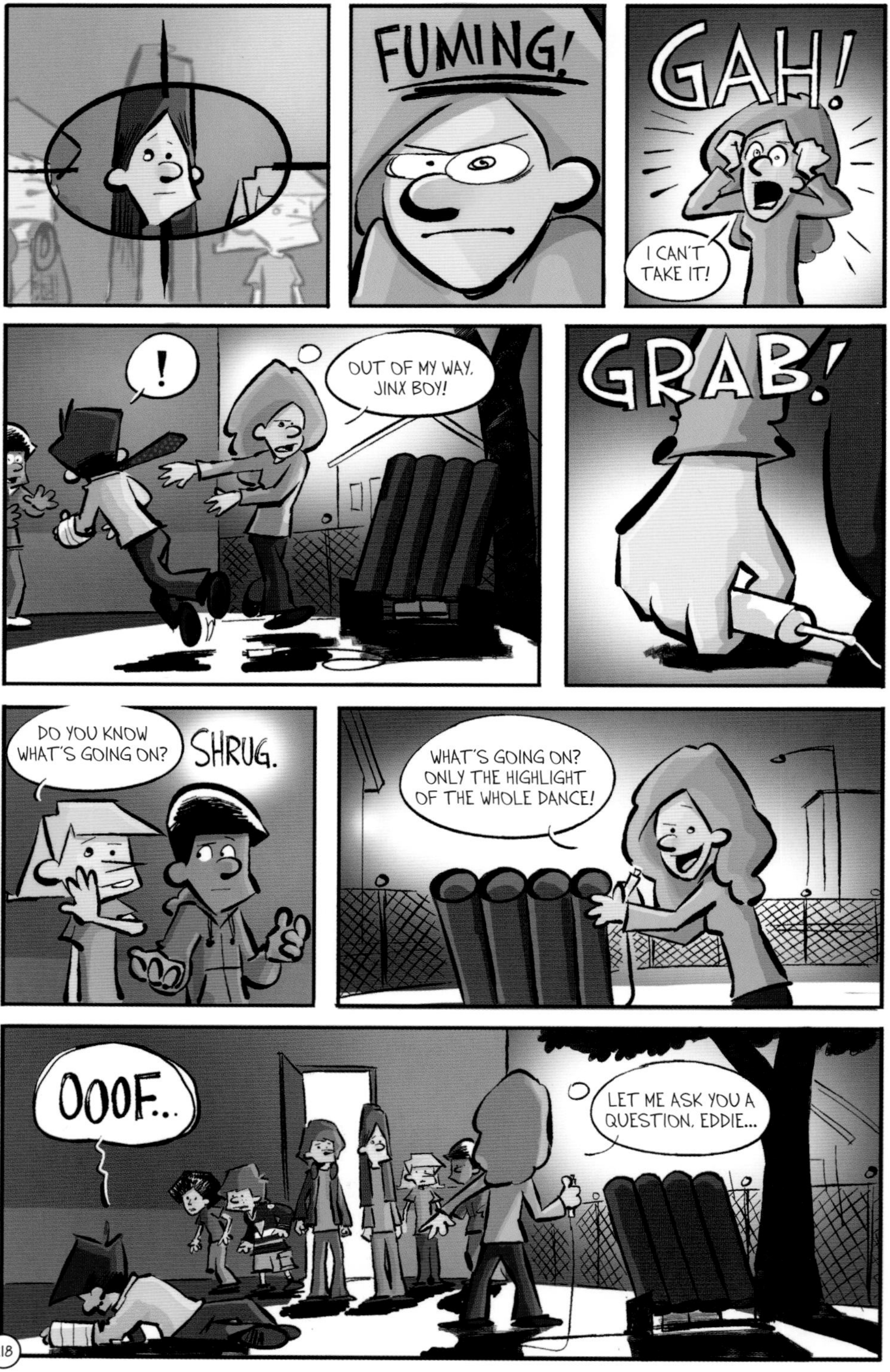
FUMING!
GAH!
I CAN'T TAKE IT!
!
OUT OF MY WAY, JINX BOY!
GRAB!
DO YOU KNOW WHAT'S GOING ON?
SHRUG.
WHAT'S GOING ON? ONLY THE HIGHLIGHT OF THE WHOLE DANCE!
OOOF...
LET ME ASK YOU A QUESTION, EDDIE...

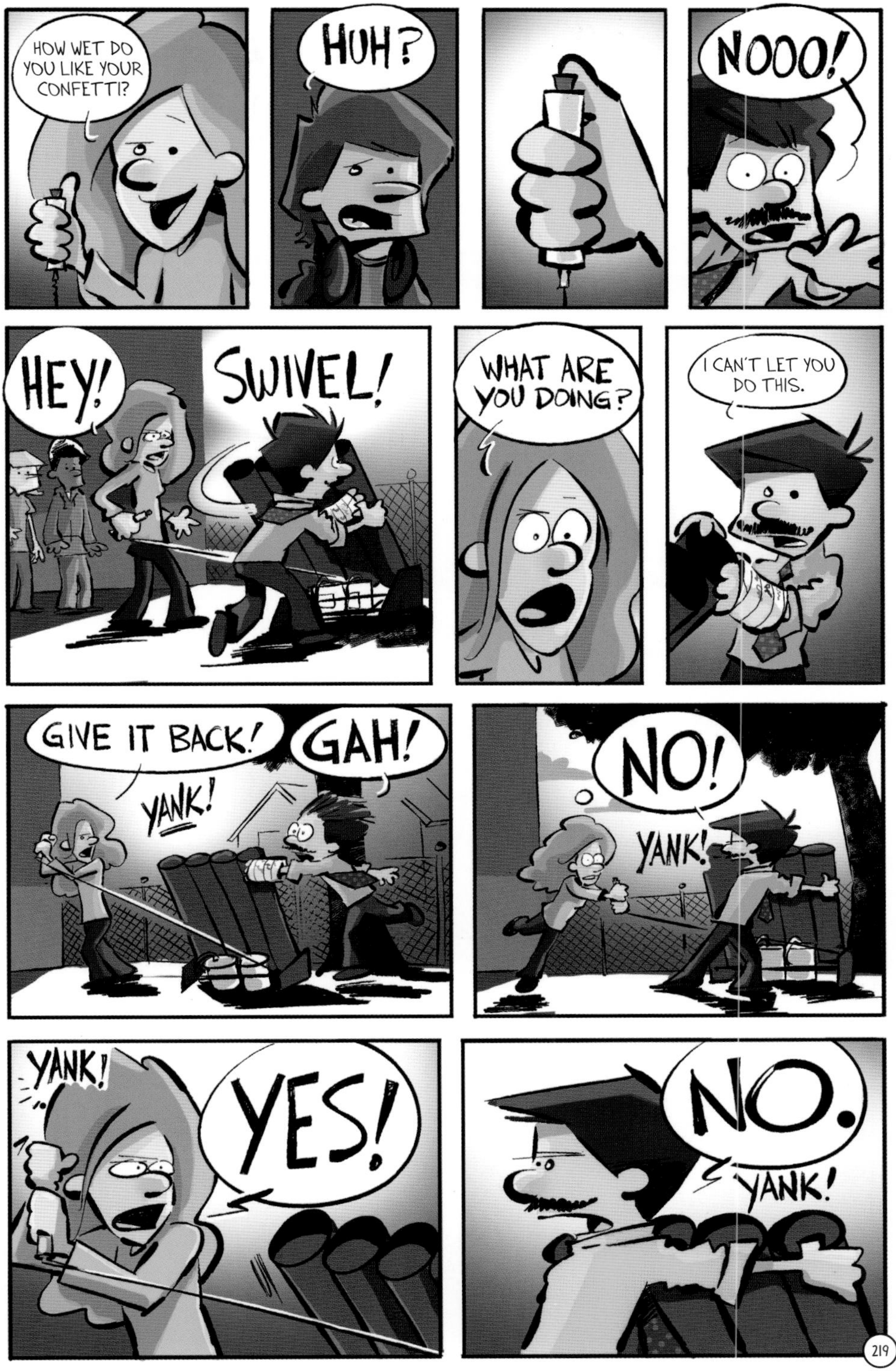
HOW WET DO YOU LIKE YOUR CONFETTI?
HUH?
NOOO!
HEY!
SWIVEL!
WHAT ARE YOU DOING?
I CAN'T LET YOU DO THIS.
GIVE IT BACK!
GAH!
YANK!
NO!
YANK!
YANK!
YES!
NO.
YANK!

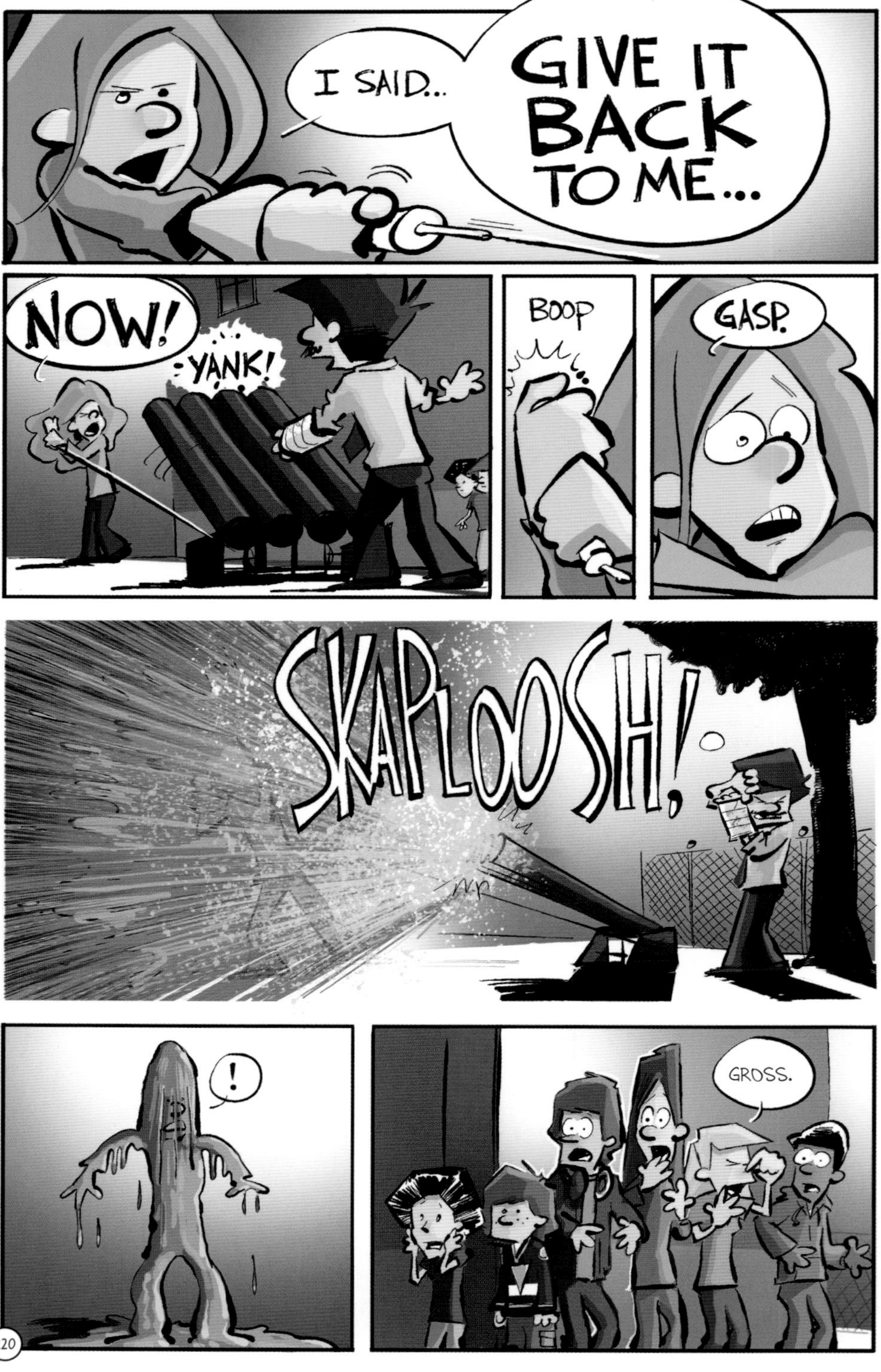
I SAID...
GIVE IT BACK TO ME...
NOW!
YANK!
BOOP
GASP.
SKAPLOOSH!
!
GROSS.

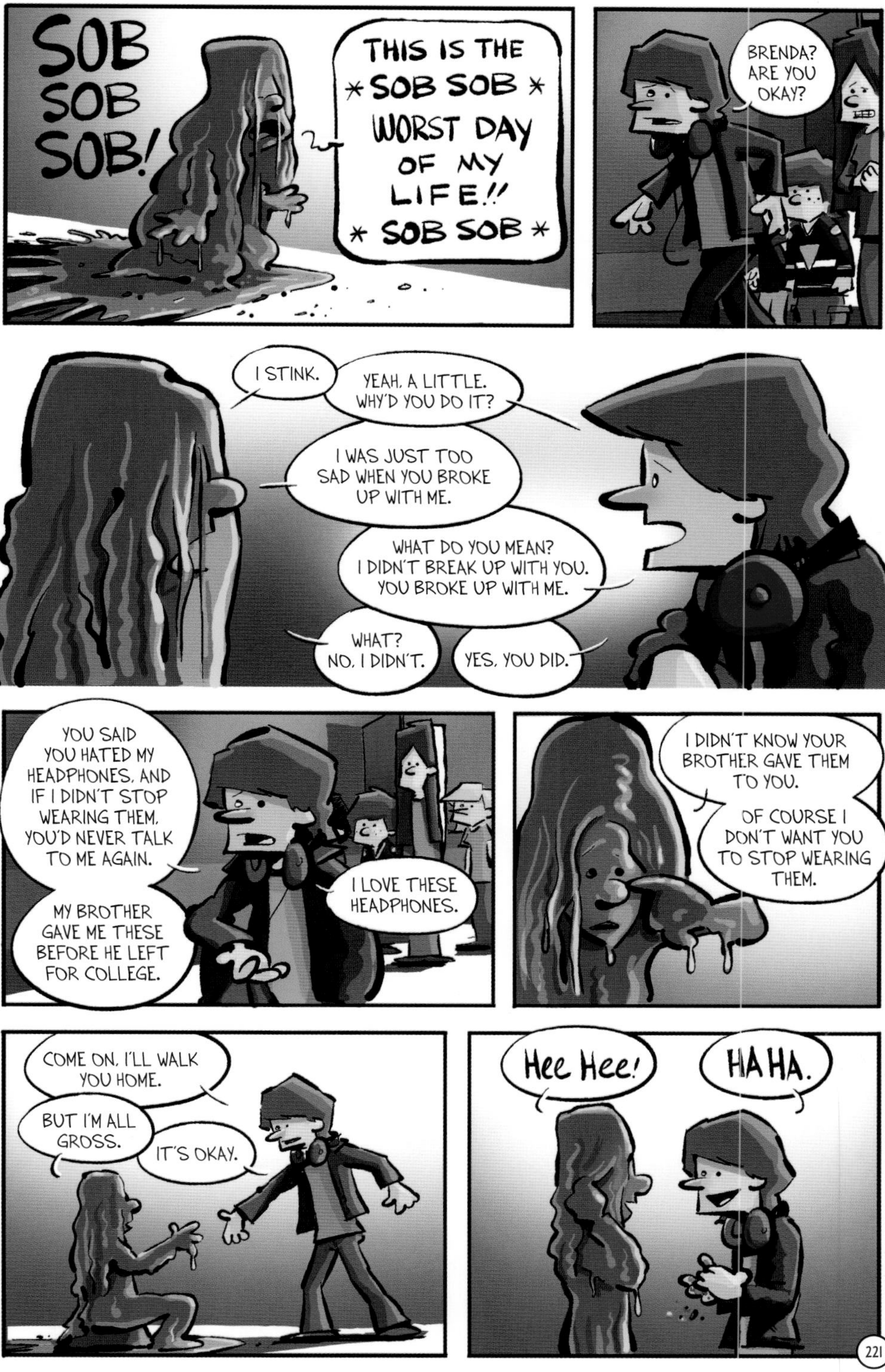
SOB SOB SOB!
THIS IS THE * SOB SOB * WORST DAY OF MY LIFE!! * SOB SOB *
BRENDA? ARE YOU OKAY?
I STINK.
YEAH, A LITTLE. WHY'D YOU DO IT?
I WAS JUST TOO SAD WHEN YOU BROKE UP WITH ME.
WHAT DO YOU MEAN? I DIDN'T BREAK UP WITH YOU. YOU BROKE UP WITH ME.
WHAT? NO, I DIDN'T.
YES, YOU DID.
YOU SAID YOU HATED MY HEADPHONES, AND IF I DIDN'T STOP WEARING THEM, YOU'D NEVER TALK TO ME AGAIN.
MY BROTHER GAVE ME THESE BEFORE HE LEFT FOR COLLEGE.
I LOVE THESE HEADPHONES.
I DIDN'T KNOW YOUR BROTHER GAVE THEM TO YOU.
OF COURSE I DON'T WANT YOU TO STOP WEARING THEM.
COME ON, I'LL WALK YOU HOME.
BUT I'M ALL GROSS.
IT'S OKAY.
Hee Hee!
HA HA.

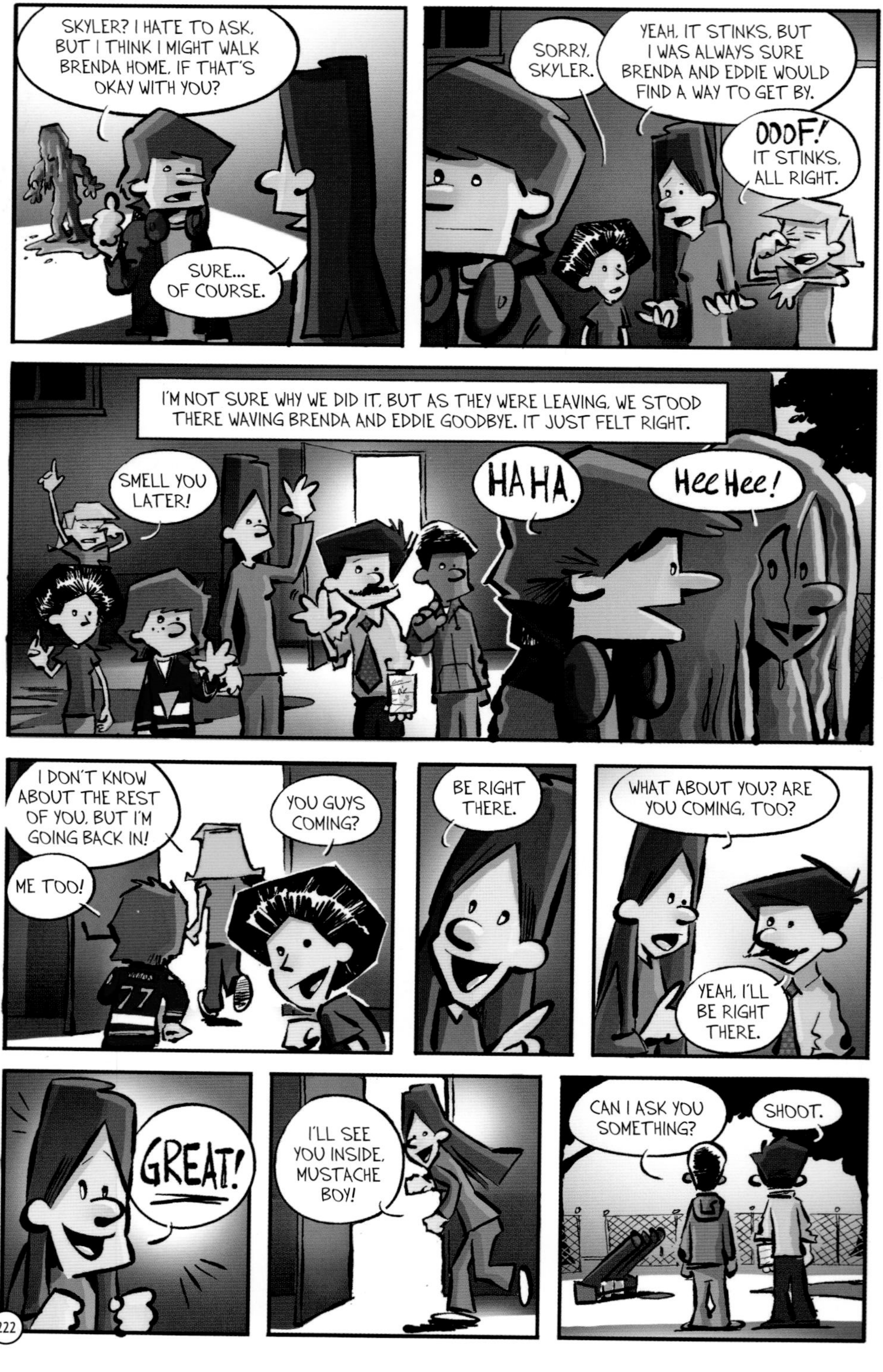
SKYLER? I HATE TO ASK, BUT I THINK I MIGHT WALK BRENDA HOME, IF THAT'S OKAY WITH YOU?
SURE... OF COURSE.
SORRY, SKYLER.
YEAH, IT STINKS, BUT I WAS ALWAYS SURE BRENDA AND EDDIE WOULD FIND A WAY TO GET BY.
OOOF! IT STINKS, ALL RIGHT.
I'M NOT SURE WHY WE DID IT, BUT AS THEY WERE LEAVING, WE STOOD THERE WAVING BRENDA AND EDDIE GOODBYE. IT JUST FELT RIGHT.
SMELL YOU LATER!
HAHA.
Hee Hee!
I DON'T KNOW ABOUT THE REST OF YOU, BUT I'M GOING BACK IN!
ME TOO!
YOU GUYS COMING?
BE RIGHT THERE.
WHAT ABOUT YOU? ARE YOU COMING, TOO?
YEAH, I'LL BE RIGHT THERE.
GREAT!
I'LL SEE YOU INSIDE, MUSTACHE BOY!
CAN I ASK YOU SOMETHING?
SHOOT.

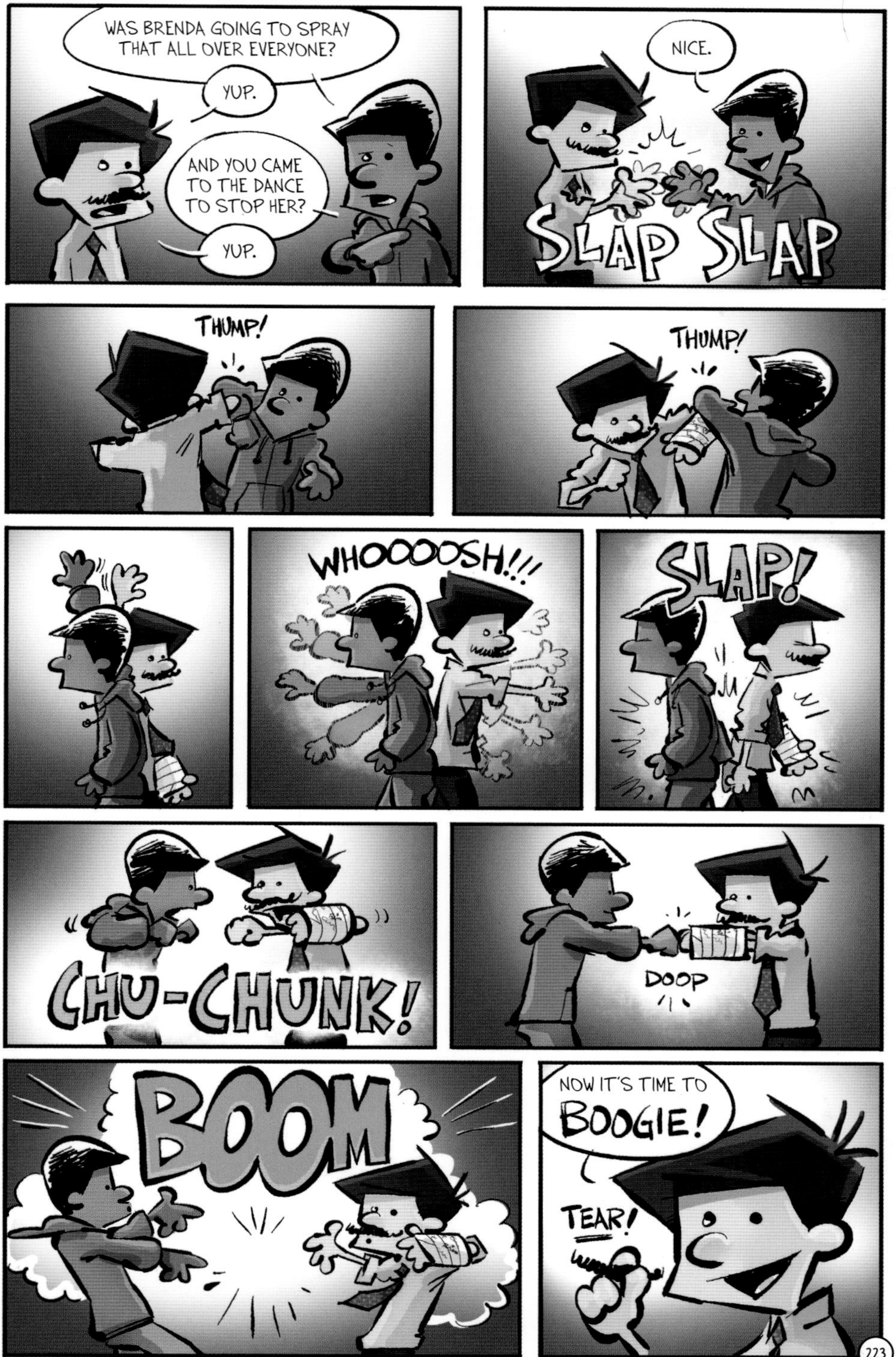
WAS BRENDA GOING TO SPRAY THAT ALL OVER EVERYONE?
YUP.
AND YOU CAME TO THE DANCE TO STOP HER?
YUP.
NICE.
SLAP SLAP
THUMP!
THUMP!
WHOOOOOSH!!!
SLAP!
CHU-CHUNK!
DOOP
BOOM
NOW IT'S TIME TO BOOGIE!
TEAR!

CHAPTER TWELVE
THE BEST SONG EVER

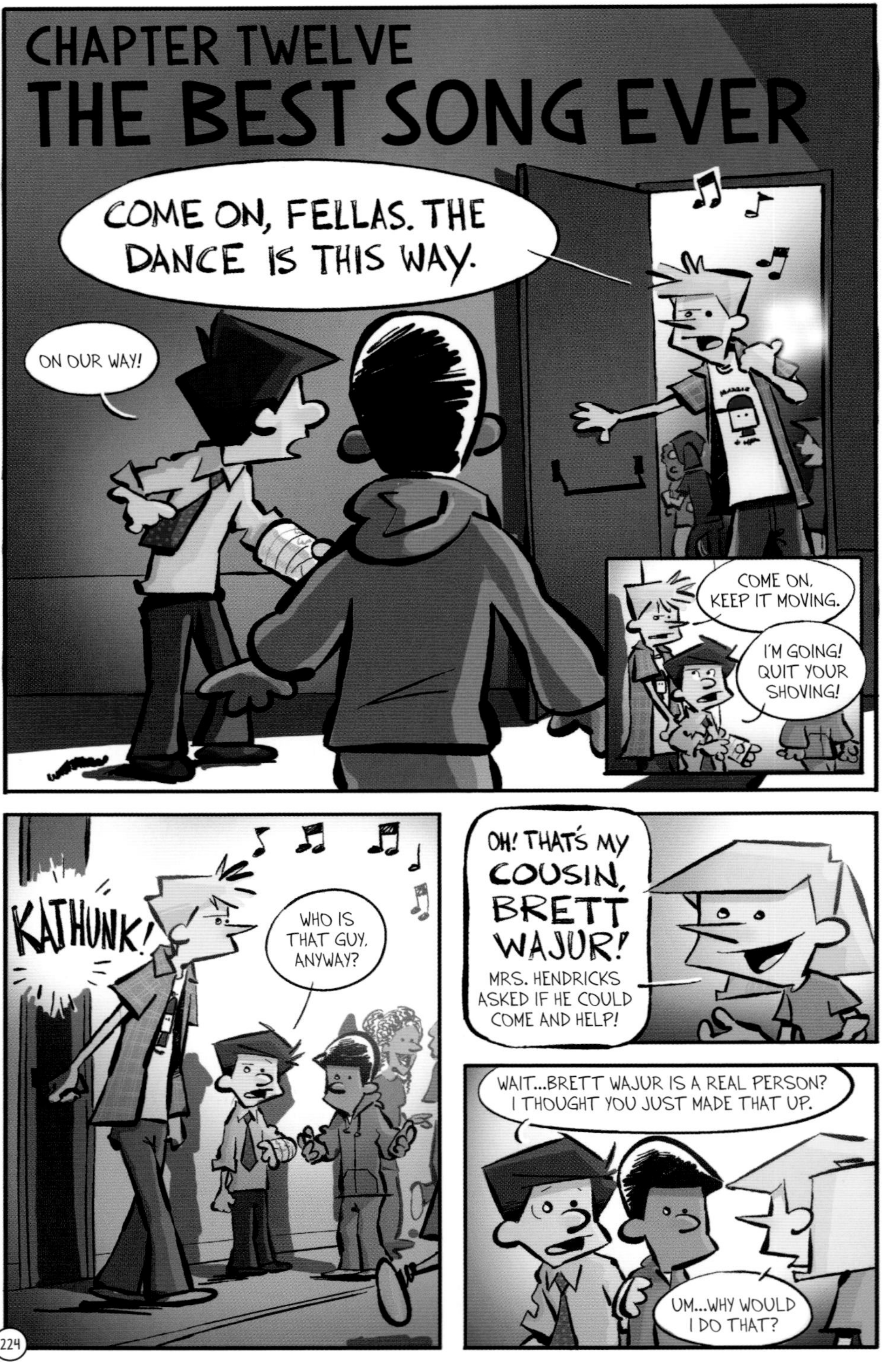
COME ON, FELLAS. THE DANCE IS THIS WAY.
ON OUR WAY!
COME ON, KEEP IT MOVING.
I'M GOING! QUIT YOUR SHOVING!
KAJHUNK!
WHO IS THAT GUY, ANYWAY?
OH! THAT'S MY COUSIN, BRETT WAJUR!
MRS. HENDRICKS ASKED IF HE COULD COME AND HELP!
WAIT...BRETT WAJUR IS A REAL PERSON? I THOUGHT YOU JUST MADE THAT UP.
UM...WHY WOULD I DO THAT?

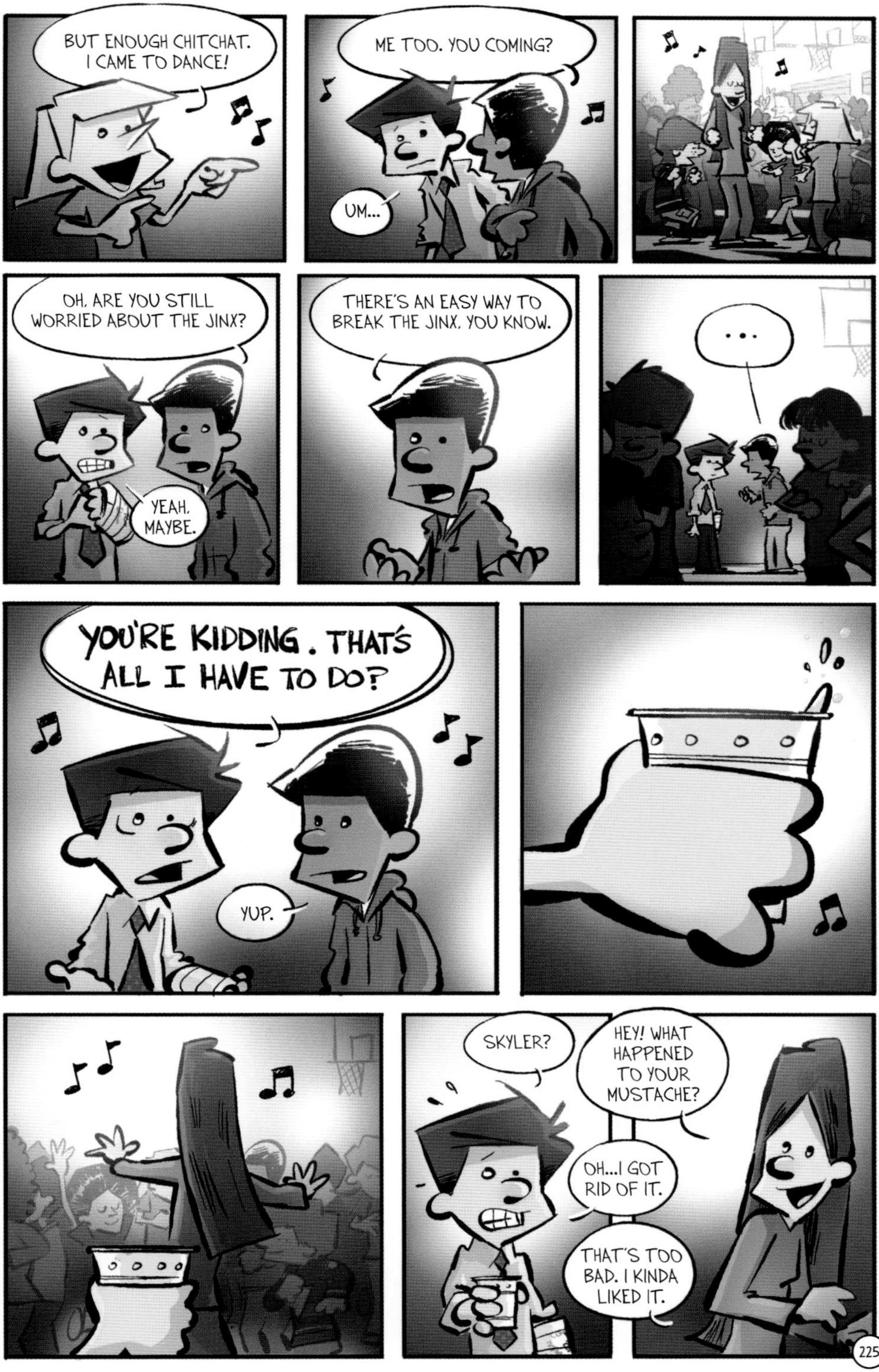
BUT ENOUGH CHITCHAT. I CAME TO DANCE!
ME TOO. YOU COMING?
UM...
OH, ARE YOU STILL WORRIED ABOUT THE JINX?
YEAH, MAYBE.
THERE'S AN EASY WAY TO BREAK THE JINX, YOU KNOW.
...
YOU'RE KIDDING. THAT'S ALL I HAVE TO DO?
YUP.
SKYLER?
HEY! WHAT HAPPENED TO YOUR MUSTACHE?
OH...I GOT RID OF IT.
THAT'S TOO BAD. I KINDA LIKED IT.

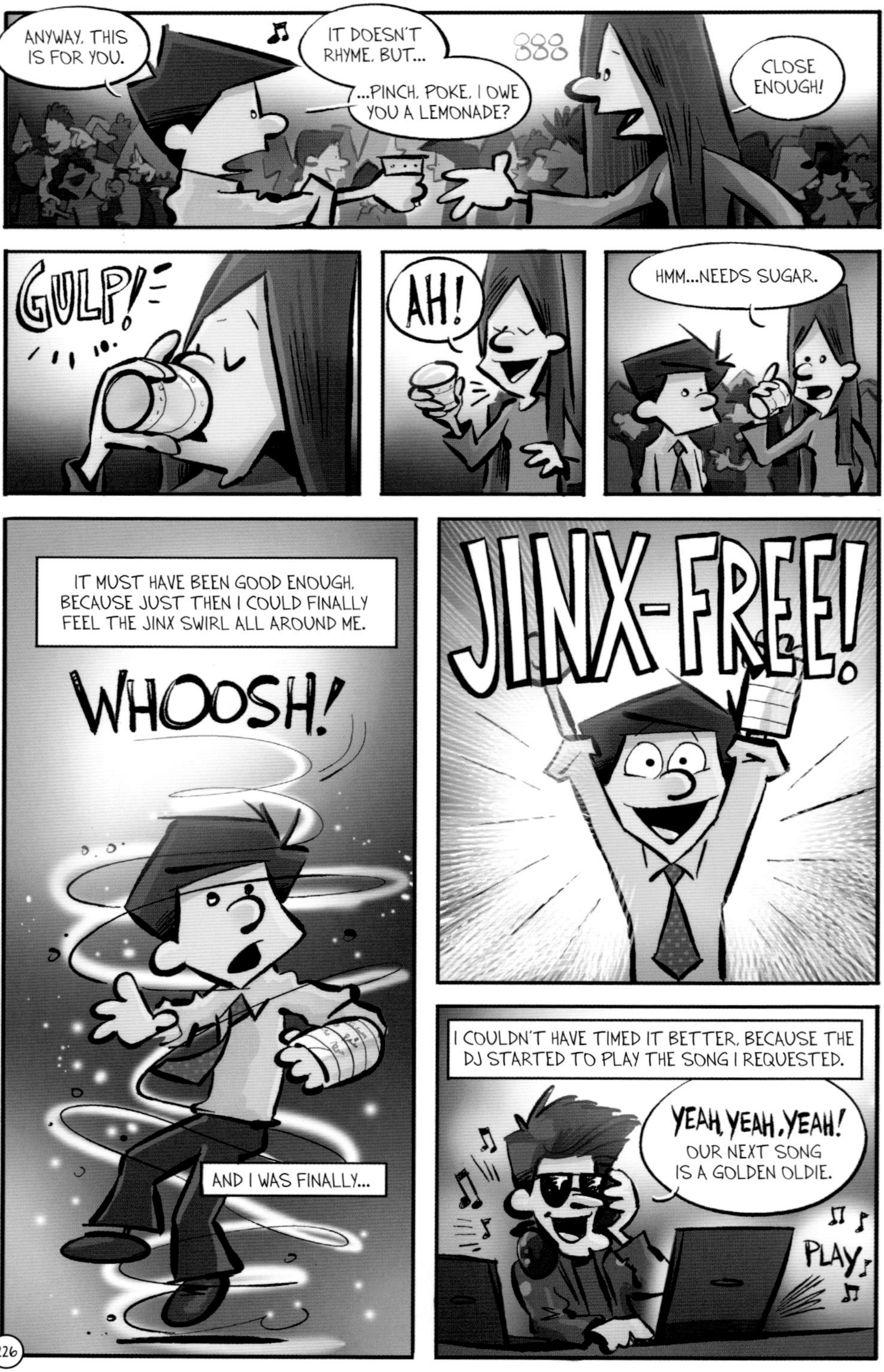
ANYWAY, THIS IS FOR YOU.
IT DOESN'T RHYME, BUT...
...PINCH, POKE, I OWE YOU A LEMONADE?
CLOSE ENOUGH!
GULP!
AH!
HMM...NEEDS SUGAR.
IT MUST HAVE BEEN GOOD ENOUGH, BECAUSE JUST THEN I COULD FINALLY FEEL THE JINX SWIRL ALL AROUND ME.
WHOOSH!
AND I WAS FINALLY...
JINX-FREE!
I COULDN'T HAVE TIMED IT BETTER, BECAUSE THE DJ STARTED TO PLAY THE SONG I REQUESTED.
YEAH, YEAH, YEAH! OUR NEXT SONG IS A GOLDEN OLDIE.
PLAY

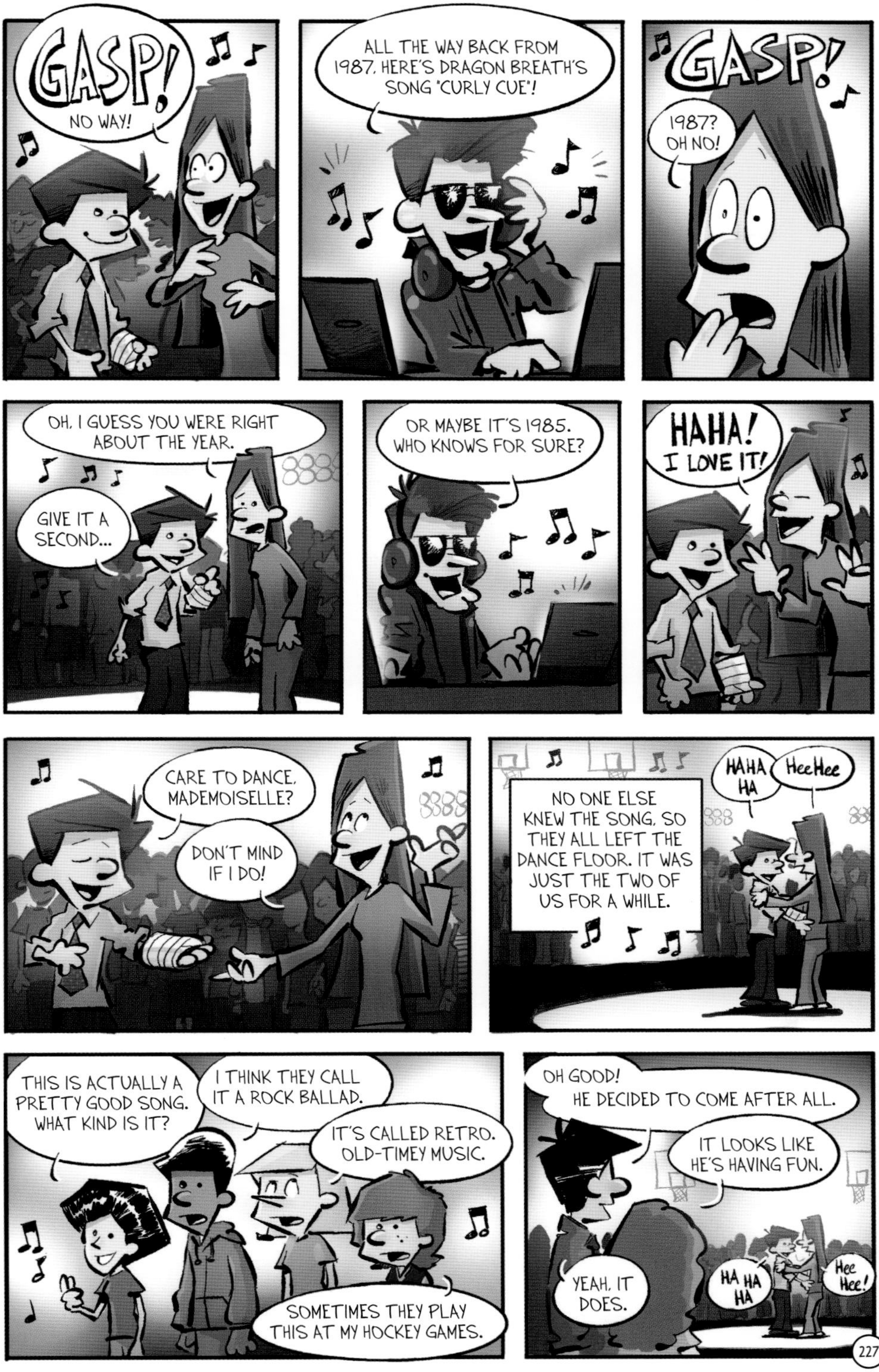
GASP!
NO WAY!
ALL THE WAY BACK FROM 1987, HERE'S DRAGON BREATH'S SONG "CURLY CUE"!
GASP!
1987? OH NO!
OH, I GUESS YOU WERE RIGHT ABOUT THE YEAR.
GIVE IT A SECOND...
OR MAYBE IT'S 1985. WHO KNOWS FOR SURE?
HAHA! I LOVE IT!
CARE TO DANCE, MADEMOISELLE?
DON'T MIND IF I DO!
NO ONE ELSE KNEW THE SONG, SO THEY ALL LEFT THE DANCE FLOOR. IT WAS JUST THE TWO OF US FOR A WHILE.
HAHA HA
HeeHee
THIS IS ACTUALLY A PRETTY GOOD SONG. WHAT KIND IS IT?
I THINK THEY CALL IT A ROCK BALLAD.
IT'S CALLED RETRO. OLD-TIMEY MUSIC.
SOMETIMES THEY PLAY THIS AT MY HOCKEY GAMES.
OH GOOD! HE DECIDED TO COME AFTER ALL.
IT LOOKS LIKE HE'S HAVING FUN.
YEAH, IT DOES.
HA HA HA
Hee Hee!

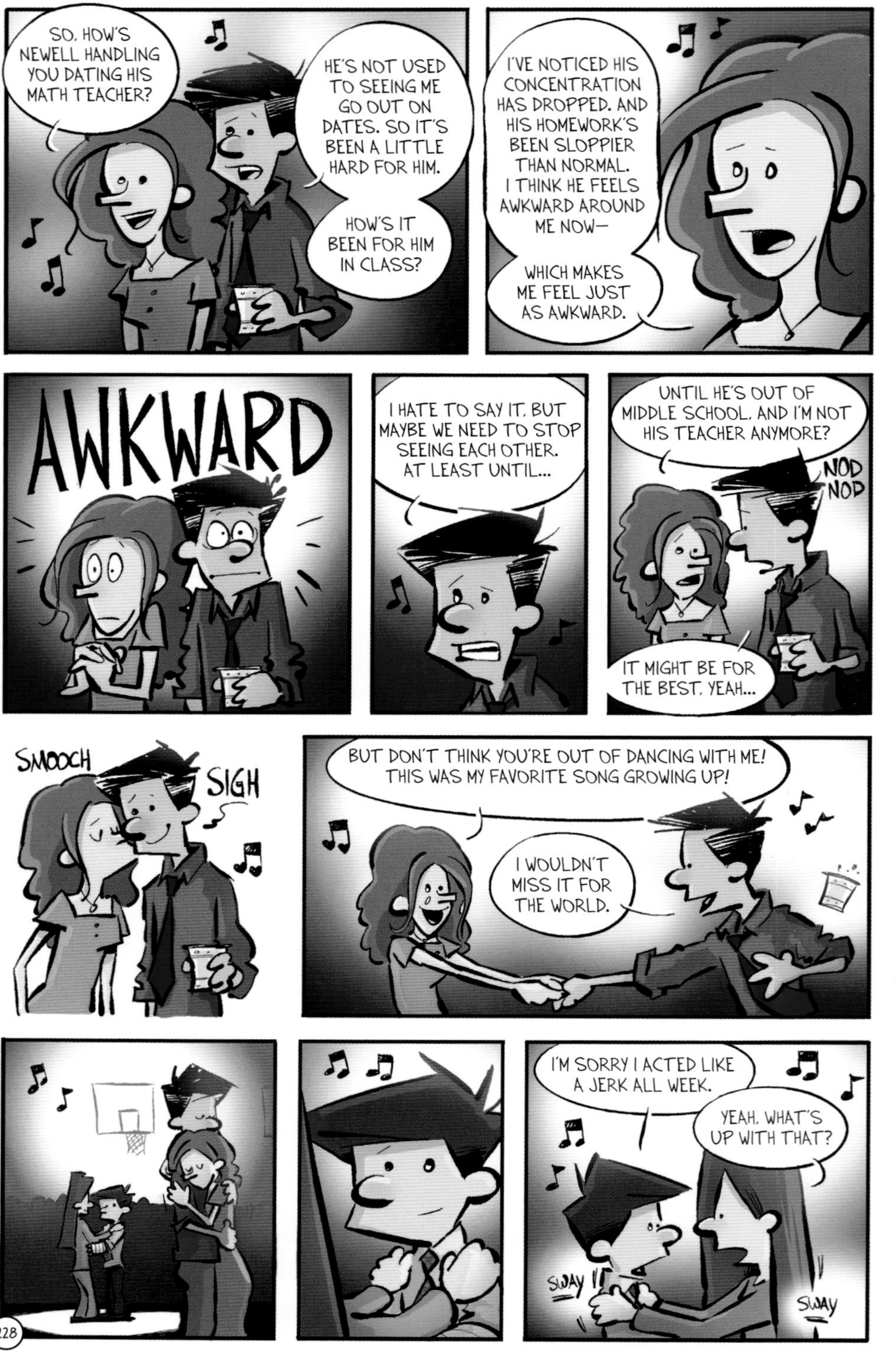
SO, HOW'S NEWELL HANDLING YOU DATING HIS MATH TEACHER?
HE'S NOT USED TO SEEING ME GO OUT ON DATES. SO IT'S BEEN A LITTLE HARD FOR HIM.
HOW'S IT BEEN FOR HIM IN CLASS?
I'VE NOTICED HIS CONCENTRATION HAS DROPPED. AND HIS HOMEWORK'S BEEN SLOPPIER THAN NORMAL. I THINK HE FEELS AWKWARD AROUND ME NOW—
WHICH MAKES ME FEEL JUST AS AWKWARD.
AWKWARD
I HATE TO SAY IT, BUT MAYBE WE NEED TO STOP SEEING EACH OTHER. AT LEAST UNTIL...
UNTIL HE'S OUT OF MIDDLE SCHOOL, AND I'M NOT HIS TEACHER ANYMORE?
NOD NOD
IT MIGHT BE FOR THE BEST, YEAH...
SMOOCH
SIGH
BUT DON'T THINK YOU'RE OUT OF DANCING WITH ME! THIS WAS MY FAVORITE SONG GROWING UP!
I WOULDN'T MISS IT FOR THE WORLD.
I'M SORRY I ACTED LIKE A JERK ALL WEEK.
YEAH, WHAT'S UP WITH THAT?
SWAY
SWAY

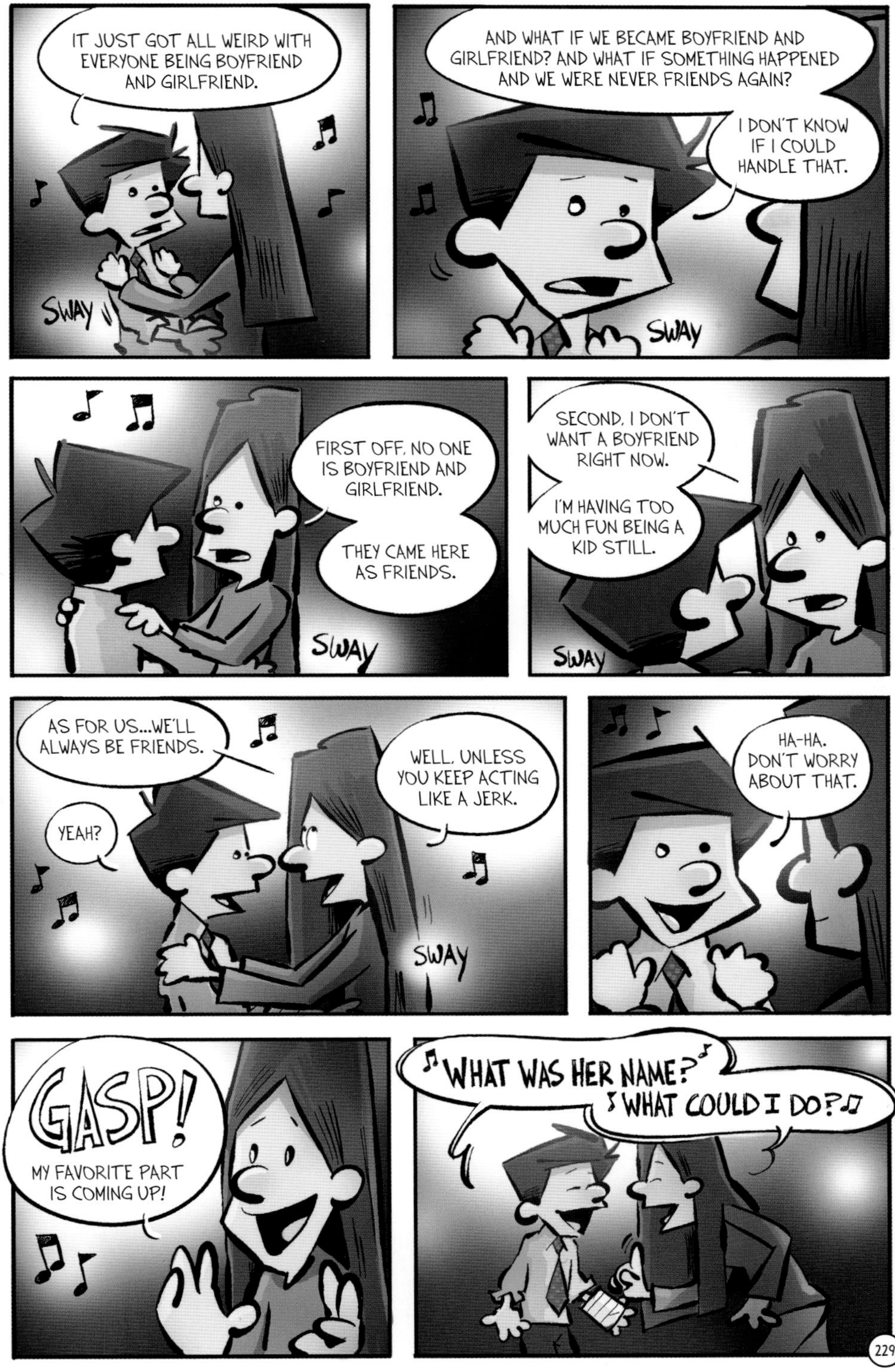
IT JUST GOT ALL WEIRD WITH EVERYONE BEING BOYFRIEND AND GIRLFRIEND.
SWAY
AND WHAT IF WE BECAME BOYFRIEND AND GIRLFRIEND? AND WHAT IF SOMETHING HAPPENED AND WE WERE NEVER FRIENDS AGAIN?
I DON'T KNOW IF I COULD HANDLE THAT.
SWAY
FIRST OFF, NO ONE IS BOYFRIEND AND GIRLFRIEND.
THEY CAME HERE AS FRIENDS.
SWAY
SECOND, I DON'T WANT A BOYFRIEND RIGHT NOW.
I'M HAVING TOO MUCH FUN BEING A KID STILL.
SWAY
AS FOR US...WE'LL ALWAYS BE FRIENDS.
YEAH?
WELL, UNLESS YOU KEEP ACTING LIKE A JERK.
SWAY
HA-HA. DON'T WORRY ABOUT THAT.
GASP!
MY FAVORITE PART IS COMING UP!
WHAT WAS HER NAME?
WHAT COULD I DO?

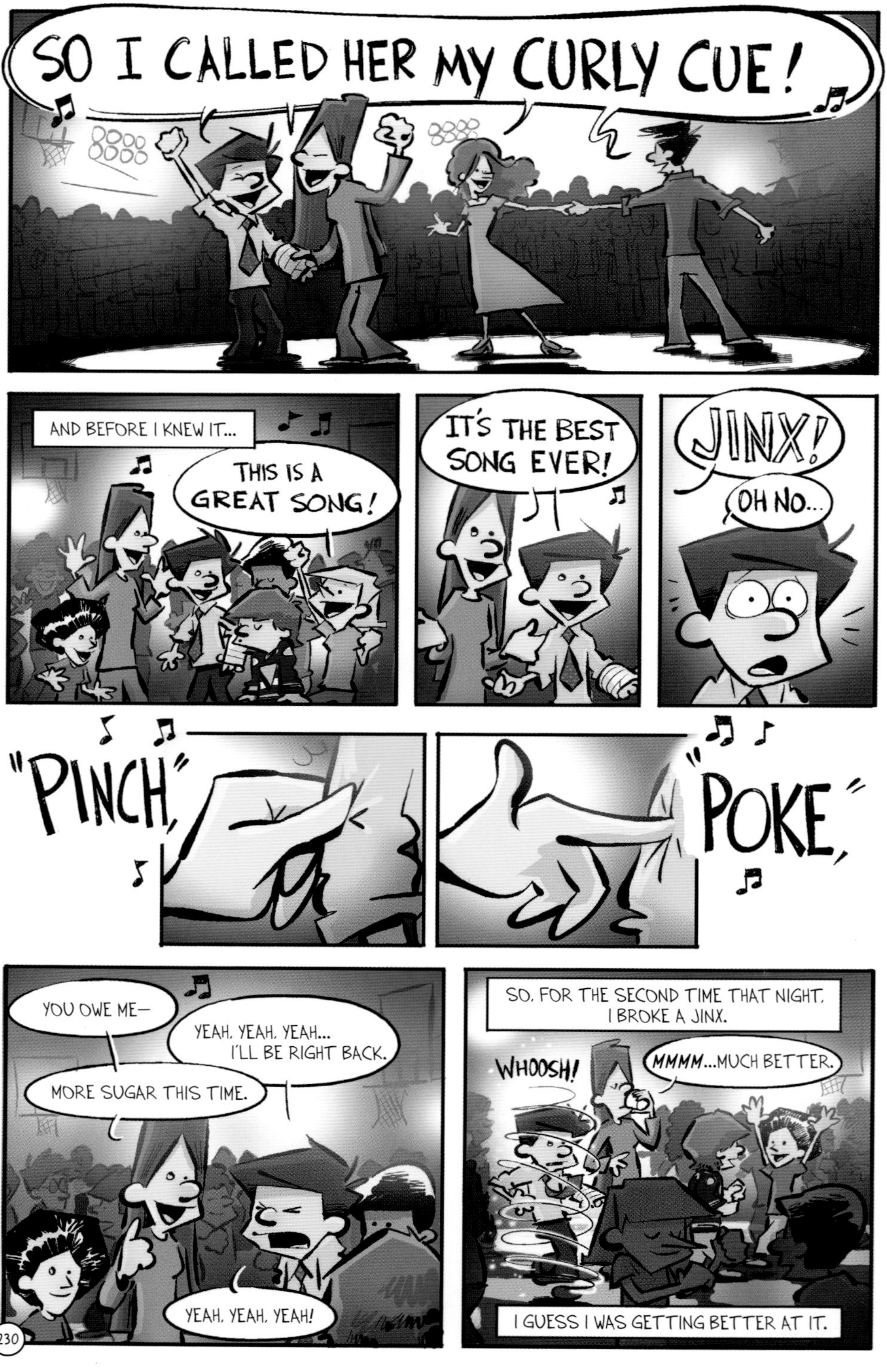

SO I CALLED HER MY CURLY CUE!
AND BEFORE I KNEW IT...
THIS IS A GREAT SONG!
IT'S THE BEST SONG EVER!
JINX!
OH NO...
"PINCH"
"POKE"
YOU OWE ME—
YEAH, YEAH, YEAH... I'LL BE RIGHT BACK.
MORE SUGAR THIS TIME.
YEAH, YEAH, YEAH!
SO, FOR THE SECOND TIME THAT NIGHT, I BROKE A JINX.
WHOOSH!
MMMM...MUCH BETTER.
I GUESS I WAS GETTING BETTER AT IT.

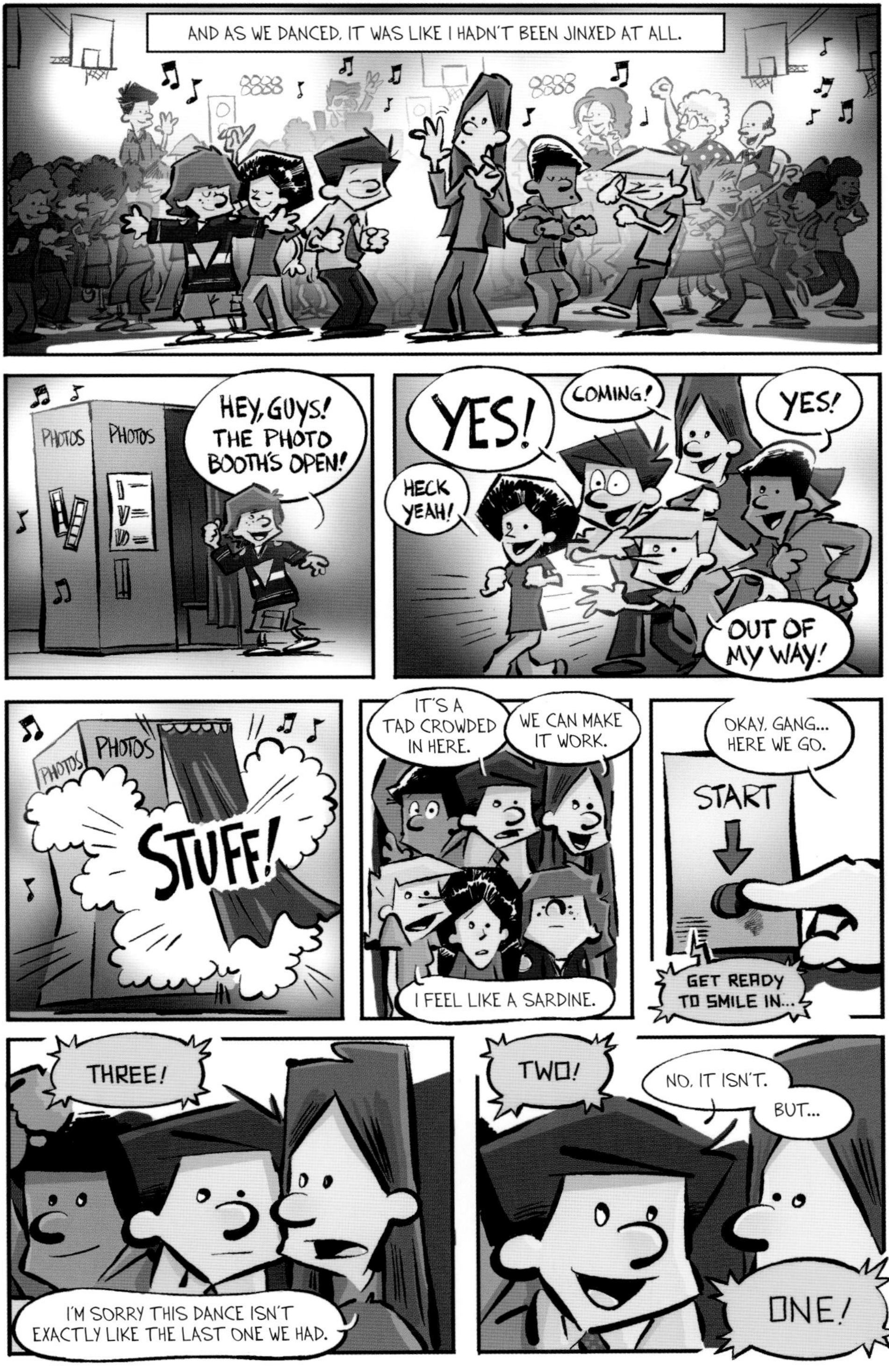
AND AS WE DANCED, IT WAS LIKE I HADN'T BEEN JINXED AT ALL.
PHOTOS
PHOTOS
HEY, GUYS! THE PHOTO BOOTH'S OPEN!
YES!
COMING!
YES!
HECK YEAH!
OUT OF MY WAY!
PHOTOS
PHOTOS
STUFF!
IT'S A TAD CROWDED IN HERE.
WE CAN MAKE IT WORK.
I FEEL LIKE A SARDINE.
OKAY, GANG... HERE WE GO.
START
GET READY TO SMILE IN...
THREE!
I'M SORRY THIS DANCE ISN'T EXACTLY LIKE THE LAST ONE WE HAD.
TWO!
NO, IT ISN'T.
BUT...
ONE!

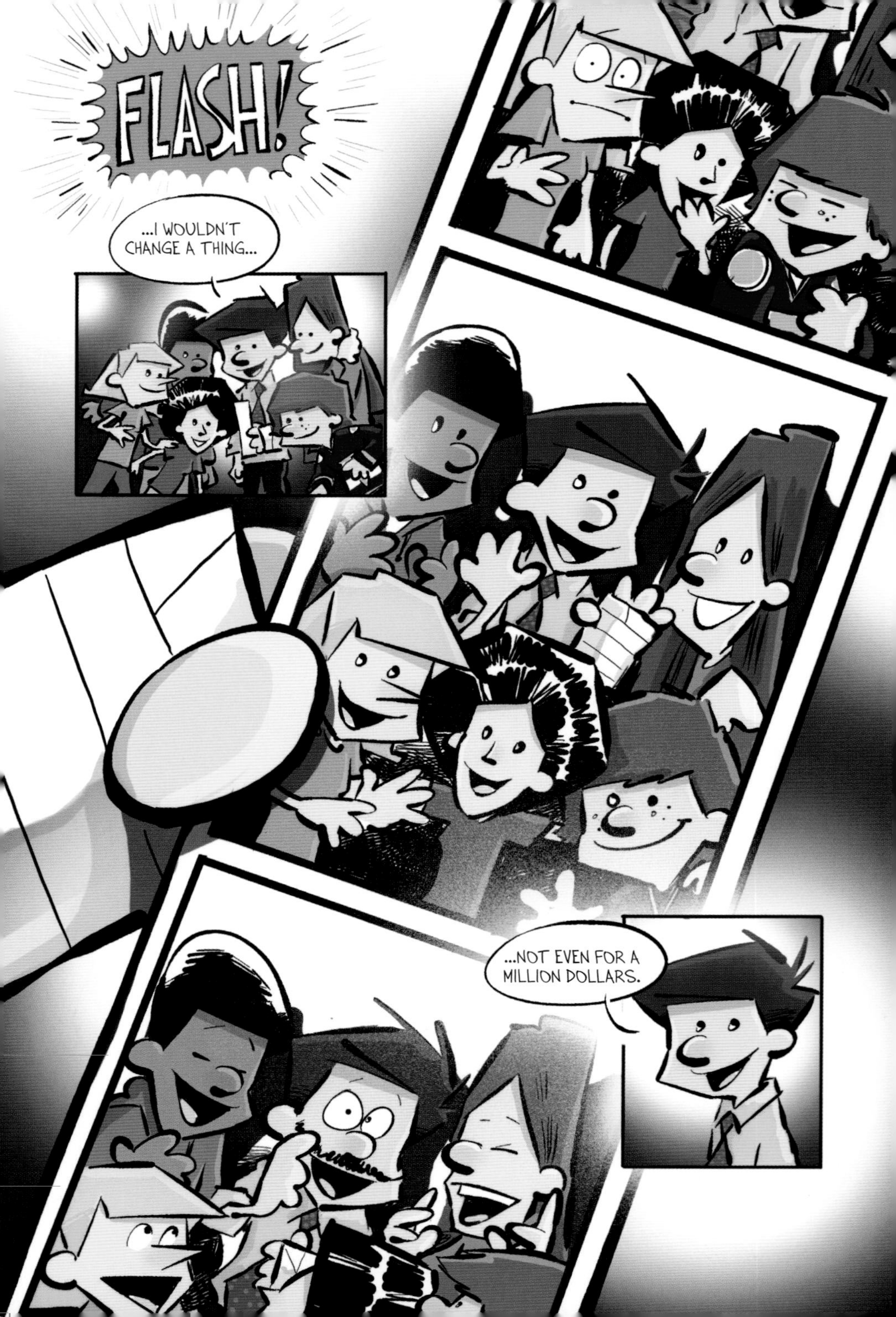
FLASH!
...I WOULDN'T CHANGE A THING...
...NOT EVEN FOR A MILLION DOLLARS.

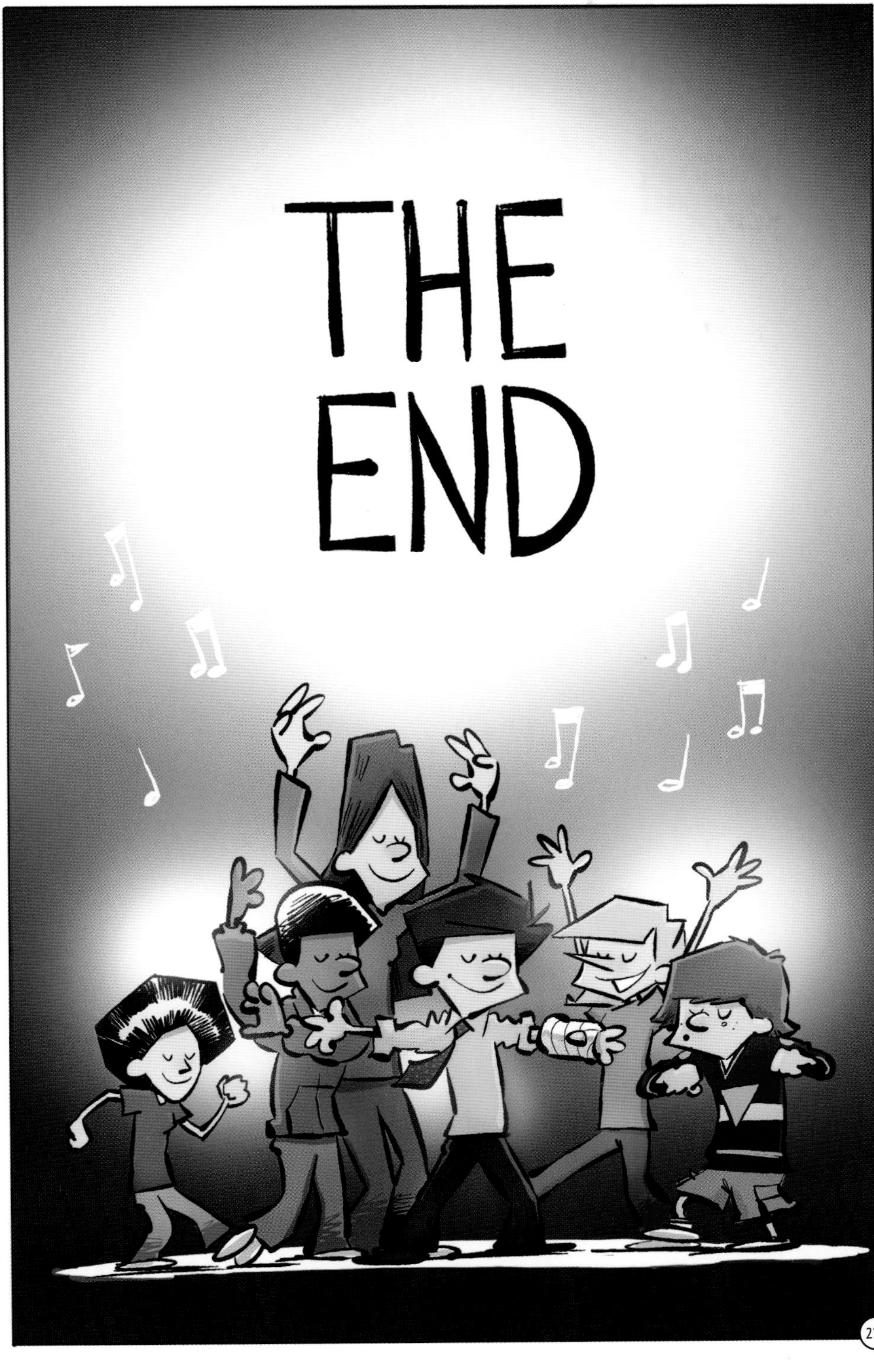
THE END

ACKNOWLEDGMENTS

* * *

MY NAME MAY BE THE ONLY ONE YOU SEE ON THE FRONT COVER, BUT BELIEVE ME, THERE ARE SO MANY PEOPLE WHO HAVE HELPED MAKE THIS MISADVENTURE HAPPEN.

FIRST AND FOREMOST, THIS SERIES WOULDN'T BE WHERE IT IS TODAY WITHOUT THE LOVE AND SUPPORT OF MY FAMILY: MY BEAUTIFUL WIFE, ERIN; MY SON, WYETH; AND MY MOTHER, KATHRYN. THANK YOU. THEY HAVE BEEN THERE FOR EVERY MOMENT OF THIS BOOK, FROM THE PENCILING AND WRITING, TO THE INKING, ALL THE WAY DOWN TO THE COLORS. WHEN YOU SURROUND YOURSELF WITH PEOPLE WHO BELIEVE IN YOU, HALF THE WORK IS ALREADY DONE. I'M A LUCKY GUY.

BIG THANKS TO MY AGENT, TIM TRAVAGLINI, WHO WAS ALWAYS THERE WHEN I NEEDED HIM AND KEPT A FIRE GOING ON THIS PROJECT.

TO EVERYONE AT LITTLE, BROWN BOOKS FOR YOUNG READERS WHO HAS HELPED SHAPE THIS BOOK. BUT MOST IMPORTANTLY TO MY EDITOR EXTRAORDINAIRE, RACHEL POLOSKI, WHOSE LAUGHTER AND INSIGHT KEPT ME ON TRACK; MY DESIGNER, MEGAN McLAUGHLIN, AND HER INCREDIBLE PATIENCE; AND MY EDITOR ESTHER CAJAHUARINGA, WHO HELPED ME ON THE FINAL STRETCH. THANK YOU.

A BIG THANK YOU TO MY SON, WYETH PLATT, FOR PERMITTING ME TO USE THE FICTIONAL PIZZERIA, MOZZIE & HAM, FROM HIS NOVELLA **THE WILL TO DELIVER: A PIZZA MEMOIR.**

EVEN THOUGH NEWELL'S MISADVENTURES THROUGH MIDDLE SCHOOL ARE FICTITIOUS, I COULDN'T HELP REFLECTING ON MY OWN JUNIOR HIGH AND HIGH SCHOOL MOMENTS WHILE WRITING THESE STORIES. SO THANK YOU TO ALL MY FRIENDS WHO HELPED GET ME THROUGH THE DAYS AT CHEWNING JUNIOR HIGH AND NORTHERN HIGH SCHOOL IN DURHAM, NORTH CAROLINA. WHO WOULD HAVE EVER THOUGHT THAT I WOULD BE MENTALLY REVISITING THOSE DAYS ALL THESE YEARS LATER?

AND FINALLY, TO ALL THE KIDS WHO'VE LAUGHED ALONGSIDE NEWELL AND HIS FRIENDS: THANK YOU. YOU'RE THE BEST.

JASON PLATT GREW UP IN DURHAM, NORTH CAROLINA, AND IS A GRADUATE OF THE SAVANNAH COLLEGE OF ART AND DESIGN IN SAVANNAH, GEORGIA. HE IS A MEMBER OF THE NATIONAL CARTOONISTS SOCIETY, AND HIS FIRST TWO BOOKS, **MIDDLE SCHOOL MISADVENTURES** AND **OPERATION: HAT HEIST!**, WERE CHOSEN FOR THE TEXAS LIBRARY ASSOCIATION'S LITTLE MAVERICK GRAPHIC NOVEL READING LIST. WHEN HE ISN'T WRITING OR CARTOONING, HE LOVES TO TRAVEL, HIKE, AND PLAY BOARD GAMES. HE AND HIS FAMILY LIVE IN DAVENPORT, IOWA.

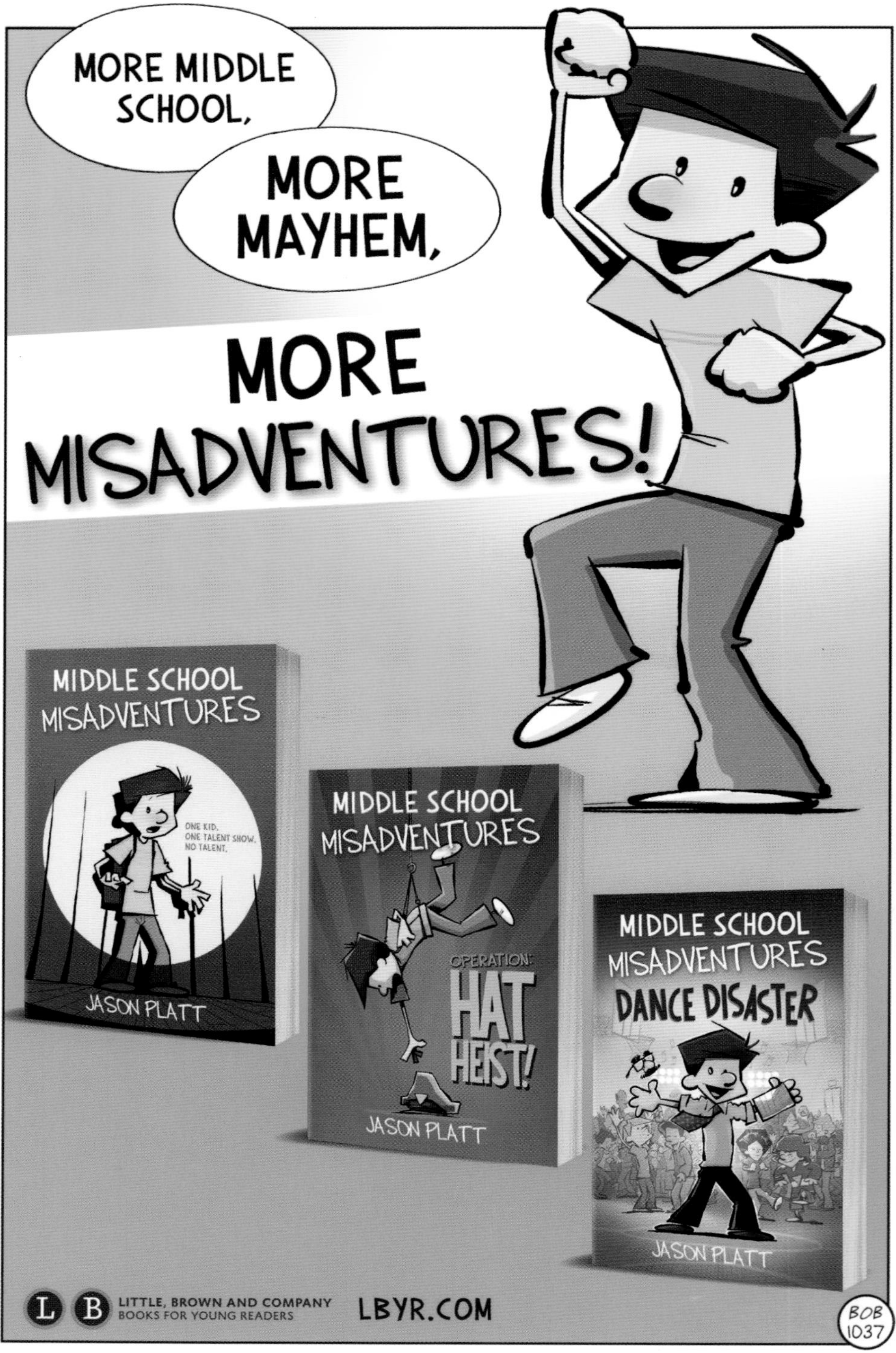
MORE MIDDLE SCHOOL,
MORE MAYHEM,
MORE MISADVENTURES!
MIDDLE SCHOOL MISADVENTURES
ONE KID. ONE TALENT SHOW. NO TALENT.
JASON PLATT
MIDDLE SCHOOL MISADVENTURES
OPERATION: HAT HEIST!
JASON PLATT
MIDDLE SCHOOL MISADVENTURES
DANCE DISASTER
JASON PLATT
LITTLE, BROWN AND COMPANY
BOOKS FOR YOUNG READERS
LBYR.COM
BOB 1037

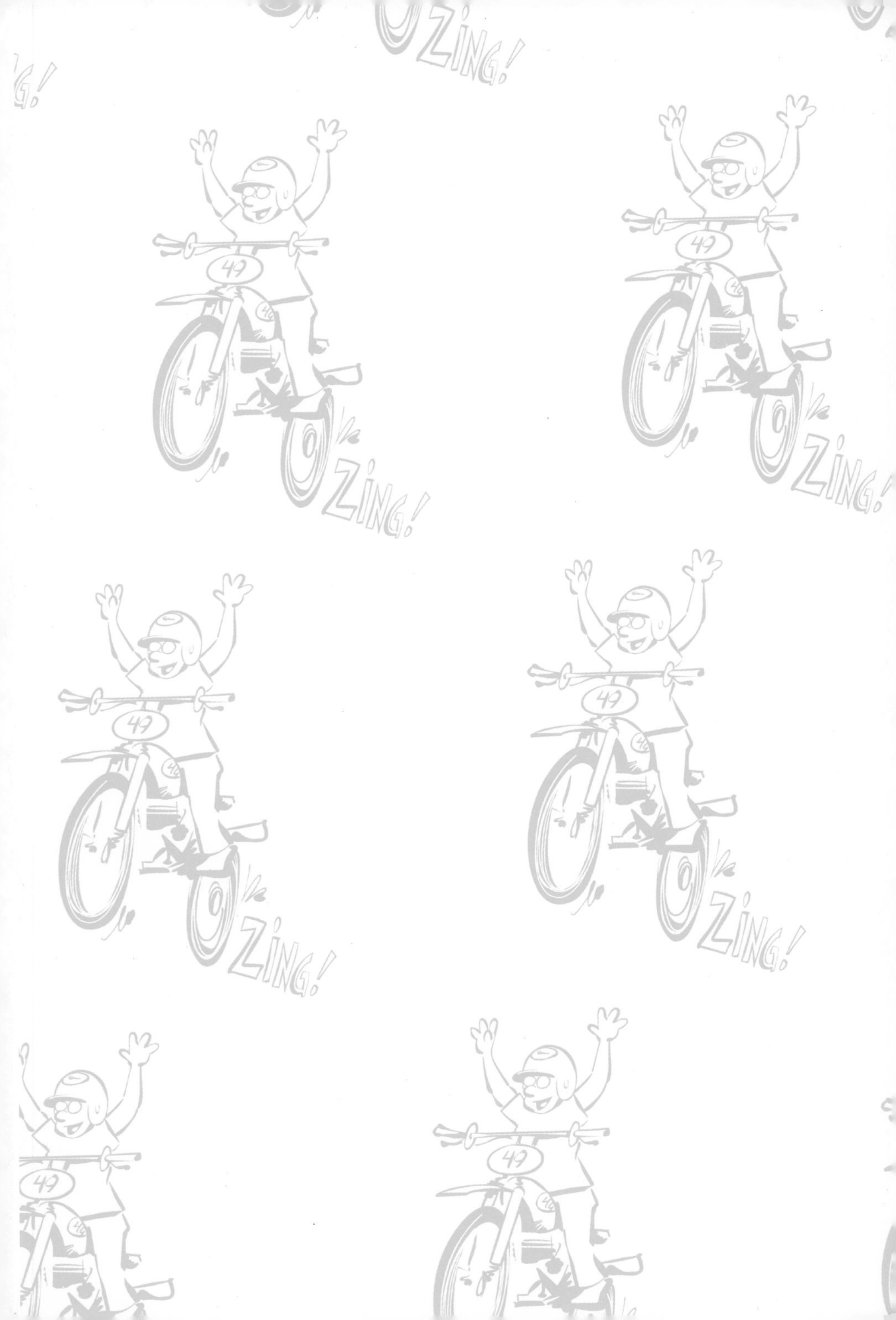
ZING!
ZING!
ZING!
ZING!
ZING!

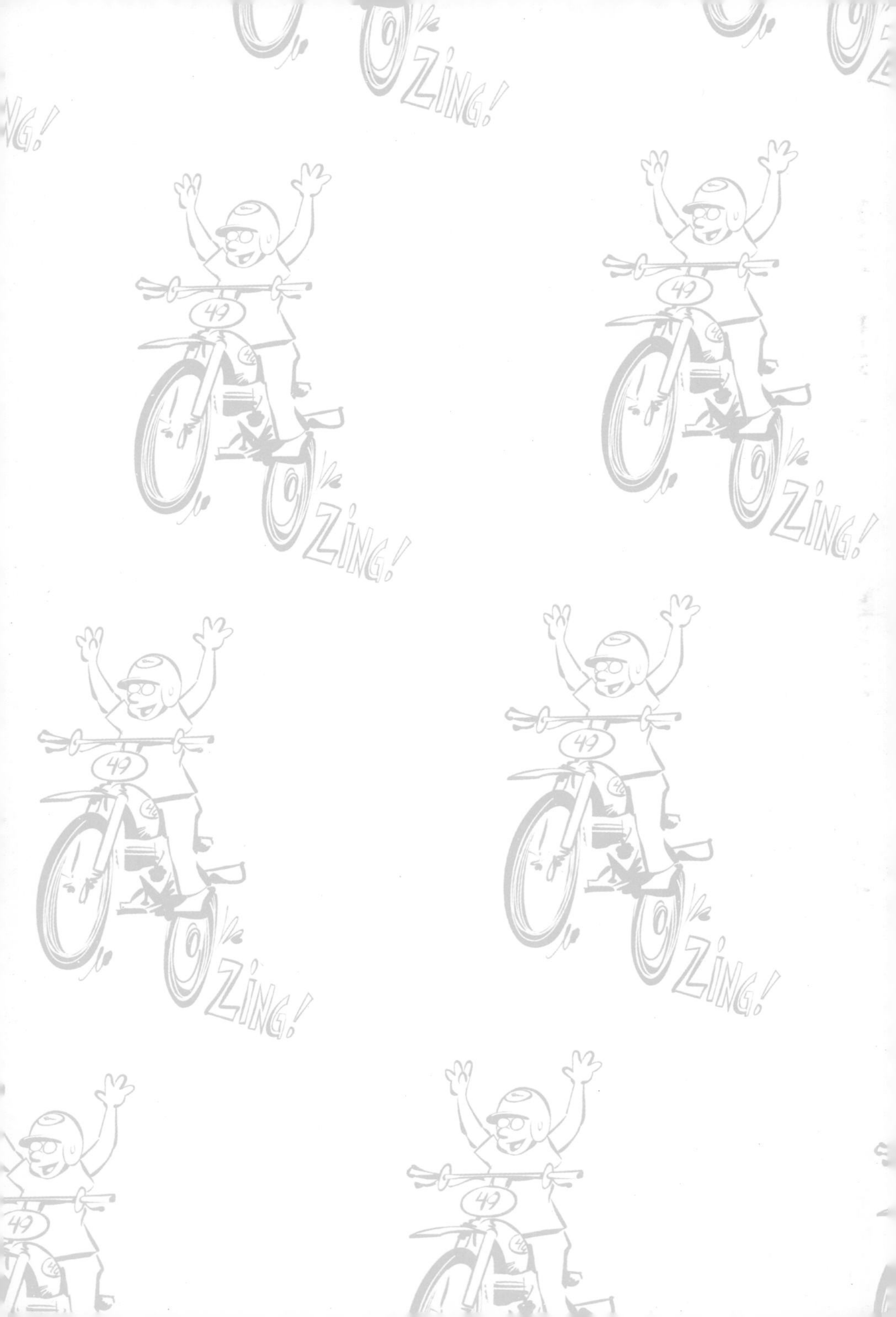
ZING!